the Farmer from CONNECTICUT

SUE TITUS

Published by N&W Press

THE FARMER FROM CONNECTICUT

Unless otherwise noted, scripture is taken from the New King James Version®. Copyright © 1982 by Thomas Nelson. Used by permission. All rights reserved.

Library of Congress Control Number: 2024924003
ISBN: 979-8-88928-047-7

Cover Design & Interior Layout: N&W Press

Printed in the United States of America
U.S. Printing History
First Edition: 2024

Dedication

First and foremost, I give God, Jesus, and the Holy Spirit all the glory!
Also, to the men and women who drive the highways and byways in their big rigs
to keep the American supply chain active. Many people need to be remembered,
including the farmers who work tirelessly day and night to make it possible for food
to be on our tables.

Acknowledgments

God has a way of directing our lives, and I truly believe He inspired me to write this book.

To Roy, my loving and wonderful husband of thirty-five years: you've encouraged me to step out in faith and allow the Spirit of God to guide me. Jesus took Roy home before he knew the success of this book. He was the love of my life, and I miss him so much.

To my children, my family, and my friends who prayed for me as I continued to write this manuscript: I wish I could name all of you.

I'm blessed to have two kindred-spirited Christian sisters, Betty Wilson and Sheila Rogers, along with many other family members and friends who have encouraged me.

Chapter One

It was a warm, mid-June day as Sally, her husband, Collin, and their two sons, Todd and Pace, were returning to Memphis on Interstate 40 from a week's vacation in the Smoky Mountains in Gatlinburg, Tennessee. Sally sat on the passenger side of the car, looking out her window at the skyline of the city of Nashville. Her thoughts were of the week spent away from home.

When the trip was originally planned several months ago, it was only going to be Collin and herself—kind of like a second honeymoon. Collin's mother, Mrs. Oldham, had gladly volunteered to keep the boys so they could go away together. Her job kept her very busy, and she had little time to spend with her grandsons. Mr. Oldham, Collin's father, had passed away two years earlier, so Mrs. Oldham tried to distract herself so as not to sink into loneliness and depression. Her week-long vacation request was granted by her boss, and she was looking forward to having quality time with Todd and Pace.

A few days before their trip, however, Mrs. Oldham fell ill with a virus and was ultimately unable to care for the boys. Of course, Collin and Sally were disappointed, but they understood that things like this happen. Sally seemed more disappointed than Collin because she had hoped this time away together would help their marriage, which seemed to be sliding downhill rapidly. She thought spending the whole week *alone* with her husband would give them much-needed time together and could perhaps change the direction of their relationship.

After thirteen years of marriage, something—or everything—seemed to be going sour, and whatever it was, Collin took it with a grain of salt. Sally had talked to Collin many times about her feelings, thinking he had noticed things weren't the same between them. All he had to say was, "It's all in your mind. Everything is OK!" She let it go for a while, thinking maybe he was right. But Collin's actions spoke louder than words, and her feelings persisted. Why didn't he seem interested in her or her family anymore? Sally knew Collin was a very hardworking man, ambitious when it came to his job. He didn't drink much, cussed a little, was a good provider for his family, and as far as Sally knew, he was faithful to her. So what could be wrong with their marriage? She did not know, but something was. She and Collin were high school sweethearts and married a year after graduation. She loved Collin very much, but it had reached the point where they seemed to only be tolerating each other.

During their trip in the mountains, Sally had an immersive opportunity to observe how Collin acted toward her and the boys, but his attitude was no different—uninterested or unwilling to participate in activities together. It was like his mind was preoccupied. The boys seemed to have a good time and enjoyed swimming in the motel pool, riding the sky lift, hiking up the mountain trails, and strolling by the mountain streams. They even played several games of miniature golf. Sally and the boys had a fun time, but Collin expressed little enthusiasm about anything they did. The trip was nothing like a second honeymoon, that was for sure.

The longer Sally thought about the trip, the more upset she became. But her train of thought was interrupted by someone laughing on the CB radio in their car. She could tell by the sound of the voice that the man doing the talking was a truck driver. Truck drivers' voices were a little different over their CBs because of the not-so-smooth ride in the cabs of their 18-wheelers. She turned to Collin and asked him what was so funny. He explained that someone was telling a good joke.

Sally noticed that they were in a convoy of several cars and three 18-wheelers. Collin would rather travel in a convoy than drive stag because he thought there was safety in numbers and he also enjoyed talking on the CB radio. He said it helped pass the time. Occasionally he would drive a tractor trailer part time on the weekends for the company he worked for, and he had the handle of "Pole Climber." He knew some of the big rig drivers and was very familiar with the language and the mannerisms of CB talk. Sally had not talked on the radio much because she was afraid of saying the wrong thing. It's not like picking up the telephone and calling someone—there's a certain way of saying things. And besides, a lot of people were listening to what was being said!

The conversation continued in the convoy, and Collin had joined in. Sally enjoyed listening. There were two young, attractive girls in a convertible going to Dallas, Texas. They were inviting the three truck drivers in the convoy to follow them and maybe enjoy dinner together later down the road. One of the truckers, "The Farmer," said he was going that direction, but his horses wouldn't be able to keep up with them. So the girls bid the truckers good-bye with a wave, pulled out of the convoy, and sped down the interstate.

After they were out of range, the Farmer said something real funny about the girls, and Sally cracked up laughing. The driver behind their car saw Sally laughing and immediately said on his CB, "There's a cute little gal in that blue and white Chevy in front of me that thought that remark about those girls was mighty funny."

Sally looked out the back window of the car and thought, *Is he the Farmer?* She saw a very handsome face smiling down at her.

Before more thoughts of him could pass through her mind, he put the CB mic near his mouth and said, "Yes, you, with the ponytails!"

Sally was embarrassed. She grabbed her ponytails and ducked down in the front seat of the car in an attempt to hide.

"Oh, come on now. Talk to me. What's your handle?"

Collin handed her the mic with a grin on his face and said, "He wants to talk to you! Talk to him."

Sally took the mic, pushed the key, and, uncertain how her voice was going to sound, she eased up into a sitting position and said, "You've got *The Cricket* here. You're the Farmer, right?"

"You've got that right. Where you be heading, Cricket?"

"That Big M Town. I know you're going to Texas, but where in Texas?" Sally inquired.

"Going to take this load to Abilene."

With curiosity in her voice, she asked, "With your accent, you can't be from Texas. Where's your Home—20?"

With laughter in his voice, the Farmer replied, "No, not Texas. Try Connecticut."

"The Farmer from Connecticut. *Wow!* You're a long way from home!" At least it seemed like a long way to Sally.

All three of the truck drivers chimed in, and Sally was involved in a lovely conversation between them all. The Farmer had given her the much-needed nudge to her confidence that she needed to talk comfortably on the CB. It wasn't so bad after all.

The weigh station sign was ahead on the interstate, and all trucks must pull over to be weighed.

"Cricket, you copy?" asked the Farmer.

"Go ahead, you've got the Cricket."

"Cricket, we've got to jump off this super slab and get these rigs weighed. We'll catch up with you in a short-short, Roger?"

Another driver came in and said, "Yeah, we've got to stay up with that Cricket. She's a cute beaver, don't ya know."

Sally was flattered and responded in a way she had heard other female CB-ers say when paid a compliment, "Thanks for those flowers, and be looking forward to talkin' to you in a short-short." The radio suddenly went quiet, and Sally felt almost alone.

The driving time from Nashville to Memphis was about three and a half to four hours, but talking on the radio had made the time go by much faster, just as Collin had said he experienced when he drove over the road. Two and a half hours had passed, and Sally almost dreaded returning to Memphis. She thought back over the conversations she'd had with those truck drivers and thought, *This trip was well worth it!* She hadn't felt that good inside in a long time. She knew it was silly, but she really felt happy, which was something Collin had not made her feel in ages. It took a complete stranger to make her feel human again.

A half hour had passed and there was still no radio transmission from the Farmer, Cowboy, or Roadrunner. She recalled there was a long line of trucks waiting at the scales, and it must be taking a while for them to get processed and back on the road again.

Heavy, thick, dark rain clouds were moving in from the northwest. Lightning streaked across the sky and down to the ground time and time again. It looked like a really bad storm, and they were heading right into it.

A few drops of rain were beginning to fall on the windshield, and drivers heading eastbound were reporting on their CBs that bad weather was ahead. One driver said that the rain was so heavy several miles back he had to pull off to the side of the highway for a while until it slacked up. Sally wouldn't take her eyes off the back window, staring down the road behind them, hoping to see the truckers.

The raindrops began to increase. Visibility out the back window became poor. Daylight grew dim as the dark clouds surrounded the car. Lightning flashed brightly; thunder crashed. Then suddenly rain came down in torrents. Collin slowed the car to a snail's pace, and even at that, the road ahead could hardly be seen. Again, the lightning lit up the sky, and the loud crashing of thunder sounded like it was right on top of them. Todd and Pace, who were asleep in the back seat, woke up frightened and startled by the horrible noise. Sally's skin crawled. She had never experienced a storm quite like this one.

The CB radio was silent, all except the static. *Where is the Farmer?* Sally asked herself sadly. Then a horrible thought hit her. *What if the Farmer and others decided to stop at a truck stop to get out of the stormy weather?* Her mind raced. *Have I seen any truck stops? No, I don't think so!* She was at the point of giving up all hope of ever talking to the Farmer again.

Collin's voice broke the silence in the car and brought reality back to her conscience. "Only thirty-five miles to Memphis!" he announced. Sally could barely read the road sign through the driving rain. Looking over at Sally, he commented, "Up until now, the weather for our vacation has been great. You know, overall, the vacation has been nice. We've had no car troubles and plenty of money to see what we wanted to see in the mountains, and you've finally talked on the CB, which I've encouraged you to do for a long time."

"Yes, Todd and Pace had a good time. The trip was exciting for them. And yes, talking on the CB was fun."

The stormy weather seemed to have passed, and the rain was more like a drizzle. Collin was able to resume normal speed. Oh, how Sally wanted to stop time and the miles from rolling away. Her hopes continued to fade of ever talking to or seeing the Farmer again.

Almost at that same moment, a voice came over the CB loud and clear, calling for the Cricket. Sally instantly breathed a sigh of relief, grabbed the mic, and acknowledged the transmission: "Go ahead, you've got Cricket."

"Sorry, Cricket. It took us so long to catch up with you, but between D.O.T. and the storm, it's just taken us a while. The storm has been so bad, we've only been able to creep along. We could hardly see a foot in front of us. How about you? Have you had to pull off the road?" The Farmer asked.

"No, we haven't had to pull off the road, but only about ten miles per hour is as fast as we've been able to go. It really was a bad storm. I was afraid y'all had pulled off the road."

Roadrunner broke in and said, "Are you kidding? We were determined to catch back up with you and lay eyeballs on you again! We had to keep truckin'."

"You've got that right, Roadrunner!" said Cowboy.

When all of them approached the Shelby County line, their speed dropped to the speed limit of fifty-five miles per hour. The Smokies were always pretty thick at the county line, and they were notorious for giving out tickets to speeders. Traffic was heavy, and Collin had reduced his speed even more because of the slower vehicles in front of him. He attempted to merge into the fast lane, but too many vehicles were passing the slower traffic and made it impossible for him to change lanes.

As Sally turned to glance out the back window to see where her truck driver friends were, she looked right up into the face of the Farmer. *He is so handsome,* she remarked to herself.

"There you are! Come on out, Pole Climber, otherwise you're going to be there a while," the Farmer encouraged. "This traffic is terrible. Where in Memphis do you live, Cricket? Will you be getting off the super slab soon?"

Sally wanted to tell him exactly where she lived, but she thought that may not be the best idea. "We get off at Exit 20 to head to the home—20," she replied.

"Well, Cricket, it's been great talking to you. You sure are a sweet thing! I hope to talk to you again. You know, I come through Memphis twice a week," the Farmer informed her.

Sally's heart seemed to jump right out of her chest when she heard those last words. She came so close to asking him when he was coming through town the next time, but she happened to catch the look her husband was giving her. It wasn't good.

Cautiously she answered, "Well, Farmer, maybe I can talk to you again. It sure has been great talking to you too. Sure hope you have yourself a good trip to Abilene, and a safe one. Cowboy and Roadrunner, I've enjoyed talking to you two, and y'all have a safe trip!"

"Yeah, Cricket, I've enjoyed jawin' with you too. Maybe catch you on the flip-flop someday," chimed in Roadrunner.

Cowboy responded, "It couldn't have been a nicer trip, Cricket, and you've made it that way! You take care, and talk to you again someday."

The sign for Exit 20 was just ahead. The three drivers remained in the fast lane, preparing to pass Sally's car as Collin drove to the outside lane to turn to exit the interstate. Sally looked out the back window and watched as they drove by. She wanted her mind to engrave in it the handsome face of the Farmer, and she hoped that she would see and talk to him again soon. She waved to each of the drivers; they waved and blew their horns. Each of them told Cricket "bye," and she reciprocated. Sally gently laid the mic down in her lap and watched the

Farmer's burgundy Kenworth roll under the viaduct and disappear out of sight, perhaps never to see or talk to him again.

Even though Sally was sad, she had found something to feel happy about. She couldn't understand it, but she knew she felt it. She was quiet the rest of the way home, letting her mind ponder the things that had been said between her and those nice truckers, especially the Farmer. Collin didn't have much to say either, but Sally really didn't care. She had something else to think about.

Chapter Two

Month after month went by, and Sally had not talked to nor seen the Farmer from Connecticut. When Collin was home, Sally often found herself lying to him about where she was going, which she had never done before, making excuses to get out of the house to give her more opportunities to drive on the super slab and call for the Farmer on the CB. She would listen intensely for his northern-accented voice, picturing his handsome face in her mind. She couldn't explain it, but she was drawn to this man. She would call for him every now and then, hoping he'd hear her voice and answer. His words "I come through Memphis twice a week" often echoed in her mind. She assumed that he meant his trips were on a regular basis, but four months had passed. To be able to talk to and to see the Farmer became an obsession—her only hope, wish, and dream.

Todd and Pace had returned to school, and the warm summer months turned to cooler autumn days. Life with Collin had not changed. He still seemed to be very disconnected from her and the boys. Sally had hoped that after their vacation, Collin would have realized there was more to life with them than his work. Their thirteenth wedding anniversary had come and gone with very little acknowledgment of their special day. No going out to dinner to celebrate, no flowers, no romantic gestures, not even a greeting card. Collin only realized what day it was when Sally handed him the anniversary card she had thoughtfully bought for him. He apologized to her, saying that he forgot and that he'd make it up to her soon. *Was this all there was to their lives?*

To add insult to injury, Collin's boss changed his hours to the night shift. He was happy about the change and was even more excited about working nights. *How could he think like that?* Sally asked herself. The boys would not see him except on the weekends, and Collin's new schedule would be leaving her to sleep alone—not that it mattered because there was no love life there either. On the other hand, Sally could go to bed thinking about the Farmer, and maybe he would visit her in her dreams.

Most mornings after Sally took Todd and Pace to school, she would not go home. Collin would sleep all day, and he wouldn't know (and probably not care) if she was there or not. She would jump on the interstate near the house and drive for several hours, calling on the CB for the Farmer and listening to hear his sweet voice.

In the many days of talking on the CB and listening to fellow CB-ers ratchet jawin', Sally had become familiar with some of the voices and handles. There were two ladies in particular she'd talk to in the afternoon when she'd go to pick up the boys from school—*Minnie Mouse* and *Lady Tiger*. After several weeks of talking to Minnie Mouse on the radio, Minnie asked Sally to come to her house the next morning for coffee. Sally accepted Minnie's invite. During their visit, Sally learned Minnie's husband, *Firecracker*, was an over-the-road truck driver. While they were talking, Firecracker came in from a run. He said he had talked to Pole Climber several times as well as the Farmer from Connecticut. Minnie spoke up and said she had heard on their base unit a driver with a northern accent calling for Cricket two days earlier. Sally suddenly felt weak and faint at Minnie's claim. Repeating her words in her head, Sally was having a hard time trying to think clearly. *Someone actually heard the Farmer calling for Cricket!* Sally was so excited.

The visit with Minnie and Firecracker was great, and Sally thought she was on cloud nine. Her hopes had been renewed. Just knowing that the Farmer had been calling for her made her want to talk to him even more. As she drove home from Minnie's house, Sally thought how nice it would be to have a base unit in the house—that way she could listen for the Farmer all the time.

That night, as she laid alone in bed, she couldn't sleep, for the thoughts of the Farmer were wandering around in her mind. She could visualize his handsome face and hear his manly voice, and she almost felt his warm touch to her face. Oh, how she longed for him.

Early one afternoon in late October, Sally was returning home from the grocery store. She had her CB on as usual and was listening to mostly I-240 traffic when suddenly the faint sound of a voice she had so desperately wanted and needed to hear appeared. Her heart nearly slid up into her throat with excitement. She could hardly believe her ears. She grabbed the mic and immediately called for the Farmer, but his voice did not return. Again, she frantically called, but nothing. She keyed the mic again to ask if anyone had heard the Farmer talking.

A man's voice returned in the CB's speaker. "Yes, I heard him."

Sally asked the man if he knew which direction he was going.

The man replied, "Westbound, I think."

Sally thanked the man and drove her car toward the entrance of the westbound lanes on the super slab. Before she realized it, she had the pedal to the medal at seventy miles per hour! She was calling every minute or two for the Farmer, but his voice never returned. She knew the mileage range for the radio was from two to five miles, and the chances of her finding the Farmer after seven miles of driving was nearly impossible. For all she knew, the Farmer could have even been going eastbound, or he may have traveled one way where I-55 and I-240 cross, and she may have gone the other way.

Sally took the next exit and drove to the side of the ramp. Tears of despair, failure, and heartbreak flowed from her eyes. She heard him; she really heard his voice. The opportunity she had waited for, for almost five months was no more.

Her dreams of talking to him and perhaps having a cup of coffee with him were gone. Oh, that chance of seeing him up close and in person, getting to know all about him, would not happen. Her heart was shattered, and her tears seemed unceasing.

After the better part of an hour, finally she was able to calm down. Sally's body was numb. The sadness she felt was indescribable. Even though her mind was dull and didn't want to think, she remembered the old sayings of "life must go on" and "in life a little rain must fall." But she felt like it had been pouring on her for such a long time. She wanted and needed a little sunshine.

As Sally began driving again, the only thought she had was that there must be another day, another time to hear, talk to, and see the Farmer.

A few mornings later, Minnie Mouse called Sally and told her she had just heard a northern-accented voice on her base unit calling for Cricket. Minnie continued, "I answered the call for you and told the northern-accented driver that I was a friend of yours. This man said he was the Farmer from Connecticut and to please tell you 'hi' for him and that he hoped to see and talk to you real soon." Minnie had told him that she would give the message to Cricket right away.

Sally quickly sat down before her weak knees gave way. Minnie couldn't have started off Sally's day any better than that! Fighting back tears of happiness, Sally thanked Minnie for calling and giving her the message. That telephone call meant so much to her. She wanted to give Minnie a message to give back to the Farmer when she heard him again, telling him to stop somewhere and she'd be glad to meet him for coffee. But she couldn't do that. Minnie didn't understand how deeply involved Sally's feelings were for the man called the Farmer. Minnie didn't know Sally's marriage was on the rocks, and she didn't feel close enough to Minnie to share with her about her situation. *Married women just aren't supposed to have feelings like this for another man to begin with*, thought Sally, so she needed to keep her thoughts to herself for now.

Several days went by, and Sally's depression was about to get the best of her. As she was preparing breakfast that morning, she decided after she took the boys to school she would go window shopping, just to have something to do and maybe take her mind off of the Farmer. Collin would be sleeping all day, so he wouldn't know whether she was home or not.

As Sally watched her sons walk through the double doors of the two-story brick school building, she thought of her plans for the day. After a quick stop at a fast food place for a cup of coffee, she ventured to a few shops where she tried on outfits; some she liked, some she didn't, none she really intended to buy. She remembered a new mall had opened across town and decided to drive there by way of the interstate. As usual, she had the CB turned on, and as always, she picked up the mic and called for the Farmer. There was no answer, but instead another trucker responded, "I'm not the Farmer, but, sweet thing, I'll talk to you. I'm *Hawk*. Where are ya headed?"

"I'm going over to Summer Avenue, Hawk. Where are you going on this beautiful day?"

"I'm going to Music City and then up to the Buckeye State. Why don't you come and go with me?"

"Oh gosh, Hawk, I'd love to, but I'd better not today. Maybe another day, OK?" Just at that moment, a fancy, dressed-out rig was passing her car. Sally looked over and saw Hawk looking down at her from his cab, waving. Sally waved back.

"Oh darlin', you're a pretty thing! You sure you can't take this trip with me today?"

Sally felt the blushing redness in her face as she answered, "Gee, Hawk, thanks for those flowers! You know how to make a girl feel good, but just not today."

"Well, Cricket, you're going to miss a great time, but I'll catch you another day," Hawk replied as he changed lanes to prepare to take the exit toward Nashville.

"Hawk, it's been nice jawin' with you. I hope you have a good day and a great trip to the Buckeye State. Catch you on the flip!"

"Yeah, Cricket, been good talking to you too. You have yourself a nice one, and I'll be looking for you on the flip!"

"Bye, Hawk," Sally said as she watched his pretty tractor trailer go down the ramp to I-40. *It must be great to travel and see all kinds of places,* she thought.

As Sally drove into the parking lot of the new mall, she decided she didn't really want to see the place as bad as she thought she did. It was a beautiful mid-November day with lots of sunshine, so she decided she'd rather just drive. Collin never mentioned just taking a drive in the country or going on a day trip with his family, and that's a shame! So she turned her car around, found the eastbound entrance to I-40, and just started driving. She rested her head on the back of her seat and thought about how good it felt to relax. There were still a lot of fall colors on most of the trees. The scenery was beautiful! There was not much traffic on the interstate and very little chatter on the CB. Several times she called for the Farmer, but there was no answer.

Sally looked at her watch, and to her surprise, she'd been driving nearly an hour. It hardly seemed possible. She wanted to just keep on driving, but she had to be back to Memphis in time to pick the boys up from school. She remembered the truck stop near Jackson, Tennessee, and decided to drive there for a bite of lunch, then start back for home.

When Sally drove into the lot of the truck stop, she looked at the trucks she could see, always keeping an eye out for the Farmer's rig, its image permanently etched in her mind. But there were times she was fooled, thinking she had spotted it. But it was not the Farmer's. Many trucks on the road looked a lot like his.

As she got out of her car and was walking to the entrance of the restaurant, she stopped. A burgundy KW was pulling into the truck stop. Her heart skipped a few beats. She stared at the truck until it disappeared out of her sight behind the building. *I wonder, could it be?* she asked herself, half-heartedly dismissing the hopeful thought.

Once in the restaurant, Sally decided against sitting at the counter and walked over to a small table with two chairs. There were a lot of truck drivers in the restaurant, and a few of them were giving her the once-over look. She always felt uneasy and uncomfortable when men stared at her, but the feeling calmed when the waitress came to her table and took her order.

Sally was sipping from a cup of coffee, staring out the back windows of the restaurant, when out of the corner of her eye she saw a man coming out of the men's bathroom. *Oh my!* she said to herself in disbelief.

The man's eyes met hers as he walked toward her. "Cricket!" he exclaimed with excitement.

"Farmer? I can't believe this!" she replied, fighting back tears of joy. The butterflies were flying around in her stomach like crazy. He was so handsome!

As she stood to meet him, the Farmer took Sally's hands in his, and with a big smile he said, "It sure is great to see you again! I called for you on the CB many times when I would come through Memphis, hoping to talk to you again. Gosh, what a wonderful surprise!"

His hands felt so warm and secure to Sally. She couldn't take her eyes off of his face and his powder blue eyes. She felt her whole body tremble. Her voice shook as she said, "Farmer, it's so great to see you too. After nearly six months of wearing out my CB trying to talk to you, I'd almost given up on the thought of ever seeing you again."

They both sat down at the small table, and the waitress came and took the Farmer's order. Sally asked him how he'd been, and other than driving, what he'd been doing. He replied that driving was all he'd been doing. Wanting to find out all she could about him, Sally remarked, "I bet your wife doesn't much like you being gone all the time."

"Well, if I had a wife, she probably wouldn't like it much, but I don't have to worry about that," he responded. "Driving is my life! I guess one could say it's in my blood."

Sally breathed a sigh of relief, thrilled at the news that there wasn't a woman waiting for him at home. She continued asking him questions about his life. "Farmer, I've tried to imagine what your name might be. Is it Gary?"

"No," he replied.

"Is it Tommy?"

"No," was again his reply.

"Is it Marshall?"

"Nope."

"OK, I give up. What is it?" Sally asked.

"My name is Rusty, Rusty Summers, and has been for thirty-three years."

"Hey, I like that name!" she answered. *And he is thirty-three years old!* she thought. Good to know.

Interrupting their conversation, the waitress brought their lunch, and they began to eat. Rusty looked at Sally with anticipation, thinking she would tell him her name, but she was determined he was going to have to ask her.

"Well, now you know my name. What's your name, Cricket?"

"Sally Oldham," she replied.

"Sally is one of my favorite feminine names, and it fits you too! You look like a Sally, and I'll say a very pretty Sally!" the Farmer added.

Sally blushed. "Thank you, Rusty. You're not so bad yourself."

"Ah, come on. Say, by the way, what are you doing this far from Memphis?" Rusty inquired in a curious tone of voice.

Oh, how she wanted to pour her heart out to him and tell him what she felt about him, but how silly he would think she was! Here she was, a thirty-one-year-old married woman with a mad crush on a man she's only talked to on the CB for a few hours and didn't even know his name until a few moments ago. But then again, why not be honest? What could it hurt?

"I came looking for you! For all these months, I've been nearly out of my mind wanting to talk to you again and to see your handsome face once more. There, I said it!" Sally confessed.

Rusty's look was definitely one of surprise, and he really didn't know what to say. He finally responded with a grin, "Yeah, sure you did!" He didn't believe her.

There was complete silence between them. *What did I just do?* Sally thought to herself.

"Well," he began, "I was born on May 3, 1945, in Waterbury, Connecticut, and was raised on a dairy farm located seven miles from Sandy Hook, where my Dad taught me everything he knows about the business. He plans to leave the farm to me one day, but to be honest with you, I'm not crazy about cows. My dad's worked hard and long to make the farm what it is today, but he and my mom never have any time to go anywhere or do anything special, constantly tending to the farm. Its responsibilities are endless. My mom often says that those cows are my dad's first love, and she is his second!"

Rusty went on. "Anyway, I graduated from Sandy Hook High School and then went to Danbury State College for three years. My ambition was to graduate from college, but my life became very complicated in my freshman year. I don't want to bore you with all that, though. Besides, I want to hear about you. Tell me about yourself, Sally."

Oh, but Sally *did* want to hear about how his life became so complicated! She didn't want to sound too pushy, so she decided to respond to his request. "I was born in Memphis on August 30, 1947. My father was in the Air Force, and we—my mother, my brother, and me—traveled a lot. When I was six years old, we moved to Dayton, Ohio, where my father was stationed for five and a half years. Then in the fall of 1959, my father was stationed to a military base in France. My mother and I were able to go with him, but my brother had married so he had to stay behind. When my father wasn't working at the base, we did a lot of sightseeing over most of Europe. I was twelve and thirteen years old, and I remember the great places we visited. The overseas tour was supposed to be for three years, but my father suffered a heart attack, and he was grounded from his flying command. He was the base commander over his squadron, and his next assignment was a desk job, which my father didn't want. He'd been in the military for twenty-four years, so he decided it was time to retire. After thirteen months in France, we returned to the States and moved back to Memphis. He soon after retired. Like your mom, my mother said my father's first love was flying, and she was his second love!"

Sally continued. "I graduated from Whitehaven High School. I didn't really want to go to college. So I enrolled into a business college for one year, taking subjects for an IBM course. I guess this is where my life gets somewhat complicated also." Sally paused, preparing herself for what she was going to say next. "It was shortly after I graduated from business college that Collin, my husband, and I married. We had known each other in high school, dated for several years, and then married in 1966. We have been married thirteen years. We have two sons: Todd, who is seven years old, and Pace is six years old. Enough about me, though, I would like to know how and why you started driving truck? I believe there is good money in driving over-the-road, isn't there? How long have you been driving?"

Rusty scratched his head and thought for a few seconds before he answered. "I've been driving for about eleven years. In my junior year of college, I started driving part time for the company I worked for at that time, and then, due to other circumstances, I applied for a job at a truck lines and was hired on full time. Five years ago, I bought my own tractor and sort of became my own boss. Three years ago, I took the contract for the over-the-road run that I drive now, and I've never been sorry about it! When I'm not driving, I go home to my five-acre farm my dad gave me some years ago. It's just a half mile from my folks' farm. My log cabin is tucked away off the road in the woods. I have several horses, a couple of German shepherds, and some chickens, which my folks take care of when I'm away from home. I enjoy it, and I wouldn't give it up for anything now."

Sally was trying to visualize his description of his cabin and the countryside scenery. "Boy, that sounds beautiful. How I'd like to see a place that picturesque. I know you're proud of it, and I can understand why you wouldn't want to give it up."

"You know, Sally, I'd love for you to be able to see my place also. I think you'd like it. Say," Rusty said as he looked at his watch, "I guess I better get to truckin' on up the road. I'm so glad to have seen you, more than you know. I'd like to see you again, but I guess that's impossible, you being a married woman."

Oh, what Rusty didn't know. Sally longed to tell him her true feelings for him. "Rusty," she admitted, "I really would like to see you again, married woman or not. That is, if you really want to?" She held her breath for his answer. What would he say?

Rusty's eyes lit up at Sally's words. "Yes, I do! I'll be heading this way and should be in Memphis Sunday afternoon, hopefully around 3 p.m. I don't know that much about Memphis other than the interstate highways I travel. Where can we meet?"

After nearly gasping for breath at Rusty's reply, Sally began searching her mind for a good place to meet, thinking it must be someplace easy for Rusty and his rig to maneuver, yet someplace not too close to her home. She wouldn't want anyone who knows her to see her with another man. She clicked her fingers. "I've got it!" she announced. "As you are moving westbound into Memphis and about to get on I-240 West, you'll see a Summer Avenue exit. Get off there, and right across the street is a big mall. At the end of the mall's parking lot, there is one of those postal stations where one can go inside and buy stamps from a machine. You can meet me right beside it if that sounds OK to you?"

Rusty agreed with her suggestion. "I believe I can find it OK. Have your CB on and be listening for me in case I get lost," he suggested.

"I'll have my radio on, that's for sure! But you're going to find it just fine," Sally encouraged.

Rusty and Sally got up from the table together. Rusty paid for both his and her tabs for lunch, and they walked out the doors. He took her hand as they walked side-by-side toward her car. He opened the door of her car, turned to her, and looked deeply into her eyes. She sensed he wanted to say something important, but perhaps it wasn't the right time. Instead, he said, "I'll be looking forward to seeing you on Sunday. For me, that day won't get here soon enough! I'm so glad all of this has happened today because I thought I'd never see you again!"

Whatever it was that Rusty seemed like he wanted to say couldn't have been said any better than what he just said. "Rusty," Sally replied, "I need to pinch myself to make sure I'm not dreaming! Yes, it's really been great seeing you too, and I can hardly wait until Sunday to be able to see you again. You just be very careful going home. It's a long way to Connecticut. I'll be thinking of you all the time!"

Rusty leaned forward and kissed her on her cheek and said, "You'll never be more than a thought away from me either." As he turned and began walking away, he waved and reassured her he'd see her Sunday at about three o'clock.

Rusty and Sally drove off the truck stop's lot at the same time. He and his rig were in front of her, but he was going eastbound and she was going westbound. They talked on their CBs for a few miles, then his last fading words to her were that he would see her soon.

As Sally drove toward Memphis, she had such a stirring feeling inside of her that she hadn't had in a very long time. How great it was to not feel any sadness or depression, just utter happiness. She felt like a new, revived woman! This part of her dream had come true, and she couldn't wait to continue her dreams in five days.

Chapter Three

S ally thought the next five days were the longest days of her life, but finally Sunday had arrived. She was trying very hard to be her normal self and not act any differently, but inside she was excited and nervous at the same time. Even Collin remarked that she seemed different that day, happier or something. Sally thought, *It certainly isn't because of anything you've done!*

The weather had gotten pretty bad outside and had been that way for several days. A cold front was moving in from the northwest and causing snow in Missouri and Arkansas, but the northern states were getting their share of snow also. Sally hoped Rusty wasn't running into any of that mess. It scared her to think of it because she knew from several experiences that Collin had had with big rigs that snow and ice don't mix. She tried forcing the thought out of her mind.

After about the millionth time looking at the clock that day, it was finally time for Sally to leave for the mall and see Rusty. Collin and the boys were watching television, and she wouldn't be missed by leaving. She told Collin she was going out to do some shopping. He, for the first time in a long time, seemed concerned she was going out in such bad weather. He asked her if she couldn't put off the shopping until another day when it was not so nasty outside. She tried to be as cool as possible so as not to raise any suspicions in his mind. "I'll be very careful, and I won't be gone long." No more was said, and she bid them farewell as she walked out of the house. Sally was so glad Collin didn't have anything else to say about her not going out. She would not have known what to say. She truly didn't expect him to care; he never had before. And of all days for him to seem concerned about her. . . .

Getting into her car, Sally immediately turned on the CB and headed toward the interstate. There was lots of chatter on the CB about the weather conditions. One man was coming in from Nashville and was reporting that the weather and road conditions were getting bad and that the rain was turning into snow in northern Kentucky. "Oh no!" Sally gasped. She wasn't sure which route Rusty would take, but she wondered if he would be driving through Kentucky. *I do hope he is OK*, she thought.

Sally was nearly at the Summer Avenue exit when she called for the Farmer on the radio. The voice she so desperately needed to hear did not return in the CB speaker. She called again, but nothing.

As Sally turned off the interstate and headed to the mall, all kinds of thoughts were racing through her mind, everything from bad to worse. She had the mall parking lot in sight, then the postal station, but there wasn't a big burgundy rig parked there. She quickly glanced at her watch. *Ten minutes to three. I'm a little early. Maybe Rusty will be here in a few minutes,* she thought.

Sally drove into the mall lot and parked near the postal station. The rain was coming down hard, almost like hail on the car's windshield and roof. The wind was so strong she could feel the car rocking, and the outside temperature was dropping. Even though she had the defroster on in her car, the windows were fogging up, and she constantly kept wiping them off with her gloves as she frantically looked for Rusty's truck.

A half hour past the meeting time. An hour. Still no Rusty. Sally was becoming a nervous wreck, and the weather reports from CB-ers traveling on the roads were getting worse. Thoughts of what might have happened to Rusty took over her thoughts. *He's had an accident, or perhaps truck trouble, or maybe he changed his mind about wanting to see me again. Getting involved with a married woman might not be such a good idea after all. I sure hope the latter thought is not true*, she said to herself.

It was 4:15, and still no sign of Rusty nor a single word from him. Sally began to cry. What was she to do? Her faith in Rusty showing up was getting shaky, but she kept reminding herself to stay calm and not give up.

Suddenly and very faintly, she heard that wonderful northern-accented voice in the speaker of her radio. "Cricket, you got a copy? The Farmer's looking."

Sally grabbed the mic as she wiped the tears from her eyes and cleared her throat, hoping not to sound like she'd been crying. She excitedly answered, "You've got Cricket, Farmer. I'm so glad to hear your voice! What's your 20?"

"I'm so glad to hear your beautiful voice too! I'm turning here at the Summer Avenue exit now. In fact, I have my eyeballs on your car. I'll see you in a short-short, Baby."

All Sally could manage to say was "Roger that" in her choked-up voice as tears began to flow freely down her cheeks, and Rusty's truck came clearly into view.

Rusty parked his truck beside her car. Sally was already standing beside her car in the pouring rain, waiting for him to stop. She ran to him as he jumped from the cab of the tractor. She wrapped her arms around him as tight as she could, and he hugged her and picked her up off the ground. He whispered in her ear how much he missed her, and then he kissed her passionately.

Rain soaked through and through, they climbed into the cab of his truck. Rusty handed Sally a towel from the sleeper part of the cab to dry off her face, and then he helped her take her coat off. "I was becoming so worried about you, Rusty," she said as she took the towel and wiped his face, helping him out of his wet coat as well.

"There's lots and lots of bad weather out there. I was so afraid maybe you'd given up on me and left," Rusty answered.

Sally, now seated in the passenger seat, looked over to him and said, "Oh, Rusty, I would never have done that. I've waited five days to see and be with you. I was so afraid you'd been in an accident or maybe you'd changed your mind about seeing me again, thinking that was a bad decision."

"Sally, you're all I've thought about since the other day, and I wanted to see you with all my heart," Rusty confessed.

Sally began to cry, for those words meant so much to her, especially since they were coming from the one she cared very deeply for.

Rusty noticed her tears and said tenderly, "Hey, what's this? Isn't it bad enough it's pouring outside without it pouring in here too?"

Sally couldn't help it, though. She was so happy. Rusty put his arm around her and pulled her close to him. "Don't cry, Sweetheart. It's OK now," he said, trying to comfort her. He took her hand, and with his other hand he wiped her tear-stained face. He slid his hand down her cheek to her chin and pulled her even closer toward his slightly opened lips. His kiss was so warm and gentle. Sally put her arms around his neck and returned the kiss passionately. That kiss was telling her so much of Rusty's feelings for her, and she was hoping her kiss to him was telling him a lot too.

The two of them sat and talked a while, mostly about the weather. Every second was precious to them. Sally knew Rusty's time with her was limited because of his time schedule for his run, and the weather had already made him late.

They spent an hour together, and to them it seemed like only minutes. It was so hard for them to say good-bye to each other, but Rusty was coming back through Memphis again two days later, so they made plans to see each other again.

As Rusty followed Sally down the interstate on her way home, he told her on CB channel twenty-three, a less-used channel and one that's not so public, that she was wonderful, and he wanted to see her a lot more in the future. Sally's feelings were the same, and she told him so.

She waved good-bye to Rusty as she drove off the interstate and threw him a kiss. He waved and pulled the cord on his air horn. He told her on the CB the loud blast was the same as the word *good-bye*. They talked a few more moments until their voices became faint, but their last words to each other were "see ya Tuesday!"

As Sally drove the last mile to the house, she thought her feelings for Rusty were growing so much. Was it possible? Rusty was so great; did he feel the same way about her as she did for him? She certainly hoped so, and she believed he did!

With this newfound love, Sally's mind turned to something she hadn't thought about in years: birth control. During Sally's pregnancy with Pace, only three months after Todd was born, her health took several bad turns. She had morning sickness for four months, then terrible headaches, even a few blood clots that had to be treated. And she gained so much weight as well. When she was pregnant with Todd, she had no sickness and felt good the whole nine months.

It wasn't even until her eighth month of pregnancy when folks knew she was pregnant. But with Pace, Sally was miserable! It was all she could do to take care of Todd. Collin felt like he was being placed on the back burner, or he was on the outside looking in. Sally didn't feel like giving him too much attention. He became very restless and maybe even reckless. Sally wouldn't see him for several nights a week after her fifth month of pregnancy, and when he was home, he would rant in anger and complain all the time about not being able to make love to her.

Sally suspected Collin was seeing someone else when she found a condom in his pants pocket on wash day. She struggled with the thought of his unfaithfulness, but after Pace was born, Collin told her that he didn't want to take the chance of her getting pregnant again and that several months before Pace was born, he had gone to the doctor and had a vasectomy. Sally was surprised Collin had the surgery, but in a way, she was very relieved.

Sally needed to take protection into her own hands. The next morning after Todd and Pace went to school, she called her gynecologist to make an appointment for that day. She believed the timing was right to go on the pill. The doctor cautioned her to be careful for the first month, then after that, she would be protected from becoming pregnant. Sally didn't know if her relationship with Rusty would ever go all the way, but she thought about it. And if they ever did, she wanted to be able to relax without fear of getting pregnant.

The latter part of November, Sally was able to see Rusty three more times. He was so fun to be with, he had a wonderful personality, and Sally was falling deeper and deeper in love with him each time they were together.

Pace turned seven years old on November 19th, and on November 30th, Todd was excited to be eight years old. Sally made sure their birthdays were happy and memorable. Collin did not show too much enthusiasm in his sons turning another year older. He didn't seem to care.

Collin's mother, Mrs. Oldham, invited the family to come to her home for Thanksgiving, but Collin could not come because of work.

It was hard for Sally to believe that when she turned the calendar page over to December, Christmas was less than a month away! The year was flying by.

Chapter Four

The month of December was passing quickly, as did six meetings between Rusty and Sally. Each time the two met, their love for each other grew stronger and deeper, although neither one of them had said that it was. Sally was so happy, and she could tell Rusty was too. *When was the time to say, 'I love you'?* Sally wondered. She never thought she could love anyone so much. Yes, Collin was her first love and her only love until Rusty came into her life. She just didn't feel like she fit into Collin's life anymore. What was she to do?

The Christmas spirit was in the air, and many holiday shoppers were at the mall. Rusty had a harder time maneuvering around the mall parking lot with his big rig because of so many vehicles, but he managed. Their time together was limited that day due to a problem with Rusty's load. It was a "hot" load, which meant it was needed in Abilene as soon as possible. Sally understood the situation—hated it, but understood. A little time with Rusty was better than none at all. Within thirty minutes of arrival at the mall, Rusty and Sally were back on the highways and byways.

"This traffic is terrible, Rusty. Please be very careful. Some people drive so crazy and take unnecessary chances," Sally remarked.

Rusty replied, "I will. You be careful too. Hopefully the traffic will be better in three days. Look forward to seeing you then. I'll miss you in the meantime!"

"I'll be missing you too, Rusty," she answered.

Rusty pulled the cord on his truck's air horn, and Sally threw him a kiss and a wave as they departed in different directions. The ride to her house was just a few short miles, but it gave her time to think about her time with Rusty. It was wonderful, and so was he.

As Sally drove into the driveway of her house, she almost dreaded going inside. If it weren't for Todd and Pace, she could so easily just leave because there was nothing keeping her there.

When Sally walked into the house, Collin was watching television, as usual, but the look he gave her was one of daggers. Without even a "hello," Collin immediately questioned, "What in the world took you so long, and where have you been?"

Sally turned to him and said sarcastically, "Since when do you care? For your information, it's getting near Christmastime, and I've been out looking for toys and gifts so it will be a nice Christmas for the boys and other members of this family!" Sally hadn't meant to come on so strong and lose her temper, but never before had he questioned her on how long she had been gone or where she'd been. That was very unusual.

Sally walked off into the kitchen, trying to act unphased by their conversation. She reached into the refrigerator to get the pot full of homemade spaghetti she had made the night before. As she turned to put the pot on the stove to warm for supper, Collin appeared, standing between her and the stove. He was staring at her with a look that could kill. He took the spaghetti pot from her hands and sat it on the stove. He then turned to her, put his hands on her shoulders, squeezing rather tightly, then calmly but directly asked her, "Who is it?"

"Who is who, Collin?" Sally replied as innocently as she could.

"I want to know who it is that you've been seeing. You go out for hours, supposedly shopping, but yet you come home empty-handed. Come on, Sally. I wasn't born yesterday!" Collin yelled.

"Collin, I don't know what you're talking about. Now let go, you're hurting me!" Sally spoke loudly, but she panicked at the thought that maybe Collin had found out about Rusty. Could someone have seen Rusty and her together and told him?

Having heard the commotion in the kitchen, the boys ran from their bedroom to find out what was going on. Collin and Sally hardly ever raised their voices at each other; perhaps that was because they saw very little of each other, but also Collin always seemed so disinterested in the family.

Pace, the younger of the two boys, grabbed his daddy's arm, trying to pull it away from his mother. "Let go of Momma! You're making her cry!" Pace yelled.

Collin released Sally's shoulders and raised his hand to swing down to hit his son, but a loud knock came to the front door of their home. Instead of Collin striking Pace, he grabbed Pace's little arm, shook him, and said very sternly, "You stay out of this. It's just between your mother and me."

Todd reluctantly opened the front door. It was his friend, Tommy, from next door, wanting him to come outside. He turned to see if his parents objected, and then he bolted out the door with Pace right behind him.

Sally could see the boys were relieved to be away from their argument. She wished she was too! She didn't know what was going to happen next, but trying to remain calm, she went right on preparing supper.

Collin re-entered the kitchen and laughed. "Well, you may think you're getting away with seeing another man, but you're not. The least you could do is tell me so I could start seeing another woman."

Sally turned to Collin with a glare. "That's about right. If I were seeing another man, or you really thought I was, just to get even with me, you'd go out and find another woman instead of trying to find out what's going wrong with our marriage."

Sally had no sooner said those words when Collin grabbed his coat and walked toward the front door.

Sally shouted, "Where do you think you're going?"

"Out . . . to do some shopping!" Collin yelled and slammed the door behind him.

Sally just stood and stared out the window in her living room and watched Collin drive away. She was beside herself. She was shocked and somewhat numb. Collin had never acted like that before. She wondered what could have prompted Collin's strange behavior. She returned to the kitchen and continued warming the pot of spaghetti.

A few minutes later, Sally heard the front door open. She looked around the corner of the kitchen to see who was coming in, thinking it might be Collin, but it was Todd and Pace.

"We saw Dad leave," Todd said. "Where did he go? He sure was mad!"

"I'm not sure where he is going, but he'll probably be home in a little while," Sally said trying to reassure the boys that all was OK. "Y'all go wash your hands. Supper is almost ready."

Supper was good, and the boys just chattered away like they have always done. Then they took their baths, put on their PJs, and sat down to watch television.

The evening was passing by, and Collin had not returned home. Sally was becoming concerned and thought about calling his mother, but she thought better about making that call. She did not want to alarm his mother to their argument and Collin leaving the house. Besides, Collin may have gone to his mother's home, and if that was the case, then she already knew about the argument between Collin and her.

"OK, boys, it's time for bed," Sally announced.

"But Dad's not home yet. You said he'd be back. I wonder where he is, Mom. Has he called you?" Todd questioned.

Sally answered with hope in her voice. "No, he has not called, but maybe he will soon. You know, he might have just gone on to work. I bet that's what he's done."

Sally followed her sons to their bedroom, tucked them in, gave them their good night hugs and kisses, and recited their nightly saying, "Y'all sleep tight, and don't let the bedbugs bite. I love y'all bunches."

Sally returned to the living room and sat down on the couch. She wondered, *What is going on? Why hasn't Collin returned home? Why hasn't he at least called? Where could he be? His actions were so out of character!* She didn't know what to do. Her thoughts were consumed more by Collin than Rusty in that moment.

About midnight, Sally gave up hope that Collin would come back home, and she went to bed. Her bed seemed lonelier than normal, and sleep alluded her for the longest time. After tossing and turning many times, she finally drifted off to sleep, only to be awakened by the alarm clock at 6 a.m. the next morning.

Sleepily, she rose up, slipped on her robe, and ambled slowly to the kitchen to prepare the coffee to brew. Then she made her way to the boys' bedroom.

"It's time to rise and shine," she announced as she walked to their clothes closet to choose the school clothes they would wear that day.

"Is Dad home?" Todd mumbled as he was waking up.

"No, Todd, he isn't," his mother replied softly. "Please help Pace get up while I go and get breakfast started."

Sally tried to put her heart into preparing their breakfast, but the enthusiasm wasn't there. She felt like she was just going through the motions—scrambling the eggs, cooking the grits, and toasting the bread. The boys entered the kitchen all dressed for school, poured their milk in their glasses, and took their places at the table as their mother served them their breakfast.

One could hear a pin drop. Everyone and everything was so quiet. It was very unusual that Todd and Pace were not talking about one thing or another. The air was so thick, it could be cut with a knife.

"Mom, are you OK?" Todd broke the silence.

"No, I'm very concerned about your dad," Sally answered. "But I'm sure he is OK, just busy at work." She tried to sound convincing. "Since y'all are finished with your breakfast, please go brush your teeth so I can take you two to school."

The boys obeyed their mother. Sally cleared the table of the dishes and placed them in the kitchen sink to be washed. Something she would do after she took them to school. She placed food items in the boys' lunch boxes and walked out of the kitchen. After Todd and Pace had brushed their teeth, it was time to go. They slipped on their coats, put their hats on their heads, and slid their gloves on their hands.

It was a cold, December day, and the north wind was blowing, which made it feel even colder. Once they were in the car, Sally started the engine and backed out of the driveway. After a few blocks, the heater in the car began warming them up from the bitter cold. In less than ten minutes, they had arrived at school, and Sally told her little sons, "Good-bye, and have a good day. See y'all later." She watched them walk to the school door, wave, and throw a kiss, and then they disappeared as the doors closed behind them.

Sally returned home, hoping to find Collin home from work, but in her hopefulness, he was still not there. She was really becoming concerned. *Where is he?* she wondered. *OK, should I call his mom? I don't really want to,* she said to herself. *What do I do? What should I do? Maybe nothing! Collin started this mess . . . or did he? Is she to blame? Maybe . . . or maybe not!* So many questions were going round and round in her head.

I know what I'll do, Sally told herself. *I'll do the dishes and clean up the kitchen, then I'll decide.*

After Sally's work was done, she grabbed her winter coat, put it on, and out the front door she went. She had decided to spend the whole day shopping.

Christmas was two weeks away, and gifts from Santa needed to be bought. She would not come home "empty-handed!"

The day was full of going to one store after another. Sally found some bargains and plenty of good buys. She felt good about saving some money on sale items and loved those *buy one, get one free* sales.

When she picked the boys up from school, they were most inquisitive as to what all was in the many bags that were in the back seat of the car. The "Santa gifts" were stored away in the trunk of the car, so the boys had no idea of the rest of the *good stuff* she had bought.

Once home, right away they noticed that their dad's car was not in the driveway. Todd said in a concerned voice, "I wonder why Dad is not coming home. Mom, what happened between you and Dad?"

Sally hesitated before she answered, thinking seriously how to respond to his question. "Well, Todd, I think your dad believes I'm away from home too much and wonders where I go when I am away. Your dad and I are just having some husband and wife problems that we are trying to get worked out. Hopefully we'll get it settled soon. Your dad leaving is part of trying to make our lives better." She wondered if what she said made any sense, and, more importantly, did it make any sense to *him*? Todd was so young; could he understand?

The boys helped their mom bring all the bags from the back seat of the car into the house. Sally asked the boys to put the bags in her bedroom. Once they were secured there, the boys placed their backpacks on the dining room table, opened them up, and began their homework while their mother began preparing supper in the kitchen.

The telephone rang.

Sally dropped the stirring spoon in the sink and ran to answer the telephone, anticipating the call was from Collin. "Hello?" she answered.

The voice on the other end of the call replied, "Hi, my dear. I haven't talked to y'all in a while and thought I'd call. How are all of you doing?" Mrs. Oldham said.

Sally was stunned, almost fearful to talk. "Hi, Peggy. How thoughtful of you to call. We're doing OK. How are you?" Sally was trying to sound cheerful but wondered why she was really calling. Had Collin informed her of their argument, and was Peggy interceding a call to her on Collin's behalf to check on them? Perhaps she shouldn't have such a suspicious mind!

"I'm doing fine. Just getting in from work and thought I'd give y'all a call. Is Collin home or is he still at work? I can never keep up with his changing work hours."

OK, where is this conversation heading? Sally asked herself. "I thought he might be with you, Peggy. Have you talked to him?" Sally asked.

"No, he isn't with me, and I have not talked to him. Why do you ask?" Peggy replied innocently enough.

Sally wanted to believe her, but then where was Collin? "Peggy, Collin and I had a disagreement yesterday, and he left the house very upset. I have not seen nor heard from him. I had hoped you would have." Sally wondered if she should have told Peggy about the situation.

"No, I haven't. I'm very sorry to hear about the problem. Are you and the boys OK? I know you are very worried about him. This is not like Collin! Have you called his work?" Peggy asked cautiously.

Why hadn't Sally called Collin's work? Shouldn't that have been something she should have done? She honestly hadn't thought of it, or maybe she didn't want to. The argument with Collin was not of her making, and she sure didn't tell Collin to leave the house. Peggy was right, the situation was not like Collin. He had never acted like he had yesterday.

"No, I haven't called his work. I thought that when Collin calmed down, cooled off, and realized leaving the house was not a good idea, he would come home or at least call," Sally responded.

Peggy was silent for a moment, then said, "I don't mean to interfere, but please let me know if there is anything I can do. And please, keep me in your thoughts as I will keep you and the boys in my thoughts. I hope Collin will be home soon and you two can mend this hurt and make up." Peggy sounded sincere.

Sally and Peggy said their good-byes, and the call ended. Sally continued to stand in place with the telephone's handset still in her hand, wondering what to do next. She slowly replaced the handset on the base of the telephone and made her way back to the kitchen to resume preparing supper for her and the boys.

"Who was that on the phone, Mom?" Todd asked.

"It was your Grandmother Peggy," Sally replied.

"Had she talked to Dad?" Todd inquired.

"No, she had not," Sally answered. Changing the subject, she suggested to her young fellas, "What do y'all think about setting up the Christmas tree tonight and doing some decorating?"

Almost at the same time, the boys replied joyfully, "YESSSSSSS!"

After supper, the table cleared and dishes done, Sally took the stepladder from the hall closet and placed it below the attic opening in the hallway ceiling. The boys held the ladder for her as she stepped up several steps, removed the covering from the attic opening, then took a few more steps to put half of her body through the attic opening. She looked around the attic area to find the Christmas boxes. Usually Collin would do this, but she had seen him do it several times, and she sort of knew what to do. He made it look so easy, but she found it wasn't as easy as he made it look. She took another step up higher and was able to lift her body up to the edge of the opening.

After sitting at the opening for a few moments, she exclaimed, "I see the boxes!" Then she disappeared from their sight.

"Momma, are you OK?" Pace squealed in a high-pitched voice.

Even though Sally was out of sight, the boys heard their mother say she was OK. As the boys concentrated their eyes on the attic opening, they heard noises. Then their mother said, "OK, look out below. Here comes a box!" Sally lowered box after box through the ceiling hole until all the Christmas boxes were gathered. She began the feat of putting herself through the opening and climbing back down the ladder. It wasn't easy, but she accomplished the task and was thrilled she had done it. Her sons were such a terrific help. She could not have done it without them.

Todd and Pace were eager to get the Christmas boxes open and begin decorating. The tree was first and looked beautiful when Todd pressed the button to turn on the lights of their finished project. They placed a few more decorations around and admired how pretty the house looked.

"OK, boys, it's past time for bed. Please, go brush your teeth and put on your PJs. I'll be in your bedroom in a minute to tuck y'all in," Sally instructed.

When Sally walked into their bedroom, she found Pace crying. "What's the matter, Baby Son? Why are you crying?" She sat down on the bottom bunk beside him and took him in her arms.

"I miss my daddy," he sobbed.

"I know, so do I," Sally said softly, hugging him tightly. "It'll be OK. Hopefully he will be home soon."

By then, Todd had climbed down from his top bunk and sat beside his mother. He stated, fighting back tears, "I miss him too. He has always helped us put up the Christmas tree. Where is he? I want him to come home!" He cried in Sally's arms.

Sally laid down in Pace's bed and gathered her sons next to her with her arms wrapped around them until they fell asleep. She was heartbroken for her little guys.

Sally gently rose from Pace's bed, trying not to disturb the sleeping boys. She remembered she needed to get all the Christmas toys from the trunk of her car. She slipped on her coat and opened the front door quietly. When she stepped onto the front porch, the cold wind took her breath away. *Could be frosty in the morning,* she remarked to herself. She had to make several trips to and from the car to retrieve all the special gifts. Once back in the house, she hid the bags in her closet for safekeeping.

It had been quite a busy day, and Sally was tired, but there was one more thing she needed to do—or that she should do. She closed the boys' bedroom door and walked to the telephone. She tried to convince herself that the next thing she was about to do was the right thing. She dialed Collin's work telephone number and waited. The telephone rang four times.

"BEDON Warehouse," a male voice answered.

"Yes, could I speak to Collin Oldham, please?" Sally asked.

"Sure, hold on a minute," he said as the telephone made a cling sound as if the handset had been set on something metal. Sally tried to plan her words for when Collin answered. Nervously she waited.

"Ma'am?"

"Yes?"

"I'm sorry, but I'm being told Collin is out on a run tonight. Can I take a message for him?" the man asked.

Stunned by his reply, yet relieved, she answered, "No, but thank you anyway." She slowly replaced the telephone's handset on its base. Not moving, Sally wondered, *Was Collin there and refused to accept her call, or was he really out on a run?*

That question continued to swirl around in her head as she got ready for bed. As she laid her head on her pillow, she convinced herself that she had made the right decision to call Collin at work. Whether he was there or not, she will never know, but the call was a good thing. She then allowed her thoughts to be flooded with visions of Rusty. How she longed to see and be with him.

The next day was much like the day before. Still no news from or about Collin, and the boys went to school. Sally removed the shopping bags from her closet and chose which colorful wrapping paper to use to wrap the gifts. She gathered up tape, ribbons, bows, and scissors, and began the holiday tradition.

The day passed quickly for Sally. When the boys entered the house from school, they were pleasantly surprised to see all the wrapped presents under the Christmas tree.

"Gee, Mom, you've been busy! It all looks so Christmassy!" Todd expressed.

The boys got down on their hands and knees to look for their names on the name tags stuck to each gift.

"That's my name!" exclaimed Pace. "Here's one for you, Todd."

It was great to see the boys happy and excited. That helped Sally feel some joy too.

Chapter Five

T he evening before was good for Sally and her sons. Todd and Pace had fun trying to guess what their gifts were under the Christmas tree. But by nighttime, there was no relief for Sally as to where Collin was; he sure wasn't at home, nor had he even called his family.

Sally woke to the sound of music playing from her alarm clock, and it was time to put her tootsies on the floor again. But this morning brought new and good feelings for her. In a few short hours, she would be in her lover's arms. She wondered, *Is it wrong to feel excited about being with Rusty when Collin is behaving the way he is? Well, now, wait a minute! Didn't Collin say when he so abruptly left three days ago that he was going to go find another woman? Maybe he is in the arms of another woman!* With that thought, Sally straightened herself up, put on a no-guilt mindset, and proceeded with her morning routine.

Todd and Pace were up, and breakfast had been prepared and eaten. While the boys brushed their teeth, Sally packed their lunchboxes, and then they were out the front door. The windshield was very frosty, and it took Sally a few minutes to scrape off the icy mess, but she still managed to get her sons to school on time.

Once she arrived back home, Sally cleaned up the kitchen, showered, and dressed in clothes that she hoped would be pleasing to Rusty. She always wanted to look nice for him. She glanced at the wall clock in the living room. *Time to go!* She slipped into her coat and closed the front door behind her. As she walked to her car, her eyes scanned her surroundings for anything that looked out of place. Could Collin be watching her? Nothing looked unusual. She got in her car, started the engine, and backed out of the driveway. Driving slowly to see if any vehicle moved near her on the street, she felt paranoid and foolish at the same time. She saw nothing suspicious as she turned the corner onto the main street.

Before she drove too far, she turned the knob on for the CB. A lot of chatter sounded from its speaker.

"Good morning, Cricket. I just passed you on the street," came a voice.

Sally recognized the voice. "Good morning, Minnie Mouse! How are you?"

"I'm good. I haven't seen or heard from you in a while. You OK?" Minnie Mouse inquired.

"Yes, I'm OK, just busy with the upcoming holidays. How's Firecracker? Been busy?" Sally continued.

"Oh, he's doing fair. He's been driving in a lot of bad weather up north, and he's thinking about taking off work until the New Year. Oh, I'm about to lose you. Merry Christmas! Hope to see ya soon." Minnie Mouse's words were trailing off.

"Y'all have a Merry Christmas too!" Sally said, not knowing if Minnie Mouse could hear her response. It had been a while since she last visited with Minnie Mouse, but ever since she started spending time with Rusty, Sally wasn't out and about or on the CB as much as she had been.

As Sally was nearing the mall, she heard Rusty's voice. Oh, he sounded so good. How she had missed him!

"Go ahead; you've got Cricket," Sally answered into the CB mic.

"What's your 20, Little Lady?" asked the Farmer.

"Around the corner from you, Farmer. I have my eyeball on ya!" Sally announced.

"I see you now too!" the Farmer replied.

Still a little cautious about her surroundings, Sally glanced one more time in her rearview mirror to make sure she was not being followed. All looked OK as she drove beside Rusty's truck. Excitement leaped inside her as she saw him standing outside his truck. She stopped her car, jumped out, and ran into his open arms. He embraced her tenderly, and their love spilled over for each other into a very passionate kiss. Rusty helped her into the cab of his truck, and immediately they made their way into the sleeper area where their kissing continued.

"Oh, it's so good to see you, honey. I have missed you so much. I have come to the conclusion that I miss you more and more when we're apart," Rusty confessed.

"Rusty, dear, I feel the same way," Sally agreed as she looked into his dreamy powder-blue eyes.

"So how have you been, Sally?" Rusty asked.

Sally hesitated.

"What's wrong, sweetheart?" Rusty asked, taking her hands in his.

"When I came home from seeing you last time, Collin accused me of seeing another man. He started yelling at me, demanding me to tell him who I was seeing! He has never acted like that before. I thought he was going to hit me. He was so angry. If it hadn't been for someone knocking at the front door, I don't know what he would have done or, what more, what he would have said. But after Todd answered the door, Collin put on his coat and left the house, saying *he could find another woman too*. That was three days ago, and I have not heard from or seen him," Sally explained in tears.

Rusty took her in his arms and held her tightly. "Oh, honey, I'm so sorry, but I'm very glad he did not hurt you. How do you think he found out about us? What can I do?" Rusty attempted to make her feel better. He was concerned. He knew she was concerned too and perhaps confused about what she was feeling.

"Do you remember when we met at the truck stop last month, and you were asking me lots of questions about my life?" Rusty inquired.

"Yes, I do," Sally admitted.

"And I told you I had reached a point in my life's story that I had rather not get into because it was complicated?" Rusty continued.

"Yes. . . ."

"Well, this seems like a good time to tell you," he began. "Late in my freshman year of college, I met who I thought was a wonderful and beautiful girl. Her name was Holly. It was almost like love at first sight for me. When we were together, it was like heaven, and I never wanted to leave her after each date. I remember I dreaded to see the spring semester end at college because I had promised my dad I would come home for the summer and work on the farm, doing some special projects we had planned to do together. My dad and I had made these plans before Holly and I met, but I was so crazy about her I wanted to spend every minute I could with her. Fortunately, after school was out, she moved back home with her parents in Waterbury, which was only twenty miles away, so we still saw a lot of each other that summer."

Rusty continued. "I was so proud of her, and I wanted my mom and dad to like her too. Several times that summer, I brought her to my home, and I thought the visits with my folks went smoothly, but I found out later that they didn't go as smoothly as I thought. I guess I was so in love with her, I really couldn't see the true person she was. However, I did enjoy being around her parents. They reminded me of an old-fashioned couple who wanted the best for their little girl. Of course, I knew I was the right man for their Holly, and I treated her the best way I knew how. Her folks were a well-to-do family. Her father was the owner and president of the largest chemical factory in the area. Sure, they had lots of money, but I wasn't interested in Holly for her money." Rusty paused for a moment. "Am I boring you, Sally?" he asked.

"No, not at all, Rusty. Please continue," Sally encouraged.

"OK. Well, the fall semester started at Danbury, and we both enrolled as sophomores. There was hardly a night that went by that we weren't together studying or eating dinner or just being together. I wanted to marry her, and I talked to my mom and dad about it. They never said *no*, but they did ask me to wait a while and get to know her better. I didn't understand what they meant, and I got hot-headed about it and told them I knew her well enough, and I was going to buy an engagement ring that day, give it to her that night, and plan a Christmas wedding—which was only three months away. My mom cried. I thought it was because of my temper. I had never spoken to my folks that way before. I wanted and needed encouragement from them. I just wish I had listened to them.

"But anyway, Holly and I became engaged. We were so happy, at least I was. Several weeks before our wedding day, Holly's father approached me about going to work for him. He explained it would be a good job with good hours after school and good pay. I accepted his job offer because the part-time job I had in Danbury was paying very little, and with added responsibilities of a wife and family, the extra money would be needed." Rusty stopped, needing to collect his thoughts.

"The big day came. It was a huge wedding; at least five hundred people attended. The honeymoon at Niagara Falls was a blast. Upon our return, Holly insisted on us living in her folks' summer house instead of getting a place of our own. She said it would save money. The summer house was part of the ten acres Holly's father owned and was lavishly furnished and beautifully landscaped, even with a swimming pool. I agreed to live in the house for a while. The idea of saving money was most attractive. We only had one car, and since Holly and I were traveling farther to school and my job, Holly's parents bought us—really *her*—a new car. They said it was a wedding gift!" Rusty looked into Sally's eyes. "You OK? You want me to go on?"

"I'm OK. Tell me more about Holly," Sally insisted.

"We finished our sophomore year of college, and I went to work full time for Holly's dad for the summer. I worked eight to ten hours a day, and the summer was over before I realized it. I didn't see my folks much at all after the wedding. Of course, my dad wasn't wild about the idea of my job with Holly's dad because it took time away from us working together, but he tried to understand. I tried to call them often, but I had no idea how much I was hurting them. And because of more and more social events most every weekend, I hardly even saw Holly. It upset me that she was gone so much, but I tried to accept it since her family was so well-to-do and was used to being in the social limelight. Holly invited me to go with her very few times, which was OK with me. I didn't care much about being with all those high-class folks anyway. I found out later that Holly was glad I didn't go to those parties and other gatherings. How did I know our marriage was already on the rocks?"

Sally's curiosity mounted as she listened intently to Rusty.

"Holly and I returned to Danbury College that fall for our junior year. I wasn't real sure how either one of us passed our sophomore year, but we did. I went back to working part time, but after several weeks, I realized the pay wasn't going to be enough to make ends meet. Holly had become somewhat of a drinker, and she went on too many shopping sprees. We began to get into many arguments about both situations. I wanted to be fair about her wanting new clothes, but she was buying outfits from the finest shops that cost way more than they needed to. She kept telling me she had to look nice for all the parties she was invited to and that her daddy and mommy would be very upset and ashamed of her if her husband didn't buy her decent clothes to wear to all the events she had to attend. Needless to say, I hit the ceiling and told her to stay home. That way she wouldn't have to worry about the darn clothes! But my words were all in vain, for she continued going to parties and wearing expensive clothes. I often thought I'd go to some of those parties when I was least expected to, just to see what went on, but then I'd feel guilty about doing such a thing, so I wouldn't go. I trusted Holly. What a fool I was!"

He continued. "I switched a few of my college classes around so I could extend my hours at work as much as possible, and it was then that I started driving trucks. One evening, I was asked by the foreman in the warehouse to go with one of the new drivers to a location in the city. Watching the driver operate that rig was fascinating, and the idea of driving a truck got the best of me. So the next day, I asked the foreman if someone would train me in driving and operating a tractor trailer. Within an hour, I was learning! It was exciting, and I really enjoyed it—and still do. In two weeks, I had my commercial driver's license and was making short runs out of town several days a week. When Holly found out I was driving a truck, she was overjoyed because that meant more money for her to spend!"

Rusty added, "I guess one of the final events that broke our marriage happened Thanksgiving Day when I pressed Holly to go with me to see and visit my mom and dad. I had promised my mom we would share the day with them. When we arrived, my folks greeted us at their front door with open arms. Holly was unfriendly and rude to them, and she knew I was not happy about her attitude. Mom had dinner ready, but before we sat down to eat, she said that she and dad had a wonderful surprise for us. Mom handed us our coats, and Dad directed us to his car. We drove about a half mile down the road from their home and turned off onto a small, newly-cut gravel road that led off into the woods on the east side of Dad's farm. He stopped the car just short of what looked like a clearing ahead and asked us to walk the remainder of the way. As we walked into the clearing, there stood a beautifully built, large, log cabin. Once inside, we saw a large living room with a stone fireplace, a huge country kitchen, three bedrooms, and two baths. All the conveniences of home. We then stepped out into a screened patio where we saw in the distance a corral and a red barn. My mom explained that my dad had worked on building the structures for hours, both day and night since early spring, to be able to have it ready for us to move into for our one-year anniversary, which was the following month. I could hardly believe it. It was a wonderful surprise and just what Holly and I needed: a place of our own. I hugged my mom and dad and told them I couldn't thank them enough for all they had done. But Holly's reaction was less than positive. She showed no enthusiasm, no gratitude, and just turned and walked back to the car. I was so angry! I felt instant disdain toward her. I realized then the mistake I had made in marrying her. The hurt in my mom and dad's eyes was a stab in my heart. I would make sure it would never happen again."

Rusty paused. "You OK?" he asked Sally.

"Yes, but I am so sorry. How horrible!" Sally anguished for Rusty. "So what happened?"

"Well, I deeply expressed to my folks how sorry I was for Holly's terrible attitude, and we left. For days, Holly and I did not speak to each other. That Christmas and our anniversary came and went, unnoticed. Holly did as she pleased; there was no stopping her. I tried my best to continue with school and work. I began driving longer hours and farther distance runs. Holly and I hardly saw each other, and that's the way we both wanted it. The dreams I had had for us a year earlier had turned into nightmares. Our love had turned to loathing. I wanted to divorce her, but I continued to hold on to the hope that things would change and be like it had been when we were first married. However, before I moved to the log cabin, I came home from work on New Year's Day at about one o'clock in the morning. The summer house was dark, and I walked quietly to our bedroom. I heard faint sounds, and when I turned on the light, to my shock, Holly and some other man were in *our* bed! I didn't want to believe that was happening, but there it was, right in front of me! I turned off the light, walked out of the house, and drove to my folks' house. I was so humiliated, hurt, mad, and distraught. I didn't want to believe it."

Looking down, feeling the old heartache rushing back to him, Rusty continued. "The very next morning, I went to see an attorney and filed for divorce, and I quit working for Holly's dad the same day. Four months later, it was final. I bought furniture for the log cabin and moved in where it was quite comfortable and ever so quiet. I needed to be alone and have time to get my head back on straight. I tried to concentrate on school. I finally finished my junior year, but I barely passed. I had had enough of school! During those last five months, I hadn't done much driving. I began to realize how much I missed it, and in June, I applied for a driving job at one of the local truck lines. I was hired right on the spot and started to work that same day."

Rusty raised his eyes to meet Sally's. "The rest of the story you know. I wanted to tell you about Holly a long time ago, but I've come to realize how much I really love you, so I want you to know everything there is to know about me. I've had feelings for you ever since that first time I talked to you on the CB radio—you and your ponytail," Rusty said with a smirk. "But I thought that was crazy. I didn't even know you, and there could have been a big possibility I would never see you again. However, fate dictated our paths otherwise, and I'm so happy it did. Having said all that, I want to tell you I understand your concern for Collin. My concern for Holly and our marriage after that Thanksgiving Day was constant. I was so confused, and I didn't know what to do. It was driving me out of my mind. I had hoped so much we could have worked out our problems, but I had done all I knew to do, and Holly made no effort to change the destiny of our doomed marriage. Maybe that's the way it is with you and Collin. You've tried to set things right and let him know things are not good in your marriage, but he hasn't listened. What do you think he will do next, Sally?"

Sally was overcome with emotion. She had often wondered about that time in his life that he was so mysterious about, so she was relieved that he felt safe and close enough to her to share that part of him. But she was even more overcome by the fact that she had just heard those previous words that she had so longed for him to say. *He loved her.* She could hardly believe her ears.

Sally reached for his hands. "Rusty, I'm so sorry for what Holly did to you and for the terrible way your relationship ended. You tried your best to make your marriage work, and that's all you could have done. Love can be confusing, and situations and decisions related to it can be so difficult. Yes, I seem to be in a similar situation now in my marriage. I don't know what to do, and I don't know what the future holds with me and Collin. But one thing I do know is that I love you too," she said as she began to cry. "Please hold me," she pleaded.

Rusty took Sally in his arms. "I'll hold you, sweetheart, until the end of time." He held her face close to his and kissed her with a soft and gentle kiss. He laid her tenderly on the sleeper bed and poured out his love for her.

Time was slipping away, and Rusty, as reluctant as he was to leave Sally in the situation she was in with Collin, had to be truckin' on down the road. However, he told Sally that he would stay over a day or two if she wanted him to, just in case Collin tried to hurt her, but she insisted on him going on and that she'd be OK.

"Rusty," Sally began, "would it be OK if I gave you my phone number? I believe I would feel better if you have a way to call me if you need to."

"I think that would be an excellent idea," Rusty agreed. "I wish there was a way for you to call me."

"Yes, me too," Sally agreed. She wrote her phone number down on a piece of paper Rusty had in his truck cab.

"Thank you," Rusty said as he took the paper and put it in his shirt pocket.

"You got to go, Rusty. I don't want you to, but I'll see you in two days. I love you, and please be careful," Sally said as she leaned toward him and kissed him one last time. They both got out of the truck and walked toward Sally's car, and Sally got inside.

"I love you too, and you be careful. See you on Friday, sweetheart," Rusty replied as he closed her car door.

With tears in her eyes, Sally watched him climb into the cab of his truck. Rusty followed her out of the mall parking lot and onto the interstate. As she turned off the interstate at Exit 20, she heard his air horn, and she threw him a kiss and a wave as he passed her car. Their voices faded on their CBs as miles came between the two of them.

Sally picked up her sons from school, and they spent a quiet evening together. Collin had not called nor come home. The uncertainty of his absence was haunting her, but her wonderful thoughts of the time spent with Rusty that day warmed her body and took over the daunting absence of Collin.

The next morning, after Sally had taken the boys to school, she was drinking her second cup of coffee while reading the *Help Wanted* classified ads from that morning's newspaper when the telephone rang. She answered it and recognized the voice on the other end. A flash of surprise and relief passed through her body. It was Collin! He said he was at work and that he had been out of town on a run. He told Sally that he was sorry for the way he acted and the horrible things he said to her. He knew she was a faithful wife, and the few days that he'd been away from her and the boys he had realized how much his family meant to him. He apologized and asked Sally to forgive him.

Sally was stunned, but she couldn't help but feel callous at his apology. She was suspicious and wondered if he was telling her the truth or if he just felt bad for disappearing. Her heart was not in a forgiving mood.

"Well, Collin," she began, contemplating what to say in return, "the boys have missed you, and I've been concerned about where you have been. Seriously, no telephone calls? You hurt us, Collin, but I want to believe you when you say you have realized your family means a lot to you. If you really mean that, then I accept your apology," she said half-heartedly.

"Thank you, Sally. Would it be OK if I come home today? I asked my boss if I could go back to my day shift, and he agreed. I want to spend more time with you and the boys at night."

Sally tried to comprehend what Collin had just told her. Should she say *yes*? He could come home? Was Collin really saying he wanted to spend more time with her and his family? That's a drastic change! "OK, Collin. We'll see you soon," she replied.

"Thank you, sweetheart. I love you!" Collin said gratefully. The call ended.

Sally had to sit down. *What just happened?* she asked herself. Collin's words echoed in her mind: *I love you, and I know you're a faithful wife.* Oh boy, what a mess! She did not expect this at all. Her love for Rusty was real, and he cared deeply for her too. She just couldn't turn away from him. But what if Collin was sincere about improving their marriage? What would she do, and how would she handle this? What if it came down to choosing between Collin and Rusty? What would she do? *Well, I guess I would stay with Collin, for the boys. But on the other hand . . . oh, I need to quit this! All I'm doing is getting myself frustrated over things that haven't happened yet! I'll just have to cross that bridge when I get there.*

A few hours later, Collin came home as he said he would and brought with him a dozen beautiful red roses for Sally. She was very surprised. She walked to the kitchen to place them in a vase, and Collin followed her, put his arms around her waist, and told her again how sorry he was about his actions and what he said a few days prior.

"I love you, Sally, and I don't ever want us to quarrel again," he said in a kind voice. He then turned her around to face him and kissed her passionately.

All Sally could see, think, and feel was Rusty.

Todd and Pace were in the backyard throwing a ball back and forth to each other. They suddenly stopped when they saw their dad through the back window, and they ran toward the door. Collin opened it, and the boys jumped into his arms.

"Oh, Dad, you're home! We have missed you so much!" yelled Todd as he hugged his dad tightly.

Pace chimed in and said, "Daddy, I missed you too!"

"Boys, I missed y'all bunches too!" Collin rejoiced with tears in his eyes.

"Come in here, Dad. See the Christmas tree!" Todd and Pace grabbed their dad's hands and pulled him to the living room. "Mom helped us put it up."

"Wow! It is so pretty! Y'all did a great job. And look at all the beautifully wrapped presents under it. It's all so nice!" Collin said.

Sally was taken aback by Collin's change in attitude and actions, especially by the kiss he gave her. Where did that come from?

That evening, Collin was so kind to Sally and the boys. It was like being in the house with a different man. When bedtime came, Collin *romanced* Sally. He was very passionate and gentle as he held her in his arms—more so than he had been in a very long time. This intimacy with him was so unexpected.

The next morning found Sally nervous and rather sick to her stomach. She was doing her best to hold herself together so Collin and the boys wouldn't think something was wrong with her. She prepared breakfast for her family, trying to keep her mind off of the complicated predicament she was in. After the boys ate and brushed their teeth, Collin helped Sally clear the table of the breakfast dishes before he left for work. As Sally turned to walk out of the kitchen, Collin gently pulled her to him and took his hands and cupped them around her face.

"Sweetheart, I love you so much," Collin spoke softly, looking into her green eyes, kissing her tenderly.

Should I embrace him and return the kiss as tenderly? she thought. *After last night and the love he gave to me, I definitely should.* She held onto the kiss for a moment longer.

Collin decided he would take the boys to school on his way to work. How different that was. How different everything was! Sally sat on the living room couch with her head in her hands. She had a splitting headache and was very nauseated. She was a mess, but she had to pull herself together. She needed to get ready to see Rusty. How was she going to handle that? *Come on, Sally. Snap out of this. Chase these guilty feeling away! Get up and get going! You're got to face Rusty and be yourself,* she thought as she jumped up and walked to the bathroom for a bit more extra strength headache medicine. She took a quick shower and dressed. Looking at her face in the bathroom mirror as she applied her make-up, she thought, *Oh, Sally, try to make yourself as attractive as possible for Rusty.*

In her car, Sally merged onto the interstate. She found herself becoming so nervous and wishing time would stand still. What would she say or tell Rusty about Collin? She had the CB on, and for the first time, she was petrified to call for the Farmer.

Sally was two miles from the mall when she heard the Farmer's voice over the two-way radio. "Breaker channel one-nine for the Cricket. You got your ears on?"

Sally's heart flew into her throat, and she froze. She couldn't muster the courage to reach for the mic.

Again he called, "How about you, Cricket? You got a copy on the Farmer?"

Sally's hand shook badly as she forced it toward the mic. She hesitated. *I've got to sound calm and act normal. I don't want Rusty to think anything is wrong before I see him.* She held the mic to her mouth, pressed the key, and began speaking. "Breaker channel one-nine."

"Go ahead, Breaker," a voice returned, giving her the OK to talk on the channel, as that was proper procedure on the CB.

"'Preciate the break. How 'bout the Farmer from Connecticut. You got a copy?" Sally continued as if she had not heard the Farmer's first call for her.

"I sure do, Cricket! You're soundin' good! What's your 20?" the Farmer asked, wanting to know her location.

"Hi, Farmer! I'm about a mile from the mall. I'll be seeing ya in a short-short," she replied, knowing that with each tenth of a mile that rolled on the car's odometer, she was feeling more and more tense.

"Let's go to our channel, Cricket. OK?" the Farmer suggested.

"OK, Farmer. On my way," Sally replied as she reached forward to turn the CB's dial selector to channel 23.

"Are you there, Cricket?" the Farmer inquired.

"Ten-four, Farmer," Sally answered.

"What's your 20 now, sweetheart?" the Farmer's voice came back in the speaker.

"I'm just right around the corner from you. I should have you in my sight in a few seconds," Sally said as her voice became shaky, realizing what she had just said. A knot of fire leaped in her stomach. She started to sweat, her hands became clammy, she felt dizzy, and her heart was about to pound right out of her chest. She couldn't dare let Rusty see her like that!

"Well, just come on, Cricket, and bring your pretty little body on over here to me. It seems like a long time since I've seen you," the Farmer said in an anxious voice, which made her more nervous than ever.

Sally cleared her throat. "I've got my eyeball on you, Farmer, and am headin' your way," she remarked, seeing his burgundy rig sitting in the mall parking lot.

"Yip, yip, yip, I see you too. I'm goin' ten-seven," he said, signing off the air.

When Sally arrived beside Rusty's truck, he was standing outside waiting for her. He walked over to her car and opened the door for her as she turned the car's key to the off position. When she turned, she looked up into Rusty's handsome face. She felt his arms around her as he lifted her up from the car and passionately kissed her. Her anxiety instantly melted away.

Without a word, Sally and Rusty walked hand-in-hand to the driver's side of the tractor cab, climbed inside, and sat down on the sleeper bed. He turned to Sally, took her face in his hands, and drew ever so close to her with his lips slightly apart. He began kissing her as he'd never kissed her before. He kissed her cheek and down her neck.

"Sweetheart, I love you so much," Rusty whispered softly in her ear.

"I love you too, baby," Sally whispered in return as they both continued kissing each other.

Sally put her hands on Rusty's broad shoulders. "Honey, please slow down. I need to catch my breath," she said, nearly breathless. She knew where things were heading, and she wasn't sure she wanted to today.

A look of concern came across Rusty's face. "What's wrong, baby?" he asked. "Are you OK?"

Sally didn't want to beat around the bush by saying anything other than the facts. "Collin came home yesterday."

"Ohhhh. And . . . ?" Rusty leaned back away from Sally, concerned about what else she was about to tell to him.

"Well, yesterday morning, I was drinking my second cup of coffee, looking at the *Help Wanted* classified ads because I need to find a job, when Collin called. He apologized for all the things he said and for his actions. He asked me to forgive him, and he asked if he could come back home. I reluctantly accepted his apology, and I told him he could come home," Sally explained.

"And did he tell you where he'd been for those three days after he left the house in a huff?" Rusty questioned.

Sally could see Rusty's anguish and could hear in his voice a hint of hostility. "He said he had been out of town on a run for work."

"And you believed him? Oh, come on, Sally!" Rusty responded.

"I'm only telling you what he told me. I'm sorry, Rusty. I told you the other day when you asked me what I thought Collin would do next. I didn't know, but this is what happened," she explained.

"So, how was he when he came home? All lovey-dovey?" Rusty asked with a slice of jealousy.

Oh boy, Sally should have known that question was coming! Should she tell the truth or not? "Well, a little," she managed to say, not mentioning the beautiful roses Collin brought her or the very romantic night. No, no, no, she did not want to say anything about those things. "He was glad to be home, and the boys were excited their daddy was with them again," she added, hoping that would satisfy Rusty's inquisitive mind.

"So, what's next for us, Sally? Do I still have you and your love?" Rusty questioned.

Good question, she thought. Sally scooted closer to him. "Rusty, honey. *Yes,* you still have me and my love! Collin returning home has not changed that. I love you, Rusty." She needed him to believe her. She reached out her hands for his.

Rusty took her hands and pulled her on top of him and kissed her tenderly. "Sweetheart, I was so afraid you were going to tell me we were over! My heart was beginning to break. I love you so much, and I don't want to lose you."

They held each other tightly and immersed themselves in their love.

Several hours had passed, and departing was bittersweet. Rusty was returning home and would not drive again until after the first of the New Year. He gave Sally his telephone number with the instructions to call him when or if she needed him.

They both jumped down from Rusty's tractor cab and walked to Sally's car. Rusty opened the door for her. Sally turned and looked at Rusty with tears in her eyes.

"I won't see you before Christmas, honey, but I'll be thinking about you all the time and missing you more than you'll know," Rusty expressed. "I hope your holidays will be good and you will be safe." He wanted to say more, but he kept his thoughts to himself, wondering if he would ever see Sally again. With Collin home and back in the picture, he just didn't know what might or could happen to Sally's love for him.

"Dear Rusty, you won't be but a thought away from my mind. I will miss you so very much too." Sally cupped her hands around his face, drew near to his lips, and kissed him tenderly. "Merry Christmas, sweetheart. I love you."

"I love you too, sweet Sally. Merry Christmas," Rusty replied.

Sally sat down in her car, and Rusty closed the door behind her and walked back to his truck. He disappeared from Sally's sight for a moment, but then there he was, sitting behind the steering wheel. Sally threw him a kiss and a wave.

They drove off the mall lot together, and their words of love and affection toward each other faded on the CB as they drove off in different directions.

Chapter Six

Sally stopped at a restaurant for a bite for lunch after departing from Rusty. As she looked out the window, she still felt so warm inside from all of Rusty's love and was already missing him. It could be at least three weeks before she would be with him again. That's a long time! Should she feel guilty for loving Rusty so much? Then she asked herself, *Is what I feel for Rusty really love, or is it just lust?* As she reasoned with herself, she wondered how it could be lust when they didn't make love to each other the first time they met up. Now, truth be told, she thought about it, but it didn't happen then. They had waited until their seventh meeting. So, she thought, *Surely it's not lust. It should be love. It just has to be love. Yes, it's love!* she managed to convinced herself.

Shortly after picking up the boys from school and returning home, Sally saw Collin drive into the driveway. She looked at the wall clock and walked to the living room window. "What's your daddy doing home from work this early?" She continued looking out the window as Collin helped his mother out of the car. Maybe Collin invited her to have dinner with them?

As Collin and Mrs. Oldham entered the house, Sally greeted them. "Hi, Peggy. What a surprise! Collin didn't tell me you were coming over."

Collin spoke up. "That's because it is a surprise for you, Sally dear!"

"What do you mean?" Sally asked.

Mrs. Oldham then took hold of the conversation and replied, "You and Collin are going away for the weekend, and Collin asked me to watch the boys."

Sally was so shocked, she had to sit down on the couch. "Going out of town!? Where? When? I don't have anything packed; we couldn't possibly go," she rattled on nervously.

Collin took her hands, pulled her up off the couch, and led her to the bedroom. Opening the closet door, he said, "There's the suitcase, and all our clothes are right here. Please pack a few nice pantsuits for you, a pretty dress, and all you will need to go with those clothes. Then, please pack for me two pair of slacks with matching shirts, my black sport coat, and the other items you know I will need. Here, I'll help you."

Sally was stunned. She couldn't process what was happening. She just did what Collin told her to do and packed as fast as she could.

As Collin zipped the suitcase closed, Sally asked, "Where are we going?"

"It is a surprise, but I can tell you that our plane leaves in an hour and a half," Collin informed her.

"Our plane!?" shrieked Sally. "Collin, what has gotten into you? We can't afford a plane trip!" she reminded him.

"Don't worry about a thing, darlin'. You're going to have a great time. I'm going to see to it," Collin assured her. "There is that little train case on the floor of the closet. Please put it on the bed. I'm going to get the necessary toiletries I need, then you need to get yours," he said as he walked into the bathroom.

Sally and Collin quickly changed clothes and packed the remainder of the needed items all in record time. It was time for them to leave for the airport. They bid their farewells to the boys and Mrs. Oldham, who wished them to have a great time.

The airport was twenty minutes away, and Collin and Sally arrived in plenty of time to check their luggage. Collin took Sally's hand, and they walked down the concourse to their flight's designated boarding gate. Before sitting down in the gating area, Sally read the destination display while Collin verified their reservations with a flight attendant at the gate counter. "This plane is flying to New Orleans!" Sally exclaimed out loud.

"That's right, honey. We're going to New Orleans!" Collin confirmed as he walked up behind her. "It's time I take you on that second honeymoon you've been wanting to go on for such a long time," he explained. "It's a new beginning for us."

"Oh, Collin, what a wonderful surprise!" Sally exclaimed again.

"I hoped you would like it, sweetheart," Collin said as he kissed her on her cheek.

Within a few minutes, the flight attendant announced it was time for the passengers going to New Orleans to board the plane. They walked the boarding ramp, entered the plane, found their seats, and sat down. Sally's head was spinning at the wonder of what was happening. Rusty would probably come unglued if he knew what was happening, but maybe it would be better if he did not ever know.

Sally and Collin settled into their seats and waited for the plane to take off. Sally couldn't stop wondering how Collin was able to make this trip happen. "Collin, this is all so very nice and exciting, but you know we don't have the money for such luxuries."

Collin leaned forward to remove his billfold from his back pocket. He opened it and removed a green slip of paper. As he unfolded the paper, Sally saw the word *BEDON*, Collin's employer's name, written on it. When he had completely opened the paper, he handed it to her. She saw that it was a check stub. Collin was grinning from ear to ear!

"My boss gave me a bonus! Do you see how much it is for?" he asked Sally.

Sally had to do a double take. "What? Really?! You were given a bonus of fifteen hundred dollars? Oh, Collin, that's wonderful!" she shrieked. She was so happy for him, and she flung her arms around his neck and gave him a big kiss before she realized what she had done. "Wow! Collin, that's great!"

"That's the most money the company has ever given to me in a bonus. When I saw the amount, I told myself that I wanted to share it with you and do something you've wanted to do for a long time. I want to make you happy, Sally." His hazel eyes looked deep into Sally's eyes, and he gave her the feeling that he really meant what he just said. Her heart fluttered in a long-familiar way.

As the plane was up, up, and away, heading for their destination, Sally was overwhelmed with Collin's thoughtfulness. She didn't want to be skeptical, but she wondered where all of his newfound kindness had come from. Saying things like *he wanted to make her happy*, and *he wanted to share with her*. She wasn't sure, but she decided that maybe she should just enjoy his new attitude and be happy with him. Things hadn't been this way in a very long time.

Sally and Collin chatted about the boys, his work, her considering looking for a job, and what Collin had researched about New Orleans. The three-and-a-half-hour flight seemed very short to them, and the next thing they knew, the plane had landed at the New Orleans International Airport.

Once off the plane, the two gathered their luggage and slowly walked the terminal halls. There were beautiful Christmas decorations everywhere as well as lots of shops and restaurants all through the terminal. Since they were only served snacks during their flight, they were hungry, so they decided to grab a bite of food before going to their hotel.

After their meal, Sally and Collin walked outside the terminal doors. For it being 10 p.m. near the middle of December, the temperature was decently warm, and the sky was filled with stars. Collin hailed a taxi. The driver secured their luggage in the trunk as they seated themselves in the back seat.

"Where to, folks?" the driver asked, getting back into the car.

"The New Orleans Marriot, please," Collin said.

"That is an excellent choice! One of the finest hotels in New Orleans," the driver expressed as he gave a thumbs up. "Where are you young folks from?"

"Memphis," Collin answered. He added joyfully, "My wife and I are on our second honeymoon!"

"Well, congratulations! That's wonderful!" the driver exclaimed.

"We're only here for the weekend. Any special places you can suggest we see or go to?" Collin asked.

"Oh gosh, New Orleans has so many awesome places to see, but y'all might be interested in seeing the aquarium or taking a tour cruise of the river. Definitely take a carriage ride . . . gee, the list can go on and on."

"We have never been to New Orleans before, so we appreciate those suggestions," Collin said.

A few moments later, the driver pulled in front of the hotel. "Well, here we are at the Marriott. Y'all enjoy your stay. It was a pleasure talking to y'all."

"Yes, thank you! And to you as well, sir." Collin paid the driver as he handed them their luggage.

Sally looked at the hotel in awe. "Collin, this is a beautiful place!"

"Only the best for you, my lady!" Collin charmed. He took Sally's hand, and they walked into the luxurious and most stylish hotel either one of them had ever seen.

Sally was amazed! She felt like she needed to pinch herself because she thought she had to be dreaming. They approached the check-in counter where a well-dressed female employee was waiting.

"Yes, sir, I'm Margo. Can I help you?" she asked.

Collin began, "We are the Oldhams from Memphis. We are on our second honeymoon and have requested reservations for the honeymoon suite for two nights."

"What!? Collin, the honeymoon suite?" Sally exclaimed. *I've really got to be dreaming!* she thought.

"Yes, sir, I have your reservation right here. Here is your key. Your suite is on the forty-second floor, room 4201. If y'all need anything, please, just let us know, and please, enjoy your stay with us. We're happy that you have chosen our hotel for your stay in New Orleans." She rang a bell, and a young man came to the lobby and took their luggage.

"Collin, pinch me! I've got to be dreaming! Not only a fine hotel, but the honeymoon suite? This is better than any dream. Thank you, Collin," Sally said sincerely.

"You are so welcome. You deserve this and more, sweetheart," Collin said, sensing her sincerity.

They followed the bellhop to the elevator and up to the forty-second floor. The elevator door opened, and straight ahead was suite 4201. The bellhop took the key from Collin and opened the door to their suite. Sally stepped into the suite and instantly gasped for breath. It was overwhelming!

"I hope the suite meets your approval, ma'am?" the bellhop asked.

"Oh, yes, most definitely," Sally joyfully answered.

"It's absolutely beautiful! I don't think it could be any better," Collin said. "What's your name, sir?" he asked the bellhop.

"George, sir," he replied.

"Well, George, I think you work for a pretty amazing company. Thank you very much for helping us," Collin affirmed as he handed George a tip for his services.

George wished them a wonderful evening and closed the door of the suite as he left.

Sally had wandered over to one of the many windows in the suite and was completely taken by the view. "Collin, look."

Collin walked toward her. The view of the city and its lights below were so stunning. "It is beautiful, but not as beautiful as you are," he said, taking Sally in his arms. He leaned into her and began kissing her.

The romantic mood of the suite was set with hearts, flowers, Cupid figurines, and colors of red and pink. Even the bed was heart shaped with matching pillows. As the two continued kissing, feelings and desires awakened in Sally that she hadn't felt for Collin in a long time. He picked her up and carried her over to the bed, her arms clinging around his neck. He laid her down gently, and their kissing sank them deeper into love as all their inhibitions went away.

The next morning found the lovers still embracing each other. Their night was full of love. Sally slowly opened her eyes and saw Collin facing her, still asleep. She looked into the face of the man she had once loved with all of her heart. As she thought about what the last night held, she couldn't help remembering what they had been like when they were first dating—back in high school. What fun they had learning about each other and then falling in love. Oh, those Friday night dates in the latter half of their senior year—they couldn't wait to be together. Before those evenings were over and Collin took Sally home, they always managed to find a steamy place to enjoy each other. It was shocking that they never got pregnant! Their parents would have been so mad. *How foolish we were,* she thought.

She remembered graduation night; they had stayed out all night hanging with their friends on a boat cruise until 2 a.m. Afterward, they drove to their "deep in the woods" spot and stayed in each other's arms until the sun came up. Oh, her Mom was so mad at her!

Several months later in October, they were engaged, and not long after they received earth-shattering news—Collin had been drafted and would leave for boot camp in January. Sally was devastated. And then she learned Collin was thinking about signing up to go fight the war in Vietnam. She cried a lot then but tried to focus on her classes at the business college she was attending. In the end, Collin came home in June, and they married in October of that year: 1966. The years since then had been good and bad, but the bad times seemed much more prevalent. They both stopped trying, and their love had become stagnant.

Her thoughts returned to the present as she looked at her husband, sleeping so peacefully.

And now there's Rusty. . . .

Collin began to stir and opened his eyes to find Sally looking at him. "Good morning, sweetheart. Oh, what a night. You were wonderful, like the days of old. It was like we couldn't get enough of each other!" He was very delighted. "How are you this morning?" he asked, getting out of bed, his nude body on full display.

Sally rolled to the edge of the bed and sat up. She walked over to Collin and took him in her arms, her hands running down his bare back as he caressed her soft body. "I'm feeling fine," she said, nibbling his ear.

"Yes, you sure do," he replied, snuggling in her neck. "We should get moving, but I'll save this moment until later," Collin suggested.

"That sounds inviting to me," Sally said.

Collin took Sally's hand and led her to the bathroom where they both showered. Then they dressed for the day. While Collin was putting on his shoes, Sally looked out one of the many windows of the suite again. The view was just breathtaking. The Mississippi River ran forever, and in the opposite direction, she felt like she could touch the sky. She still thought she had to be dreaming, but this was really happening.

The solitude of her moment was interrupted when Collin asked, "Are you ready, sweetheart?"

"Yes, I am, honey," she replied.

They grabbed their light jackets, walked out of their suite, and approached the elevator. Upon reaching the ground floor, Collin saw an employee with the name tag *Kasey* at the customer service desk. He asked her for a map of the city.

As Kasey handed him a folded piece of paper, she asked, "Can I help you find some place y'all are looking for?"

Collin, still looking at the map, said, "Yes, can you tell me where the Cafe Beignet is on Royal Street?"

"Of course!" she said, taking the map from Collin's hand and circling the restaurant's location. "Can I circle any other locations for you?" she politely inquired.

"Well, yes. I appreciate your help. How about the aquarium, the Superdome, the Riverwalk area, Felix's Waterfront Restaurant, and . . . where is the best location to catch a carriage ride?" Collin asked.

"All great places to go and things to do," Kasey remarked. "OK, I've circled those locations for you. Y'all have a wonderful day!"

Collin and Sally were grateful for Kasey's help, and they thanked her as they turned and walked through the gorgeous lobby toward the front doors of the hotel.

The Cafe was only a few blocks away from the hotel, and instead of calling for a taxi, they just decided to walk. The air was a little cool, but the sun was shining, and it felt warm.

They enjoyed their breakfast at Cafe Beignet, and Sally commended Collin for his fine restaurant selection. Neither one of them had eaten a beignet before, and they were very good!

After leaving the Cafe, they walked a short distance to the aquarium, where they spent hours walking through, looking at, and admiring their beautiful surroundings. So many fish displays. They walked through tunnels with water over their heads, with all kinds of fish swimming above them—just amazing! There were smaller displays of creatures from the oceans, some exotic, some scary looking, and some so fascinating to watch. Sally had never been to an aquarium before, and she was so happy that Collin took her there.

On their walk to the Superdome, Collin and Sally stopped to grab a bite of lunch at a little corner walk-up-and-order vendor. The coney dog was tasty but rather messy, but that was OK because they enjoyed cleaning the mustard and ketchup from each other's faces, adding in a few sweet kisses.

The Superdome was *huge* from the outside, but once inside, it was *even bigger.* They decided to pay to go on the tour of the stadium, which was worth every penny. They walked the concourse, which was like the halls of the building, and they were able to see the inside of the stadium as well. Sally thought, *Oh my gosh, there are seats for thousands and thousands of fans!* The playing field was immaculate. Seeing the Saints games on television paled in comparison to what they were seeing in person.

When the tour was over, they visited the gift shop where they bought a few things for the boys and looked at all the Saints memorabilia. Collin had outdone himself. What an experience!

The afternoon was waning, nearing early evening, and the sun was setting. Sally and Collin debated walking back to the hotel to change into more appropriate evening attire, but they decided to just head to dinner—at Felix's Waterfront Restaurant. While they waited for their table to be ready, they sat next to each other at the outside bar and sipped on a glass of wine. It was a little chilly outside, but the wine went down warm. Collin held Sally close and whispered in her ear that he sure did love her. Sally looked into his eyes and whispered back that she loved him too. At that moment, she felt special to Collin. Did he really love her? She felt content. Or was it the wine that had her thinking that?

"Oldham, a table for two is ready," the hostess announced over the loudspeaker.

Collin helped Sally to her feet, and they walked hand in hand into the restaurant. They were seated at a cozy table in the back corner of the restaurant by a window looking out over the water.

How perfect, Sally thought. Collin sat close to her as both of them watched the activity on the water through the window.

The waitress approached them, sat down two glasses of water, and asked, "What can I get you two to drink?"

Collin answered, "I'd like to have a glass of wine, please."

Sally chimed in, "Would you make that two, please?"

"Yes, I'll bring those wines right out," replied the waitress.

Sally hardly ever drank alcohol, but tonight she was in the mood.

Sally and Collin looked at the menu. Sally really liked shrimp; Collin was more a steak guy. When the waitress returned with their wine, she took their food order.

Sally turned and faced Collin. "Honey, you have planned our trip so well, and I thank you for all the fun things we did today. You have made me very happy. I hope you have enjoyed the day as much as I have."

"I have, but do you think this is what you could have wanted for a second honeymoon, sweetheart?" Collin asked. "I so much wanted it to be very special for you."

"And it has been, Collin. I really wouldn't have known what to expect because our wedding night and honeymoon weren't extravagant, since we just didn't have the money. If it hadn't been for your sister giving us a wedding gift of a one-night stay at the Holiday Inn, we would have spent our wedding night in our apartment! So all we have done and seen on this trip has been wonderful. Thank you very much," she said as she kissed him.

"Thank you for making me happy," Collin responded. "I, too, really didn't know how to plan a second honeymoon, but I believe it has turned out very nice." Collin was relieved that Sally approved of his efforts for a memorable weekend.

The waitress brought their meals, and they ate while enjoying the solitude of being together at their quiet, little cozy table. Once they were done, they decided to take a walk along the Riverwalk. Hand in hand, they walked slowly, observing other couples and some children enjoying their evening. It was a beautiful, relaxing time. It felt like Sally and Collin were in another world. Tomorrow, they would return home and back to the routine of their normal lives, but Sally hoped that her life with Collin would continue in this way—with love and thoughtfulness for each other's feelings.

But then she remembered . . . Rusty.

"Let's do one more special thing, Sally," Collin suggested as he spotted the horses and carriages. There was one covered carriage like right out of a movie. They approached the driver and Collin asked, "Sir, could we rent this beautiful carriage so my beautiful lady can feel like the princess that she is?"

The driver, dressed in a black top hat and a red coat with tails, answered, "You certainly may. I'd be happy for you and your lovely bride to allow me to escort y'all on the streets of New Orleans. I'm McHenry, and this here is Annabelle. We are at your service," McHenry said as he patted the mane of his beautiful white horse standing next to him.

"Thank you, McHenry and Annabelle," Collin replied. He held Sally's waist as she stepped up into the fable-like covered carriage. Collin turned to pay McHenry and then stepped up into the carriage and sat close to Sally. She felt like one of those fairytale princesses—just like Collin had said he wanted.

The carriage made its way through the streets, beautifully lit with thousands of colorful Christmas lights and holiday decorations. This was the perfect time of the year to visit New Orleans. Sally and Collin snuggled together to stay warm as they relaxed and enjoyed the scenery.

After a while, McHenry asked which hotel they were staying at.

"The Marriott on Canal Street," Collin answered.

"If you desire, at the end of your ride, Annabelle and I can drop you off there?" McHenry suggested.

"That sounds perfect, McHenry. Thank you," Collin replied.

The wonderful carriage ride came to an end as they approached their hotel. The hotel doorman stood in front of the hotel, and before Collin helped Sally down from the carriage, he asked if he could take a picture of the couple. Collin agreed and handed the doorman his camera.

"Thank you, LeMonte," Collin said, reading the name tag on the doorman's jacket lapel. "That was most thoughtful, and we appreciate that!"

Collin helped Sally down from the carriage, then turned and thanked McHenry and Annabelle for a very special carriage ride. The ride was the highlight of their evening. Collin and Sally wished the driver and his mare a wonderful night. McHenry wished the couple the same and gently instructed Annabelle to trot ahead.

As Collin retrieved his camera from LeMonte, Sally remarked to Collin that the evening was still young and that she would like to walk down Bourbon Street before going to their room. Collin took the map out of his pocket, opened it, and exclaimed, "Bourbon Street is only a block away! Let's go!" he said as he grabbed her hand and began walking.

A lot of folks were walking on one of the most popular streets in New Orleans—sort of like Beale Street in Memphis. There were lots of bars, restaurants, and even clubs. Collin and Sally enjoyed the music they heard from the street, so they went into a few of the bars to listen and dance to the music.

Some people were drinking from a signature souvenir glass. "I wonder where they are getting those glasses?" Sally asked Collin.

About that time, a couple was passing by, so Collin asked, "Excuse me, my wife was wondering where y'all found those glasses? She'd like to take one home with her."

The young man answered as he pointed, "Go two blocks that way to the bar on the corner. You can find the glasses there."

"Thank you very much," Collin gratefully replied. "Come on, Sally. Let's go get those glasses!" Collin excitedly wrapped his arm around her waist and walked in the direction the man indicated.

They walked two short blocks and found the bar, walked in, and sure enough, there were the glasses. Collin and Sally moved slowly through the crowded room to get to the bar. A bartender approached them.

"What can I get for the two of you tonight?" he asked.

Collin glanced at Sally. "We'd like to have two of your souvenir glass drinks," Collin requested.

"Comin' right up," the man replied. And within a few minutes, the bartender returned with two souvenir glasses in his hands and handed one to each of them. "That will be twenty dollars, sir," the bartender said.

Collin removed his billfold from his back pocket, opened it, and pulled out a twenty dollar bill along with two one dollar bills for a tip. After Collin thanked him, he took Sally's hand and carefully maneuvered to the entrance of the bar. It was elbow to elbow full of folks, nearly suffocating, but finally, they were back outside and could breathe again. They strolled the street, taking small steps, sipping on their drinks, and just enjoying their last few moments together on the streets of New Orleans.

The hotel was in sight. Both were somewhat glad because their alcoholic drinks were having an effect on them. LeMonte opened the hotel door and said, "Y'all have a good evening!"

"Thank you, and you too, LeMonte," Sally and Collin both said to him in unison. They walked through the lobby to the elevator, and once on the elevator, Collin pressed the forty-second-floor button. During the ride up, they kissed passionately with their arms locked around each other tightly. When the elevator door opened, they stepped out into the hallway, walked to their suite, unlocked the door, and entered the room.

The fragrance of the beautiful flowers in the room filled the air. Collin helped Sally take her coat off, and she, in turn, helped Collin take his off. She took Collin's face in her hands and expressed, "It has been an awesome and wonderful day today, sweetheart, and I thank you from the bottom of my heart. I just don't think it could have been any better!"

"I'm very glad it's been a wonderful day for you, honey, because it's been a great day for me too. I'm sure we could have done more to have made it more memorable, but the memories we made today I'll remember always. Thank you for making our trip so special." And with that, he sealed it with a very meaningful kiss.

Their evening ended with romantic snuggling as they fell asleep in each other's arms.

Morning found Collin and Sally getting ready for their trip home. They ate breakfast in the hotel restaurant, gathered their luggage, and checked out of the hotel. Kasey was on duty, and she remembered the Oldhams.

"Sure do hope your stay with us was a good one," she commented.

"It was definitely more than we anticipated, and everything was very special. Thank you for making our stay most memorable," Sally expressed gratefully.

"We appreciate you saying that! Wishing y'all a safe trip home, and please, come and see us again. Our shuttle is waiting out front to take y'all to the airport," Kasey said with a wave goodbye.

Collin and Sally exited the hotel and stepped into the shuttle, which took them to the airport. Arriving in plenty of time for their noon flight back to Memphis, they strolled slowly through the terminal after checking their luggage.

Nearing 11:15 a.m., they walked into the boarding area and found a place to sit. Not long after, the flight attendant announced, "It's boarding time for those passengers bound for Memphis." Collin gave Sally his hand, and they walked the boarding ramp, stepped into the aircraft, and found their seats.

The plane was nearly full of passengers. The *please fasten your seatbelts* sign began flashing, and the voice of the plane's captain announced, "The weather conditions between here and Memphis are clean and green. So relax and enjoy your flight."

Sally and Collin felt the motion of the plane as it left the gate. Soon, they were in the air, flying high above the earth.

Chapter Seven

Early the next morning and before the daily routine began, Sally was sitting halfway up in bed. She pondered over the past weekend with Collin. They had had so much fun—more fun together than she could ever remember having, even more than their Florida trip five years earlier. The plane flights were exciting, the hotel was fabulous, the places they went and all the different things they saw and what they did were very special. If there was one place or one thing about the trip that she had to say was *the best,* she wouldn't be able to say. All of it was just wonderful. And in every aspect, the trip was like a honeymoon.

As she was getting up out of bed, Collin pulled her back toward him. "Good morning, sweetheart. I wish we had another day together."

"I know," Sally agreed. "But we all must get up and get ready. You for work, and the boys for school," she said as she kissed him and proceeded to get out of bed.

"Yes, I'm getting up," he grumbled.

Sally walked from their bedroom to the boys' bedroom and woke up Todd and Pace. "Good morning, my little sons. Time to rise and shine. Just one more week of school and then y'all will be out for Christmas break! This week should be a fun week doing Christmas things at school," Sally said enthusiastically as she laid out their clothes to wear to school. "I'm going to go start breakfast while y'all get dressed."

"OK, Mom," Todd responded sleepily. "Come on, Pace, you gotta get up too," he said, coaxing his little brother.

Not long after Sally entered the kitchen, the smell of coffee brewing was in the air. Then, the smell of bacon frying. The eggs were ready to be scrambled, and the water was boiling for the grits.

Collin rounded the corner of the kitchen. "Somethin' sure is smellin' good," he said as he poured coffee into his cup. "Can I pour you a cup of coffee too?" he asked Sally.

"Yes, that would be great. Thank you. Todd, Pace, breakfast is almost ready. Y'all makin' it OK in there, or do y'all need some help?"

"No, Mom, we're almost ready," Todd said loud enough for his mom to hear.

Sally placed the food on the dining room table, and all her family sat down to eat.

As Collin began to eat, he addressed his sons. "So did y'all have a good time with your grandmother while your mother and I were gone?"

"Yip! She took us to the park, and we fed the ducks," Pace excitedly answered. "That was fun!"

"Yea! Then, on the way home, she picked up pizzas for us to eat. And then after pizza, we played games. We had lots of fun!" Todd added.

"Well, it sounds like y'all had a good time. I'm glad," Collin said delightfully.

"But we sure did miss you, Daddy and Momma," Pace said sadly. "So happy y'all are home."

"Little buddies, we missed y'all too. Sure hope y'all like the toys we brought y'all?" Collin inquired.

"Yes, I really like the dinosaurs! They are so cool lookin'. Thanks again," Todd expressed.

"And I really like playing with the 18-wheeler," Pace replied.

"Time to brush your teeth and be off to school," Sally said as she checked the time. "Your father said he was taking y'all to school this morning, so move along."

After teeth were brushed, Sally helped the boys put their coats on, handed them their lunchboxes, gave them and Collin kisses, and out the front door they went. "Love y'all bunches, and have a good day," she told them with a wave and closed the front door.

As Sally returned to the kitchen to do the morning dishes, the telephone rang. "Hello?" she answered.

"Good morning, Sally dear. Hope I'm not disturbing y'all this early," Mrs. Oldham replied.

"Good morning, Peggy. No, you're fine. Collin just left. He's taking the boys to school and then he'll go on to work," Sally said. "How are you this morning?"

"I'm doing OK. Thanks for asking. I forgot to tell you yesterday when y'all got home about a telephone call for you. There was just so much excitement. I'm sorry," Peggy apologized.

"That's OK, Peggy. Don't worry about that. Who was it, and did I need to call them back?" Sally asked.

"I wrote the telephone number down on a piece of paper and placed it by the telephone. It was a rather strange number, and it was a Mr. Summers. He was calling about a job offer for you. Are you looking for a job, Sally?"

As Peggy continued to tell Sally about the telephone call, Sally found the piece of paper. She had to sit down on the couch as she felt weak in the knees. The strange telephone number Peggy wrote down was Mr. Rusty Summers' telephone number!

"Dear, did you find the piece of paper?" Peggy asked. "Sally, are you there?"

"I'm sorry, Peggy. Yes, I'm here." Sally finally managed to respond. "Yes, I'm considering taking a job. With both boys in school now, I thought it might be a good idea. And yes, it is a strange telephone number. Certainly not local! Thank you for taking down the information and telling me about the call. Do you remember anything else about the conversation?" she asked Peggy, but she didn't want to sound too pushy.

"Well, let's see. The gentleman was very nice. He just asked if Sally Oldham was available to take his call. I told him you were out of town with your husband on your second honeymoon and would be returning Sunday afternoon. Then I asked him what the call might be concerning. He said it was about a job inquiry you had made. I suggested I take his telephone number and that I would have you call him when you returned from your trip. I think that's about it. Did I do OK, Sally? I didn't do anything wrong, did I?" Peggy asked nervously.

Sally felt sick. Peggy had told Rusty way too much. She wasn't going to mention the trip to him at all! It would make matters worse for her and Rusty's relationship . . . or whatever it would continue to be after this last weekend's events. What he didn't know wouldn't hurt him, right? But now the cat was out of the bag. And she was more confused than ever.

"No, Peggy, you did just fine. I appreciate you sharing with me the conversation you had with Mr. Summers. I will give him a call in a little while. Thank you again for watching the boys while we were away. The boys told us this morning that they had lots of fun with you. You have a good day, Peggy. Talk to you again soon. Love ya," Sally said as she ended the call.

Sally reached over the arm of the couch to hang up the handset on the telephone's base. She still could not believe all that Peggy had told Rusty. *Why did she do that?* she thought to herself. *Was she just not thinking? Who would give out that kind of information to a stranger on the phone? Now what do I say to Rusty? I need to call him!*

Sally's mind ran in circles as she pondered the words she would say to Rusty. She still felt sick to her stomach and as nervous as a leaf on a tree branch on a windy day. She reached to grab the telephone's handset, placed it next to her ear, and dialed Rusty's telephone number. Her heart sank as the phone began to ring in her ear. She wondered what was about to happen.

"Hello?"

Rusty's voice took her breath away. "Hi, Rusty. It's Sally. How are you, dear?" she asked in a chipper voice, trying to pull off a cheerful attitude. "Is this a good time to call you?" she continued.

There was silence on the other end of the line.

"Rusty, are you there?"

"Yes, I'm here, Sally," Rusty finally answered. "How was your second honeymoon, sweetheart?" he asked sarcastically.

"Rusty, that trip was a total surprise. Collin came in Friday afternoon with his mother and announced that he and I were taking a trip and that his mother was going to watch the boys while we were away. We quickly packed our luggage, went to the airport, and took a plane to New Orleans. We came home yesterday. Collin's mother just called me and told me she forgot to tell me that on Saturday a Mr. Summers called about a job, and you had left your telephone number to call you. I was going to call you this morning anyway, trip or no trip. I know you are upset, ticked off, and very hurt, but Rusty, please understand, the trip was not my idea!" Sally explained frantically.

"Well, the word *honeymoon* can mean many things in my mind. Was Collin all lovey-dovey, keeping you in bed the whole time? You know intimacy is a big part of a *honeymoon*. Yes, I am very upset, more than ticked off, and *hurt* doesn't even come close to what I feel! Sally, how could this happen?" Rusty exclaimed in anger.

Sally was fighting back tears. Her mind was racing, trying to find the right words to say to him so he would understand that the situation was not her fault. Her thoughts were distorted and confused. She felt so guilty. She was an unfaithful wife to her husband and now she felt so unfaithful to her lover whom she loved deeply. If Collin was really trying to make their marriage better, to be the husband and father that he should be, she should give him the chance, then it would be over between her and Rusty. Her heart and mind were going in two different directions.

Tearfully, Sally said, "Rusty, I'm so very sorry. I hope you know I would never do anything to hurt you. I love you so much. I'm sorry." Sally couldn't manage to speak any more words as she began to cry.

"Oh, my dear Sally, I'm sorry too. The thoughts of Collin holding you in his arms and making love to you just tore me up on the inside of my body. He was holding *my girl*. My mind has tormented me since Saturday when your mother-in-law told me about you going on this second honeymoon with your husband. Sally, I was crushed!" Rusty admitted his heartbreak as his voice waned in sadness. He struggled to speak when he asked, "OK, so where do we stand with each other? I've got to know. Has this trip revived your love and your desire and devotion for Collin? As much as I hate to say this, if Collin is committed to becoming a better husband to you and a better father to his sons, then I don't want to be the one to keep that from happening. But if there is any shadow of a doubt in your mind, then I'm still here for you. I love you that much, Sally."

The silence was deafening. Sally wanted to speak, but what was she to say? She couldn't know for sure if Collin had really changed for the better or if this was just temporary. Only time would tell. As far as her feelings for Collin, well, they were mixed. She was glad he acted like he cared for her again, like the old Collin that she used to know and love, but for her to know beyond a shadow of a doubt . . . no, she didn't know yet. And this is where her strong feelings came in for Rusty. Her heart couldn't bear the thought of not having him in her life. She began, "Rusty. . . ."

"I tell you what, Sally," Rusty interrupted her, "we have almost three weeks to think about our situation. I'll be here if you want or need to talk to me. I really don't want us to make any rash or quick decisions about our relationship right now. We're both too emotional to think very clearly. Within these coming days and weeks, we'll have time to evaluate the situation, our thoughts, and our feelings for each other," Rusty said. Then he added, "Just know that I love you with all my heart, and I miss seeing you very much. I might call you, if you want me to."

Sally nodded her head, as if Rusty could see her. She finally was able to answer. "Yes, I would like for you to call me. I still want you in my life, Rusty. I love and miss you too." She broke down in tears again.

"OK, Sally. We'll talk again soon. You take care of yourself for me, sweetheart," he told her, and the call disconnected as Rusty hung up.

With Sally's head in her hands, she cried like she hadn't cried in a long time. Her heart was breaking—not only for herself, but for Rusty. She never meant to hurt him or for this to have happened in the first place.

Sally had a hard time focusing on anything the rest of the day. She sat on the couch a lot, thinking about her conversation with Rusty, and when she did feel like moving, it felt like she was moving in slow motion.

Finally, Sally dressed to picked the boys up from school. Several hours later, Collin came in from work. She tried so hard to be herself and to be happy. To not let on to the turmoil that was overtaking her mind and heart.

That evening after supper, Sally was trying to keep her mind occupied by reading the newspaper. It was warmer than normal outside for mid-December, and the boys were playing in the backyard. Collin was sitting in his favorite chair, reading a letter he had received that day from his sister and brother-in-law who lived in Brandon, Mississippi, a small town about fifteen miles east of Jackson.

"Hon, it's been a long time since we've been down to see Ellen and David," he said. "Let's call and see if it's convenient for us to go down this weekend. I'd love to see them," Collin suggested.

"That'll be fine," Sally answered, not really paying too much attention to what he had said.

Collin got up from his chair. "Their telephone number is in the blue telephone book, isn't it?" he asked Sally.

Sally was staring out the window, her mind elsewhere. When she came to, she realized Collin had asked her a question. "I'm sorry, Collin, what did you ask me?"

"Ellen's telephone number. Is it in the blue telephone book?" he repeated.

"Yes. Are you going to call her?"

"Yes. I thought we'd go visit with them this weekend, if they don't have anything planned," Collin suggested again.

Before Sally could say anything, Collin was in the process of dialing their telephone number. Sally thought to herself, *Gosh, not another weekend away from home. Maybe they'll have something planned, and we won't be able to go.*

All Sally could hear was one side of the conversation between Collin and his sister.

Then, finally, "That's great! We'll see y'all late Friday night, and I'll bring Mom," Collin joyfully said as he hung up the telephone. "Well, she said she'd be happy for us to come down, and I'll get Mom to go with us," he said excitedly. "I know it would be a little early, but maybe we can celebrate Christmas with them. What do you think, Sally?"

"Oh, that sounds good," Sally said, trying to be enthusiastic about the trip. "I'll need to buy some Christmas gifts for your sister and her family. Maybe I'll do that tomorrow. That will give me time to wrap the gifts before Friday," Sally said.

Immediately, Collin called his mother and told her of the conversation he had just had with his sister. "Mom, we would like for you to go with us."

There was a pause.

"That's wonderful! I'll call you later with more details. Sally and I thought that we'd celebrate Christmas a little early while we are visiting with them. How does that sound to you?"

Another pause.

"OK, super! Later, Mom. Looking forward to the trip. Love ya." And the conversation ended.

"Mom is going to be able to go with us! Sally, this is going to be a great trip!" Collin excitedly announced.

Sally wasn't so sure. Shopping for people she hadn't seen in a long time might not be so easy. She decided to temporarily dismiss the situation from her mind. She was in no mood nor in the frame of mind to think about all of that. Tomorrow's another day, and maybe she would feel better.

After what seemed like a very restless night, with thoughts of her and Rusty's conversation replaying time and time again in her mind, Sally attempted to make the next morning her normal routine. After getting her family up, fed, and off to work and school, she laid down on the couch. She was tired and had a splitting headache. She rested with an icepack on her head and drifted off to sleep. An hour later, the telephone rang, startling her from her sleep. Her first thought was of Rusty. Was he calling her?

"Hello?" Sally answered in a sleepy voice, still not completely awake.

"Oh my. Dear, did I wake you? I'm so sorry. I thought you would be up and at 'em this morning." Peggy's voice sounded so loud in Sally's ear.

"Hi, Peggy. That's OK, I just didn't sleep very good last night. Are you OK? Are you at work?" Sally asked concerningly.

"Yes, I'm fine, and I am at work, but I'm thinking about taking the afternoon off to do some Christmas shopping for Ellen and her family. I was wondering if you'd like to join me? We could do lunch and then shop for several hours before you pick the boys up from school? I could pick you up about noon. It's almost 10:30 now," Peggy said.

Sally didn't really feel like getting out yet or even being sociable, but she did need to shop for gifts, and Peggy talked often to Ellen, so she would know more about what she and Collin could give her and her family. "Peggy, I'd like that. You can give me some gift ideas. Thank you, and I'll see you at noon," Sally said, accepting Peggy's invitation.

As Sally hung up the telephone, she wanted so badly to call Rusty, just to hear his sweet voice. But she thought better about it. *Not yet. Give us both a little more time to think. The old saying, "absence makes the heart grow fonder"—what? What has that got to do with this situation? We both know we love each other,* Sally admitted to herself.

Sally dressed, threw on some makeup, and greeted Peggy at noon at the front door of her home. They both liked barbecue and enjoyed lunch at a popular local restaurant. Then it was on to a nearby mall to do their shopping. Peggy was a huge help to Sally in purchasing gifts for Ellen, David, and their two children. Peggy indicated she had bought a few things for Todd and Pace, but Sally helped her with a few more ideas for the boys. It was a refreshing afternoon, and Sally enjoyed spending time with her mother-in-law. They seldom saw each other let alone shopped together.

The hours had too quickly passed, and it was time to pick the boys up from school. Todd and Pace were very surprised to see their grandmother at pickup. Sally explained to them that she and their grandmother had been out doing some shopping together. All the way home, they talked about their day at school, giggling and laughing as they recounted the events. Sally loved to hear her sons being so happy. It turned out the day was a good day for all.

Once at home, Peggy left, and Todd and Pace began their homework on the dining room table. Todd complained that his teacher was giving too much homework. He said the teacher told his class that they had to make up some schoolwork before Christmas break in four days. Sally tried to help him and Pace with some of their work before starting supper.

When Collin came in from work near 5:30 p.m., he was upset and rather rude to Sally and the boys. She asked Collin what was wrong, but all he would say was that he didn't want to talk about it and for her not to ask him again.

After supper, the boys finished their homework and spent the rest of the evening in their room. They told their mother that because their father was upset, they felt better to just stay in their room. Sally was perplexed. She really wanted to know what was wrong with Collin. He had the television on, but he was not watching it. He wasn't talking. Soon he just went to bed—much earlier than normal.

What was going on?

The next morning, Collin was up before Sally. He dressed and told her he had to go to work early. Without a kiss or a goodbye, he left the house. Sally was very concerned about Collin, his attitude, and his actions. *What could have happened? What could be wrong? Why wouldn't he talk to me about this?* Sally wondered.

Sally woke up Todd and Pace, laid out their clothes for school, and began preparing breakfast for them. After eating breakfast, the boys finished getting ready, and Sally took them to school. On the way home, she stopped to visit with Minnie Mouse. Firecracker was home through the holidays. Over coffee, they talked about many things, especially plans for Christmas. Minnie asked about the Farmer from Connecticut. She said that she hadn't heard him very much on their base station lately. Sally shared with Minnie that she had had lunch with the Farmer a while back, and he was a very nice man. Sally didn't feel comfortable telling her any more than that about Rusty. At the end of their nice visit, they all wished each other Merry Christmas.

It was good for Sally to visit with her friends. It took her mind off of Collin and what was going on with him . . . and also Rusty. But once back at home, her mind returned to Rusty. She wanted to call him so badly. If she did, what would she say? She needed to get busy doing something. She decided to wrap the Christmas gifts that were bought yesterday for Ellen and her family. That would keep her occupied for several hours.

She was able to wrap all the gifts before it was time to get the boys from school. The boys had more homework, and they needed to study for tests that they were going to have to take tomorrow and the next day. Sally helped where she could and then began preparing supper.

The telephone rang. Sally froze for a moment. *Could that be Rusty?* she wondered as she walked toward the phone.

"Hello?" Sally answered.

"Sally, it's me," Collin said. "I'm still at work. I'm not going to be home for supper, and I don't know what time I'll be home. Gotta go." The call ended.

Sally stood in place for several moments, trying to absorb what had just happened and what Collin had said. "What is going on with Collin?" she said softly out loud.

"Mom, are you OK?" Todd asked as he broke her concentration.

"Well, I don't know, Todd. That was your father, and he said he didn't know what time he was going to be home tonight," Sally responded.

"He sure did act weird last night. Kinda scary," Todd remarked.

"Yes, I know," she said and returned to the kitchen. "Supper's almost ready. Please clear the table of y'all's books, and go wash your hands," Sally instructed.

After supper, the boys finished their schoolwork, then slipped into their PJs to watch a little television until it was time for bed. Sally tucked her little sons into bed and reminded them, "Sleep tight. Don't let the bedbugs bite. I love you two bunches."

"Nite-nite, Momma. Love you too," they both said at the same time.

The hour was getting late, and Sally was feeling more and more concerned about Collin. She decided to call his work. She needed to know he was OK.

"BEDON, this is Stephen. How can I help you?" the voice answered.

"Hi, Stephen. This is Sally Oldham. Could I please talk to my husband, Collin?" she asked.

"Hi, Mrs. Oldham. Collin isn't here," Stephen answered.

Sally hesitated, then said, "OK, maybe he just left and he's on his way home. Thank you, Stephen. You have a good night."

"Wait, Mrs. Oldham. Collin left several hours ago," Stephen informed her.

"Oh?" Sally expressed with a surprised tone. "OK, well, thank you, Stephen. I appreciate you telling me."

Sally sat down on the couch. She really didn't know what to think. She was concerned, bewildered, and somewhat upset with Collin for this whole situation that began last night. *What is going on with him?* she asked herself over and over again.

The clock on the wall above the couch showed its hands near midnight. Sally had the television on, but the station she had it tuned to had gone off the air, and the screen was showing snow with accompanying static noise. As she got up from the couch to turn off the television, she thought she heard a car door slam. Maybe it was Collin! She looked out of the living room window, but Collin's car was not in the driveway. She wondered, *If it were Collin, how would I handle the situation? Would or should I attack him like he attacked me with his words previously—*"where have you been," or "who have you been with all evening?" *How would he respond?* That last thought scared her, remembering what happened the last time she came home from seeing Rusty, and Collin confronted her with those same words. She didn't want another shouting match, physical harm, or Collin storming out of the house! She decided the best idea was to go to bed and *not* address his late-night adventures until the time seemed more reasonable and appropriate.

When Sally woke up the next morning, Collin was in bed with her. She was surprised! He must have been as quiet as a mouse getting into bed because Sally didn't know when he came home last night. He probably didn't want there to be a scene if he had woken her up. As she laid in bed a few more minutes, she decided to just pretend all was OK. It was 6:30 a.m., so she would just get up and go about the normal morning activities.

"Good morning, sweetheart. It's time to wake up," Sally cheerfully announced as she gently shook Collin's shoulder. Then she walked down the hall to the boys' room and gave the same announcement. Once Todd and Pace's school clothes were laid out for them, she entered the kitchen and began breakfast.

After about ten minutes, Todd rounded the corner of the kitchen. "Good morning, Mom," he greeted her as he took the container of milk from the refrigerator and poured him and Pace a glass.

"How are you this morning?" Sally asked Todd.

"I'm OK," he answered.

"Where's your brother?"

"I'm right here, Momma," Pace exclaimed as he ran into the kitchen.

"And how are you this morning?" Sally asked.

"I'm good. And how are you, Momma?"

"I'm good too. Thank you for asking! Y'all hop up at the table. Your breakfast is being served," Sally announced as she sat their breakfast plates in front of them. "I'll be right back. Gonna check on your father," she said as she left the table.

Sally walked to the open door of the bathroom and saw Collin shaving. "Just wanted to let you know your breakfast is ready."

"Thank you, Sally, but I'm going to have to skip breakfast this morning. I need to get to work. I'll grab something on the way," Collin said as he washed the shaving cream from his face.

Sally so badly wanted to ask him about last night, and now, why he couldn't eat breakfast with his family. But she let it slide, again not wanting to have a confrontation with him. Maybe soon he would be ready to share with her what's going on with him.

"Are you taking the boys to school this morning?" she asked.

"No, I can't do that either. I've got to go!" Collin said as he grabbed his coat. "See y'all later," he said as he hurried out the front door.

"Momma, what's wrong with Daddy?" Pace asked concerningly.

"I don't know, Son." After a moment, she added, "Everything will be OK." She tried to sound convincing. She fought back tears as she left the dining room and entered her bedroom to get dressed. She was so stressed, but she didn't want to let the boys see her cry.

Once dressed, she prepared Todd and Pace's lunchboxes and helped them put on their coats. It was a cold December morning, and heavy frost covered everything. It took a few minutes to clear the windshield, but Sally managed, and the boys arrived at school with little time to spare.

Once back home, Sally washed the breakfast dishes and began a load of clothes in the washing machine. She wanted to wash them today so she could have all clean clothes to pack tomorrow for their trip to Brandon. With Collin's behavior, she wasn't sure if the trip was still planned, but she had to act like it was and be ready to go.

Sally missed Rusty so much. With all that was going on in her life with Collin, she just wished she could step out of this world and into Rusty's—and especially into his loving arms. Should she call him? What would she say to him? She sat down on the couch and looked at the telephone, thinking about the sound of Rusty's voice. After a minute, she convinced herself. *I'm going to do this!* She picked up the handset and dialed Rusty's telephone number.

There was a very quiet hesitation on the phone line. She thought, *It's not too late . . . you can hang up!* The ringing began. *Too late! You're committed now.* Five times it rang. Ten times it rang. Twenty times it rang. Sally's heart sank as she lowered the handset to disconnect the call. Her emotions gave way to tears. She laid down on the couch and sobbed. She was so tired from lack of sleep the night before, and she drifted off to sleep.

Several hours passed, and Sally woke up abruptly. She got up from the couch, walked to the kitchen, and fixed herself a cup of coffee and a sandwich. While she was eating, she attempted to reason with herself about Collin's attitude and how drastically it changed from last weekend's romantic getaway. They had such a great trip together, and now he was acting even worse than before. *What happened?* All her thoughts came up with blank. "I have no clue!" she said out loud.

In desperation, Sally returned to the telephone. She looked at it for a moment, then reached her hand down, picked up the handset, and dialed Rusty's telephone number again. The ringing sound began. Sally held her breath.

Five rings. Ten rings . . . .

"Hello?"

Rusty's voice.

Breathe, Sally, breathe. . . .

"Rusty, it's Sally," she managed to say nervously.

"Sweetheart, are you OK? I've been so concerned about you. I've wanted to call you, but I didn't know if I should. I'm so glad you called. I've been doing a lot of thinking about us, and I'm so sorry I said the things I did. I know you had no control over that trip with your husband. I was, and in a way I still am, afraid of losing you. I love you, Sally."

Sally broke down crying, sobbing uncontrollably. Hearing Rusty's words meant everything to her. "Rusty, it's so good to hear your voice," she was finally able to say through her tears. "Thank you for understanding, and thank you for still loving me because I love you too, honey, and I miss you so much."

"Oh, Sally dear, I miss you too. I long to see you and wrap you up in my arms. Are you OK?" Rusty asked her again.

"Yes and no. I'm not sick or anything; just seems like I'm going through the motions of each day and doing what I need to do. How are you? What have you been doing?" Sally asked.

"I've been helping my dad with a few projects of his and going several places with my mom and dad, getting ready for Christmas. I helped Mom decorate the Christmas tree and also helped her and Dad put up all the many decorations. My mom loves to decorate for Christmas. What about you? What have you been doing?"

"The boys have had a lot of homework this week and tests yesterday and today. They're excited about tomorrow being their last day of school until after the holiday break, January 7th, I think. They helped me put the Christmas tree up and decorate the house. Gifts are all wrapped and under the tree; now we're just waiting for Santa to come in a few days." She thought better of telling Rusty of the trip Collin planned to go see his sister and her family this weekend. There should be no way of him finding out—Mrs. Oldham will be with us (the phone messenger). "I wish I could be with you too, sweetheart. You are always on my mind," Sally responded.

"You said the boys won't go back to school until the 7th, right?" Rusty inquired.

"Yes," Sally answered.

"My first run to Abilene will be on January 1st, weather permitting. It doesn't sound good for us to see each other when I come through Memphis on January 3rd, since the boys will still be home, but maybe on the 6th. Gosh, that seems like such a long time away!" Rusty sounded bewildered.

"I'm sad to say, yes, the 3rd is out, and depending on the situation here, I'm not sure about the 6th. It is a Sunday, and most of the time, Collin is home, but he's been acting really weird since last Tuesday. When he came home from work, he was very upset about something. When I asked him what was wrong, he told me he didn't want to discuss it and for me not to ask him again. Since then, he's not been at home a lot. I don't know what's happening with him, and I'm not going to ask because I don't want him to get upset with me. I don't want or need him to get violent like he did several weeks ago. That was scary and really scared the boys," Sally said.

"No, please no, don't get him angry. I do not want him hurting you or the boys. Sally, I wish you would let me come and get you and the boys. I don't mean to put more on your plate, but I'd rather you be away from him and the three of you be with me," Rusty suggested with concern.

"Oh Rusty, thank you for your kindness and your thoughtfulness. You're so sweet. But, honey, that's a lot of responsibility to take on yourself. Besides, I don't know how that would work." Sally was grateful for Rusty's admirable gesture.

"I know how it would work. I come and get you and the boys, bring you all home with me to live, and then you can file for divorce," Rusty suggested.

"Oh, sweetheart, you make it sound so simple . . . and *so* inviting!" Sally remarked softly.

"I know several attorneys, and I'll do some checking into what we need to do to make this happen. You would leave Collin, wouldn't you?" Rusty questioned.

Wow. This was a lot for Sally to take in. Her mind was racing. Rusty's question demanded an answer. Her heart was elated and excited and was ready to say *yes,* but her mind wasn't so sure. Too many things to consider, and the uncertainty of how everything would work out. But it was too early for her to think about this now. How wonderful it would be for her to step into Rusty's world. Her heart overruled her mind and her hesitation, and she had her answer. "Yes, I would! I want to be with you!" she affirmed.

"Sally dear, you have made me very happy. Thank you! I love you so much. I will make you happy and give you and your sons a good life. I will start the research for our solution right away. I wish we were together right now. I'd take you in my arms and hug you so tight!" Rusty was overjoyed.

"I'll take bunches of your warm kisses too, OK?" Sally said.

"You've got 'em, sweetheart! All the time."

"And I'll give them right back to you," she responded.

There was a silence.

"Rusty, are you still there?" Sally asked.

"Yes. I'm just thinking. I don't want to put our journey together on hold, but with Christmas just a few days away and businesses here closed down for the holidays, it may take me a while to have a chance to talk to the attorneys I know. But I'll do my best to get the ball rolling," Rusty said.

"I know you will. I, too, don't want to put our journey together on hold, but I believe we'd better wait until after Christmas too. So please take your time. I'm here, and I'll be waiting for you. I don't know any attorneys, but I have some friends who I might be able to talk to also, if that's OK with you?" Sally suggested.

"Yes, of course. That would be helpful to get as much information as we can on how to handle things. Good idea, my dear."

"I'm so glad I called you, honey. You have given me hope. Your love for me is very special," Sally gratefully said. She looked at the wall clock. "Rusty, I need to go. I don't want to, but I must go and get the boys from school. We'll talk again soon. I love you more than you'll ever know. Take care and stay safe."

"I love you too. You take care and stay safe. If you can, stay cool with Collin. I don't want him hurting you or the boys. Talk to you later, sweetheart," Rusty said, and the call ended.

Sally didn't have time to sit and ponder over her conversation with Rusty. The boys would be waiting for her. She threw on her coat and ran out the front door. It was cold as the north wind blew, but Rusty's words kept her warm.

The boys were waiting for Sally at the school's front door. They ran to the car and climbed into the back seat.

"I'm sorry I'm late, guys. Y'all OK?" she said apologetically.

"That's OK, Mom. We hadn't been outside but a minute. I'm OK," Todd answered.

"That's good. How about you, Pace? You OK?"

"Yes ma'am, I'm good," Pace replied.

"How do y'all think you did on your tests today? Did your teachers say how y'all did on your tests from yesterday?" Sally asked as she began driving home.

Pace began, "Well, nothing on the tests from yesterday, but today, I made a hundred on my spelling test. The other test, I don't know. It was kinda easy; maybe a hundred."

"Oh, that's great, Pace! I'm proud of you. Good job! Todd, how about you?" Sally asked.

"My teacher passed out the graded math tests from yesterday, and I made a ninety-five on it. Also, on my English test, I made a ninety. It was hard! I don't know my grades for today's tests, but I think I did OK," Todd replied.

"Now that's my Todd! I like those grades too. Very good! Well, no more tests for a while, kiddos. Tomorrow, y'all will only be in school for half a day. Then we'll leave in the afternoon for your cousins' house for a few days. That'll be fun!" Sally pulled into the driveway. "How about some cookies and hot chocolate? That sound good?"

The boys jumped out and ran into the house excitedly.

As Sally folded the washed and dried clothes, the boys enjoyed their hot chocolate and cookies. She sat some of the clothes to the side of the bed so she could pack them for their trip. If she thought about her conversation with Rusty too much, she would not get the things done she needed to do for the trip. She was excited about their plans, but she had to stay focused on the here and now.

"How about bacon, egg, and cheese sandwiches with chips for supper tonight? How does that sound?" she asked her sons as she walked back into the dining room.

"That sounds really good, Momma," Pace responded.

"Mom, do we have any tomato soup?" Todd asked.

"Yes, I believe we do."

"Could I have some soup with my sandwich?" Todd requested.

"Absolutely."

Even though it was cold outside, Todd and Pace wanted to play in the backyard. Sally dressed them warmly with all their winter clothes, and out the back door they went. "Y'all can only play for a little while. It's cold!" She didn't know if they heard her, as they were already yelling excitedly and jumping off the back deck.

Sally shivered from the cold air as she closed the door. Even though it was still a little early to prepare their supper, she made sure she had a can of tomato soup.

About thirty minutes later, the boys came in from playing. Chilled to their young bones, they needed to warm up. Sally suggested that they take a hot bath to chase the chills away, and that way they wouldn't need to take baths that night. They liked that idea. Sally helped them take off their layers of clothing while the hot water ran in the bathtub. Then away they went to play in the tub.

Normally Collin would leave work at 5 p.m. and be home near 5:30. The hands on the wall clock indicated it was 5:45 p.m. Not wanting to delay dinner, Sally began to prepare the food.

The phone rang.

"Hello?" Sally answered.

"Hi, Sally. It's Peggy. How are you?" Mrs. Oldham asked.

"Hi, Peggy. We're doing good, just fixin' supper. How are you?"

"I'm OK. Just hadn't heard for y'all about our trip. Are we still going? And what time do I need to be at your home, or are y'all picking me up?" Peggy inquired.

"I wish I had the answers to your questions, but I don't. Collin planned this trip, so I guess you might need to ask him those questions. He should be here, but he hasn't come in from work yet. As soon as he gets home, I'll have him call you. I'd like to know the answers to those questions too. He's been working a lot of hours this week. I just hope he remembers the trip!" Sally said with dismay.

"Yes, Sally. Please have him call me. See y'all soon." And the call disconnected.

Sally went back to the kitchen and continued preparing supper. Todd and Pace came into the kitchen all bathed and warm in their flannel PJs.

"Supper's almost ready. What do y'all want to drink?" Sally asked.

"Milk for me," Pace answered.

"Me too. I'll get our glasses and pour it," Todd chimed in.

"Thank you for helping, kiddos," Sally responded gratefully.

The boys carried their glasses of milk to the table, and Sally followed them with the food. They chatted about their upcoming trip and talked about the games the boys would take to play during their road trip.

Near 8 p.m., Collin walked through the front door. Sally and the boys were watching television.

"Hi, y'all. Sorry I'm late," he said. "Work has been crazy," he added as he took off his coat and hung it on the coat tree in the living room.

"Your mother has called asking questions about the trip tomorrow. She needs for you to call her. Are we still going?" Sally asked, trying not to sound aggravated with him.

"Yes, we are still going. I'm tired, Sally. You call her. I'm going to take a shower and go to bed. I have to be back to work at 6 a.m. tomorrow." Collin's words were stern.

"Collin, I don't know the answers to her questions. You planned this trip, and you have all the information. I don't!" Sally retorted. Then she quickly reminded herself, *Be nice. Don't upset him!* "OK, I'll call your mother," she agreed in quiet frustration.

"Thank you. I appreciate that," he replied and walked out of the living room to their bedroom.

Sally, as frustrated as she was with Collin, called Peggy and arranged for her to come to their home and they would leave for Brandon at 3 p.m. tomorrow afternoon. Sally thought if things worked out that way, great! If not, well, so be it!

Sally sat down on the couch with the boys and continued watching television until 9 p.m., and then they all went to bed.

At 5 a.m., Sally woke up and saw Collin getting ready for work. "I told your mother to come here to the house and we would leave at 3 this afternoon," she informed him.

"That's fine. I'll try to be home by 3," Collin halfway assured Sally. "See ya later," he said as he left the room and walked out of the house. He drove Sally's car to work and left his car for her to pack for their trip.

Sally laid back down in bed and thought, *If this is the way it is going to be with Collin after he made his new commitment to me that he was going to be a better husband and father, then his commitment doesn't mean a thing! The sooner I can leave him, the better off I and the boys will be!* She rolled out of bed, too upset to go back to sleep.

While the morning coffee was brewing, she took the luggage from their closet, opened it, and began packing their clothes and other things for their trip. As she looked at the luggage she remembered just a week earlier, the happiness she had with Collin on their getaway. How could their situation have changed so much in one week? Sally felt so sad and again wondered just what had happened to make things change so quickly.

The morning activities went normally, and Sally returned home from taking the boys to school. Reluctantly, she continued packing. She wondered how the trip was going to go. Would Collin's attitude be any different? How much Christmas spirit was really going to be evident? She really didn't feel like going, but to help represent the family, she had to go.

The morning passed quickly, and it was time to get the boys from school after their half day. She had packed all she was going to pack.

When they arrived back home, they ate lunch, packed their games in a small bag, and waited for Grandmother to arrive. At 2:30 Peggy pulled in the driveway. Sally helped her put her things in their car, and they went inside to wait for Collin.

Soon after, Collin pulled up at 2:55, parking on the street outside the house. He hurried into the house, greeted his mother, and quickly acknowledged Sally and the boys in the living room before going straight to the bedroom. He changed into more comfortable clothes for the drive, then appeared back in the living room where everyone was waiting.

"I'm ready! Let's go!" he announced as he opened the front door and headed to the car, the others following.

Chapter Eight

By 3:15 p.m., they were on the road to Brandon. The weather was nice—sunny but cool. Sally sat in the back seat with the boys who were already playing one of their road trip games. She hoped they would be occupied with their games for the whole trip. She tried to be pleasant and congenial with Peggy, who was sitting in the passenger seat next to Collin. Sally thought she would be more comfortable in the front seat than in the back seat with her feisty grandsons. Collin made conversation with his mother, and all seemed fine, to Sally's surprise. Collin wouldn't speak to Sally or the boys, but he was Mr. Chatty with his mom!

The little over three-hour trip to Brandon was uneventful. When Collin drove into Ellen and David's driveway, they, as well as their two children, Brad and Tammy, walked to the car and greeted them with hugs. It was a joyous reunion. The men brought in the luggage, Brad and Tammy took Todd and Pace to the basement to play, and Ellen showed Peggy and Sally their new home—every nook and cranny. She had it beautifully decorated with Christmas décor from floor to ceiling. The house was definitely ready for the holidays!

Ellen had prepared a delicious dinner for the family, which everyone enjoyed. After the table was cleared and the kitchen was cleaned, they all retreated to the den where snacks of every kind and delicious drinks were waiting to be consumed. They talked for hours, catching up on all the latest news about the family. It wasn't until the wee hours of the morning before the house was quiet and all were asleep.

The next morning, Sally was awakened by the aroma of coffee brewing and the smell of bacon frying. She glanced at the clock on the nightstand and saw that it was 7:30 a.m. After only five and a half hours of sleep, she really wanted to stay in bed!

She rolled over to wake up Collin, but she found his side of the bed empty. Sally laid in bed for a few more minutes as her mind turned to Rusty. She wondered what he might be doing today and pictured him, the best she could from Rusty's description of his home, in his kitchen eating breakfast.

Suddenly, Sally's train of thought was interrupted.

"Sally, are you awake?" Peggy softly asked as she gently opened the door.

"Yes ma'am. Good morning, Peggy." Sally wondered why Peggy had come to wake her up instead of Collin.

"Good morning. I thought you might like some coffee before breakfast," Peggy suggested.

"That sounds good. I'll be downstairs in a few minutes."

Peggy left the room, and Sally slowly rolled over and found the edge of the bed. She slipped into her long, blue, velvet robe and slide her feet into her matching slippers. She walked across the hall to the bathroom where she ran a brush through her hair. She looked at her reflection in the mirror and said quietly to herself, "That will just have to do for now!"

As she walked down the hall to the stairs, she heard giggling coming from behind the closed door of the room she had just passed. She stepped back a few steps, knocked on the door, and slowly opened it. As soon as Todd and Pace saw her, they greeted her. "Good morning, Momma!"

"Good morning, kiddos. Y'all are up early too. What are y'all doing?" Sally asked them.

"Watching cartoons on the television," Pace answered.

"Oh, how fun! It'll be time to eat soon. Don't forget to wash your hands before coming downstairs," she reminded as she continued her walk down the hall. When she reached the bottom of the stairs, a glass window curio caught her attention. She knew that Ellen was a collector of blown glass and had been for years, but since the last time she'd seen Ellen's collection, it had grown to many more beautiful pieces. As she admired the pieces, the curio's inside light came on, and the pieces just sparkled.

"They are beautiful, aren't they? Much prettier with the glow of the light!" Ellen remarked as she walked beside Sally and looked with pride at her huge collection.

"They are beautiful! You have added a lot to your collection."

"Yes. Whenever we go on vacation or a long weekend trip, I always look for blown glass. I'm fascinated by its beauty," Ellen admitted. "Come on in the kitchen and grab you a cup of coffee. Breakfast is almost ready," she said, ushering Sally along. Then she turned toward the stairs and said in a louder voice, "Time to eat, children!"

Immediately the children bounced down the steps and ran into the kitchen. In the back of the kitchen was an eating area that included a picnic table set up for the kids to eat their breakfast so the adults could be together at the dining table.

David asked everyone to form a circle in the kitchen, join hands, and pray, and he thanked the Lord for the meal and for the family and asked for blessings for the day ahead.

The four children crawled up on the benches of the picnic table, and the five adults sat at the dining room table. Ellen had outdone herself with every kind of breakfast food one could think of eating and more than plenty to go around. Everything was so delicious, and everyone enjoyed being together.

After the wonderful meal and the kitchen was all clean, the family decided to celebrate their Christmas. The night before, David and Collin had brought in all the gifts and placed them under and around the Christmas tree. The children sat around the tree and took turns handing out the presents, one at a time. Then everyone watched while each person opened their gifts. It took a while, but it was the family tradition. There were lots of nice and special gifts given, and it was great family time.

Ellen served coffee and sweet rolls after the celebration. David explained that for dinner, he and Ellen were taking the family to a nice supper club in town.

Sally could hardly hold her eyes open, and since the dinner arrangements were several hours away, she asked to be excused to take a little nap. Todd and Pace were in the basement playing with Brad and Tammy, so they were preoccupied, but Ellen said she'd keep an eye on them while Sally rested.

Sally went upstairs to the room she was staying in, and not long after she had laid down, she fell asleep. Several hours passed before she finally woke up, feeling rested and somewhat revived. She decided to get dressed for the evening's dinner. As she walked down the hall, she could hear voices talking softly downstairs. It was Collin.

"Sally doesn't know, and I don't want her to know!" Collin said. "That's the reason I took her on that so-called *second honeymoon* last weekend—to make it up to her and get her back to where I wanted her. I could have spent the money in so many other ways. To me, it was a waste of money!"

"Collin, that's not fair to Sally. When are you going to tell her?" Sally heard Ellen respond with concern.

Sally listened intently as she stood ever so still, almost holding her breath, wondering what Collin's mysterious secret was that he wanted to keep from her.

"Probably after Christmas because I'll need time to start packing my things for the trip."

"Son, I know you think it's a great opportunity for you, but I think you need to consider your family," Peggy chimed in.

"No, Mom, I'm going for it. I may never have another chance like this again. BEDON has been great to me, and even if the position takes me farther away from the family, then so be it. Besides, the fringe benefits could certainly be very attractive. I'd be around a lot of different people and new women to look at and admire. I'm looking forward to it, personally. Sally's *old stuff* anyway. I need something new to look at during the week. Then on the weekends, I can stomach her," Collin said with a little laugh.

Sally's hand flew to her mouth to quiet her mortified shock and urge to scream out. Tears suddenly welled up in her eyes. She fought to hold them back.

"When do you leave and start this new job?" Ellen asked. "Do you know how long you'll be gone?"

"I'll leave January 1st, drive to Houston, and check in with my new boss on January 3rd. It can't be soon enough. I'm so excited. Sure, I'm going to miss the boys, but over the last several months, with all the time I've spent at work getting trained and ready for this move, I've hardly seen them anyway. They'll be OK. Sally will see to that," Collin said. "I don't know how long it will take to start from the ground up with the new warehouse. People will be hired, the warehouse will need to be set up with racks, storage bins, equipment . . . and I'll be in charge of all of it. I could be gone for six months or longer. Then, if the boss wants me to become the warehouse manager, who knows, I could be there for a long time," Collin explained.

"Surely you'll want Sally and the boys to move to Houston?" Peggy questioned.

"No way, Mom! I'm ready for a change, and it does not include Sally," Collin responded with irritation in his voice.

"Collin, you're terrible, and you should be ashamed of yourself! You know Sally is a good woman. She's made for you a great wife all these years. You're supposed to be a family man. Don't start messing up!" Ellen said forcefully.

"I'm not messing up, Sis. Sally can handle it. She can keep on tending to the boys and the house while I advance my career and hopefully have some fun too. Our days of serious romance are over. We have so little love for each other, especially in the bedroom. I'm sure I can find someone new to romance," he said, laughing again.

Sally couldn't stand to hear any more. She quietly hurried back to the bedroom and closed the door. She sat on the bed, tears streaming down her face. She laid down and buried her face in the pillow and cried.

Eventually the tears stopped. Sally's mind and body were numb; her heart was totally broken. Collin's cold-hearted words continued to ring in her ears. She guessed hearing the conversation the way she did was what cut her so deeply. There truly was no love left in him for her or in their marriage. And what's even worse was that he said all this in front of his family. What were they going to think of her now?

"I need you, Rusty!" she softly cried out. "I want to be with you now more than ever!"

She laid motionless on the bed for a long while, staring at the ceiling. She realized she was going to have to pull herself back together as much as she could. She needed to be strong enough to get through tonight and tomorrow's trip back home without letting on to Collin or his family that she heard that whole conversation.

Sally slowly rose up from the bed and started toward the door to go to the bathroom to wash the tears from her eyes and face. When she opened the door, Collin was standing in the doorway. She immediately felt the urge to throw up.

"I was just coming to wake you up, but you are already up and dressed. I was going to help you get dressed," Collin said, walking toward her.

Sally turned cold.

Collin closed the door behind him. "Is there anything I can help you with, sweetheart?" he said, drawing closer to her.

"No, there isn't, Collin. I'm not feeling well. Please, go," Sally said softly.

Collin reached for her.

"Collin, what are you doing? I asked you to go! Now, go!" she screamed. At this point, she didn't care if anyone heard her or not.

Collin stared at her, expressionless. "OK," he said as he turned and left the room.

Sally wept in her hands silently from both anger and humiliation. Nearly blind from tears, she staggered to the side of the bed. As she wiped the tears from her face, she wondered how she could go on knowing Collin's true feelings for her. She hated him! So much for being strong, as she had hoped she would be. She felt sick when Collin came near her.

Again, there was a knock on the door.

"Yes?" Sally answered.

"It's me. Can I come in?" Ellen asked.

Oh my gosh. Now what? Sally thought. "Sure, come in," she said as she attempted to wipe any trace of tears from her face.

The door opened, and Ellen stepped into the room. "Collin said you weren't feeling well. So I brought you a small glass of orange juice. It might help you to feel better. It's probably because you've not had enough sleep. Can I get you anything else, Sally?" Ellen asked concerningly.

"No, but thank you."

"We'll be leaving soon for the supper club. You rest, and I'll be up to get you when we get ready to leave, OK?" Ellen said.

"OK," Sally replied and watched Ellen leave the room.

Sally continued to sit on the side of the bed while she drank the orange juice. She felt like she needed something much stronger. She wondered what Collin said to Ellen after he left the room, but then, did she really care? She sat the glass on the nightstand and made herself get up from the bed. She walked across the hall to the bathroom, took a washcloth and washed her tear-stained face, and combed her hair. While she was touching up her makeup, both of her boys burst into the open door of the bathroom.

"Momma, come on! We're ready to go to dinner!" Pace shouted.

"I'm starved! Hurry, Mom!" Todd exclaimed, and both of them took Sally by the hand and nearly dragged her out of the bathroom.

As Sally emerged downstairs, Peggy said, "There she is! Are you feeling any better, my dear? We are hoping that you are."

Sally realized they were all trying to make her feel better, and she appreciated it. She needed the attention and to know that someone cared, or at least acted like they cared. She knew Collin didn't.

"Yes, thank you, Peggy. I am feeling somewhat better. And Ellen, the juice was good. Thank you," Sally expressed.

The group made their way out the door. The night air was crisp, and the north wind was sharp to their bare faces. David had warmed the van in advance for the trip to the supper club, and it was warm and cozy. Sally kept her distance from Collin, as their sons sat between them in the back seat.

After a twenty-minute drive, they arrived at the supper club. The parking lot was full of vehicles, and there were lots of people inside. It was a very nice place. The hostess seated the group, handing them their menus. The smell of food suddenly made Sally hungry.

The waitress returned with their beverages and began taking their orders. When she walked away, David rose from his chair and stated, "There is a cheese and cracker table in the corner by the door we came in. Their cheeses are really good. Please, help yourself. I am," he said, getting up from the table. "Coming, Ellen?" Ellen rose from the table, followed by Peggy and Collin, and walked over to the cheese table.

"You kiddos want to try the cheese and cracker table?" Sally asked the boys. They shook their heads *no.* "I don't blame y'all. I think I'll pass too."

The others returned to the table with small plates full of different cheeses and crackers. Ellen lagged behind a few moments, as she saw a woman she knew and stopped to chat. Several men in the club recognized David, and they visited with him for a few minutes also. The waitress had brought the children a small package of crayons and a coloring page, helped them pass the time before their meals were served.

After about a twenty-minute wait, one by one, the meals were brought to the table. When David saw that Sally had chosen the prime rib, he remarked that she had made a good choice—that the supper club's prime rib was delicious. She hoped it would be. She cut a small piece to taste, and David was right! It was scrumptious.

Sally was helping prepare the boys' burgers when David asked if he could say a quick prayer for the food. When he finished, everyone dug in. The table was very quiet as everyone enjoyed their food selections.

The waitress came to take their dessert orders. The children ordered ice cream, and the adults chose a selection of pies and cakes, including Sally's favorite: creamy coconut cake.

Everyone's tummies were more than full. It had been a delightful evening, and a good distraction from Sally's reality. Going to the supper club was an excellent decision—pricey, but very good. Sally saw Collin hand David some money to cover the tab, which was the proper gesture. She was glad he thought to do that, all things considered.

When they arrived back home, Sally was thankful. The whole day had created lots of good memories for the family—and some bad ones she would never forget. She was thankful that she had pulled herself together and enjoyed the evening, but she was concerned what the night was going to bring. She did not want to be in the same room with Collin and definitely not the same bed. But how could she avoid that situation without causing any suspicion regarding Collin's earlier conversation with his family? She sure did not want Collin to think she knew his secret.

Once inside David and Ellen's home, everyone agreed the hour was late, and it was near bedtime. Sally followed the boys upstairs and helped them get ready for bed. After they brushed their teeth, she tucked them into bed, and as always, she said, "Sleep tight. Don't let the bedbugs bite. I love y'all bunches," as she kissed them good night and left the room.

Collin was standing at the door of the boys' bedroom. Sally cringed.

"Coming to bed, dear?" he asked suggestively.

Sally glared at him, having the urge to slap him. "No, I'm not ready for bed yet. You go ahead. I'll be there in a little while." She tried to sound normal, like nothing was bothering her. As much as she now hated him, she needed, to a point, to play along with his stupid game so he wouldn't think she knew his secret. She disliked playing emotional games, but if that's what she needed to do until Collin spilled the beans, then that's what she must do.

Sally walked down the stairs quietly to the kitchen and poured herself a glass of water. When she turned around, Ellen was standing at the entrance of the kitchen.

"I'm sorry, Ellen. I was trying to be quiet. I didn't mean to disturb you. I wasn't ready for bed yet, and I thought I'd sit in the den for a while near the fireplace. I thought it might be relaxing for me, listening to the wood crackling and watching the dancing flames," Sally explained, trying not to reveal the true sadness she was feeling.

Ellen sat down beside her on the couch. "Sally, you didn't disturb me. I wasn't ready to call it a night either. I know we, as sisters-in-law, don't know each other as true sisters do, but I've always loved you as a sister. It might be because we're near the same age and our interests are about the same. When Collin married you, I was so delighted in his choice for his wife. I know the Lord put y'all together for a reason, but now I feel a real need to pray for you."

Sally was thankful for Ellen's concern for her because she really didn't know what to do about her situation with Collin. Sally also knew that Ellen and David were people of faith, and praying was an important part of their lives.

"I feel that way too, Ellen," Sally responded. "I wish we had been able to spend more time together in the years that Collin and I have been married. I truly would appreciate your prayers for me. Thank you, Ellen."

"You got 'em, girl. I'm going to let you enjoy the fire, and I'm going to leave on the Christmas tree lights also. You rest. I've got some praying to do. I love you, Sally." Ellen left Sally's side and disappeared into the darkness as she walked into her bedroom.

Sally was deeply moved by Ellen's words. How precious she really was! As Sally stared into the low-burning fire and the blinking of the Christmas tree lights, there came a calmness over her that she couldn't explain. She laid down on the couch, totally relaxed, and fell asleep.

Early the next morning, Ellen and Peggy were in the kitchen brewing coffee and preparing breakfast.

"I feel so sorry for Sally and the boys. I wish Collin would come to his senses and reconsider his new position with BEDON," Peggy lamented.

"I know, Mom. I do too, but he sounds like he's made up his mind. I just don't know how Sally is going to take this news and his plans to practically move away and out of their lives. His attitude about Sally is surprising. I thought they were happy and very much in love. Collin doesn't deserve Sally. She is a sweet girl." Ellen continued. "Last night I prayed to our Lord that He would give Sally the strength to guide her through the days ahead of her . . . and the boys too. Collin's absence will greatly affect Todd and Pace." Ellen poured two cups of coffee.

"I, too, have lifted up prayers for Sally and the boys. I'm glad I live close. I'll be there for them," Peggy assured Ellen.

Sally was still lying on the couch, but she awoke when their conversation started and listened intently. She was grateful for their concern for her and the boys, and she wanted to know more about how *praying* worked. She didn't want them to know she had overheard their conversation, so she coughed several times to alert them to her presence. About the same time, Todd and Pace bounced down the stairs.

"Good morning, Momma," Todd and Pace greeted as they ran and hugged Sally.

"Good morning, my little boys. Did y'all sleep good?"

"Yip, sure did," they answered.

"Good morning to y'all too," Peggy said as she stepped from the kitchen to the den.

"Good morning, Grandmother Peggy," Todd and Pace replied.

"Would you like some coffee, Sally?" Peggy asked.

"Got it right here for her," Ellen announced as she handed Sally her cup of morning joe.

Sally reached for the cup. "Thank you." She took a sip. "Mmm, that's good. Nothing like a good cup of coffee to begin the day! I'll take a few minutes to freshen up and then come to the kitchen and help with breakfast," Sally suggested as she stood up, her coffee cup still in her hand, and walked up the stairs and into the bathroom.

As Collin opened the bedroom door, he found the bathroom door closed. He waited a few moments, then the door opened. "Sally, you never came to bed last night. I missed you."

Sally, somewhat startled by his appearance, veered past. "Yip, I relaxed by the fire last night and enjoyed falling asleep on the couch," she remarked as she continued to walk down the hall and down the stairs.

The preparation for breakfast was well underway when Sally entered the kitchen. "It sure is smellin' delicious in here, ladies. What can I do to help?" Sally asked.

"Well, you can pour the juice and milk and put the jams and jellies on the tables; that'll help," Ellen replied. "Mom, while Sally is doing that, would you please put a stick of butter on two plates and put them on each table? The biscuits are done. Please take them out of the oven and place them in the basket warmers for each table."

Collin had come downstairs, and he and David both entered the kitchen. "Breakfast is almost ready, kiddos," David announced.

All the children ran to the kitchen and climbed onto the picnic table benches, ready to eat. Sally placed the bowl of scrambled eggs on the table with a plateful of crisp bacon. Peggy came in behind Sally with a bowl of hot, buttery grits. David asked for all to join hands so he could pray a blessing over the meal.

After the dishes were washed and the kitchen was cleaned, Sally and the boys went upstairs to pack up their things to head home. Collin was already dressed and was waiting for Sally to finish packing. He watched her intently from the edge of the bed but did not offer to help her.

"You know, honey, I really do appreciate you agreeing to take this trip. It's been great to visit with my family. I don't know when we'll get to see them again, with the way work has me burning the candle at both ends. So thank you very much. I love you, sweetheart." Collin almost sounded grateful.

Sally was about to rage, but she didn't want to cause a scene. What she would say to Collin would not be very nice, and she was sure their voices would be heard by the rest of the family. "You're welcome, Collin," she said as calmly as she could.

Collin rose up from the bed and walked toward Sally. "Baby," he said, reaching out for her.

Sally's stomach churned at his words and the thought of him touching her. She stepped back. "Not now! We need to leave." She grabbed her purse from the dresser and walked toward the door. "Would you please bring the luggage downstairs?" she asked as she exited the room.

Collin stood in place, bewildered at what had just happened. He thought he had control of his relationship, but Sally was acting strange. He grabbed the luggage and walked out of the room.

David, Ellen, and Peggy were in the den with the four children. "Sure wish y'all would stay a little longer and go to church with us," David said.

Collin quickly responded, "No, but thanks for the invitation. We need to be gettin' on home, David. We thank y'all for the wonderful visit and all the great food and especially allowing us to share an early Christmas with all of you. It was a special time!"

"Yes, we, too, have definitely enjoyed y'all's visit with us. Celebrating Christmas together was so great. We haven't done that in ages, have we, Mom?" Ellen responded.

"That's right, Ellen, It's been many years. It was so nice," she agreed as her eyes welled up with tears.

They all walked toward the front door. Peggy wrapped one arm around Ellen and the other around Brad and Tammy. "I'm going to miss my grandchildren," Peggy admitted, again fighting back tears as she bent down and hugged and kissed them.

"Mom, we'll come for a visit with you this spring when the kids get out of school." Ellen drew a tissue from her pocket and handed it to her mother.

"Oh, that would be great! I'm already looking forward to that visit," Peggy said gleefully.

Sally, Collin, and the boys said one last goodbye as they approached their car. "Don't know when I'll get to see y'all again, but stay safe and well. Love y'all," Collin said as he shook David's hand, then hugged Ellen and the kids.

As Ellen hugged Sally, she whispered in her ear, "I'll have you in my prayers, and if you need anything, you just call me. I love you."

Sally's eyes welled up in tears at Ellen's words. "Thank you very much. I love you too." Sally opened the car door and sat down in the back seat.

Ellen hugged Todd and Pace before they climbed into the back seat with their mother. "Love you, kiddos. Great to see y'all," she said.

"Love you too, Aunt Ellen and Uncle David. Bye, Brad and Tammy. We had fun!" Todd and Pace said.

"Bye, Todd and Pace. Hope to see y'all again soon," Brad said as he and Tammy gave them a wave.

Ellen turned to her mom, the last to get into the car. "We sure did enjoy your visit with us, Mom. Thank you for everything. Hope to see you soon, but if not, we'll definitely see you this spring. We love you!" Ellen motioned to Brad and Tammy. "Kids, come and give your grandmother a big hug and thank her for your great Christmas presents."

They did as they were told.

"I love all of you too. Great visit, and thanks. . . ." Peggy couldn't finish her sentence as she fought back tears. She quickly got into the passenger seat of the car and closed the door.

"Y'all have a safe trip home, and please give us a quick call when you get there," David requested.

Collin started the car and lowered the windows. Arms and hands waved as they drove away. "Merry Christmas, y'all!" everyone said to one another.

"It was a great visit, don't y'all think? I'm glad we made the trip. Mom, are you OK?" Collin asked his mother who had tears rolling down her cheeks.

"I will be. I'm just sad to leave," she expressed as she took a tissue and dried her eyes. "Yes, it was very nice to see my daughter, son-in-law, and grandchildren. I've reached the age where I know time is growing short for me, and goodbyes are just sad," Peggy explained.

"Oh, Mom, you've got a lot of time left in you. It's OK; you'll see them again," Collin reassured her.

The drive home was uneventful. Todd and Pace played their road games while Sally watched, and Collin had surface-level conversation with his mom. Once home, Sally asked Peggy to stay a while for coffee or just to visit, but Peggy elected to go on home.

"Peggy, I'm happy that you were able to go see your family. I hope you enjoyed yourself," Sally told her.

"I truly did, and I thank y'all for asking me to join y'all."

"We'd like for you to be here for Christmas tomorrow . . . unless you have other plans. We don't want you to be alone," Sally said, wrapping her arms around her.

"I'd like that. About noon?" Peggy responded as she returned Sally's hug.

"That sounds great. We will see you then. Love you, and be careful driving home." Sally turned to Todd and Pace. "Go hug your grandmother and tell her bye."

The boys did as their mother asked them, then ran up the steps of the porch and disappeared into the house. Sally followed while Collin remained with his mother.

Once in the house, Sally watched out the living room window at a distance so as not to be seen. She would love to be a fly on the roof of Collin's car and be able to hear their conversation. Peggy looked distressed as Collin appeared to be agitated in what he was saying to her. Soon she turned and got into her car and left. She looked to be upset. Sally wondered what Collin had said to her.

Sally quickly walked into the boys' bedroom and began unpacking their bags of Christmas presents and their road trip games. She didn't want Collin to know she was watching him and his mother from the living room window. She needed to look busy.

Collin entered the house and walked into the boys' room. "You boys really did get some nice Christmas presents from your aunt and uncle, but tonight is the *big night*. Santa arrives! Are y'all excited?"

"YES!" Todd and Pace exclaimed. "Are we going to leave him some milk and cookies too?" they asked eagerly.

"We always do!" Sally chimed in.

"Santa is so busy, and I know he'll be hungry, so that'll be good for him," Pace said joyfully.

"What's for lunch, Mom? I'm hungry!" asked Todd.

"I need to go to the kitchen and see what we have to eat," Sally answered.

"Never mind. I'll run to a fast food place and get us some lunch. How's that? Does that sound OK?" Collin suggested.

The boys were excited! "Burgers and fries, please, Dad, for Pace and me."

"Yea, Daddy, that's what I want! Burgers and fries!" Pace echoed with excitement.

"Sally, what do you want?" Collin asked.

"Burger and fries for me too," Sally answered.

"OK, I'll be back in a bit," Collin said as he walked out of the room.

Sally was relieved he was going to be away from the house for a while because she had no idea how the rest of the day was going to be. She immediately went to the Christmas tree and removed all of the presents she had bought for Collin. Under the circumstances, she decided he didn't deserve the nice, thoughtful gifts. However, she did leave the gifts from Todd and Pace—not that he deserved those either, but she could not take that joy away from her boys.

"Momma, what are you doing?" Pace asked when he saw his mother taking some of the presents out from under the Christmas tree.

Surprised by his question, Sally wasn't sure how to answer. After a moment, she replied, "Truthfully, I've thought better about giving these gifts to your daddy. I'll give him something else. You might not understand, but it's OK, little Pace," she answered him honestly. She then took the presents and hid them under her bed. The day after Christmas, she would return them for the money. With Collin presumably leaving town, she wasn't sure if or when Collin would be giving her any money.

Sally had time to unpack the remainder of her and the boys' luggage and start a load in the washer before Collin returned with their lunch. When he came in, she wanted so desperately to ask him what took him so long, but she didn't want to ruffle his feathers or make him upset. Rusty's words echoed in her mind: *Don't let him get upset with you.*

Placing the food on the table, Collin said, "Man, it's a mess out there! Traffic is terrible. I had to go to five different places. Almost all the fast food restaurants are closed, and the one I did find that was open, the cars were lined up onto the street trying to get into the parking lot! But I finally made it. So let's dig in. I'm starving."

As Sally listened to Collin's words, she couldn't help but wonder if he was telling the truth. On the afternoon of Christmas Eve, she figured lots of places would be open, with last-minute shoppers looking for something to eat.

After finishing his meal, Collin got up from the table and went to the bedroom, then emerged moments later in just his underwear as he walked across the hall to the bathroom. Sally heard the shower start. She stood up and walked over to the desk and pulled out the telephone book and started looking through the yellow pages for restaurants. Her finger slid down the page to a nearby fast-food location, and she took the telephone's handset and dialed the number.

Someone answered.

"Hi! How late is your location open tonight?" Sally asked.

"Until midnight," the employee responded.

"OK, thanks," Sally said and hung up.

Sally continued to call three more nearby popular fast-food locations and was told the same thing: *midnight. Why did Collin lie about the delay in his return home?* she wondered. As she walked to their bedroom, she saw Collin's clothes lying on the bed. She picked them up to put in the dirty clothes hamper, but a sweet smell caught her attention. She raised his shirt to her nose and breathed in. There was a *sweet* smell all right, and it was not the smell of the detergent she used. It had to be perfume!

"What are you doing, Sally?" Collin surprised her, but she did not turn around to look at him.

"Why, I'm smelling your shirt. Strange; it doesn't smell like the detergent I use. I wonder why?" Sally remarked, turning to look at him with his bath towel wrapped around his waist. "Do *you* know why?" She walked passed him, laid the shirt across his naked shoulder, and exited the room.

Sally walked to the dining room and cleared the table of lunch remnants. Todd and Pace were watching television, so she decided to join them. Moments later, Collin entered the living room all neatly dressed and put on his coat.

Todd recognized that his dad was leaving. "Dad, where are you going? It's Christmas Eve! We always spend Christmas Eve together doing things. Will you be gone long?" he asked concerningly.

Collin opened the front door. "I'm sorry, son." Then he looked at Sally and said, "I'm going to find the *smell*." And with that, he walked out the door.

Todd turned to his mother. "Where is Dad going? It's Christmas Eve! He's supposed to be here with us, isn't he?" Todd had tears in his eyes, unable to understand and confused as to what was happening.

"I'm not sure, but yes, he should be home with us," his mother answered. She felt so sad for her boys. They didn't know it, but their world was about to fall apart.

Hours went by, and Collin did not return.

Todd and Pace took showers and put on their flannel PJs. "Mom, can we go ahead and put out the cookies and milk for Santa Claus?" Todd asked.

"Can we, Momma, can we?" Pace added excitedly.

"We sure can. Come on."

Sally pulled herself up from the couch and took her boys by the hand, and they walked to the kitchen. "Todd, you choose the glass for the milk, and Pace, you choose the plate for the cookies. I'll get the goodies out." They walked to the dining room table—Todd poured the milk into the glass, and Pace opened the bag of cookies and placed them on the plate.

"Looks good! I know Santa Claus is going to enjoy y'all's snacks you're leaving for him." Sally was delighted with her sons' enthusiasm in making sure Santa was fed.

"Mom," Todd began, "can we sing some Christmas songs before we go to bed?"

"Yes, I think that is an excellent idea! To help us, I'll put a Christmas record on, and we can sing along," Sally suggested. She walked over to the record player cabinet, pulled out an album, and placed it onto the turntable. The needle arm slowly came down on the edge of the record, and the music of "Silent Night" began to play. Sally sat down on the couch between her boys and put her arms around each of them. They began to sing.

They got through the whole album, up to the last song, "Santa Claus Is Coming to Town." What a perfect song to end the night!

Sally looked at the clock on the living room wall. "Oh my. It's time for bed! Santa won't come unless you two are asleep! So it's off to bed. That was so much fun singing. Thank you, Todd, for your suggestion."

"It was fun! Thank you, Momma. Let's do it again next year," Pace suggested.

"Sounds like a plan to me! Good idea, Pace!" Todd said.

Sally followed the boys into their bedroom and tucked them in. "Y'all sleep tight, and don't let those bedbugs bite. And especially tonight; y'all have sweet dreams. I love y'all bunches. Merry Christmas Eve!"

"Love to you too, Momma," Pace responded.

"I hope you have sweet dreams too, Mom," Todd said, hugging his mother.

"Thanks, my little guys." Sally turned to leave the room with tears in her eyes. She was so grateful to have such wonderful sons.

When she got back to the living room, she sat on the couch with her head in her hands, tears streaming down her face. Maybe she should not have made an issue out of the smell on Collin's shirt, and maybe he would still be home for the boys. What did she do? But then, she might as well get used to being alone because come January 1st, Collin would be gone for days at a time, according to what she had overheard. She thought about calling Rusty, but it was late, and she was too upset. She sure didn't want to upset Rusty, especially on Christmas Eve.

It was near midnight. Still no Collin, and Santa needed to do his work. Sally went to the bedroom closet and took out the toys Santa was bringing the boys. Quietly, one by one, she took the toys to the living room and sat them around the Christmas tree. When they were all placed, she took a step back and admired her work. She was very tired, so she decided she would just go to bed. As she made her way toward the hall, she stopped dead in her tracks. *Santa's snack has to be eaten!* she remembered frantically. She rushed to the dining room and consumed the cookies and milk, making sure she left some crumbs on the plate and a drop or two of milk in the glass. *OK, Santa, now it's time for bed.* Very quietly, Sally walked to her bedroom, took off her slippers, and crawled into bed, remembering Todd's words: "You have sweet dreams, Mom."

About four o'clock the next morning, Christmas Day, Sally was awakened by a noise. She laid still in bed for a few moments. Then, another disturbance. She thought maybe Todd or Pace might be up, checking out what Santa had brought them. She slowly got out of bed and walked to the bedroom door. Opening it quietly, she peered around the corner into the living room. She was shocked to find not Santa nor one of the boys but Collin, lying on the couch. Sally stood still, staring at her sleeping husband. She fought mixed emotions. As mad as she was at what he was about to do to the family, she was relieved that he was OK and home for Christmas—especially for the boys. Breathing deeply and steadying her heart, Sally gradually tip-toed back to bed.

Sally woke up a few hours later and eased out of bed. She wondered why Todd and Pace were not up yet. She moved slowly to the door of their room and saw both of them still lying in their beds. She stepped closer.

"Todd, Pace, Merry Christmas!" she spoke softly so as not to scare them.

They began to stir in their beds. Then suddenly, Todd sat up. "It's Christmas!" he shouted. "Good morning, Mom. Is Pace up yet?" He leaned over his bed to try to lay eyes on his brother.

From the bottom bunk, Pace exclaimed, "Yes, I am! Come on, Todd, get down!" and the race was on for both of them to get to the living room.

Their excitement filled the air with shouts of joy and laughter as they dashed from one gift to another. Sally's heart was full of happiness as she watched pure, childhood elation.

The boys didn't even notice their father lying on the couch until he sat up and uttered, "Merry Christmas, boys."

"Hey, Daddy! Merry Christmas!" both boys said at the same time as they continued to open the gifts that Santa had brought them.

Sally grabbed her camera from the closet shelf and took pictures of Todd and Pace enjoying their Christmas morning. She watched them for a little while, then drew their attention to the dining room table. "Santa must have liked your snack because only cookie crumbs are left!"

Todd and Pace rushed to the table to see. "He sure did!" Pace exclaimed as he looked at the empty plate and glass.

"I hope our snack gave him enough energy to reach the next house's snacks," Todd expressed.

Sally picked up the empty plate and glass and carried them to the kitchen. It was definitely *coffee time*, so she began the process of brewing the coffee and getting breakfast started.

Collin entered the doorway to the kitchen. "Good morning, Sally. Merry Christmas."

Sally had no desire to look at him, but she calmly acknowledged his greeting. "Morning, Collin," she said as dryly as she could.

"I'm sorry about not being here last night. I should have stayed home. I noticed you really did do a great job putting out Santa gifts, and the boys seem happy with everything. You did good! Thank you, Sally," Collin affirmed her.

Sally took what Collin had to say with a grain of salt. She knew how he really felt about her, so why was he acting like he cared? She really wanted to rip him open, but what was the sense in that? It was Christmas Day, and it was supposed to be a day of joy. She needed to make it that way, even if it was only for the boys.

"I wish you'd talk to me, but I understand if you don't," Collin admitted, then turned and left the kitchen.

As Sally continued to prepare breakfast, she remembered that Ellen had told her she would pray for her. She couldn't help but wonder *how* Ellen prayed. She'd heard about people praying, but she had never done it herself. She always relied upon her own instincts. Was she wrong to do that? Who was David and Ellen praying to? Did it help? Sally was in a very hard place in her life, and she wasn't sure what to do next.

Pausing her train of thought, she announced, "Breakfast is ready," as she sat the food on the dining room table. "Be sure to wash your hands, boys," she reminded them.

As the family sat around the table, Sally remembered David saying a prayer before they ate their meals. "It's Christmas Day! Shouldn't we say a prayer or something?" she asked.

Collin and the boys looked at her with blank stares.

Finally, Collin broke the silence. "Nah, that's just not necessary. Besides, I'm hungry, and everything looks delicious. I'm digging in. Come on, boys, fill your plates," he quickly said, rejecting the idea.

The boys talked about their new toys the whole time they ate. They were so excited! Sally and Collin ate in silence, with nothing to say to each other.

When everyone had finished eating, Collin said, "I have something I need to tell y'all."

Sensing what he was about to tell them, Sally interrupted. "If what you are about to tell us has anything to do with Houston, I highly suggest you wait until after Christmas is over. I want the rest of today to be happy for the boys."

Collin was speechless! He couldn't believe Sally's spunk.

"Todd, you and your brother are excused from the table," Sally said. "I know y'all want to go play with your new toys. Your father and I will be there soon, and you can open the presents from us. OK?"

The boys agreed and ran into the family room.

Collin stayed frozen to his seat as Sally took the dirty dishes to the sink. When she picked up the last of the dishes from the table, Collin followed her into the kitchen and approached her side.

"How did you know?"

"You talk to me quietly," she whispered emphatically. "I do not want the boys to hear this conversation. I heard everything, and I mean *everything*, you told your family about you taking a new position with BEDON and you being relocated to Houston to start up a new warehouse from the ground up. That you would be gone during the week and home on the weekend."

"Sall—"

"No, no, you wait. I'm not finished," she said, cutting him off. "You told your family that our 'honeymoon' trip to New Orleans was just a way to get me back to you, but that the trip was a waste of time and money. That *I didn't really mean anything to you* and *there was no love between us anymore.*"

Collin tried to turn and walk out of the kitchen, but Sally grabbed his arm.

"No, no, there's more, Collin. You said that I was 'old stuff' and you would be looking for a new romance! That on the weekends you were home, you'd just have to 'stomach' me. That you knew I'd take care of the house and the boys while you were out having *fun*." Sally looked at Collin with daggers in her eyes. "How could you, Collin? As far as I'm concerned, you do not need to wait until January 1st to leave this house. You can leave tonight. I wish you the best of luck in your new life. Now, you don't need to say anything to me because you have said enough. Besides, I'm nothing to you anyway."

Collin was shocked to learn Sally had heard his conversation with his family. The cat was out of the bag. She was right, he had nothing to say that would make anything better, but he tried. "Sally, I'm so sorry."

"Oh, Collin. Don't keep lying. Let's just get through today, and then you can go your merry little way, OK? I'm as sick of you as you are of me."

"Hey, Mom. Is it time to open our presents yet?"

Sally saw Todd appear in the kitchen doorway.

"It sure is, son. Let's go!"

Sally and Collin followed Todd into the living room and joined Pace who was sitting on the floor by the Christmas tree. Todd sat down next to Pace, Sally sat on the couch, and Collin rested his back against the front door.

"OK, who wants to be the first to hand out a present?" Sally asked.

"Pace, you go first!" Todd pointed at his little brother.

"OK!" Pace reached for a present from under the Christmas tree and looked at the name tag. "It's for you, Todd. From Momma," he announced and handed it to his brother.

Todd tore the wrapping paper from the box and opened the lid. He pulled out a bright blue long-sleeve shirt. "Oh, Mom, it's nice. I really like the color. Thank you."

"I'm glad you like it. You're welcome."

"OK, Todd. Your turn," Sally instructed.

Todd took a bigger box from the side of the tree. "It's for you, Dad. From Pace and me."

Collin walked over to Todd and took the box. "Wow, I wonder what's in it?" He ripped the wrapping paper off from the side of the box and opened the top. He saw it was a throw blanket with cars imprinted on the fabric. At the bottom, it read, *To Daddy, from Todd and Pace.*

"Do you like it, Dad?" Todd asked.

"We picked it out for you all by ourselves," Pace added.

"I love it, my sons! Thank y'all very much. I will treasure it, that's for sure!" Collin bent down to hug them and thank them for their wonderful gift. Sally saw tears in his eyes. She knew he was emotionally moved by their thoughtful gift.

"OK, Momma. This one is yours," Pace said as he handed her a package.

"Oh my, what could it be?" Sally asked as she took the gift. She looked at the name tag. "It's from you and Todd!" She opened the wrapping paper and pulled the lid off the box. It was a throw blanket, but it was different from Collin's. This one had many hearts imprinted all over it, and at the bottom was written, *To Momma, from Todd and Pace.* Sally lowered herself to the floor and crawled over to hug her boys. "Thank y'all. I love it. It's so special to me."

Todd grabbed the last box and handed it to Pace. "It's from Dad."

Pace quickly opened the present, lifted the box lid, and saw a red and black plaid shirt. "Thank you, Daddy. I like it!"

"We hope your Christmas has been good," Sally said to her sons as she stood to her feet. "How about some hot chocolate and cookies?" she asked.

"*Yes!*" the boys cheered.

As Sally walked toward the kitchen, the telephone rang.

"Hello? Hi, Peggy, and Merry Christmas! How are you this morning?"

"Merry Christmas to y'all also," Peggy responded. I was planning on coming over to your house today, but I'm not feeling good. So I'm going to stay in and watch the parade. Are the boys having a good Christmas?" Peggy asked.

"Yes they are! But I'm so sorry you are not feeling well. Sure hope you feel better soon. Do you need anything?" Sally responded.

"No, I have what I need, thanks for asking."

"OK, but if you do need anything, please call. Enjoy the parade!" She hung up the phone and turned to inform Collin. "That was your mother. She is not feeling good, and she won't be coming over today," she said and then turned and walked into the kitchen. She prepared the hot chocolate and put the cookies on a plate. "Here ya go, kiddos. Enjoy!" she said, placing the goodies in front of them while they admired their gifts.

Sally turned the Christmas parade on the television. The boys were sitting on the floor, and Collin was on the couch. She didn't really want to sit near Collin, so she took her cup of hot chocolate and two cookies and sat at the dining room table where she could still see the television.

A short while later, the telephone rang again. Sally answered.

"Hello?"

"Hi, sweetheart!" Rusty greeted. "I know you're not alone and cannot say very much, but I just wanted to call to tell you Merry Christmas, I love you, and I miss you. I wish we were together," his voice uttered tenderly from the other end of the line.

As soon as Sally heard Rusty's voice, she turned away from the living room and walked quietly into the dining room. She was startled but so pleasantly surprised. "Hi, honey, and Merry Christmas to you," she spoke just above a whisper. "What a wonderful surprise. I love and miss you too. I can't talk long. Collin is here."

"I figured he might be, but I had to call you. Call me when you can. I love you," Rusty said.

"I will call you soon. I love you too." Oh, how Sally did not want to hang up. She had so much to share with Rusty and just wanted to talk to him, but hopefully she would get that chance later.

Collin came into the kitchen to get a glass of water. "Was that Mom on the telephone again?" he asked.

"No," Sally answered.

"Anyone I know?"

"I don't think so," Sally replied.

"I was just wondering. You were whispering to the person, like you didn't really want me to hear your conversation," Collin said sarcastically.

"It was just a friend wanting to wish me a Merry Christmas. Satisfied?" Sally snapped.

"Yea, whatever! Say, Sally, when do you want me to tell the boys about Houston?"

"Are you leaving tonight?" Sally exclaimed.

"I'd rather leave tomorrow. I need to pack, and I didn't want to do that today," Collin said.

"Tomorrow? OK. I guess in the morning. The shock of the news will be better tomorrow than today. Agree?"

"Yes, I agree," Collin admitted.

"Before you leave, I need a telephone number and an address ASAP in case I need you. And what about money? How are you going to continue to help us with finances?" Sally urged.

"I'll get you that information as soon as I have it. As far as the money, I'll be home every weekend."

"What if you decide you don't think you can stomach me, and you decide to stop coming back home? Or you find a 'new romance' and want to stay with her instead? Then what?" Sally pushed him a little harder for an answer.

"Dang it, Sally! I don't know. It doesn't really matter!" Collin slammed his hand on the kitchen counter.

"Yes, Collin, it does matter! I need to put food on the table for your boys, buy them clothes, pay for gas . . . the list goes on and on. I need to know what you plan to do!" Her voice was louder as she demanded answers. "I did not put us in this situation. *You* did."

"I'll get you some money!" he blurted as he walked out of the kitchen. He wanted so much to just leave the house, but instead, he went to the bedroom closet, grabbed his luggage, and threw it on the bed.

Todd rushed to the kitchen, "Mom, are you OK?" he asked. "What's wrong with Dad? He's really mad!"

Before Sally could answer, the telephone rang again.

"Hello?" she answered.

"Is Collin there?" a female voice asked.

"Who's calling?" Sally inquired.

"Is this his wife?" the woman responded.

"Who's asking?"

"A friend. A very personal friend. I'd like to talk to him." The woman tried to sound like someone *really* important.

Sally shouted, "Collin! A friend—no, a *very personal* friend—who won't tell me her name is on the telephone for you. She wanted to know if I was your wife. You want to take the call, honey?" She couldn't resist a sarcastic attitude.

Collin stepped out of the bedroom into the hall and stared at Sally.

"Well, here's the telephone!" Sally said as she tossed the handset on the couch.

Collin rushed angrily into the living room. "Hello?" he answered.

A two-second pause.

"I've told you not to call me at home! Why are you calling me?"

Another few-second pause.

By this time, Todd and Pace had hurried to their mother's side in the dining room with their little arms around her waist. They were frightened by their father's actions.

Suddenly, Collin slammed the handset down on the base of the telephone. He was furious. He looked up and saw Sally and his sons staring at him. There was fear in his boys' eyes.

"Well, Collin, say something!" Sally urged.

"Todd and Pace, I wasn't going to tell you two my big news until tomorrow, with it being Christmas and all, but it appears that now is the time to tell y'all. I've been given a huge opportunity to further my career with the company I work for, and I need to pack and leave for Houston, Texas, today," Collin explained.

"Why can't we go with you?" Todd asked with tears in his eyes.

"Because, right now, y'all need to stay here with your mother."

"No, Daddy! Don't go!" Pace cried as he ran to his daddy and hugged his legs.

"Hey, little buddy, I'll be home to see y'all on the weekends. Come on, now. Don't cry." Collin bent down and embraced his little son. "I'll tell ya what . . . y'all come and help me pack. That would be a big help to me."

"No! I'm not helping you!" Todd blurted out as he ran to his bedroom. "Just go! I don't care!" he screamed as he slammed the door behind him.

Confused, Pace cried even harder. Sally approached him with open arms, and he grabbed her legs and held on tightly. Sally looked up at Collin and quietly said, "I hope you're happy now. You could have handled this situation so much differently. You are so selfish. See what you've done? Please, just pack and go. The sooner, the better." Sally picked Pace up in her arms and walked to the boys' bedroom to join Todd.

After much crying, Todd and Pace fell asleep out of pure exhaustion. Sally wished she knew how to pray and ask for her little children's pain to go away, and that somehow they would understand what was happening.

Several hours later, Sally heard the front door open and close multiple times. Then she heard a car engine start, then fade into the distance. Collin was gone. Tears welled up in her eyes, then streamed down her face. Why? She wasn't sure.

Sally stayed with her sons until they began to stir. They got up and walked into the living room. The house was so quiet. Todd looked out the window.

"Mom, Dad's car is gone," he said, fighting back tears. "Why does he have to go?"

Sally stepped behind him as he continued looking out the window. She could give him an honest answer by telling him that his father didn't love her anymore, and he left to find a better life for himself, but that answer would be very cruel, making it sound like his father didn't love *him* anymore either. So what does she tell him? She took him by his hand and led him to the couch where they sat down beside Pace.

"It's like your daddy said. BEDON has offered him a better-paying job overseeing the building and setting up another warehouse in Houston, Texas. It's a huge responsibility, and BEDON believes your father is the man to do the job. True, he will be away from home a lot, and when the job is completed, he could come back home. He needed to leave because he has to find a place to live before he reports to work soon after New Years."

"Is Houston very far away? Can we go and visit him?" Pace asked.

"Houston is a good ten-hour drive. I kind of doubt we'll go visit him. Besides, he is going to be very busy." Sally tried to change the subject. "Hey, how about some supper? Y'all hungry? I thought I'd fry some chicken with mashed potatoes. How does that sound?" Sally suggested.

"I'm not real hungry, Mom, but I'll eat some. Can we help you?" Todd replied.

"Sure. That would be great! I can always use y'all's help!" The three walked to the kitchen, but Sally stopped short. On the dining room table was an envelope with Sally's name written on it. She slowly reached for the envelope, picked it up, and opened it. There was a piece of paper folded up inside. She unfolded the paper to find Collin's handwriting. It said,

> *I'm sorry, Sally.*
> *Look in the top drawer of the dresser.*
>
> *—Collin*

Her hands shaking, Sally told the boys she would be back in a few minutes. She walked to her bedroom, which looked so bare with Collin's things gone, opened the top drawer of the dresser, and found another envelope. She opened it, and to her surprise, she found five-hundred dollars. Clipped to the money was a note from Collin, saying that he would send more money soon. All things considered, Sally was grateful. She put the money back in the drawer and returned to the kitchen.

After supper was over, Sally and the boys rested on the couch, watching television. Christmas Day was fading away. The hour was late, but there was no school for the boys tomorrow, so they could all sleep in for a change. They climbed into bed, and Sally covered them up. Before turning out the light, she said, "Sleep tight. Don't let the bedbugs bite. I love y'all bunches. Night night, my little sweethearts." She shut off the light and quietly closed the door behind her.

Through all the commotion of the day, Sally had forgotten to call her brother, Matthew, and her sister-in-law, Jodie, who lived in Dallas, Texas, to wish them a Merry Christmas. It was late, but better late than never, she thought. She had always called them on Christmas Day. So she dialed their telephone number, and the ringing sound began.

"Hello?" her brother answered.

"Merry Christmas, brother dear! How are you and Jodie?" Sally asked. "I'm sorry it's so late. Is this a good time to talk?" she continued.

"Hey, sis. Merry Christmas to you and yours too! Your timing is good. We're good. How about y'all?" Matthew asked.

"I'm glad y'all are doing OK. Here isn't so good. Collin's company is sending him to Houston to oversee the building of a new warehouse, which is going to take a while. He left today. And the bottom line is that I don't know if he will be back. His departure was not so friendly," Sally said sadly.

"Oh, Sally! I'm so sorry. So you and the boys are not going with him? What are you going to do?" Her bother's voice showed concern.

"No, he informed me that he was starting a new life, and it did not include me and/or the boys. Our love has disappeared for each other, and our marriage has been in a rut for a while. I'm not sure how it all will work out. He said he would send us money, but I'm not holding my breath. I'm considering seeing an attorney and filing for divorce. I don't know. It's so much to take in."

"I am so sorry to hear this terrible news. Jodie and I will be praying for you and the boys. This will be hard on them. Just know we are here if you want to talk, and you're always welcome to come here for a while to sort things through."

"Oh, Matthew, you are so kind. I appreciate your thoughtfulness." Sally cleared her throat as she changed the subject. "How was y'all's Christmas?"

"Our Christmas was very good. Some of the children were here. Chad and Darlene are still in the service and stationed in different places in the world. Reed, Karen, Rita, and Leah were here. The day was wonderful! Lots of family fun and delicious food, and many memories were made. Sure wish y'all could have been here too."

"Sounds like a very happy day for everyone. Yes, being with y'all would have been special. We haven't been together for Christmas in a long time. Maybe next year," Sally wondered hopefully. "By the way, I plan on going to the cemetery on the 27th to leave flowers on Daddy's grave. It's hard to believe he's been gone five years. And Mother, ten years! Where does the time go?"

"Yes, it is hard to believe," Matthew agreed. "Mom and Dad were taken from us way too soon, but God has a reason. There's reason for everything! Be careful going to the cemetery," he cautioned. "Please tell Mom and Dad we miss them, and even though they are not here anymore, they are not forgotten."

"I sure will, Matthew." She looked at the clock on the wall. "It's late. It's been good to talk to you. I'll keep y'all posted on the situation here. Again, Merry Christmas to everyone. Love and miss y'all."

"Please, do let us know what's happening. And Merry Christmas to you and the boys. Love and miss y'all too. Bye for now."

Sally hung up the handset and sat on the couch for a few minutes, pondering the conversation she had just had with her brother. It was good to hear his voice. She sure wished they lived closer to each other.

Sally was exhausted from all the activities of the day, so she decided to head to bed. As she laid in bed, she thought how hard it was for her to imagine all that had happened that day. But the most pleasant surprise for her was hearing Rusty's wonderful voice. How sweet it was for him to have called her. Dangerous, but very sweet. She looked forward to talking to him the next day.

Sally woke up to the sounds of giggles. She heard Todd say, "Shh, Pace! You'll wake up Mom. Just be quiet."

She looked over at the clock on the nightstand: 7:30. How nice it felt to sleep in, but it was time for her to get up and get going. She quietly got out of bed and walked to her bedroom door, opening it slowly to peer down the hall. In the living room, she saw her boys playing with their new toys next to the tree. *How precious,* she thought.

"Good morning, my two little men," she said softly.

"Good morning, Mom! I hope we didn't wake you up. We were trying to be quiet so you could sleep," Todd explained.

Pace jumped to his little feet and ran to his momma and hugged her. "Did you sleep good?" he asked.

She bent down to kiss his forehead. "I sure did. What about you? And you, Todd? Did you sleep good?"

The boys shook their heads *yes*.

"Do you know what time y'all got up?" Sally asked.

"I think it was seven o'clock," Todd answered.

"Y'all haven't been up too long. Say, who's hungry?"

"We are! I'm starving!" Todd exclaimed.

"Me too!" echoed Pace.

"OK! Y'all continue to play, and I'm gonna start our breakfast," Sally said as she walked toward the kitchen. Right away she began brewing coffee, then put the bacon in the skillet to fry. The eggs came next to scramble, and then water in a saucepan to boil for the grits.

As they sat down to eat, only minutes passed before Todd asked, "I wonder where Dad is?"

Sally looked at Todd who was fighting back tears. "I don't know, Todd, but he said he would call us."

"I miss my daddy," Pace expressed sadly.

"Everything will be OK," Sally assured them. Down deep within her, she hoped that would be true.

When they were done eating, Sally cleared the table. "Y'all go play. I need to call your grandmother and see how she is feeling," she said. Sally dialed Peggy's work telephone number.

"Good morning, this is Globe Incorporated. Judy speaking. How may I direct your call?"

"Good morning. This is Sally Oldham, and I'd like to speak to Peggy Oldham, please." Sally thought it was very strange because Peggy is the person who normally answers the company phone.

"I'm sorry, but Mrs. Oldham is not in today," Judy informed her.

"OK, thank you," and Sally ended the call. She thought that it was very unusual for Peggy to miss work. She hoped Peggy wasn't feeling worse. She decided to call her home number.

"Hello?" Peggy answered.

"Hi, Peggy. It's Sally."

"Hi, Sally. How are you?"

"I'm OK. I called your work, and I was told you were not there. Are you OK?" Sally inquired.

A long pause.

"I'm not sick, just heartbroken. Collin came to see me late last night to tell me he was leaving for Houston tomorrow or the next day. He also told me that you and he had an argument, and he packed and left the house. I'm so sorry, Sally."

"Thank you, Peggy. I feel so bad for you too. It was a shock for us to learn Collin would go so far away from home and leave his family." Sally paused for a moment. "I will share this with you because I feel like you should know. The Saturday we were at Ellen and David's, I was going to come downstairs when I heard Collin's voice. He was telling you and Ellen all about his new job and that I did not know yet. I heard him tell you all how he felt about me. I was so hurt and humiliated. I am so concerned about how you and Ellen now feel toward me. I couldn't believe Collin could say such hurtful things. I've always tried to be a good wife to him, but the way I feel now, I don't have any feelings left for him. I'm sorry, but that's the way I feel."

"I can understand, Sally, and I know you have made Collin a good wife—better than he deserves, that's for sure! And, child, I don't feel any different about you than I did before Collin said all he said. I still love you like a daughter. Sunday, when we came home and I was about to leave, I told Collin that I thought he was making a big mistake by leaving his family and going to Houston. He fired back at me like I've never seen him before. He told me that his mind was made up, and nothing that I could say would change his mind. Then he told me to 'just butt out of his life.'" Peggy's voice broke as she began to cry.

"I'm so sorry, Peggy. I was watching from the living room window, and the conversation didn't look like it had gone well. I wish Collin had been more considerate toward you."

"I wanted to come over yesterday and spend Christmas afternoon with y'all, but I just couldn't do it," Peggy muttered, fighting her tears.

"I was afraid it was something like that," Sally admitted.

"And I just could not make myself go to work this morning. I'm just so sad and hurt. I hurt for you and the boys too, Sally."

"Well, we're not OK, but it's going to be OK. You rest, and later, if you feel up to coming over, you come on. We love you, and we're here for you."

"Thank you, Sally. I'll see how I feel later. Thank you for calling. Talking to you has helped me. Love ya," Peggy said, and the call disconnected.

Sally continued to sit in the chair for a few minutes, thinking about the conversation she had just had with Peggy. How cruel Collin had become. He should never talk to his mother that way. She wished there was something she could do for Peggy. She wanted to call Ellen and share with her what had happened between Peggy and Collin, but first she wanted and needed to call Rusty. She had so much to tell him.

Sally dialed Rusty's telephone number and walked back to the dining room chair and sat down. The ringing sound continued for what felt like an eternity. Then, an answer.

"Hello?"

It was not Rusty's voice that she heard.

"Hello. This is Sally. Is Rusty there?" she asked.

"Hi, Sally. This is Russell, Rusty's dad. Rusty has told us so much about you. How are you?" he asked cheerfully.

Oh, dear! What had Rusty told them about her? "Well, hi, Mr. Summers. I'm doing good. How are you?" Sally replied.

"I'm doing good, and please, call me Russell. I'm helping Rusty with a project in his kitchen, and he asked me to answer the telephone for him. But he's right here. It was nice to talk to you, Sally. Take care."

Sally was pleasantly surprised by her positive interaction with Rusty's father.

"Hi, sweetheart. How are you? I'm so glad you called. How was Christmas? I have so many questions, but first, I need to tell you I love you and I miss you!" he said joyfully.

"Oh, Rusty, you are so sweet. I love and miss you too. I am delighted I got to speak with your father! It was a very pleasant surprise. He said you had told him about me. Do I need to know what you said?"

"I told my mom and my dad that I met someone, I have fallen in love with her, and that she and her two sons might be coming to live with me." Rusty put his hand over the handset as he acknowledged his father: "OK, Dad. I'll see you in a little while." He removed his hand and returned to his conversation with Sally. "Sorry, Sally. My dad wanted to give us some privacy. I'll catch up with him after a while," Rusty explained.

"What did they say when you told them?"

"Well, they were a little concerned. They thought this relationship had just happened recently and I was acting too impulsively. I explained to them that we had been seeing each other for a while, have grown to know each other, and have both fallen in love with each other. I mentioned there were some problems in Memphis and that I had suggested you and the boys move here and live with me. Since Dad has now heard your voice and seen how sweet you are, he will tell Mom he has talked to you, and they will feel better about the situation," Rusty encouraged.

"I hope so, honey. If not, you definitely need to let me know. I do *not* want to cause any friction between you and your folks," Sally said with concern.

"No, all will be OK. So now, how are you, and how was your Christmas?" Rusty asked again.

"Lots has happened here. I know you're busy in your kitchen; do you want to call me when you finish your project?"

"No, I'm good. What's going on? Are you OK?"

"I don't know that I would say I'm OK, but I'm not sick. You remember I told you that Collin was acting really weird last week? Being rude, telling me not to ask any questions, and keeping very strange hours that were supposedly work related?"

"Yes. . . ." Rusty said.

"Well, I found out some of what was going on with him last Saturday. He wanted to go see his sister and her family in Brandon, Mississippi, to celebrate Christmas with them since it had been years since they'd been able to do that. And we would invite Peggy to come along. Collin barely said a word to me on the way there, but when we arrived at his sister's house, he turned on the charm and was very sociable with her family. The next day I took a nap before dinner, and before I came down the stairs afterwards, I heard Collin talking. He was saying that he was going to Houston, Texas, to start up a new company warehouse. He told them he had not told me yet, and he didn't want me to know. That he wasn't going to be taking me or the boys with him. That he had fallen out of love with me a long time ago and was looking forward to being away from me and finding a new romance. Also, he told them I could continue taking care of the boys and the house while he was out having fun." Sally continued. "I couldn't stand to hear any more, Rusty. I ran back the bedroom and cried. I was so hurt and humiliated."

"Oh, Sally, honey, I am so very sorry you had to hear his garbage and all that blabbing about you to his mom and sister. He is such a jerk. The sooner I get you and the boys out of that mess, the better it will be for you all," Rusty said with determination.

"There's more!" Sally urged.

"*More?*" Rusty exclaimed.

"Yes! We came back home on Christmas Eve, and before Peggy and us parted ways, I looked out the window and saw Collin and her having what looked like a heated conversation. Then, Collin offered to go get us something to eat from a fast-food place for dinner. He was gone for an hour! When he came back, he made excuses as to what took him so long. I could tell he was lying. Later I saw his clothes on the bed, and I picked them up to put them in the hamper. When I did, I could smell perfume. He came into the bedroom and asked me what I was doing. I told him I could smell perfume on his shirt, and I walked out of the room. Collin came out of the bedroom a few moments later with fancy clothes on and said he 'had to go find *the smell*.' And he left the house." Sally paused. "Am I keeping you too long, Rusty?"

"No. I need to know what's going on! Did he come back home?"

"Yes, at about four o'clock the next morning. He was very quiet coming in, and he laid on the couch in the living room. The boys were so upset when he left, though! So I tried to make them feel better by singing Christmas songs, and we put out cookies and milk for Santa Claus. The next morning at breakfast, Collin was about to break the news about Houston, and I stopped him. I told him I knew and that he needed to wait and not ruin Christmas. He was shocked that I knew! When the boys had left the table, I told him that I overheard his whole conversation with his sister. He had nothing to say, of course." Sally continued. "Then the phone rang, and I heard a most welcomed voice on the other end. I was so glad you called me! When we hung up, Collin came in and asked who I was whispering to . . . like he deserved to know. I changed the subject to ask when he was planning to leave for Houston. It got heated, and I told him to go ahead and just pack and leave." Sally could barely muster the courage to continue. "He walked out of the kitchen and told the boys he was leaving. They were so confused and heartbroken, and Todd ran to his room crying! I told Collin that he should be ashamed, and I left to go comfort the boys. Not long after, Collin walked out the front door."

Sally took a long pause as she contemplated what she was saying. "It's peaceful and quiet now, but the boys are sad. I don't think Collin will be back. That's OK for me, but it'll take a while for the boys to understand what's happened."

"My dear Sally, you are so brave. You stood strong for yourself and for your sons. I'm proud of you! Are you sure Collin is gone? He's not coming back?"

"I believe he is gone for good. There is nothing for him to come back to. As far as I'm concerned, he's off to make a new life for himself," Sally said.

"Do you want me to come and get you and the boys now?" Rusty asked.

"As much as I would love for you to do that, I need to stay here for a while. I plan to start my search for an attorney tomorrow and find out information about divorce, leaving the state with the boys, and anything . . . everything I need to know. I'll let you know what I find out. Are you sure you want to take on the responsibility of me and my two sons?" Sally stated. "Before you answer, please think about it. It'll be a *big change* for you."

"I have given a lot of thought to you and the boys coming to live with me, and I'm positive that is what I want to do. Sure, it will be a change for all of us, but I believe the change will be for the better. Please let me know what you find out from the attorney. I want to send you some money. I know attorneys are not cheap. What is your address?" Rusty offered.

"How about I find an attorney first, talk to him or her, and get a fee quote before you send any money? I don't want to impose on you, and I'm not crazy about taking money from you, Rusty. I would feel so bad."

"You would not be imposing on me. Hey, *we*—that's you and me—are on this new journey together. So please, trust me, and let me help you," Rusty said persuasively.

"I love the 'you and me' and especially 'this new journey together,'" Sally said smiling. "Thank you, sweetheart. There is a lot ahead of us that will need to be accomplished, and I need your confidence, for I am treading on ground I have never been on before."

"You'll be fine, honey," Rusty said reassuringly. "I just wish I could be there with you to see you through the process of everything you need to do."

"Me too. But just to know you are just a telephone call away is good for me. By the way, I will be out of pocket for a while tomorrow. The boys and I will be taking some flowers to the cemetery to place on my father's grave." Sally remembered she hadn't yet told Rusty about her father's death. "Five years ago, he passed away," she said. "I will also be making telephone calls to search for an attorney. I will call you and let you know what I find out. I'm sorry for keeping you so long from your dad and your project. Have fun, and I love you," Sally said tenderly.

"You're not keeping me. We have all day to do the project. You be careful out and about. I'll talk to you soon. I love you, too, sweetheart."

Their call ended.

As Sally hung up the handset, she noticed Todd and Pace sitting on the couch, looking bored.

"Say, kiddos," she began, "your Grandmother Peggy was sort of down in the dumps when I called her a while ago. What do y'all think if I called her again and ask her to go to lunch with us? She needs to get out of her house, and so do we!"

"That's a great idea, Mom!" Todd exclaimed.

"Hey, call Grandmother Peggy! Let's go!" Pace chimed in excitedly.

"OK!" Sally picked up the telephone handset and began dialing Peggy's number. "Hi, Peggy. It's Sally. How would you like to do lunch with the boys and me?"

A pause.

"Great! We'll be by to get you in twenty minutes. See ya soon!" She turned to the boys. "It's a *go*, boys! Go get dressed. Hurry!"

Todd and Pace dashed to their room to get dressed, and moments later they were out the door.

When Sally drove into Peggy's driveway, Peggy was waiting for them by the front door. She got into the car and the two ladies shared a knowing look. There was lots of chit-chat, laughter, and smiles on their way to lunch, which was really good medicine for all of them. After lunch, they visited a few stores looking for after Christmas sales. They found some bargains for them and the boys, which made everyone excited. The whole afternoon was just what they all needed.

Chapter Nine

December 27th had become a sad day for Sally. She, Todd, and Pace slept in, and then Sally wanted to honor her dad's passing by having breakfast at one of his favorite places. They got dressed, brushed their teeth, and braved the cold as they headed out of the house. A little snow had fallen during the night, which made for a beautiful landscape view.

They arrived at the C&B Restaurant about twenty minutes later. It wasn't too busy, so they were seated right away. The waitress brought glasses of water and took their orders: short stacks for the boys and two buttermilk biscuits smothered with sausage gravy and covered with two scrambled eggs on top—her dad's favorite meal there and the only one he ever ordered. It didn't matter what time of the day it was; that's what he ate.

About fifteen minutes later, the waitress brought their meals.

"How are y'all's pancakes?" Sally asked.

"They are *so* good!" Todd said with a mouth full of food.

"It's *deeeeelicious*, Momma," Pace emphasized, clearly enjoying his meal.

"I'm so glad! So is mine!"

After they had eaten their final bites of food, they left the restaurant, and Sally headed down the road toward Interstate 240. The cemetery was on the south side of Memphis. The traffic wasn't too bad, and within thirty minutes, they arrived at the location where her dad was buried. It was a big cemetery with several drives to different sections of the grounds. Sally took the first right and drove up the hill. Her dad's grave was on the west side in the Masonic Gardens section. Sally stopped the car, picked up the bouquet of flowers that were lying on the front passenger seat, and exited the car with her boys.

"The snow is a little deeper here. We should have worn our boots!" Sally realized. "Y'all follow me. We need to be careful where we walk," she instructed as they began walking toward the gravesite.

"It's farther than I remember," Todd commented.

"Are we there yet, Momma?" Pace inquired.

"Almost. We'll turn here and walk toward the brick wall," Sally informed her two snow-trudging warriors.

Finally, they arrived at Sally's mom's and dad's graves. The boys watched their mother as she bent down and brushed away the snow from their shared headstone so their names could be seen.

"Well, Mom and Dad, it's me again," she said. "Todd and Pace are here too, and we've brought some flowers for you." She looked at her dad's name. "Daddy, it sure doesn't seem like five years since your passing. I sure do miss you." She shifted her gaze to her mom's name. "And Momma, I miss you too. I know Matthew and Jodie are thinking about y'all today too. We love y'all bunches." Sally had tears in her eyes as she placed the bouquet of flowers in the vase attached to their headstone. "Sure wish both of you were still here with us." Raising her hand to her lips, she kissed her fingers and placed them on the headstone. "Love y'all so much," she whispered softly. "I'll see y'all again in February for your birthday, Momma." Sally took a few steps back so that her boys could take their turn. "Y'all, tell your grandparents bye and that you love them," she encouraged.

"Bye, Grandpa and Grandma. Love y'all." Both boys did what their mother had asked, but neither really understood the sentiment.

Sally wiped the tears from her eyes, gave a little wave toward her parents' grave, and then took the hand of each of her sons as they walked back toward the car. The snow crunched under their feet with each step; other than that, silence filled the air as they walked. All of a sudden, the sky above them filled with the roar of a passenger airliner. They stopped to watch the low-flying aircraft; the boys were in awe!

"*Wow!* Look at that!" Todd exclaimed. "It's huge!" He was overwhelmed with excitement.

Pace grabbed Sally's legs. He was scared. Sally bent down and took him in her arms. "Don't be afraid, sweetheart. Your granddaddy used to fly one similar to that one years ago when he was in the service. He wasn't scared; he loved it! He wouldn't want you to be scared of it either," she said, hugging her boy tightly.

Sally opened the car door for the boys, making sure they didn't track too much snow in. As she walked around the car to her door, she looked in the direction of her parents' graves and said softly, "Daddy, that fly-over was just for you! Perfect timing, wasn't it?" Because the cemetery was just a few miles from the airport, the planes flew over often. But this one, she thought, was special.

She got in the car and drove out of the cemetery. She had every intention of going straight home, but then she had an idea. Instead of turning right out of the cemetery, she turned left.

Soon, from the back seat, Pace shouted, "Momma, look! Another airplane!" The Memphis International Airport runway was just to their right.

"Gosh, look at that! Mom, how do airplanes fly?" Todd asked.

"Well, there's a lot of this and a lot of that that makes airplanes do what they do. We could go to the library and see if there is a book that can help you answer that question if you'd like?" Sally suggested.

"That would be great! Can we?" Todd replied.

"We sure can. We have lots of time to do some research since y'all are out of school. But first, let's look at the airport a little more closely." She pulled into an airport parking lot. "Come on. Let's go in!" she said excitedly. The boys had never been into an airport before, and she knew they would just love it.

The three walked toward the big terminal doors and entered. The boys immediately gasped, their faces exuding awe and wonderment. Their mouths dropped open, and their eyes widened as they looked all around them.

"Wow! What a place!" Todd was shocked at what he was seeing.

Pace was so amazed, he couldn't even talk. Sally was full of joy, watching the excitement in her boys' eyes. There was so much more to this world, and this was a good time to let them see some of it.

Sally took her sons by the hand and began to walk the lobby, then down one of the concourses. There were so many shops and restaurants. The concourse windows were huge, and the activity taking place outside of them captured the boys' attention. A passenger airplane was parked near the window, and the ground crew was riding around in tugs, pulling trailers full of the passengers' luggage. They watched the men place the luggage piece by piece on a conveyor belt that fed into the belly of the airplane.

"Look at that, Mom! That's amazing!" Todd exclaimed.

"What happened? Where did the luggage go?" Pace was concerned.

"Well, fellas, there are other men inside the plane, and they take the luggage, then store it in a different area of the bottom of the airplane," their mother explained. "When all the luggage is on the airplane and the passengers have boarded, the airplane takes off! When it lands, the passengers get off, the crew unloads the luggage and brings it into the airport terminal to where the passengers can pick it up."

"When I grow up, I want to do that!" Pace announced with determination in his voice.

"It looks like it would be a fun job," Todd commented.

"Y'all will have many opportunities for job decisions when the time comes," Sally assured them. "I guess we need to be going. I hope y'all enjoyed seeing the airport!"

"I sure did. Thanks, Mom, for bringing us. What did you think, Pace?"

"I loved it! This has been fun," Pace said as he hugged his momma. "I'm not afraid anymore!"

"I'm glad, my little man," Sally said as she hugged him back. "Let's go home."

When they arrived back home, Sally began to prepare lunch of peanut butter and banana sandwiches. Todd poured some milk for them to drink, and Sally tore open a fresh bag of potato chips. While they sat around the table and ate together, the boys talked and talked about their adventures of the morning. It was heartwarming for Sally to know they had such a good time.

Then, she remembered the library idea. She got up from the table and took the telephone directory out from under the telephone. She opened the book, found the library listings, and announced, "I found the library I want us to go to. It's the one I went to when I was in high school!" She walked back to the telephone and picked up the handset, then dialed the number for the library. "Yes, what are your hours today?" she asked. "What about tomorrow?" Sally wrote down what had been told to her. "OK, thank you."

"What did they say, Mom?" Todd asked anxiously.

"It closes today at three o'clock. It's nearly two o'clock now, so we will go in the morning and take our time looking for a book that tells us all about how an airplane flies. How does that sound?"

"Sounds good to me," Todd answered.

"After I clear the table, I have a few telephone calls I need to make. I think it's still too cold for y'all to go outside and play. Will you two play in your room for a while?" Sally asked.

"Sure, OK," Todd and Pace both agreed.

As Sally cleared the table, she pondered how she was going to approach talking to an attorney. She never dreamed she'd be thinking of such a situation. She took the telephone book in her hands and turned to the letter *A*. So many names were listed, and she didn't recognize any of the law firms. How would she know which one could be better than another? Then she thought, *Of course, I'll call the Better Business Bureau.* She turned to the letter *B* and found the number. She had the handset in her hand, but she paused. *Am I really going to do this?* she asked herself. *What do I say?* She looked up, but she didn't know why. Perhaps she was searching for words to pray? But she didn't even know how. She needed help. Abruptly she stated out loud, "OK, let's do this!"

Sally dialed the telephone number for the Bureau, and the phone began to ring.

"You have reached the Better Business Bureau. This is Betty. How can I help you today?" a woman's voice said.

Sally hesitated for a moment, thinking she had to be in a bad dream. "Yes. I would like your suggestion as to a good divorce attorney," she asked, not really knowing what exactly had come out of her mouth.

"Oh, sure. Let me find some information for you. With divorce attorneys, there are many to choose from. There are some who specialize in divorces particularly with no children involved, and there are those who specialize in divorce including custody matters for children." Betty paused. "Let me ask you a few questions. First, financing can sometimes be an issue. Are you looking for a less expensive attorney? Second, do you have children? Third, is the marriage irreconcilable? Fourth, is your husband going to contest the divorce? I'm sorry to be so personal, but I want to make sure I'm directing you to a suitable attorney for your situation," she said.

Sally sat stunned by all the questions Betty had asked her, but she knew those questions needed to be answered. "Don't apologize. I understand. I just appreciate you helping me. I never thought I would be talking to someone regarding a divorce attorney. To answer your questions, yes, money is an issue, and yes, we have two sons. My husband has taken a job in Houston, Texas, and I do not expect him to return home. I would say the marriage is irreconcilable because he no longer wants a life with me. I doubt if he will contest the divorce. Also, I would like to leave the state and move north. Will that be possible, and if so, when?" Sally breathed deeply after unloading all the details of her situation.

"Wow, bless your heart. I'm so sorry for your woes," Betty commented. "Yes, I would say that it is time for you to move on with your life too. I know you are experiencing a huge shock to your life . . . and your children are too. OK, I have a few names for you. Do you have something to write with? If I may ask, what is your name, please?" Betty inquired.

"My name is Sally. Yes, I'm ready to write. Go ahead."

"It's called the Cut and Dry Law Firm. Believe it or not, the names are for real." Betty provided Sally the address and telephone number for Sally to write down. "Their first consultation is free, and they aren't too expensive. Another one is Douglas Law Firm. Their first meeting is also free, and their divorce rates are comparable. Now, if you don't get any satisfaction from either one of these two law firms, call me back, and I'll give you more information."

"Thank you very much for all your help and also for your encouragement," Sally responded. "You've been most thoughtful."

"Sally, I wish you well and I will keep you in my prayers," Betty said compassionately.

After ending the call, Sally felt numb and drained. She was thankful she had that conversation behind her. But it was only the beginning.

A knock came at the front door. Pace ran to the living room. "Is it Daddy?" he asked innocently.

Sally didn't say anything but got up from the couch, walked to the door, and opened it. "Ah, Peggy. Come on in. We're glad you decided to come over today," she said, standing aside to let her in.

Pace ran to his grandmother and gave her a hug. Todd entered the room and also gave her a hug.

Peggy handed Todd two big boxes. "I hope it's OK if I brought pizza for us to eat for supper," Peggy commented. "I tried calling you earlier, Sally, but you didn't answer. I did some shopping and decided to just pop over. I hope it's OK?"

"It's absolutely OK! Isn't it, boys?" Sally joyfully answered.

"Yes, Grandmother Peggy. You know we love pizza!" Todd expressed with delight and took the pizza boxes to the dining room table. "I'll get some paper plates and drinks, Mom, and we can eat. I'm hungry, and the pizzas are smelling delicious!"

Sally took Peggy's coat and hung it on the coat tree, then they both walked to the dining room. "Thank you so much for the treat. It's a very nice surprise," Sally said appreciatively.

"Well, I sure didn't want to come empty-handed!"

While they ate, the boys told their grandmother all about the adventures they had that day. When they were done, the boys retreated to the living room to watch some television. Sally and Peggy continued to sit at the table.

"Have you talked to Collin, Peggy?" Sally asked.

"No, I haven't. Have you?"

Sally answered, "No, but I don't really expect too. His mind is made up, and he will forge forward with his plan. I know I probably shouldn't say what I'm about to say, Peggy, but Collin leaving, even though it's sad, especially for the boys . . . it's a good thing, maybe even the best thing to happen. Our marriage has been in trouble for years. I expressed to Collin many times that I thought we needed to get help, but he always said that my feelings were just in my mind and that all was OK. But it hasn't been OK for a long time." Sally hesitated a moment. "I have given what I'm about to say some serious thought: I plan to call a divorce attorney tomorrow."

"Oh no, Sally! Are you sure that's a good idea?" Peggy questioned with concern.

"I don't know, but I and the boys can't go on thinking Collin is coming back home or that he is going to fall back in love with me. He has said terrible and hurtful things, and besides that, he is seeing another woman!"

"No, really!?" Peggy was shocked.

"Yes! She called my house on Christmas Day, wanting to talk to Collin. She called herself a 'very personal friend' of my husband. I was furious! When Collin spoke to her, he asked her why she was calling because he had told her to *never* call him at home."

"Oh dear, that is terrible! I am so sorry, Sally. I never would have thought Collin would do something like that." Peggy was ashamed by her son. "Well, in light of his actions, and as much as I dislike the thought, I will not hold it against you for seeking an attorney and filing for divorce. Collin has destroyed any trust you might have in him. I understand your decision."

"Peggy, you know I never wanted Collin and me to end up in this situation. I loved your son very much at one time and have for a long time, but now, I feel nothing for him but pity. Thank you for understanding my dilemma. I love you, and I do not want to hurt you, but I believe this is the best thing for me to do." Sally was grateful that her mother-in-law supported her decision.

"Oh my, I remember another reason I wanted to visit with all of you this evening!" Peggy said abruptly. "I'll be right back." Peggy slipped on her coat and went out the front door to her car.

"Where is Grandmother Peggy going?" Pace asked.

"I'm not sure . . ." Sally answered.

Both boys and Sally were looking out the living room window while Peggy took bags out of her trunk.

"Y'all open the screen door for your grandmother," Sally told the boys as Peggy made her way back toward the house.

"Grandmother Peggy, what's in these bags?"

"Well, my Christmas presents for y'all are better later than never!" she explained excitedly as she sat the bags down by the Christmas tree.

"More presents!?" Pace exclaimed.

"Pace, you and Todd come sit on the couch. Let Grandmother Peggy have the floor!" Sally said.

Peggy began opening the bags and pulled out a few gifts. "Pace and Todd, close your eyes," Peggy instructed them.

"OK . . ." the boys replied, obeying the instruction.

Peggy picked up each of the three gifts and placed them one by one in front of Todd, then Pace, then Sally. "OK, open your eyes!"

Todd and Pace wasted no time tearing the wrapping paper from the gifts. Sally and Peggy had their eyes fixed on the boys, anxiously waiting to see the expressions on their faces when they saw their new toys.

"Oh boy, Grandmother Peggy, I love it!" Todd shouted as he discovered the big box contained a small-scale pinball machine. He jumped up, ran to her, and gave her a big hug.

"Look, Momma! I got a little basketball goal!" Pace exclaimed loudly. He, too, ran to his grandmother and hugged her.

"I sure hope y'all like your gifts. They look like they would be lots of fun." Peggy turned her eyes to Sally. "OK, Sally, open your present."

Sally carefully removed the wrapping paper to find a good-sized, heavy box. Sally's eyes grew extremely wide and bright as she looked inside. "Oh my gosh, how beautiful!" she exclaimed.

"Momma, what is it?" the boys yelled.

Sally lifted out of the box an exquisite-looking lighthouse, and then she began to cry. "It's absolutely beautiful, Peggy. Thank you *so* much. I love it," Sally expressed with tears streaming down her cheeks. She got up from the couch and bent down toward Peggy with open arms. You shouldn't have, but thank you very much." Sally was most grateful for the perfect gift.

"When I saw it, I thought it had your name written all over it. I know how much you like and admire lighthouses. I just couldn't help myself; I had to buy it for you. It even has a light inside! The beacon light turns, and there is a foghorn sound too," Peggy informed Sally.

Sally admired her gift as she wiped her tears.

"Well, kiddos, it's late, and I need to get on home and get ready for bed. Six o'clock in the morning will come early, and I'll need to head to the *salt mine* to do another day's work. I'm thinking retirement soon," Peggy admitted half-heartedly.

"Really? That'd be great! I hope you can, Peggy. You deserve it," Sally encouraged.

Sally helped her mother-in-law with her coat and gave her a big hug. "Thank you for everything. I love you."

"I love you too, Sally. Keep me posted about your situation. Call me if you need my help with anything . . . I mean it," Peggy whispered softly.

"I will. Boys, break away from your new toys for a minute to say bye to your grandmother," Sally instructed.

"Thank you bunches, Grandmother Peggy. Our toys are *great*!" they said as they embraced their grandmother.

Sally opened the front door and waved good-bye as Peggy left.

Closing the door and looking back at her boys, Sally said, "It's almost bedtime, fellas. Y'all go take your baths."

"Ah, Momma. Can we play just a little while longer? We love our new toys! Please, Momma?" begged Pace.

"OK, just a while longer, then," Sally said, caving in to their wishes. "I'm going to make a phone call, but I'll be here in the dining room if y'all need me." With the telephone handset in her hand, Sally dialed Rusty's number. On the fourth ring, she heard Rusty's voice.

"Hello?"

"Hi, honey! It's me. Am I calling you too late?" Sally asked.

"Hi, sweetheart. It's never too late for you to call me. How are you? Are you OK?" he inquired.

"You are so sweet. I'm good. I'm sorry for calling so late, but it's been a busy day. How are you?" Sally asked.

"I'm OK. I've been busy too. Dad and I finished our project in the kitchen yesterday, and today, I helped both Mom and Dad take down the Christmas decor and the tree. Then, I helped Dad with the farm chores. It's been cold and snowy here, and it's always harder for him to do the chores that need to be done daily when the weather is bad," Rusty said. "So what's been keeping y'all busy?"

"Oh, where do I begin?" Sally said, laughing a little. "The boys and I went to one of my dad's favorite places to eat for breakfast, then to the cemetery to put flowers on his grave. Then I had the spontaneous idea to take the boys to the airport, just so they could experience its magnitude! They had never been there or seen anything like it before. They were completely awestruck!" Sally was so thrilled with how the day had gone, knowing how joyful her boys were. Then, she decided to share the important update she had for Rusty. "I made a phone call this afternoon and asked for recommendations on divorce attorneys. I have two firms I plan to call tomorrow. Hopefully I can arrange for a consultation appointment soon. I'll keep you updated on that." Sally continued. "My mother-in-law, Peggy, surprised us with pizza this evening! We were able to talk about Collin and my plans moving forward. Believe it or not, she understood and agreed. I was so relieved."

"Wow, what a day. Please, let me know what you learn from the attorneys tomorrow," Rusty requested.

"Of course I will. Do you have any plans for tomorrow?"

"I will probably help my dad some more. I'm going to wash clothes and begin to get my gear ready to travel on the first of the New Year. The weather forecast is looking good—no snow! Since Collin will be in Texas, is there any chance I can see you on the 3rd?" Rusty asked hopefully.

"Honey, I just don't know right now. The boys will still be home for Christmas break. We'll have to play that one by ear. I want to see you. I'm missing you like crazy, but we'll just have to wait and see. Please understand," Sally said apologetically.

"I miss you so much too, and seeing you is at the top of my list. But I do understand," Rusty reassured her.

"I'm tired, and it's late," Sally said. "We can talk tomorrow. I'll let you go so you can get a good night's rest. I love you."

"I love you too, Kitten. You said you'd 'let me go,' though—please don't let me go too far!" Rusty added with a little chuckle.

"Oh you're only a heartbeat away, my dear," Sally said as she threw a kiss into the telephone.

"I caught that kiss!" Rusty said. "Thank you. I'm throwing my kiss right back at you." There was a slight pause and a quick pecking sound. "Did you catch it?"

"I sure did! Thank you. You take good care of yourself for me. Good night, my love."

It wasn't but a few moments after the call ended when Pace rushed into the dining room and asked, "Who was that you were talking to, Momma?"

"A very dear and sweet friend. Maybe one day you'll get to meet him," Sally answered with a smile on her face. "It's time for baths now, kiddos. We have a busy day tomorrow."

After baths, the boys put their PJs on and got into bed. Sally leaned over to give kisses and hugs to her little boys. As she began to say what she says every night, the boys chimed in: "Sleep tight, and don't let the bedbugs bite!" and all three of them laughed.

"We love ya bunches, Momma."

"I love y'all bunches too!" Sally turned off their light and walked out of their room. She was worn out by the day, so she got ready for bed too, turned the light off on her nightstand, curled up under her covers, and bid the day 'farewell.'

"Come on, Pace. Mom's still asleep. Crawl slowly. Don't shake the bed!" Todd whispered as he and his brother crawled into bed beside their mother.

"Are her eyes open?" Todd questioned softly.

"No."

"Shhh! Be still!" Todd scolded.

Sally stirred. Her eyes opened, and to her surprise, a pair of eyes were looking back at her. She broke into a big smile as she removed her arms from the covers and inched them toward Pace to tickle him. Todd jumped right beside Pace and helped his mother tickle him. Pace kicked and squirmed and giggled until he managed to escape.

"What a wonderful way to start our morning!" Sally exclaimed as she rolled to the edge of the bed. "Hey, we slept in again this morning! Doesn't that feel so good?" She stretched as she stood up, then reached for her robe.

"Come on, Todd. Let's get this day moving. We have things to do, places to go, and people to see. I hear the library calling us, don't you?" Sally questioned with excitement.

"Yes ma'am," he answered as he followed her to the kitchen.

Sally began brewing coffee and preparing breakfast. How about some French toast this morning?"

"That sounds great!" Todd replied. "Hey, Pace," he yelled as he ran to their bedroom. "You want some French toast for breakfast?"

"Yea! Yum!" Pace exclaimed.

Sally placed some sausage patties in a skillet, then scrambled the eggs for the French toast. After several turns of the bread in the skillet, Sally said, "Breakfast is on the table, boys. Come and get it!"

After breakfast, the boys didn't waste much time getting dressed and ready for the library. Old Man Winter was blowing a cold north wind, and the three of them shivered as they got into the car and cranked up the heat.

The library was on the south side of town and about a thirty-minute drive from the house. It had been a long time since Sally had been in that part of town, but the years had not changed it too much. They arrived at the library and went inside. The boys were amazed as they looked at row after row of shelves and all the thousands and thousands of books on the shelves.

Sally and the boys approached the service desk. A lady looked up and asked, "May I help y'all?"

"Yes. Where can we find a book that could tell us how airplanes fly?" Sally asked.

"Let me go to the file and see. I'm sure there are books on aviation. Let's see." She paused as she looked through the files. "Yes. Follow me," she said, motioning to them.

Sally sensed something very familiar about this lady. She wondered where she knew her from. Her thoughts were interrupted by the woman's voice.

"Here we are. There are books about airplanes in general, learning how to fly an airplane, being an airplane mechanic . . . you name it, it looks like it's here," the lady explained. "You're more than welcome to look through some of the books to see which one or ones might help you," she told the boys.

The more Sally heard this woman talk the more confident she was that she had heard her voice before. "I feel like I know you," Sally said to her.

"I thought the same thing when you walked in," she said.

"Are you from this area?"

"Yes. Where did you go to school?" the lady asked.

"Whitehaven."

"So did I. What's your name?"

"Sally Sullivan. What's your name?"

"Audrey Sims. We were in homeroom together in most of our years of high school!" she exclaimed.

"Audrey! Wow, how have you been?" Sally inquired.

"I've been good! How about you? Did you marry Collin Oldham? Y'all were *such* a cute couple in high school," Audrey said, smiling.

"Yes, Collin and I did get married. We have two sons, Todd and Pace. Collin has recently accepted a job transfer to Houston, Texas." Sally paused for a moment, unsure of the extent of her situation that she wanted to share. "Our marriage is going through some difficult changes right now," Sally replied.

"Well, y'all have two good-looking boys. Sure hope and pray all works out for you and Collin. Do you still live in the Whitehaven area?"

"Thank you. No, we moved about five years ago to the Getwell/Park area. Do you still live in Whitehaven?"

"Yes, not too far from here. I married, and I also have two children," Audrey said, looking at the two boys.

"Do you see any of our other classmates?" Sally inquired.

"Yeah, every now and then I'll see some of them. How about you?"

"Before we moved, I'd run into a few at the grocery store from time to time." At that, Sally noticed the time. "I better let you get back to work. It sure was great running into you!" She turned to Todd. "Did you find a book or two you'd like to check out and take home?"

"Yes ma'am. These two," he replied, holding up his two finds.

"Come on, Todd. I'll help you get those books checked out," Audrey said. "Now, you have two weeks before you'll need to return them. Sally, do you have a library card?" she asked.

"No, I don't."

"That's OK. I just need you to fill out this form, and then y'all will be good to go." Audrey handed Sally the library form and a pen. As Sally filled out the form, Audrey asked, "Todd, where do you go to school, and what grade are you in?"

"I'm in second grade at Southview Elementary School, and Pace is in first grade," Todd answered.

Sally finished filling out the form and handed it to Audrey. "OK, that should be it. Did I miss anything?"

"Everything looks good! You're now a member of the library system in Memphis," she said, handing Sally her new library card. "Here are your books, Todd. Enjoy them! Sally, it was so good to see you again."

"Thanks for helping us!" Sally and the boys turned to leave, and then Pace paused, turned, and waved to Audrey.

On the way home, Sally could hear the boys in the back seat oo-ing and ahh-ing at the pictures in one of the books. "Is that a cool book, fellas?"

"It sure is! I like this book. Thanks for taking us to the library, Mom," Todd exclaimed.

"You are very welcome!"

They arrived at home, and Sally sat on the couch with her boys to look at the books with them. After a while, she knew she needed to make a telephone call. "I'll be back soon. I need to do something. I need for y'all to be a little quiet, OK?"

"OK, we will," both boys said.

Sally picked up the telephone and carried it to the table. She grabbed the paper with the law firm information she got from Betty at the BBB and stared at the names and telephone numbers for a moment. She wondered, *What do I say? How do I ask the questions I need answers to?* Sally took a very deep breath and dialed the first number.

"Good afternoon. This is Mary with Cut & Dry Law Firm. I hope I can help you today. May I ask who I'm speaking with?"

Sally thought that was a lot for a receptionist to say when answering the telephone for a company! "Yes, my name is Sally Oldham."

"Well, hi, Ms. Sally. May I call you Sally?" Mary asked.

"Yes, that's fine."

"How can I help you today?"

"Mary, I'll be honest with you, I really don't know where to start this conversation because I've never had to do this before."

"I understand, Ms. Sally. OK, let's begin with why you are calling?" Mary requested.

"I need information on filing for divorce and how much it will cost, plus I have more questions too," Sally blurted out.

"OK, this law firm can definitely help you with your divorce and answer all your questions. We always prefer to have a consultation meeting with a potential client to talk about what's going on and which direction is the right way to go to help. This meeting is free of charge. If you like us and we feel we can help you resolve your situation, then we can go forward with your case. At that time, many issues will be addressed, including the fee for the proceedings. Can I schedule an appointment for you to see one of our attorneys?"

"I have two young sons. Do you make appointments on Saturdays so my mother-in-law could watch them for me?" Sally inquired.

Mary paused for a moment. "Usually we don't make appointments on Saturdays, but in your situation, we can probably make an exception. However, this coming Saturday is New Years weekend, and the office will be closed. We could schedule an appointment on January 6th at 11 a.m. Would that work for you?"

"I believe so, Mary." Sally's mind started racing.

"If there is a problem, just call us, Sally, and we can reschedule for you," Mary encouraged. "We'll see you on the 6th of January at 11 a.m.!"

Sally slowly hung up the telephone and breathed a sigh of relief. The call was difficult to make, but she was hopeful with the information she had been given and the progress she had made. She had to call Rusty to fill him in, so she dialed his number; she knew it by memory now. The phone rang six times before he answered.

"Hello?"

"Hi, honey. It's me."

"Hi, *me*. How are you?" he said with a chuckle.

"I'm good. Won't keep ya but a minute. I wanted to let you know, I just got off the telephone with a law firm, and I have an appointment on January 6th. It's a free consultation, and I'll know more about many of my questions after I talk to them," Sally explained.

"That's great news! The ball is rolling. I wish it could be sooner, but, hey, that's OK. I'm proud of you, sweetheart. All the law offices here are still closed for the holidays, so I haven't had a chance to ask any questions. How was the trip to the library this morning?" Rusty asked.

"Ahh, thanks for remembering! It went well. In fact, better than I expected. The lady that helped us was a classmate of mine in high school. Her name was Audrey. She helped Todd find the aviation section, and he had his choice of many good books. She and I talked and caught up on each other's lives since high school. It was really good."

"Hey, that's pretty cool! I bet Todd is looking at every page and taking it all in. Never know where his new knowledge might lead him. It's super that he's interested in such topics this early in his life," Rusty said emphatically.

"You're right. His interest in aviation might mean more later on in his life. We'll be excited to see where that goes!"

"Yes, *we* will! So are you OK?" Rusty asked.

"Yip, just a little tired. Is all going well for you leaving on your run in a few days?" Sally asked.

"Still helping Dad with those cows and the farm chores. Mom's a little concerned about him and all the work that he has to do. She says that he's not a spring chicken anymore, and the chores seem to be taking more of a toll on him lately. I'm just glad I've been home these last two weeks to help him."

"Yes, me too, and I know he appreciates you helping him. I miss seeing you, but it's been important for you to be there. I better get going. Time to make some vittles! I love you, and we'll talk tomorrow," Sally said.

"I miss you too, sweetheart, but with the boys home for Christmas break, we would not have been able to see each other anyway if I were making runs. It's all good. Yes, let's talk tomorrow. You guys enjoy your . . . *vittles*? Is that right?" Rusty laughed.

"Yes, that's right!" Sally laughed too. "Bye, sweetheart." She threw him a kiss into the telephone.

"Right back atcha, honey!" Rusty said, returning the kiss.

"Are you off the telephone, Mom?" Todd asked, peering around the corner.

"Yes, I am," Sally said as she took the telephone back to its little table in the living room. "What's ya got, kiddo?" she asked, sitting down on the couch beside the boys.

"Look at this, Mom." Todd showed her a page in one of the books. "The picture describes all about the different parts of an airplane, and here," he pointed below the picture, "the words tell what all these parts do to help the airplane fly!" he explained with excitement.

"How about that! That's great, Todd. You chose just the right book to get the answers you were looking for."

"Yeah, but some of these words I can't pronounce, and I don't know what they mean. Can you help me?"

"I will try. I'll go get the dictionary, and we'll look up the words," Sally said, making her way to the hall closet. Before she got there, the phone rang.

"Hello?"

"Mrs. Oldham, this is Rebecca Pierce from Southview Elementary School. How are you today?"

"I'm OK, Rebecca. How can I help you?" Sally asked.

"I'm calling all the parents of the students who go to our school to inform you that the Board of Education has changed the date for students to return to school for the new semester. Your sons will need to report back to school on January 3rd instead of January 8th. I'm sorry for the inconvenience this may cause, but the Board elected for the students to come back earlier," Rebecca explained.

"Thank you for letting me know. The boys will be back to school on the 3rd," Sally replied. When she hung up the phone, she walked back to the hall closet, grabbed the dictionary off the shelf, and brought it to Todd. "I'll be back in a few minutes, and we'll look up some of those words. But first, I need to make another quick telephone call."

"Try not to be long, Mom!" Todd expressed earnestly.

She picked up the handset and called the law firm back to reschedule her appointment for January 4th. With the boys going back to school earlier, she wouldn't need her mother-in-law to watch the boys, and she could come earlier for her consultation. That might hurry the process along of getting the divorce paperwork started.

"All right. I'm ready for a word!" Sally exclaimed, emerging back into the living room.

Todd began reading the words below the airplane's diagram. Sally was surprised when he got up to grab some paper and a pencil to write down things he was learning. They looked up words for nearly an hour until Sally had to start preparing dinner. Todd continued his research at the dining room table.

When supper was ready, Sally asked Todd to move his notes off the table. "We can continue working on your project after supper, if you want to!" she encouraged him. "You've been working hard. Are you finding the words in the dictionary OK and understanding the meanings?" she asked.

"Kinda. I have some I need to ask you about. I wrote a star next to them so I would remember," Todd said.

"Hey, that's a good idea. We'll look at those after supper. Let's eat before our supper gets cold."

The hot tamales and chili hit the spot on that cold evening. The temperature outside was dropping, and the poor old floor furnace seemed like it was working overtime to heat their small house. Sally suggested the boys go ahead and take their baths and put on their flannel PJs so they would stay warmer. While they were in the tub, Sally called Rusty.

"Hi! I won't keep you but a minute, but I have some news," Sally announced.

"What is your news, honey?" Rusty asked curiously.

"The boys' school called me this afternoon and informed me that students would be going back to school earlier on January 3rd. If all goes well with the weather, and you are making your run, hopefully we'll be able to see each other that day! However, I'll need to pick up the boys from school at three o'clock," Sally said, excited about the possibility of seeing her man.

"Oh, sweetheart, that *is* news . . . *good news!* I have missed you *so* much. I'll take you in my arms and love you to pieces!" Rusty was near ecstatic over Sally's news.

"There's more news. Because the boys are going back to school sooner, I rescheduled the attorney's appointment for January 4th. The sooner the better, right?" Sally chuckled.

"Wow! That is better news too! All this news makes me very happy, Sally."

Sally heard the sound of the water draining in the tub and the commotion of the boys rummaging through their drawers. "The boys are done with their baths, so I need to go. I love you bunches," Sally said and threw him a kiss.

"I love you, too," Rusty said.

Sally heard Rusty's kiss being thrown to her just before the telephone call ended.

Todd and Pace were all snuggled in their warm flannel PJs and sitting on the couch. Sally went to her room to change into her warm velvet robe, then came back and sat with the boys, wrapping a cozy blanket around all three.

"Do you want to work some more on your notes, Todd?" Sally asked.

"No, I'll do more tomorrow. Will you be able to help me?"

"You betcha, I will," Sally answered. She and the boys snuggled on the couch for a while, watching TV. Before too long, it was near ten o'clock, and the boys were having a tough time staying awake. Sally turned off the television and helped her boys to their beds. She whispered low, "Sleep tight, and don't let the bedbugs bite. I love both of y'all bunches." She turned out their bedroom light, quietly walked down the hallway to her room, and got in bed after another long day.

It was a lazy morning for the Oldham household. When Sally looked at the clock on her nightstand, it was shortly after eight o'clock. She sleepily sat up, slipped her slippers on, and grabbed her robe. She walked from her room to the doorway of the boys' room. They were still sleeping, so she wandered into the kitchen and began making coffee. Reaching into the cabinet for her mom's cookbook, Sally found the recipe for pancakes. She knew homemade pancakes probably wouldn't taste as good as C&B's pancakes, but she decided to give it her best shot.

Suddenly, Sally heard a noise coming from the boys' bedroom. She ran down the hall to find Pace crying, and Todd had climbed down from his bunk bed to see what was wrong.

"Pace, honey, what's the matter? Why are you crying? Are you hurting?" Sally asked anxiously, sitting down beside him.

"Pace, talk to Mom! What's wrong?" Todd said, leaning closer to his brother.

Pace could barely talk, he was crying so hard. "I had a bad dream about Daddy! Momma, where is Daddy?" he said in a near scream.

Sally took Pace in her arms and hugged him tightly as tears began to stream down her face. She felt his pain. "Oh, Pace, I'm so sorry. I wish I could take away your bad dream. I want to make you feel better."

Todd was now crying as well as he hugged his brother. "I miss him too, Pace. Please, don't cry," Todd urged him.

"Todd, please stay here with your brother. I'll be right back," Sally instructed. She went into the bathroom, took a clean washcloth from the towel shelf, dampened it with cold water, and took it to the boys' room. "Here, let's wipe away those tears, little man." The cold cloth felt good to Pace as she tenderly washed his small face. "Feel better?" she asked.

"Yes, ma'am. Thank you, Momma," Pace replied.

"I thought about making some homemade pancakes for breakfast. How does that sound?" Sally cheerfully said, trying to change the subject.

"That sounds pretty good. Can we help, Mom?" Todd asked.

"Y'all sure can. Come on. Let's go to the kitchen and get a-cookin'!" Sally said as she stood up from Pace's bed.

The boys followed their mom into the kitchen. "The recipe calls for milk," Sally began, reading the ingredients from the cookbook.

"I've got the milk." Pace ran to the refrigerator.

"While you're in the fridge, we'll need one egg too. Todd, you can get the canisters of flour and sugar from the countertop. I'll get the baking powder and the salt." Sally found the skillet and the mixing bowl along with the measuring cups and spoons. "OK, Todd, you can take this measuring cup and pour one cup of milk into it, please. Pace, after I crack the egg into the mixing bowl, you can stir it up real good." Sally watched as her boys followed the steps one by one. "You both are doing *so* good!" she encouraged. She measured out the rest of the ingredients and stirred it all together. "It's time to pour the batter onto the hot skillet!"

Todd and Pace watched their mother intently as she poured little silver-dollar dollops. They already looked delicious!

"One of you, please put the syrup and butter on the dining room table because these pancakes are about to be ready to eat!" Sally said as she put the first batch on a plate.

After breakfast, Todd grabbed his library books, some notebook paper, and a pencil, and camped out at the dining room table. Pace climbed back up in his chair and watched his brother, asking a lot of questions. Sally looked up words for Todd in the dictionary and explained each one to him. Todd amazed his mother with how interested he was in what he was learning. She was very proud of him.

After a while, Sally said, "Let's take a break and rest. Y'all want to go for a ride and get out of the house for a little while?" she asked. The boys agreed. They had had a really lazy morning and were still in their night clothes! So they all got dressed and ready and were out the front door in no time.

The sun was shining, and the temperature was delightfully warm for that time of the year. "Any place y'all would like to go?" Sally inquired.

"Since it's warm, can we go to the park?" Pace asked.

"Yea, that sounds like a good idea," Todd chimed in.

"I think that is an excellent idea! And with these warm temps, we don't need our coats. This is crazy weather!" And off to the park they went.

There were not many people nor ducks at the park, so they nearly had the place to themselves. They walked around the lake and down a few paths. The boys played on some of the playground equipment, laughing and giggling together.

In no time at all, Sally looked at her watch. They had been playing for nearly two hours! She was shocked. "Boys, I think it's time to leave. How about some burgers and fries? Does that sound good?" Sally asked her sons.

"Burgers and fries always sound good, Mom," Todd answered cheerfully.

"Let's go, Momma," Pace yelled as he began to run to the car.

They arrived at the restaurant and ordered their food. "Our lunch should be ready in a few minutes," Sally announced as she sat down at the table with her sons. "Listen for our number. It's 1130."

"Hey, that's a great number!" Todd remarked. "That's my birthday!"

"It sure is. That's a lucky number!" his mother agreed.

Soon, number 1130 was called, so Sally approached the counter to retrieve their food.

"Yum yum," Pace exclaimed.

Sally sat the tray down on the table and handed the food out. The boys quickly opened up the paper wrappings and began eating. Sally sat their cup of fries beside them, and they scarfed them into their mouths as well.

When they were done eating, Sally said, "Maybe tomorrow, depending on the weather, we can plan to do something special again. It'll already be Saturday! On Wednesday, y'all will be going back to school. Time is flying by!" Sally said to the boys.

"Where can we go, Momma?" Pace asked.

"Well, let's see. We could go to a movie or to the museum, go bowling, or go to the zoo? Can y'all think of other places to go?"

"No, not really, but I'd like to go to a movie," Todd said.

"Me too, Momma," Pace agreed.

"OK, then it's off to the movies tomorrow. I'll look in the newspaper to see what's showing and what time would be best for us to go," Sally said as she gathered up the boys to head home.

Todd sat his library books on the dining room table and continued to read about airplanes, Pace retreated to his bedroom to play with some of his new toys, and Sally poured herself a cup of coffee and grabbed the newspaper. She found the page that listed movie showtimes, and her eyes scanned the options.

"Hey, boys, you've seen the advertisements on television about *The Rings*, haven't you?" Sally asked.

Pace came into the living room, and Todd looked up from his work. "Yes," they answered.

"Do y'all think you'd like to see that movie?"

"I like the commercials about the movie. Yes, that would be a good one," Todd responded.

"Me too, Momma," Pace said.

"OK, that's the one then! I believe the best showtime for us will be at one o'clock. We'll need to leave here by noon or a little after," Sally explained. "Todd, would you like me to help you?" she asked, walking over to him.

"Yes, please. I have some words I need help with."

Sally realized it was nearly time to start supper, so she walked over to the pantry to see what options there were. "Todd, let me see what vittles I have to fix for supper, then I'll be right there to help you." She looked in the pantry, then the fridge, then the freezer. *OK, I have an idea!* she thought. Then she walked back over to Todd. "I can help you for a little while, Todd, but then I need to start our supper." Sally sat down at the table beside him.

"While you are helping Todd, can I turn on the television, Momma?" Pace asked.

"Yes, dear, but don't have it too loud, please."

"OK, I won't," he answered.

"Whatcha got, kiddo?" Sally leaned closer to Todd.

An hour went by, and Todd and his mother had made some great headway on his project. "I need to start our supper now. You can continue working if you want to; it'll take me a while to cook our food," she explained. Sally began peeling and cutting potatoes and placing them onto a hot, oiled skillet. She took the ham from the refrigerator and cut off a chunk of it and put it in a baking dish, placing it into the oven. She grabbed a can of green beans and a small can of crushed pineapples from the pantry. She poured the green beans in a saucepan to warm and placed the pineapples into a small bowl.

"Something sure is smelling good, Mom," Todd commented as he closed his library book and began removing his project from the table. "Can I help you?"

"Yes. Thank you. You can get what you want to drink and ask your brother what he wants to drink. That would be most helpful." Sally was appreciative of Todd's offer.

Todd came into the kitchen and poured two glasses of milk and took them to the table.

"Supper is almost ready. Y'all go wash your hands," Sally announced. She placed their supper on the table and they sat down to eat.

Later that evening, the telephone rang. The boys watched their mother anxiously as she moved toward the phone, hoping it was their dad calling.

"Hello?" Sally answered.

"Hi, sweetheart. Is this a good time to call?" Rusty asked.

"Hi, dear! Yes it is, but hold on a minute," Sally said, lowering the phone from her mouth. "I'm sorry, boys, it's not your dad," she said to them. She saw the sadness on their faces. "Y'all can watch television if you want to. I'll be a few minutes." Sally walked to the dining room table so she could talk to Rusty a little more privately. "I'm sorry, Rusty. The boys have not heard from their dad since he left, and they were hoping the call might be from him. How are you?"

"I'm OK, just missing you! I am sorry Collin has not called. That's really low of him. How are you?" Rusty asked.

"I'm OK. I'm missing you too. Really looking forward to seeing you next week. How is the weather looking?"

"So far, so good, and I'm praying it stays that way. I want to wrap my arms around you!" Rusty expressed.

"I can almost feel you near me. Your precious words mean so much to me," Sally expressed back to him.

"Have you and the boys had a good day today?"

"Well, it started out rough with Pace having a bad dream about his daddy. It really scared him, and he cried hard. But the day got better." Sally continued. "We worked on Todd's airplane project for several hours after breakfast, then we took a break and went to the park. It was a beautiful day here, but unseasonably warm. Could be setting the area up for some bad weather. How about your day, dear Rusty?"

"It was not as exciting as your day, that's for sure! Mom asked me up for breakfast, I helped Dad with the cows, I had to go into town for some supplies, and then I packed a little more gear in preparation for my run on Monday."

"Are you getting excited about getting back to work?" Sally asked.

"Yes, I am. I've missed making my runs, but I miss seeing you most of all! It was important for me to be home and help Mom and Dad, but it's time to get back to work." Rusty paused. "Dad just walked in, hang on." He covered the mouthpiece of the phone with his hand. "I'll be ready in a minute, Dad. I'm talking to Sally." Rusty removed his hand. "Dad and I have an errand to run. I love and miss you bunches, and we'll talk again very soon. You guys have fun tomorrow, and please, be careful."

"Tell your dad I said *hi*! Love you too." Sally smiled as she lowered the telephone from her ear. She was very happy Rusty called her. She walked back to the living room and placed the handset on the telephone's base. The boys had turned on the television, so Sally sat down on the couch beside them.

Todd looked at his mother with tears in his eyes and asked, "Why doesn't Dad call us? Is he mad at us? I sure do miss him."

"I do too, Todd." Pace leaned over and laid down in his mother's lap.

"Boys, your dad is not mad at y'all, and no, I don't know why he hasn't called to talk to you two. I guess he's just busy and hasn't had time," Sally responded, but the answers did not ease their pain. She wished Collin knew how much sadness he was causing his little sons. She guessed Collin just didn't care. His *new life* was more important. She knew she needed to make up for the emptiness they felt by filling the role of both mother *and* father to the boys.

The rest of the evening was quiet, even though the television was on. Sally wished there was a way to call Collin, but she didn't know where he was. Maybe at work, maybe at *the other woman's house,* or maybe on the road heading to Houston. She wasn't sad for herself, but she sure was sad for her sons.

"I guess it's time for bed, fellas. I'll run your bath water if y'all will go get ready," Sally instructed.

"OK, Mom," Todd replied as he walked to his room, Pace following him.

While they bathed, Sally went into her room and sat on the bed, thinking about all they had planned for tomorrow. *I sure hope the fun movie makes the boys feel a little better,* she thought. After a few moments, she grabbed the boys' bath towels and walked into the bathroom.

"All right, all dry!" she said, finishing drying little Pace off. "Let's go get those PJs on."

The boys ran to their room and dressed in their PJs, then jumped into their bed.

"Y'all sleep tight. Don't let the bedbugs bite. I love both of you bunches. Night night," Sally said, kissing their foreheads.

"Love you too. Night night," they responded.

Sally turned their light off and shut their door, then slowly walked to her bedroom, slipped on her night gown, and tucked herself into bed.

The morning of December 30th brought bad storms. A very loud clap of thunder woke all three of them suddenly. Todd and Pace ran into their mother's bedroom and jumped into her bed. Sally gathered them up beside her and held them tightly. They could see the bright lightning flashing through the window, and the thunder sounded like it was right on top of their house. The wind blew the rain hard into the side of the house, and pellets of hail hit the windowpanes. Then, the tornado siren screamed. Sally immediately grabbed up the boys, and they huddled down in the hallway. Sally was scared, but she held her terrified boys and tried to comfort them, breathing words of protection over them.

After what felt like an eternity, the tornado siren stopped blaring, the wind ceased, and the pounding rain stopped.

"Are y'all OK?" Sally asked her boys, still in clear shock from the storm.

"I think so," Todd answered.

"Momma, I was *so* scared!" Pace's voice quivered.

"Thank goodness we're OK!" Sally said gratefully as she looked up. She slowly stood up and walked to the living room window with the boys right behind her. "Oh my! That storm was bad," she remarked, seeing the damage in the front yard. The boys peered around their mother to look out the window.

"Our little tree is laying on the ground!" Todd exclaimed. "And look across the street! More trees are down! Oh my, what's wrong with that house?" he said, pointing down the street.

"That house has lost its shingles from off the roof! Not good. I sure hope our roof is OK. We need to get dressed and go outside to see if we have any damage," Sally suggested. They got dressed, put on their raincoats, and went out the front door. The porch was covered with leaves that had blown off the nearby trees, and branches were down in their driveway, in their neighbors' yards, and in the street. Sally walked out to the sidewalk in front of their house, then turned to look back at their home. From her viewpoint, the roof looked good. She would need to check the back of the house.

Pace had walked over to the little tree. He bent down to lift it up and started to cry. Sally rushed to him and took him in her arms. Through his tears and crying, he struggled to say, "Daddy helped Todd and me plant this little tree, and now it's broken!" He was crying so hard. Todd came to Pace's side and held him too as he began to cry also. That little tree meant a lot to Todd and Pace.

Several of Sally's neighbors had come out to survey the damage to their homes as well. There was a partial roof in the street from someone's house down the road.

"I'm going to the backyard. Come on, y'all, come with me," Sally insisted. She opened the gate to the backyard and immediately saw shingles lying on the ground. She looked up to the roof, but to her surprise, she didn't see any shingles missing. It must have been her neighbor's roof.

"Everything looks good back here, Mom! I don't see any damage," Todd said with relief.

"I don't either. That is great! I think, to be on the safe side, I'm going to call the landlord and ask him to check for any damage. I'd rather be safe than sorry! I think we best go back inside the house. It's starting to rain again," Sally said, ushering the boys back toward the house. "Let me have your raincoats before you go into the house. I'll shake the rain from them."

When they were back in the house, Sally noticed the electricity was off. "We have no power, boys," she announced. "That means I can't fix us any breakfast, but we do have cereal! Do y'all still want to go to the movie today?"

"Can we?" Todd asked. "Will the theater have electricity?"

"That's a good question! I'll get the newspaper, find the telephone number for the theater, and call. But first, let's eat some cereal. Todd, when you get the milk out of the fridge, please, do it quickly. We don't want too much cold air to get out of it!" Sally walked into the kitchen and took the cereal bowls from the cabinet while Pace picked up the cereal box from the pantry and Todd quickly retrieved the milk. It was a different kind of breakfast, but it just had to do.

After they finished their breakfast, Sally called the theater and confirmed they had power and the movie was a *go*! The boys were so excited, and they all rushed out the door.

As Sally drove down their street, they saw more damage, including a broken traffic light. Carefully she drove down main street, taking in all the damage the storm had done to the town. By that point, the rain had stopped, and the sun was trying to peek through the clouds.

When Sally drove into the theater parking lot, she noticed that not many others had chosen to come see a movie that day. Maybe they would have the whole theater to themselves! As they entered the theater, the smell of freshly popped popcorn filled the air.

"Mom, can we have some popcorn?" Todd asked anxiously.

"Please, Momma!" Pace begged.

"Yes, I'll buy us some popcorn, but first, I need to buy our tickets to the movie," Sally said as she approached the ticket booth. "One adult and two children, please," she requested, handing the agent $2.00. He gave Sally the tickets, and then Sally and the boys walked to the concession counter. "I'd like three bags of popcorn and three small cups of pop, please," Sally told the clerk behind the counter.

"Coming right up!" the young, pleasant-voiced man responded. He handed the bags of popcorn to Todd and Pace and sat the cups of pop on the counter. "That will be $1.25, please," he said.

Sally handed him the money, then grabbed the drinks and ushered the boys toward the theater room. They climbed the steps to a little more than halfway, stepped in front of the row of seats, and sat down.

"Wow! I forgot what it's like to be in a theater," Todd remarked.

"That's right. It's been several years since we took you to your first movie. Pace, you weren't but three years old when we brought Todd. You probably don't remember being at the movie, do you?"

"No, I don't remember. It's kind of scary in here," Pace said, looking around. "But I think I like it!"

"That's good. I don't want you to be scared," his mother said, wrapping her arms around him.

As they waited for the movie to start, they munched on their buttered popcorn and sipped on their drinks. Then the lights dimmed, and a cartoon appeared on the big screen in front of them.

"Look, Momma! It's like on television!" Pace yelled out.

"Shhh! Pace, you are to be quiet in a movie theater," Sally whispered, giggling slightly by his pure joy. "You can talk, but you need to whisper, OK?"

"Oh, OK," he whispered back to her.

After a few minutes, the movie started. The music was louder than the boys expected, but they reveled in the experience of it all; they were glued to the screen. They laughed, they stared in wonderment, and they grabbed their mother's arms and wiggled in their seats at a few scary parts. Sally was overcome with joy at the boys' priceless reactions.

After the movie was over, the boys sat quietly in their seats.

"Are y'all OK?" Sally asked.

After a moment of hesitation, Todd said, "Yes. That was a good movie! But I didn't want it to stop. I want to see more movies!"

"I'm sure we can arrange that. I'm very glad you liked the movie. It wasn't too scary, was it?" Sally asked.

Pace quickly answered, "I was a little scared. I didn't like that one guy in the movie."

"But are you OK now?"

"Yes, I'm OK," Pace said, nodding.

By the time they walked out of the theater, the temperature had dropped, and Old Man Winter was blowing his north wind. They hurried to the car and the promise of the warm heater.

After a quick stop at a grocery store, they were on their way home. The debris still looked pretty bad around their street, but at least the neighbor's partial roof had been taken off the road. Men with chainsaws were cutting up the fallen trees. It was such a sobering sight.

Once in the house, Sally was thankful to see that electricity had been restored and the floor furnace was working properly. She took the grocery bags to the kitchen and put away the items she had bought while the boys went to their room to play. Sally then called the landlord and explained to him about that morning's storm and the damage it had caused in the neighborhood. She told him that she hadn't seen any damage to her house but asked him to come assess it himself. He agreed and said he would be there in an hour.

In the meantime, Sally worked on some chores that she needed to do—change the bed sheets, wash clothes, and vacuum the floors. Suddenly, there came a knock at the front door. Todd and Pace ran to the doorway of their room, waiting anxiously to see who was at the door—still hoping for a visit from their dad.

Sally opened the door. "Hi, Mr. Waddell. Please, come in," she said to the landlord.

"Hi, Sally. Boy, that storm did a number on your street. So many trees down and property damage," he said as he stepped into the living room. "I want to go into the backyard and look around. I didn't see any damage to the roof or any part of the front of the house. Everything looks good. Does everything inside the house seem to be working OK?" Mr. Waddell asked.

"Yes, sir, it does," Sally answered.

"Good. I'll go check out the back of the house and the roof. I'll be back," Mr. Waddell said as he opened the front door and stepped out on the porch.

Todd came into the living room. "Who is he?"

"He is Mr. Waddell. He owns this house. We are renting from him, and he is responsible to repair any problem we might have with the house. Say the floor furnace stops working; I would call him, and he would need to get it fixed. Understand?" Sally explained.

"Yes, I think so."

"It's not your worries, little man. I'll handle any situation that comes along," Sally reassured him.

Mr. Waddell knocked on the door again, and Sally quickly opened it. "I don't see any damage of any kind, Sally, but thank you for calling me so I could check. Just glad you and your family are unharmed. How is Collin? Working, I guess?"

"I'm glad all is OK, and thank you for checking it out for us. Collin is OK. Yes, he is at work," Sally decided to say. She did not want Mr. Waddell to know anything about their situation—at least, not yet.

"Well, good. Call me if you need anything," he said as he walked out.

As Sally closed the door, Todd asked, "Is Dad at work?" Todd had heard what his mother had told Mr. Waddell.

Sally was unsure how to answer. "Todd, honestly, I don't know where your dad is, but I could not tell Mr. Waddell that. He doesn't need to know the problems that your dad and I are having. I didn't mean to lie about your dad, but I just thought it was best that Mr. Waddell did not know the truth. Do you understand?" She looked into Todd's eyes. "Lying is not good. Do you think I should have told Mr. Waddell the truth?"

Todd hesitated, then answered, "No. I think I understand." But Sally was unsure that he did. How could she better explain the situation without confusing him even more? Todd turned and walked back to his room.

Sally walked to the kitchen to prepare supper. The situation with Todd concerned her and would not leave her mind. She felt like she needed to say more to him, but what?

Her train of thought was interrupted when Pace asked, "What's ya fixin' for supper, Momma?"

"Well, little one, with the chill in the air, I thought about servin' up hot dogs, chili, and tater tots. How does that sound?"

"Yum yum good! Hey, Todd, Momma's fixin' some good food for supper," he yelled as he ran toward his bedroom.

Supper wasn't much, but it hit the spot. Chili is always good in cold weather! As Sally cleaned off the table, she suggested, "How about a game of cards after I wash up the dishes?"

"Yes! I'll go get the cards," shouted Pace.

"I'll get the paper and pencil so we can keep score," Todd added.

Within a few minutes, the three of them were sitting at the table again. The game went on for nearly two hours!

"Gosh, Mom, that was so much fun! Let's do it again real soon," Todd exclaimed.

"Yeah, Momma, let's do this again!" Pace agreed.

"I believe that's an excellent idea, kiddos!" Sally said.

"Todd, tomorrow, if you want to, we can work on your airplane project some more. You'll only have three days left before you go back to school, and you might not have time to work on it once you're back in school," Sally reminded him.

"Yes, I probably should. Soon the books will need to be returned to the library. I don't think I have much more to read. We can go to the library before I go back to school."

"We might. We'll see how it goes tomorrow. Do y'all want to watch television? Y'all can see what's on? Or do y'all want to play in your room before bedtime in an hour or so?" Sally inquired.

"I'll see what's on television," Todd answered. "Come on, Pace. Let's check it out." Pace followed Todd to the living room.

In the darkness of the dining room, Sally carried the telephone to the dining room table. Taking the handset in her hand, she dialed Rusty's telephone number. After the fifth ring, he answered.

"Hello?"

"Hi, honey. It's me," Sally said softly.

"Hi, sweetheart. How are you?" Rusty asked.

"Well, it's been another one of those crazy days. A very bad storm woke us up this morning, then the tornado siren started blasting. We huddled in the hallway until the storm passed."

"Oh my. Are you guys OK?" Rusty asked eagerly.

"Yes, we are, but our little tree in front of the house was blown over along with many of our neighbors' trees. But worst of all, our neighbor at the end of our street lost most of his roof! Thankfully there didn't seem to be any damage to our house."

"That is too close for comfort. So glad you all are OK. That had to be scary!"

"Yes, it was," Sally confirmed. "How's your weather?"

"It's cold, but no snow and none predicted for several days. So Monday should be OK for me to leave and head your way. Thank goodness today is over, but tomorrow will probably drag by. I can't wait to see you and hold you in my arms again. It seems like forever!" Rusty said tenderly.

"It does seem like forever, honey. I want your arms to wrap around me, and I want to wrap my arms around you! I miss you so much. I am glad to hear the weather is cooperating for your departure. You just be very careful. By the way, the boys and I were still able to go to see the movie despite the terrible storm. It was good, but a little scary for Pace. It was his first time at a theater, that he can remember. By the way, last night, while we were talking, your dad came into your home, and you needed to go. Is everything OK?" Sally inquired.

"Yes. He and Mom were having a hard time putting a new box of Christmas ornaments in the attic, and he needed my help. Unfortunately both of them are getting to the age where they aren't able to do the things they used to be able to do. My dad, especially, is having a hard time dealing with that. He's always been able to do anything he's wanted or needed to do, and now, it's really bugging him that he can't. I feel bad for both of them because they've always had very active lives. I'm sorry. I didn't mean to go on about that situation," Rusty apologized.

"No, please don't apologize. I can hear in your voice that you are quite concerned about your parents. I'm happy that you are, and most of all, that you do care so much. You're a good son. You know, when the boys and I move there, hopefully we will be able to help them too," Sally reassured him.

There was a deafening silence.

"Rusty, are you still there?" Sally asked with worry.

"Yes, sweetheart. I'm here. What you just said is the first time you have really acknowledged that you and the boys would be here with me. That means everything to me, Sally." Rusty was struggling to speak as he fought back tears. "I love you so much."

"Sometimes, Rusty, I feel like I'm already there. I want that so much. I love you too, my love." Sally looked at the clock on the wall. "It's late, and I need to get Todd and Pace ready for bed. You sleep tight tonight. Don't let the bedbugs bite, and I'll see you in my dreams. Love you bunches!"

"Thank you, Sally. I'll see you in my dreams also. I love you."

Their call ended.

Sally continued to sit in darkness for a few moments, thinking about how so very much she loved that man.

When she walked into the living room to set the telephone on its table, she found both of her little boys asleep on the couch. She gently picked up Pace and carried him to his bed, still in his day clothes, and covered him up. She walked back to the living room to get Todd. He was too big and too heavy for her to pick up, so she lifted him from the couch and tenderly woke him, just enough for her to help him walk to his room. He very sleepily climbed the ladder to his bunk bed and laid down. She stood on her tip-toes to pull the bed covers over him.

"Night night, sweet son. I love you."

Todd mumbled back to her, "Love you too."

She turned out the light and took two steps out of their room, then turned to face them and threw both of them her good night kisses.

Walking into her room, Sally slipped between the sheets of her bed and breathed deeply. Her last thoughts before drifting off to sleep were the words she had told Rusty: "I'll see you in my dreams."

The last day of the year began like most other days of that year. Sally was up at seven o'clock, but she let Todd and Pace sleep in. She meandered to the kitchen to brew the coffee, and while she waited for it to be ready, she turned on the television to watch the news and weather. *HEADLINES: Iran has a new Premier; Taiwan's final day of diplomatic relations with the United States; in Memphis, the high today is in the mid-60s with the low tonight in the mid-30s.* According to the National Weather Map, the northeast would be sunny and cold. She thought about Rusty, hoping the good weather would hold out for him as he started on his run tomorrow morning.

The morning coffee tasted good as Sally took her first sips. She looked in the refrigerator and the pantry for something she could make the boys for breakfast, but nothing jumped out at her. She decided on sausage, egg, and cheese omelets with toast. Now that sounded good, and it was different!

"Good morning, Momma," said a sleepy-voiced Pace as he entered the kitchen and hugged his mother's waist.

"Good morning, my little man. You still sound sleepy. Are you OK?" She bent over to hug him and kissed the top of his head.

"Yes, a little. I'm OK. Maybe hungry. My tummy is growling. Hear it?" he asked, drawing closer.

"Well, we'll just have to do something about that, won't we?" she responded. "Is your brother up yet? Let's go see." Sally walked from the kitchen to the boys' bedroom. Pace followed her.

Pace climbed only two steps up the ladder (that was as far as he was allowed to climb) and peeked over the footrail of the bunk bed. "I think he is still asleep, Momma," he whispered.

On her tip-toes, Sally peeped over the side railing at Todd. Suddenly Todd opened his eyes and yelled, "*Boo!*"

He caught Sally off guard, and she jumped back and laughed. "You stinker! You scared me!"

Pace laughed. "Todd, you scared Momma! Shame on you!" He stepped carefully off the ladder as Todd scooted down to the foot of the bed.

Sally met him and hugged him. "That was funny, Todd. But you've heard about paybacks, right? I'll get you when you least expect it, so watch out!" Her hand ruffled his hair as she walked away from him. "How about some breakfast?"

"Sounds good! I'll be there in a minute to help you," he remarked as he walked into the bathroom.

Pace followed Sally into the kitchen. "Can I help too, Momma?" he asked.

"You sure can. You can get the milk and eggs from the fridge. Oh yeah, I need the sausage too. Can you get that too?" Sally requested.

"OK, I'm here. What can I do?" Todd said, walking into the kitchen.

"You can get the milk glasses down and fill them up. It's going to take a little while before breakfast is ready, so y'all can rest." Sally scrambled the eggs in a bowl while the sausage was browning. Then she mixed them together into one large omelet, topping it with cheese and placing it on the table. She took the toast out of the toaster, slathered some butter on the top, and set it on the table next to the eggs. "Breakfast is ready!"

The boys rushed to the dining room table and sat down.

"This looks good, Mom," Todd expressed.

"I don't remember what this is?" Pace was puzzled.

"It's a sausage, egg, and cheese omelet. I hope y'all like it!"

After a few bites, there was a look of delight on the boys' faces. "Very good, Mom!" Todd said.

"Yes, Momma, it's delicious!" Pace agreed.

"Good! I'll make this more often."

When they had finished eating, Todd brought his library books to the table and opened the one he was working from. "Mom, I have a few starred words for you to help me with when you have time," he asked.

"I'll be there when I finish in the kitchen. What is Pace doing?" Sally asked.

"He is watching cartoons," Todd answered.

Sally finished the dishes, then sat down with Todd at the table. "Which words do you need help with?" she asked.

"There are five of them. Here's the dictionary." Todd opened the book to the letter "E." The first starred word was *empennage.*

"OK," Sally said as she began reading the definition. "It is another phrase or word for the tail of an aircraft, which provides stability during flight." They both looked at the picture in the dictionary.

"Say the word again, please. How is the word pronounced?" Todd asked.

"It's *em-pen-nage*." Sally spoke the word slowly, emphasizing each syllable. "Now, you say it."

"*Empennage?*" Todd repeated.

"Very good, son! What's another word?"

After nearly an hour, Todd had gone through his whole list, taking a lot of notes. "I think I have finished my project. I have learned a lot about airplanes and sort of understand how and why they fly," he said as he closed his library book.

"I'm very proud of you, son. You have worked hard on this. Tomorrow's a holiday, but on Tuesday we can return the books to the library. Then we'll go to the airport where you can put your new knowledge into practice. How does that sound?" Sally suggested.

"Oh, I'd like that very much! I'll take my notes with me so I will have them to help me." Todd rejoiced!

"Is anyone hungry for lunch? I thought I'd fix peanut butter and banana sandwiches. What do y'all think?"

"Sounds OK," Todd said.

"Mmm-mmm good, Momma!" exclaimed Pace.

Sally proceeded into the kitchen to prepare their sandwiches. Todd joined her and poured two glasses of milk. Pace bounced into the kitchen too and asked, "Is it all right if I eat some potato chips with my sandwich?"

"It sure is. I'll get them for you. Would it be OK with you if Todd and I eat some potato chips too?" Sally asked with a smile.

"Absolutely!" he answered happily.

Lunch was ready, and each one enjoyed their sandwiches and potato chips. When they were done, Todd sat a few games on the table that he had taken from the coat closet. The boys and Sally spent the next two hours playing games together.

Then the telephone rang.

"Hello?" Sally answered.

"Hi, dear. How are you and the boys?" Peggy asked.

"Hi, Peggy. We are doing good. How are you?"

"I'm OK. I was wondering . . . if you and the boys aren't going anywhere to celebrate the New Year, I could bring lots of pizzas, and we could celebrate together? Are y'all doing anything or going anywhere?" Peggy asked.

Sally did not hesitate. "We have no plans, and we'd enjoy seeing you. But I can prepare supper for us. No need for you to bring pizzas," Sally suggested.

"No, no, I want to bring pizzas. I know the boys love pizza. If it's OK, I thought I would stop by one of those places that are selling fireworks and pick up some sparklers for the boys. Would that be OK?" Peggy continued.

"Well, OK, pizza it is! Thank you. And, yes, the sparklers sound fun. I remember my folks always had sparklers for me when I was the boys' age. That would be special!" Sally reminisced for a moment.

"OK, great! I'll see y'all in about an hour."

Sally hung up the telephone. "Grandmother Peggy is coming over and bringing pizzas for supper! Not that the house is a mess, but let's pick up the toys in the living room and take them to your bedroom. I'll make sure all else is looking nice," Sally instructed.

An hour later, Peggy arrived with two big boxes filled with pizza.

"Peggy, those pizzas are smelling ever so good," Sally remarked. "Please sit the boxes on the dining room table. I'll get paper plates and napkins. What would you like to drink?"

Peggy sat the boxes down and took off her coat. Todd took her coat and hung it up on the coat tree. "I guess I'll drink a soft drink, Sally."

"Boys, what would you like to drink?" Sally asked.

"Soft drink too, Mom," Todd answered.

"Yip, me too," Pace chimed in.

All four of them took their seats at the table. Peggy asked to say the blessing for their supper, and they obliged. Then, she said, "OK, who wants the first slice of pizza?" as she reached into one of the boxes.

About halfway through supper, the telephone rang again. Sally excused herself from the table and went to answer the call.

"Hello?" Sally said.

"Hi, sweetheart. How are you?" Rusty's voice echoed in her ear.

Pleasantly surprised by his call, Sally walked to the couch and sat down. "Hi, honey. I'm OK, but Peggy is here, and we're eating pizza," she said in a near whisper. "Are you OK?"

"Uh oh. I'm sorry. I won't keep you. I'm going to bed soon, and I wanted to call and tell you Happy New Year, sweet darling. My run is scheduled, and I'll leave at four o'clock in the morning. I'll call you mid-morning tomorrow when I stop for a break," he explained.

"I hope you sleep well, and please be super careful on the road. Happy New Year to you, also, honey! I'm sorry I can't talk longer, but I'll be looking forward to talking to you in the morning. I love you, my dear. Sleep tight and sweet dreams," Sally said in a hushed tone.

"I love you too, baby." And Rusty hung up.

Sally held the handset a few moment before she placed it on the telephone's base. She had to regroup herself. She definitely did not want her mother-in-law to notice anything different about her as she returned to the dining room table. "I'm sorry. That was a friend wishing a Happy New Year to me. They were about to leave town and wouldn't be able to call me," Sally explained, hoping that what she said sounded convincing.

"Well, that was nice of them. Good friends are hard to come by," Peggy commented.

Most of the pizza had been eaten, and the boys left the table to go play in their room. Sally stood up to clear the table when Peggy said, "Wait a minute, Sally. I need to talk to you while the boys are out of the room. Collin came to see me today. He is leaving for Houston in the morning." She reached into her sweater pocket and pulled out an envelope. She extended her arm out to Sally and handed it to her. "Collin asked me to give this to you. He said he would rather give it to me to give to you than come by the house and upset you and the boys."

Sally took the envelope from Peggy. "Thank you. So he really is going?"

"Yes, he is. And Sally, I get a feeling that he isn't coming back," Peggy admitted sadly.

Sally took a moment before she said another word, letting Peggy's words sink in. "I really thought as much. There has just been too much bad stuff between us for him to want to come home. It will be OK."

"There is money in the envelope. I don't know how much, but he did tell me to tell you that more money would be coming when he received his next paycheck. I do want you to know that I am here for you, Sally—you and the boys."

"Thank you very much, Peggy. I appreciate you saying that. You are such a sweetheart," Sally said, her eyes filled with tears.

"I'm so sorry, Sally. Collin has changed so much. His father would be so ashamed of him, as I am." Peggy shook her head.

"I guess I should get serious about finding a job. I'm sorry to say this, but I don't feel like I should rely on or even trust Collin to send me money. And even if he does, will it be in a timely manner? I do have an appointment on Thursday to see a divorce attorney, and hopefully they will have the answers to my questions," Sally said, confiding in Peggy.

"I wish I also could have faith in Collin to do the right thing for you and his sons, but I can't. Please, continue to keep me in the loop about the attorney. I don't believe there are any job openings available at my work, but I'll check to see and let you know," Peggy offered graciously.

After they had finished clearing the table, Peggy realized how late it was. "The time is getting away from us, and I probably should be thinking about heading home. I want to be home before the New Year's Eve celebrators are out on the road. I did buy a few packs of sparklers, though. Would it be OK if the boys brought in the New Year a little early?"

"Yes, let me get the boys, and we'll go outside. Thanks for thinking of that idea. I really hadn't given too much thought on celebrating today. To me, today just seems like another day," Sally said with a frown as she walked down the hall to the boys' room.

"Todd, Pace . . . Grandmother Peggy bought some sparklers for y'all to help celebrate the New Year. We need to put on our coats so we can go outside," she announced.

"Oh, wow! Thank you Grandmother Peggy!" Todd shouted. "Come on, Pace! This is going to be fun!" He grabbed his little brother's hand and ran to the living room.

Peggy already had her coat on and was holding the boys' coats in each of her hands. Sally slipped hers on as well and out the door they went. The night air was cool, and the smell of wood burning was present.

"It's a nice night to have a fire burning in the fireplace," Peggy remarked as she took a deep breath.

"Who has the matches?" Todd asked loudly.

"I do," answered Sally, pulling them out from her pocket.

Peggy opened one of the boxes of sparklers and handed two to each of the boys. Pace stared at the sparkler in Todd's hand and watched intently while his mother lit the match and held it under the end of it. Instantly the glow of the sparkler burst into a brilliant shower of sparks. Pace was mesmerized by the colorful explosion.

"That is so pretty. Momma, will you make my stick light up like Todd's stick?" he exclaimed eagerly.

"I sure can! Hold still now," Sally instructed him as she struck the match on the side of the matchbox and took its flame under one of the sparklers Pace was holding. Again, he watched with amazement as his stick was engulfed in flaming sparks. His facial expression was priceless!

Todd pressed his sparkler to the other stick he was holding, and again, the sparks flew! Pace saw what Todd had done and did the same thing. His excitement erupted again.

The boys' eagerness to continue lighting each sparkler lasted for a good ten minutes until Peggy handed them the last two. When the sparks stopped and the glow burned out on each of the last two sticks, the boys' joy faded.

"Oh boy! That was great, Grandmother Peggy!" Todd said as he hugged her.

"I loved that. I wish we had more!" Pace said sadly.

"I wish we did too, Pace," Peggy agreed. "Both of you boys seemed like you really enjoyed the sparklers. We will definitely do them again!" She looked at her watch. "I guess I better run on, kiddos. It's getting late. I sure did enjoy our visit. Thank you for allowing me to come over and for helping me ring in the New Year. It's been great!" Peggy said, grateful not to be spending the evening alone.

"No, Peggy, thank *you* for a wonderful, fun-filled evening. The pizzas, the sparklers, just the whole evening. You have been most kind and thoughtful." Sally and the boys all hugged her and walked her to her car.

After she had driven away, Sally and the boys walked back into the house and hung their coats in the closet. Sally listened to her sons talk excitedly about the sparklers and how pretty they were. She was happy that Peggy thought about something that was so simple yet brought so much enjoyment to Todd and Pace.

"Boys, I'd like for y'all to take your baths and put on your PJs. That way, when it comes time for y'all to go to bed, that will already be done," Sally suggested.

"OK, Mom. Come on Pace," Todd said as they walked toward their bedroom. Sally walked to the bathroom and began to run the bath water. Soon, the bath water and the boys were ready, and in they went.

As Sally returned to the living room, she remembered the envelope from Collin that Peggy had given her. She picked it up and opened it. A note was wrapped around the money that was enclosed. Sally began reading:

Dear Sally,

I'm leaving for Houston the morning of January 1st (Monday), and I should arrive there late that night if I drive straight through. I don't know when I will have a permanent address, but as soon as I do, I'll let you know. I will call you and give you a telephone number where I can be reached in case you need me. I don't anticipate coming to Memphis for a while, but I will send you money when I receive my paychecks. I hope the money I've enclosed will last you a while.

I know we had our good times, and they were good, but things have changed between us, and those changes are not for the good. In my opinion, I don't know that we can or even want to mend our difference or our marriage. This time away from one another might help us . . . I don't know . . . determine if we even want to try. Personally, I don't know that I even love you anymore, and the way we act toward each other, I don't think you have much love left inside of you for me either.

I will miss Todd and Pace, but they are better off with you. I don't have much time to spend with them, and the future for me is not looking too promising for me to see or be with them anytime soon. I'm not the "father figure" they need.

Sally, I wish you well. We had a good run for a while, but it's over.

—Collin

Tears rolled down Sally's cheeks and fell onto the note. She knew Collin's feelings for her before she read his note, but reading his words made the whole situation feel so much more real. Her heart hurt as she looked at the words again: *It's over.* She buried her face in her hands and wept.

Todd and Pace emerged from the bathroom with bath towels wrapped around their little bodies. They saw their mother sitting on the couch, crying. They looked at each other. Pace whispered to Todd, "What's wrong with Momma? Should we go see?"

"No, not yet. Let's put on our PJs, then we will," Todd answered as he pulled his little brother by the arm into their bedroom.

"But what's wrong?" Pace was concerned.

"I don't know. Maybe we just need to give her a few minutes, Pace. Here's your PJs. Put them on."

After the boys dressed in their PJs, they peeked around the corner of the door. "Where is Momma?" Pace whispered.

"She could be in the kitchen. Come on," Todd motioned to Pace.

Slowly they stepped around the corner into the living room. They saw the kitchen light was on, so they ran toward it. "Hi, Momma. We're finished with our baths. Can we have some popcorn to eat?" Pace promptly asked.

Sally quickly wiped the tears from her eyes as she turned her gaze from the darkness outside the window toward her little boys. "Look at the two of you. In PJs and asking for popcorn! That really sounds good to me too. I'll get the popper out and whip it up." She was trying desperately to overcome the shock of Collin's note. "Y'all want sodas to drink?"

"Yes! I'll get the glasses. You too, Mom?" Todd asked.

"Yes. I'll get the ice out of the freezer. Pace, you want to get the sodas from the pantry?"

"OK, Momma," Pace answered.

The popcorn had begun to pop . . . faster and faster . . . until it popped no more. Sally removed the popper pan off the burner and poured the popped corn into a huge plastic bowl. She had the butter already melted, so Todd poured it over the popcorn and Sally flavored it with a little salt.

"It's all ready, kiddos!" she announced. "Here, Pace, you can carry the popcorn bowl, and Todd, can you get your drink as well as your brother's? I'll carry my drink and the napkins." Sally turned off the kitchen light, and they all carefully walked to the living room. Sally turned on the television and found the channel the boys wanted to watch. Then they all partook of their stack as they snuggled together on the couch.

It was near eleven o'clock, and the television screen turned snowy as the channel they were watching went off the air. The boys were trying so hard to stay awake to see the New Year in, but they fell asleep thirty minutes shy of midnight. Sally managed to get Pace into his bed. She kissed his sweet cheek, told him she loved him, and whispered, "Sleep tight. Don't let the bedbugs bite. And Happy New Year." She knew she could not help Todd get into his top bunk, so she took a blanket from the hall closet and covered him up as he continued to sleep on the couch. She kissed his cheek and said quietly, "Sleep tight. Don't let the bedbugs bite. I love you, and Happy New Year." She picked up Collin's note and the thousand dollars he left her in the envelope and walked to her bedroom. She sat on the edge of the bed and reread the note. Then, she laid back on her pillow and thought about what this new year would bring for her. She thought, *OK, so Collin said, 'it's over.' I should feel more free to seek a divorce from Collin and feel less guilty about my love for Rusty.* She breathed a big sigh of relief.

Suddenly the quietness was interrupted by the thundering fireworks, vehicle horns, and some of her neighbors yelling and celebrating the incoming New Year.

Chapter Ten

As Sally woke up to the first day of the New Year, her thoughts immediately turned to Rusty. She recalled him telling her he would be leaving home with his load that morning at 4 a.m., and he would call her when he stopped for his break. She wasn't sure when that might be, but she was planning on being home all day so she wouldn't miss it. Recent prayers she had heard her family pray came to mind. They had asked God to "watch over them and keep them safe." Sally bowed her head, closed her eyes, and folded her hands in front of her as they had done. She whispered, "God, I don't know You, and because of that, I don't even know if I have the right to talk to You. But please, watch over Rusty, and help him to be safe. Thank You, Lord. Amen." As she opened her eyes, she felt an amazing peace come over her. It was almost like she wasn't alone; she felt the closeness of something invisible. She eased herself slowly to the side of her bed and sat very still for a moment, basking in the peace she felt. It was an eerie yet pleasant feeling— something she didn't want to dismiss quickly.

Sally pulled up the bed sheet and blanket to make her bed, and she saw Collin's note lying beside her pillow. She opened the nightstand drawer and dropped the note in it, closing the drawer swiftly. She felt a slight hint of sadness flash though her mind as she remembered he was leaving today for Houston to start his new life. She fought back those thoughts by reminding herself that she was beginning a new life as well, and that put a smile on her face.

"Good morning, Mom, and happy New Year!" Todd greeted. "I thought I heard you getting up. Pace and I were trying to be quiet so you could sleep."

"Well, y'all did a good job. I bet y'all are hungry, aren't you? I know I am. What do you think you might want for breakfast?" she asked.

"Hi, Momma. Did you sleep good?" Pace asked as he ran to his mother and hugged her.

"Hi to you too! I did sleep good, especially after all the noise from outside calmed down. Did all the fireworks and horn honking wake y'all up? Folks were bringing in the New Year in a loud way!"

"No, I didn't hear anything," Pace answered.

Todd shook his head.

"I asked your brother what he would like for breakfast. What would you like?" Sally asked Pace.

"Hey, Todd, you want some French toast?" Pace asked.

"That sounds good! Mom, could you make us French toast this morning?" Todd asked.

"I believe I can, and that's a good choice," Sally said as she walked toward the kitchen.

Right away, Sally began brewing her coffee. Then she took the eggs, milk, and sausage patties from the refrigerator.

"Can I help?" Todd asked.

"You can. I need the bread and a fork," Sally requested as she took a skillet from the cabinet. "I have the milk out if you want to pour you a glass . . . and a glass for your brother, please."

"Yes, ma'am, I can do that," Todd joyfully answered.

"Hey, Momma, have you beaten the eggs yet?" asked Pace as he entered the kitchen.

"No, I haven't. Would you like to do that for me?"

"I sure would," he agreed.

Within minutes, breakfast was ready and placed on the dining room table. Todd and Pace took their seats, and as Sally sat down, she paused for a moment before taking her first bite. She had never done that before, but she felt that incredible, invisible closeness again.

"What's wrong, Momma?" Pace asked his mother.

"Are you OK, Mom?" Todd asked, noticing his mother's stillness.

Sally looked at her sons. "I know we, as a little family, have never prayed before meals, or as far as that goes, we've not prayed at all. I'm not sure how or what to pray, but I'd like for us to start saying grace before our meals."

The boys looked at each other, then back to their mother with puzzled looks on their faces. Finally, Todd said, "That's OK with me, Mom."

"Yeah, me too, Momma," Pace agreed.

"OK, thank y'all. Let's fold our hands in front of us, bow our heads, and close our eyes. *Oh Lord, please, hear this prayer as we ask You to bless this food before us. Allow us to stay well, and help us in all things each day of this New Year. Thank You, Lord. Amen.*" Sally looked up at her boys. "I want to learn more about praying so I can teach y'all to pray. In fact, I want to learn much more about God so I can share what I learn with both of you."

"I'd like that, Mom. A girl at school, Barbie, prays every day before she eats her lunch. She's a very sweet girl. I like her. You know, Mom, Grandmother Peggy prays. I bet she could help us!" Todd suggested.

"You have a wonderful idea, Todd! After breakfast, I'll call her."

"This is a delicious breakfast, Momma. I think the Lord already blessed it! It's really good! Sometimes Grandmother Peggy says, 'Praise the Lord.' Can I say that too?" Pace inquired excitedly.

"I'm sure you can, Pace, but I'd like to know more about why people say that before we start saying it, wouldn't you?" she asked.

"Yeah, I guess so."

"OK, if y'all are finished eating, go brush your teeth while I clean up. I need to call your Uncle Matthew and wish him a happy birthday, and I need to call your Grandmother Peggy. Then, we need to take down the Christmas tree and all the Christmas decorations and put everything away."

"Wow! We are going to have a busy day!" shouted Pace as he and Todd ran to the bathroom to brush their teeth.

While Sally washed the dishes, she glanced at the clock on the stove. It was near 10 a.m. She realized that Rusty had been on the highways and byways for six hours by now, and he could be calling soon. She wanted to wait for his call before she made her own telephone calls. She didn't want to miss his call.

Once she finished cleaning up in the kitchen, she helped the boys get dressed. She asked them to go to the storage building in the backyard and get the Christmas boxes. The air was still very chilly, but with their warm coats on, the boys made the necessary trips to and from the building, bringing in the boxes and setting them in the living room.

One by one, the boys handed their mother the Christmas decorations from around the house. Sally wrapped them carefully and placed them in the boxes.

"Say, let's take a break before we start taking down the Christmas tree. How about some hot chocolate and a few cookies?" Sally suggested.

"Oh, that sounds really good, Momma!" Pace replied excitedly.

"I'll help," Todd said as he walked toward the kitchen.

"I appreciate that, Todd," Sally said as she patted him on his shoulder.

Within ten minutes, Todd was adding marshmallows to their hot chocolate. Then Sally took the cups to the dining room table, and Pace carried the bag of cookies. As they sat down to enjoy their treat, the telephone rang.

Sally hurried to answer in the living room. "Hello?"

"Oh, your voice sounds like an angel to me!" Rusty said. "How are you, my love?"

Sally sat down on the edge of the couch. "Oh, listen to you! You know how to brighten my day. I'm good, sweetheart. How are you?"

"I look forward to brightening each and every one of your days very soon, honey. I'm good too. What's going on over there?" Rusty asked.

"Can't be soon enough! We have begun taking Christmas decorations down. Right now, the boys and I are taking a little break, drinking some hot chocolate and nibbling on some cookies. How does it feel to be back on the road? How's the weather?" Sally inquired.

"Mmm-mmm, hot chocolate and cookies sound really good. Have some for me too! Oh, baby, it feels great to be driving again. I have certainly missed it. The weather is cold, and so far, there's no snow on the roads. When I turn south tomorrow, I figure there will be less snow and warmer temps. How is it there?"

"I wish you were here and I could fix you a cup of hot chocolate and feed you some cookies! As much as you enjoy driving, I know you are glad to be at it again. I'm happy to know the road conditions are in good shape. Just, please, be careful. It's chilly here with a little bit of sun, but no snow in the forecast for this area. Sure hope the roads will remain clear all the way for your trip. As far as you know, all is good for us to see each other on Tuesday?" Sally asked.

"It's coming up clean and green, sweetheart! It seems like forever since we've seen each other. I can hardly wait to hold you in my arms. I should be coming into Memphis about 11 a.m. Still meet you at the mall?" Rusty inquired.

"Sounds *wonderful*. It has been *forever!* At least, it sure does seem like it. Holding you in my arms already feels *so good!*" Sally said, envisioning the embrace.

"Is it all right if I call you tonight?" Rusty asked.

"Of course! Any time," Sally answered.

"Well, I'm going to hit the road. I hope your hot chocolate didn't get cold. I love you, honey. You be careful, and I'll call you later," Rusty said.

"I love you too, sweetheart. *You* be careful too. Already looking forward to talking to you later, love." Sally's words echoed as she threw him a kiss.

Rusty threw Sally a kiss in return, and the call ended.

As Sally approached the dining room table, she saw that Todd and Pace had finished their hot chocolate and cookies.

"Are y'all ready to get back to our project?" Sally asked.

"Yes, ma'am," both boys answered. The boys took turns taking off ornaments from the tree and handing them to their mother. Sally wrapped each one in tissue paper and placed it neatly in the ornament box. This process took a while, but it ensured the ornaments would not get broken. The silver tinsel came off next. There was never a year that all the tinsel could be taken off the tree. Sally always bought an extra box or two of tinsel each year to make sure they had enough to put on and spread the silver strands over the whole tree. She helped the boys with the many strings of lights that encircled lots of branches of the tree from the top to the bottom.

It took nearly three whole hours to finish packing up all the Christmas decorations. Sally set up the ladder, and with *lots* of help from Todd and Pace, she placed all the boxes in the attic. Then the ladder was put away for another year.

Worn out from all the heavy lifting and walking up and down the ladder, Sally rested for a little while. When she had recovered a bit, she decided to call her brother. She reached for the telephone and dialed his number.

He answered.

"Happy birthday to you, happy birthday to you, happy birthday, dear Matthew, happy birthday to you," Sally sang.

"Well, thank you very much, sis! That was so sweet," Matthew replied cheerfully.

"Happy New Year, too! I sure hope you are having a wonderful day to start off y'all's New Year. How are you and Jodie doing as well as all the kiddos?"

"We all seem to be doing good. How about you and your family? How's your situation with Collin?" Matthew asked with concern.

"We're hanging in there. Peggy, Collin's mother, came over yesterday to celebrate the New Year with pizza and sparklers for Todd and Pace. She brought with her a note from Collin to me. It said that he was leaving for Houston today, he'd send money when he received his paycheck, and he was moving on with his life. He said that we were over." Sally's voice cracked as she choked out those last few words.

"I'm so sorry, Sally. I know this news has just devastated you and the boys. To ask you what your plans are right now is probably an impossible question. Just remember, we are here if or when you need anything, and we will continue to have you and the boys in our prayers," Matthew reassured his sister.

"You know, right here at Christmastime, it was a hard pill to swallow. But I keep telling myself that if Collin wants to move on with a new life, then so can I. I'm definitely not sure how it will come about or what's going to happen, but I need to pull the pieces of my life back together and move on. The boys do too. As Momma used to say, 'You can't cry over spilled milk.' So I cannot change what has happened, and I want to learn how not to be upset over the situation. I appreciate you saying you'll keep us in your prayers, though. I've heard you and Jodie talk about the Lord, and you thank Him for the blessings He has given to y'all. How do you know Him?" Sally wondered.

"Jodie and I have been Christians for a long time. I guess, close to twenty years now. You remember when we lived on Harris Street, and Mom and Dad took us to that church off of Jackson Boulevard? I never received any spiritual guidance from that preacher's services, but when Jodie and I started dating, she and her family invited me to go to their church . . . and *what a difference!* Only after a few Sundays of listening to their preacher, my life was changed forever. I accepted Jesus Christ into my life, and He became my Savior! In the Bible, in the first book, the book of Genesis, it tells how God made heaven, earth, as well as Adam and Eve. Throughout the Old Testament, many things happen, including predictions of a Savior who comes to earth. In the New Testament, in the books of Matthew, Mark, Luke, and John, the story is told about the birth and life of Jesus Christ. God sent His only Son to earth." Matthew stopped himself for a moment. "OK, sis, it starts with and is a matter of *faith* . . . F-A-I-T-H. Do you want me to go on, Sally?"

"Yes, please," Sally anxiously answered. "I'm going to get a piece of paper and a pencil. Hold on." Sally searched for what she needed to take notes. "OK, I'm ready."

Matthew began,

"'F' is for *forgiveness*. Everyone has sinned and needs *God's forgiveness*. Romans 3:23 says, 'All have sinned, and come short of the glory of God.' Also, God's forgiveness is in Jesus *only*. Ephesians 1:7 says, 'In whom we have redemption through his blood, the forgiveness of sins, according to the riches of his grace.'

"'A' is for *available*. God's forgiveness is *available for all*. John 3:16 says, 'God so loved the world that he gave his only begotten Son, that whosoever believeth in him should not perish, but have everlasting life.' Another verse is found in Matthew 7:21: 'Not everyone that saith unto me, Lord, Lord, shall enter into the kingdom of heaven.' God's forgiveness is available but not automatic.

"'I' is for *impossible*. According to the Bible, it is *impossible* to get to heaven on our own. Ephesians 2:8-9 says, 'For by grace are ye saved through faith; and that not of yourself: it is the gift of God: not of works, lest any man should boast.' So how can a sinful person have eternal life and enter heaven? Only by Jesus!"

Matthew paused. "Sally, I know some of this is confusing to you. All I ask of you is that you go over your notes time and time again. Each time, ask Jesus to help you understand it more and more. If you know someone who knows Jesus as their Savior, talk to them, and ask them to help you understand it. Of course, you can always call and ask me, but someone sitting beside you and personally talking to you would be best. Do you have a Bible?"

"Yes, I do. Somewhere. I'll find it. I believe Collin's mother is a Christian. I can talk to her," Sally suggested.

"That's great! She would be a good person to talk to because you know her, and she would want to help you. Do you want me to go on with the remaining F-A-I-T-H letters?" Matthew asked.

"Yes, please," Sally replied anxiously.

"'T' is for *turn*. Let's say . . . if you were going down the road, and someone asked you to turn, what would that person be asking you to do? The answer would be, *change direction*. *Turn* means to repent. Turn away from sin and self. Scripture says in Luke 13:3, 'Except ye repent, ye shall all likewise perish.' Turn to Jesus alone as your Savior and Lord. In John 14:6 Jesus says, 'I am the way, the truth, and the life: no man cometh unto the Father, but by Me.' You need to be willing to repent. That means ask forgiveness and confess your sins to Jesus.

"'H' is for *heaven*. Heaven is a place where we will live with God. Jesus says in John 14:3, 'And if I go and prepare a place for you, I will come again, and receive you unto myself; that is where I am, there ye may be also.' You see, eternal life begins with Jesus. He tells us in John 10:10, 'I am come that they might have life, and that they might have it more abundantly.'"

Matthew paused for another moment.

"Sally, you can have God's forgiveness, eternal life, and heaven by trusting in Jesus as your Lord and Savior. You can follow these steps of F-A-I-T-H and be one of God's children. He loves you. Knock on His door, and He will answer. I want to take a moment and pray for you, sis.

"Our most heavenly Father, You know Sally, You love Sally, and You know her burdens. She needs You in her life, and I pray she accepts Your invitation of salvation to know You as her personal Lord and Savior. Lord, please guide her as she has decisions to make about her future and her young sons. Just wrap Your loving arms around her, and let her know You are there with her. I ask all these things in your holy and precious name. Amen."

Sally was moved to tears as she listened to Matthew's words of prayer. She felt that very same invisible closeness she had felt before, but this time it was strong. Her heart wanted to yield to the beckoning calling, but she was uncertain what all of the words meant that Matthew had prayed. "Oh, Matthew," she cried, "I don't know what to do."

"The Holy Spirit is dealing with you, Sally. What I want you to do is hang up the telephone, go to a quiet place, and on bended knees, ask Jesus to forgive you of your sins and to come into your heart. Will you do that for me?"

Sally didn't know what to say.

"We'll talk later. I love you, baby sister, and I'm praying for you." Matthew hung up the phone.

Sally slowly lowered the handset onto the telephone's base. She continued to sit on the couch for a few moments.

Todd, hearing his mother crying, came from his bedroom and sat down by her side on the couch. "Mom, what's wrong?"

Pace then crawled up beside her. "Momma, why are you crying?"

"I'm not real sure. I don't know if I'm crying because I'm confused or because I'm happy that Jesus wants to come into my heart," she admitted the best she could through her tears.

"Jesus wants to come into your heart?" Pace asked, stunned.

"Your Uncle Matthew was telling me about who Jesus is and giving me verses in the Bible that will help me to know Jesus. He prayed for me, and all of a sudden, I felt this invisible closeness of something that I've never felt before," Sally explained.

"You think it might have been Jesus, Mom?" Todd was amazed.

"I don't really know, Todd," Sally answered. "But I feel like I know everything is going to be OK for us. I feel stronger and more confident, and I have a positive attitude." She looked up and whispered, "I thank You, Lord, for this feeling."

"As Grandmother Peggy would say, 'Praise the Lord'!" Todd rejoiced.

"Yes, praise the Lord!" Sally echoed.

Sally glanced at the clock above the couch. "Oh gosh, it's nearly four o'clock! Where has this day gone?"

"We've been *very* busy, Momma!" Pace exclaimed.

"No wonder I'm hungry! The hot chocolate and cookies have run out!" Todd chimed in.

"What do y'all think you'll want for supper?" their mother asked.

"I don't know. Todd, what do you want?" Pace asked his brother.

"I'm thinking. Give me a minute, Pace," Todd answered his little brother. "Mom, do you have any suggestions?"

"No, not right off the top of my head. I know tomorrow we need to go to the grocery store after we take your books by the library. Todd, don't forget to take your airplane notes with you. Would you still like to go to the airport and use your notes to put them in visual context?" Sally inquired.

"Yes, I sure would like to do that. That would be swell!" Todd replied excitedly.

"Y'all be thinking about what foods y'all would like to take for your school lunches. Y'all go back Wednesday, that's just the day after tomorrow!"

"Oh, already?" Pace groaned.

"I'm looking forward to going back to school and seeing my friends, but not the homework!" Todd remarked.

"Well, maybe look at it like this: one half of the school year is over!" Sally said. "OK, fellas, what's for supper?" Without an answer from her sons, Sally snapped her fingers and exclaimed, "I got it! How about some hot tamales and chili? Today is a good day for a meal like that!"

"That sounds good, Mom. We haven't had that in a long time," Todd agreed.

Sally looked at Pace who was making a weird, sort of scrunched-up face. "What's wrong, my little son?"

"I can't remember ever eating ta . . . whatever you said, and chili," Pace reacted to his mother's suggestion.

"The best I remember, you liked them. I'll fix the meal, and if you like it, great, but if not, I'll fix you something else. How's that?"

"OK. I'll try to like it!" Pace replied.

Sally headed for the kitchen and began supper. As she opened the can of tamales and the can of chili, her mind drifted in two different directions. Rusty should be calling her soon. His suppertime was getting close. And then she wondered where Collin could be on his trip to Houston. She was surprised that Todd or Pace had not asked her about their dad.

"Supper's almost ready," Sally called to the boys. "What do y'all want to drink?"

Both boys ran into the kitchen. "I'd like some soda. I'll get it. What do you want, Mom? Pace, you want soda too?" Todd asked, being so helpful.

"Soda sounds good to me," Sally agreed.

"Me too," Pace chimed in.

Todd grabbed the ice cube tray from the freezer and twisted the plastic container. Out popped the ice cubes. He picked up some cubes and placed them in their glasses. Pace handed him the soda bottles from the pantry, and Sally took the bottle opener from the kitchen drawer and popped off the bottle caps. Todd slowly poured the soda into the glasses so the liquid would not foam too much. Todd and Pace carefully carried their drinks to the dining room table.

"Good job, you two. Y'all have helped me so much. Thank y'all!" Sally commended her young sons as she followed them to the table. She handed each of them a plate full of tamales and chili.

"Could I have some bread and ketchup, Mom?" Todd asked.

"Sure thing. I'll get them." Sally walked back to the kitchen.

"I remember the tamales and chili now, and I do like them!" Pace exclaimed after he looked at his plate full of food.

Sally sat the bread and ketchup on the table. "I'm so glad you remembered!" she happily replied. Sally sat down at the table and said, "Let's hold hands and pray. *God is great, God is good. Lord, we thank You for this food. Amen.*"

"I like that prayer, Mom. It would be easy for me to remember and to say. We can even say it together!" Todd suggested.

"I think that is an excellent idea, Todd. Thank you for suggesting it." Sally smiled at her son and thanked the Lord for Todd's thoughtfulness.

The three of them enjoyed their meal, and afterwards, the boys helped their mother clear the table and wash, dry, and put away the dishes.

"Now that the kitchen is all clean, would y'all like to play a game or watch television?" Sally asked them as she removed her apron from her waist and hung it up on the back of the pantry door.

"Let's watch television. That Western we like is on tonight," Todd voiced.

"OK, that sounds good." So Sally, Todd, and Pace curled up on the couch and got comfortable. The local news was still on the channel the Western would be on, but soon the Western began.

Near eight o'clock, the phone rang.

"Could that be Daddy?" Pace quickly asked.

Sally was surprised at his question, but even to her wonder, could it be Collin?

"Hello?" Sally answered with anticipation.

"Hi, honey. It's me," Rusty said, sounding very tired.

Sally got up from the couch and walked to the dining room away from the boys. "Oh, sweetheart, are you OK? You sound so tired."

"Yes, I'm OK, just beat. I guess my time off from driving has me out of shape!" Rusty explained. "So how has the rest of the first day of your New Year been?"

"The boys and I finished taking down the Christmas tree, I called my brother to wish him a happy birthday, and I also wished all of them a happy New Year! We had a very good conversation. I'll tell you about it on Wednesday. So where are you? How's the weather?" Sally asked.

"I'm in Columbus, Ohio, and the weather is good. I'll be spending the night here. Then in the morning, I'll jump back on the super slab and will make my way closer and closer to you. I can't seem to put the miles behind me fast enough. I'm so looking forward to seeing and being with you, baby," Rusty lovingly expressed to her. Then he asked, "How's your brother and his family? I look forward to you telling me more about you and your brother's conversation."

"Honey, I too want those miles to melt away so you can be in my arms. I miss you so much. Just please, be careful," Sally expressed.

"I miss you too, my love, more than you know. Is it OK for me to call you tomorrow?" Rusty asked.

"Absolutely! But we have some running around to do. We have books to return to the library, we're going to the airport for a little while, then we need to go to the grocery store. We probably will leave at about ten o'clock in the morning," Sally explained.

"Wow! You guys are going to be busy tomorrow. Will calling you about 8:30 in the morning be too early?" Rusty inquired.

"No, that should be perfect," Sally answered.

"OK, I'll talk to you then. I'm going to go eat some dinner and then hit the hay. You sleep good tonight and have sweet dreams. Sweetheart, I love you."

"Sounds good. I look forward to talking to you in the morning. You enjoy your supper, and you sleep good too. I hope you see me in your dreams, as I'll be dreaming of you. I love you too, darlin'. Till tomorrow. Good night." Sally blew him a kiss into the telephone.

"Good night, Sally dear." Rusty ended the call as he returned his kiss to her.

Sally lingered for a moment as her mind clung to Rusty's words. How precious he was to her! As she moved slowly toward the living room, she breathed a brief, yet meaningful prayer: *Please, Jesus, watch over Rusty.*

When Sally sat down on the couch, Todd looked up to her and asked, "When is Dad going to call us?"

"Oh, Todd, I wish I knew. He left for Houston this morning. I don't believe he'll get there tonight. That's a long drive. Hopefully he'll call tomorrow," his mother said, trying to sound encouraging.

"I miss him!" Todd said with tears in his eyes.

"I do too, Momma." Pace's sad voice was sincere.

"I know y'all do, but I'm here. It might only be the three of us to take care of each other. With God's help and guidance, I'll try to do my best to take good care of the both of you," Sally said with hope in her voice and tears in her eyes.

They sat close to each other on the couch for a while. Sally wondered if Todd and Pace understood what she said and what she meant about "it might only be the three of them taking care of each other." She really didn't know how to tell them that their dad wasn't coming back home—or back to them at all. Her heart broke for them. She would just have to pray hard for her little boys.

"Mom, is it OK if I take my bath and go to bed?" Todd asked sadly.

"Yes, it's OK. Are you feeling all right?" Sally asked.

"I'm just tired," he answered as he stood up and walked toward his bedroom with Pace following behind him.

"You too, little Pace?" Sally asked.

"Yes, Momma," he answered, just as sadly as his brother.

Sally bowed her head, closed her eyes, and asked the Lord to comfort her little sons. She then walked to the bathroom and began running their bath water. Soon both boys had bathed, dried off, put their PJs on, and crawled into their beds. Sally tucked them in and kissed them good night. "Y'all sleep tight. Don't let the bedbugs bite. I love both of you very much. Sweet dreams." She could hardly hear their reply. Sadness filled their room. She didn't know what else to do for them. She turned out the light and left their room.

Even though it was nearly nine o'clock, she walked to the telephone and dialed Peggy's number.

Peggy answered on the second ring. "Hello?"

"Hi, Peggy. It's Sally. Happy New Year to you! Am I calling you too late?"

"Hi, Sally. No, it's not too late, dear. How are you? What's up?"

"I'm not real sure how we are doing. Peggy, I believe you're a woman of faith, and I'm asking you to please pray for Todd and Pace. Collin still has not called them yet. When the telephone rang earlier this evening, they thought it was their dad, but it wasn't. They don't understand, and I don't have the heart to tell them their dad will not be coming home and that he doesn't even want them in his life anymore. I did tell them, after the call, that it was not their dad. I told them that it might only be the three of us to take care of each other from here on out. My words were about as close as I could come to telling them the truth," Sally explained.

"Oh, Sally, I'm so sorry that Collin has created problems for you and the boys. I always have had the three of you in my prayers, but yes, I will pray harder. So nothing from Collin yet? Me either. You know, Sally, Collin might come back home. Do you really think he won't?" Peggy tried to sound optimistic.

"I can't imagine that would happen after I read the note you gave me last night from Collin. It pretty much spelled it out. He wrote that he wanted to get on with his life and that I should too. He went on to say that since he hadn't been seeing much of the boys in a long time, his absence in their lives would probably not even be noticed. Then his last words were, 'Our lives together are over.' I believe he is telling me that he has no intentions of coming home or being a father to his sons."

"Wow. Collin wrote that to you? That's just horrible! I wish Collin wasn't being so foolish and selfish. You truly don't deserve this behavior from him, and neither do those sweet boys." Peggy grieved for them.

Sally said, "I want to share something with you that happen to me this morning. When I went to bed last night, I reread Collin's note again. I must have fallen asleep with the note in my hand because, when I woke up this morning, the note was beside my pillow. I looked at it again. I'm not a praying person—in fact, I'm not sure why people pray or to whom they pray—but for some reason I bowed my head, closed my eyes, and prayed. When I opened my eyes, I felt an invisible closeness to me, and a peace came over me that I had never felt before. It was an eerie, yet pleasant feeling."

Peggy interrupted Sally with joy in her voice. "Sally, that was God's Holy Spirit drawing near to you! Oh, how wonderful, dear! Then what happened, Sally?" Peggy wanted to know more.

"The boys and I had just sat down to eat breakfast when I felt that invisible closeness with me again. I asked the boys to pray with me over our breakfast, as

I have seen you do. Both of them wanted me to pray. Later today, I called my brother and his family to wish them a happy New Year and to say 'happy birthday' to my brother. He asked me how we were doing, and I told him Collin had left for Houston, and according to him, he was starting a new life. My brother was very saddened by the news, and he told me he and Jodie would pray for us. I asked him right then, 'When you pray, who do you pray to?' Peggy, he began to tell me so many things about God and His Son, Jesus Christ. Things I never knew! It was *wonderful!*" Sally continued to share her experience with Peggy.

Peggy asked Sally, "Have you ever heard the phrase *born again*?"

"No, I haven't," Sally answered. "What does it mean?"

"I want to tell you a New Testament Bible story from the book of John. Nicodemus was a highly moral man who obeyed God's law. He was a respected leader of the Jewish community. No doubt he was a fine man, yet he felt something was lacking in his life. Nicodemus sought out and approached Jesus one night, and he curiously asked Jesus about the kingdom of God. Jesus told him: 'Except a man be born again, he could not see the Kingdom of God.' Nicodemus responded, 'How can a man be born when he is old?' This story is found in John 3:3 and 3:4. The answer to Nicodemus' question is lifesaving. New birth begins with the Holy Spirit convicting a person that he or she is a sinner. Because of sin, we are spiritually dead. Spiritual birth, as Jesus described it, is necessary. God loves us and gives us spiritual birth when we ask Him for it. You see, Jesus Christ was with God the Father before the world was created, but He had to become human. He came to earth to show us what God was like. Jesus lived a sinless life, showing us how to live, and He died upon a cross to pay for our sins. God raised Him from the dead, He ascended to heaven, and now He sits with His Father in heaven. Are you following me, Sally?" Peggy asked.

"I'm trying to, Peggy. I know at Christmas we celebrate the birth of Jesus, and that's His birthday. His mother was Mary, and He was born in a manger. All the other things that you're telling me is new and foreign to me, especially about being *born again* and the *forgiveness of sin*," Sally admitted.

"Sally, were you ever in church when you were a child?" Peggy inquired.

"Yes, but I was young. I remember Mom and Dad taking me to a church in Memphis, but it didn't mean much to me. When we moved up north, I was seven years old, and I don't believe we attended church. I was twelve years old when Daddy was stationed in France, and still, no church. When we returned to the States and moved back to Memphis, every now and then we'd go to the same church we did before we moved North, but the services did not make much sense to me. Collin and I married in that church, but we never attended any services there. Collin was not interested in attending church, so we never went. You know, come to think of it, neither my mother nor my father ever talked about God or Jesus. Please tell me more," Sally asked Peggy.

"I can tell the Holy Spirit is working. You are experiencing the edge of salvation! Stay with me, Sally. You need to admit to God that you are a sinner, and you want to repent and turn away from sin. Everyone has sinned. By *faith*, believe in Jesus Christ as God's Son, and you will receive Jesus' gift of forgiveness from your sin. Now understand, we have done nothing to deserve God's love, but He does love us. He wants to save us through salvation. Jesus took the penalty of your sin by dying on the cross. You need to confess your faith in Jesus Christ as your Savior and your Lord. Sally, I want you to pray this prayer with me, OK?" Peggy requested.

"OK," Sally agreed.

"Repeat after me. 'Dear God,'"

"Dear God,"

". . . I know you love me."

". . . I know you love me."

"I confess my sin, and I need Your salvation."

"I confess my sin, and I need Your salvation."

"I turn away from my sin,"

"I turn away from my sin,"

". . . and place my faith in Jesus,"

". . . and place my faith in Jesus,"

". . . as my Savior and my Lord."

". . . as my Savior and my Lord."

"In Jesus' name I pray. Amen."

"In Jesus' name I pray. Amen."

"I sincerely thank the Holy Spirit for guiding you, Sally. For your decision to ask Jesus for His salvation and for Him to come into your heart. I pray your faith will always continue to grow and become more real to you each and every day. I would love and enjoy for you, Todd, and Pace to join me at church on Sunday. The sooner y'all become involved, the more you will learn about the love Jesus has for the three of you. I'll be happy to come by and pick y'all up, and we'll walk into church together. Sally, thank you so much for calling me. I have loved sharing Jesus with you. You call me anytime. Are you OK? I know I've talked and told you a lot," Peggy rejoiced.

"Yes, Peggy, I'm OK. I thank you for all you've told me, and yes, we would like to join you for church on Sunday! Thanks again, Peggy. I love you. Sleep well. Bye for now." Sally placed the handset on the telephone's base. She felt renewed within her inner self, almost like a clean feeling, like she had been washed from the inside out. It was a refreshing feeling. She didn't really understand it. She wondered, *Have I just been 'born again'?* she whispered to herself. *If that's the case, thank You, sweet Jesus!*

As Sally laid down in her bed and pulled the bed covers over her body, she asked the Lord to watch over her through the night, and she thanked Him for His love and salvation.

Chapter Eleven

S ally woke up refreshed and feeling good. Before her tootsies touched the floor, she gave thanks to the Lord for watching over her through the night and blessing her with another day. There was lots to do that day; it would be a busy one for her and the boys.

As she sat on the edge of the bed and slipped her feet into her slippers, she glanced at the clock on her nightstand. It was 6:45. She thought, *Not too early nor too late*. She glanced in the boys' room on her way to the kitchen. They were still asleep, and that was OK. Tomorrow, they would be up early for the first day back to school from their Christmas break.

Sally prepared the coffee pot to begin brewing. She walked to the kitchen door and looked outside into the backyard. Several squirrels were chasing each other on the electrical lines, and five robins were on the ground, looking for their breakfast. She thought, *It's early for robins to be in the area*. Then she remembered what her mother had said: 'Once one sees a robin in the wintertime, spring can't be too far behind.' She wished that would be the case. Warmer temperatures and sunnier days would be nice.

Sally turned back to get her coffee cup from the cabinet and the milk from the refrigerator as the coffee was about ready to pour. Out the window over the kitchen sink, she noticed her neighbors leaving for work. She wondered how soon she should tell her friends the situation between her and Collin. Maybe after she had seen the attorney in a few days would be a good time to share the news with them.

The coffee was ready to pour. She added a little milk and some sugar and carried it to the dining room table. She sat down and pondered over the day's activities. She noticed the time on the clock. Rusty should be calling soon. She prayed that he was OK and that he would have a good day. She wondered what the next several months would bring and how her and her sons' lives would change. Her thoughts made her warm inside, thinking she might be with Rusty. But a lot of things needed to be addressed before those thoughts could become reality.

The sound of the telephone ringing startled her. She quickly walked to the living room. "Hello?"

"Good morning, honey. I hope I'm not calling too early," Rusty said tentatively.

"No, not at all, sweetheart. In fact, I had just looked at the clock and remarked to myself that you should be calling soon. How are you?" Sally asked.

"I'm good, but I'll be even better tomorrow when I see you and will be able to take you in my arms!"

"Hey, that sounds like an excellent plan. I'm looking so forward to seeing and holding you too, my love. You just be so careful getting here! How's the weather there?" Sally inquired.

"It's a little cloudy, but no rain, at least not yet. How is it there?" Rusty asked.

"It's partly sunny and cool, but I saw robins this morning for the first time this winter, and that's supposed to mean spring isn't too far away. I sure hope that is true!" Sally answered.

"Robins, eh? Yes, I sure hope you seeing them is so. We could use some spring-like weather! Well, listen, sugar, I need to be getting on the super slab. I didn't realize when I told you yesterday that I'd call you at 8:30—that's *your* time. That would be *9:30* my time. So, hope calling you an hour early didn't mess you up," Rusty said apologetically.

"No. I was just drinking my first cup of coffee. The boys are still asleep. I thought I'd let them sleep in this morning because it's gonna be up and at 'em early in the morning to get them ready to head back to school. When do you think you'll be here tomorrow?" Sally asked.

"I should be at the mall about ten o'clock. Is that a good time?" Rusty inquired.

"Yes, that'll be great. I can't wait! I'm so looking forward to seeing you! It's been so long!"

"Yes, it has been too long, babe! Please be careful out and about today as you'll be running your errands. I sure do love you, Sally. See you tomorrow," Rusty said and then blew her a kiss.

"I love you too, Rusty dear. You be careful too. Till tomorrow." Sally blew him a kiss back, and the call ended.

As Sally hung up the handset, she heard giggles coming from the boys' bedroom. She walked in the direction of those giggles and saw both boys sitting on Pace's bed.

"Good morning, you two! How did it feel to sleep in this morning?" she asked.

"It was good, Momma!" Pace announced.

"I think I could have slept longer, but the telephone rang, and I woke up. Pace and I have been talking about today and all the places we plan to go. We're excited, Mom!" Todd exclaimed.

"Well, all right then. Let's get up, get dressed, and go! Since this will be our last day together before y'all go back to school tomorrow, I thought I'd treat y'all to a C&B breakfast. How does that sound?"

"Oh, yum! Come on, Pace. Let's get our teeth brushed and get dressed before Mom changes her mind because we are too slow!" Todd encouraged his brother.

"On my way!" Pace yelled as he jumped out of his bed and ran to the bathroom.

"Hey, wait for me!" Todd slid to the edge of the bed, landed on his feet, and was right behind Pace, racing to see who could get to the bathroom first.

While the boys were brushing their teeth, Sally laid out their clothes. Then she walked to her bedroom, found the clothes she would wear, and dressed.

When Sally walked back to the boys' room, she found Todd dressed and helping Pace get dressed. "Wow! Look at the two of you. I'm proud of y'all! Todd, thank you for helping your brother get dressed," she said. "OK, if we are ready, I'll get our coats. Todd, please don't forget your airplane notes," Sally reminded him.

"I've got them, Mom."

Sally helped her sons on with their coats, and out the door they went.

C&Bs wasn't too busy, and the hostess seated the three of them soon after they arrived. The waitress came to their table and took their orders. All three of them wanted pancakes. Within ten minutes, the waitress returned with their meals. Sally helped Pace cut up the big, steamy pancakes, then she poured the hot syrup over them.

The three of them held each other's hands, and Sally blessed their breakfast.

After Todd took his first few bites, he rolled his green eyes and said, "Mom, these pancakes are delicious. Thank you for bringing us here for breakfast!"

Pace chimed in. "This couldn't be better. Thank you, Momma."

Sally smiled. "Y'all are so welcome. I'm glad the pancakes are good. Mine are too!"

After the last forkful of pancakes was eaten and Sally had paid for their meal, she took their small hands, and they walked to the car.

"Where to next, Mom?" Todd asked.

"The library. We need to return the airplane books. I'm so glad the books gave you a better insight into how airplanes fly. I, too, found it very interesting."

"Me too!" Todd exclaimed.

The twenty-minute drive to the library quickly passed as the three of them chatted away about one thing or another. Sally parked the car, and they entered the library. Audrey, Sally's high school friend, was sitting behind the service desk. Upon hearing the small bell ring above the library door, Audrey looked up from her work and saw Sally.

"Hi, Sally. How are y'all?" Audrey asked.

"Hi, Audrey. We're OK. Good to see you again. How about you? Are you doing OK?" Sally asked.

"Oh, yeah. The good Lord has given me another day. I'm blessed. So, Todd, how did you like those books you checked out? Did you enjoy reading them?" Audrey inquired.

"Yes, Ms. Audrey, I sure did. I learned a lot about airplanes. The main thing I learned was how they fly! It's really amazing. I wrote lots of notes to help me remember what I read," Todd explained.

"Wow! You have been busy. Well, if you ever need to research again, the books will be here for you, plus many other books about airplanes. I'll be happy to help you any time," Audrey said with a smile.

"That's good to know. Thank you, Ms. Audrey. After we leave here, my mom is going to take us to the airport to look at the airplanes again. I brought my notes so I can look at the airplanes and understand my notes better," Todd added.

"That's called *practical application*, Todd. Another way to say it is you're using your notes to see and understand more about what you've read in the books. You're teaching yourself from your notes. Those are excellent study skills. I'm proud of you," Audrey commented and patted him on his shoulder. "Do you want to see if there are any other books you'd like to check out? How about you, Pace? Any books for you?"

The boys looked at each other, then looked at their mother. "It's OK. Go ahead," Sally nodded. And both boys walked fast toward the rows of bookshelves.

"You have some super kiddos, Sally. I know they are such a joy to you," Audrey said to Sally.

"Yes, they are, Audrey. Thank you for your kind words, especially to Todd. He really worked hard on writing his notes. He was so taken by what he was reading. I'd never seen him so excited or so interested by anything as much as he has been with those two books. And in a way, his interest in the books took his mind off of the situation at home. Collin did leave us and has moved to Houston. It's been hard on us," Sally admitted.

"Oh, Sally, I'm so sorry. I wanted to ask, but I didn't want to impose on your personal life. Maybe he'll come back home," Audrey encouraged.

"No, I don't believe he will. He told me he was starting a new life and that I needed to do the same thing," Sally confessed.

"Sally, that's a hard pill to swallow. What do you think you'll do?" Audrey looked concerned.

"Well, I've thought about looking for a job. I also need to come to terms with the fact that a divorce is the most likely next step. And there are so many other things on my mind too. The boys go back to school tomorrow, and I'll have more time to really think about my future," Sally said, trying to be modest with the details she chose to share.

"Sally, I'll be praying the Lord will show you the right direction for you and your boys to take in these upcoming days and weeks. It's a lot to take in and a lot to consider." Audrey sympathized with Sally and gently hugged her.

"Thank you so much, Audrey. I truly do appreciate your prayers. I, too, am praying. I'm asking God for strength and guidance. I guess the boys and I need to be going. Thanks again, Audrey. I'm not sure when we might be back in, but you take care of yourself. It was good to see you again." In a little louder voice, Sally called to her boys. "Todd, Pace, we need to go. Tell Ms. Audrey 'bye,' and thank her for her help."

The boys rounded the corner of the bookshelves and stopped by their mother's side. "Thank you, Ms. Audrey," the boys said.

"Bye, boys. Come see me again soon. Bye, Sally. God bless you."

Audrey watched the three of them turn and walk away. As Sally opened the library door, they waved to Audrey, and Audrey waved back. When the door closed, Audrey wiped tears from her eyes, as she felt sadness and heartache for her friend and her boys.

When Sally drove toward the exit of the parking lot, the library door swung open, and Audrey rushed out. Sally quickly stopped the car, and Audrey ran to the driver's side of the car. Sally rolled down the window.

"Here, Sally. I want you to have my telephone number. Please call and stay in touch with me!" Audrey said, slightly out of breath, as she handed Sally a piece of paper. Audrey then handed Sally another piece of paper. "Please write your telephone number down for me, if you don't mind."

Sally took the paper and wrote her number down and handed it back to Audrey. "I'll call you. Thank you, Audrey. You're so kind; you always have been. Take care, my friend."

"You too, Sally." Audrey waved as Sally began to drive away.

"Ms. Audrey is such a nice lady. I like her," Todd remarked.

"I like her too, Momma," Pace agreed.

"Yes, she is a special person," Sally said as she nodded her head. "OK, we're off to the airport. It shouldn't take us but a few minutes to get there."

The traffic was light, and within minutes they were entering the airport property. A few airplanes were taking flight over their heads as Sally parked the car.

"Wow!" Did you see that, Pace? I could have jumped up and touched it!" exclaimed Todd.

"I saw that, Todd! Maybe someday we can take a trip and be inside one of those big airplanes. That would be something," Pace wished.

"You never know, but maybe, kiddos," Sally said, smiling at the thought.

Sally took the hands of her boys, and they walked through the doors of the airport terminal. Again, the boys' eyes got big as they looked around at the size of the huge building and watched all the activity going on in the terminal. Sally walked slowly with them, soaking in their excitement. Soon they entered the concourse hallway with large windows overlooking the ground below where employees were scurrying around doing their jobs.

"Look, Mom. An airplane is sitting just feet from this window. I wonder what kind of airplane it is. I think that will be my next project, being able to know the different airplanes." Todd pointed toward the airplane.

Behind them came a man's voice. "That's a DC-9, young man. You sound very interested in airplanes."

Sally and the boys turned around and were surprised to see a tall, professional-looking man in a pilot's uniform.

"Hi. My name is Captain Hall, and that airplane is a DC-9. I'll be flying that airplane from here to Chicago in a few hours. What's your name?" The Pilot directed his question to Todd.

"My name is Todd, and yes, sir, I am very interested in airplanes. You really can fly that airplane?" Todd couldn't believe he was talking to a real pilot.

Captain Hall broke into a big smile. "Yes, I really can, and I've been flying for the airlines for ten years. Is this your mother and brother with you?"

"Yes, sir, it is," Todd answered, looking at his mother.

"Hi, Captain Hall. I'm Sally, and this is Pace."

"It's very nice to meet all of you. Your Todd reminds me of myself when I was his age. I loved airplanes, and I wanted to learn all I could about them. I guess I get it, honestly. My father was an Air Force pilot, and he began teaching me how to fly when I was ten years old. By the time I was sixteen, I had enough flying hours to be certified. I passed the necessary tests and received my pilot's license. After I graduated from high school, I enlisted into the Air Force, and after basic training, I began the process to qualify for aviation school. When I graduated, I flew the F-100 jet fighter. Gee, I didn't mean to go into my life's history. I'm just excited to see your young man so taken by airplanes. How old are you, Todd?" asked Captain Hall.

"I'm eight years old, sir," Todd answered.

"I have arrived a little early today, and I have a few minutes before I need to check in. How would you, your mother, and brother like to see the inside of that airplane? If it's OK with your mother?"

Todd's face lit up. "Mom, can we, please? Mom?" Todd begged.

"Oh, Captain Hall, I believe you have just made Todd's day the best ever! Are you sure it's OK for us to do that?" Sally inquired excitedly.

"Yes, it is OK. Come on with me." The captain waved his hand in a forward motion.

Giddy with excitement, they followed the captain. Todd ran up and walked beside him. They walked to a tunnel-like hallway, and at the end of the tunnel, they stepped through a doorway and emerged inside the airplane. Sally wished she had her camera for this once-in-a-lifetime experience. She felt Todd and Pace's excitement, plus a fair share of her own!

Captain Hall began to explain what they were looking at. "We are near the nose section of the airplane. To our left is the cockpit where I'll be, along with my first officer. Then to our right is where the passengers will be seated. The scheduled airline stewardess will help our passengers get settled into their seats, make sure their seatbelts are fastened, and after the flight is in the air, will serve our passengers beverages and snacks. Now, if y'all will step this way." He turned toward the cockpit, opened a small door, and walked through.

Todd stepped into the cockpit first behind the captain. His eyes grew to the size of quarters. Sally and Pace squeezed into the cockpit behind them. What a sight! They took in the whole scene—the seats where the officers sat, the instrument panel, all the gauges, the view out the front windshield and side windows . . . all of it. Wow!

"Todd, would you like to sit in the officer's seat where I will be sitting?" the captain asked.

"Could I?" Todd was just beside himself. Was this really happening to him?

"You certainly can! Go ahead. Take the seat," the captain encouraged Todd.

Todd stepped carefully and eased down into the captain's seat.

"Go ahead, take the yoke. Get the feel of it. That steers the airplane. Put your right hand on the throttle. That is the airplane's engine power, and it controls the amount of fuel provided to the engines. When the airplane is in the air, all the gauges in front of you are registering lots of information, such as air speed, altitude, whether the airplane is climbing or descending as well as turning and banking, plus lots more. I and the first officer wear headsets so we can communicate with the air-traffic controllers in the towers who are giving us instructions about which runways to taxi the airplane on before take-off or landings. They also give us weather information and anything they believe they need to tell us. There is a lot to flying an airplane, but Todd, if you have the ambition and a strong desire, and maybe even the dream of flying in the clouds, you're on your way to a fun and rewarding career. I hope this little tour has been inspirational and also has given you an experience you'll always remember." The captain looked at his watch. "I could just go on and on about flying, but it's time I check in and get ready for my next flight. Todd, you continue to learn all you can about flying, and who knows, you could be taking my place one of these days!"

Todd rose up from the captain's seat and, with much gratitude, hugged the captain. "Thank you so much for all this. It's been *great!* I never dreamed I'd have the chance to see all I have seen today. Thank you very much!" Todd rejoiced.

"Yes, Captain Hall, you have been most gracious, and I appreciate you being so kind to my son in taking your time to show Todd all you have. This experience means so much to him as well as to Pace and me," Sally said gratefully.

The four walked back into the main section of the airplane, stepped through the doorway, and walked through the tunnel to the concourse hallway.

"I would like to say I'll see you again, but it was by God's divine grace that we happened to be at the same place at the same time, and that I heard the words from a young child who has such interest in airplanes and flying. You take care and God's blessing to the three of you, always." And Captain Hall walked away.

Sally and the boys stood in awe, watching the captain disappear behind a closing door. Todd looked up at his mother and asked, "Have I been dreaming, or did this really happen?"

Sally stooped down to Todd's eye level. "No, son, you are not dreaming. You just experienced something that you will never forget. What a special man, Captain Hall is. What he did with you was God sent!"

The afternoon was already half over, and grocery shopping was still to be done. Sally took her sons' hands and walked back through the concourse hallway, through the terminal, and out the doors of the building. They walked in silence toward the car.

Once in the car, Todd broke the silence. "Mom?"

"Yes, Todd?"

Sally saw in his face that he was deep in thought. "Do you know anyone who could teach me more about airplanes and flying?" Todd asked.

"No, I don't, but I can do some checking and asking around to some folks. That's a great idea, Todd! I'll see what I can find out."

"OK, thanks, Mom. I didn't use my airplane notes, but I think I learned more from Captain Hall than I would have from my notes," Todd remarked.

"Your notes were more about the outside of the airplane's operations, but you were rewarded with a bonus today. Seeing the inside of an airplane's cockpit, up close and personal, was pretty darn special. What a learning experience you were given, Todd! In my search to find someone, let's pray that person will be as willing to help you and teach you as Captain Hall was. That would be just an answer to prayer," Sally said. Then she looked at her youngest boy. "Pace, you're very quiet. Are you OK?"

"Yes, I'm OK. I'm just thinking about how excited I'll be tomorrow when I tell my friends at school that I was in a real airplane cockpit, and we talked to a real-life pilot! They will be so surprised!" Pace exclaimed.

"You are right. They will be so surprised and think you are one lucky guy!" his mother boasted. "We're almost to the grocery store. Please be thinking what you both will want to take to school for your lunches so I can buy it."

"Probably peanut butter and something like jelly or bananas," Todd suggested.

"I wish I had something to use to keep your lunches cool. I'd buy some bologna or mix up some egg salad. I need to think on that." They pulled into the grocery store parking lot. "OK, here we are. Let's go buy some vittles!" Sally said as she and the boys got out of the car.

Once inside the grocery store, Todd grabbed a grocery basket, and Pace helped his brother push it. Sally pulled from her purse a written list she had prepared to help her remember the items she needed. One by one, she placed the grocery items in the basket. One of the grocery aisles she walked down had a display of school supplies. She hadn't written any school supply items on her shopping list, but she thought she needed to grab several tablets, a few pencils, a package of erasers, and two small bottles of glue. She thought that if the boys needed more items, she could stop by the store and get them. She spotted a lot of lunch boxes near the school supplies as well. She saw something she had never seen before, and it was an answer to the cooling problem. She picked up the small package, and within the packaging was a small ice bag. She read the writing on the packaging. *This could work!* she thought. Two of the ice bag packages went into the basket. Sally then back-tracked several aisles to the meat counter and asked the butcher for six thin slices of bologna.

Sally doubled-checked her shopping list. "OK, fellas, I think we have what we need. Let's head for the clerk at the register."

The clerk greeted them with friendly words and began ringing up the items in the basket. Another person bagged the items and placed the paper bags in the shopping basket. The clerk totaled the price for the purchased items, and Sally removed her billfold from her purse, took out the money, and paid the clerk. The person who was bagging Sally's groceries pushed the basket out of the store and to Sally's car. After the grocery bags were transferred from the basket to the back seat of the car, Sally handed him a quarter and thanked him for helping her. He walked away, and Sally and the boys got into the car and started for home. Todd and Pace helped their mother bring the groceries into the kitchen, and Sally put them away.

Sally glanced at the clock on the stove. "It's five o'clock already! Are y'all hungry?" Sally asked.

"Yes, ma'am!" Todd and Pace answered at the same time.

"OK. Let's see what I can stir up for us to eat," Sally responded. She pulled out meat from the refrigerator, a few cans of vegetables from the pantry, and a skillet and saucepan from under the counter. Thirty minutes later, the food was ready.

Sally blessed their supper, filled their plates, and they all began eating.

"It has been quite a day . . . one I feel like we will always remember. How about y'all's thoughts for today?" Sally asked.

"I think it was absolutely, positively a wonderful day!" Todd expressed.

"I do too, Momma. I think I'll always remember Captain Hall. He was such a nice man," Pace commented.

"How about you, Mom? What are your thoughts?" Todd asked.

"Well, I believe the Lord gave us such a blessed day from beginning till now. Our breakfast was delicious, seeing Audrey at the library was good, and the biggest and best was experiencing the airport and Captain Hall. God has been so good to us today!" Sally said joyfully.

"And we say, praise the Lord!" Todd added.

"Yes, yes, praise the Lord!" Sally and Pace echoed.

When supper was finished, and the dishes were washed and put away, the three sat down on the couch to watch television. After a little while, Sally said, "It's time for your baths. Y'all will be getting up early in the morning. It's the first day back to school."

"What is it you say, Mom? 'All good things must come to an end'? Well, I guess this is it!" Todd said.

"Ah ha, you do pay attention to what I say? You did good, Todd." Sally laughed.

"Come on, Pace. We gotta take a bath!" Todd reluctantly stood up from sitting on the couch and walked to his bedroom with Pace following behind him.

Sally, too, stood up and walked to the bathroom and started running the boys' bath water. Then the telephone rang. "I'm going to answer the call. The bath water is running," she informed the boys.

"Hello?" she answered.

"Sally, it's me. Just wanted to call you and let you know I made it to Houston. I have a telephone number and address to give to you. You want to write it down?"

"Yes, Collin, just a minute." Sally laid the handset on the couch and went to get a piece of paper and a pencil.

Todd heard his mother say his dad's name and ran to pick up the handset. "Hi, Dad! When are you coming home? I sure do miss you!" he said.

Sally did not know Todd had heard her say Collin's name, and she didn't get to the phone in time to stop him from jumping on the phone. She could tell by the expression on Todd's face that the conversation was not going well.

"OK, here's Mom." He threw the handset on the couch and ran to his room crying.

Before Sally went back to Collin, she ran to the bathroom and turned off the bath water, which had already reached the top of the tub. She walked back to the living room and picked up the handset. "OK, I have pencil and paper. What did you say to Todd? He ran to his room crying!" she asked.

"I just told him I was in Houston, and I was not coming back home. Then I told him to put you back on the telephone." Collin proceeded to give Sally his new telephone number and address in Houston. "You got that, Sally?" he asked.

"Yes. Do you want to talk to Pace?"

"No. One more thing, Sally. I won't get a paycheck for two weeks. Then, I'll send you some money. I need to go."

"Collin, I need to tell you I'm going to see a divorce attorney this Thursday. I don't see any need to prolong this relationship, do you?" Sally asked.

"No, I don't. I'm glad you are going to file for divorce, Sally. I wanted to do it this week, but I must be a resident of this county for six months before I can file for divorce. There is no need to wait. I won't come back to you. Let me know what the attorney fee is, and I'll send you what money I can to cover the expenses. As far as custody of the boys, you can have full custody, and I will pay child support."

"I'm sure the attorney will want to know all this information. I doubt if he will just take my word for what you've told me," Sally said cautiously.

"Just have your attorney send me whatever he needs to. I'll confirm my request. I have to go, Sally." And the call ended.

Sally was stunned and couldn't move from the couch, trying to wrap her mind around what had just happened. After a few moments, she slowly stood up. "Lord, please help me," she whispered to herself. She slowly walked to the boys' bedroom. What she saw broke her heart. Both boys were hugging each other and crying. Sally walked to the side of their beds, knelt down, and took them into her arms. They cried together.

After a while, the boys were nearly asleep from the exhaustion of crying. She covered them up in Pace's bed, prayed for them, and quietly left their room. She emptied the water out of the bathtub and walked to the living room. Before she sat down, the telephone rang again.

"Hello?"

"Oh dear, what is wrong? I can tell by the sound of your voice you're upset," Rusty said tenderly.

"I'm so glad you called. I'm just so perplexed. The boys and I had a great day with lots of exciting experiences, then Collin called from Houston. He really upset the apple cart for the boys by telling Todd he was not coming back home, and he did not even want to talk to Pace. He is such a rotten jerk! I told him I was going to file for divorce. He told me to do it. He was intending to file there, but he can't for six months. Also, he told me he did not want any custody of the boys, and he would pay child support. And then he gave me his new telephone number and address. I wish he had not been so cruel to Todd and Pace. They cried so hard that they fell asleep! I feel so bad for them," Sally explained.

"Boy oh boy. That is terrible, Sally. Collin really is a rotten bum and a whole lot more. I am so sorry you and the boys have to go through such traumatic ordeals with him. I hope, soon, you, Todd, and Pace will be away from all those bad times. I'll be so happy when you all are with me! I wish I could be with you three right now. I want to hold the three of you and take care of you!" Rusty said.

"I wish you were here too, but hopefully soon. Are you OK? Where are you?" Sally asked.

I'm in Nashville. Just a little over three hours from you. I'm so close to you, yet so far away. Is it still OK to meet you at the mall at ten o'clock in the morning?" Rusty paused for a moment to think. "In fact, Sally, I could drive over tonight, and I'd be there with you now. Would you like for me to do that?"

"Oh, Rusty, that is so sweet of you to think of that, and I would love for you to be here with me. But I think we best wait. I have a lot going on in the morning with getting the boys ready for school. But yes, sweetheart, ten o'clock will be good. I'm ready to hold you in my arms. Please be so careful," Sally urged.

"I will. You sound tired. I'm about to go to bed. You too?" Rusty asked.

"Yes, I am tired. You sleep well, my darling, and have sweet dreams. I know I will. I'll be dreaming of you. I also will have you in my prayers. I love you, honey," Sally tenderly spoke to Rusty and then blew him a kiss through the telephone.

"I will be dreaming of you too, baby, and I will keep you in my prayers as always. I love you bunches." Rusty felt her kiss and blew his own. Then the sweethearts ended the call.

Tears welled up in Sally's eyes. That was the first time either one of them had told the other that they were praying for each other. That was very special to Sally.

Sally rose from the couch and meandered toward her bedroom. She briefly stopped and glanced in the boys' room. They were sound asleep. She quietly stepped around the floor furnace and entered her bedroom. She slipped into her nightgown and crawled between the sheets. When her head was on her pillow, she folded her hands under her chin and prayed, asking God to watch over her sons as they slept and for them to have good attitudes when they woke up in the morning. She wished for them to be happy as they prepared to go back to school. She also prayed for Rusty to have safe travels for his trip tomorrow. She was so excited to be able to see and be with him. She then prayed for herself that the Lord would give her the knowledge and strength she would need to get her through the upcoming days.

The alarm clock was punctual as the music clicked on at 6:30 a.m. the next morning. Sally rolled over in bed and pressed the button to turn off the music. She laid there for a few moments, thanking the Lord for another day. Then she stretched her body before throwing the covers back and extended her legs and feet to the floor. With her feet in her slippers and her robe on, she walked to the boys' bedroom and to Pace's bedside. Both boys were snuggled up warmly with each other, and she hated that she had to wake them up. Sally bent down and placed her hand on Pace's arm. "It's time to rise and shine, little ones," she softly announced. "Time to get dressed for school."

"Good morning, Momma. You know I want to sleep longer, don't you?" Pace informed her with his eyes barely open.

"I know, but in a few days, it will be the weekend, and you can do just that!" she replied.

"OK, I'm getting up. Come on, Todd, time to get up," Pace said, looking at his brother.

"Good morning, Todd. Can you open those green eyes of yours?" Sally asked.

Todd popped his eyes open, smiled at her, and replied, "Yes, ma'am. I can." He scooted to the edge of the bed and hugged her.

After both boys were up, Sally looked in their closet for their school clothes. She pulled out two long-sleeve shirts and two pairs of corduroy pants. "I'll be back to help y'all with your shoes, but I need to get in the kitchen and get breakfast started," Sally said as she quickly left their bedroom. She was thankful the boys were in a good mood after the bad scene last night.

Sally prepared her coffee, put the skillet on the stove burner, and took the bacon and eggs from the refrigerator. As she rounded the corner of the kitchen to go back to the boys' room, she found them in the living room with their shoes on, watching a children's show on the television.

"You fellas are just too fast for me! Got those little shoes on already? Thank y'all," Sally said as she turned back toward the kitchen. While she was watching and waiting for their breakfast to cook, she prepared their lunchboxes.

When breakfast was ready, Sally called the boys to the dining room table. They blessed their meal and dug in. When the boys had finished their last bites, Sally cleared the table while the boys brushed their teeth and combed their hair. Sally checked the time and hurried to get herself dressed. She then helped the boys get their coats on, and out the door to school they went.

The drive wasn't bad—very little traffic—but the school's car line for drop-off at the entrance was long. After a few minutes, it was Todd and Pace's turn to hop out of the car.

"Y'all have a good day. I'll be praying for y'all. I love y'all," Sally said as the boys exited the car.

"Love you too," they yelled as they closed the car door and began to walk the short distance to the school's entrance. Sally watched for a moment and waved to them as they walked inside the building. She breathed a sigh of relief. She feared she wasn't going to get the boys to school on time. She felt like the morning had been so rushed; she needed to plan the school mornings a little more efficiently so they wouldn't be in a hurry.

Her thoughts shifted to Rusty, and excitement leapt within her. She longed to see him, for him to hold her, and for him to kiss her tenderly.

When Sally arrived home, she finished cleaning up the kitchen then took a shower. With the bath towel wrapped around her body, she searched in her closet for the *perfect* outfit to wear. She wanted to look her best for Rusty. She spotted a silky blue blouse and pulled it out, then grabbed a pair of tight-fittin' jeans from her drawer. She whispered to herself with a smile, *this should do it*, and began to dress. She looked in the bathroom mirror as she applied a little makeup to her face and combed her long auburn hair. As she peered at her reflection in the mirror, she hoped that Rusty would like what he saw.

Sally walked to the living room and looked at the wall clock. It was nine o'clock. She had a few minutes before she would need to go to the mall. She then thought of something she had meant to do for several days but hadn't taken the time to do it.

Where would I have put my mother's Bible? Sally asked herself. She looked on the top shelf of the coat closet, but it wasn't there. *OK, maybe it's in the hall closet.* But it wasn't there either. *It wouldn't be in the kitchen or the boys' room, or the dining room.* She looked in the bottom drawer of her nightstand, and there it was, along with her mom and dad's picture. She gently took it from the drawer and carried it to the dining room table where she laid it down.

Sally sat down in one of the chairs and stared at the book in front of her. She wondered how many times her mother opened her Bible, and when she did open it, what book or which pages she looked at. She touched the book with reverence, knowing that within these pages were God's words. She carefully opened the cover, and there on the first page she found four four-leaf clovers wrapped in a very old tissue. Sally remembered her mother always enjoyed finding four-leaf clovers, and she saved them. The number four was her mother's favorite number because there were four members in her family.

As Sally turned the pages, she found more treasures her mother had tucked away inside—such as her mother's parents' newspaper obituaries. The clippings had turned yellow from age. A little further along in the Bible, Sally found an obituary for one of her mother's five brothers, which was incased in plastic. Almost halfway through the Bible, Sally found a picture of her mother, father, and brother. It was an old picture and had been taken when her brother was maybe six or seven years old. How precious!

Suddenly Sally jumped to her feet. She looked at the clock. *Oh my goodness, I have to go!* She didn't realize how long she had been looking through the Bible. She threw on her coat and ran out the front door. Once in the car, she turned the knob of the CB to the *on* position and immediately began hearing voices. She made the necessary turns to get on the super slab and headed for the mall and to Rusty. She couldn't put the miles behind her quick enough, but she didn't want to go too fast and be pulled over by the police. It was almost 10 a.m., and she was still a few miles from the mall.

Through all the chatter from the CB's speaker, Sally could barely make out that northern-accented voice calling for the Cricket. Her heart was beating overtime as she grabbed the mic. "Breaker 1-9 for the person who is calling for the Cricket," she broadcasted. But the Farmer didn't answer. She thought that she might still be too far away, and he couldn't hear her yet. She called again. This time her call was heard.

"Cricket, where are you? I'm at our spot." Rusty's voice was getting clearer and louder as Sally turned the last corner before driving into the mall's parking lot.

"I'm at the mall. I see that beautiful KW of yours," Sally excitedly told him.

"Yes, I see you too! Come bring your sweet self on over here to me!" Rusty exclaimed.

"I'm on my way, sweetheart!" Sally shouted, and within a few moments, she had driven up beside Rusty's truck. She jumped from her car and ran to Rusty's open arms. They embraced each other and kissed passionately.

Rusty took his hands and cupped them around Sally's face. He drew her close to him. "I love you, and I have missed you so much." He kissed her again. "Come on, let's get in the truck," he said as he took her hand in his.

Rusty opened the truck's driver-side door, and both of them climbed inside the cab. Sally immediately stepped into the sleeper, and Rusty followed her. He helped her off with her coat, and she laid back on the sleeper bed.

"Come here, you handsome hunk!" Sally enticed him as she pulled him toward her. "I have missed you so very much, sweetheart."

Rusty snuggled close to Sally, holding her tightly and kissing her over and over again. Sally's fingers ran through his thick hair as she pulled herself even closer to his body. Through Rusty's heavy breathing, he asked Sally, "Do you want to make love, baby? I do, but is it safe?"

Sally knew it was wrong to have an affair with Rusty, but the thought vanished as she found herself unbuttoning Rusty's shirt. "Yes, honey, I do," she said. "And we are good."

They kissed slowly and passionately and whispered tender words until their passion consumed them both.

After a while, they just laid still in each other's arms. Sally's head rested on Rusty's shoulder, and her fingers gently ran over his manly chest.

"I could stay like this forever. I feel so relaxed, so safe, and so satisfied with you. I hope you feel that way too, sweetheart," Sally whispered.

"I sure do, honey. I'm so content with you. Better than I ever imagined. I love you so much, Sally. I truly hope you know that and believe it," Rusty whispered back.

"I do believe you, Rusty. You're wonderful, and I love you very much too. I long to be with you, take care of you, and be yours for the rest of our lives together," Sally said as she leaned up on her elbow and looked directly into Rusty's blue eyes.

"I definitely want and long for our love to be that strong too, Sally," Rusty expressed. "And the sooner the better!"

Sally reached for her blouse and began to dress. "Rusty, honey, you told me last night in our conversation that you would pray for me also after I told you I would have you in my prayers. What does that mean to you?"

Rusty looked at Sally as he buttoned his shirt and answered, "That means that I believe you were asking God to watch over me, just as I ask God to watch over you and the boys."

"Then you believe in God?" Sally inquired.

"Yes, I do. Don't you?" Rusty responded.

"Yes, but not until this week. When I woke up Monday morning, I said a prayer, not really knowing how to pray or even to whom I was praying. Peggy, my mother-in-law, always prays before she eats a meal, and she has mentioned many times the saying, "Praise the Lord." And especially lately she'll tell me she'll be praying for us. And my brother uses the phrase "we'll be praying for you." So with all that's going on in my and the boys' lives, I thought I'd pray for us. After I prayed and I opened my eyes, I felt this invisible presence around me. I also felt at peace and that everything was going to be OK. I told my brother about it when I called him to wish him happy birthday, and he was very elated, telling me that the invisible presence was Jesus' Spirit who was inviting me to become a Christian. He gave me different Bible scriptures to look up and read. Also, that day, I talked to Peggy and told her about my experience, and she asked me about going to church when I was growing up and if I had ever heard the phrase "born again." I told her I had not. She told me a story about Nicodemus asking Jesus about being born again. She agreed with my brother that the Holy Spirit was dealing with me, and she has invited the boys and me to go to church with her on Sunday," Sally told Rusty.

"Wow! Sally, I sure would agree with those folks that God's entreating you. Have you asked Him to forgive you of your sins, and have you accepted Jesus as your Lord and Savior?" Rusty asked.

"I think so. Peggy had me recite a prayer with her that sounded like what you just asked me. I do feel different, but how do you know for sure, Rusty?" Sally tried her best to explain her complicated feelings.

"As a child, my mom and dad took me to church for years, but I never let the words of God sink into my mind, and it wasn't until Holly and I divorced that I was at the lowest point in my life. My mom and dad encouraged me to go back to church with them. I wasn't crazy about the idea, nor was I interested, but I went. It was Easter Sunday. The preacher seemed like he was talking directly to me. He taught me that Jesus was the only Son of God, that Jesus lived a life of love, grace, and trust, and that He died a horrible death for *me* because of my sins. That struck such a cord with me. As the preacher continued to preach, such a guilty feeling came over me. I felt like I heard Jesus say to me, *Come, ask forgiveness for your sins, and be saved. I will give you eternal life.* I walked to the front of the church, got on my knees, asked God to forgive my sins, and asked Jesus to come into my life. The next Sunday I was baptized and began praising the Lord for all His blessings. Hopefully I'm living a life of service for Him." He looked into Sally's eyes. "Sally, having Jesus in your life is a wonderful thing, and I do believe you are being *born again*. Going to church will help you understand and teach you more about Jesus and the life of a Christian. Do you have a Bible?" Rusty asked.

"Yes. I found my mother's Bible this morning. When I get home, I want to start reading it, especially the verses that my brother and Peggy have given me to read," Sally said.

"I believe that is an excellent idea. I want to add one more thought to your plan. After I was baptized, my preacher urged me to read the Bible too, but he asked me to begin by reading the book of John first. I did, and it opened my eyes to the life of Jesus so clearly. Oh, and one more suggestion. Before you begin to read God's words, pray for Him to open your mind and heart to what you are reading. The Holy Spirit that lives inside your heart will do the rest for you." Rusty took Sally's hands, bowed his head, and prayed: "Dear Father in heaven, Jesus, my Savior and Redeemer, and my Holy Spirit, I ask You to touch Sally's heart and allow her to know You in a very special and deep way. Let her feel Your presence so that she would believe You are her Savior. Please, Lord, guide her and protect her and her boys. Lord, You know I love this lady with all my heart, and I pray that soon You will allow her to be my wife. We know that in all situations, You are in control, and You know all things. I ask You to forgive us of our sins, even today's sin. But Lord, I truly love this woman. I ask You, Lord, that in the coming days and weeks, Your guiding hand will be upon us in all things. My Savior, I ask You all these things in Your sweet and holy name. Amen." Rusty felt tear drops fall on his hands. He looked at Sally.

"Oh, Rusty," Sally sobbed. "Thank you. That was a beautiful prayer you've prayed for us. I do want to believe I feel the power of the Lord. I want what you feel and believe!"

Rusty took Sally in his arms and held her. "You will, honey. Jesus will show you more and more about Him and His genuine love for you. Soon you will wonder how you could have ever lived without Him in your life. He is wonderful!" He took Sally by her shoulders and kissed her nose. "Are you OK, my baby girl?" Rusty took a soft cloth from the pocket next to the sleeper and gently wiped away the tears from Sally eyes.

Sally held Rusty's hands after he wiped her tears and brought them to her lips and kissed them. "You are so wonderful, sweetheart. I love you more today than I ever thought I could. You will be my strength with your thoughts and prayers."

"God has both of us in His hands, and He will provide. He is our strength. Always remember that, my love," Rusty encouraged Sally.

"I will. Thank you so much, darlin'," Sally said.

Rusty looked at his watch. "Dear Sally, I don't want to leave you, but we'll see each other again in a few days. Maybe search out another place for me to park Buster that is closer to your home now that we don't need to be so concerned that Collin or someone else might see us and give you a problem," he suggested.

"That's a great idea. I will. Then I can drive over, get you, and bring you to the house. I'll work on that!" Sally agreed excitedly.

Rusty helped Sally out of the sleeper and down from the cab. They held hands as they walked to Sally's car. Before Rusty opened the car door for Sally, they held each other one last time and kissed good-bye.

"I love you so much, Sally. I'll call you later tonight. Be careful, and I will have you and the boys in my prayers. See you on Friday," Rusty told her.

"I love you more today, Rusty, than I did yesterday. Remember that. I'll be waiting for your call. Oh yeah, I have an appointment with the attorney tomorrow at eleven o'clock," Sally reminded him.

"I'll definitely be praying for and about that appointment. I hope you can be given a divorce soon so we can *always* be together," Rusty exclaimed.

"Yes, me too! I long to be with you. Gotcha in my prayers, honey, and thank you for your prayers for us. Friday can't get here soon enough," Sally exclaimed back.

Rusty gave Sally a quick kiss and helped her get in her car, then quickly walked to his truck.

Sally watched him climb into his rig, and she saw the black puffs of smoke belch from the truck's stacks when he cranked up the engine. He slowly drove off the mall parking lot, Sally driving close behind.

The CBs were on, and Rusty and Sally talked to each other until their voices faded away as the miles grew between them. She was happier than she had ever been in a long time. Rusty's prayer to the Lord had boosted her spirits and given her more confidence that she had indeed been born again. She was so warm inside and really felt good.

As Rusty drove farther and farther away from Sally, he was more and more convinced that Sally was the right woman for him, and he looked forward to having her for his wife. The memories of that day would stay with him forever.

It was lunchtime, and Sally decided to stop by the local bar-be-que restaurant and pick up a sandwich. When she arrived at home, she prepared her soda to drink and chips to eat, then sat down at the dining room table and prayed, thanking the Lord for her food and asking Him to bless her boys and keep Rusty safe on the highways and byways. She gently slid her mother's Bible near her and began turning its pages again. She found more four-leaf clovers wrapped in wax paper and a little greeting card that appeared to be very old. She tenderly picked it up. A cute little girl with blonde hair was painted on the front of the card. At the top was the word *HELLO*. Sally carefully opened the card. At the top of the inside was written, *To my daddy.* The verse read, *Roses are red, violets are blue, sugar is sweet, and so are YOU!* At the bottom of the card was written, *I miss you so much. —Shortie.* Instantly tears formed in her eyes as she remembered the card. She had sent it to her father when he was in Korea in 1951. His nickname for her was "Shortie" because she was a very little child. She was so touched that her mother had saved the card.

After Sally finished eating her bar-be-que sandwich, she careful picked up the Bible and walked to the living room and sat on the couch. She placed the Bible ever so gently on her lap and paged through to the book of John. She bowed her head, folded her hands, and prayed like Rusty suggested. She wanted so desperately to understand and learn from what she was reading.

Sally read for several hours. The scriptures she couldn't understand, she reread several times to try to discover the meaning of God's words.

All of a sudden, she looked at the wall clock behind her. *Oh gosh, I must go get Todd and Pace from school!* In a panic, she threw on her coat, and out the front door she flew. *OK, Lord, please don't let me be late,* she prayed. All the traffic lights she had to go through were green, and she made it to the school right as the children were getting out. *Thank You, sweet Jesus.* She was grateful.

Sally drove behind the last car in line and slowly inched her way up to the boys. Finally the school attendant opened the back door of the car, and Todd and Pace stepped inside. Once the boys were safely seated, the attendant closed the door.

"Hi, kiddos! How are y'all? How was school?" Sally asked.

Todd and Pace began talking at the same time to answer her questions: "You first, Todd," Pace said.

"I'm feeling good, and school was good! But I do have a little homework. It was great to see all my friends again," Todd replied.

"Yeah, I liked seeing my friends again! I told them about Captain Hall and being in the cockpit of an airplane. They thought that was pretty cool! I helped the teacher some, and I was happy about that. How was your day today, Momma?" Pace inquired.

"Oh, my day was good," Sally thought, thinking of her time with Rusty. "But it was too quiet without you two being in the house or us going places. I missed y'all, and I'm glad to see y'all! How did the little ice packs do in your lunchboxes? Did they keep your lunches cold?"

"I thought it worked good. My sandwich was cold," Todd answered.

"My lunchbox was still cold too," Pace replied.

"That's great. I'm glad I found those ice packs. Say, how about some cookies and milk when we get home?"

"That sounds good!" both boys said at the same time.

They arrived back home, and the boys put their schoolbooks on the dining room table, took off their coats, and helped their mother with the milk and cookies. They sat at the table, and the boys told their mother all about their day at school. She was so happy that the situation with their father the evening before was a thing of the past. She was concerned that they were sad and troubled. That prayer was answered. Praise the Lord!

While Sally started preparing the meatloaf for supper, Todd began his homework. Pace didn't have any homework and asked if it was OK for him to watch television.

"Yes, that will be fine, but do it quietly so Todd can concentrate on doing his homework," she requested.

"OK," Pace agreed.

Sally opened a can of green beans and poured them in a pan, adding a teaspoon of bacon drippings as she sat the pan on the stove's burner. She opened a can of apple sauce, poured the sauce in a bowl, and placed it in the refrigerator to chill. Next, she took her mother's cookbook down from the shelf above the stove and turned to the page for cornbread muffins. She gathered the necessary items and stirred everything she needed in a mixing bowl.

Todd entered the kitchen. "Can I help, Mom?" he asked.

"You sure can. Homework all done?"

"Yes ma'am," he answered.

"That's great. That didn't take you very long at all. You can get the muffin tin from the bottom drawer of the stove if you want to, and then get the little can of shortening from the pantry along with a paper towel. I'm ready to pour the cornbread mixture into the tin," Sally instructed.

Sally took the lid from the shortening can, applied some of its contents on the paper towel, and swirled the shortening into each muffin cup. "There, that should do it! You want to put some mix in each cup?'

"Sure!" Todd said excitedly.

"Be careful now. Easy does it. You're doing a great job, Todd," remarked his mother.

"What great job is Todd doing, Momma?" Pace overheard them talking from the living room and ran into the kitchen to see what was happening.

"I'm helping Mom fix cornbread!" Todd exclaimed.

"Supper sure is smellin' good, Momma! I'm hungry!" Pace shouted.

"I'm glad you're hungry. The cornbread takes twenty minutes to bake, then everything else should be ready to be put on the table. In the meantime, we can get our drinks, plates, silverware, the butter, the catsup, and whatever else y'all might want to go along with your supper."

The timer went off that signaled the cornbread and meatloaf were ready to come out of the oven. Sally placed a hot pad on the table for the meatloaf, poured the green beans in a bowl, dropped the muffins in a warming basket, and took the applesauce from the fridge and placed it on the table.

"Please, go wash your hands. Supper is served," Sally announced.

The boys ran to the bathroom, washed their hands, and zipped back to the table, all in record time. They sat in their chairs, folded their hands, and bowed their heads to bless their supper. Sally smiled at her sons as they ate. Their appetites were good, and they all enjoyed the delicious meal.

After supper, the table was cleared, and the dishes were washed and put away. Then Sally ran the boys their bath water. She had enjoyed Todd and Pace being home from school on Christmas break, even though some of the time was nightmarish, but they did have some good times together too. However, getting back into a normal routine was going well and felt good.

"Y'all's PJs are laying on Pace's bed," Sally told the boys who were getting out of the bathtub. Sally had decided to allow the boys to take on a little more responsibility by having them dry themselves. Todd was already doing that, but Pace needed to begin drying himself too. Of course, she was nearby just in case he needed her help. "Please pull the tub stopper so the water can drain," she instructed.

"It's done," Todd said in a raised voice so his mother could hear him from the bathroom. Stepping from the bathroom to the doorway of the hall and living room, wrapped in his towel, Todd asked, "Mom, can we watch a little television before we go to bed?"

Sally was sitting on the couch in the living room. As she glanced up to answer Todd, she saw Pace streak by Todd in his birthday suit, heading to his bedroom. Sally laughed, "That little brother of yours is something else! Ah, yes to the television, but only for a little while."

With their PJs on, the boys snuggled up on the couch by their mother and watched their favorite western show on the television. Then it was off to bed. Sally watched Todd climb the ladder to his bunk bed and made certain he was secure.

She stood on her tip-toes as she helped him pull the covers over him. He leaned forward and kissed his mother.

"What do y'all think about bringing the top bunk bed down to the floor? Todd, would you like to be down here?" she asked.

"I think I'd like to try that. If I don't like it, can we put it back?" Todd responded.

"We sure can. After school tomorrow, let's see if we can take your bed down." Sally leaned over Pace, covered him up, and kissed him. "Y'all sleep tight, and don't let the bedbugs bite. Have sweet dreams, you two. I love y'all bunches."

"Love ya too," both boys said simultaneously.

Sally turned out the overhead ceiling light and left the room with a prayer to Jesus to watch over them through the night. Then, her prayers turned to Rusty as she walked to her bedroom. She glanced at the clock on the nightstand and wondered when he might be calling her. She undressed and slipped into her nightgown and robe. As she was stepping into her slippers, the telephone rang. She flipped out the bedroom light and ran to answer the call.

"Hello?"

"Hi, baby. It's me. How are you?" Rusty's manly voice touched her ear.

"Hi, sweetie. I'm OK now that I'm hearing your voice." Sally sighed as she reclined on the couch. "How are you?"

"I'm good too. Just hearing your sweet voice makes *all* things right. I have had you on my mind the whole trip. Our time together this morning has made my day so wonderful. I'll just be so glad when each day is full of you," Rusty softly said in a seductive tone.

"Oh, listen to you, making me all warm inside. This morning was beautiful. I love you so much, my love," Sally swooned. "Where are you?"

"I'm between Dallas and Fort Worth at a nice truck stop. I just finished eating, and I'm about to slip back on the super slab and roll on to Abilene. I should be there before midnight. How was the rest of your day?"

"It was good. I looked more at my mother's Bible, picked up the boys from school, fixed supper, and spent a little while with the boys watching television before I put them in their beds," Sally explained.

"I wish you were here to put me in bed. I would love that," Rusty hinted.

"Oh, aren't you such a bad boy! There ya go, making me all warm inside again."

"Well, you can probably guess what it's doing to me, baby . . ." Rusty claimed. "OK, I'd better go before I just turn this rig around and come see you."

"That'd be OK! Come on. I'm already laying on the couch. I'll be waitin' for ya," Sally enticed him.

"Oh, you're not making it easy on me, you know that, don't you?" Rusty said, wanting to give in.

"I guess we'll just have to wait until Friday. Then, I'll see what you've got for me, Mr. Summers!" Sally spun the web.

"I bet you could handle it, sweetheart," Rusty spun right back. "OK, I'm out of here. I can't handle this temptation anymore. Shame on you, Sally dear!" Rusty chuckled.

"I'm sorry . . . no . . . no, I'm not!" Sally teased him. "Before we kiss and kiss and kiss good night, please don't forget. Tomorrow at 11 a.m. I go to the divorce attorney. Say a little prayer for us," Sally added.

"That's right. I'll be praying. I love you, and you be careful. I'll call you, probably tomorrow afternoon. Oh yeah, be thinking of a parking spot closer to you, OK?" Rusty reminded her.

"OK, I will. Please be careful. Gotcha in my prayers. Love ya bunches, honey," Sally said, throwing Rusty a long kiss.

"Wow! I really did feel that one! Love you too, kid." He threw Sally a long kiss back. And the call ended.

Lord, You know how much I love that man. Thank You for him, and please, please watch over him and keep him safe, Sally prayed. She didn't want to move. She was so comfortable, curled up on the couch as she embraced all of Rusty's loving words. It really had been an awesome day. *Thank You, Lord.*

Chapter Twelve

Rusty arrived at the truck terminal in Abilene just before midnight. The gatekeeper of the facility checked Rusty in and directed him to drive his truck to West Dock 5. The property was well lit, and being that Rusty had been to this location a number of times, he knew right where he was to go. One of the dock employees met him at Dock 5 and, using his lighted wands, guided Rusty into the numbered parking slot. With Rusty's excellent backing skills, it only took him one time to back his truck to the dock.

Rusty shut the rig's engine down and jumped from the cab. The dock employee approached him to retrieve the load's manifest.

"Hey, Rusty. How are you doing tonight?" the man asked.

"I'm doing good, Carl. How about you?" Rusty chatted with the man as he handed him his manifest. "Any fresh coffee brewed?"

"Yes, sir. I just made a fresh pot not twenty minutes ago. Go help yourself, Rusty," Carl encouraged.

"I believe I will, along with a bag of chips. Then I'm going to call it a night," Rusty added. "Unloading and loading time good tonight, Carl?"

"We are on time. We should have you out of here around 7 a.m.," Carl answered.

"Sounds good to me. Thank you." Rusty was pleased with the schedule.

The two men walked into the terminal. Carl went to his desk, and Rusty walked to the men's room, then to the vending machine, then to the open coffee table and poured a cup of coffee. As he walked out of the terminal, he wished Carl a good night.

The night air was refreshing and cool to Rusty's face. He slowly sipped the coffee from the tall cup as he walked to his truck. He stood by the cab door for a few moments and thanked God for a safe and good trip. He also thanked Him for Sally. As he opened the cab's door and stepped on the running board, Rusty had a flashback of the beautiful day he had with his Sally. She meant everything to him. When he laid down on the sleeper, he pictured her beside him with her lovely green eyes looking at him and her flowing auburn hair hanging down across her shoulders. He drifted off to sleep with her image on his mind.

"Rusty, Rusty, come on, man! You got to wake up! Rusty, wake up! It's very important!" Carl yelled, banging his hands on the driver's door.

Finally Rusty heard the commotion and rose up from the sleeper. He struggled getting to the driver's seat after being awakened from a deep sleep. He opened the door. "Carl, what is it, man?" he said, trying to wake up.

"Your boss, Mr. Walker, is on the telephone. It's an emergency. He needs to talk to you right now!" Carl urged.

"All right. I need to put my shoes on." Rusty hurried and jumped from the cab. Then he and Carl ran to the terminal. Rusty grabbed the telephone from Carl's desk.

"This is Rusty."

"Rusty, this is Nash Walker. I hate to give you this news, but your mother has called me and said I needed to get you home. Your father has had a heart attack and is in intensive care at the hospital. He isn't doing well. Carl is going to take you to the airport in Abilene where a private plane is going to be waiting for you. We will fly you home, son."

"What? Oh my gosh! Not my dad! OK, Mr. Walker. I appreciate this. Please let my mother know that I'll be home as soon as possible. What about my truck?"

"I will tell your mother. Don't worry about your truck. I'll have another driver at the Bridgeport Airport, and he will fly back to Abilene. He will bring your truck home. Right now, we just want you to get here," Mr. Walker encouraged.

"Thank you, Mr. Walker." Rusty hung up the telephone, ran to his truck, and grabbed some of his personal things. Carl was waiting with the car. Rusty quickly got in the car, and Carl drove fast to the airport. When they arrived, the plane was being fueled for the trip. Rusty had to take a minute and call Sally.

Still curled up on the couch, Sally jumped when the telephone rang at 5 a.m. She scrambled to answer the telephone in her sleepy state. She thought that nothing could be good when the telephone rings at this hour.

"Hello?" Sally answered as she cleared her throat.

"Sally, Dad's had a heart attack and is in bad shape. He is in the hospital. The company is flying me home. I wanted to let you know. I've got to go. The plane is waiting for me. I love you. Please pray! I'll call you later, sweetheart." And he hung up.

Sally fell to her knees, crying, and she started praying. *Oh, Father in heaven, please help me to know how to pray for this situation. Please be with Rusty and his airplane trip home. Please be with his father. Allow the doctors to know what to do to sustain Russell's life, and please be with Rusty's mother. I lift her up to You. Lord, I've been told You are in control, and You know all things. With this, I believe You know what's happening. Please, Lord, please, let all this be OK.* She cried for the Lord to hear her prayer.

Sally sat on the living room floor motionless. She watched the hands on the wall clock move slowly, and she wondered what was happening in Rusty's world. How long would it take for Rusty to fly to the Connecticut airport? Which hospital was Russell taken to? Is he still alive? Is anyone with Mrs. Summers? She wished Rusty were able to call her again.

Sally heard her alarm clock begin to play music. She grabbed hold of the edge of the couch to help her stand up. Her legs were very wobbly, and she had trouble walking to the boys' room. She was trying so hard to get her mind focused. Under her breath she asked the Lord to give her strength to do whatever He needed for her to do because she felt like she was a mess.

"Hey, little boys, it's time to get up and get ready for school," Sally announced as she gently touched each one of her sons' arms.

The boys stirred and stretched their arms in the air, then rubbed their eyes with their hands.

"Good morning, Momma," Pace greeted. "Is it time to get up already?"

"I'm afraid so. Is Todd thinking about getting up?" Sally teased.

"I think he might be, Mom," Todd answered as if he was someone else speaking for Todd.

"You could tell him to hurry!" Sally pretended to play along with Todd's game.

"OK, I will," Todd replied.

Sally walked to their closet and selected the clothes she wanted them to wear to school. When she turned around, both boys had left the room, and she heard them in the bathroom. Sally walked from their room toward the kitchen. "Your school clothes are laying on Pace's bed," she yelled to them. "I'm going to start our breakfast." Sally turned on the oven to preheat for the biscuits she was going to bake. Then, she prepared her coffee to brew. She removed the eggs and sausage patties from the refrigerator and placed a skillet on the stove. She laid six sausage patties in the skillet to cook.

Wondering how the boys were fairing by dressing themselves, she walked to their room quietly and peeked around the corner. She smiled. The boys were completely dressed and were putting on their shoes.

"Look at you two! I am so proud of both of you," she said as she walked over and hugged both of them. "That's a job well done. Breakfast will be ready soon."

"Can we watch television until breakfast is ready?" Todd asked.

"Sure, that'll be fine," she agreed as she walked back to the kitchen. Within a few minutes, their breakfast was on the dining room table. The boys came to the table and took their seats as Sally sat their milk and juice on the table.

"Sausage, egg, and cheese biscuits with orange juice? Mom, this is great!" Todd exclaimed loudly.

"Looks delicious, Momma!" Pace was excited too.

"I thought it would be a nice change. Let's join hands, bow our heads, and thank the Lord for our breakfast: *God is great, God is good. Let us thank Him for our food. Amen.*"

"I like that prayer, Momma," Pace commented.

"I remember when I was a little girl, I used to say that prayer. Maybe we can say it together before every meal from now on. Whatcha think?" she asked.

"I like that idea, Mom," Todd answered.

"Me too," Pace agreed.

The time was running thin again, so the boys hurried to brush their teeth while their mother dressed. The boys put on their coats and got their schoolbooks as Sally grabbed their lunchboxes.

"Do we have everything?" asked Sally as Todd opened the front door.

"I think so," the boys answered together, and Sally closed the door behind them.

There was a mist in the air from a settling fog. Sally needed to drive carefully, as her vision out the car's windshield was obscured. The traffic lights were all fuzzy looking due to the dense moisture in the air. She was relieved when the school finally came into view. The drop-off line was only a few minutes.

"Oh, Mom. I forgot to give you this yesterday," Todd said as he handed her a piece of paper. "Pace, do you have one too?" Todd asked his brother.

"Yes, I do. Here, Momma." Pace also handed her a paper.

"What is this?" she asked.

"A list of school supplies we need," Todd answered.

"OK. I don't know if I can get to the store today, but we can definitely go this weekend. Will that be OK?" she asked.

"I think so," Todd agreed.

The school attendant opened the car door, and the boys scooted across the back seat and stepped on the ground. Sally wished her sons to have a good day and told them she loved them. They waved and disappeared as the school door closed behind them.

Sally drove carefully and was thankful when she arrived home safely. Her mind was on Rusty, and she wondered how and where he was. She breathed a prayer for the situation. She hadn't taken the time to clean up the kitchen before leaving to take the boys to school, so she quickly did that chore. She looked at the stove clock. Nine o'clock. She needed to allow at least forty-five minutes to drive downtown to the attorney's office.

Suddenly a thought crossed her mind. She had to pay her bills! Collin always took care of the household finances, so she never had to think about it. She remembered he stored the paperwork in a box that he kept on the shelf in their bedroom closet, so she went to find it. No bills had come in the mail since Collin had left, so she had no idea what even needed to be paid. She took the box to the dining room table and opened it. What was she even looking for? Slowly she removed the top envelope that said *Work Pay Stubs*. Under that envelope were other envelopes. Each one had a *month* written on it. She opened December's envelope. There were four money order stubs inside—one for utilities, one for rent, one for the telephone, and one for insurance. Each one had attached to it a statement, except the rent stub. It occurred to her to check the dates on the stubs. It was January 4th. The money order stub for the rent was dated December 1st.

The rent is due! Oh dear. What do I do? Where did Collin buy his money orders? Sally asked questions she had no answers for. Then she saw a small notebook under December's envelope, and she opened it. She found a list of information dating back to 1975 that looked like a record of all the bills that were paid. She turned the pages to January 1979. There, she located more information that would help her know how Collin maintained their finances. She lifted up more envelopes until she reached the bottom of the box. She found January 1975's envelope.

At the bottom of the box was a larger brown envelope curled up around the sides of the box. It was marked *Tax Returns*. Sally removed the envelope and peeked inside. It contained paperwork from filing taxes.

The clock was ticking away. She wished she would hear from Rusty before she left for the attorney's office, but if not, she'd just keep on praying that all was good. She took a quick shower, dressed, and gathered up the financial box just in case the attorney needed to know about their expenditures. She didn't know what all the attorney would need or ask for, but it would stand to reason that the attorney would need to know this information. She put the two notes Collin had left her in her purse as well. At least she would have proof that Collin doesn't intend to return and his encouragement for her to move on with her life.

As she opened the front door, she looked at the telephone, wishing it would ring. She closed the door behind her and got in her car. Sally remembered there was a Memphis City map in the glovebox of the car. She reached for it and opened to the city street index and found Hickory Street. *D-6*, she uttered to herself, then turned the map over so she could view the city street. *There is D, and there is 6.* She ran her index fingers across the map until they met. *There is Hickory Street! Now which way is the best way to get there?* she asked herself as she studied the streets from her house to the attorney's office.

Satisfied with her driving plan, she cranked up the car, backed out of the driveway, and was on her way. She was glad the fog had cleared and the sun was shining. She prayed for a safe trip downtown and that she would not get lost attempting to locate the attorney's office.

About thirty minutes later, Sally arrived at 662 Hickory Street and saw the attorney's sign board above a door, on it written, *Cut and Dry Law Office*. She parked the car at the curb in front of the office, breathed a sign of relief for her arrival, and asked the Lord to help her know how to do what she was about to do.

As Sally stepped into the office building, a small bell rang above her head. A lady at the desk in front of her looked up.

"Good morning. Are you Sally Oldham? If so, we've been expecting you. Please, come on in. I'm Mary," the lady welcomed her with a smile.

"Hi, Mary. Yes, I am Sally Oldham."

"You can have a seat, and I'll let Mr. Hugh Cut know you are here," Mary said and disappeared around the office wall. A few moments later, she reappeared. "Mr. Cut will be with you in a minute."

Sally nodded as she sat down in the waiting room.

Moments later, a dark-haired, medium-built man appeared from around the wall and approached Sally with his right hand extended.

"Good morning, Mrs. Oldham. I'm Hugh Cut. Welcome."

Sally stood up and shook his hand. "It's nice to meet you, Mr. Cut."

"Oh, please call me Hugh. Is it all right if I call you Sally?"

"Yes, sir. That's all right," Sally confirmed.

"Let's go to my office and talk about your situation, Sally. I understand you're seeking a divorce from your husband." Hugh talked as he led Sally to his office. Upon entering his office, he invited Sally to sit down in the plush chair in front of his large desk.

"Yes, sir. That is correct," Sally answered as she casually glanced around Hugh's office. She was impressed with its décor and found it all very appealing. She felt more comfortable than she had anticipated.

"Sally, whatever you tell me is strictly confidential, and if I feel like I can help you in your quest, I will sincerely do my best to achieve your goal. This consultation session is at no cost to you. Upon our discussion today, you will determine if you want to go forward with my services. Then we can discuss my fee. But first, let's start by you telling me about yourself and your situation. I'll be taking notes if that's OK?" Hugh said, grabbing his notebook and pen from his desk.

"Notetaking is fine with me," Sally said. "I'm not real sure where you want me to begin. . . ."

"I'll start with some basic information. I need your full name, date of birth, address, social security number, your husband's name, his date of birth, when you two got married, and if there are any children."

Sally answered all his questions.

"OK, now that we have that much out of the way, do you think this marriage is reconcilable? Do you think he will change his mind and want to remain married?" Hugh asked.

At this point, Sally opened her purse and pulled out the two notes Collin had written to her. "Collin has very clearly expressed his feelings and desired outcome about us and our marriage in these two written notes he gave me. When he called me the evening of January 2nd to give me his new address and telephone number, he told me again that we were over, and he did not want any custody of his sons."

After the attorney read the notes, Sally noticed his facial expression. "Wow, this dude is more than rude and crude; he is very socially unacceptable. You definitely have grounds for divorce, alimony, and child support. You're right, there is no reasonable expectation of reconciliation from this man. I will need his address and telephone number so I can send him registered mail documents to fill out, get notarized, and send back to me. After I receive the paperwork back from Collin, I can file the paperwork for your divorce with the court. He really left you holding the bag of total responsibility. You have a lot on your shoulders, Sally. I'd be happy to take your case. Once I explain to the judge your petition of complaint for divorce, I wouldn't be the least bit surprised if the judge doesn't throw the book at your husband!" Hugh chucked a little as he looked at Sally. "When Collin gets these documents and sends them back to me, I believe this case will move right along. But please, keep in mind, lots of folks are getting divorced, and the docket can hold just so many cases in a day's time. To get your case on the docket might take a while. I'm talking three to four months. It's one thing we attorneys and clients cannot rush. My fee for your case is five hundred dollars. Do you want to go for it, Sally?" Hugh asked.

"Yes, sir. Let's do it," Sally said with confidence. She gave Hugh Collin's address and telephone number.

"OK then. Let's get into the household finances and see what we have." Hugh was ready to tackle the rest of the business at hand.

Sally laid the box of statements, receipts, and tax returns, and all of Collin's bookkeeping information on Hugh's desk. "It's all in this box."

Hugh opened the lid of the box and began to look through its contents. "Collin sounds like a terrible husband, but he was a man of good recordkeeping! From all of this, I will be able to discern the amount of alimony and child support you should receive," Hugh stated confidently.

"When it's time for the divorce to come to court, will Collin be required to be there too?" Sally asked.

"Not really. Don't worry, Sally. He is not going to contest this divorce. He wants out in the worst way. I'm just sorry that you have had to deal with such a ruthless man. You seem way too nice to be treated the way he has treated you and those two young boys." Hugh straightened up in his seat. "Do you have any other questions?" he asked.

"Yes. When do I pay you?"

"I usually ask for one half of the fee upfront. What can you pay today?"

"I can pay one hundred dollars. I still have some money from what Collin left me, but I don't know when or if I'll get anymore from him. I need to get a job, at least a part-time position, so I can bring in some money. Will one hundred dollars be OK today?" Sally pleaded.

"Yes. That's fine. Thank you, Sally. We'll deal with the rest in time," Hugh responded kindly.

"Thank you so much, Hugh. I truly appreciate your help," Sally replied gratefully.

Hugh came out from around his desk and took Sally's hand as she stood up. "It's nice to meet you, Sally, and again, I'm sorry for all you're going through. But if we can help or more questions come to mind, please call me. I'll be in touch and keep you informed as to what's happening. Everything will be OK, Sally," Hugh reassured her.

"Thank you again, Hugh." Sally turned and walked from his office to Mary's desk where she paid the agreed upon upfront fee. Then she left the office and began driving home. Sally felt so relieved. She thanked the Lord for His strength in getting her through that meeting. She was happy with Hugh as her attorney and believed he would help her through the next very difficult steps.

Sally wasn't very hungry because of her nervous stomach, but she decided to stop by her favorite bar-be-que restaurant for some sandwiches for her and the boys. She also wanted to invite Peggy over so she could tell her the news about her appointment with the attorney.

It was almost two o'clock when Sally arrived home. She placed the sandwiches in the fridge and rested for a moment. She had about forty-five minutes before she needed to get the boys from school, which gave her time to briefly call Peggy. She didn't want to be on the telephone long in case Rusty had a chance to call her. She really wished she would hear from him soon.

Sally dialed Peggy's work telephone number. After the first ring, a voice answered that Sally recognized. "Hi, Peggy! It's Sally."

"Hi, Sally. How are you, my dear? I've been meaning to call you. What's happening?" Peggy asked.

"We're as good as we can be. I've been meaning to call you too. Do you have any plans for supper tonight? I had to go into town this morning, and on the way home, I stopped by our favorite bar-be-que place and picked up some sandwiches. How about you come over, and I'll bring you up to speed on the latest news?" Sally proposed.

"You know how I enjoy those bar-be-ques! Yes, I'd love to join y'all for supper. What time?" Peggy happily accepted Sally's offer.

"You can come right after you get off work, if you want too."

"Perfect. I'll see y'all about 5 p.m. or so."

Sally was happy the conversation went well, and Peggy would be able to join them for supper. She strolled into the kitchen and took one of the sandwiches from the fridge. Her stomach was feeling better, and she was a little hungry. She had eaten a few bites when the telephone rang. She ran to the living room.

"Hello?"

"Hi, honey. I'm glad I reached you. I've called several times. I know you had an appointment with the attorney. How did that go?" Rusty asked.

"Oh, sweetheart, the appointment went good. But first, how are you, and how is your dad? You sound so tired," Sally anxiously asked.

"Well, I'm a wreck. I'm so worried. The doctor is telling Mom and me that Dad is touch and go. Surgery is scheduled in a few hours to repair his heart. Dad is on oxygen and has tubes running everywhere. We really don't know much and understand less. Mom is trying so hard to hold herself together. A few church friends are here with us as well as our preacher. Just a lot of praying going on. We know Dad is in God's hands," Rusty struggled to get his words out.

"I sure wish I were there with you, Rusty. I've been doing a lot of praying too, especially for healing for your dad and strength for your mom and you. I'm glad other folks are there with y'all. That's important," Sally said thoughtfully.

"I wish you were here too!" Rusty paused a moment. "I need to go. I'll call you later when I know more. I love you." Rusty's voice broke.

"Please, call me . . . anytime. Know my arms are around you, holding you tightly. I love you bunches." And the call ended.

Sally's heart was breaking for Rusty and his family. She really wished she were there with them. She folded her hands and bowed her head. *Please, Lord, allow Rusty's dad to survive his surgery. Make the doctor's hands steady, and give the doctor the knowledge he needs to perform a successful surgery. Also, please, Lord, give Rusty and his mom peace, and help them to feel Your presence. Amen.*

It was time for Sally to pick the boys up. As she drove to the school, she continued to pray. Her car was tenth in line for pickup, and many vehicles were pulling in behind her. Soon her boys emerged from the building and ran to the car. The school attendant opened the back door, and the boys slid into the seat, along with a gust of cold air.

"Hi, my sons. Gosh, it is getting colder, and those dark clouds look threating. Could be some bad weather moving in. So how are the both of you? How was school?" Sally inquired as she turned the heat up in the car.

"Hi, Momma! I had a good day, but I have homework. Maybe you could help me with it?" Pace eagerly asked.

"I bet I could help you. How about you, Todd? How was your day?" Sally looked in the car's rearview mirror at Todd. "I see you smiling. What's up, kiddo?"

"Mom, do you remember me telling you about the girl who prays before she eats her lunch?" Todd began.

"Yes, I do. Barbie's her name, right?"

"Yes, her name is Barbie. Well, I sat with her at lunch, and guess what? We prayed together before we ate lunch!" Todd rejoiced.

"I think that is wonderful, Todd!" Sally exclaimed.

"I was nervous, but I asked the Lord to give me the nerve to sit with her. Then she asked me to pray with her. I was so surprised and happy at the same time. She is so sweet, and I really like her! If I get her telephone number, would it be OK with you if I called her sometime?" Todd suddenly sounded like a love-sick boy.

Sally swallowed hard before she could even answer his question. Finally, she said, "You'll have to let me think on that question for a little while. You might be just a wee bit too young to be calling a girl just yet. We'll see." Sally certainly wasn't expecting that question from her eight-year-old son. "By the way, Grandmother Peggy is coming for supper tonight. Pace, we need to start your homework right away so we don't have to do it after she leaves."

"OK, Momma," Pace agreed.

As soon as they arrived home, Todd and Pace put their schoolbooks on the dining room table and started their homework assignments.

"Here's my spelling words, Momma," Pace said as he handed Sally a sheet of paper.

Sally sat down at the table and looked at the list of twenty words. "OK, you ready?"

"Yip!"

"The first one is *earth*."

"E-A-R-T-H," Pace spelled.

"Correct. Very good! OK, *high* is the next word. Like how *high* is the tree?"

"H-I-G-H. Right?" Pace asked.

"Yes. Super!" Sally continued the rest of the spelling word list, and Pace spelled each one of his words correctly. "You should make a *100* on your test tomorrow!" Sally proudly announced. "How are you doing, Todd? Need any help?"

"Nope. I'm almost finished. Mine was circling the correct multiple-choice words for sentences for English," Todd explained.

"That sounds like fun," Sally commented. "Since y'all are about finished with your work, let's clear the table. Your Grandmother Peggy should be here in thirty minutes or so. If y'all want to change from your school clothes to your play clothes, that would be OK. It's getting cooler in the house. Y'all dress warm. What is the temperature outside?" Sally asked.

Todd was still in the dining room, so he looked at the round temperature gauge hanging from a metal brace outside the window. "It's forty degrees, Mom, and the wind is really blowing."

"Thank you, son. At 5 p.m., let's turn the television on to the news and see what this weather is doing," she suggested.

"Is it OK if I turn on the television after I change clothes, Momma?" Pace asked.

"Yes, that's OK," Sally answered as she sat down on the couch to rest before Peggy arrived. The boys ran back into the living room and turned on the television. "Wow! That didn't take long. Are y'all warm enough?"

"Yes, ma'am," both boys answered at the same time.

The telephone rang.

"Hello?" Sally answered.

"It's me, Sally dear," Rusty said. "I won't keep you but a minute. Just wanted you to know Dad has just been taken to surgery. I asked the doctor how long the surgery might be, but he couldn't tell me. Mom and I are going downstairs to the café to get something to eat. Neither one of us are really hungry, but we need to eat something. Are you OK? How did it go with the attorney?"

"As you were talking, I breathed a prayer for your dad . . . and for you and your mom. I can only imagine what y'all are going through. My heart is breaking for y'all. The attorney was very nice, and he assured me that the divorce would be no problem. He will be sending documents to Collin for him to fill out, sign, and return, then he can start the divorce process. He said it could go to court in three to four months," Sally explained.

"Well, three to four months isn't too bad, but I wish it could take place sooner than that. Did he say what his fee would be?" Rusty asked.

"Me too, honey. The sooner the better! His fee is five hundred dollars. Usually he asks for half of the fee to be paid on the front end, but he allowed me to pay just one hundred dollars today. He said he would inform me of any updates along the way," Sally said.

"I'll send you some money, Sally. You have no idea when or if Collin will send you any," Rusty offered generously.

"Listen, Rusty. Please, you just take care of yourself and your family. Don't be concerned about me right now. I'm OK. I still have some money that Collin left for me. You are so kind and sweet, and I appreciate you offering to send me some money, but seriously, I'm OK right now," Sally insisted.

"OK, but we will talk about this in a few days. Mom is standing here waiting for me, so I need to go. I love you, Sally."

Sally hung up the phone.

"Mom, you look sad. Are you OK?" Todd asked as he glanced at his mother.

"I am sad, Todd. A very good friend's father isn't doing very well. He is having an operation right now, and we're praying he will be much better very soon," she explained.

"Momma, look! The weatherman is talking about snow!" Pace exclaimed.

"What!? No way!" Sally rushed into the living room to watch.

"Beware, folks, we are expecting three to five inches of the white stuff by morning, and more snow throughout the day tomorrow. Totals could range up to a foot of snow in most areas before this weather system moves on to the south."

There was a knock on the door. Sally walked over and opened it.

"Hi, Peggy. Come on in here out of the cold! You're just in time to hear the news. A storm is coming, and it's to leave behind a foot of snow by tomorrow night," Sally informed Peggy as she walked in the door.

"What? Oh my goodness. I know it has gotten very cold outside, and the wind is a monster! When is it to start snowing? I need to get home before it starts," Peggy anxiously stated.

"Pace, did you hear when it's supposed to start snowing?" Sally asked.

"No ma'am, I didn't, but he might tell the weather again in a few minutes. I'll keep listening," Pace responded.

Sally hugged Peggy and helped her with her coat. After they walked to the kitchen, Sally took the bar-be-que sandwiches from the refrigerator and placed each one of them on its own plate. Peggy sat the plates on the table and asked the boys what they wanted to drink. While they were getting supper ready, Sally told Peggy about her appointment with the divorce attorney and about Collin's telephone call on Tuesday night. How he had upset the boys by not wanting to talk to them. She told her how Collin said he didn't want custody of them in the divorce either.

Peggy was visually upset by what Sally was saying. "I am so sorry, Sally. I don't know what's wrong with Collin. Thank you for telling me about Collin because he has not bothered to call me. He has just gone off the deep end." Peggy just shook her head.

"Come on, fellows. Time to eat. Grandmother Peggy needs to get home before it starts snowing," Sally announced.

The boys ran to the table, sat in their chairs, and waited for their grandmother to bless their supper.

"Gee, Mom! Bar-be-que sandwiches for supper. How special!" exclaimed Todd.

"Mmm-mmm, good," Pace's said.

Todd and Pace told their grandmother all about their first two days of school, and Todd even told her about Barbie. Sally reminded the boys about their trip to the airport, and they shared with their grandmother about their meeting with Captain Hall.

"Oh, wow! Y'all have had a very exciting start to your New Year. How awesome! I think I'll hang out with y'all more often. Y'all just have so much fun!"

After the table was cleared and the dishes were put away, Peggy picked up her coat. "I have truly enjoyed supper. It was delicious and hit the spot. I do hate to eat and run, but I better get on home. Boys, Grandmother loves y'all, and I really did like you telling me all about your adventures so far this year. I look forward to hearing more. Sally, thank you for our talk. Please keep me in the loop. If you need anything, please call me. By the way, have you talked to Ellen lately?"

"No, I haven't. I've intended to call her but just haven't. I need to call her soon. Thanks for coming over, and be careful going home. Please call me when you get home. If it snows, be careful going to work in the morning," Sally cautioned Peggy.

As Peggy opened the front door, she reassured Sally she would not be going to work in the snow. "Oh my word, it is so cold out here, and it feels like it's spitting snow," Peggy yelled as she ran to her car.

Sally and the boys yelled and waved to Peggy as she drove away.

"Man, it is really cold outside," Sally said as she closed the door. "If it does snow, and especially as much as the weatherman was saying, you two probably won't be going to school tomorrow. We'll have to check in the morning. I could just let y'all sleep in in the morning. How does that sound?" Sally asked with a tinge of excitement.

"That would be OK with me. Does that mean we can stay up a little later tonight?" Todd asked.

"Well, maybe. We'll check the weather again and see what it says." Sally didn't want to commit to staying up later just yet.

Sally pulled a blanket from the hall closet and wrapped it around the three of them as they sat on the couch to watch television. The program they were watching was interrupted by a "Weather Report." The weatherman showed a map of their local area, and there was a lot of *white* on it, indicating snow. He reported that the snow was already falling in parts of the city, and it would continue all night with accumulations up to an inch an hour. He also advised people to stay home and not drive on the slippery roadways.

"Gee, Mom. We could get a lot of snow!" Todd remarked.

"We are going to have so much fun playing in it tomorrow, Todd!" exclaimed Pace.

"Yes, it does sound like a lot is coming. It sure does look like y'all are going to have a snow day tomorrow, and playing in it is going to be at the top of your list!" Sally was excited for them.

Peggy called to report she had made it home OK, but the roads were getting a little icy. Sally was glad she was home safe and sound.

It was nearly nine o'clock, and the telephone rang. Sally hurriedly threw back the blanket and reached for the handset. "Hello?" she answered.

"Hi, honey. I hope I'm not calling too late," Rusty said with a raspy voice.

"No, not at all. You call me anytime, sweetheart. How's your dad?" Sally asked concerningly.

"He's been out of surgery for thirty minutes and is in recovery. We really don't know how he is doing other than the doctor has told us the surgery went well. The surgery took four hours, and the procedure is called a *coronary angioplasty*. I need to read up on what the surgery really means. The doctor explained a little bit about it, but I'd like to know more. All of us are so exhausted, but Mom will not leave. She needs to be near her husband. So we will remain here at the hospital tonight. According to the doctor, Dad will be in intensive care for at least four days. Depending on how he is tomorrow, I need to go home and take care of the cows. One of the church members has been taking care of them today. He is also a dairy farmer. Several other men have stepped forward to say they will help me over the next several days and weeks. Baby, I'm so tired. I'm going to see if I can lay down somewhere and get some sleep. I love you, and I miss you, Sally. I don't know when I'll get to see you again. Please take good care of yourself and those little boys. I will worry about all of you." Rusty's voice was so weary.

"Oh, my darlin'. My heart is breaking for you and your mom. I wish I could help. I'm so thankful the surgery went well. My prayers have been answered. I don't know much either about that kind of surgery. I'd like to know more also. I'm happy there are other men who are helping you with the farm work. Yes, it could be a while before we will see each other again, but sweetheart, I'm not going anywhere, and I definitely understand the position you are in now. You've got to take care of business and be there for your family. I will continue to pray for all of you. Please, try to get some rest and sleep. You've got to stay well and healthy. I look forward to talking to you when you are able to call me the next time. According to the weatherman, we are about to get lots of snow. So I'm staying right here. I miss you, my love. I love you bunches and bunches, with all of my heart. My arms are around you and hugging you tightly, Rusty. You sleep well. I will see you in my dreams." Sally blew him a long kiss before hanging up the handset. Under her breath, she prayed, *Lord, please allow Rusty to get some sleep.*

Seeing tears in his mother's eyes, Pace asked, "Momma, are you OK?"

Sally took him in her arms and kissed his forehead. "Yes, I'm just very concerned about someone I care about very deeply. I'd like to help him and his family, but I can't. He lives too far away." Looking at him, she said, "I love you, my little son. Thank you for caring," and she hugged him.

A chill had taken over the house, and they all snuggled back under the blanket once more. As the night grew later and later, they began to yawn and rub their sleepy eyes. It was time for bed, but they all wanted to take a look out the living room window to see if any snow had fallen. They were tickled to see that almost everything was covered by a white blanket. Oh, how beautiful it looked!

Chapter Thirteen

S on, your dad's awake." Rusty's mother, Mandy, softly spoke into his ear as he slept on the couch in the ICU waiting room at the Danbury Memorial Hospital. "Rusty, can you hear me? Your dad is alive and awake!" Mandy spoke a little louder.

"Mom, is that you?" Rusty struggled to open his sleepy eyes. "Did you say Dad was awake? God allowed him to make it through the night? Hallelujah and praise the Lord!" He rejoiced at his mother's words and sat up on the edge of the couch.

"Yes, son. Our prayers were heard and answered. Your dad's been awake for several hours, but since the nurses have been tending to his needs, I decided to let you sleep a little longer. You needed your rest. At 7 a.m., the nurses left his room, and it was time to let you know that your dad is much better."

Rusty slipped on his shoes and stood up. "Come on, Mom! I want to see him!" Rusty took his mother's arm, and they walked together to his dad's room.

Upon hearing the sliding hospital door open, Russell looked toward the sound.

"Hi, Dad! How are you feeling?" Rusty excitedly asked.

"Hi, son. I feel like I've been hit by a big rig. But other than that, I feel pretty good." Russell laughed.

Rusty walked over to the side of his dad's bed and took his hand. "You gave us one heck of a bad scare. But praise God, you are still with us. Lots of prayers answered, Dad." Rusty's eyes teared up.

"Hey, it's OK. The Good Lord still has a reason for me to be here." Russell tightened his hold on his son's hand. "I see a pretty lady behind you. Come on over here by me, sweetheart."

Mandy walked to the other side of the hospital bed and carefully took her husband's hand, which had an IV line stuck in the top.

"Russell, dear, we are so thankful for the immediate care that was given to you when the ambulance arrived here. The Lord had Dr. Harrison on call at the hospital and his team right where He wanted them to be able to give you the medical attention you needed. You are very blessed because this part of your journey could have been so different," Mandy said teary-eyed as she bent down and kissed him.

A nurse came into the room to take Russell's vitals. "Blood pressure is good, temp is normal, and your heart is sounding very good," she informed them.

"So when do I get to eat? I'm hungry!" Russell exclaimed.

"Dr. Harrison is in the process of making his rounds. He should be in soon, and he can better answer your questions, Mr. Summers," the nurse replied as she left the room.

"After we talk to the doctor, and if all is good, I'm heading to the farm to take care of the cows. Or as you refer to them, Dad, your 'ladies.'" He chuckled. "I sure do appreciate Allen and Tom stepping in to care for them yesterday. That was a huge help for us."

"Yes, those two men are outstanding people. Great friends," Russell replied.

The sliding door opened, and Dr. Harrison entered the room. All eyes were focused on him. "Good morning, Russell and family," he greeted as he walked toward Russell. He unwrapped the stethoscope from around his neck and inserted the earpieces into his ears. He bent down to listen to Russell's heart. After listening for a few moments, he stood up straight, removed the earpieces, and remarked, "Your heart is sounding very good and strong. It was a rough surgery, Russell, and we lost you twice, but our Lord allowed you to see another day. The new technology of coronary angioplasty we doctors have today does help save lives, and you are living proof! Now, what I'm about to tell you does not paint as pretty a picture as I wish I could make it. You will remain in this Intensive Care Unit for at least another two days. You will be on a soft food diet for today. We'll see how your digestive tract handles the food. If all works well, then regular food can be ordered tomorrow. The nurses will begin moving you today and will have you sit in a chair and do a little bit of walking. Once you are moved to a regular room, you will be doing some rehab along with more walking and sitting in a chair each day for five days. This will build up your strength and get you ready to go home." The doctor paused for a moment as he looked at Russell. "Now that's the easy part. I know you are a very active man and a dairy farmer, but for the next six to eight weeks, you must not do any physical work. I realize this is hard to hear, but you maintaining an easy day-by-day activity routine will sustain your life. We fixed your heart, but it will never be like your God-given heart was. You will need lots of rest because you will tire easily and quickly at first. Your strength will gradually come back to you, but it could take a year for full recovery. I'm going to prescribe a heart medication that you'll take once a day. Your diet will change, but not too drastically." He looked over at Mandy. "I'll give you a list of foods he should and should not eat. Try to get him to stick to it. Coffee tomorrow, but none today. Any questions?"

"You covered a lot of information, Dr. Harrison." Mandy's facial expressions indicated she was slightly overwhelmed. "I don't know the questions to ask right now, but as time goes on, I'm sure I will have some. Rusty, do you have any questions?" his mother asked him.

"Yes, I do. As you know, I make my living as a truck driver. I will be taking care of the farm while my dad recuperates, but I need to give my boss a time frame for how long I'll be off work," Rusty asked in a concerned voice.

"With some rehab and proper care of himself, I'd estimate at least six months. Your dad is fifty-five years old and is a healthy man. The time could be a little less, but with the heavy machinery that dairy farmers use and the exhausting endless chores that have to be performed each and every day, it could take him every bit of six months to partially manage the work. You know, Rusty, as a member of your church family, I know your dad better than most people. He and I have worked together on many church projects. He is a strong-willed and conscientious man. When he sets his mind on doing something, no matter how difficult the project is, he's the one that finishes what he starts. Now, Russell, you're hearing me, and I pray you prove me wrong, but people, men and women, who have heart problems like heart surgery, statistically show a declining rate of life's normal activities. It's like their *get-up has got up and gone!* I'm shooting you straight, Russell. I don't mean to discourage you, but life changes. I'll be back later and check on you." Dr. Harrison turned and left the room.

Rusty followed him and closed the sliding door behind him. "Dr. Harrison, may I have another minute of your time, please?"

Dr. Harrison stopped and turned around. "Yes, of course."

"I'm trying to absorb all you just told us. Like you said, you know my dad very well. Do you really think my dad fits your statistics? If so, and it's true he won't really be up to running the farm, then my family may need to sit down and talk about changes for our futures. I can help my dad—I don't have a problem with that—but I don't see myself taking care of milk cows for the rest of my life. I've witnessed the struggles my mom and dad have gone through and the sacrifices they have made day after day for their farm that has left them no time to enjoy life. I really don't want that life for me," Rusty explained.

Dr. Harrison listened intently to Rusty's words and understood his dilemma, then he offered his advice. "Rusty, your mom and dad have operated under *old school* rules and reasoning for their entire lives. Your parents really would not have changed anything about the way they have lived. As you know, your dad took over the farm where your grandfather left off when he passed away, and your mom married into the business. She was familiar with the hardships since she came from her parents' farming business. She loved it and wanted to continue that life when she married your dad. The love they have had for each other all these years has carried them through the good times and bad times. They wouldn't have had it any other way. You're a different generation with different ideas and different ways of thinking. Your dad wants to leave you the farm, but you may not be interested in taking that path for your life. Let me add this, maybe just give your dad some time and see what happens. I pray he will surprise all of us and prove those statistics wrong! Then life can return to normal for everyone." Dr. Harrison extended his right hand to Rusty.

Rusty reentered his dad's room.

"Is everything OK, dear?" his mother asked.

"Yes, just asking a few more questions. Mom, will you be OK with Dad? I need to go to the farm and take care of business," Rusty told her.

"Sure, son, I'll be fine. Oh look, Russell. Here comes some breakfast!" Mandy announced. "You go ahead. I know you have work to do."

"OK. I'll be back later. Bye, Dad. Enjoy your breakfast. Mom, be sure and get you something to eat too." Rusty squeezed his dad's hand and kissed his mom's cheek, then walked toward the door, closing it behind him as he walked out.

So much was going through Rusty's mind as he left the hospital and drove his dad's pickup truck sixteen miles to the farm. He prayed God would show him how to handle the responsibilities of the farm and help him cope with the thought of dealing with the cows. His real desire was to get in his big rig and hit the road, but most of all, he wanted to be with Sally. Thinking of not being able to see her was heartbreaking for him. If only she and the boys could be with him *now*. That would be a great help, but he knew she could not make that move yet. There was too much going on with her in her life.

Instead of turning off the highway to go to his folks' farm, Rusty decided to go to his home first. As he drove up the road and parked the truck, his two German shepherds came around the corner of the house. They were glad to see him, their tails wagging and literally jumping for joy. He immediately let them into the kitchen and fed them. Then he wasted not another moment and called his Sally.

Sally was in no hurry to get up, and she didn't mind sleeping in a little while longer. Since the boys would not be going to school, why be in a rush? She sat up on the edge of her bed. Out of habit, she looked at the clock by the bed: 7:30. She bowed her head and prayed for Rusty, his dad, and his mom, and thanked the Lord for giving her another day. Her feet found her slippers, and she stood up. A chill surrounded her, and she quickly wrapped up in her robe. She stepped into the hallway and checked the floor furnace. Yes, it was on, but she raised the thermostat lever up a few degrees to get the house a little warmer before the boys woke up. She glanced in the boys' room as she was on her way to the kitchen. They were still sleeping.

From the kitchen door window, she saw nothing but *white*—and the snow was still falling. *Maybe six inches or more*, she thought. She turned to the sink and filled the coffee pot with water, then poured the grounds into the coffee basket and plugged the cord into the wall socket. Within a few moments, the coffee was brewing. She was taking her coffee cup from the cabinet when the telephone rang. She ran to the living room and answered the call.

"Hello?"

"Good morning, honey. This is your *missing you lover*! How are you? Are you missing me too?" Rusty said, trying to sweet talk Sally.

"Good morning, handsome! Yes, I am missing you too! How are you? How is your dad?"

"I'm OK, just very overwhelmed. Dad is awake and seems to be much better. The doctor was in to see him before I left the hospital, and he shared with us that the surgery was rough, and Dad's heart stopped twice," Rusty explained.

"Oh, how scary! But prayers were answered, and he is on the mending road. Did the doctor say when he could go home?" Sally asked.

"Maybe in a week. A few more days in ICU, then he'll be moved to a regular room for several days. He'll be doing some rehab, plus walking and sitting in a chair. The doctor needs him to be strong enough to be able come home," Rusty answered.

"That sounds good. I know he will be glad to get home. It'll probably be a while before he'll be healthy enough to run the farm again. Did the doctor say when that might be?"

"Six months. I don't like it, Sally, but I have no choice. According to the doctor, Dad won't be healed enough to take on the grueling responsibilities of taking care of the farm for a long time. I miss you so much, and the thought of not seeing you for that long is driving me crazy! I sure wish you and the boys were here." Rusty was so dismayed.

Sally fell silent. She was not expecting that their absence from one another would be so long, but she had to say something encouraging. "It's OK, sweetheart. I miss you very much, but I understand. You must do what you've got to do. Your mom and dad need you more than ever now. It would be wonderful if the boys and I were there. We could help you too, but it's impossible for me to leave right now. I've got to see this divorce through and get it behind me so you and I can start our lives together. So please know I love you, and even though there's a few miles between us, we're going to be OK. You hear me, Mr. Rusty Summers?" Sally stressed to him.

"Yes, I do hear you, Sally. I do love you so, and I love that you understand. I've heard long-distance relationships make the heart grow fonder and stronger. I believe our love will carry us through this situation." Rusty was grateful.

"Oh, I hear my little fellows. They're just now waking up. Snow is falling, and they are out of school today. I'm sure that after breakfast it will be time to go make a snowman!" Sally said.

"They will have a lot of fun. You all be careful. I'll be at the farm most of the day. I'll call you again before I go back to the hospital. I love you, babe, and thank you for understanding. That means so much to me." Rusty threw his kiss to her.

Sally threw her kiss back. Then she sat on the couch for a moment, thanking God for allowing Rusty's dad to pull through the surgery. She also asked God to be with Rusty as he tends to the farm.

The boys were giggling down the hall, so Sally walked into their room to see what the fuss was all about. They were thrilled about all the snow that had fallen as they stood gazing out their bedroom window.

"Look at all the snow, Mom!" Todd exclaimed.

"Momma, I want us to go make a snowman! With all this snow, we could make a bunch; we could make a *snow family!*" Pace said joyfully.

"A snow family would be fun to make!" Sally said. "But first, I need to make us some breakfast. What would y'all like to eat?"

The boys glanced at each other. Pace leaned over to Todd and whispered in his ear. Todd smiled as he looked back at his little brother and nodded his head. "We would like sausage, egg, and cheese biscuits, please, Momma," Pace responded.

"All right! Sausage, egg, and cheese biscuits coming up! Excellent choice, fellows," their mother replied cheerfully as she walked toward the kitchen.

Within twenty minutes, Sally had their meal prepared and sitting on the dining room table. Todd and Pace had helped her get their milk, and Sally poured another cup of coffee to enjoy with her breakfast.

After she sat down in her chair, she remembered the jam. "I'll be right back, boys. I forgot something," Sally said as she hurried to the fridge. "Y'all might want some jam for your biscuits. OK, are y'all ready to pray?" she asked.

Both boys answered, "Yes," at the same time. They joined hands, bowed their heads, and prayed: "God is great, God is good, let us thank Him for our food. Amen."

"Mmm, that was good, Momma. Thank you," Pace said as he rubbed his tummy.

"Yes, it was very good. I'll help you clear the table, Mom. Then can we get dressed and go outside?" Todd asked.

"Thank you for helping me. Yes, I'll help y'all get dressed after the two of you brush your teeth."

The boys hurried along, and Sally dressed them with clothes that would keep them warm, at least for a little while.

"Hurry, Mom! Get dressed!" Todd urged.

"OK, I will. I don't want y'all to get too warm waiting for me. Go ahead and go in the backyard, and I'll be there in a few minutes," she said.

"Come on, Pace. Let's go play in the snow!" Todd excitedly shouted, and they both ran to the back door. The wind blew snow into the kitchen as it had fallen over the top of the step out the back door.

"Please be careful," Sally cautioned them as she watched them trudge through the deep snow halfway covering their little legs. "I'll be out soon!" she said as she quickly closed the door.

Sally hurried into her bedroom, found the warmest clothes she could find, and got dressed. Then she went to the coat closet and put on her winter coat along with her wool scarf and gloves. She slipped on her winter boots. *I think I'm ready*, she said to herself as she walked to the kitchen, opened the back door, and felt the chill of the north wind on her exposed face.

"OK, boys. Are y'all ready to build our snowman family?" she asked.

"Yes, ma'am!" both boys shouted.

"OK. First we need to form a snowball and then add more and more snow to make the ball bigger and bigger," Sally instructed.

The three of them picked up a handful of snow and each began making a snowball. Once the balls got too big for them to handle, they sat them down on the snowy ground and added more and more snow. They continued packing the snow for the middle section of their snowmen. They were already getting cold, but they worked on. Finally, the head sections were placed on top of the second section. They found some fallen twigs they could use as arms for their snowmen, and they found a can of collected rocks sitting beside the house that they could choose from for the snowmen's eyes. Todd broke another twig in pieces and formed mouths for the snowmen. By this time, all three of them were shivering from the cold, and they were ready to go inside. From the deck, they turned to look at their creations, and they all agreed their snowman family looked pretty good!

Sally opened the back door, and they all stepped into the kitchen. They were covered from head to toe with caked-on snow. She asked the boys to undress there so as not to track the snow any further into the house. She then hurried to the bathroom and began to run water in the bathtub to warm the boys up. Soon the boys were splashing around in the warm water, and the chill they felt earlier was all gone.

While the boys had fun in the bathtub, Sally mopped the kitchen floor to clean up all the melting snow. She glanced out the back door window and smiled. The snowmen were really cute, and she had a lot of fun building them with her boys. *I need to take a picture,* she thought. She found the camera in the coat closet on the shelf and carried it with her to the back door. She quickly stepped out on the back deck and aimed the camera at the snowmen. "Gotcha, snowmen! Now we'll have y'all forever," she exclaimed as she stepped back into the kitchen.

Pace was standing at the kitchen door with his bath towel wrapped around his shoulders, watching her. "Whatcha doin', Momma?"

"The thought occurred to me to take a picture of our snowmen so we would always have it to look at and remember the fun we had," Sally answered.

"That's a great idea! I'm glad you did that, Momma," Pace said.

"You're glad Mom did what, Pace?" Todd had overheard the last part of the conversation.

"Momma took a picture of our snowmen with her camera so we would always know what they looked like," Pace told him.

"Wow! Yes, that was a great idea because they will melt, and they will be gone. Thank you, Mom!" Todd was glad his mom had thought about that.

"Y'all need to get dressed with some warm clothes. It is still cool in the house," their mother advised. Sally thought she ought to do the same, so she walked to her bedroom and dressed in a sweatshirt and a pair of heavy-weight jeans along with a pair of knee-high socks. As she passed by the boys' bedroom, she peeked her head in to check on them. "Y'all doin' OK?"

"We are," they answered.

"I need to make a telephone call, boys. Will y'all stay in your room for a few minutes, please, while I make this call?" Sally asked.

"OK," Todd responded.

Sally took the personal telephone book from the cabinet drawer and found Mr. Waddell's number. She sat down on the couch, breathed a quick prayer asking the Lord to help her with this conversation about the house rent and Collin's moving out, then dialed his number.

"Hello?" a man's voice answered.

"Is this Mr. Waddell?" Sally asked.

"Yes, it is," he replied.

"Hi. This is Sally Oldham. How are you today?"

"Hi, Sally. I'm doing good, except for all this snow! How are you?" Mr. Waddell asked.

"Well, sir, I have been better. I need to let you know that Collin has left, and he has moved to Houston, Texas. He told me he was not coming back and that he wanted both of us to start new lives," Sally explained.

"Oh, Sally. I am so sorry to hear that. Y'all seemed like a forever couple. How can I help?" Mr. Waddell sympathized.

"Thank you for saying that, Mr. Waddell. I thought so too, but not anymore. I appreciate your thoughtfulness to help, but the boys and I are OK for now. Collin did leave some money for me to continue to supply for our needs. I was planning on purchasing a money order and sending you the house rent payment this morning, but unfortunately, the snow has stopped me from getting out and going to the post office. Tomorrow might be a better day, but I can definitely get it to you next week. I'm sorry for the delay. Collin always took care of the household finances, and I'm still trying to figure out what to do," Sally expressed.

"Sally, you take all the time you need. I definitely understand, and again, I'm just so sorry Collin has left you and your sons in this dilemma. Do you have any plans for you and the boys?" He sounded concerned for them . . . or was he more concerned about his investment? Sally wondered.

Sally paused before she answered, wondering what to say. Should she tell him everything or just a little? "Mr. Waddell, I truly wish I knew. I've prayed about our situation, and I know God is in control. It's just one day at a time right now."

"You are in a tough spot, but yes, God is in control, and He will see you through this situation," Mr. Waddell reassured her. "Just remember, if there is anything I can do, please call me, Sally." Mr. Waddell ended the call.

Sally took a deep breath. She was glad that conversation was behind her. She thought it went well and thanked God that Mr. Waddell understood . . . or at least he sounded like he was OK with her situation.

"OK, fellas, I'm off the telephone if y'all want to watch television. I do need to call Grandmother Peggy and make sure she is OK," Sally said to Todd and Pace.

"OK, Mom. We will later. Pace and I are playing a game right now," Todd responded.

"Y'all have fun," she replied. Then she called Peggy.

"Hello?" Peggy answered.

"Hi, Peggy. It's Sally. Just callin' to check on you. Are you OK?"

"Hi, Sally. Yes, I'm OK. Can you believe all this snow?"

"I know. It's a lot! The boys and I were out in the backyard earlier, and we made a snowman family. We had fun, and the snow people look great! I took a picture of them so we could always remember making them," Sally told Peggy.

"With all the snow, y'all had plenty to make many snowmen," Peggy laughed. "I'm glad you took a picture. Y'all made memories this morning. I listened to the weather report a little while ago, and the temperature is supposed to start rising this afternoon and start melting the snow, but it's going to take a while for it to be gone. I just hope the roads will be OK for us to go to church Sunday morning. The snow removal equipment is out in full force, clearing the streets. Are y'all still planning on attending church with me?" Peggy asked.

"Yes, if that's still OK, and if the streets are drivable," Sally answered.

"Yes, most definitely! I do want you and the boys to go. I'll keep an eye on the travel conditions and let you know if church will be having Sunday service," Peggy said. "By the way, have you heard from Collin?"

"No, not since Tuesday when he called to let me know he was in Houston. Just to keep you in the loop, I did keep the appointment yesterday, and I saw the divorce attorney. I didn't tell you yesterday what all the attorney told me, but he is sending Collin paperwork, and as soon as the attorney receives the papers back from Collin, he will file it with the court. He said it could take three to four months before the petition would come before the judge," Sally explained.

"Well, Sally, I hate that it has come to that, but I do understand that you need to do what you need to do. I have not heard from Collin either. Are you still doing OK financially?" Peggy asked.

"I'm still OK with the money Collin left me, but a few bills are due. I'm budgeting the best I can. Thank you for asking. Collin said he would send more money after he gets his first paycheck, but that won't be until the middle of the month. I think next week I'll start looking at the classified ads for employment. I need to know I have some money coming in. I know God has a plan," Sally confided in Peggy.

"Yes, God is always with us, and He will help you find your way. I do hope Collin will send you money when he gets paid. I'll do some checking on the employment opportunities for you too," Peggy said.

"Thank you, Peggy. I would appreciate that very much. We'll talk tomorrow about the weather and church. You have a good day, and stay warm," Sally encouraged.

"Yes, y'all too. Talk tomorrow." Peggy ended the call.

Sally left the living room and entered the boys' room. "Y'all having fun? What are y'all playing?" she asked.

"We're playing Mr. Stud Head," Pace answered.

"After I do some Bible reading, would y'all like to play cards or another game?" she suggested.

"That's sounds good, Mom," Todd responded.

"OK. I won't be too long," Sally said as she walked from their room into her bedroom where she picked up her mother's Bible from the nightstand and sat down on the edge of her bed. She bowed her head, closed her eyes, and prayed the Lord would allow her to understand His words from the book of John. She opened her eyes and opened the Bible to the bookmarked page. She began reading chapter 5. Jesus was in Jerusalem when He moved through a sheep market. A lot of hurting people were waiting near a pool where healing took place when the water was stirred. Jesus noticed a lame man close to the pool, but he never could get into the pool because other people moved quicker than he could. Jesus, knowing all about the man, told him to "Rise, take up your bed, and walk," and immediately the man was made whole and was healed. But because this event happened on the Sabbath, the Jews were not happy, so they rebuked Jesus. His words back to them were that He was doing the work of His Father. In chapter 6, Jesus fed the great multitude of five thousand with only five barley loaves and two small fishes that a young lad had with him. Jesus gave thanks for the food. After everyone had their fill, Jesus asked His disciples to gather the fragments that remained, and they gathered twelve baskets full of food fragments. His disciples were amazed by that miracle.

Sally was beginning to understand and believe more that Jesus is "the Son of God." The book of John had opened her mind to wonderful insights she never knew. Her prayer for knowledge and understanding was being graciously answered.

Suddenly, Sally sensed four little eyes peering around the corner of her bedroom door. "I see you two. Are y'all ready to play some games?" she asked them.

"Yes, ma'am!" both boys answered at the same time.

"OK, let's go play." She closed the Bible carefully, placed it back on the nightstand, and joined her sons at the doorway of her room. The three of them walked to the dining room table where the boys had already set several board game boxes and playing cards along with pencil and paper.

"Look at y'all. Everything is ready! Do y'all want a snack while we play, or do we want to do lunch first? If it's lunch, what about hot dogs and chili?" she suggested.

"Yeah, hot dogs and chili sounds good!" shouted the boys.

"OK. I'll prepare the dogs and chili, if y'all want to get the drinks and chips," Sally prompted.

"Sure thing, Mom," Todd agreed.

Within fifteen minutes, lunch was ready and on the table. They prayed and enjoyed their lunch. It wasn't much to clear the table, and then it was game time. First, they played a board game with dice, and each at their turn moved their token around the board. Todd rejoiced at his win! Pace chose for them to play cards next. They took turns dealing the cards to each other, discarding the unwanted cards from their hands. Pace surprised himself by winning not once but three times. Each win deserved a clap of their hands!

Sally then decided they would play a game they hadn't played in a long time. She took the paper and pencil and drew dashed lines that would eventually have letters to spell a very simple word (or words). Todd and Pace took turns guessing a letter from the alphabet. When they guessed a letter that was in the word, Sally would write it on the dashed line, but if the letter was not in the word, a body part of a "stick man" was drawn next to the word. The game ended with all the letters filled in to make the mystery word, or all of the stick man's body was completely drawn. They played that game for an hour, and all three of them won three times.

"That game is so much fun. I hope we can play it again soon," Todd remarked.

"I liked it too, Momma. Maybe we can play it again tomorrow!" Pace suggested.

"I believe we might be able to arrange that," Sally said, giving a thumbs-up. "It's getting close to suppertime. What are y'all hungry for?"

"Ah, gee, Mom, I don't know. Pace, what do you think?" Todd asked his brother.

"I don't know either. Surprise us, Momma!" Pace exclaimed.

"Well, OK. I'll think on it, fellas." Sally scratched her head and walked into the kitchen.

"Is it OK if we turn on the television?" Todd asked.

"Sure," Sally replied as she opened the fridge and surveyed the prospects for their meal. She saw a hunk of ham and some ears of corn. She turned and opened the pantry door, spotting the sweet potatoes on the floor and the cornbread bag on the shelf. All that sounded pretty good to her. It took a while to prepare the meal, but in an hour, Sally sat their supper on the dining room table.

"Supper's ready. What do y'all want to drink?" Sally asked the boys.

"I'll get some milk. Pace, you want milk too?" Todd asked.

"Yes. I'll help." Pace jumped up from sitting on the living room rug and ran to the kitchen to help.

"Supper sure does look good, Mom," Todd expressed as he and Pace sat down in their chairs.

"Well, I sure hope it tastes good too. Let's thank the Lord for our supper." They bowed their heads and prayed their blessing over the food.

After only a few bites, Pace looked at his momma and said, "Thank you for this delicious food. You did good choosing the best things to fix."

"Yeah, Mom. It's a really good supper," Todd agreed with Pace.

"Thank you, kiddos. That's very sweet of y'all to say that." Sally was grateful for their thoughtfulness.

After supper and all was cleaned in the kitchen, all three of them looked out the back door window at their snowmen. They were still standing and looking . . . *cold!* The snow was no longer falling, and the sun was setting. They sat and rested on the couch in the living room and watched television.

Near seven o'clock, the telephone rang. Sally answered.

"Hello?"

"Hi, sweetheart. How are you?" Rusty sounded so tired.

"Oh, my dear. I'm fine, but you sound exhausted. How was the rest of your day?" Sally asked.

"Yes, I am tired, but I wanted to call you before I go back to the hospital to visit with Dad for a little while. The day was long, but Dad's workers and I got the job done for another day. I forgot how much work there was to keep up with the cows and all that goes along with them. There's not only the process of milking them twice a day, but there's the cleaning up after them in the parlor and in their stalls, making sure they have the right mixture of food they need to eat, keeping the necessary records . . . plus, there were two calves born today! I'm just glad Dad doesn't have more cows than he does. I don't see how bigger farms with more cows get all the work done. More space is needed as well as many more workers who know what they are hired to do. I'm thankful Dad has six good hands who know how to do their jobs. How's the day been for you and the boys?"

"After breakfast, the boys and I made three snowmen. We had so much fun! After lunch, we played games for a few hours, then had supper. We're just relaxing now. The snow has stopped falling, but we probably got about eight or more inches of the white fluffy stuff! It's so pretty! How is your weather?" Sally asked.

"Oh, it does sound like y'all had a super good day. It's cold here, but no snow, and we don't need any either. I sure do miss you, honey. My thoughts of you through my day today kept me going. I sure wish I could see you. The horrible part about this is I just don't know when I'll be able to be with you again. I love you so much, Sally," Rusty lovingly expressed.

"Rusty, my love, I love you, and I long to see you too. I wish we knew how much longer it might be before I can hold you in my arms again, but I keep telling myself to be patient. We will be together again when it's time. I'm just so thankful your dad is doing better. Please be very careful going back to the hospital tonight and coming back home. Call me in the morning. I'll be looking forward to talking to you. And tell your mom and dad *hi* for me. I have all of you in my prayers. I love you, sweetheart. Sweet dreams," Sally told him.

"I will, and you sleep good too. Talk to you in the morning. I love you, babe." Rusty blew her his kiss.

Sally blew him her kiss. Then there was a click, and Rusty was gone. For a few moments, Sally felt all alone, yet she knew she had Rusty's love. She sure did miss him.

When she turned from hanging up the handset, she found the boys sound asleep—Todd on the couch, and Pace on the rug. It had been a busy day, and they played hard outside in the snow. She helped Pace to his bed, tucked him in, and kissed his cheek. She returned to the living room and covered Todd up with a blanket and kissed his cheek. Then it was off to bed for Sally.

Sally, Todd, and Pace woke up to a very sunny morning, with the sun reflecting off the snow. It was hard on their eyes as they looked out the windows.

"Wow, Mom, I don't ever remember it being so light outside!" Todd exclaimed. "And the snow is melting, but our snowmen are still standing," he added as he stared out the back door window.

"With the snow melting that means the temperature is above freezing, which is a good thing. The snow needs to melt off the streets. I need to go to the store later today. Also, we want to go to church tomorrow with Grandmother Peggy!" Sally said to the boys.

"Oh, that's right, Momma! I want to go to church," Pace excitedly remarked.

"I need to call your grandmother and ask her what time we need to be at the church. But first we have some things to do. What do y'all want for breakfast?" she asked.

"Is it too much trouble to fix French toast?" Todd asked.

"Yeah, that sounds really good. Momma, can we?" Pace agreed with his brother's suggestion.

"Absolutely, kiddos! French toast, coming up," Sally responded as she headed for the kitchen.

It was Saturday, so cartoons were on television. Todd and Pace sat on the living room rug and watched the animated characters, giggling as they watched.

As Sally prepared their breakfast, she prayed for Rusty. She missed him so much and wondered what would be next for them. Would their relationship slip away from them as time went on? The saying, *Absence makes the heart grow fonder*—does it really? She sure prayed it would. She knew Rusty loved her, but being separated for what might be six months was a long time. She prayed Russell would recover from his surgery much faster than six months. By then, her divorce could be final, and hopefully Rusty's plans for them to live with him would come true. She knew it was a possibility that Collin might not send her any more money, and she really did not want Rusty to feel obligated to support her. Sally prayed for the Lord to open the door of opportunity for her to find a job and, perhaps pushing the envelope, a job that would work around school hours. There was just so much to pray for and so much uncertainty.

Sally's train of thought was interrupted when Todd came into the kitchen and asked, "How's breakfast coming along? Can I help, Mom?"

She snapped out of her deep thoughts and prayers and answered, "It's almost ready, and yes, you can get your milk and Pace's too. Thank you for helping me," she politely replied.

"Hey, Momma, can I help too?" Pace asked as he entered the kitchen.

"Well, let me see. You want to get the syrup and the butter? Maybe also get three forks and three knives. Oh yeah, maybe a few napkins?"

"Yes, ma'am, I'll get them," Pace said.

Sally took three plates from the cabinet and put the French toast on them along with the sausage patties. Todd and Pace carried their plates to the dining room table, and Sally followed them with her plate and cup of coffee.

"Would y'all like some orange juice to go with your meal?" Sally asked.

"Yes, ma'am," they both answered.

Sally walked back to the kitchen. She took three small juice glasses from the cabinet, took the juice container from the fridge, and poured it into the glasses. "Here ya go. I think that is it," she said as she sat down in her chair. "Let's say grace." They joined their hands and prayed. As they began eating, Sally reminded the boys of something they were going to do a few days earlier and they forgot to do—move Todd's top bunk down to the floor. "Do you still want to do that, Todd?" she asked him.

"Yes, I sure do! I can't believe I forgot about that. Thanks for remembering, Mom." Todd was happy.

"OK, after I get the kitchen cleaned up, we'll do that. We need to rearrange a few things before we take the bed down so we can just set it right where you want it," Sally suggested.

Breakfast was over, and the kitchen was cleaned up. Sally and the boys walked into the boys' bedroom and began moving a few pieces of furniture around to make room for the upper bunk to be put where Todd wanted it. They stripped the bed of its linens, removed the mattress with a bit of a struggle, and moved the headboard, footboard, and rails down onto the floor.

"Gosh, there's a lot to doing this, but hey, we did it!" Sally exclaimed. "I think we should rest a minute. We've been working hard!"

"It might not have been so hard if Daddy had been here to help us," Pace sadly said.

His remark and sudden sadness surprised Sally. She quickly thought, *Say something encouraging!* She said, "Well, I know, Pace, but aren't we a *team*? I think we are, and we're a really *good* team. We worked hard, and we got the job done!"

"That's right, Pace. We are a team!" Todd agreed, trying to cheer up his brother.

"You're right. We *are* a team!" Pace shouted happily.

To keep the happiness going, Sally suggested, "To celebrate our good work, how about some hot chocolate and cookies?"

"All right! Sounds great!" Todd clapped his hands and ran toward the kitchen. Again, the three of them worked together to prepare the treat and rescue Pace from his sadness.

As they were enjoying their hot chocolate and cookies, the telephone rang. Sally walked to the living room and answered.

"Hello?"

"Hi, darling. Are you busy?" Rusty's voice was sweet music to Sally's ears.

She sat down on the couch. "Oh, honey, it's so good to hear your voice. I miss you! The boys and I were just taking a break from disassembling Todd's top bunk and setting it up on the floor," Sally explained.

"Oh my. That must have been a job. I wish I could have been there to help you and the boys. Is it still snowing there?" Rusty asked.

"You are so sweet. Thank you. I wish you could be here too, baby. No more snow, and it's warmer today, so the snow is beginning to melt. We're hoping the streets are clear enough so we can go to church with Peggy tomorrow. How are you? How is Russell?" Sally inquired.

"Hopefully the streets will be drivable, and you three will be able to attend church. I know you want to go. Just please, be careful. I'm tired but OK. I was up at four o'clock this morning so I could be up at the barn at 4:30 a.m. to start my day with the cows. I came home for lunch and wanted to call you before I head back up to the barn. Dad was feeling good last night, and when I talked to Mom this morning, she said the doctor will move him to a regular room today," Rusty informed her.

"That's great! That's got to mean he is doing good. I'm happy for you and your mom. How is she doing? You know, in all the months we have been together, you've not mentioned your mother's name, and I haven't asked," Sally said.

"I thought I had, I'm sorry. My mother's name is Mandy. Come to think about it, you've not told me your mom and dad's name either. I guess because they've passed away, we never discussed their names," Rusty said.

"*Mandy.* That's a pretty name. My mother's name is Lois, and my dad's name is Matthew Sr. My brother is a Jr., and his wife's name is Jodie," Sally answered.

"You have talked about your brother and sister-in-law, but I didn't know their names either. I need to know more—no, I need to know all about you and your family. One of these days, and I pray it will be soon, I'll be a part of your family. I long for us to be married, sweetheart—that is, if you still want me," Rusty hinted.

"Oh, darlin', more than anything I want to be a part of your family. But more, I want to be your wife and you to be my husband! I love you so much." Sally hoped she gave him a very affirmative response.

"Sally, you are so precious," Rusty tenderly spoke. "You have definitely made my day, sweetheart. I could talk to you the rest of the day, but I guess I better go. I want to go see Dad later this afternoon. I'll call you after I get home and before I go to bed. Have a good day. I love you, babe." He blew her a kiss.

"Please be careful. I love you, too, honey." She blew him a kiss back. Then she hung up the handset and turned back toward the dining room where the boys sat, still munching on their cookies. "You boys ready to finish our project?" she asked.

"Mom, who were you talking to?" Todd asked.

Sally was caught off guard by Todd's question. Does she come clean with the truth, or does she give him an answer that will satisfy him for now? "Well, Todd, I have a very dear friend who is concerned about us, and he calls often to check on us and make sure we are OK. He is very nice, and I'm glad we have someone like him who cares. Maybe someday you'll see him, and I can introduce him to both of you. OK?"

"I'm glad he is nice and he cares about us. I'd like to meet him." Todd sounded so grown-up.

Sally was surprised by his answer but so pleased. She turned away quickly so Todd would not see the tears in her eyes. She wanted them to know and like Rusty, as he could be their new stepdad. "Come on, boys. Let's finish your room." She walked to the boys' bedroom, and they followed.

Picking up where they left off, they set Todd's bed up in the other corner of their bedroom. Sally remade his bed with clean linens. "OK, how does it look? Is this the way you want it, Todd?"

"Yes, ma'am. It's great! Thank you." Todd hugged his mother.

"I'm happy if you're happy. Now, we need to get dressed. I hope we can make it to the store," Sally stated as she walked to the living room window. She was surprised when she saw that their street had been plowed. "Come look, boys! Our street is nearly free of snow. I think we can make it to the store. Let's get dressed so we can go." Sally laid out warm clothes for the boys to wear, then she dressed. They put on their coats and snow boots. Todd opened the front door, and they exited the house. The snow wasn't too deep on the porch, but the walkway to the car was deeper. The boys took their place in the back seat. As Sally walked around the car, Wendy, her neighbor, was coming out of her house and saw Sally.

"Hi, Sally," she partly yelled and gave a wave. She walked toward Sally. "How are you?"

"Hi, Wendy. Oh, so-so, I guess. How are you and Greg doing? Did y'all have a nice Christmas?" Sally asked.

"We're doing good! Our Christmas was nice. How was your family's Christmas?" Wendy continued.

"Well, our Christmas was different. I've been meaning to tell y'all that Collin has taken a permanent job in Houston, Texas. He won't be returning here, and I'm in the process of filing for divorce," Sally explained.

"Oh, Sally, I'm so sorry. I told Greg last week that I thought something was not right at the Oldham's house. Collin's vehicle was gone, and you were the one taking care of business. How are the boys handling all this change?" Wendy inquired.

"They don't really understand why their dad is gone. They are hurting, but school is helping them stay busy. We are just living one day at a time. We're asking God to see us through this new journey," Sally said.

"Prayers will be answered, Sally. We'll be praying too. I'll catch you later. I have an appointment. If you need anything, Sally, please call us." Wendy waved and walked away.

As Sally sat down in the car, she was thankful she had the chance to see and tell Wendy about what was going on with her.

The car was cold and still covered with snow. She started the engine and reached under the driver's seat where she kept a snow brush. She got out of the car and began sweeping away the snow. Once back in the car, she slowly and carefully backed the car out of the driveway. They could hear the snow crunching under the tires. Sally reached the end of the driveway without any problems and began driving down the street. The two main streets Sally needed to drive on were mostly clear of the snow, and arriving at the store was easier than she thought it would be.

The parking lot left something to be desired. Snow was in clumps and was very slippery, so they had to walk into the store very carefully. Once inside, Todd grabbed a grocery basket, and Pace helped Todd push it. Sally walked ahead of them and selected the items she needed. After she and the boys checked out, Sally walked to the customer service counter and asked to purchase several money orders. She took the needed money to pay for the money orders and cringed when she took notice to what little money was left in the envelope. But she was doing what she had to do. She needed to make sure her boys had a roof over their heads and stayed warm. That was very important. It was a sure thought that she needed to find a job, and quick!

Being very careful not to fall, they were relieved to be back in the car. Sally had thought earlier about going to a fast-food restaurant for lunch, but peanut butter and jelly sandwiches were less expensive.

Sally breathed a sigh of relief and thanked the Lord for a safe trip home as she drove into the driveway. The temperature outside was rising, and more snow was melting. The front porch was almost clear. Once in the house and the groceries were put away, Sally made their lunch. It wasn't burgers and fries, but the peanut butter and jelly with chips and milk tasted pretty good to them.

"I need to make a few telephone calls. Afterwards, depending on what time it is, we can play some games . . . if y'all want to," Sally suggested.

"OK, Mom. Can we watch television if we're quiet?" Todd asked.

"Sure, that's fine," Sally replied. She looked in her personal telephone book and found Ellen's number. She took the handset in her hand, dialed the number, and waited for someone to answer as she walked to the dining room table to sit down.

"Hello?" a female voice answered.

"Hi, Ellen. This is Sally. Have I caught you at a good time?" Sally asked.

"Oh, hi, Sally. Yes, this is a good time. I've been thinking about you and meant to call you. How are you and the boys? I've talked to Mom a few times, and girl, I feel so bad for you. My brother is just so stupid. He is now in Houston, right?" Ellen talked on.

"Yes, he is. The boys and I are OK. We try to stay busy to keep our minds occupied, but there are times Todd and Pace are sad. I'm happy that school is back in session. Between their schoolwork and their friends, they seem like they are doing good. We're going to church with your mom tomorrow, and they are excited about that. I am too," Sally replied.

"I'm praising the Lord for y'all going to church. Mom was telling me about your wonderful experience with the Holy Spirit. Just gives me chills thinking about how you must have felt! Welcome to the family, sister dear. I know you're learning many new things about being a Christian, and believe me, one never stops learning. God is still teaching me new lessons all the time. And going to church will also open up a whole new world of God's Word to you and the boys. I'm so excited for y'all!" Ellen encouraged Sally.

"Oh, thank you, Ellen. That means so much. I also wanted to share with you, and you may already know, but I saw a divorce attorney day before yesterday. When the attorney receives the paperwork back from Collin, then he will begin the divorce filing procedure. It could take three to four months before it will be final. Collin really left me no choice. He is moving on with his life, and he told me to do the same. He said he was *not* coming back to me. He doesn't even want any custody of his sons. So I must move on, Ellen. I hope you don't think bad of me, but I feel like I need to do what I need to do," Sally explained.

Ellen's silence was concerning to Sally. She thought that maybe she had said too much . . . after all, this was about her brother. Finally, Ellen's voice broke the silence. "I'm sorry, Sally. I just said a quick prayer for God to help me say words of encouragement to you. I've never been in your position or faced these challenges. David and I have always loved each other deeply, and the few problems we have had to face, well, God helped us figure them out. Collin does not believe in God nor does he have the virtues of a Christian man. I believe you were the best person that came into Collin's life; you made a wonderful wife, and you are a great mother to those two little boys. I have no idea what has further turned him from the near perfect life he could have had. So Sally, no, I do not hold any ill will toward you and what you need to do about your life and your two sons' lives. I believe you have gone to the Lord in reverent prayer and asked Him for His help in giving you guidance, strength, and most of all, wisdom to get you through the days and months ahead. My prayers will always be with you, my dear Sally. I wish I was there to hug you tightly. I love you." Ellen's voice broke.

Sally fought back tears, but one by one, they fell from her eyes. Ellen's words were heartfelt. She couldn't have been more encouraging, and Sally needed to hear her words. Sally grasped for composure so she could speak, but she failed.

"It's OK, Sally. I'm right here with you, and I always will be. Take your time." Ellen was steadfast and patient so Sally could recover from her tears.

Still with a broken voice, Sally said, "Thank you so much, Ellen. I love you too."

"You are so welcome. You call me anytime. I'm here for you. And know, you and the boys can come here anytime y'all want to. We'd love to have y'all," Ellen invited.

"We'd love to visit with y'all. Thank you." Sally was grateful for Ellen's open arms.

"David and I have some shopping to do. I'm so glad you called; let's talk again soon. Remember Philippians 4:13: 'I can do all things through Christ who strengtheneth me.' Write that verse on your heart and mind, Sally. Y'all enjoy your time at church tomorrow. I love you, and hug those little boys for us."

"Thank you again, Ellen. I love you too," Sally said as she hung up the telephone.

Todd quietly came into the dining room. "Are you OK, Mom?"

"Yes, I'm OK," she told him. "Your Aunt Ellen and I were talking."

"I was wondering if it would be all right if I got Pace and me a glass of soda?" Todd asked.

"Yes, Todd. That would be fine. Just please, y'all don't spill it. Do you want me to help you?" she asked.

"No, ma'am. I can do it," Todd replied. "Still making calls?"

"Yes. I hope to be done soon," Sally replied as she dialed another number. A male voice on the other end answered.

"Hello?"

"Mr. Waddell, this is Sally Oldham. I'm sorry to bother you, but I need your address. I was going to put the rent money in the mail on Monday, but I discovered I don't have your address. Collin always took care of the bills, and he's not here." Sally was embarrassed.

"Sally, after I talked to you the other day, I decided to allow you to forego the rent this month. You save your money. Perhaps your circumstances might be better next month. I want to help you, and I hope that saving that money will help," Mr. Waddell expressed.

Moved to tears again, Sally could hardly manage to respond. "Thank you so much, Mr. Waddell. That is most generous of you, and I greatly appreciate your kindness." She grabbed a napkin from off the table and wiped her eyes for the second time. *Thank You, sweet Jesus!* she whispered with her eyes looking up.

OK, one more call to go, she thought. She took in a big breath and dialed the last number. She needed to call Peggy.

"Hi, Peggy. It's Sally. How are you?"

"Hi, Sally. I'm OK. How about y'all?" Peggy responded.

"We're OK. The snow is melting and looks good for going to church tomorrow morning. You still going?" Sally asked.

"Absolutely! I'm thrilled to hear y'all are going. Do you want me to pick y'all up?"

"That would be great if you're OK to drive. If not, tell me what time, and we'll pick you up," Sally offered.

"No, the streets look good, and I think I'll be good to drive. I'll pick y'all up at 10 a.m. I usually go to Sunday school, but not tomorrow morning. The boys can come into service with us, but there is also children's church if they want to go there. When we get to church in the morning, I'll show you and the boys where children's church is held and introduce y'all to the boys' teachers. Now, dress comfortably, nothing fancy. We are just kind of like an old-fashioned church. Any other questions?" Peggy asked.

"No, ma'am, I think we've got it. Looking forward to being with you and going to church. See ya in the morning!"

"Me too! Love y'all," Peggy said, and the call ended.

"Kiddos, I'm off the telephone, at least for now. Who wants to play games? Or do y'all want to go outside and play in the snow one last time before it's all melted?" Sally offered.

Pace looked at Todd, "Come on, brother. Let's go play in the snow!" he shouted anxiously.

"OK, Pace! Let's get some warm clothes on. Mom, are you coming too?" Todd asked.

"No, not today, but I'll watch y'all from the window," she said. "I'll help y'all get dressed."

The boys ran to their bedroom and dressed in warm clothing. Soon, they were out the back door. Right away, they noticed their snowman family was much smaller, so they tried to patch them up with more snow. Sally grabbed the camera and took a few snapshots of their hard work.

After about thirty minutes, the boys were cold and wanted to come back inside their warm home. Sally helped them with their wet and snowy clothes.

"You two did a great job patching up the snowmen. Now they will last a little longer! I'm going to run some bath water so y'all can get warmer faster," she said as she walked from the kitchen toward the bathroom. The boys followed her, and soon they were soaking up the warm bath water.

"How about some hot chocolate to warm those tummies of yours?" Sally asked.

"That sounds yummy, Momma!" Pace joyfully shouted.

"Me too, Mom!" Todd chimed in.

"OK then. I'll go fix it. Y'all be careful getting out of the bathtub," she cautioned as she walked toward the kitchen.

It didn't take the boys long before they were in the kitchen with their mother, dressed in their flannel robes and flannel-lined slippers.

"Don't y'all look so cozy and warm!" Sally told the boys that Grandmother Peggy was going to be picking them up in the morning and taking them to church, and she explained to them about children's church. They were excited about meeting other children and making new friends.

Todd and Pace played in their room while Sally started preparing supper. It would take her a while as she was going to fry chicken, boil and mash potatoes, slice tomatoes, and fix gelatin for dessert.

An hour and a half later, supper was on the table. It was later than normal, but the boys didn't mind. Their mother's supper was good, and the gelatin topped with whipped cream was delicious.

When the dishes were washed and put away, they snuggled up together on the couch and watched a bit of television together. Then, the phone rang.

It was Rusty. He was exhausted and about ready to go home. He told her that his dad was feeling better and was enjoying being in a regular hospital room. The weather was threatening, and it might even snow, which would make his work at the farm more challenging. Sally was so glad to hear his voice once more that day.

At 10 p.m., the television was turned off, and it was time for bed. The three of them knelt down beside Todd's bed and prayed their nightly prayer. Todd was excited about not having to climb up the ladder to get into his bed and that he could now look over at his brother from across the room. It was a pleasure for Sally to just bend down to tuck Todd into his bed instead of having to stand on her tip-toes to be able to reach him. She tucked Pace into bed, kissed both of them good night, and recited their *bedbug* wish.

"I love you, Todd. I love you, Pace. See y'all in the morning," she said as she turned out their bedroom light.

"Love ya too," the boys answered together.

Sally slipped into her nightgown in the darkness of her bedroom and laid down on her pillow. She turned her head and envisioned Rusty lying beside her with his eyes looking into hers. She so longed for his gentle touch and warm embrace. She closed her eyes and prayed for Rusty's safety. She asked God to give Rusty His strength to do what he needs to do to keep the farm running in his dad's absence and for Rusty's dad to continue to heal and recover from his surgery. She also prayed for God to protect her and her little boys, and she thanked God for all His blessings. As Sally drifted off to sleep, she hoped she would have sweet dreams of Rusty.

Chapter Fourteen

Sunday morning, and the beginning of a new and different journey for the boys and me, was the first thought Sally had when she sat up on the edge of her bed. She bowed her head, closed her eyes, and prayed: *I thank You, my Father in heaven, my Savior Jesus Christ, and Your Holy Spirit whom You have given to me to live inside of me, for this new day, and how special this day is! Lord, the expectation of my sons and me going to Your house and being able to worship You is exciting to me, and yet I feel nervous at the same time. Lord, please allow us to know and do everything we should as we go into unfamiliar surroundings. Let Todd and Pace be excited too, and please, open their young minds to what they are being taught about You. Also, please be with Rusty and his family. Lord, thank You for everything. Amen.*

The clock on her nightstand read 7:30. Plenty of time to eat breakfast, get dressed, and be ready for Peggy to pick them up at ten o'clock. But still, Sally wasted no time in preparing her coffee, waking up the boys, and starting their breakfast. She noticed out the kitchen's back door window that the snow had continued to melt during the night, and not much of the snowman family was left. Sally felt a little sadness as she peered at the three piles of snow—like memories were literally disappearing. She was so glad she had taken pictures of the creations they had made.

The telephone rang. Sally quickly walked from the kitchen to the living room. "Hello?"

"Hey, Sally. Is everything still a *go* for church this morning?" Peggy inquired.

"Yes, ma'am. I'm fixin' breakfast, the boys are up, and we're excited. How about you? All OK with you?" Sally asked.

"Yes. Praise the Lord, the streets are looking good. I'm happy to hear all is good there too. See y'all at 10."

Sally, still holding the handset to her ear, was stunned. That had to be the shortest conversation ever with Peggy!

Todd and Pace were sitting on the couch watching cartoons on the television. Todd saw the expression on his mom's face and asked, "Are you OK?"

Sally turned to look at him and replied, "Yes. That was your grandmother checking to make sure we were still planning on going to church this morning. That call had to break a record of being the shortest call from her! OK, fellas, breakfast will be ready soon," she informed them as she walked back to the kitchen and turned the sausage patties over as they fried in the skillet. "Would y'all like to come and get your glasses of milk? If y'all want some orange juice, that can be poured too."

The boys ran to the kitchen and helped their mother. Moments later, breakfast was on the table. As Todd sat down in his chair, he noticed out the dining room window that the snowman family was now only a few mounts of snow. "Man, the snowmen have really melted!"

"Let me see!" Pace rushed to the window. "Oh, Momma, they are almost gone! I hope it snows again soon so we can make more snowmen," he exclaimed.

"It could happen, Pace. We never know about our sometimes crazy weather," she said.

The three blessed their breakfast and ate. When they were done, they helped their mother clear the table.

"Will you boys go brush your teeth while I make a telephone call?" she asked them. The boys ran to the bathroom.

Sally walked to the living room, picked up the handset, and called the telephone number to get information about the weather forecast for the day. She listened for a minute and hung up the handset. "It's going to be near fifty degrees for a high today. That will help me know how to have y'all dress for church," she commented as she walked to the boys' bedroom. She opened their closet door and intently looked for the appropriate clothes for them to wear to church.

While she helped the boys get dressed, she asked Todd, "How did you sleep last night? Did sleeping in your bed in the new place in your bedroom make a difference?"

"You know, it did. When the bunk bed was above Pace's bed, I was not really afraid of falling, but now that I am sleeping on the floor, well, sort of, I think I slept better," Todd explained.

"I never knew that, Todd. I'm sorry. If I had known that, I would have brought your bed to floor level long before now," she said apologetically. Stepping back and looking at her sons, she said, "Boy, you two little men look so handsome. Y'all can watch more cartoons if you want to, but don't get musted up. I'm going to go get dressed."

The boys ran to the couch, sat down, and began watching television. As Sally walked toward her bedroom, the phone rang again. She hurried to answer the call.

"Hello?"

"And good morning to you! This is your ever-so-lonely farmer from Connecticut. I sure do miss you, sweetheart. Just checking in. How are you and the boys this morning?" Rusty asked.

"Good morning, my love. I'm so lonely and miss you like crazy! We're OK. Getting ready for church. Peggy is picking us up at ten o'clock. The snow is melting fast, and the street should be good for travel. How are you? How is your dad and mom? How's the weather?" Sally had so many questions.

"Y'all be careful going to church. I know this is a very special day for you and the boys. I will be praying for you three as you enter on this new path with God. I'm tired, but I slept better last night. I dreamed about you, that's why!" he said coyly. "Dad is making progress. Mom is tired, but she went home last night, and that helped her a lot to sleep in her own bed for a change. It's getting cloudy and turning colder here. Could get snow tonight," Rusty responded.

"I slept better last night too because, before I went to sleep, *you* were lying beside me. Oh, I long for your loving arms to hold me. I'm glad you slept better and your dreams were sweet. That's great news about your dad. And your mom needed a good night's rest. I'll be praying the weather doesn't get bad. Things don't need to get worse for you and the farm." Sally tried to sound encouraging.

"I've already called Allen and Tom and asked them to be on standby to help me if the weather does get bad. They both said they would help." He paused for a moment. "Well, I need to get back to work, but I wanted to call you before you all headed to church. My prayers are with you, honey. I love you, Sally, very much. I'll call you later," Rusty lovingly said.

"I'm glad you have backup coming if you need them. Please be careful, and stay warm. Thank you for your prayers; I have you in my prayers too. I love you more than words can say, darlin'." She blew him a kiss.

"Bye, babe," Rusty said, blowing her a kiss.

Sally replaced the handset on the telephone base and breathed a prayer, asking the Lord to please watch over Rusty. She glanced at the wall clock: 9:30. She hurried off to her bedroom to look for something to wear. She selected a navy blue skirt with its matching jacket along with a lacy-collared, white blouse. She found her navy blue heels and a handbag of the same color. She dressed quickly. Then, from her mother's jewelry box, she found the accessories she wanted to wear. She walked into the bathroom and applied her makeup and brushed her hair. As she looked into the mirror, she thought what she did would pass in a pinch, but when she walked into the living room, her boys' facial expressions were priceless.

"Wow, Mom! You look great!" Todd shouted.

"Momma, you are beautiful!" Pace exclaimed.

Sally was very surprised by their reaction. She didn't dress up nicely very often, but today was an exception. She hoped she didn't look too dressy. Peggy said to dress comfortably—nothing fancy. Maybe she was dressed too fancy, but it was too late to change. Peggy would be at the house soon.

"Thank you, Todd and Pace. I guess it's been a while since y'all have seen me dressed in a suit. You think it's too much?" she asked.

"No, ma'am," they answered at the same time.

"It's almost 10. Let me get your jackets so we can be ready to put them on when your grandmother gets here," Sally suggested.

"She's here, Momma!" Pace shouted. He had been standing at the living room window watching for his grandmother.

Sally opened the front door so that Peggy knew they were coming. She helped the boys on with their jackets and grabbed her handbag, then all three of them exited the house and got into Peggy's car.

"Good morning, y'all. So wonderful to see the three of you! And don't y'all look so nice," Peggy greeted them joyfully.

"Thank you! It's good to see you too. I like the perfume you are wearing . . . very nice," Sally said.

"Good morning, Grandmother Peggy," Todd politely greeted her.

"Yeah, and the same thing that Todd said, Grandmother Peggy!" Pace excitedly expressed.

Peggy slipped the gear shift in reverse and began backing out of the driveway. "The streets are mostly clear, and with the warmer temps today, I believe the snow could be gone by tomorrow," Peggy shared.

"Grandmother Peggy, our snowman family that we made is melting away, but I hope it snows again so we can make some more," Pace expressed.

"Yes, warmer temps are very hard on snowmen, but you are right. The next snow fall we have, you can create more of those cute white creatures!" Peggy tried to sound positive.

It wasn't but a five-minute drive to Cherish Baptist Church. It was an average-sized church building, and the parking lot was filled with lots of vehicles. Peggy parked her car, and as Sally helped Todd and Pace out of the back seat, she asked them, "Are y'all OK?"

"I'm fine, Mom," answered Todd as he took his little brother's hand.

Pace walked beside Todd. "Yes, but I'm a little scared, Momma," he admitted, looking up at her.

"It's OK, Pace. I'm right here with you," Todd encouraged his little brother.

Sally took Pace's little hand too and told him everything was going to be all right.

Peggy said hi to many people as they walked toward the church doors. She had been a member of the church for years, and most of those years she and her husband were very active, serving on many of the church's committees. But ever since Mr. Oldham's death, Peggy had become less active.

They entered the church doors and looked around. It was beautifully decorated with pictures and flowers, and it felt very warm and safe. There were a lot of people standing and talking to each other. Children were hurrying along, first one way, then another, avoiding the small groups of folks gathered in the area. Many of those folks looked up and saw Peggy and waved or said hello. Sally and the boys followed Peggy as she walked toward a doorway.

"This is where Todd and Pace will have children's church," Peggy explained. "You'll enjoy being in this room, boys," she said as she looked at them.

Several ladies were in the room and approached them.

"Hi, Jan and Becky. This is Sally, Todd, and Pace. Sally is my daughter-in-law, and these two young men are my grandsons. Boys, this is Jan and Becky. They are your teachers for children's church."

"It's nice to meet you Sally. And we are very happy to see you, Todd and Pace. We look forward to having you two in our church," Jan said sincerely.

"Yes," Becky began, "it's special to meet Peggy's family! Welcome. How old are y'all?"

Todd answered quickly. "I'm eight."

"I'm seven years old," Pace announced bravely.

"Thank y'all for taking a minute for me to introduce you to my family. We'll be back in a little while for children's church," Peggy said, ushering them out of the classroom. "We should make our way to the sanctuary," Peggy told Sally. "I'd like to find our preacher. His name is Brother Hal Hogan. We call him Brother Hal."

Sally took Todd and Pace's hands and followed Peggy into the sanctuary. Peggy's eyes searched for the preacher while Sally, Todd, and Pace took in the grandeur and beauty of the sanctuary.

"Wow! Mom, this is something!" Todd expressed with very wide eyes.

"Momma, is this the church?" Pace reacted with surprise in his voice.

Sally bent down to her sons' eye level and said softly to them, "Yes. This is God's house. It is truly awesome."

Peggy touched Sally's shoulder, and Sally looked up. "Brother Hal sees us, and he's walking our way."

Sally stood up and saw a man walking toward them. He was a nice-looking man, about six feet tall, well built, and had black wavy hair. He shook a few people's hands as he approached them.

"Hi, Ms. Peggy," he greeted with an extended hand. "It's great to see you! And this must be your family you have told me about."

"Yes, Brother Hal. This is Sally, my daughter-in-law, and this is Todd and Pace, my grandsons." Peggy turned to her family as she introduced them to her preacher.

"It's a pleasure to finally meet y'all. Peggy has shared her thoughts of love for the three of you with me. Welcome to Cherish Baptist Church. Sally, I'd like to talk to you after the service if you have a few minutes," Brother Hal said politely.

"It's nice to meet you too, Brother Hal," Sally responded as she shook his hand. "Peggy, since the boys and I rode with you this morning, would I detain you too long if I talked to Brother Hal after the service?" she asked.

"No, dear, that's fine. The boys and I will wait for you," Peggy answered.

Sally turned to address Brother Hal. "My chauffeur for this morning's drive has graciously said she will wait for me, so yes, sir, I'll be able to see you after the service."

"Great. I'll see you later." Brother Hal turned and began walking toward the front of the church.

Peggy took Todd by the hand, and Sally took Pace by his hand. They walked up the main aisle of the church to a pew Peggy chose for them to sit in. After being seated, Todd leaned over to his mom and commented on how comfortable the bench seat was. She whispered back to him that the church bench seat was called a *pew* and that she too thought it was very comfortable. Pace squirmed a little bit as he looked all around him at his new surroundings. He told Sally that God sure did have a pretty house!

People took their seats in the church as the choir filed into the choir loft from both sides of the front of the sanctuary. The singers wore long, light blue choir robes with dark blue satin stoles. Todd and Pace were mesmerized as they watched the choir. Once the choir members were in their places, the choir director walked up the five steps to the top center of the stage that stretched from one side of the sanctuary to the other. He greeted the people in attendance, then asked the people to stand and turn in their hymnals to page 234.

"Let's sing praises to God with this song, 'Sweet Spirit.'" Then he turned to face and direct the choir.

The people stood up, opened their song books to the mentioned page, and began singing as the organ started. Peggy held the book for Todd, and Sally held the book for Pace. The boys weren't sure what was happening and didn't know what to do. They just watched their grandmother and their mother.

As Sally began to sing the words of the song, something stirred within her. *Could it be the Holy Spirit?* she thought. She couldn't help but notice the facial expressions of the people standing near her. She believed they, as she did, felt God's presence too, and everyone in the church was being filled by His love. Folks were lifting their hands toward heaven and praising the Lord for His blessings. She had the most incredible feeling of joy leaping inside of her.

The choir director turned and faced the congregation and said, "There are blessings you cannot receive till you know Him in His fullness and believe: You're the one to profit when you say, I am going to walk with Jesus all the way. If you're not saved from your sin, you're bound by Satan and cannot enter into heaven. But you can make it right if you will yield, then you'll enjoy the Holy Spirit that we feel." He then asked the people to be seated. He asked the congregation to sing a hymn about the greatness of God on page 115. He turned back to the choir, the organist began playing, and the people sang loudly.

The song was poignant, and the words were powerful, capturing Sally's emotions. She pictured God creating the universe with His hands, and she thought about all the wonders He has done.

The choir director turned to the congregation and spoke these words: "And when I think that God did not spare His only begotten Son, but sent Him to bleed and die on the cross to take away my sin. Yes, stop and think, how great is my God." He turned back to face the choir, and the singing continued.

Sally listened to the words of the song. She heard that one day Christ will come to Earth, and He'll take her home to heaven. *Yes,* she thought, *I shall be humble, and I will bow to Him in gratefulness! What a wonderful song.*

The next song was called, "The Names Are Called." The choir sang the hymn with perfection, and the congregation enjoyed it so much that they clapped their hands and waved their arms in the air. Sally, as well as Todd and Pace, were quite taken by the congregation's enthusiasm. It was such a display of rejoicing and praising the Lord.

The choir was seated in their chairs in the choir loft, and Brother Hal approached the pulpit. "Wow! I am energized! That was great singing, choir. The Lord certainly blessed us today with some super special music. Can I hear an *amen*?"

The congregation clapped enthusiastically and very loudly shouted, "Amen!"

"Those of you who are going to children's church may be excused," he instructed.

Peggy leaned over to Sally. "I'll take the boys if that's OK?"

Sally looked at the boys. "Y'all OK?"

"We're good, Mom," Todd agreed and took Pace's hand. They followed their grandmother as she walked toward the back of the sanctuary. Sally prayed a quick prayer that her little boys would be OK and would enjoy the new experience of children's church. Then she turned her attention back to Brother Hal.

The preacher opened his Bible and placed it on top of the pulpit. He began speaking. "Please stand. Let's bow our heads, close our eyes, and ask for a blessing over our message today. *Dear heavenly Father, we approach You with praise and thank You for this day that You have given to us. We thank You for Your Son, Jesus Christ, and for allowing us to have Your Holy Spirit living inside of us. Please bless the words of this message that they will fall on each person's ears with Your understanding and teachings it possesses. Lord, I thank You for those who are in Your house today. Thank You for Your loving-kindness that never fails us. Allow us to bring You glory through our thoughts and actions. Strengthen us and fill us with Your peace. I ask these things in Jesus' holy name. Amen.*" The preacher raised his head and picked up his Bible. "If you'd like to follow the reading this morning, please turn in your Bibles to 1 Peter, chapter 1, verses 1–5. Please continue standing, if you are able, for the reading of God's Word."

As Sally was turning the pages in her Bible to the reading, Peggy stepped back in beside her.

"This writing of Peter's is titled, 'Greeting to the Elect Pilgrims.'" And he began to read:

Verse 1: Peter, an apostle of Jesus Christ, To the pilgrims of the Dispersion in Pontus, Galatia, Cappadocia, Asia, and Bithynia,

Verse 2: elect according to the foreknowledge of God the Father, in sanctification of the Spirit, for obedience and sprinkling of the blood of Jesus Christ: Grace to you and peace be multiplied.

Verse 3: Blessed be the God and Father of our Lord Jesus Christ, who according to His abundant mercy has begotten us again to a living hope through the resurrection of Jesus Christ from the dead,

Verse 4: to an inheritance incorruptible and undefiled and that does not fade away, reserved in heaven for you,

Verse 5: who are kept by the power of God through faith for salvation ready to be revealed in the last time.

Brother Hal paused, then continued, "*Lord, we thank You for these verses Peter wrote per Your instructions. Amen.*" He looked up. "Please be seated."

Sally whispered to Peggy, "Did the boys seem to be OK?"

"Yes, they walked right into the room with the other children. They'll be OK," Peggy assured her.

Brother Hal's eyes looked out over the congregation, and he smiled. "If you're already having a stressful week, stop for a moment and think about all the blessings that surround you. You have the blessings of family, friends, and neighbors. You have the blessing of knowing Jesus as Lord and Savior if you have put your trust in Him. You have the blessing of being assured of an eternal home forever with Jesus in heaven. So take a deep breath, and count your blessings."

He continued. "If you have taken a moment this morning to look at the pages of the church bulletin, you may have noticed that I have titled this sermon after the expression, *Too blessed to be stressed.* Let's take another look at verse 3 because I truly believe this saying could apply to this situation. 'Blessed be the God and Father of our Lord Jesus Christ, who according to His abundant mercy has begotten us again to a living hope through the resurrection of Jesus Christ from the dead.' In today's passage, the Apostle Peter assured the stressed Christians in his day about the blessings of being saved. Talk about stress! These dispersed, persecuted Christians were in danger daily of being killed for their faith. Today, as a body of believers, we may be ridiculed and attacked for our faith. We can become discouraged into not continuing the work God has given us. But just as discouragement is meant to take our focus away from the Lord, our faith calls us to depend on Him. May God be glorified through our faithful prayer, perseverance, and sacrifice to work diligently for Him."

Brother Hal looked pointedly at the congregation. "If you think you cannot take another stressful moment today or this week, stop and read the blessing in this key verse that we just read, and perhaps continue reading beyond verse 5 for more blessings. We can all thank God for His blessings. As scripture reminds us, we can bless Him for the greatest blessing of all: the gift of salvation through His Son. We are absolutely too blessed to be stressed. One day this past week, I was looking through some paperwork in my office desk drawer that had accumulated over the last several months, and I found this saying I'd like to share with you: 'Heaven is where Jesus is . . . where worship fills every breath, where light fills every heart, where peace fills every soul, where joys never cease. Heaven is our forever home.' Isn't that a beautiful place? We wonder what heaven will be like. Through the indwelling Holy Spirit, we have confidence we'll be at home with the Lord. Jesus offers us an invitation to come just as we are. Are you weary from living a busy life without focus on the Savior? You're not only tired physically and emotionally, but spiritually you are weary from the dailiness of survival that steals our strength as we strive to make it on our own. The world diverts our attention and beckons us to look at the glitter of a sometimes-pretentious society, and we allow it to take away our source of true peace and joy."

He continued. "But Jesus beckons us all to come! The Savior's invitation is for everyone—regardless of our sin, financial situation, place of birth, or social standing—for we all become heavy-laden by things of this world. In John 3:3, Jesus replied, 'Very truly, I tell you, no one can see the kingdom of God unless they are born again.' In John 14:6, Jesus replied, 'I am the way and the truth and the life. No one comes to the Father except through me.' My friends, I find nowhere in the Bible where Jesus changes His mind. So please, God loves you and wants a relationship with you so much that John 3:16 says, 'For God so loved the world, that He gave His only begotten Son, that whosoever believeth in Him will not perish, but will have everlasting life.'" He looked down at his Bible and said, "Please stand. The choir will sing our closing hymn, and while they are singing, don't fight the feeling that the Holy Spirit is dealing with you. Luke 11:9 says, 'And I say unto you, ask, and it shall be given you; seek, and ye shall find; knock, and it shall be opened unto you.' Listen, is Jesus knocking on the door of your heart? If so, repent and ask forgiveness of your sins, and ask for Jesus to come into your heart and know He is your Savior."

Sally knew the Holy Spirit was calling her to make this decision. She stepped in front of Peggy and began walking to the front of the church toward Brother Hal. She approached him and leaned toward him, expressing that she wanted to accept Jesus as her Lord and Savior.

"Oh, Sally. That's wonderful," Brother Hal reacted joyfully.

A lady came to Sally and walked with her to the front pew, asking her what her name was. There, Peggy was waiting for Sally and sat down beside her. They both prayed with Sally, helping her confess her need for a Savior and ask for God's forgiveness of her sins. She prayed that God would come into her life and change her heart and that she would honor Him with her life.

Another person came to the front of the church and spoke to Brother Hal. This man was also brought to a pew and prayed over. When he was done, Brother Hal motioned for Sally and the man to come and stand beside him. Those who had prayed with them gave the preacher their names, and he said, "Ladies and gentlemen of the congregation, I am pleased to introduce to you two folks who have asked forgiveness of their sins and have asked Jesus for His salvation. This is Sally Oldham and Bret Levy. Can I hear an *amen*?"

The congregation said loudly, "Amen!"

"Please, church, join us up front and greet our new members," he encouraged. Then he turned to Sally and Bret and shook their hands, welcoming them to the church. He stepped back to Sally and reminded her that he still would like to see her before she left.

Many people came to the front of the church and congratulated Sally and Bret. Peggy reappeared with Todd and Pace, who waited patiently to run and hug their mother. They didn't really understand what was happening, but they were glad to see her.

As the crowd died down, Sally saw Brother Hal at the back of the church. She, along with Todd, Pace, and Peggy, walked toward him.

Brother Hal approached Sally and said, "I won't keep you long, but Peggy and I have been talking about your situation. God works wonders, and He does answer prayers, that's for sure. This is one of those times that makes me feel so blessed. I understand you're seeking employment? The young lady that is employed to operate our church office is going on maternity leave for several months, and I'd like for you to consider filling in for us in her absence. The work consists of answering the phone, filing paperwork, and other simple-to-learn responsibilities that need to be performed. It's a Monday through Friday job, and with your children, your hours can and would be flexible. The pay would be $3.00 an hour. If you would like to think about it, I do understand," he explained.

Sally was caught off guard and was very surprised. She really did not need to think about it because this was a wonderful opportunity to go to work and a prayer answered. "Brother Hal, I'm honored to be asked to fill the position, and I'd like to accept. However, yes, my sons need to be at school by 8:30 each morning, and I would need to pick them up at 3:30 in the afternoon. Will getting to work at 8:45 be too late?" Sally inquired.

"No, not at all. The office doesn't open until nine o'clock, and you leaving around 3:15 p.m. will work out OK too," Brother Hal replied. "When can you start, Sally?"

"Would Tuesday be OK? One more thing I do need to share with you, and Peggy may have told you, but I have filed for divorce. I don't expect too many office visits with my attorney, but I hope that won't be a problem."

"I don't see a problem with that at all. We'll see you on Tuesday. By the way, would you like to be baptized next Sunday?" Brother Hal asked.

"Yes, that would be special! Thank you! And thank you so much for the job," Sally excitedly answered. She walked toward the lobby and joined Peggy and the boys.

"I see you smiling from ear to ear," Peggy observed. "What's up?"

Sally continued her smile as she answered Peggy. "I owe you a *big* thank you. I appreciate you sharing with Brother Hal my situation of seeking employment. I start work on Tuesday in the church office!" she announced joyfully. "Certainly, prayers answered! Thank You, sweet Jesus!" she rejoiced.

"Mom, you're going to work? You're going to be working at this church? Wow!" Todd was excited for his mom. He knew she had been talking about finding a job.

"But Momma, that means you won't be at home with us anymore," Pace said, nearly in tears.

"No, no, Pace. I'll be home with you. I'll be working when you're in school. Don't cry! It's OK." Sally took Pace up into her arms and comforted him. He wrapped his arms around her neck and held her tight. So much newness. It was overwhelming to him. But by the time the four of them walked to Peggy's car, Pace felt better.

"Is anyone hungry?" Peggy asked once all of them were in her car.

Instantly the boys shouted, "YES!"

"What would y'all like to eat?" Peggy asked.

She had hardly spoken the question when both boys shouted, "Burgers and fries!"

"OK, burgers and fries coming up!" Peggy agreed. She started the engine of the car and drove out of the parking lot, and they were on their way to the fast-food restaurant.

The wait wasn't too long at the restaurant, so they got their food rather quickly. They chatted and chatted while they ate. Sally told them she would be baptized the following Sunday, and between Peggy and Sally, they explained to the boys what it meant to be baptized.

They arrived back home after lunch, and Peggy needed to get going as she had some errands to run. It was nearly one o'clock. Right away, they all changed out of their church clothes. Sally couldn't help but wonder what she would need to wear to her new job. In an office environment, she probably would be expected to wear professional-looking clothes. She looked through the clothes in her closet and chose an empire-lined, blue, long-sleeve dress with matching blue heels and a handbag. *This might do,* she thought. But she had a whole day to think about it.

Sally's train of thought was interrupted when Pace entered her room and asked, "Can we play games this afternoon, Momma?"

Sally peered around the corner of the closet door and answered, "Sure. That sounds like a really good idea. Did you ask Todd if he wanted to play? And if so, what do y'all want to play?"

Pace dashed from her room and yelled, "Hey, Todd! Wanna play some games?"

"Sure! That sounds like fun! Is Mom gonna play too?" Todd asked.

"Yip. She said she would. Whatcha want to play?"

"Anything, everything, I don't care! I'll help you pick out the games," Todd suggested.

So the games were chosen and brought to the dining room table, and all three of them began to play. First one game, then another. They had fun. Midway through their game playing, Sally popped some popcorn and served up soda to wash down the buttery treat.

The hours of the afternoon ticked away quickly, and it was already close to 6 p.m. Then the telephone rang. Sally walked to the living room and answered.

"Hello?"

"Hi, sweetheart. I don't have but a minute. Dad is back in ICU. Mom and I are heading to the hospital now. I'll call you later. I've got to go. I love you, Sally," and Rusty was gone.

Sally fell to the couch and immediately bowed her head and began praying. Her heart was pounding so hard, she could hear it. Anxiety welled up inside of her for Rusty and his mom. She thought to herself, *Russell was doing so well. What could have happened? Lord God, please allow Russell to be OK*, she prayed.

"Mom, are you OK?" Todd asked as he walked from the dining room to the couch in the living room.

"Not really, Todd. My friend's father was doing better, but now he just told me something has happened, and he isn't doing very good. I was lifting them up in prayer," she explained.

"That's not good. Can I sit beside you and pray for them too?" Todd caringly asked.

"You sure can. That would be very thoughtful of you. Thank you, Todd."

Todd sat down beside her, and Sally leaned over to him and put her arm around his shoulders as they bowed their heads and prayed. Soon, Pace sat on the other side of his mother, and he held her arm. He prayed too.

Several long, agonizing hours passed. Sally wanted to hear from Rusty so badly. She had prepared a quick supper for the boys, and then they took their baths to get ready for bed. Before Sally tucked them into their beds, they got on their knees and prayed a new prayer: "*Now I lay me down to sleep, I pray the Lord my soul to keep. Please, angels, watch over me through the night, and keep me safe till morning light. Amen.*" Sally hugged and kissed the boys good night and told them to not let the bugs bite. "I love you, Todd. I love you, Pace," she told them.

"Love you too," they told her.

As she left their bedroom, she turned out the light.

Sally returned to the couch and prayed until 10 p.m. She knew she needed to get ready for bed, but how could she go to sleep with what felt like a very dark cloud over her? She was so concerned for Russell.

At 10:30, she forced herself to get up from the couch. She hadn't taken many steps into her bedroom when the telephone rang. She ran to answer it, praying it was Rusty and that he had good news about his dad.

"Hello?" she answered anxiously.

"Hi, honey. I know it's late, but before it got any later, I wanted to call you. Dad is still in ICU. The doctor is running tests on him to find out what happened to him. He was feeling good and was up walking around as the doctor instructed him to do. One of the nurses found him lying on the hallway floor not too far from his room. He was unconscious and was barely breathing. From what Mom and I have been told, they rushed him to the ICU and took his vitals and oxygen and examined him for injuries from the fall. They gave him injections to stabilize his blood pressure, which was very low. The doctor told us he could have had a blood clot. The hospital staff have taken him to X-ray now. Mom had come home to do laundry and other chores when they called her. She ran to the parlor where I was cleaning up after milking the cows and told me about Dad. I ran back to the house with her and cleaned up quickly, and here we are. I know you are praying for us, and we appreciate those prayers. We still don't know very much, but when we do, I'll call you and let you know," Rusty explained in a very tired and worried voice.

"Oh, sweetheart. I am so sorry. I wish I was there, if just to hold you in my arms and comfort you. Is Russell awake?" Sally asked.

"He is in and out of consciousness. I wish you were here too, Sally." Rusty's voice broke. "I'm going to go. You need to get some sleep. I'll call you in the morning after you take the boys to school. Will that be OK?"

"Yes, absolutely. Thank you for calling because I was getting quite concerned. I'll be praying the tests will soon reveal the problem so the doctor can begin treating your dad and he will be better quickly. I love you, Rusty."

"I love you too." Rusty's voice faded, and then there was a click as he disconnected the call.

Sally just sat there. The conversation drained her mentally.

"Mom, was that your friend?" Todd startled her. He had ever-so-quietly walked into the living room and stood beside her.

"Yes, it was. His name is Rusty," she told him, deciding it was time he knew the name of her friend. "His dad took a bad fall and is back in the Intensive Care Unit at the hospital. That's the part of the hospital where very sick people are taken. I'm sorry the telephone woke you up, but thank you for caring. Come on now, I need to put you back to bed," Sally said as she stood up from the couch and took Todd by his little hand and walked with him to his room. She tucked him in and kissed his forehead. "Night night, my sweet son," she whispered.

"Night night, Mom," Todd whispered back.

As Sally laid down in her bed, she hoped her mind would calm down. She was tired but not very sleepy. There was so much she wanted to share with Rusty about her day, but it had to wait. Russell was more important now. She prayed many times before falling asleep that God would allow Russell to be OK.

Sally heard the music playing from her alarm clock, but she was far from ready to wake up. She turned over in bed to turn off the alarm, then slowly sat up on the edge of her bed. Her first thoughts were of Rusty and his family, so she said a quick prayer for him. Then she continued out loud, "And thank You, Lord, that my tootsies are on the floor again this morning." With her slippers and robe on, she hurried to wake Todd and Pace up. Todd was groggy, but Pace hopped out of his bed and ran to the bathroom. Sally needed to encourage Todd to get up. She felt bad for him for not getting a good night's sleep, but she was proud for his reaction to Rusty's late-night call.

"Come on, my son. It's time to get up and get ready for school," she said as she slowly uncovered him. "OK, let's first move this leg to the edge of the bed. Now, this leg. You're halfway up, Todd! You can do it the rest of the way. I know you can!"

About that time, Pace ran into the room and jumped up on Todd's bed. "You gotta get up, sleepyhead!" Pace shouted.

"OK, OK, I'm gettin' up!" Todd's legs slid off the bed, and he stood up on the floor in front of his mom. She hugged him.

"Go on to the bathroom, and I'll lay out y'all's clothes for school. Then y'all get dressed while I start breakfast," she stated. She headed to the kitchen and started brewing her coffee. That morning's breakfast was going to be cereal and bananas. Quick and easy. She prepared the boys' lunches, then grabbed cereal bowls, milk, and the cereal boxes and placed them on the dining room table.

The boys entered the room and sat down at the table.

"Well, don't y'all look so nice! Excellent job dressing yourselves," their mother said proudly.

The boys quickly ate their cereal then rushed off to brush their teeth. Sally washed up the dishes and tidied up the kitchen. The boys watched a children's program on the television while Sally got dressed.

"It's 8:10 and time to go to school. Now tomorrow morning, everything should be the same as this morning, except after I drop y'all off at school, I'll be going to the church to go to work," Sally explained as they slipped on their coats and walked out the front door.

As Sally was backing the car out of the driveway, Todd asked, "Mom, will you be able to pick us up after school as usual?"

"Yes. I'll be able to leave work at 3:15 and be at school at 3:30," she explained.

"But Momma, what happens if we are out of school? Will you be home with us?" Pace inquired.

"Well, you know, that's a good question, Pace. I guess I'll need to take off work, or maybe your Grandmother Peggy might be with the two of you." Sally paused. "You know what?"

"What?" both boys said at the same time.

"We'll cross that bridge when we get to it. How's that?" she said.

"OK. That'll work." Pace was satisfied with his momma's answer.

Sally approached the school's parking lot. There were no other cars in line, so she stopped the car near the school's front entrance. "I'll see y'all later. Have a good day. I love y'all," she told the boys as they kissed her cheek.

They exited the car with an "I love you too."

Sally was able to watch her young sons open the school's door. They turned and waved to her, she waved back, and then they disappeared as the door closed behind them. She uttered out loud, "Please, Lord, allow them to have a good day."

Sally drove straight home. She knew Rusty said he would call her after she took the boys to school, and she sure did not want to miss his call. As she walked to the front door, she raised the lid on the mailbox. Inside was an envelope, which she took and brought into the house. She laid her coat on the chair and opened the envelope. It was the utility bill. She remembered Collin always took the bill to a store and paid the bill with cash, but which store was it? He might have taken it to the drugstore or the grocery store. She looked at the bill again. She saw a telephone number on it. She called the number and asked where she could pay the bill. It was the drugstore. She thought to herself, *I'll stop and pay the bill this afternoon on the way to pick up the boys from school.*

Sally gathered the dirty clothes from the clothes hamper and took them to the washing machine to start a load. It was a good time to vacuum the house, but as she took the vacuum cleaner from the coat closet, the telephone rang. She was only steps away from the telephone.

"Hello?"

"Good morning, my love. How are you?" Rusty greeted her cheerfully.

"Good morning, honey! I'm OK. How are you, and how is your dad?" Sally eagerly asked.

"It is a good morning. Your voice is music to my ears. I miss you so much. I'm better. Still very tired, but because Dad is much better, Mom and I are better. He is still in ICU, but the doctor said he may be able to go to a regular room later today," Rusty explained.

"Oh, praise the Lord! Prayers are answered! I've been so concerned about him. Has the doctor told y'all what happened? I guess your dad is conscience and awake?" Sally asked.

"Yes, he is awake and talking. Prayers are being answered indeed. The doctor believes Dad's blood pressure dropped due to a small blood clot. Then, due to low blood pressure and the blood slowing to the heart, Dad fainted or passed out. When Dad passed out, he did suffer a slight head injury. The doctor is telling us that he will be OK. It was quite scary!" Rusty further explained. "So what is going on with you? Did y'all make it to church yesterday, or did the snow keep y'all from going?"

"Scary is right! I'm happy he is improving. Well, yesterday was a very good day. The boys and I did go with Peggy to church. The church was beautiful, and the boys and I were in awe of everything—the people, the singing, the preacher, children's church . . . just everything. I did go to the front of the church to make a profession of faith, and I agreed to be baptized next Sunday," Sally joyfully expressed.

"Oh, baby, that's wonderful! God's Spirit within me just jumped for joy at your news. How exciting! I wish I was there to give you a huge hug," Rusty said lovingly.

"Oh, Rusty, I wish you were here too. I miss you and love you bunches. But there's more! After the service yesterday, Brother Hal, the preacher, shared with me that the lady that works in the church office is going on maternity leave, and he asked me to temporarily take her place and work in the office while she's out. I start tomorrow. I'll work Monday through Friday from 9 a.m. to 3:15 p.m. I'm so excited!" Sally exclaimed.

There was silence.

"Rusty, are you there?" Sally asked.

"Yes, I'm here," Rusty answered slowly.

"What's wrong? What's the matter?"

"Well, you do sound happy about the job, but I thought we agreed you would not go to work and that I would send you money to help you with expenses. And what if Dad gets well enough where he can start working the farm again, and I go back on the road? When will I get to see you if you're working?" Rusty sounded disappointed.

"Rusty, I know we talked about me not working and you sending me money, but, sweetheart, you've taken your dad's place right now in running the farm, and you're not driving nor are you earning any money. Right now, the doctor says it could be as long as six months before your dad could even think about working the farm, so that means you won't be driving for maybe that long as well. You know how much I appreciate you offering me your money, but it could be money you don't have right now. I didn't want that put on your shoulders. Please understand. I'm doing this for both of us, and if the job gets in the way of us, then I'll quit. I would never *not* want to see you nor be with you if you go back to driving. You are the one person who has kept me going all these months . . . you, your love for me, my love for you. I would never do anything to hurt you or us. I'm sorry if I have hurt you or if I have made you feel like I've not trusted you. Besides, when the divorce is final in hopefully four months, I want the boys and I to be with you. If you still want that too," Sally said softly.

Rusty was silent again, but then responded. "Sally, I can tell you have thought this situation out. I'm still so upset about this whole health thing happening with Dad, and I've tried not to be angry. Having a heart attack certainly wasn't his idea and wasn't the way he wanted this part of his journey of life to happen, but it did. And God has His reasons, I know that. But it has interfered with my life with you. I hate it! But what you said is true about the money. No driving, no money. I'm still good, but with no extra money coming in, finances are thinning. It hurts me. I feel like I have let you down. I told you I would send you money, and now I can't. And yes, you're right about me still running the farm for Dad, and I will for as long as it takes until he can be well enough to be able to do it himself. I'm the one who is sorry, Sally. I understand that you are trying to look out for us. And yes, after the divorce, I *do* want you and the boys to be with me; there is no doubt about that! We're good, babe. You are the one who keeps me going too. Can you forgive me for being so hard on you?" Rusty asked.

"Yes, my darlin', but there really isn't anything to forgive you for. You were just showing your sweet and generous ways of wanting to help me and caring for me. Are Tom and James helping you with the farm? Did you get any snow?" Sally asked, changing the subject.

"Sally, you are so kind; I can't wait to make you mine. Oh, I'm a poet, and didn't know it!" Rusty chuckled. "But it's true! I do want you to be mine. I so look forward to that day. Yes, Tom and James are at the farm. If Dad is able to go to a regular room today, then I'll be able to go back to the farm. I really do appreciate their help. When all of this is over with, I need to do something special for them. We did get a dusting of snow, but thank goodness, it wasn't so much that it disrupted the work at the farm." Rusty paused for a moment. "I guess I better get back to Dad's room and see what's happening. I'll be thinking about you and praying for you. I'll call you tonight. I won't be able to call you in the mornings anymore, but it'll be extra sweet when we talk to each other in the evenings," Rusty said.

"You're right, extra sweet. Thank you for your prayers. I'll be praying all will continue to go well for your dad. Please tell him and your mom I said *hi*. Please be careful in all you do. I'll be praying for you too. I love you bunches." Sally blew him a kiss.

"I love you with all my heart, Sally dear." And Rusty blew her a kiss.

That was the hardest conversation Sally and Rusty had had in a long time, but it turned out OK. Sally walked to the washing machine and took the clothes out and tossed them into the dryer. It would be a while before they would be dry. She went into the bedrooms and stripped the beds of their linens and took them to the washer to begin another load. Her bowl of cereal hadn't gone very far in keeping her from hunger, so she prepared herself a sandwich for lunch.

The afternoon seemed to go quickly, but Sally was pleased with all she had accomplished. The laundry was finished, beds were remade, the house was cleaner, and it was near time to pick the boys up from school. On the way, she stopped by the drugstore and paid the utility bill. She then picked up the boys. They said they had a good day but had some homework to do.

The evening went like most days—homework, dinner, baths, television, then bed. Not long after she tucked the boys in, the telephone rang. It was Rusty! He updated Sally on his dad, who had been moved to a regular room and was feeling much better. Rusty and his mother had returned home, and it would be back to farm work tomorrow. Rusty and Sally longed to see each other, but there was no way for that to happen yet. Telephone calls would have to be enough right now to continue their relationship and help their love to grow.

Sally had set her alarm clock for fifteen minutes earlier than normal to give her extra time to prepare herself for her first day of work. As she sat on the edge of her bed, she prayed the Lord would guide her through the next few hours of her morning. She slipped into her robe and made her way to the kitchen. She brewed her coffee and made the boys' lunches. Then it was time to wake up the boys.

As she entered their bedroom, she began singing,

> *Good morning, good morning!*
> *The best to my little boys this morning!*
> *It's time to rise and shine.*
> *Be careful, and don't let the sun outdo ya!*

"Good morning, Momma. That sun isn't going to outdo me. I'm up!" Pace shouted as his little feet hit the floor, and he ran to the bathroom.

"Hi, Mom. I enjoyed your singing. I slept good last night. How about you?" Todd asked.

Sally opened the boys' closet, searching for their school clothes for the day. "I slept pretty good. Thanks for asking. I'm glad you did too." She turned around with their clothes in her hands. "Here are your clothes for the day. I'll lay Pace's clothes on the end of his bed." She pulled the linens of Pace's bed up to the top of the bed and asked Todd to help his brother get dressed.

"Sure, Mom. I'll help him." As Sally started to leave the room, he said, "Mom. . . ." A slight pause. "Would you let me start choosing my clothes to wear to school?"

Sally stopped abruptly in her tracks, as if she had just laid on the brake of a car. Before she answered, she thought to herself, *Is this a growing-up moment for him?* She turned to face him. "Well, I guess you can. We can certainly try it." She hoped her response wasn't too protective; she was caught so off guard with his question. She didn't know whether she should address the situation more or leave it alone. "I guess I better get our breakfast started. Call me if y'all need any help," she said as she walked toward the kitchen, still somewhat rattled by Todd's request.

Ten minutes later, the boys walked into the kitchen and helped their mother with their glasses of milk and juice. Sally placed the fried eggs on their plates carefully so as not to break the yolks. She sat a small bowl of buttery grits beside the eggs along with some bacon, and she placed a piece of toast with jam next to it.

"Here's y'all's breakfast," she said as she walked back to the table and sat the two plates of food in front of her sons. "I'll be right there. I'm going to get my cup of coffee and my plate." They then blessed their food and began eating.

Midway through their meal, Todd asked his mom, "Are you excited about starting to work today?"

"Yes, I am, but I'm a little nervous too. I haven't worked in years—almost nine years. I just hope I can do the work OK," she confessed.

"Oh, Mom, you'll do just fine. I'll say a prayer for you. God will help you," Todd reassured her as he touch her hand.

"That's very sweet, Todd. Thank you." Sally fought back tears, hearing his kind words.

"Me too, Momma. I'll say a prayer for you too," Pace chimed in.

"Thank you too, Pace. Both of you are such sweethearts. I love y'all bunches," Sally expressed as she wiped her tears away.

When they had finished eating, they cleared the table of the breakfast dishes and placed them in the kitchen sink. Sally noticed the time on the stove clock and realized she didn't have time to wash the dishes just yet.

"Y'all brush your teeth; we need to get going," Sally instructed as she walked toward her room to get herself dressed. She applied a little make-up to her face and combed her hair. When she was done, she entered the living room. "Do I look OK, boys?"

The boys looked at their mother. "Yes, ma'am!" they said excitedly.

"Thank you, fellas. I need your vote of confidence. I have a few minutes. I think I'll clean up the kitchen. Then, we need to go."

The kitchen was clean, coats were on, and the three of them were out the front door. They chatted on the way to school. The car line was short, and no other cars were behind Sally, so she was able to have a minute longer with her sons. As they exited the car, they wished their mother of have a good day at work. They waved to each other, and the boys entered the school building.

Sally drove out of the school's parking lot and onto the main street. She turned on the CB radio, which she hadn't done in a long time. Right away, she heard voices. It sounded mostly like interstate traffic. She stopped at a red light, then made a left turn onto the street where the church was located. As she turned, someone came over the radio.

"Cricket, is that you? If it is, Minnie Mouse is behind you. I'm flashing my headlights at you."

"Hey, Minnie Mouse! Yes, it's me. I'll pull over to the curb. I have a minute to talk. Do you?" Sally asked.

"Yes, I do," Minnie Mouse replied, and both drivers pulled over to the curb.

They exited their cars and walked to the sidewalk to get out of the street. They greeted each other with a hug, then the rattle of questions started. They asked each other how they had been, how their Christmases were, and how their husbands were. Minnie Mouse told her that Firecracker was back on the road after a nice break from driving through the Christmas holidays. Cricket told her that her husband had transferred to Houston, Texas, and when he left, he told her he wasn't coming back. Cricket mentioned the pending divorce and explained to Minnie Mouse she was on her way to the first day of her new job. She wanted to tell Minnie Mouse about the Farmer from Connecticut, but maybe another time. She needed to get to work. They parted with promises to each other that they would get together soon, hugged good-bye, then re-entered their cars and drove away.

Sally was glad she had taken the time to talk to Minnie Mouse. She'd been thinking about her for a while but just hadn't taken the time to call her.

The church was in sight, and suddenly Sally grew more excited and nervous at the same time. She drove into the parking lot and parked the car near the church office door. It was nine o'clock. She stepped out of the car and began walking to the office door. She prayed the Lord would help her through all things that day. When she opened the office door, Brother Hal was waiting for her.

"Good morning, Sally! Welcome to the Cherish Baptist Church office," he greeted her with a big smile.

Sally was surprised by his pleasant introduction and replied with a joyful smile, "Well, thank you, Brother Hal. I'm very happy to be here."

"How are you this morning?" he asked.

Sally wanted to say she was nervous, but instead she answered, "I'm good and most grateful for the opportunity you have given me."

"You are so welcome. All things work for the glory of God. The timing was in His hands!" Brother Hal turned slightly and pointed in the direction where a big, dark-colored desk was sitting. "This is where you'll be working. Patty, the lady who is on maternity leave, left you some notes and her telephone number just in case you have some questions. She wanted you to feel free to call her."

Sally stepped closer to the desk and saw the handwritten notes lying in the center of the desk. "That's great! I appreciate her doing that for me."

"Make yourself comfortable. I need to get the employment form from my office, which you will need to fill out. I'll be right back." Brother Hal walked down the short hall, then disappeared through a doorway.

In Brother Hal's absence, Sally pulled the black leather armchair away from under the desk and sat down. The high-back chair was very comfortable. She snuggled up to the desk and looked over the information Patty had left for her. Most of it was Greek to her and was very confusing. She wondered, *Have I agreed to do something I don't know how to do?* She knew she was definitely going to need help.

Brother Hal re-entered the hallway and approached Sally. He handed her the paperwork that she needed to fill out. "Take your time, and when you're finished filling in the blanks, please bring it to me. My office is down the hall and to the left." He turned around and walked back down the hallway.

Sally found a ballpoint pen in the center desk drawer and began filling out the form. A few questions she wasn't sure how to answer because of her pending divorce. But when she had finished filling most of it out, she stood up and walked down the hall to Brother Hal's office. He looked up from what appeared to be a Bible on his desk.

"I'm sorry. I did not mean to disturb you," Sally apologized.

"No, no, you're fine. I was just reading God's Word, asking Him to direct me on what He would like for me to preach about this Sunday. Did you have any trouble with the paperwork?" he asked.

"It's been a long time since I've applied for a job, so I do have a few questions. I did mention to you that I have filed for divorce," Sally said, ensuring he remembered her situation.

"Yes, you did."

Sally handed him the form. "I wasn't quite sure how to answer the *withholding* information."

Brother Hal looked at the section of the form she hadn't answered. "You've marked *Single*. OK, you have two children, right?"

"Yes," Sally answered.

"I've marked two dependents, and your income will be three dollars an hour. So to make sure you won't have to pay the government more money at tax time, I'm going to write in 15 percent toward your *withholdings*. Depending on Patty's maternity leave time, you may not even need to file taxes at all because you haven't made enough money. Now, once Patty returns to work, you most likely will be searching for another job, and the salary you'll earn will put you into a higher income tax bracket. But for right now, let's take care of today, and tomorrow will take care of itself. That's Matthew 6:34." He finished his notes on the form and looked up. "OK, I believe that's that. Now, a little instruction time. When the telephone rings, please answer promptly and address the caller with, 'Good morning' or 'Good afternoon, thank you for calling Cherish Baptist Church. This is Sally. How may I help you?' Your friendly voice will be pleasing to the caller. When someone comes into the office, greet that person in a similar manner. Usually, I'll be the only one in the office, except on Wednesdays. Maggie Harper, our church hostess, and Dennis Miller, our minister of music, will be in and out of the office preparing for that night's service. Maggie oversees the kitchen and the personnel who prepare our Wednesday night meals. She's in early those mornings to pick up money to go grocery shopping for the food items and other items needed for her cooks to start cooking by eleven o'clock. On Tuesday mornings, she will bring to the church office the menu for the Wednesday night meal for the week after the upcoming Wednesday supper so we can add it to the following Sunday morning bulletin. She was in yesterday to leave the menu because she had a dentist appointment this morning. I'll give it to you shortly. Oh, just a head's up. Maggie is in charge of all the activities that involve the kitchen—like the ladies' luncheons, wedding or baby showers, wedding receptions, etc. She is a busy lady, so don't be surprised if she approaches you to assist her from time to time with an event. You're not obligated to help; however, if you do, you will be paid extra for your time from her budget. Speaking of the kitchen, you have access to it. You can bring your lunch and put it in the refrigerator. Being that you'll be here from nine o'clock until 3:15, I'll pay you for a twenty-minute lunch. Does that sound fair?" Brother Hal asked.

"Yes. More than fair. Thank you," Sally answered gratefully.

"Two other things. I know all this sounds like a lot, but after a few times of doing the work, it'll be a snap for you. I'll have paperwork for you to file from time to time. I'll show you the file cabinet when the time comes. And last but not least, every Tuesday you will be helping me with each Sunday's church bulletins." Brother Hal reached for and handed Sally the Sunday church bulletin from two days earlier. "We need to get started on next week's bulletin. Also, here is the Wednesday night menu. You will be able to use the typewriter near your desk. The typing paper is in a desk drawer. Here's a list of songs Dennis has given to me for Sunday's song service. Just type the bulletin the way you see it from last week. I believe that's it for now, but if you have any questions, I'll be ready to answer them for you."

Sally thanked him and walked from his office back to her desk where she sat down. She opened the bulletin from last Sunday and pondered how to do what she needed to do. After a few minutes, she found the typing paper, slid a sheet into the typewriter, and began to type next Sunday morning's bulletin. She calculated every keystroke, measured each margin, and followed and typed each entry from the previous bulletin onto the typing paper. This new experience took her a while, but after several hours, she mastered the task. She took the finished product to Brother Hal to proofread.

After Brother Hal starred at the new bulletin for a few moments, he seemed to be extremely pleased. "OK, great job, Sally! Now, we take this to the printer located on Park Avenue. Would you like to take it? If you do, I'll add a few more dollars to your paycheck," Brother Hal said.

"Sure, I'd be happy to. What's the address?" Sally agreed, as she thought a few more dollars would be nice.

Brother Hal wrote down the address on a piece of paper and handed it to Sally.

"Thank you, Brother Hal. I'll be back soon." As Sally walked past her desk, she grabbed her purse and left for the printers. When she arrived, the clerk knew exactly what needed to be done. Within fifteen minutes, the bulletins were printed and the fee charged to the church's account. On her way back to the church, she stopped at a fast-food restaurant for a quick bite to eat. She grabbed a burger and a drink and ate it as she drove back to the church.

Back at her desk, Sally folded the bulletins in half and rubber banded them neatly for Sunday morning's service.

Sally's first work day went quicker than she expected. In no time, the little clock on her desk said 3:10. She walked to Brother Hal's office and told him she was leaving. He gave her a thumbs-up, and she was thrilled.

As she drove to the boys' school, Sally replayed her workday in her mind. She was proud of herself and thought that her first day had gone really well. She thanked God for a *blessed* day.

Sally waited in the car line, and soon Todd and Pace emerged from their school and got into the back seat. They immediately asked their mother how her first day of work was. She explained to them all she did, and they were excited for her. They praised the Lord together.

Once at home, Sally prepared a small snack for her sons while they began their homework. Then she changed from her work clothes to more comfortable lounging clothes.

The evening seemed to rush by. Supper had been prepared and eaten, a little television had been watched, and bath time for the boys had come and gone.

"I can't believe it's time for y'all to go to bed!" Sally expressed as she followed Todd and Pace into their bedroom. They knelt beside Pace's bed and prayed. Then Sally kissed them and tucked them into their beds. Standing in their bedroom doorway, Sally tenderly told them, "I love y'all. Sleep tight, and don't let the bedbugs bite. Have sweet dreams, my sons."

"Good night, Mom. Sweet dreams to you too," Todd replied.

"Night night, Momma. You have sweet dreams too," Pace echoed.

"Thank y'all. See y'all in the morning," Sally said as she switched the overhead light off.

Sally had just sat down on the couch when the telephone rang. She expected Rusty to call her, so she answered with joy in her voice.

"Hello?"

"Is this Sally?" a male voice asked.

Recognizing the voice, her countenance dropped as she responded. "Yes."

"Well, it didn't sound like you. I wanted you to know I received the divorce papers. I have filled them out, and I will Express Mail the envelope back to the attorney in the morning. I asked my boss for a particle advance from my upcoming payroll check for next week. I'm sending you some money. I'm sure you're needing it. I called several times today. Where were you?" Collin inquired.

Sally hesitated to answer, wondering why he cared where she was. "Thank you for returning the paperwork so quickly to the attorney. I appreciate it. And thank you for sending some money; I could definitely use it. I've been in and out of the house several times today taking care of business," she told him. She wasn't about to tell him she was working. "Do you want to know how your sons are doing?"

"Oh, sure. How are they?" Collin reacted with little to no concern.

"They are doing good. I've got to go, Collin. Thank you again." And Sally hung up. She muttered to herself, *Collin, you are such a jerk!*

A few seconds later, the telephone rang again. *Is he calling back?* Sally asked herself, annoyed.

"Hello?" she snapped.

"Oh my, you're upset! What's wrong, sweetheart?" Rusty could tell by the tone of her voice that something wasn't right.

"Honey, I'm sorry. Collin just called, and as usual, he ended the call by being a real jerk!" Sally apologized.

"No apology needed, dear. What did he want?"

"He wanted to tell me he had received the divorce paperwork and will put all of it in the mail tomorrow morning. Plus, he is sending me some money. Then, he asked me where I'd been all day because he had called several times, and I did not answer the telephone. I wasn't about to tell him I was working!" Sally sounded upset again.

"It's none of his dang business as to where you were!" Rusty popped off in disgust. "However, I'm glad about the divorce papers and the money. I still feel bad about not sending you any money, but hopefully soon I can. Dad is doing better, and the doctor thinks he might be able to come home this weekend, barring no complications," Rusty said, happy to be giving some good news.

"Oh, that's wonderful news! That means he is getting better, and that's very important," Sally replied joyfully.

"Yes, it is great news. But he still has a while before he'll feel like running the farm. I wish everything here could get back to normal so I could get back in my K-Whopper and be back on the road. I know it's only been a week since we were together, but I miss you so much, and I long to see you. I need to hold you in my arms and kiss you all over!" Passion rose in Rusty's voice.

"My Rusty, your endearing words are making me tingle all over. I want all that too. Golly, how I miss you too. I wish I could reach through this telephone and give you a big juicy kiss!" Even as she said the words, she heard a still small voice whisper that this was wrong. She was still married to another man. But she continued on. "I can almost feel your arms around me and the warmth of your body next to mine. I daydream about our time together in your sleeper all the time. I long for that time together with you." And this was true, but she knew it wasn't right. Not yet.

"Babe, the thoughts of us being together soon is what keeps me going from day to day. Waiting is *so* hard," Rusty confessed.

"I know. Waiting is hard for me too! I pray our time apart will go by quickly." Sally took a long breath. His words and her feelings were making her crazy.

"Sally, are you still there?" Rusty said, interrupting the silence.

"Yes, I'm here, Rusty dear. I needed a moment to clear my head. It was spinning with the wonderful thoughts of us wanting to be together. So anyway, are you feeling OK? How is the farm work going?" Sally said, changing the subject.

"I'm feeling OK. The farm is the same. How was your first day at work?"

"I enjoyed the day, and working felt good. I just hope all my workdays are as good as today," Sally replied.

"I'm glad your day was good. I prayed it would be a good day for you," Rusty said, wanting Sally to know he was thinking of her.

"You are such a sweetheart. Thank you."

"Well, darling, it's late, and we both need to get to bed. I sure wish you were going to be lying beside me. I hope to see you in my dreams. I'll be praying for you. Please stay safe, and I'll call you tomorrow night. I love you, my Sally girl," Rusty tenderly said.

"I wish I was going to be lying beside you too, my love. Let's meet in our dreams! I have you always in my prayers. I love you too, Rusty. Good night," Sally replied as she puckered her lips and threw him her kiss.

"Got it! Good night, baby." Then Rusty ended the call by blowing a kiss to her.

As Sally returned the handset to the telephone base, she smiled happily. She loved that man so much, and she was thankful he was in her life.

Sally was tired. It had been a long and exhausting day for her. She quietly walked to her bedroom, slipped into her nightgown, and crawled into bed. Moments later, she turned out the light on the nightstand, briefly prayed her good-night prayer, and drifted off to sleep.

The next two days were as busy as Tuesday, with Sally getting the boys to school, working, picking up the boys from school, their homework and evening activities, and then Rusty's loving phone calls.

Friday was a good day—even better because, at the end of the day, she had been given her first paycheck. Sally was so happy. Once she was in her car, she opened the envelope that Brother Hal had given to her, and she smiled from ear to ear. She had earned seventy-five dollars! *Thank You, sweet Jesus!* she rejoiced as she cried.

When she picked up the boys from school, she excitedly told them about her first paycheck. They were so happy for their mother.

Not long after Sally and the boys arrived home, the telephone rang.

"Hello?" Sally answered.

"Is this Sally Oldham?" the male voice asked.

"Yes, it is," Sally replied.

"Hi, Sally. This is Hugh Cut, your attorney at Cut and Dry Law Office. I wanted to let you know we have received the paperwork back that we sent Collin to fill out. I need for you to come into the office and sign a few forms, and then I can take your petition for divorce to the courthouse. When can you come in? The sooner, the better."

"That's wonderful! Will you be in your office tomorrow? It's Saturday," Sally asked.

"Yes, until noon. Can you be here near eleven?" Hugh asked.

"Should it take very long?" Sally asked, then continued. "I'll have my two sons with me. Will that be OK?"

"Maybe fifteen minutes is all. And yes, I'd like to meet your boys. So y'all come on! See ya in the morning." And Hugh hung up.

Sally stood by the phone table with the handset still in her hand. *Lord, what just happened?* she thought.

"Is something wrong, Mom?" Todd asked.

Sally slowly returned the handset to the telephone's base, looked at Todd, and answered, "No, not really." Deep down inside of her, though, she felt like the pieces of her future were finally coming together. "We will need to go downtown tomorrow, so we won't be able to sleep in too long in the morning."

"Downtown? Where is that, Momma? Have we been there before?" Pace inquisitively asked.

"No, y'all have not been downtown. We usually don't have any reason to go in that direction. We'll make it a fun trip," Sally explained.

"I think I just heard the mailman at the mailbox. Is it all right if I check?" Todd asked.

"Sure!" Sally agreed.

Todd opened the front door, pushed open the screen door, and reached into the mailbox. "Yip, we got mail!" he announced as he re-entered the house. "Here, Mom," and he handed her three envelopes and one magazine.

"Thank you, Todd," she said as she patted his head. "Let's see," Sally remarked as she opened the first envelope. "This one is an advertisement. Now, what is this one? It's the telephone bill. Uck! But the amount due is not too bad. And this one . . . oh my." She stopped talking suddenly.

"Who is it from, Mom?" Todd anxiously asked.

Sally could hardly believe her eyes. "It's from your father! He did what he said he would do! He sent us some money!" Sally counted five, one-hundred-dollar bills in the envelope. Also enclosed was a short note that Collin wrote, stating he would send more money soon. *Thank You, our dear Lord!*

"I'm glad he sort of remembers us! I miss him. I hope he is OK," Todd sadly said.

"Me too, Momma. I'd like to see him," Pace added.

"I know, fellas, but hey, he is thinking of us by sending us this money. That should count for something, right?" Sally quickly stated, trying to make it sound like their father was doing this for the boys. "OK, time's getting away. What would y'all like for supper?"

"Hey, Todd, you want some hot dogs and chili?" Pace suggested to his big brother.

"I think that sounds pretty good, Pace. Mom, what do you think?" Todd turned the suggestion to her.

"I like that idea. I'll get to work on it right after I change my clothes," Sally agreed as she walked to her bedroom, still holding Collin's envelope in her hand. Once in her bedroom, she glanced at the money again and thanked God for allowing Collin to do the right thing for his family.

After supper was eaten and all was cleaned up in the kitchen, the three of them settled down on the couch and watched television.

Near eight o'clock, Rusty called. He had news that his dad was coming home tomorrow, and it would be a busy but exciting day. Sally was so happy for Russell and his family. She told him about going to the attorney's office in the morning, and they were another step closer to being together. Rusty was overjoyed about her news.

Several hours later, the television was turned off, the kiddos were tucked into their beds, the lights were out, and slumber ensued for all.

Chapter Fifteen

Sally and the boys enjoyed sleeping in on Saturday, and once they arose, they quickly headed out for their day. Sally surprised them by going to a fast-food restaurant nearby and treating them to breakfast before heading downtown.

They soon arrived at the attorney's office, and Hugh Cut joyfully greeted them as they walked in the building.

"Hi, Sally! This must be Todd and Pace." Hugh extended his hand and shook their little hands. "I'm Hugh Cut, your mother's attorney. It's nice to meet the two of you."

Shy and cautious of this stranger, Todd was a little apprehensive about shaking his hand. Pace, on the other hand, was happy to shake this new person's hand.

"Hi. It's nice to meet you too," Pace politely said.

"Y'all come on back to my office and sign the paperwork," Mr. Cut said, leading the way. "All the paperwork Collin signed looks fine. This shouldn't take too long. Are y'all doing OK today?"

"Yes, sir. We're doing good. Thank you for arranging to do this today," Sally said with appreciation.

"Oh, you are so welcome. Just glad we can now move forward with your petition for divorce," Mr. Cut said confidently.

They entered Mr. Cut's office, and Todd's eyes grew big as he looked around.

"Mr. Cut, do you live here?" Pace asked inquisitively.

Hugh laughed. "Well, Pace, no. I don't live here, but some days, I spend more of my time here than I do at home. But that's OK because at home, it's just me and my pooch."

Pace looked at his mother, leaned toward her, and asked, nearly in a whisper, "What is a pooch?" He had never heard that word before.

Sally smiled at him and whispered, "That's another word for *dog*."

"Oh, OK. So you have a dog? We've never had a . . . *pooch*," Pace exclaimed.

"What kind of dog do you have, Mr. Cut?" Sally inquired.

"Duke is a Great Dane," he answered as he reached for a picture frame that was on his desk. "Here's a picture of him."

Todd glanced at the picture for a second, then he did a double take. "Wow, he is huge!"

"Yes, he is! He's almost two years old, and he weighs almost one hundred and fifty pounds and is as tall as I am," Mr. Cut said.

"Golly, Duke is a pretty dog," Pace admired.

"How did it come about that you chose a Great Dane?" Sally asked.

"Well, my Duke is from Germany. My folks, as well as I, are of German heritage. My parents and my grandparents raise Great Danes in Germany. I don't raise them—well, not yet, but I'm thinking about it."

"That's quite a family history and especially about the Great Danes in your family," Sally commented.

"I wish I could see him," Pace added.

"Oh, Pace," Sally said, hushing him.

"No, that's OK, Sally. Maybe you can sometime. I'd like for you to see him," Hugh said, smiling at Pace. "All right, getting to the paperwork. Here's a pen, Sally. You need to sign here," he said, pointing to a blank line. "By signing this document, you are giving me permission to file this petition with the courts."

Sally nervously signed her name. She knew she was doing the right thing, so she didn't understand why she was so nervous. This is what Collin insisted on doing, and this is what she wanted to do to be able to move on with her new life with Rusty.

"OK, one more form. This one is stating that everything you have told me is the truth . . . and I know it is," Hugh assured Sally.

"And nothing but the truth, so help me God. Right?" Sally added.

Hugh laughed. "That's right, Sally! You are so clever."

"It just popped out," she admitted, slightly embarrassed.

Hugh laughed again. "OK, I'll file this on Monday. Any questions?"

Sally thought for a moment. "Yes. Do you still think it will take four months before the divorce will be final? And will Collin need to be here for court?"

"It could be sooner, but that's not likely. I'm sorry. And no, Collin will not be required to be present in court. If you think of any other questions, please call me. I'm here for you," Hugh told her, giving her an odd smirk.

Sally felt weird by how Hugh was looking at her. *Is he coming onto me? Surely not—*, she thought. "OK, Mr. Cut, I will," she responded.

"Oh please, call me Hugh. Mr. Cut sounds so formal. You have a good day. Thank you for coming in so promptly and signing the paperwork. It's to your advantage. The sooner, the better," Hugh remarked as he patted Sally on her shoulder. "And it sure was nice to meet you, Todd and Pace. Y'all are good kiddos." Hugh shook both the boys' hands.

"OK, boys, let's go so Mr. Cut—ah, Hugh—can get on with his day. Thank you for everything. Have a good day," Sally said gratefully as she and her sons walked out of Hugh's office.

"You guys have a good day too, and stay safe," Hugh said, ushering them toward the front entrance.

Sally and the boys walked to the car. She was relieved the divorce paperwork was signed and would be taken to the courthouse in two days. She smiled as she thought of being free from Collin so she could finally be with Rusty.

Once in the car, Sally began driving toward the Mississippi River. She noticed the eerie silence from her boys. "Are y'all OK? Not a word has been spoken since we got in the car," she asked, looking at them in the rearview mirror.

The boys looked at each other, then Todd spoke up. "I've heard the word *divorce*, but I'm not sure what it means."

Sally thought for a moment before she spoke. So many difficult things had happened in her marriage, and she wasn't sure how to present all this. She didn't want to say anything bad about her husband or her own infidelity, so she decided to just describe to the boys what the word *divorce* meant. She said, "When a married man and woman fall out of love with each other, they will sometimes meet with a person like Mr. Cut to fill out some paperwork to legally end their marriage. Does that help you understand?"

"So you and Dad don't love each other anymore? And y'all don't want to be married?" Todd asked, trying to understand.

"Yes, Todd, that's correct. I'm sorry that it has come to this, but we have made this decision. We both want to move on with our lives."

"There is this girl at school who lives with her mom but sees her dad every other weekend. I guess her parents are divorced. I wish we could see our dad every other weekend," Todd sadly admitted.

"I know, kiddo. I wish y'all could too." It hurt Sally to know that Collin didn't want to see them, but she dared not share that with them. It would hurt them so much. They love their dad, and they would not understand.

As Sally turned the car onto Riverside Drive, Pace exploded with excitement. "Wow! Look at all that water! Look at the boats! Where are we, Momma?"

"You're looking at the mighty Mississippi River on the banks of the Memphis Bluffs. Those boats are called *riverboats* or *barges,* and those other little boats are called *tugboats*. You can also see a paddlewheel riverboat. It takes passengers out for river cruises, floating up and down the river for entertainment. The little tugboats help navigate the barges on the river. This river is one of the busiest rivers in the United States," she told them, continuing to drive down the road.

"What are barges?" Todd asked.

Sally pointed. "See that line of things on the river coming toward us, going under the bridge? Those are barges. Sometimes they can be two or three barges wide and as many as ten to fifteen barges long. The tugboats, sometimes called towboats, guide the barges. There is a bigger, master tugboat that pushes the barges along the river. It's serious business!"

"What do they do?" Todd wanted to know more.

"Each barge can carry different things like wheat, corn, other grains, coal, gravel, timber, fertilizer . . . just about most anything," she explained as she drove into a parking area so they could watch the barges travel the river, being pushed and towed by the different boats.

The boys' eyes were glued to the river's activity. Pace finally broke the silence. "The barges don't look very big."

"Looks can be deceiving, Pace. You're seeing only the top part of the barge. What you can't see is the other five to nine feet below the surface of the water. Each barge is probably close to two hundred feet long and at least thirty or more feet wide," Sally added.

"They really are big!" Todd's eyes grew wide as he and his brother intently watched the barges being pushed farther north.

As Sally drove out of the parking lot, Todd asked, "Where are those barges going?"

"That's a good question, Todd. There are a lot of major cities along the Mississippi River between here and its origin in Minnesota, like St. Louis, Missouri, Davenport, Iowa, and then north past St. Paul in Minnesota. Plus there are several large rivers off the Mississippi River that the barges could use to navigate to other ports like the Ohio and Missouri Rivers. Barges can go all over the United States," Sally continued.

"Hey, Momma, can you fish in the Mississippi River?" Pace asked as he settled back in his seat.

"I'm sure people do, but carefully. The water currents and whirlpools in the Mississippi River can be dangerous," she replied.

After a little while, Sally and the boys arrived in the parking lot of Air Memphis.

"Mom, what is this place?" Todd asked.

"Look at all the little airplanes! They're our size!" Pace exclaimed.

Sally said, "Remember several days ago when we were at the airport and you mentioned to me that you'd like to learn how to fly? Well, I wondered if this flight training school was still here, and it is! Come on; let's go in!" Sally encouraged, ushering the boys out of the car. Todd couldn't contain his excitement.

Sally approached the desk in the main office. "I'd like some information about flight school. My son, Todd, is interested in learning how to fly," she continued as she placed her hands on Todd's shoulders.

At that moment, another man entered the office area from a door in the back. Pace bolted from his mother's side. "Captain Hall!" he shouted loudly as he ran and hugged the captain's legs.

"Well, hello Pace! It's so good to see you!" Captain Hall said, surprised to see the young boy. He reached down and hugged Pace, then looked up and saw Todd, who also ran to him. Sally was in total shock as she stood staring at Captain Hall.

"Sally! What a wonderful surprise. How are you and the boys?" Captain Hall asked as he began walking toward Sally, holding the boys' hands.

Sally struggled to compose herself. "Well, hello there! The boys and I are good. We're here to inquire about flying lessons for Todd. How are you?"

"I've been good, but seeing y'all has made my day! So, Todd, you're serious about wanting to learn how to fly?" Captain Hall squatted down in front of Todd to be at eye level with the youngster.

"Yes, sir. I sure am," Todd answered eagerly.

Captain Hall patted Todd on the head and stood up. He looked at the man behind the counter and said, "Evan, I'd like to help these folks. Is that OK with you?"

Evan smiled at the captain and replied, "Yes, sir. That's fine with me."

Captain Hall motioned with his hand to Sally and the boys. "Y'all come on and follow me." He opened the door he had just walked through, and Todd and Pace immediately froze at what they saw. They had entered into an airplane hangar where many small airplanes sat. The looks on the boys' faces were priceless. Sally caught a glimpse of Captain Hall as he smiled at the boys, and she thought, *He's a very handsome man in or out of his uniform. . . .* Then she said, "Captain Hall, do you work here?"

Captain Hall hesitated for a moment, then answered, "Yes. Matter of fact, I do. I'm one of the flight instructors."

At that statement, the boys came out of their trance and looked at the captain. Todd couldn't help himself. "You must be really smart! You can fly the big jets, and you can also fly these little airplanes?"

"Well, Todd, no matter the size of the airplane, the concept of flying is basically the same. Come on. Let's get closer to them," he said, leading the way.

As they walked closer to the small aircraft, Captain Hall pointed out the different makes of them, using names like *Diamond, Piper, Cirrus, Beechcraft,* and *Cessna.* Todd and Pace were like little sponges, soaking everything in.

Captain Hall stopped beside a white-trimmed red airplane. "This is my baby," he said, looking at his aircraft. "It's a Cessna 172 Skyhawk. I've had it for several years, and I enjoy flying it."

"Wow! That's nice," Pace shouted. "Maybe you could take us flying sometime, Captain Hall."

"Pace! That's not polite," Sally scolded.

"You never know, Pace. Maybe someday," Captain Hall quickly said, hoping his words might sooth the scolding. "How about you, Todd? How do you feel as you see all these aircrafts?"

Todd was silent for a few moments. Sally could tell he was in deep thought. He looked at Captain Hall with tears in his eyes. He struggled to talk. "Captain Hall, I'm just so excited to see all this, and it makes me want to learn to fly even more!" he expressed as tears flowed down his little cheeks.

Captain Hall bent down to hug Todd. "Don't cry, little man. I feel your excitement, and I understand your enthusiasm in wanting to learn how to fly. I've been there!"

Sally noticed the tears in Captain Hall's eyes. She saw and felt the compassion he had for Todd—how sensitive he was. Captain Hall seemed to be an incredibly special man.

"Can I talk to your mother for a minute?" he asked Todd. He took a handkerchief from his pants pocket and gave it to Todd to dry the tears from his eyes.

Todd muffled, "Yes, sir."

When he stood up, Captain Hall approached Sally. He wiped the tears from his eyes. "Sally, I'm sorry for the tears, but Todd's expression and desire for flying brought back memories of those days in my young life. I'm going to ask something that may be off the wall and inappropriate, but if you have time, if you trust me, and if you feel OK with this, I'd like to take Todd for a quick flight in my airplane. Now, if you prefer I don't, I understand. I'd just like to know exactly where his thinking and desire truly is in learning how to fly."

Sally was so surprised at the captain's request. "Oh, Captain Hall, I don't know. I'm certain Todd would be over-the-top with excitement and appreciation for the opportunity you'd be giving him, but as a mother, I'm reluctant to agree to this idea. What if something happens? Please, Captain, give me a minute." Sally looked at the boys and told them she'd be right back and to stay with Captain Hall.

Right away Todd and Pace began talking to the captain. Sally stepped away from the three of them behind a nearby airplane. She was desperate for an answer to her prayer request to God about this situation. *God, my Father in heaven, I don't want to deprive Todd of this opportunity, but I'm concerned for his safety with a man I barely know. If this flight is Your will, please give me peace. I ask this in Your Son's name. Amen.* Instantly a calm flowed over her, and she knew her prayer had been answered. She walked toward Todd, Pace, and Captain Hall with a thankful heart. She looked at the captain and said, "It's OK."

Captain Hall was elated and turned to Todd with a big smile. "Let's go flying, master Todd!"

"What? Really?" Todd rejoiced. "Mom, is it OK?" he asked excitedly.

"Yes, my son," Sally answered with tears in her eyes. She hadn't seen him so happy in a long time.

The captain asked an employee to pull his airplane out of the hangar. He explained to Todd about the checklist that needed to be fulfilled before entering the aircraft. Then Sally and Pace watched as Todd and the captain climbed into the front seat of the airplane. Another checklist was performed. Then both signaled a thumbs-up as the captain engaged the single-engine propeller. The Cessna slowly rolled away, taxied down the runway, and then turned around. After a few moments, the aircraft moved forward faster and faster, then lifted off the ground and was airborne. Sally and Pace watched wide-eyed until the airplane was out of sight. Sally wondered what Todd was thinking, what he was saying, what he was seeing, and how he was feeling. What a special time for him.

The employee who pulled the captain's aircraft out of the hangar passed by Sally and asked, "Is that your son with Captain Hall?"

Sally answered, "Yes, it is."

"Well, your son is flying with one of the best pilots there is. He's a lucky young man," he said.

Sally was reassured by the man's confidence in Captain Hall. She was also surprised by Pace's attitude about Todd being allowed to fly with the captain. He was not upset that he didn't get to go; he was extremely happy for Todd.

After a brief flight, the Cessna landed and taxied back to the hangar. Todd and the captain exited the airplane at the same time, then Todd broke into a sprint toward his mother and brother.

"Oh, Mom, it was wonderful! Thank you for letting me go! I even flew the airplane for a few minutes. It was something to look down to the ground from way up in the sky. Everything is so small . . . so different." Todd was so excited. He turned and hugged Captain Hall and thanked him for taking him flying.

"You are very welcome, Todd. I'm glad I could. Maybe someday, you'll take me flying with you in *your* aircraft!" he said joyfully.

"That would be really swell, Captain Hall," Todd answered.

Looking toward Sally, Captain Hall said, "I don't have any other students to train today. Would you and the boys like to go to dinner with me?"

Sally was shocked and flattered at the same time. She wanted to take him up on his invitation, but she knew she shouldn't. "Oh, Captain Hall," she began, but he stopped her.

"Sally, I'd like for you to call me by my first name, please. It's Bruce. Captain Hall seems to be too formal. I'm sorry for interrupting you. You were about to say you'd join me for dinner, right?"

"Well, Bruce, actually . . . no. It's very nice of you to want us to have dinner with you, but the boys and I need to be getting home." Sally took the boys' hands and began walking to the office door. "We've already taken up too much of your time today. It was such a surprise to see you here, and then the *biggest* surprise of all was you taking Todd flying. It truly has been such a grand day. Thank you so much, Captain—ah, I mean, Bruce."

The captain opened the office door for her and the boys, and they all walked to Sally's car. She helped the boys into the back seat. Then Todd rolled down his window and said to the captain, "Thank you again for taking me flying!"

The captain waved. "You're welcome, Todd."

Bruce walked Sally to the driver's side of the car. He put his hand on the door handle but paused before opening it. "Sally, I need to confide in you that I feel strongly about Todd's enthusiasm and eagerness to learn how to fly. I'd like to be the one to teach him, but not yet. Mentally he has at least another year of growing up to do. However, I would still like to work with him and teach him the fundamentals of flying through book work, but only on ground level. Do you understand what I'm talking about?"

"Yes, I do understand. Todd is still a playful boy, and another year of lessons would be better for him. But, Bruce, I must be honest with you. I don't have a lot of money. How much would this teaching cost?" Sally asked.

Bruce placed his hand on Sally's shoulder and moved a little closer to her. "There is no cost. Todd reminds me so much of myself when I was his age. I want to do this for him. I own this business, and I can make those decisions. So there is no cost. Will you help me to help him? I really want to do this. Besides, I will get to see you more often." Bruce gave Sally a coy smile.

Immediately Sally was uncomfortable with how this conversation was going. She wanted Todd to have this opportunity, but it felt wrong to her, like the captain was expecting something in return. "Oh Bruce, your offer is so overwhelming, and I'm honored you want to do this for Todd. But if you're doing this to see me more, I can't be in a relationship with you. I'm getting a divorce from my husband right now, and being with someone else is not what I want." Sally was upset.

Bruce removed his hand from Sally's shoulder and stepped away from her. "I'm sorry, Sally. I guess I came on too strong. Please forgive me. I like you and just wanted to be your friend."

"And what did you want from me in return, Captain Hall? No, thank you." Sally opened the car door and got in. "Good-bye, Captain Hall." She shut the door, started the engine, and drove out of the parking lot. She was speechless. She felt humiliated and used. Was he really using her son this whole time to get to her?

"Mom, is there something wrong? You seem upset," Todd asked, noticing her change in demeanor.

What was she to say to him that would not ruin his near-perfect day? "I know you have had a wonderful and special time today, and you made lots of memories you'll never forget. I'm very proud of you. It was great for me to see you so happy. Captain Hall expressed to me that you have great potential, and he wants to see you through this stage of your life, but he thinks it would be best that you wait at least another year so that you can grow a bit more mentally mature before he can train you to fly. Do you understand?" Sally held her breath for his answer.

"Yes, I think I do. It was a great day, and yes, I believe I'll remember this day all my life. But from what Captain Hall said when we were flying, I do have a lot to learn. I think waiting a year would be good. That's OK. I can wait," he replied with certainty in his voice.

His response to his mother was more grown-up than she expected. Perhaps he really did understand. But does she tell Todd that Captain Hall said he would train him through this year of waiting? She didn't want to take away that opportunity for him to learn more about flying, but the captain had put her in an awkward position. She just didn't like the idea of seeing him on Todd's time. Besides, why even think about this opportunity? In, hopefully, four months, the divorce would be final, and she and the boys would be with Rusty. She just wanted to forget the whole conversation with Bruce.

Sally glanced at Todd in the rearview mirror and proudly said, "I believe you've made the right decision, Todd. At your age, one year can make a big difference in growing up. Say, all this excitement has made me hungry. Are y'all hungry?"

"I sure am, Momma," Pace shouted.

"Yeah, I'm pretty hungry too," Todd chimed in.

"OK, then. How about a large pizza or maybe two of them?" Sally suggested. Both boys echoed in mutual agreement.

They stopped at the pizza parlor and grabbed a few to bring home. They ate till they were satisfied, then the boys took their evening baths and then sat on the couch to watch some television. As they were watching, the telephone rang.

Rusty called to check in on Sally and the boys. His dad was enjoying being home, but he was tired from all the excitement of coming home. He asked how the time went at the attorney's office. Sally told him all the paperwork was signed, and Mr. Cut would be filing the petition on Monday. Rusty didn't ask about the rest of that day, and Sally elected not to tell him just yet. It would only upset him. She reminded him of her baptism at church the following day, and he told her he wished he could be there with her but that he would have her in his prayers, as always.

Bedtime called, so the television went off, Sally and the boys prayed, and the boys jumped into their beds. Sally slipped into her nightgown and snuggled up in her bed covers for the night.

Sally's alarm clock played music at 7 a.m. Their Sunday morning routine went well. The three of them were dressed and ready to walk out the door when Peggy arrived to take them to church.

There were lots of folks at church, just like last Sunday. Everyone was friendly, and more members introduced themselves to Sally and the boys. Brother Hal instructed Sally to go to the baptismal room to change into a gown that was provided, and Lois would help her. Peggy took the boys into the sanctuary and sat in the same pew as they did the week before.

Soon the service began. Brother Hal stepped down into the baptismal pool at the front of the church behind the choir loft. The lights in the church dimmed, and a bright light shone over the pool. Brother Hal began to speak.

"Today is a special day." He turned and extended his hand up. Sally placed her hand in his and stepped down into the pool. "Sally Oldham has come on profession of faith to be baptized," he said.

"That's my momma!" Pace blurted out.

"Yes, that's right little, Pace! This is your momma!" Brother Hal declared.

The congregation broke out in laughter as Grandmother Peggy encouraged Pace to be quiet.

"She is a very special momma who has accepted the Lord Jesus Christ into her life as her personal Savior." He turned and looked at Sally. "Upon your profession of faith, I now baptize you, my sister, in the name of the Father, the Son, and the Holy Spirit. Buried in the likeness of His death," he said, lowering Sally backward into the water, "and raised to walk in the newness of life." He raised her up out of the water and steadied her on her feet. "May God always bless you, Sally." Brother Hal held Sally's hand and helped her to the baptismal steps, and the congregation clapped their hands in celebration. "This is always a beautiful occasion, obedience in baptism. Because of Sally's decision, her name has now been written in God's Book of Life."

The baptismal curtain closed, and Brother Hal exited the pool as the choir director walked to the front and asked the congregation to stand and turn in their hymnals to page fifty-three. The choir stood, and the singing began.

Lois helped Sally get dressed and dried her hair. Soon Sally joined her sons and Peggy. Sally smiled at them as she felt a certain refreshing feeling inside of her body.

At the conclusion of the church service, Sally, Peggy, and the boys went out to lunch for some burgers and fries. Peggy stayed with them for a while afterward, sharing a cup of coffee at home while the boys played in their room. They talked about several different things, but then Peggy asked if Sally had heard from Collin.

Sally answered, "Yes. Have you?"

"Only one time, which was last Tuesday," Peggy replied. "He asked me if you were OK. He said he had been attempting to call you most of the day, and you weren't answering the telephone."

"Peggy, what did you tell him?" Sally quickly asked as she was anxious to hear the answer.

"Well, I told him I did not know. I wasn't about to tell him you had started to work. I thought that was none of his business!" Peggy responded.

"Oh, thank you, Peggy. I don't want him to know, at least not yet. That's my feeling exactly. It's none of his business. He called me that night and asked me where I'd been all day. I told him I had places to go. He wanted to tell me he had signed the divorce papers and was putting them in the mail. My attorney called me Friday to tell me he had received the paperwork. I went to his office yesterday to finish signing, and the attorney will take the petition tomorrow to the courthouse," Sally explained.

"So it really is happening? I'm just so sorry for you and the boys. I would never have dreamed that Collin would be so cruel." Peggy teared up.

"It's OK, Peggy." Sally tried to console her. "It's for the best. I feel like it was going to happen sooner or later. Collin has changed so much," Sally admitted.

"How is your new job?" Peggy asked.

"It's good. I like it. Again, thank you for talking to Brother Hal. God answered that prayer. And thank you for your prayers too." Sally raised up from her chair at the dining room table and hugged Peggy. "More coffee?"

"No, dear. But thank you. I should be going. I have several places I need to go," Peggy said as she walked to the boys' room to kiss them good-bye. Sally opened the front door for her, and Peggy walked out to her car, the three of them waving from the door.

The rest of the afternoon consisted of playing games and watching television. Rusty called as well, and he and Sally told each other about their day. Soon it was bedtime and lights out.

The third week of the New Year started and ended the same as the week before, with school, work, and Rusty's telephone calls each evening. Rusty's father's health was improving, but Rusty was discouraged that the progress wasn't happening fast enough. Sally understood because both of them were so anxious to see each other again. However, they both knew that God was in control, and their time together would be in His timing. The lovebirds just had to be patient.

That Saturday morning around eleven o'clock, there was a knock on the front door while Sally was washing the breakfast dishes.

"Mom," Todd said, running into the kitchen, "someone's at the front door. Do you want me to open the door?"

"Sure, that's OK. I'll dry my hands and be right there."

Todd dashed out of the kitchen. A second knock sounded as Todd began to unlock and open the door.

"Captain Hall! Mom, it's Captain Hall!" Todd shouted.

Sally lost her breath and grabbed the edge of the kitchen sink, thinking she might faint.

Todd ran back into the kitchen. "Mom, did you hear me? Captain Hall is here! Come on! He's in the living room! Come on!"

Sally's body was numb; her head felt like it was spinning. She thought, *How could this be happening?* Todd pulled on his mother's arm. She felt herself moving toward the kitchen door. "OK, Todd. I'm coming." *OK now, pull yourself together. Be nice!* she told herself.

"Well, Captain Hall. What a surprise!"

"Hi, Sally. I wasn't sure if I had the correct address or not. I'm sorry for coming unannounced. I hope it's OK," Bruce said apologetically.

Sally was trying to be polite but was very uneasy about him being there. "And yet, you are here. I did not give you my address. How did you find us?" Sally asked inquisitively.

"Please, don't be upset, but when you left the other day, I remembered your car's license plate number. I asked a friend to get your address for me. I wanted to bring Todd some basic training books for him to read and study. Is that OK, Sally?" Bruce asked.

Immediately Todd said, "Really? Wow! Thank you, Captain Hall." He reached his hand out to take the bag that Captain Hall was handing to him.

"There are three books inside the bag. I have marked each one with a number in the order as to which you should read and study them. I believe you'll find them easy to read and understand, but I've enclosed my telephone number on a sheet of paper in the bag. So please, feel free to call me with any questions you have, and we'll discuss them—if, of course, that's OK with your mother," Captain Hall added as his eyes turned to look at Sally.

"Is it OK, Mom? Please say yes!" Todd begged anxiously.

Bruce had done it again. He put Sally in the middle. She felt so uncomfortable. "Bruce, what are you doing? I told you about my situation, and it feels like you are using my son to get to me. I know I should be grateful for your generosity and interest in Todd, but I think you have ulterior motives behind your actions."

"Sally, can you step outside with me for a moment?" Bruce said, taken aback. "Todd, please let me know if you need any help. Call me. Pace, it was good to see you again," he said as he opened the front door.

Sally walked outside with Bruce. Bruce turned and looked her directly in the eyes and stepped closer to her. "Sally, I don't deny I'm attracted to you, and I'd enjoy a relationship with you, but I promise, I'm only trying to help Todd achieve what he believes to be his dream. Please believe me." He took Sally's hand. "Please, let me help Todd. If he has a question or wants to talk, please allow him to call me. Please," Bruce pleaded.

Sally was confused by the feelings she was having. She wanted to pull her hand out of Bruce's hold, but she didn't. She wondered, as she looked back into his mesmerizing eyes, was he being truthful with her? Or were his efforts in wanting to help Todd only to gain her affections for him? She didn't know!

Bruce drew closer to Sally, and before she knew it, he kissed her. Then he stepped away and said, "Call me when you have it figured out. Todd has my telephone number." He stepped off the front porch, got into his car, and drove away.

Sally was bewildered by what had just happened as she watched him drive away. Slowly her fingers touched her lips. "He kissed me," she uttered softly to herself. "How did that happen?" It had to be a moment of weakness, but she didn't even see that coming. What did it mean to her? Oh, how she needed Rusty! She wanted and needed that kiss to have come from him, not from someone else. Tears came into her eyes. How did she let that happen? Sally made herself move. She needed to get in the house and out of the cold air.

As she walked inside, the boys were looking at her.

"You tell her, Todd!" Pace whispered.

"No, I don't want to! You tell her, Pace!"

Sally looked at her sons. "What?"

"We saw him kiss you, Momma," Pace half-shyly stated.

"Oh, y'all did? Well, that was a surprise I didn't want nor need. That man is full of surprises! Todd, he is very interested in your dreams coming true of becoming a pilot, and he wants to help in any way he can. These books can be a real start!" Sally conceded that Captain Hall had gotten his way . . . at least for now.

Todd took the bag of books and went to his room, Pace went back to watching television, and Sally slowly strolled to her bedroom. She sat down on the edge of her bed and replayed the events that had just transpired. She thought, *Why does he think he can just come into my life and practically take over? He has some nerve! He is so manipulative. I just don't like him. There is no place and no reason for Bruce to be in my life, but here he is! The only reason I'm not pushing him away is because of Todd.* Sally forced herself to turn her thoughts to Rusty. She laid back on her bed and closed her eyes. She imagined him laying beside her, remembering the warmth of his embrace. She longed for his arms to hold her and for his lips to kiss hers. How much longer would it be before she would see him again?

The telephone rang, interrupting Sally's precious thoughts of the one she loves. She ran from her bedroom to the living room.

"Hello?" she answered.

"I was thinking you might not be home. Hi, honey. How are you?" Rusty's voice sounded like music to her ears.

"Hi, sweetheart. Yep, we're here. We're good. How are you?" Sally asked, not wanting to think about Bruce and his kiss.

"I'm great now that I'm talking to you. I sure do miss you. Sometimes, I feel like I'm stuck in a trap, and I can't get out. I want to see you, be with you, hold you . . . well, you know the rest," Rusty said longingly.

"I want all that too, my love, and yes, I do know all the rest. Just moments ago, I was wondering when we were going to see each other again. It seems like forever since I saw you last. I have to remind myself that your dad and the farm come first. How is you dad?" Sally inquired.

"It does seem like forever, but baby, I am so glad you feel the same way I do about my dad and the farm. As much as I hate to say it, right now, it is my life. I appreciate you understanding my commitment to my dad and the farm. You know, I'd rather be with you than stuck here. I don't believe many women would understand, but I'm proud you're standing beside your man. I love you so much, Sally. Dad is getting a little better, a little stronger each day. He even walked with his walker out to the parlor yesterday for the first time since his heart attack. Praise the Lord! I truly believe being home from the hospital has been the best medicine for him." Rusty was thankful.

"Please tell him and your mom I said hi, and I'm continuing to pray for them as I always pray for you. I know you were excited for him when you saw him out and at the parlor. That is great and a *huge* praise. And darlin', I will always be by your side. I better get going. OK to talk tomorrow?" Sally asked.

"You betcha! We'll talk then. I love you, and I'll see you in my dreams, babe," Rusty said and blew her his kiss.

"I love you too, honey. Be careful, and I'll see you in my dreams too." Sally returned a kiss back to Rusty.

As Sally slowly placed the handset on the telephone base, she thought, *How could I think of any other man? Rusty is the only man for me.*

Pace was still watching television. Sally walked to the boys' bedroom door. Todd was sitting up in his bed with his back up against the wall.

"How are you doing? Are these new books interesting?" Sally asked him.

"Yes, ma'am. Lots of picture of airplanes and their parts. I really haven't started reading yet," Todd answered.

Sally stepped a few steps away from him and looked at how he was sitting. "You know, you don't look real comfortable, leaning up against the wall. Have you ever thought about getting a desk? You could sit at it and read your books. In fact, you might want to do your homework on it or even work on a project. What do you think? Would you like a desk?"

"Yes, I think so. Where would we put it?" Todd inquired.

Sally looked around the room. "Well, we could move your dresser in front of the window and put the desk where the dresser was."

"Or, depending on the size of the desk, it could go in front of the window, and I'd have the daytime light from outside," Todd remarked.

"Yes! An excellent idea. I like the way you think! Maybe buy a lamp to put on the desk for working at night," she suggested.

"Yes, I might need a lamp," Todd agreed.

"Let's get dressed and go shopping!" she shouted with excitement.

Pace ran into the room. "What's all the shouting about?"

Todd said with joy, "We're going shopping! Get dressed, little brother!"

Soon they were dressed and out the door. They went from one store to another. Yes, they found desks, but either they were too big or too expensive or just not to Todd's liking. Then finally, at a discount store near the Tennessee/Mississippi state line, close to where Collin used to work, they got lucky.

"Mom, I really like this one," Todd said. "I like the color and the size. It has several drawers and even a matching chair to go with it!"

Sally liked it too. She looked at its price tag. "And it's affordable! We'll take it. You've got yourself a new desk, kiddo!"

After Sally paid for their new purchase, a sale's clerk helped her put the desk in the trunk of her car. Its legs stuck out, but after the man tied the trunk lid down to the bumper of the car, they were good to go.

Sally drove extra slow and carefully all the way home. Once home, Sally and Todd, with a little struggle, managed to get the desk inside the house, into the boys' bedroom, and placed in front of the window.

Todd stood back and admired his new furniture. "It's perfect, Mom! Thank you so much!" He hugged her tightly.

"You are so welcome. I'll get the chair. I'll be right back," she told him.

The telephone rang. The boys looked at each other.

"Go answer it, Todd!" Pace shouted.

"No, Pace. You answer it. Just say *hello!*"

Pace ran to the living room. "Hello?" he said, looking at Todd. There was silence on the other end of the line. "Nobody's there."

"Say it again," Todd encouraged.

"Hello? Is anybody there?" Pace asked.

"Pace, is that you? This is Grandmother Peggy. Is everything OK?"

"Hi, Grandmother Peggy. Everything is OK. Momma is outside. Oh, here she is now." Pace held the phone out to Sally. "Here, Momma, it's Grandmother Peggy."

"Thank you, Pace. Hi, Peggy. Can I call you back?" Sally asked.

"Sure, dear. Is everything all right?" Peggy asked.

"Yes, all is good. I'll call you back in a few minutes." Sally handed the handset back to Pace, and he put it back on the base.

"Well, how was that? You answered the telephone for your mother. Thank you! That is a first! I'm proud of you. More surprises . . . my sons are growing up!" she stated with admiration. She carried the chair into the boys' room and placed it on the floor next to the desk. "OK, Todd. Take a seat. Try it out."

Todd sat down, grabbed the sides of the chair seat with both hands, and scooted the chair under the desk.

"Well, how does it feel?" Sally asked.

"It's great! I love it. I really feel a little older," Todd exclaimed.

"I'm glad you like it. Maybe when you're not using it, you wouldn't mind sharing it with your brother. Would that be OK?" she asked, ensuring Pace would not feel left out of the new experience.

"Sure, that would be fine," he replied.

"Super. I appreciate that. Maybe tomorrow, we'll get you a nice lamp," Sally added. "OK, I need to call your grandmother back." She walked back to the telephone and dialed her number. "Hi, Peggy. I'm sorry I couldn't talk to you earlier. We went shopping for a new desk for the boys' room. We were getting it inside the house. What's up?"

"I'm OK. Just calling to check on y'all and see if y'all were going to church tomorrow? I'll pick y'all up," Peggy said.

"Yes, you can pick us up for church. We appreciate that," Sally responded.

"Not a problem. How do the boys like their new desk?"

"I believe they like it. It's nice and a great place for them to do their homework or anything they want to do."

"I'll give you some money to cover the cost of it. I want to help you," Peggy offered.

"Oh, Peggy, you're so kind, but I got it. It was reasonably priced. Thank you for your thoughtfulness." As she noticed the time, she said, "I need to get supper started. We'll see you in the morning. You have a nice evening."

"See y'all tomorrow," Peggy replied.

Sally entered the kitchen and prepared their supper. About thirty minutes later, she walked to the boys' bedroom door and found both boys sharing the one chair and looking at the pages of a book Bruce had brought to Todd. She wanted to etch that sight into her memory forever. How precious was that!

"I hate to interrupt your enjoyment, but supper is almost ready. Please wash your hands and come to the table," she instructed.

"OK, we will," the boys answered together.

Sally returned to the kitchen and put their supper on the table. After blessing their meal, they chowed down their food.

The next morning, the boys showed their maturity by getting up and getting dressed on their own. Sally was happy about their achievement, but she was sad at the same time—they truly were growing up.

Peggy was on time to pick them up for church, and even though it had only been three weeks of attending church, the family enjoyed their new routine.

The message Brother Hal preached was a blessing from Proverbs 3:5-6. "Trust in the LORD with all your heart, and lean not on your own understanding; in all your ways acknowledge Him, and He shall direct your paths." His last words before closing the message were very meaningful to Sally. "We can always trust that God will lead us in the right direction." She needed to hear those words. And the boys were excited about what they had learned in children's church as well.

Upon leaving church, Sally mentioned to Peggy that she needed to go buy a lamp for the boys' new desk. Peggy said she would go with them after lunch.

The burgers and fries tasted good and satisfied them all. Peggy drove them to a few stores, and at their second stop, the perfect lamp was found. She also found an alarm clock radio for the boys' room. She believed that Todd was ready to have one.

Peggy surprised Sally by paying for the items. Sally urged her not to buy them, but her plea was to no avail. Sally was most grateful.

On the way home, Todd told his grandmother about Captain Hall's visit at their home the day before and about the flight training books that he brought him. Peggy could hear the enthusiasm in his voice. "Todd, I think that is wonderful. Your mother will need to tell me more about this Captain Hall," she said as she looked toward Sally in the passenger seat.

"And you know what, Grandmother?" Pace asked sheepishly.

"No, what?"

Sally knew what was coming, but before she could stop Pace, he let the cat out of the bag. "He kissed my momma!"

Sally held her breath. There wasn't any sense in scolding him, which was her first instinct. She just swallowed hard as she saw the incredible glare Peggy gave her.

"Now, I really do want to know more about this man!" Peggy exclaimed.

Sally cringed and even squirmed a little. She was thankful Peggy was driving into the driveway of her home and prayed Peggy would not want to stay. But, oh no, that wasn't the case.

"I'll help you inside with your bags," Peggy insisted.

"Oh, there's no need. There are only two bags. You might need to get home. We've kept you way too long today."

"Sally, you're not getting off that easy!" Peggy sounded very determined.

As Sally stepped out of Peggy's car, she thought, *Oh boy, I know I'm about to get grilled about Bruce.* She unlocked the front door, and they all entered the house.

"Todd, please take these bags into your room. You want some coffee, Peggy?" Sally asked, trying not to look reluctant to be sociable.

"Oh, that sounds good. Thank you."

Sally took the boys' coats and hung them in the coat closet. She took Peggy's coat and laid it on the arm of the chair.

Peggy followed Sally into the kitchen like a shadow. "So, you want to tell me about this Captain Hall?" Peggy asked pointedly.

Sally began the coffee-making process. "Well, there's really not too much to tell." She chose her words carefully. "The boys and I met him at the airport about a month ago. He is a pilot for one of the major airlines. He was passing by us as we were looking at an airplane out the window. Todd was talking about how he wished he knew more about airplanes and that one day, he'd like to learn how to fly. Then Captain Hall introduced himself to us. We talked, and then he took us inside an airplane cockpit and showed Todd a lot about the airplane's controls. He was very interesting, and he took a lot of interest in Todd. When we left the airport, I told Todd I'd check into flight training school one day soon. Well, that time came last weekend. I took Todd and Pace to the flight school business across from the airport, and we were surprised to see Captain Hall there! He showed us around and explained to Todd about the different airplanes. Then he asked me if he could take Todd for a quick flight in his airplane. I reluctantly agreed, and Todd was more excited than I had seen him in a long time. It made me feel good. So Captain Hall offered to teach Todd more about how to fly, and in the process, he would get to know me better." Sally stopped and poured herself and Peggy some coffee. "At this point, I felt used. How could he use Todd to have a relationship with me? I even told him that. We left the building and walked to the car to leave, and he followed us. He apologized and admitted he did like me. But he also said he would teach Todd for free. That he owned the flight school and could make those decisions. When he told me this, I figured he thought he could get his payment by getting cozy with me! Then he showed up on my porch yesterday to give Todd easy-to-learn flight training books that would help Todd understand more about airplanes and flying. It would be a year of helping Todd before he could start teaching him how to fly. I know Todd has a dream of one day flying, and I'm proud of him and his dream, but I just don't appreciate the game that Captain Hall is playing. He is putting me in the middle of Todd's dream. If I don't go along with his game, then Todd doesn't get the training; if I do agree, then I feel like I'll be at his beck-and-call.

Peggy listened intently. "That does put you in an awkward position. But Sally, what about the *kiss*?"

"I told him I was in the process of a divorce, and I was not interested in a relationship with him. He asked me if I'd step outside with him, which was fine with me; the boys didn't need to hear the conversation. On the porch, he reassured me he understood my situation and my feelings, but all he wanted to do was help Todd. I told him I couldn't give him an answer. The next thing I knew, he kissed me, looked me in my eyes, and told me to think on it. Then he left. That's it!"

Peggy stared at Sally for a moment as if wondering what to say. Sally looked away and sipped on her coffee.

Finally, Peggy spoke. "Gosh, what a story! I just prayed to God for you and also for me to say the right words to you. I understand you want to help Todd fulfill his dreams. You would feel guilty if you held him back. I believe God has a reason for you meeting this man. I give him credit for his tenacity and persistence in winning you over to him. He must like you a lot to go to all this trouble! How did he find out where you lived?" Peggy asked.

"I asked him the same question. He said he remembered my car's license plate number from when I drove away last week. He asked a friend to find my address, and then he found me," Sally answered.

"See. That's what I'm saying. He is determined! I don't know, Sally. Maybe let him help Todd, but keep your distance from him," Peggy suggested.

"But then, am I not playing right into his game? He is just so forward. It's like he gets what he wants, no questions asked." Sally was so perplexed and upset. "I don't want to talk about this anymore. I just feel like I'm getting into something over my head. I know Collin and I had our problems, and in the end, it was terrible. But this is crazy! I don't know how to deal with it." She wanted to blurt out Rusty's name and claim that he would be taking her away from all of this madness in just a few months, but she couldn't. She did not want Peggy to know about him . . . yet.

Peggy was quite subdued when she prepared to leave Sally's home. She told Sally she would have her in her every prayer. The boys came out of their room to hug their grandmother and then waved goodbye as she left.

Sally didn't feel much like fixing a big supper, so she made grilled cheese sandwiches and tomato soup. The boys were happy enough. After they ate, they took their bath and put their PJs on. Rusty called at his normal time, and it was so good for Sally to hear his voice. She attempted to sound cheerful so he would not suspect anything was wrong. And she succeeded.

Chapter Sixteen

S ally's alarm clock radio abruptly woke her from a deep sleep. After lying in bed
for a few moments, she suddenly remembered that she forgot to help Todd
set up his new lamp and clock radio. She had been so preoccupied and upset
about Peggy asking so many questions about Bruce. She felt terrible. She was
determined to help Todd set everything up after the boys got home from school.

Sally sat on the edge of her bed and prayed, asking God to be with the three
of them and Rusty throughout their day. Then she scurried around to get the boys
up, dressed, fed, and to school on time. As she made her way to work after school
drop-off, she took a deep breath.

The work day Sally started as usual: opening the mail, preparing next
Sunday's bulletin, and making copies of letters for Brother Hal. Around lunchtime,
Maggie, the church hostess, came into the office.

"Hi, Sally! I know I'm early giving you next Wednesday night's meal menu,
but I hope that's OK? Also, I have a bridal shower coming up next month. If you
can, I'd like for you to help me prepare for it. I know it's a month away, but I'm
one for planning ahead. You don't need to give me your answer now, but think on
it, and let me know within the next two weeks." Then out the office door she went.

Sally sat at her desk, stunned, and stared at the closing door. She wasn't sure
what she should be thinking.

"Sally, are you OK?" Brother Hal asked. Sally was unaware he had walked
to her desk. "Did I hear Maggie's voice?"

Sally looked up at Brother Hal and answered, "Yes, you did. She gave me
Wednesday night's meal menu for the bulletin, but she also asked me to help
her with a bridal shower next month. I have no idea what I'm supposed to do,"
Sally admitted.

"Ah, don't worry. Maggie will talk you through the event. She's hosted many
social gatherings. And don't forget, if you agree to help her, she will pay you for
your service," Brother Hal reminded her, and he returned to his office.

Sally thought to herself, *The extra money would be nice, especially if I take a
trip to Connecticut on the boys' spring break!* With that thought, she raised up from
her desk and walked to Brother Hal's office. She politely knocked on the door as
she looked in.

"Yes ma'am?" he said, gesturing for her to come in.

"I don't know how appropriate this is, and please, forgive me if I'm out of
line," Sally began.

Brother Hal's forehead wrinkled as he looked over the top of his eyeglass frames. "OK . . . well, it can't be that bad! Whatcha got, Sally?"

"OK, here it goes. My sons are out of school for spring break from March 10th to the 14th, and I'd like to know if I can be off work during that time to take a trip out of town?" Sally was nervous to make such a request.

"That's it?" Brother Hal questioned.

"Um, yeah . . . ."

Brother Hal laughed. "Oh, Sally. You had me concerned there for a minute. You asked very professionally! Let me see." He paused as he flipped through his calendar to the month of March. "Palm Sunday is not until March 30th, and Easter is April 6th. A lot of activities go on here at the church during that time. The boys would be back in school March 17th, and you would be back to work the same day, I assume. So yes, that will work."

Sally smiled. "Thank you very much, Brother Hal," she said gratefully as she left his office and walked back to her desk, thanking God for the positive response. She was able to finish out her day with so much joy, excited that in a little more than six weeks, she would be in Rusty's loving arms.

When Sally and the boys returned home after school, Sally said, "Come on, kiddos. We have work to do!"

The boys followed their mother into their bedroom, and they began to unpack their purchases from the day before. Todd placed the lamp on the new desk and plugged it in.

"Oh, it looks so nice, Todd. What do you think?" Sally asked him.

"I think it's swell! What do you think, Pace?" Todd asked his brother, not wanting to leave him out of this happy time.

"I like it too!" Pace shouted with delight.

"OK, let's take the clock out of the box. Save the instruction sheet. It will help us know how to operate it," Sally said.

After all the wrapping had been removed from the clock, Todd asked, "Can I plug it in the outlet?"

"Sure," Sally agreed.

"Something's flashing, Momma," Pace excitedly said, pointing at the numbers on the clock's time display.

"Let's see what we need to do to set the time." Sally picked up the instructions. She read and explained each step to Todd, and he followed them precisely. Once the time was correctly set, the instruction sheet showed how to set the alarm. The last step was explaining the operation of the radio. "This knob turns on the radio, this knob is for the volume, and this knob is for channel selection. When you turn it, you'll hear different stations, mostly music. Sort of like the television. You just find what you want to listen to. Now the alarm is set for a wake-up time of 6:30 each morning, but you must remember to push this button to "ON," and the radio will turn on automatically to wake you up. The radio will continue to play until you press this button." She pointed to the "OFF" button. "The radio will shut off when you push this. I believe we're done! Good job!"

"I know I'll need your help until I get used to it, Mom, but thank you so much." Todd hugged his mother. He was so happy.

"I've got some homework. Can I use my desk?" Todd asked.

"Absolutely, you can. Go for it, kiddo! Do you have homework, Pace?" she asked.

"Yes, ma'am, I do."

"While I fix supper, you can use the dining room table, OK?"

"Yip," he answered. He picked up his book bag and headed for the table.

Sally prepared supper, and as they ate, she thought about telling them about the trip she hoped to plan. But she decided to wait for now. The evening continued as usual with bathtime followed by some television. Rusty called and told her a big storm was predicted to roll in tomorrow, and he wasn't looking forward to the problems it could cause with the farm. Sally told him she'd be praying hard for God's hedge of protection to be around them. She wanted to tell him about her plans to see him in March, but there was concern in Rusty's voice about the storm. She could tell him later. They kissed each other through the telephone and said good night.

Sally sat at the table for a moment when Todd, dressed in his PJs, walked over to her from the living room. "Mom, can I ask you something?"

"Sure."

"You like Rusty, right?" Todd softly asked.

Todd's question caught Sally off guard. She wondered where his question came from and where the conversation was heading. She looked at Todd and answered honestly. "Yes, I do."

"Y'all talk to each other every night, and you always tell him you love him and put a kiss through the telephone. Does he tell you he loves you and do the kiss thing too?" Todd inquired.

Sally could feel the seriousness of his questions. "Yes, he does."

"Will we ever meet him? I think I'd like him too. He seems to make you happy. I like to see you happy, Mom."

"Rusty does make me happy, son. I hope y'all can meet him soon," Sally expressed.

"Captain Hall doesn't make you happy, does he?" Todd asked more cautiously than curiously.

"No, he doesn't," she said sternly. "I'm sorry, Todd. I should not have answered you like that. It's just, I believe he wants to be in control. I do appreciate all he is doing for you, and I'm happy for you, but I don't like the way he is approaching the situation."

"It's OK, Mom." Then he hugged her and walked toward his room.

Sally was amazed. Tears rolled down her face. Todd showed her a caring side that she had not seen before. He was so thoughtful and observant. She thanked God for him and his tender heart.

As they knelt beside their beds, Sally and the boys said their nighttime prayers. She tucked them in, kissed them good night, and told them to sleep tight and not let the bedbugs bite. Then she turned out the light and left their room. She slowly walked to her bedroom and changed into her nightgown, crawled between her bed sheets, and turned out the light. As she laid there, she could hear Todd's words in her mind. She prayed to God to let Todd's reaction be a good start to his and Rusty's relationship, which would hopefully begin in the near future.

The two-day Connecticut blizzard impacted Rusty and the farm in a big way. He told Sally about the freezing temperatures, with wind chills below zero, high winds with gusts of fifty to sixty mph, and many inches of heavy snow that collapsed barns and other buildings. They lost many cows who suffocated in the snow drifts, and others were killed when barn roofs fell on them. The roads were impassable, and cows could not be trucked to other locations for warmth and safety. The cows' milk had to be dumped because there was no way for it to be transported. Many dairy farms as well as other farms and businesses in the area were devastated. So much shock and grief.

Rusty still called Sally every night to let her know he was OK, and she needed to know that he was. Many nights, their conversations were short. She could hear in his tired and exhausted voice that the twenty-hour days were taking a toll on him. He tried to remain optimistic and hopeful, but Sally could tell he was struggling. The days of recovery turned into weeks of hard work, with clean-up, rebuilding, and re-stocking. Sally prayed and prayed hard for Rusty, his father, and the farm.

In the meantime, Sally continued thanking God for allowing her to put one foot in front of the other day after day. Rusty was also constantly in her prayers. She was so concerned for his health, his welfare, and his and his dad's business.

Over the next few weeks, Todd had called Captain Hall several times, and he even came to the house once. But Sally avoided him by asking Peggy to come for a visit while he was helping Todd, which worked out perfectly.

The weekend before Valentine's Day, Sally and the boys decorated the house to celebrate the day. Sally bought candy and a box of Valentine's cards for the boys to address and give to their classmates. They spent all afternoon after church choosing just the right card for each classmate; Todd cared more about that than Pace did.

Hugh Cut called Sally several evenings before Valentine's Day to tell her he had checked on the petition for her divorce, and all was looking good. The good news was that a court date could be set for the last week of April. That was music to Sally's ears.

On the eve of Valentine's Day, there came a knock on the front door. Sally was in the boys' room, helping Todd with a math problem. She walked to the living room window to see if there was a car in the driveway, but there wasn't. Another knock. She opened the door to find a man hiding his face behind a vase of beautiful red roses with a pizza box in the other hand. Her heart started racing. Was this mystery man Rusty?

"Wow! How beautiful are these roses! And who is the bearer standing behind them?" Sally asked with excitement in her voice, ready to hug and kiss Rusty. In a conversation with him several days earlier, he told Sally that he'd love to be with her for Valentine's Day, but there was still so much work that had to be done at the farm.

"It's me," the man said as he moved the flowers from in front of his face.

Sally wanted to throw up and die. She tried to quickly compose herself. "Why, Bruce, what a surprise! You shouldn't have. Come on in."

Bruce handed her the vase. "Happy Valentine's Day," he said as he leaned toward her.

Sally quickly moved away from him before he could touch her. "Thank you, Bruce. They are lovely. Here, I'll take the pizza box and set it on the table. You can lay your coat on the chair."

Todd and Pace ran into the living room. "Captain Hall! I thought I heard your voice," Todd said excitedly.

"Hi, Captain Hall!" Pace chimed in.

"Hi, boys. I hope y'all like pizza," he declared.

"Oh yeah," both boys answered at the same time and hurried to the table to take their seats.

Sally went to the kitchen and returned to the table with their drinks and paper plates.

"Sally, do you have a can of beer?" Bruce asked. "I like beer with my pizza. Don't you?"

Sally frowned at Bruce. "No, no beer. And no, I don't like beer with my pizza."

Before Bruce could react to Sally, there was another knock on the door. Sally quickly walked over to the door and opened it. She saw a young man holding another vase of flowers. "A delivery for Sally Oldham," he announced.

"That's me," Sally replied as she opened the screen door and took the vase of flowers from him. "Thank you very much."

"You're welcome, and happy Valentine's Day!"

Sally closed both doors and walked to the kitchen with the flowers and sat them on the countertop. She opened the small envelope, pulled out the card, and, from the dining room light, saw the writing.

HAPPY VALENTINE'S DAY to my SWEETHEART VALENTINE!
I wish I could be there with you. ALL MY LOVE, RUSTY.

Sally held the card to her heart, and tears streamed down her face. She silently said to herself, *I wish you were here too, my love.*

"From an admirer, I suppose. But *carnations? Really?*" Bruce commented snidely.

Sally wiped the tears away, turned, and retorted, "This person knows that my *favorite* flowers are carnations, not roses." She took the roses from the vase Bruce had brought, carried them to the front door, and threw them as far as she could into the front yard. Then she turned to face Bruce. "I'm about tired of you, and unless you want to be treated the same as your distasteful roses, I suggest you get your sarcastic and rude self out of my house."

Bruce raised up from the table. "Now, Sally," and began walking toward her.

Sally grabbed his coat from the chair. "Don't 'now, Sally' me! Here's your coat. Leave, and please, don't come back."

Bruce snatched his coat from her hand and walked out the front door. Sally slammed the door behind him and said loudly, "Good riddance!"

After a moment or so, Sally turned away from the front door. She saw Todd and Pace staring blankly at her, afraid to move.

"I guess I got really mad at him, didn't I? I'm sorry," she apologized as she walked toward them. She sat down in her chair at the table, bowed her head, and prayed. "Lord, I am so sorry I got so upset with Captain Hall. I should have controlled my anger, especially in front of Todd and Pace. I ask You and my sons to please forgive me." Tears flowed from her eyes.

Both boys got up from their chairs and went to their mother. "Don't cry, Momma," Pace said, hugging her.

"It's OK, Mom. We forgive you." Todd hugged her too.

Sally put her arms around her boys and sobbed. "Thank you both."

After a moment, Pace looked up at his mother and said to her, "I didn't like those roses either, Momma!"

All three of them laughed and smiled at each other.

"Mom, would it be OK if I brought the carnations in here and set them on the table? They're from Rusty, aren't they?" Todd realized.

"I'd be happy if you sat them on the table. Yes, they are from Rusty."

As Todd carefully brought the flowers to the table and sat the vase down, he looked at his mother and said, "He really does love you, doesn't he?"

With tears in her eyes again, she answered, "Yes, he does."

"They sure are pretty flowers, Momma," Pace said as he pressed his nose into several of the carnations to get a good smell.

Then the telephone rang. "I bet that's Rusty!" Todd suspected. "Come on, Pace. We need to study." Both boys walked to their bedroom.

Sally walked from the table to the telephone. "Hello?" she answered.

"Happy almost Valentine's Day! I love you, sweetheart," Rusty said in his sweet, loving voice.

Sally's eyes filled with tears. "I love you too . . . so much, honey."

"What's the matter, Sally? What's wrong? Are you OK? Why are you crying?" Rusty said, concerned.

Sally took a tissue and wiped her tears. "Oh, Rusty, the carnations are beautiful, and I pressed the words on the card to my heart. I sure wish you were here so I could take you in my arms, hug you tightly, and kiss you all over your sweet lips. I miss you so very much!"

"Baby, I love you too, and I miss you more than you know. I wanted the carnations to send all my love to you," Rusty expressed.

"And they did, over and over again. Thank you, and happy Valentine's Day to you too! How are you, dear?" Sally asked.

"I'm good, now that I hear your sweet voice. Hearing your words of love always energize me. The day has been good. The parlor and the milking stations are working, the new cows are adjusting, and the milk is once again being processed and delivered. A few of the damaged buildings are still being worked on and should be finished tomorrow. Other farmers are waiting for the rebuilding crews to finish here, and then the crews are going to them. It's been rough, but God has been with us and showing us the way. With us now having more up-to-date machinery and equipment, the milking process will be easier and quicker. New procedures have been introduced as well. Most importantly, my dad, who does not like change, is onboard with everything. His happiness makes it all worth it!"

"You know, God does work in mysterious ways. Maybe the storm was His way of making new improvements to make life better for you, your dad, and the farm," Sally suggested.

"That sounds right because if it had not been for the storm, we'd still be doing things the old way. Good point, my Sally dear. Hey, it's getting late. I wanted you to start celebrating your Valentine's a little early because when I call you tomorrow night, the *happy* day will be almost over. Is everything OK there? Are you and the boys OK? Any plans for tomorrow?" Rusty asked.

"I'm thrilled about our early celebration! Thank you. All is good. Todd and Pace have their six-week tests tomorrow, plus Valentine's cards will be handed out and there will be a cupcake party. Busy day for them! I don't know if we'll do anything after school or not. We'll just have to wait and see. You be careful, and I'm glad the farm is returning to more normal activities. It took a while, but God got y'all through it. Thank you again for your thoughtfulness with the beautiful carnations and the loving words on your card. We'll talk tomorrow. I love you, miss you, and always have you in my prayers. I seal all this with my kiss to you," Sally said, blowing him her kiss.

"Sweet dreams, my love. I love and miss you too and, as always, prayers for you and the boys. Sealed with my kiss to you." Rusty kissed her through the telephone in return.

Sally hung up the phone, then she walked down the hall to the boys' room. They were both sitting on the chair by the desk. "Hi, boys. I see the pizza box! Glad y'all ate it. Are y'all studying? It's almost bath and bed time."

"Yes, ma'am. Just last-minute study time. I've been helping Pace with his spelling words list, but we're finished," Todd explained.

Sally ruffled his hair as Todd stood up from the desk. "Thank you for helping your brother, Todd. I'll be praying for both of you tomorrow for all your tests."

After their baths and their PJs were on, they knelt by their beds and breathed their nightly prayers. They then jumped into their beds, and Sally covered them up, kissed them good night, and told them not to let the bedbugs bite. And it was lights out.

Before Sally walked away, she added, "I love both of you. Thank you for tonight. Sweet dreams."

"Love ya too, Momma," Pace said sleepily.

"Sweet dreams too, Mom," Todd thoughtfully replied.

What a day, Sally thought as she turned out the light next to her bed. She voiced her prayers to God in silence and then drifted off to sleep.

The next morning, Sally was up and at 'em at her normal time. The boys were up and dressed for school, the coffee was brewing, and she had breakfast started when Todd and Pace burst into the kitchen.

"Happy Valentine's Day!" they both shouted as they waved their hands above their heads, each holding an envelope.

"Well, happy Valentine's Day to both of you!" Sally rejoiced back to them. "What are y'all holding?"

"Your cards! Here, Momma." Pace excitedly handed her his Valentine's card.

"Here's mine, too, Mom!" Todd slipped the card into her open hand.

"Ahh, you two are so sweet," she gratefully said as she took their cards. She opened Pace's envelope first and took out the small card and read it out loud:

You know, you're the sweetest Valentine! Love, Pace.

With tears in her eyes, she bent down and gave Pace a big hug. "Thank you. I love the card, and I love you." Sally then opened Todd's envelope, pulled the card out, and read again:

Please be my Valentine because you are so special! To Mom, from Todd.

With more tears, she reached for her son and hugged him tightly. "Yes, I'd be honored to be your Valentine. You are special too! Thank you both for thinking about me with your great cards. I'm going to put them on the dining room table so I can easily see them. Now, I need to finish our breakfast. It'll be ready in a few minutes.

The boys left the kitchen, and soon their meal was on the table along with a little surprise Sally had planned of her own for Todd and Pace. "Breakfast is ready," she said, calling for the boys.

As soon as they began to sit down in their chairs, the boys saw on each of their placemats small heart-shaped boxes and big red envelopes. When they opened the boxes, they found them full of candy. Then, each of them opened their envelopes, and when they opened up their cards, a big red heart unfolded and popped up in front of them. They had never seen a card like that before. They were so surprised and happy! It was a wonderful start to their day.

As they pulled into the school parking lot, Sally wished Todd and Pace a good day, and she told them she would be praying for them and their tests. She waved good-bye as they ran toward the school and disappeared as the door closed behind them. As she drove out of the school parking lot, she prayed, asking God to allow them to make good grades on their tests and have a special Valentine's Day. The moments she had with them that morning flashed through her mind, and she smiled.

Sally arrived at work, and when she opened the office door, right away she saw a vase of multi-colored flowers sitting on her desk.

"Happy Valentine's Day, Sally!" came a voice from the hall. Brother Hal appeared. "I thought it was appropriate to honor you with flowers today. I hope it's OK?"

"Brother Hal, they are beautiful. I appreciate your thoughtfulness. Thank you very much. And Happy Valentine's to you as well! However, I did not get you flowers or even a card. I'm so sorry. . . ." Sally apologized.

"I'm happy that you like the flowers. You giving flowers to your boss was not expected, so you're good. Oh yes, Maggie is in the kitchen. She would like to see you," Brother Hal said.

"Should I go now?" Sally asked slowly.

"I would think so. Go ahead. I'll answer the telephone if it rings."

"OK. Thanks." Sally walked down the hall to the church kitchen. As she stepped in, she saw Maggie. "Hi! Brother Hal said you wanted to see me?"

"Good morning, Sally," Maggie greeted her. "Yes . . . are you going to be able to help me with the bridal shower on the 24th?"

Sally answered, "Yes, I would like to, but I have no idea what to do."

"I was hoping you would say yes. Thank you," Maggie expressed gratefully. "Have you ever been to a bridal shower?"

Sally thought for a moment. "Yes, I have been to several. Before I married, my mother and several of my friends gave me showers," she explained.

"Oh, that's perfect! Then you may remember the preparation involved. The girls that are giving the bride-to-be's party will be doing the decorating. Being that this is an afternoon event, there will not be a meal; however, there will be punch to drink. The punch bowl and glass cups will be provided by the church as well as special glass bowls for the nuts and mints, plus small glass plates for the cake that will be brought in by the girls giving the shower."

Sally listened intently to all of Maggie's instructions. She thought her responsibilities for helping were not too many and not very difficult. She could handle it.

"Sally, the shower begins at 2 p.m. and should be over by 4 p.m. I don't know how much help we'll get from the party givers, but we need to do the clean-up afterwards. Well, that's about it. Any questions?" Maggie asked.

"Yes. What time should I arrive to help you, and what is the proper dress for the occasion?" Sally responded.

"Time? Maybe 1:15. And dress nicely—something like you'd wear to church. Sally, you're going to be fine. I'll be right here with you," Maggie said with confidence. She turned out the lights in the kitchen and thanked Sally for taking her work time to spend with her. They walked together to the church office, and then Maggie left.

Sally sat down at her desk, and Brother Hal approached her.

"That wasn't too bad, was it?"

Sally looked at him. "No, not bad. Just a lot to remember and to do, but it should be easy enough."

"Good. OK, I'll let you get to work," he said, walking back to his office.

Before Sally knew it, it was time to get the boys from school. As they jumped into her car, Todd and Pace revealed hands full of Valentine's cards, and they had big smiles on their faces. They excitedly chattered about their day, and Sally had a hard time keeping up with how quickly they were talking.

On the way home, Sally stopped at their favorite bakery, and she bought heart-shaped sugar cookies with red icing and white sprinkles. A sweet treat for them to eat when they got home.

Once they arrived at home, the boys quickly grabbed their cookies. "Oh, Momma, these cookies are *so* good!" Pace said as he took another big bite.

"Thank you so much for them, Mom. They hit the spot!" Todd chimed in.

"Yes, they are really good! Maybe sometime we can make some sugar cookies. Whatcha think?" she suggested.

The telephone rang.

"When y'all are finished, y'all can watch television." She walked toward the phone. "Hello?"

"Well, happy Valentine's! How's my favorite family?" Peggy said.

"Happy Valentine's to you too! We're doin' good. How about you?"

"I'm good. What are y'all doing? I was wondering what y'all are doing for supper," Peggy said.

"We haven't really talked about it. Whatcha got in mind?"

"*Pizza!* That's what I'm thinkin'. Does that sound good?" Peggy asked.

"It sounds delicious," Sally responded. Pizza two nights in a row was just fine with her!

"OK then. I'm on my way. See ya in thirty," Peggy said.

Sally walked back over to the boys and said, "Grandmother Peggy is bringing pizza for supper!"

"Oh boy. *Yum!*" Pace shouted loudly. He could always eat pizza.

"She should be here in about thirty minutes. I'm going to change my clothes. By the way, how do y'all think y'all did on the tests today?" she asked.

"I think I did OK," Todd answered.

"Me too, Momma," Pace told her.

"Oh, good. When I come back in the living room, I want to see all your Valentine's cards from your classmates," she said as she disappeared around the corner of the hallway. She changed her clothes quickly and then walked out of her room. Just as she did, the phone rang again.

"Hello?"

"Happy Valentine's Day, sweetheart!" Rusty greeted happily.

"Ah, baby. Happy Valentine's Day to you also. How are you?"

"I'm good. I wanted to call you early. I thought you and the boys might go out for dinner. You OK? How did the boys do on their tests today?" Rusty asked.

"Well, Grandmother Peggy is going to be here soon with pizza for supper. The boys told me they did OK on their tests. Are you doing anything special for tonight?"

"I'm wishing I could be with you and the boys! But second best, Mom is preparing some special dinner for Dad and me. But hey, please take a bite of pizza for me. I love pizza!" Rusty said.

"I'm sure your mom's dinner will taste much better than pizza! But yes, I will take a bite of pizza for you," Sally said with a laugh. "Please tell your folks I said *hi*. How's it going with the farm?" Right then, Peggy appeared at the door. "Oh, sweetie, Peggy's here. I need to go. I'm sorry. Maybe call me later. I love you!" Sally didn't wait for Rusty's reply before she hung up.

Todd already had the front door open for his grandmother as Sally put the handset on the telephone base. She hated that she hurried the end of her and Rusty's call, but she needed to protect her secret from Peggy for now.

"Hi, Peggy! Here, I'll take the pizza boxes. Todd, please help your grandmother with her coat. Pace, would you like to help me with the drinks?" Sally said.

"OK, Momma," Pace answered and followed his mother into the kitchen.

When the drinks and plates were placed on the table, they all sat down, prayed the blessing over the meal, and began eating. The boys chatted about school, and Sally told them about the bridal shower she was helping with at church and the flowers Brother Hal surprised her with that morning.

"Speaking of the bridal shower, Peggy, would you be able to watch the boys for three or four hours the afternoon of the 24th?" Sally asked. "That's a little over a week from today."

"I don't believe I have anything going on that day. So, yes. I'd be happy to sit with the boys," Peggy answered.

"Oh, that's great. I sure do appreciate you," Sally replied gratefully.

The evening passed by so quickly, and Peggy hugged everyone before she left. Then Todd and Pace showed their mother all the Valentine's cards they had received from their classmates.

"Oh, Todd, this one is so sweet. It looks very special and is different from all your other Valentine's cards," she commented.

Todd glanced at the card his mother was holding in her hand and said sheepishly, "Yeah, that one is from Barbie. She likes me!"

"Isn't she the girl that prays before she eats her lunch?" Sally remembered.

"Yes. Sometimes I sit with her at lunch, and we pray together." Todd smiled.

"Oh, Todd, that's wonderful! You like her too, don't you?"

"Yes. She really is a nice girl," Todd remarked, and Sally could see he was thinking about her.

Sally put her arm around his shoulder and said, "Thanks for sharing your thoughts with me, Todd. OK, boys, time to get ready for bed."

The boys took their baths, got in their PJs, and called their mother as they were ready to say their nightly prayers. Sally tucked them into bed, kissed them, and said she loved them. "No bug biting tonight! And thank y'all for a super Valentine's Day." Sally walked out of their room and turned out the light.

Sally sat in the living room for a while, waiting for Rusty to call again. But the telephone did not ring. So she took matters into her own hands and called him. It was late and even an hour later in Connecticut, but she took the chance, hoping Rusty wasn't in bed yet.

After the fourth ring: "Hello?"

"Rusty, is that you?" Sally asked, not sure she had the correct telephone number.

"Hi, Sally. What time is it?" Rusty asked sleepily.

"It's ten o'clock here, eleven your time. You sound sleepy. I'm sorry, did I wake you?" Sally apologized.

"Gosh, I fell asleep after I talked to you. I'm the one who's sorry. I was going to call you back an hour ago. How was the pizza?" Rusty asked.

"The pizza was good, and I took several bites for you! I'm sorry for the way I had to hang up earlier, but Peggy was nearly walking in the door, and I didn't want her to see me on the telephone. She might have asked questions. You are still a secret to her," Sally explained. "But I was concerned about your feelings."

"Hey, babe, all is good. I understand. No problem. Me still being a secret is probably for the best. Soon she will find out, but not yet. If it's OK, honey, I'm going to go to bed. I'm beat. I love you, and we'll talk tomorrow." Rusty threw her his kiss through the phone, and Sally threw him her kiss back. Then the call ended.

Sally felt bad that she had woken Rusty up, but she was relieved he wasn't upset with her. She could sleep peacefully.

The rest of the week, the weekend, and the following week passed quickly and was uneventful, other than Sally receiving money from Collin just in time to pay the monthly bills that were due.

Late Saturday morning, Peggy arrived at the Oldham's home to watch the boys while Sally served at the church for the bridal shower.

When Sally drove into the church parking lot, she noticed several vehicles were there. She knew one of them was Maggie's, and the others were probably the ladies who were giving the shower. As Sally entered through the church door that led to the dining and kitchen area, she heard voices.

"Hi, Sally," Maggie greeted. "Good to see you! Thanks for helping me today. Abbey, Crystal, Karri, this is Sally. She will be helping us today."

"Hi, Sally! It's nice to meet you," the ladies all said, looking up from their decorating project.

"Hi! It's nice to meet y'all too." Sally glanced around the dining area. "Everything is looking very pretty. I'm sure the bride-to-be will be so pleased."

"Come on in the kitchen, Sally. We need to get busy," Maggie suggested.

Sally followed Maggie into the kitchen, and she began showing Sally what to do. Sally was a little nervous about doing what Maggie instructed, but after a short while, her nerves calmed. She just wanted to do her best for Maggie.

The finishing touches had been completed, and people began arriving for the shower. The bride-to-be was surprised and delighted with the beautiful decorating by her friends.

Abbey, Crystal, and Karri facilitated the shower with fun games, gift openings, and serving the guests cake and punch. Lots of pictures were taken, and there was plenty of fellowshipping between family and friends. Sally thought it was a wonderful shower.

After the shower and the guest were leaving, Sally and Maggie began the clean-up. Sally and Maggie washed the dishes while the hostesses took down the decorations and swept the floor. Soon, everything was put away, and all was back to normal.

"Sally, you did an excellent job helping me. I appreciate you very much. I'll be in the office on Monday to pay you for today," Maggie told Sally as both of them walked down the hall to exit the church.

"Thank you, Maggie, for asking me to help you. It was fun, and I enjoyed it a lot." Sally appreciated the opportunity to serve.

"You're welcome, Sally. We'll do it again. Lots of events happen in the spring and the summer!" Maggie explained. "See ya at church tomorrow," she said as she walked to her car.

"Bye, Maggie." Sally waved as she opened her car door. As Sally drove home, she thought about Maggie saying she would need more help in the spring and summer. By that point, she hoped she'd be in Connecticut with Rusty!

Todd and Pace greeted their mother as she walked into the house, and Peggy came out of the kitchen. "How was the shower?" Peggy asked.

"It was very nice. Lots of family and friends were there to celebrate the upcoming wedding," Sally explained. "Hope the boys were good for you."

"Oh, yes. We played games and had a good time. Oh yeah, Collin called. He wanted to know if you received the money he sent you. He was surprised I answered the telephone. He wanted to know where you were. I told him you were helping out at the church. That was OK, wasn't it?" Peggy asked.

"Yes, that was fine. Did he say anything else? Did he talk to the boys?" Sally asked.

"No, he didn't talk to the boys. I asked him if he wanted to, but he said *no*. Other than that, he just said he was OK, and work was keeping him busy."

"I wish he had talked to the boys. But then, maybe it's better that he didn't. We did get some money from him yesterday, which was good. I have bills to pay," Sally commented.

"Yes, I know. Talking to their dad might have done more harm than good at this point. But at least I did get a minute to talk to my son. He never calls me," Peggy said sadly.

"I'm so sorry, Peggy. He should not do his own mother like that!" Sally voiced sympathetically.

Peggy agreed.

"I'm going to start supper. You will stay, won't you, Peggy?" Sally asked.

"You know what? Better idea. Let's go out. My treat!" stated Peggy.

"I think that's a great idea, but it should be my treat! You watched the boys for me. The least I could do is buy our supper," Sally said.

"Well, OK. We'll see. Let's go!" Peggy announced.

Everyone slipped on their coats, and they were out the door.

Several hours later, the family was back home after their delicious meal. Sally and the boys waved goodbye to Peggy as she drove away.

Sally suggested the boys get their baths, put on their PJs, and watch some television for a while. An hour later, Rusty called. Sally walked from the living room to the dining room so their conversation would be more private. Among other topics of conversation, Sally mentioned that in thirteen days, the boys would be starting their spring break from school, and she was wondering if it was still OK for them to come up and visit with him and his family. Rusty exclaimed a resounding *yes!* Excitement was in the air.

That night, it was hard for Sally to sleep with all of her happy thoughts jumping through her mind.

The next ten days couldn't go fast enough as Sally tried desperately to keep her mind on her work at the church office and keep her secret trip plans from the boys. But on the evening of March 4th, Sally broke the news to the boys.

"I'm thinking about us taking a trip while y'all are on spring break. How does that sound to you, fellas?" Sally asked.

"I think that would be great!" Todd expressed.

"Where would we go?" Pace quickly asked.

Sally held her breath as she said, "To Connecticut to see Rusty."

"OK! We are finally going to meet Rusty! That's great, Mom!" Todd was overjoyed.

"Meet Rusty? Yeah! Is Connecticut very far, Momma?" Pace asked.

"It's a good day's drive and then some, but we'll be OK. I'm excited about y'all meeting Rusty too," Sally said with a big smile. "We'll start packing tomorrow after school. We'll leave right after y'all get out of school on Friday and drive into the night."

The rest of suppertime and all evening, the boys and their mother talked about the trip. She answered tons of questions the boys asked.

Rusty called, and Sally told him their secret was out and the boys were very excited about the trip and were looking forward to meeting him. Rusty was very delighted about the news and could hardly wait to see Sally and meet the boys. Rusty gave Sally directions to his farm, and she wrote them down. He suggested she might want to buy an atlas to help her on the long trip.

The boys' excitement spilled over into the next morning and all the way to school. Sally was sure the boys would tell all their classmates and friends about their upcoming trip.

Sally pressed hard at work to keep her mind focused on her job. Brother Hal thought ahead and brought her work to cover the days she'd be away.

That evening, the boys were so excited to pack. They got games together they could play during the road trip, and Sally did laundry so they could make sure to pack everything they needed.

"Well, boys, we've done very well. We'll finish up our packing tomorrow night, and that'll be it. But now, it's bedtime. I don't know about y'all, but I'm tired!" Sally took a deep breath. "Y'all go take your baths and get into your PJs."

Rusty called, and Sally told him they had started packing and would finish up tomorrow night. He told her to be sure to bring their winter coats because it was still chilly there, especially at night. He also shared with her some plans he had thought of for them to do. He had already asked a few extra men to cover for him while she and the boys were there. He said he wanted to spend all his time with her and the boys. Sally expressed her thanks for all he was doing to make their visit as perfect as possible. They were just beside themselves to know they were soon to be together again.

The boys hopped into their beds, and Sally slipped into her nightgown and covered herself up in her bed. True, it wasn't Christmas, but visions of Rusty danced in her head.

Thursday was a *go* day all day. After picking up the boys from school, Sally stopped at the store and bought an atlas. After supper, packing was completed. While the boys watched television, Sally needed to make a few telephone calls: She had to call Peggy to let her know she and the boys were going out of town, just to get away and have some fun. She'd call her when they returned. And she also needed to call her brother. He might not call, but if he did and no one answered, he would worry about her. Her brother was glad to hear from her. They talked about their kids and the weather. Then, Sally told him she was taking the boys on a trip for their spring break. He told her to be careful and have a good time. During neither telephone call did she mention where they were going nor the purpose of the trip.

While Sally was looking at her atlas and the directions Rusty gave her, Rusty called. They mostly talked about the route Sally would take. He cautioned her several times about being careful and to call him Friday night from the place they would spend the night. He told her to listen to the voices on the CB for any problems on the road. She could hear the worry in his voice. She appreciated his concern for her safety, but she was confident she could make the trip OK.

"I'll see you soon, sweetheart. I'll be praying for a good and safe trip. I love you, babe," Rusty said.

"I love you too, my love. Can't wait to see you. I'll call you tomorrow night." Sally sent a kiss to him.

Rusty sent a kiss back to her. "Bye-bye, Sally dear."

As Sally hung up the telephone, she said to the boys, "Time for bed, my little men."

"OK, Momma." Pace sounded sleepy.

"Was that Rusty you were talking to?" Todd asked.

"Yes, and he is so excited and anxious to meet you and Pace. He told us to be very careful."

Todd hugged his mother. "Thank you for taking us on this trip. Come on, Pace. Let's go to bed."

Sally followed them into their bedroom and prayed with them. She tucked them in their beds and kissed them good night. "I love both of you. Thank y'all for helping me get us all packed. Sleep tight," she said and turned out the light.

Sally walked directly to her bedroom, changed into her gown, and crawled into bed. She was alone, but loving thoughts of Rusty would keep her warm and comfortable.

Chapter Seventeen

Friday had finally arrived. Sally, Todd, and Pace were so excited. After breakfast, Sally made a few trips to the car as she packed the trunk with their suitcases. She put their pillows, a few blankets, and the boys' bag of games in the backseat.

The boys and Sally put on their coats. Before Sally closed the front door of the house, she took one last look to make sure she hadn't forgotten anything they needed for the trip. She closed the door, put the overnight bag in the trunk, and got in the car.

On the way to the boys' school, Sally reminded them, "When I pick y'all up this afternoon, I'd like to hit the road. But if y'all think of anything we forgot, please tell me."

"OK," both boys agreed.

"I think we have everything, Mom," Todd added.

After Sally dropped the boys at school, she drove to the gas station, and the attendant filled up her car's gas tank. *Now we should be ready to go,* she thought to herself.

At work, Sally tried very hard to concentrate on her work. At eleven thirty, she finished what was left for her to do.

Brother Hal approached Sally's desk and handed her an envelope. "Here's your check for the week. You can leave now. Y'all have a great week, and drive carefully, Sally."

Sally smiled, took the envelope, thanked Brother Hal, and left the church. She drove to the store to cash her check, then proceeded on to the school to pick the boys up.

"Mom, you're early," Todd remarked as he walked into the school office.

"Brother Hal allowed me to leave work early, which is good. We can get an earlier start," she explained.

"Hi, Momma! Hi, Todd! Are we leaving?" Pace asked.

"Yes, we're leaving early! Please, get your coats. We can get started on our trip!" Sally said excitedly.

They walked quickly to the car, and Sally prayed to the Lord, asking Him to give them a safe trip. She cranked up the car's engine, and away she drove.

Soon, Sally emerged onto the super slab and headed eastbound. She glanced up into the rearview mirror, and the boys were getting settled in as they chatted away to each other. The CB was on, and lots of voices were talking. She remembered what Rusty said about listening to the drivers, especially about traffic conditions.

"Y'all doing OK back there?" Sally asked the boys.

"Yes, ma'am," Todd answered.

Without hearing a reply from Pace, Sally asked, "How about you, Pace? You OK?"

"Yes, Momma," Pace answered.

"Y'all try to get comfortable. We have a long way to go," she reminded them.

The traffic was light, and the three-hour drive to Nashville was uneventful. Before Sally turned north and headed toward Kentucky, she stopped at a popular convenience store for a potty break and some gas, and she bought each one of them a pecan log, which the store was famous for.

Back on the road again, Sally drove north on Interstate 65 through Bowling Green, driving another hour to Louisville where they stopped for supper.

The sun had set, and the darkness of night had surrounded them, but Sally and the boys pushed on northeast on Interstate 71. The CB was quiet; most truckers had probably stopped for supper.

Once past Cincinnati, Ohio, the boys were getting restless. "I know y'all are getting tired, but if we can keep going another hour, we'll be in Columbus, and we'll spend the night there. I sure am glad Rusty gave me directions, and the atlas has certainly helped me navigate our trip. Can y'all make it another hour?" Sally asked. Before they could answer, Sally suggested, "Hey, I have an idea. Let's sing! Whatcha want to sing?"

There was silence for a few seconds. Then Pace yelled, "Christmas songs!"

"It's not Christmas time, Pace!" Todd remarked.

"But, hey, we know those songs by heart, right?" Sally encouraged. "Which one can we sing first?"

"The one about the reindeer!" Pace's responded.

"That's a good one," Sally agreed.

At first, only Sally and Pace were singing, but Todd chose the next song, and the three of them sang all the way to Columbus.

"That was fun!" Sally said as they arrived in Columbus. "Praise the Lord! Now, let's find a place to sleep." Sally was grateful.

Sally saw a motel and drove into the driveway toward the main office. "Y'all stay here. I'll be right back. Lock the door, Todd, after I get out," Sally instructed as she exited the car.

Within a few minutes, Sally returned. Todd unlocked the door, and Sally sat in the driver's seat with a key in her hand. They found their room number, and Sally parked the car and grabbed the overnight bag out of the trunk. The boys held their pillows as Sally unlocked the room door, and they stepped inside their room.

"Wow! This is nice," Todd exclaimed.

"Yes, it is," Sally agreed as she placed the overnight bag on one of the two double beds. She opened the bag and handed the boys their PJs. Within minutes, the boys were ready for bed. They jumped on the bed a few times, then they settled down and Sally covered them with their blankets. Sally held their hands, and they prayed their nightly prayers.

"Y'all go to sleep. I need to call Rusty and let him know we are OK. I love y'all," she said softly. Sally picked up the handset of the telephone and dialed "O" for the operator, telling the person on the other end she needed to place a collect call to Rusty Summers in Newtown, Connecticut. The operator asked for Sally's name, then Sally heard a ringing sound. Rusty accepted the call.

"Hi, sweetheart. How are you? Where are you?" Rusty asked, relieved to hear her voice.

"Hi, honey. We're tired but OK. We stopped in Columbus, Ohio, for the night. How are you? I know it's late, but you asked me to call you," Sally said.

"Yes. Thank you for calling. My mind is at ease now! You've made good time. That's great! You are almost halfway here . . . about ten hours yet to go. I'm so excited, babe. I can't wait to see you. Depending on what time you leave in the morning, it could be late when you and the boys get here. But no matter what time, I'll be eagerly waiting for you all to arrive. I'm praying the Lord will continue to keep you and the boys safe for the rest of your trip," Rusty said with anxiousness in his voice.

"I'll be careful. Thank you for your prayers, honey. I hope we can leave at least by 8 a.m.," Sally said.

"The closer you drive to New York, the heavier the traffic might get. Please stay alert," Rusty cautioned her. "Please try to get some sleep. I'll see you all tomorrow! Our time of waiting is almost over. Oh, Sally, I love you so much!" Rusty said passionately.

"Baby, I can't wait to hold you in my arms and kiss your sweet lips. Yes, our time is so near. Sleep good. I love you, Rusty." She blew a kiss into the telephone, and he returned his kiss back to her. The call ended.

Sally laid back in her bed with a big smile on her face and breathed a long sigh. *Yes, we're almost together again,* she thought. Both boys were asleep, and she wasn't too far from sleep herself.

The telephone rang two times at 6:30 a.m., which Sally had requested from the motel desk clerk the night before. Sally thanked the Lord for another day and that she could put her feet on the floor. The boys began to stir.

"Good morning, fellas. Time to get up. I know y'all are sleepy, but we need to get back on the road," she encouraged.

Both boys headed to the bathroom. Sally brought a small bag to them that contained their toothbrushes and toothpaste. "Please brush your teeth, then get dressed," Sally instructed. She returned to the room and dressed. While the boys dressed, she finished up in the bathroom.

Everyone was ready by seven o'clock, and they were back on the super slab. A lot of drivers were on the road, and the CB was busy. The boys had curled up in the back seat, hugging their pillows. Sally decided to let the boys sleep for a little while, then they would stop for breakfast.

An hour later, the boys woke up and were hungry. They were near Mansfield, Ohio, when they saw a fast-food location. They stopped and ate breakfast. The car also needed gas. After a thirty-minute stop, their trip began again.

It was a sunny day with not a cloud in the sky. Town after town passed through Sally's rearview mirror. The scenery was beautiful with mountains and forests all around. She followed Rusty's directions and arrived on Interstate 80 in Pennsylvania. Near Milesburg, they stopped for lunch and gas. Continuing to travel on Interstate 80, they got closer and closer to Connecticut, but it was not fast enough for Sally. She made another turn onto Interstate 81. When she approached Scranton, she needed to take a break. They had been on the road for eight hours. After she filled the gas tank, they walked around for a little while before it was time to hit the road again.

Looking at the atlas and Rusty's directions, the next turn was south on Interstate 380. Then, in a few miles, Sally turned on Interstate 84. An hour later, they crossed the New York state line. After another hour, the sun was setting, and finally they crossed into the state of Connecticut. The highway sign indicated *Newtown - 20 miles*!

"Boys, we are almost there!" Sally exclaimed. "It's past supper time, and even though I am anxious to get to Rusty's, I believe we need to eat something before we get to his home." After a quick stop in Danbury for a bite to eat, they got back on Interstate 84 and on to Newtown.

Sally turned on the dome light in the car so she could see and read Rusty's directions. "Y'all help me look for Exit 10 and Highway 6, please," Sally asked the boys.

"I see the sign! Exit 10," Todd said loudly.

"Good eye, kiddo," Sally said.

"OK, now we turn left on Highway 6, which is also Church Hill Road. Rusty says it will turn into West Street." Sally continued to read the notes she wrote.

"There's the street sign: West Street," Todd pointed out.

"Super! Turn right and go to Castle Hill Road. Then take another right on Old Castle Hill Road," Sally read.

Several miles later, Todd asked, "Did we pass the road?"

"No, I don't think so. There are not that many roads. Oh, look. Is that a road sign coming up?" Sally pressed the floor dimmer switch to make the headlights change to high beam. "Yes, the sign has *Old Castle Hill Road* written on it," Sally said, turning to the right. "Rusty told me his house was the first house on the right side of the road. Let's look for his mailbox."

"There it is!" Pace yelled happily.

Sally turned onto the gravel road. She remembered Rusty's story about the long gravel driveway when she first met him. She saw the clearing ahead, then Rusty's two German shepherds ran barking as Sally drove closer to the home. It looked just like he described it to her months ago. Then she saw him coming out of the front door. Her heart started racing.

"Is that Rusty, Momma?" Pace asked.

Sally stopped the car, turned off the engine, and began to open the car door. "Yes, it is!"

Rusty ran to the driver's side of the car and immediately wrapped his arms around Sally, picking her up off the ground. As he lowered her back down, they kissed each other passionately.

Todd and Pace looked at each other in amazement and wonder. Todd stepped out of the car with Pace right behind him. The two shepherds licked their hands as both boys petted them and spoke softly to them.

Sally and Rusty, still arm in arm, looked at both boys. "Rusty, these are my two sons, Todd and Pace," Sally said, introducing the boys to Rusty.

"Hi, boys." Rusty extended his right arm to shake their little hands. "I've heard so much about the two of you, I feel like I already know you. Come on in the house where it's warm. This night air is chilly."

Sally took the boys' hands, and they followed Rusty into his home with the shepherds right behind them. Once inside, the warmth of a blazing fire was welcoming and comforting.

"Wow! Rusty, this is a huge room! I like your home," Todd exclaimed as he walked closer to the fireplace.

"Yeah, this is really nice!" Pace chimed in.

Sally was overcome with gratitude. Outside, when Rusty extended his hand to shake the boys' hands, they did not hesitate; and now, both of them accepted their surroundings so quickly. She looked at Rusty and smiled with genuine happiness. It already felt like home.

"I'm so glad you and the boys are here. I've been concerned for you driving all that way. Did you have any trouble?" Rusty didn't want to take his eyes off of Sally. He wanted so desperately to take her in his arms and tell her how much he loved her, but he felt like he had to restrain himself, at least for a while until the boys knew him better.

Sally, too, was fighting the overwhelming urge to hold him next to her body tightly and kiss him over and over, but she knew she had to give the boys time to appreciate what could be the start of their new life, and she needed to be cool. "I'm thrilled beyond belief to be here with you. I thank the Lord for a safe and trouble-free trip, but it was a long ride. I'm just so happy to be here and be with you."

"Can I get you guys anything to eat or drink? Todd, Pace, you want anything?" Rusty asked.

"No, sir, but I do need to go to the bathroom," Todd answered.

"Me too," Pace added.

"Sure. Come on; I'll show you to the bathroom." Rusty led them out of the living room area and down a hallway to the bathroom. The boys went in and closed the door.

Rusty and Sally couldn't hold in their emotions any longer, and only for a few moments, they hugged and kissed each other romantically. Soon, they heard the bathroom door opening. "I'll show you all the rest of the house." Rusty guided them from room to room. When they came to the kitchen, Sally was in awe of its size, and she noticed the nice appliances too. She was very impressed.

Moments later, the telephone rang. Rusty answered. "Hello?" There was a pause. "Oh, hi, Mom. Yes, they are here. . . . I'll tell them. . . . No, we're good, but thank you. . . . Night, Mom. . . . I love you too."

As he hung up the telephone, Todd asked, "That was your mom?"

"Yes, it was, Todd. My mom and dad live up the road. She wanted to know if you all were here yet and if we needed anything. She invited us to join them for breakfast in the morning, if that's OK with you guys," Rusty explained.

"That would be great! We want to meet your folks," Sally said, accepting the invitation. "By the way, how is Russell doing?" Sally asked.

"Dad's getting better. I'd like to say each day, but it's more like each week. I am thankful he's recovering; however, it's just slower than we thought. I'd like to help you get your suitcases from the car. I know you guys must be exhausted and close to being ready to go to bed. You put a lot of miles behind you in the last two days!"

Rusty was right about that. "I'll be back in a minute," Sally said. "Y'all stay here where it's warm. The pups look like they are enjoying their new friends!"

"What are their names?" Pace asked.

"Prince is the black one, and Princess is the tan and white one," Rusty answered, then he opened the front door and walked with Sally, hand in hand, to the car. "Sally, I'm so glad you decided to come up because I still don't know when I'll be able to get back to driving again. I've wanted to see you so bad," Rusty confessed.

"I understand your situation, and I have missed you tremendously too. But I'm here now. I love you, my darling." Sally took his face in her hands and kissed Rusty tenderly.

Rusty held her tightly to his body and whispered in her ear, "I know I should not ask, but I sure would love for you to sleep with me tonight."

Sally looked into his eyes. "Honey, I want that too, but I need to see how the boys will do in a strange house with new surroundings."

"I understand. Come on, let's get your things and get back inside." Rusty grabbed Sally's suitcases from the trunk, and she grabbed the pillows and overnight bag from the back seat. They hurried back to the house.

Todd and Pace were laying in front of the fireplace, petting the shepherds who were lying beside them. *What a precious sight*, Sally thought. "Are y'all ready for bed?" she asked them.

"Yes, ma'am," both boys answered.

"Where will the boys and I sleep, Rusty?" Sally asked, looking at Rusty and hoping he understood what she meant.

"There are two bedrooms near the bathroom. Either one of them will be fine," Rusty said.

"I'm going to help them get ready for bed, and I'll be back in a few minutes," Sally told Rusty.

"Can Prince and Princess sleep with us?" Pace asked.

"Of course they can. They will be happy to, and they will watch over you guys too," Rusty said, trying to make them feel comfortable and safe.

Sally and the boys walked down the hall to the bedrooms, and Sally let them choose which one they wanted. Soon, Todd said, "Mom, he is a nice man. I like him."

"I like him too, but I really like his dogs!" Pace exclaimed as he petted one of the shepherds on the head.

"I'm very happy y'all like Rusty because I do too!" Sally said joyfully. She helped them with their PJs and tucked them into bed after their nightly prayers. "I'll be back in a while. Y'all OK?" she asked.

"Yes, ma'am. It's almost like we're at home," Todd remarked.

"That's good. I'm very glad you think so," she said, smiling. "Night night. Love y'all," Sally said. She decided to leave a dimly-lit light on in the bedroom as she walked out and closed the door. Sally walked back into the living area and found Rusty staring into the fireplace. He turned toward Sally, and they embraced each other tenderly, kissing with fiery passion. Words of endearment passed through their lips as they expressed their love and commitment to each other.

Rusty took Sally's hand and led her to the couch where they sat down beside each other.

"I feel like I need to pinch myself, Rusty. I can't believe I'm really here with you. I've dreamed of this moment over and over again every day, and my dreams have finally come true!" Sally said as she stroked Rusty's face with her hand.

"I know. I'd sit here on this couch and picture you sitting beside me, just as you are now, so many times, wondering if that time would ever come. The good Lord has allowed for us to be together again," Rusty said as he drew near to Sally and kissed her lips softly, time and time again.

Sally whispered, "I'm going to see if the boys are asleep. I'll be right back. Don't go away." A minute later, Sally returned to Rusty who was still sitting on the couch. She bent slightly and took his hands. "The boys are asleep. I know it's not right, but I want to be with you, sweetheart."

Rusty raised up from the couch and picked Sally up in his arms. He carried her to his bedroom, closed the door, and laid her on his bed. He laid down next to her, and they kissed passionately. They embraced each other throughout the remainder of the night.

Rusty woke Sally with sweet kisses and a warm embrace. "I hate to get up. Last night was more than I could have imagined, sweetheart." Rusty kissed Sally gently.

As they got up and started dressing, Sally said, "Gosh, you are such a good lookin' man, Mr. Rusty Summers. So handsome from head to toe!"

"Yeah, right! You must still be asleep," Rusty said with a hint of embarrassment.

"Nope, I'm wide awake!"

Rusty turned around and hugged her. "I love you, Ms. Sally. I can't wait to make you my wife!"

"I can't wait to make you my husband!" Even as she said the words, the weight of what she was doing was heavy. She knew until her divorce was final, she was having an affair. That was sin in God's eyes. But she pushed the thought aside and winked at Rusty. "What time does your mom want us to come to breakfast?"

"Probably about eight," Rusty replied. "She didn't want to make it too early so you and the boys could rest."

"OK, I'm going to get the boys up so they can get ready to go." Sally walked out of Rusty's bedroom.

The shepherds had left the boys and were in the kitchen, waiting for Rusty to provide their morning meal. Sally found the boys still sleeping. The road trip had worn them out, but it was time for them to wake up.

"Good morning, my little men. You think you might want to wake up and get dressed so we can go to Rusty's folks' house for breakfast? I know y'all have got to be hungry." Sally hoped to entice them with the thought of food.

Todd stretched and voiced a sleepy, "Good morning, Mom."

Pace, hearing Todd's voice, sat up in bed, opened his mouth with a big yawn, and rubbed his eyes with his hands.

"Good morning, Pace. You hungry?" Sally asked.

"I sure am. Are you hungry, Todd?" Pace asked his brother.

"Yip!" Todd answered.

"I'll lay y'all's clothes out. Y'all need to get around," Sally encouraged them.

"Where are Prince and Princess?" Pace asked.

"They're up and maybe having their breakfast," Sally said. While the boys got ready in the bathroom, Sally changed clothes. Soon, all of them were ready to go. They loaded into Rusty's pickup truck and headed off to the Summers' home.

"You look very pretty, Sally," Rusty said. "Are you OK?"

"Thank you! I want to look nice for your folks. I'm nervous. I hope your mom and dad like me . . . like *us*."

"Don't be nervous, sweetheart. They are going to love all of you," Rusty encouraged. He turned his truck off the main road and drove a quarter of a mile before they arrived at his parents' home.

The first thing Sally and the boys noticed was all of the cows! The boys could not contain their excitement. Seeing so many cows was all new to them. Immediately the boys started asking Rusty question after question about the cows.

The truck came to a stop, and they all got out. Rusty took them to the parlor where the cows were on the milking machines. More questions ensued. Todd and Pace came up close and personal with some of the cows, their eyes as big as silver dollars. Soon, as they turned to go toward the house, they saw Mr. Summers.

"Good morning, Dad." Rusty greeted him. "Good to see you! And look who is here to meet you. Dad, I want you to meet Sally and her two boys, Todd and Pace."

"It's great to finally meet the three of you. Rusty has told us so much about you," Mr. Summers greeted them.

Sally stepped toward the elderly man who was supporting himself by a walker. As she hugged him, she said, "It's wonderful to meet you too, sir."

Mr. Summers was happy that Sally hugged him. "Please, Sally, it's Russell. Hi, boys." Russell extended his hand toward them.

Todd shook his hand. "Hi, sir."

Pace couldn't allow his brother to outdo him. "Hi! It's nice to meet you," he said as he shook the man's hand.

"Mom has breakfast ready. We best go get it before she gives it to the calves!" Rusty laughed as he helped his dad turn the walker around toward the house. Rusty held the back door open, and after Russell entered, the rest of them walked in. Soon, another door opened, and an elderly woman emerged.

"Please, come in," she said pleasantly. They waited for Russell to navigate the doorway, then the others entered the kitchen area. The aroma of food filled the air.

"Mom," Rusty began, "this is my sweetheart, Sally, and her two young sons, Todd and Pace."

"Mrs. Summers, it's a pleasure to meet you." Sally tried not to sound nervous.

"Sally, you have captured our son's heart, and I am pleased to meet you. Rusty has told us so much about you and your sons. We commend you for driving that long trip. Please, take their coats, son, and you guys come to the table. Everything is ready." Mrs. Summers was most gracious.

All of them gathered around the table and took their seats. Russell blessed their meal and thanked the Lord for Sally, Todd, and Pace.

Mrs. Summers had prepared a lot of food, and bowl after bowl full of breakfast items were passed around the table. The meal was delicious and very filling. The conversation was delightful and interesting, full of information about Rusty and his family. Sally learned so much from Rusty's mom and dad's stories. Even Todd and Pace were amused by the family stories.

An hour and a half passed in the blink of an eye. Mrs. Summers raised up from the table, taking dirty dishes to the sink. Rusty and Sally followed suit, then the boys.

"I'll help you do the dishes, Mrs. Summers," Sally volunteered.

"Oh, Sally, that's very kind, but I got this. I know Rusty wants to show you and the boys around the house and the farm. We can catch up later. And please, call me Mandy. I can tell you are a very sweet girl. Thank you for loving my son. He loves you a lot!" Mandy smiled a big smile and hugged Sally.

"Mandy, I do love Rusty very much. You are very kind as well," Sally responded.

"Thank you, Mom. That was very sweet." Rusty kissed his mother on her cheek and hugged her.

"Dad, can I get you anything before I take Sally and the boys around the farm?" Rusty asked his dad.

"No, son, but thank you. Be careful, and keep a close eye on those boys," Russell cautioned.

"I sure will, Dad," Rusty promised. "Sally, boys, come on! I'll show you around the house and get you acquainted with your surroundings." Rusty showed them room after room in the old farm house. Most rooms were just rooms, but upstairs was very different. It was a huge room. One wall was full of books. There was gym equipment, a ping-pong table, and a pool table. The boys could see themselves having all kinds of fun there. Rusty said they could come back to that room later and play, which made the boys very excited.

Next was an unforgettable journey for Sally and the boys as Rusty took them outside and they toured the workings of the farm—calves, cows, milking, processing the milk, storing the feed, how the feed is given to the cows, the birthing area, the stalls for the cows . . . so many things! Then he took them to the pasture where many cows were grazing and then to the barns where farm equipment was stored. Rusty introduced them to the men who helped keep the farm operating. What the tour ultimately showed them was that a glass of milk or a bowl of ice cream was so much more than they knew it to be.

"Thank you, Rusty, for all you've shown us. I had no idea what all a dairy farm had to do to preserve the industry. And you're just one farm! Wow, it's amazing!" Sally was so impressed.

Todd looked at Rusty and remarked, "There is so much to do. How do you do all of it?"

"That's why we have men helping us. Dad and I could never do it alone. It's a big job," Rusty said.

"I like the calves most of all. They are so cute!" Pace declared.

"Yeah, they're pretty cute. If you three are OK, I'll show you some of the town. There are a lot of small towns in the area, but we all serve each other with different amenities," Rusty explained.

They climbed into Rusty's pickup truck, and he drove through several towns where they saw food places, churches, schools, and many other businesses. The areas and their surroundings were all so charming. Everything was very convenient. Sally liked what she saw.

After several hours, they returned to the Summers' home. Mandy had prepared sandwiches for their lunch.

"I thought I'd prepare chicken and dumplings for dinner. Do you and the boys like chicken and dumplings, Sally?" Mandy asked as she put away the condiments from lunch.

"Yes, ma'am. Sounds delicious! What can I do to help you?" Sally asked.

"Not really anything right now. Maybe later. Rusty and the boys, I believe, went upstairs to play. Do you like to play pool?" Mandy asked.

"I've never tried it," Sally answered. "But I'd liked to."

"Rusty can teach you. It's fun," Mandy replied.

"I saw a piano in the living room. Do you play?" Sally inquired.

"Yes. Russell and I both do. Do you?" Mandy asked.

"No, not the piano. My father bought an organ when I was seven years old, and my mother, brother, and I learned how to play it. My brother was a fast learner. Once he played a song by reading the sheet music, he could play the song from memory. He was very talented, but mother and I had to read the sheet music to play," Sally shared.

"Would you like a cup of coffee? I'd like to learn more about your family," Mandy said.

"I'd like that, Mandy," Sally agreed. They sat at the kitchen table, sipping their coffee, and talked for several hours about Sally's life and family.

Rusty, Todd, Pace, and Russell entered the kitchen after playing several games.

"What's going on down here?" Rusty asked.

"Sally and I have been sharing about our lives with each other. Rusty, you have yourself one fine lady!" Mandy complimented.

Rusty walked over to Sally and put his hands on her shoulders. "I know it, Mom. She's a *keeper!*" Then he bent down and kissed her on her cheek. Sally's heart fluttered and skipped a beat as he kissed her.

Todd and Pace looked at each other and shrugged their shoulders as to what had just happened.

Mandy rose up from the table. "Anyone want any coffee or soda before I start dinner?"

"I'd like a soda, please," Todd asked politely.

"Me too, if that's OK?" Pace chimed in.

"Follow me to the pantry and choose which one you'd like." Mandy walked ahead of them.

Rusty walked to the kitchen counter and took a cup from the cabinet. "Dad, I'm going to have a cup of coffee. You want some?"

"Yes, son, I would," Russell replied.

Mandy began taking food items from the refrigerator to begin preparing their evening meal. Sally and Rusty helped. In an hour, the meal was being served. Sally had missed good old-fashioned homecooked meals.

Everyone helped with the clean-up of the kitchen, including Pace and Todd. Sally marveled at the family togetherness. It was a comforting feeling to her, and she thought it was for the boys too. Something they were not used too.

The day at the Summers' home was coming to a close. Rusty, Sally, and the boys gave their *thank yous* to Mandy and Russell for a wonderful day. Rusty kissed his mother's cheek and hugged his father. To Sally's surprise, the boys hugged both of Rusty's parents, and she followed their lead.

The outside air was cold, and all four of them huddled together on the bench seat of Rusty's truck. Sally certainly didn't mind the closeness to Rusty.

Within minutes, they were in Rusty's home. Prince and Princess were glad to see them. Rusty stoked the fireplace with wood, and soon there was a roaring fire warming the living area.

Todd and Pace helped Rusty feed the shepherds. "Do you like dogs?" Rusty asked.

"Yes, I do," Pace answered.

"I do too, but we've never had a dog," Todd commented.

"What about horses? Do you like them?" Rusty asked.

The boys looked at each other and really didn't know what to say. "They haven't been around horses," Sally chimed in as she walked into the kitchen.

"Well, I need to make a trip to the barn. Does anyone want to go with me?" Rusty asked.

"I do," the boys shouted together.

Rusty reached for a few blankets and wrapped them around the boys for extra warmth. He wrapped another one around sweet Sally and gave her a quick kiss on the lips. As they walked out the back door of the house, Rusty flipped a switch, and a string of lights lit up. "Let's hold hands so we can stay together on the lighted gravel path," Rusty suggested.

Sally took Todd's hand, and as she was going to take Pace's hand, he ran in front of her and grabbed Rusty's hand. Sally looked at Rusty with a big smile and with tears in her eyes. She thought, *How special!* Rusty took Sally's hand. Prince and Princess followed them.

The lights were on in the barn, and there were lots of noises coming from inside. Rusty opened the barn doors, and the shepherds ran in. In two of the four stalls, horse heads extended out of their stall doors, their eyes watching who was coming in. Both boys froze in place.

Rusty was a few steps ahead of Sally and the boys. He stopped and looked behind him. "It's OK, boys. I want you to meet Chief and Sundance. They are two-year-old twins. Come on. They won't hurt you. They're big but gentle," Rusty encouraged as he filled two buckets of horse feed.

Sally walked close to Chief and rubbed the bridge of his nose and his muzzle, attempting to show the boys the horse would not hurt her. Pace approached the horse and reached his arm and hand up to touch him, but he wasn't quite tall enough. Rusty came up behind Pace and scooped him up in his arms so Pace could be closer to the horse.

Todd, seeing that his brother was OK, walked closer to Sundance and bravely rubbed his muzzle. Sundance made a whinny sound, which startled Todd. Todd jumped back, nearly falling.

Rusty quickly stepped behind Todd to secure him. "You OK, little buddy? Sundance was saying hi to you. He likes you, Todd."

Todd looked up to Rusty. "You think he really does?"

"I'm sure of it!" Rusty exclaimed.

The horses were fed, and as the four of them walked back to the house, the boys asked Rusty many questions about the horses. Sally thanked God for all the blessed moments of the day. Everything felt so right.

The boys took their baths, slipped into their PJs, and laid on the furry rug in front of the fireplace with Prince and Princess by their sides. Sally and Rusty sat close to each other on the couch, holding hands and talking about the events of the day. Sally told Rusty that it was another beautiful night of togetherness and that she could really get used to this kind of life. Rusty smiled and told her that he could too.

The boys started falling asleep, so Rusty carried Todd to bed, then returned to the living area to pick up Pace and carry him to bed. Sally followed him, and once Pace was in bed, she covered both boys with their blankets and kissed them good night. Prince and Princess entered the room and laid down on the floor at the foot of the bed.

Rusty and Sally retreated to Rusty's bedroom and shared a nighttime full of romantic bliss. Sally knew it wasn't right, but she had lost herself in the moment and told herself they would be married soon enough.

Chapter Eighteen

Rusty's alarm clock interrupted the restful embrace of the sleeping couple. Rusty rolled over and turned off the clock then turned back toward Sally and kissed her.

"I'm going to get up, sweetheart. I need to go to B and D and get my big rig and bring it home. It's been sitting in all the weather, and it should be cleaned. Maybe you and the boys would like to help me later today," Rusty suggested.

"I would like to do that with you, and I know the boys would too. Do you want me to take you?" Sally asked.

"No, I'll drive my pickup over there. I thought when I take the big truck back to the yard, you and the boys would ride with me," Rusty said.

"Oh, how thrilling! Yes, the boys would love that!" Sally rejoiced. "Do you know how long you'll be gone? Do you want me to prepare breakfast?"

"Well, you see, that's another thing. We need to go to the grocery store. I was going to go, but I did not know what you all ate. So we need to go," Rusty confessed.

"We can do it, honey," Sally said.

"I should be back in less than an hour. I'll pick up some breakfast food on the way home," Rusty suggested as he kissed Sally and rolled out of bed.

Sally watched his naked body walk into the bathroom. She thought, *I still need to pinch myself!* Sally promptly got up when she heard the shepherds barking. Then someone knocked on the front door. She quickly ran to the bathroom. "Rusty, someone is at the door," Sally informed him.

Rusty opened the door to the bathroom. "OK," he said as he grabbed his robe from the hook on the back of the bathroom door and hurried out of the bedroom.

Prince and Princess were still barking, and Sally dressed as quickly as she could. Rusty opened the front door, and Sally could hear excited voices. He ran back into the bedroom.

"Sally, I've got to go to the farm!" he anxiously announced as he began to get dressed.

"What's wrong?" Sally asked.

"A cow is calving! I've got to go!" Rusty answered. He gave her a quick kiss as he ran out of the bedroom and out the front door.

Sally heard a voice. "Mom, is everything all right?" Todd said, running into the living area.

"I'm not sure, but I hope so," she answered with concern in her voice as she looked out the front window and saw Rusty speed away.

Pace entered the room very sleepy-eyed. "What's happening?" he asked.

"I'm not sure. Someone came and told Rusty something, and he had to go to the farm," Sally answered. "I tell ya what. Let's get dressed just in case Rusty needs our help." Sally hurried them to the bathroom. While they did their morning routine, she found the clothes she wanted them to wear, and the boys got dressed. "Todd, do you remember feeding the shepherds yesterday?" Sally asked.

"Yes, ma'am," he answered.

"Do you think you could feed them this morning?"

"Yes. Come on, Pace. You can help me." Todd grabbed his little brother's hand, and they ran to the kitchen.

While Todd and Pace fed the shepherds, Sally took a look in the fridge. She saw a carton of eggs but no bacon or sausage. Then she looked in the pantry and found a loaf of bread but nothing else she could use as food for breakfast. She found a skillet and began frying the eggs. She toasted several slices of bread and buttered them. There were a few almost over-ripe bananas in a bowl on the kitchen table as well.

"I know this isn't much, but hopefully this food will tide y'all over until later. We'll need to go to grocery store."

Not long after they ate, there was a rapid knock on the front door. Sally rushed and opened the door.

"Good morning, Sally. Rusty asked me to come and get you and the boys. He wanted you all to see another part about the farm," Mandy announced.

"OK, Mandy. Boys, put on your coats. Let's go with Ms. Mandy," Sally instructed as she put on her coat.

Mandy quickly drove back to the farm. Sally wanted to ask questions, but she chose just to keep quiet.

Rusty was waiting for them when his mom drove up. "Come on! I want you all to see this!"

They ran to a room where a cow was lying on her side about to give birth to her calf. The boys watched in awe, and Sally could almost feel the mother's labor pains as she mooed and strained. Soon, they could see a leg emerge, then the calf's face, and then another leg, until the whole calf was born. Right away, the mother began licking her new baby, and within a few minutes, the calf was struggling to stand up. The young baby staggered a bit but found its way to its mother's milk source.

Sally breathed a sigh of relief for the mother cow. "Wow! What an experience! Boys, y'all just saw a new little life being born. That's one of God's miracles! How fascinating," she said in amazement. "Thank you, Rusty, for allowing us to see this special event. Definitely a learning part of life on your farm!"

"You're welcome. Boys, what did you think?" Rusty asked.

"I've never seen anything like that before. I never really thought about it or how something is born. Very interesting," Todd expressed.

"Does it hurt the momma when her baby is being born?" Pace asked sympathetically.

"Well, yes, in a way. But normally it doesn't hurt too long," Rusty explained. "I didn't mean to run out on you this morning, Sally, but sometimes when a cow is about to give birth, there could be problems. My worker didn't want to take any chances, so he decided to alert me. Now that you all are up and going, do you want to get some breakfast and get my truck?" Rusty asked.

"That sounds great; however, I did find eggs in your fridge, and I also found some bread. So I prepared the boys something to eat already. But I'm sure they could eat again," Sally said with a giggle as she looked at her boys.

"An egg and bread isn't much, is it boys?" Rusty asked.

"No, sir!" Todd and Pace answered at once.

"OK, then. Let's go!" Rusty took the boys' hands. "Come on, Momma!" Rusty called to Sally.

The diner Rusty chose was different looking than any other place they had ever been. It looked like a very long train car! The food was served quickly and was delicious. After breakfast, Rusty drove Sally and the boys to B and D Express. He parked his pickup truck in front of the office and ran inside. A few minutes later, he came back out and motioned for Sally and the boys to get out of the pickup. All four of them walked a short distance to his Kenworth. He unlocked the passenger door and opened it. "You all climb in," Rusty invited.

Todd looked at Rusty with a priceless look of disbelief. "Is this yours?"

"Yes, it is, Master Todd. Here, let me help you. That first step is high." Rusty picked him up and placed his feet on the running board, then Todd stepped the rest of the way into the truck's cab. Rusty and Sally heard him exclaim, "Wow!"

Rusty picked up Pace and looked at his face. "What's the matter, little guy?" Rusty asked as he saw tears in Pace's eyes.

"I'm just so happy, Rusty." Pace threw his little arms around Rusty's neck and hugged him tightly.

Tears came into Rusty's eyes, and he felt something he had never ever felt before: the love of a child.

Sally witnessed the most incredible scene, and such happiness sprang up inside of her. Sally became teary-eyed too as she wondered, *Are we becoming a real family?*

"Hey, it's OK, Pace. I'm very happy too!" He looked at Sally and saw tears rolling down her face. He put his arm around her and pulled her close to him.

"Pace, are you getting in here or not? You've got to see this! Hurry up!" Todd shouted to his brother.

"I believe your brother wants you in the truck. Here you go." Rusty sat his feet on the running board, and Pace sat in the passenger seat for a moment. Then he disappeared into the sleeper.

"Sally, I can't tell you how wonderful I feel. I never imagined feeling the way I feel right now. I want us to be a family so much," Rusty declared.

Sally smiled and happily replied, "I believe we already are, my darlin'." With that, she held Rusty tightly.

Rusty helped Sally into the passenger seat, and then Sally turned to look at the boys who were laying on the sleeper bed. She never pictured this moment happening.

The driver's door opened, and Rusty climbed in and sat in the seat. When he cranked up the truck's diesel engine, the sound was more than the boys could have imagined. They *wow-d* and *woo-d* over and over again. The look on their faces was a treasure for Sally to behold. They were so excited! As Rusty drove his big rig off the yard, the boys' excitement grew. They watched intently out the wide windshield, taking in all the sights of sitting up so high off the ground. They watched Rusty shift the gears and turn the big steering wheel. It was a ride they would never forget.

Once back to Rusty's home, Sally and the boys helped Rusty wash the truck, dust off the dashboard, and vacuum the floor. Sally stripped off the covers from the sleeper and washed and dried them in the house. Then, as she remade the bed, she remembered the romance that she and Rusty created in that very bed.

Rusty climbed up in the cab. "You OK in here? You need some help, sweetheart?" He saw her sitting on the edge of the bed, looking at him with those green eyes of hers, her beautiful flowing auburn hair draped across her shoulders. Her look enticed and beckoned him, and he stepped into the sleeper and sat down beside her. He took her in his arms and kissed her tenderly, like he did the first time he kissed her months ago. He softly told her that the place they were sitting had a lot of their history. Sally agreed. Many hopes, dreams, and plans had started there. They were so happy that those hopes, dreams, and plans were coming true.

"Mom, Rusty, are y'all up there?" Todd called out.

Sally stepped out of the sleeper and saw Todd. "Yes, sir, right here."

"I believe we're done," Todd explained.

"OK, great job! We're coming down," Sally informed him. Sally backed down out of the cab, and Rusty followed. The boys had been wiping off the cleaned floor mats. Rusty praised them for all their help and hard work. The tractor sparkled again, and it was time to take the truck back to the yard. Sally and the boys again enjoyed the ride.

On the way home, they stopped at the grocery store and bought a few groceries. Rusty did cook, but not often. His mom always prepared enough food for Rusty to eat with them. Sally picked out most of the food that was bought and had a few meals in mind to prepare.

When they arrived at Rusty's home and brought the groceries inside, they noticed there was food sitting on the counter, along with a note from Rusty's mom saying that more food was in the refrigerator. He immediately called her and thanked her for their dinner. Rusty blessed their food, and each one ate a plateful of another delicious home-cooked meal.

After the kitchen was cleaned, the boys asked if they could take their baths. They were tired and soon would be ready for bed. Rusty fed the shepherds and the horses while the boys took their baths. Then the boys laid by the fireplace and chatted to their mother and Rusty about their day, telling them what a special day it was. It wasn't long before the boys and the shepherds went to bed.

Rusty and Sally prepared a small platter of cheese and crackers to eat while they sat on the furry rug, relaxing in front of the fireplace.

"Baby, I believe the boys are bonding with you very well—even more than I expected they would. Thank you for all the attention you're giving them. I think they're already learning to trust you," Sally expressed gratefully to Rusty.

"And I do want them to trust me. I was so taken by Pace this morning and his spontaneous and sincere hug. I really felt like I could be his father. It was a wonderful feeling! And Todd seems to be relying on me more to answer his questions. I feel like he's warming up to me. Bottom line, honey, is that I'm falling in love with your sons. They are great kids," Rusty admitted to Sally.

Sally's eyes filled with tears, and at the same time, she smiled a very happy smile. Rusty's words meant the world to her. "Darlin', I'm so glad you feel that strongly about my kiddos. They mean everything to me, and if they didn't liked you, I would be very sad. You have already shown them more than they have ever seen—me included. You have a wonderful life here. Your parents are great and very loving. Your home is beautiful . . . everything is perfect!" Sally said truthfully.

"But, sweet Sally, you're going to make it better because you and the boys belong here with me. I hope you feel that way too." Rusty prayed for a positive answer from Sally.

"I truly do, Rusty dear. I've not been this happy in years. I do want to make a life with you, and I believe the boys would say they would too," Sally spoke from her heart.

"My lady, you are making this man so very happy. I love you more than you know." Rusty leaned toward Sally and kissed her with the sweetest and most meaningful kiss. He stood up, took her hands, and lifted her up from the rug, and he carried her to his bedroom.

Sally was up before Rusty, so she started a pot of coffee. While she waited for the coffee to brew, she stood at the back of the kitchen, looking out the window at the woods. The birds were fluttering around, and a rabbit hopped across the gravel path. It was so peaceful and serene. She felt such contentment. She softly whispered to God, "Thank You."

Rusty quietly walked up behind her and wrapped his loving arms around her small waist. "Good morning, beautiful." He slowly turned her body around to face him and kissed her.

Sally hugged him, "Good morning, handsome. Would you like some coffee?"

"I'd rather have you than coffee, but I guess I need to settle for coffee." Rusty sounded frisky!

"Down, boy. Down! Save it for later." Sally needed to tame the beast in the man . . . at least, for a little while. She poured their coffee, and they sat at the kitchen table. "When it gets warmer, I'd like for us to sit in the screen room and have our coffee," Sally suggested.

"I do believe that could be arranged." Then Rusty paused. "I need to go over to the farm for a bit. I need to check on how things are running. I'm sure everything is OK, but the new men are used to seeing me there. I don't want them to think just because I'm not there, they don't need to do their jobs. I don't know how long I'll be," Rusty explained.

"I'll fix you some breakfast," Sally said as she raised up from the table. "Bacon, eggs, biscuits, and what else, honey?"

"All that sounds good. I bought some oatmeal yesterday. Could I have a small bowl?" Rusty asked as he walked out of the kitchen.

"Coming right up, Mr. Summers," Sally answered, thinking about the day when Rusty would call her *Mrs.* Summers. She tried to be methodical about preparing breakfast. Being in a different kitchen, with new and different appliances, trying to locate all the things she needed, was a challenge, but she managed and had Rusty's meal on the table in thirty minutes.

Rusty, all dressed and ready for the day, walked into the kitchen. "Smelling good, sweetie."

"And you're just in time. Don't you look so nice in your farm clothes! Want another cup of coffee?" Sally asked.

"Yes, I do. Thank you," Rusty answered as he poured a small glass of orange juice and carried it to the table. "Are you having breakfast with me?"

"No. I'll eat when the boys get up. Is there anything I can do while you're tending to the farm?" Sally inquired.

"No, just relax. It's going to be a beautiful day with lots of sunshine and warmer temps. When I'm done at the farm and I get cleaned up, if you and the boys want to, we can go for a drive down to the ocean," Rusty suggested.

"That sounds great! We would love to do that."

Rusty got up from the table with his plate in his hand and carried it to the sink.

"Was your breakfast OK, honey?" Sally asked. "I wish I could cook like your momma."

"Well, she has a few more years of cooking than you, sweetie, but she'll teach you. And yes, my breakfast was very good. Thank you," Rusty said. "I'm going to finish getting ready, then I'll leave."

A short while later, Rusty was ready to go. He hugged and kissed Sally. "See you later. I love you."

"Love you too. Be careful." Sally waved as he drove away.

"Morning, Mom. Where is Rusty going?" Todd startled her.

"You're just as quiet as a little mouse!" Sally said as she walked over to Todd and gave him a hug. "He needed to go to the farm for a while. Are you ready for some breakfast? Is your brother up too?" Sally asked as she walked to their bedroom.

"Yes, I'm hungry! I don't think Pace is up yet," Todd answered.

"Nope. He's still in bed." Sally walked over to her sleeping little boy and sat gently on the bed beside him. "Good morning, Pace," she whispered. "I'm about ready to fix breakfast. Your brother says he is hungry. You hungry?" Pace groaned a little but didn't respond. "I'm going to tickle you!" Sally said as she started to run her fingers over his belly.

Giggles erupted as Pace squirmed away from his mother. "Momma, don't get me! I'm getting up! Yes, I'm hungry too," he said as he wiggled off the other side of the bed.

"OK, Pace, I won't get you today, but maybe tomorrow! I'm going to the kitchen."

The shepherds were waiting to be fed. Sally asked Todd about the dog food, so Todd came into the kitchen and fed them for her. Breakfast was prepared, and the three of them sat down and ate.

"Momma, I like it here. Do you?" Pace asked.

His statement and question were music to Sally's ears. "I'm glad you like it here because I do too. Do you, Todd?"

"Yes, I do, very much," Todd happily remarked. "It's so different here than at home. So much more to do, and Rusty is very nice. I really like his folks too. I like everything!"

"You both seem happy . . . happier than I've seen in a long time. That makes me happy," Sally expressed to them.

"Do you think Rusty likes us, Momma?" Pace asked inquisitively.

"You know, after the two of you went to bed last night, Rusty and I talked about our day together. He told me he really enjoyed being around y'all, and to him, he felt like we were the family that he never had," Sally shared.

"I can tell he really likes you, Mom, and you are happy. That makes me happy too," Todd said.

"This may be hard for y'all to understand, but I love Rusty, and he loves me. And yes, he does make me very happy!" Sally confessed.

The front door opened. "I'm home!" Rusty announced loudly. "Where are you all?"

"We're in the kitchen, honey," Sally called.

"Hi, you guys," Rusty greeted as he walked into the kitchen.

Pace jumped up out of his chair, ran toward Rusty, and hugged his legs. Rusty bent down and picked him up in his arms. Pace then hugged Rusty's neck.

"And good morning to you too, little Pace!" Rusty said as he hugged the young child and walked toward Sally. He lowered Pace to the floor, leaned forward, and kissed Sally on the lips.

"Rusty, do you want to marry my mom?" Todd suddenly asked.

Rusty did not hesitate his answer. "Yes, I do, Todd. Would that be OK with you?" Rusty turned to look at Pace. "And you, Pace?"

Sally sat in awe, listening to the conversation her sons and Rusty were having. She was speechless.

"Would that make you my daddy?" Pace asked excitedly.

"Yes, I would say it would, if that's OK with you guys?" Rusty happily answered.

"Then, yes! It's OK with me for you to marry Mom. Pace, is it OK with you?" Todd asked excitedly.

"Yes, and yes, for you to be our dad! Right, Todd?" Pace voiced joyfully.

"Absolutely, I want you to be my dad!" Todd exclaimed.

Sally was overwhelmed with happiness, and she cried. She wondered what had just happened. She was overjoyed. They all cried, hugged, and kissed each other in anticipation for their new soon-to-be family.

Rusty, still wiping his tears away, told Sally he was going to go take a shower and get dressed. Sally helped the boys get dressed, then she dressed.

"OK, are we ready to go?" Rusty asked with excitement in his voice.

"I believe so," Sally answered joyfully.

"Where are we going?" Pace asked.

"Sally, they don't know?" Rusty was surprised she hadn't told the boys about the trip they'd take that day.

"No, they don't know," Sally replied.

"We're going to the beach!" Rusty exclaimed.

Todd looked at Rusty and asked concerningly, "What's a beach?"

Rusty was taken off guard by Todd's question and looked at Sally.

"They have never been to the beach before," she admitted.

"Oh my gosh! Boys, you are going to be in for a treat. Come on. Let's go have some fun!" Rusty shouted with joy.

The boys rushed out the front door and headed for Rusty's pickup truck with Sally, Rusty, and Prince and Princess right behind them. Rusty lowered the truck's tailgate, and the shepherds jumped into the bed of the truck. He opened the back door for the boys, and Sally waited for Rusty to open the driver's door for her. As he approached her, they kissed.

The four of them and the pups were settled, and Rusty began driving. The warmth of the sun raised the temperature above normal. They rolled the windows down to enjoy the fresh air.

Bridgeport was a thirty-minute drive south on Highway 25, and the closer Rusty drove to the city, the more traffic there was. Rusty turned onto Interstate 95, and the drive took them over several bridges and the harbor. The boys and Sally were in awe of the scenery. There were huge freighters navigating the harbor. They saw marinas with every size boat imaginable. And then there was the beach with the Atlantic Ocean beyond.

"Wow, it's beautiful!" Pace shrieked with total enthusiasm.

"Yes, it is beautiful, Pace," Sally echoed.

"Mom, are we living in a dream?" Todd asked in wonderment.

"No, son, this is real life! I could say it's a dream come true, but you have never thought of having a dream that included things that you've never seen before now. This is for real!"

Rusty got out of the truck and helped Sally out. He let the tailgate down, and the shepherds jumped out and started running. Once Todd and Pace saw the shepherds running, they opened the truck door and stepped onto the sand.

"Momma, I'm sinking! What is this?" Pace was scared.

"Yeah, this feels weird, Mom!" Todd stepped cautiously.

"It's OK, boys. It's called *sand,* and yes, it does feel weird when you walk on it," Rusty agreed. "You guys, the sand is not bothering the shepherds, and they would love for you to go play with them. Go get them!" he encouraged. And the boys ran off to catch the shepherds. Rusty reached in the truck's full-length toolbox and pulled out several blankets and a big picnic basket.

"And what is this?" Sally asked.

"When I was at the farm this morning, I mentioned to Mom that we were going to the beach today. As I was leaving to come home, she hailed me down and gave me the basket," Rusty explained.

"Your mother is so sweet and thoughtful. I really like your mom," Sally said. As Sally and Rusty walked across the sand toward the shore, Sally asked, "What do you think your mom and dad will say about us getting married?"

"Sally, the first time I saw you and came home after that trip, I told Mom about you and our conversation. I told her then, I sure hoped I'd see you again. Every trip after that, she would ask me if I talked to you or saw you. I'd tell her *no, I didn't.* She'd always tell me she was praying for me to see you again. The day I told her about seeing you at the truck stop, and we talked and made arrangements to see each other again, she cried. After she stopped crying, she told me that I would marry you! Little did she know that I was already in love with you, and I hoped someday you'd be my wife. So yes, my mom and dad would be very happy for us," Rusty said.

"That's an amazing story, Rusty," Sally said, helping Rusty spread the blankets on the sand. "Thank you for sharing it with me."

"God works in ways we don't understand. I don't know how my mother would have known, but she told me that God placed you on her heart. And, well, here we are!" Rusty took Sally in his arms and kissed her. "I love you so much, Sally," he said, looking deeply into her eyes.

"I love you dearly too, Rusty."

The sweethearts walked hand in hand along the shore, with the boys and the shepherds running in front of them, for a long while. Not another beach-goer was there that day; they were in a world of their own. When they returned to their blankets, they sat down, opened the picnic basket, and found it full of delicious goodies to eat.

After a wonderful few hours at the beach, the four of them returned to the pickup. Rusty secured the shepherds in the truck bed, and they were on their way home. It had been a dream of a day and a huge learning experience for the boys.

Before getting home, Sally started to feel a little unwell, so she laid down on Rusty's leg. "What's the matter, honey?" Rusty asked concerningly.

"I'm just feeling a little crampy. Could be my cycle," Sally said.

Rusty frowned as he looked down at Sally. It took him a minute. "Oh, that!" he said, realizing what she meant. "It's that time of the month. Right?"

"Maybe. When we get back, I'll take some medication. Hopefully then I'll feel better," Sally stated.

"I'm praying right now for you, sweetheart," Rusty thoughtfully said.

Once home, Sally took some pain pills and laid down for a while. Rusty took the boys with him to his parents' home to return the picnic basket, and he praised his mom for the gracious idea for their lunch. Todd wasted no time asking if it would be OK for him and Pace to go upstairs and play pool for a little while. Mandy had no problem with that, but she told them to be careful. She asked Rusty where Sally was, and he explained that Sally didn't feel well. He also told her about the blessed news that he, Sally, Todd, and Pace talked about wanting to become a family. His mother was overjoyed, and she cried as she wrapped her arms around her son. She praised God over and over for His answer to her prayers.

Rusty had an idea that he wanted to share with his mom. He wanted him, Sally, and the boys to all come over to his parents' house for an early dinner the night before they left to go back home. At that time, he'd have a surprise for Sally. With excitement, Mandy was in full agreement with his plan.

Rusty and the boys returned home. They agreed to be quiet so as not to wake their mother if she was asleep. But instead, they found her in the kitchen, pondering over what to prepare for supper—well, it's *dinner* up north!

"Hi, babe. How are you feeling?" Rusty asked as he kissed her.

"Much better, honey. Thank you. What do y'all want to eat?" Sally asked, looking at Todd and Pace. "Did y'all have a nice visit at Rusty's folks' house?"

The boys told their mother that they played pool.

"Let's hold off on dinner for a little while. Let's go check on the horses first." Rusty headed toward the back door.

Sally and the boys followed him. The boys ran ahead, and Prince and Princess followed them. Todd opened one of the barn doors and peeked inside. Pace opened the door wider and ran in.

"Pace, don't scare the horses!" Todd voiced just above a whisper.

"I don't think I'll scare them, Todd," Pace laughed.

The boys helped Rusty get the buckets of feed, and then Rusty showed them where to place the buckets in Chief's and Sundance's stalls. The boys were a little scared and timid, especially when the horses made their sounds. While the horses ate, Rusty cleaned up after the horses and showed Todd and Pace what to do to help.

Rusty opened the doors at the back of the barn, which led directly into the corral. He walked back to Chief's stall, opened the door, and led him out by his halter. He tied the horse to a post in the barn and began to put a saddle on his back. Todd, Pace, and Sally watched Rusty's every move. Next, Rusty did the same to Sundance, who showed he was excited by pawing the ground several times. Rusty had to tell him to calm down!

Soon after, Rusty asked Sally to come to him. He took her right hand and placed it under the halter so she could guide the horse out of the barn. He walked over to Chief, untied the rope, and put his hand under the halter. He began walking the horse out of the barn, and Sally followed him with Sundance. Todd and Pace slowly followed them. Sally was nervous but tried to remain calm.

Once they were in the corral, Rusty asked Todd to join him. Todd was hesitant, but he followed Rusty's instructions. Rusty then picked up Todd and sat him in the saddle. Rusty took the halter in his hand to steady the horse. He asked Todd to hold on to the horn of the saddle. While Todd was holding the horn, Rusty slowly began walking Chief. Sally watched Todd. He had never been on a horse before. She could feel how tense he was, but after one walk around the corral, she could tell he was more relaxed. Rusty stopped Chief and lifted Todd off the horse's back and let Chief walk on his own.

Rusty approached Sally and asked Pace to come to him, and Rusty did the same for Pace as he did for Todd. Sally watched and held her breath. She noticed right away that Pace seemed to be more relaxed than Todd—actually, he was enjoying riding Sundance. Then it was Sally's turn. She had to be brave. Her sons were watching her! When Sally's turn was over, Rusty helped her step down from the horse.

"You guys did great! I hope we have time to do this again. Are you OK with the horses?" Rusty asked them.

"Yes, I loved it!" Pace shouted. "Thank you, Rusty."

"I hope we can do it again. I was scared at first, but it was fun. Thank you," Todd responded.

"Like the boys, I've never been on a horse before, but it was quite an amazing feeling. Thank you for doing this for us. You are so thoughtful, and I appreciate you. There is more to you than I ever imagined. You're such a good man." Sally admired his generosity.

"Sally, I just want to show you and the boys all I can. I want you all to be happy here with me," Rusty sincerely expressed.

"And you have, my darlin'. Thank you." She stroked his face with her hand and smiled.

Rusty pulled the saddles from the horses' backs and walked Chief and Sundance back into their stalls and closed the doors.

As they all walked back to the house, Rusty suggested that, instead of fussing over preparing dinner, they go to a restaurant in town to eat. His suggestion was accepted as a grand idea.

All of them freshened up and left the house. On the way, Rusty slowed the pickup down and pointed out the school the boys would be attending once they moved there. The future all of a sudden rushed to Sally's mind; she felt weak and unprepared. In reality, that time was only six months away. But so much had to happen in six short months.

The restaurant wasn't busy and was very quiet, other than the music that was softly playing. They ordered and then talked about the wonderful day they had had. There was a small dance floor in the restaurant, and the song that was being played prompted Rusty to ask Sally to dance with him. Sally loved to dance, so she quickly accepted his invitation.

"I'm seeing another side of you, Mr. Summers!" Sally was impressed. As he circled her around a few times, she remarked, "And a very good dancer!"

"You're not so bad yourself, Ms. Sally. Just another thing I love about us!" Rusty commented.

The song ended, much to their dismay. They walked back to their table and found the boys looking at their mother and Rusty, laughing.

"What's so funny?" Sally asked them.

"We've never seen you dance before, Mom," Todd explained as he continued to laugh.

"Really?" Rusty sounded surprised.

"Ah, probably not. The other . . . ah, person didn't dance. So I guess that was one of those first-time-for-everything moments!" Sally fluffed Todd's hair as she sat down at the table.

Rusty frowned and asked Sally, "Do you like to dance? You did so well just now."

"Yes, I love to dance. When I was in high school, I was on the dance team. We had so much fun. It was a way to explore our self-expression and gain more confidence in ourselves," Sally reminisced.

"Talk about learning something new! I didn't know that." Rusty felt enlightened about Sally's younger days. Their meal soon arrived, and they enjoyed it.

Once home, Rusty and the boys fed the shepherds, then Todd and Pace took their baths. Then they rested a few minutes in front of the warm fireplace. It had been a very active day, and soon they were off to bed.

But the most important part of the day was when they decided they wanted to become a family.

Chapter Nineteen

The morning light from the sun filtered through the window above Rusty's bed. Sleepily, Sally opened her eyes, and she saw Rusty's handsome face just inches away from hers. She watched him sleep and smiled with a silent prayer on her lips, thanking the Lord for Rusty. She told God she loved Rusty with her whole heart, and she praised Him for her happiness. She felt blessed that they decided to become a family.

Rusty began to move. Soon, he opened his eyes and saw Sally looking at him. "Good morning, beautiful," he said, smiling.

"Good morning, handsome," she said, smiling back at him. She leaned forward, and they kissed affectionately.

"I have an idea," Rusty began. "Do you think you'd feel comfortable leaving the boys with my mom and dad for several hours this morning after breakfast? There are a few places we need to go, but we need to be alone."

"I guess that would be OK, but do you think your mom and dad would want the boys to stay with them?" Sally replied.

"I don't know why not, but if you'd feel better about it, I'll call Mom in a little while and talk to her about it. OK?"

"Yes, I'd like that. Thank you. You think we should get up since we have places to go, people to see, and things to do?" Sally asked.

"Yeah, I suppose we should. You want to go first or me first?"

"I'll go first," Sally decided. She got up and walked to the bathroom.

"Looking good, sweetheart!" Rusty exclaimed, giving a wolf whistle.

"Watch it, kid!" Sally reacted.

"I always am," Rusty assured her with a smirk.

Once she was done in the bathroom, Rusty took his turn. When he walked out, Sally asked, "Ready for coffee?"

"Sounds good," Rusty answered.

They both walked to the kitchen, and Sally prepared the coffee while Rusty called his mom. At the end of the conversation, Rusty joined Sally at the kitchen table.

"Mom said she'd be happy to watch the boys for us," he said. "Sally, let's walk to the barn while we drink our coffee. I need to talk to you about something that's on my mind."

Sally agreed, but she wondered what he wanted to talk about. It sounded concerning.

They wrapped themselves in blankets, joined hands, and walked the gravel path. Birds sang their songs as they perched high in the tops of the trees.

"It's a beautiful morning. Don't you think so, sweetheart?" Sally broke the silence between the two lovers. "Rusty, are you OK? You're so quiet." Sally stopped walking and pulled on Rusty's arm. "What's wrong?" *Now* she was concerned.

Rusty took her in his arms and looked upon her face and into her eyes. "Sally," he began, "we don't have much time left to be together before you and the boys leave to go home. I miss you guys already! There is still so much I want to show you, to take you to, and do with you. I want to believe I know you, but I have concerns for you about how it is so different here in the north than down south. Not to short-change the northern people, but we are not as friendly as the people are in the south; we are not patient, and sometimes we may seem downright rude! I want you and the boys to understand those differences. It's going to be a big adjustment for you all. You and the boys have lived in the south a long time. I just need to know that you will be happy here."

Sally listened to Rusty, and she could feel the concern in his words for their well-being and their upcoming life in a brand new environment. She wondered, and she had the same concerns also. "Rusty dear," she paused, "I want my words to sound right. Yes, I have considered the entire change we would be facing, and I have prayed about this situation because we would be moving away from everything we have ever known. But then I think, there really isn't anything holding us in Memphis. There are a few people who we will miss, like Peggy, my mother-in-law, and a few school and church friends the boys have, but you know, the boys are young enough, and they can make new friends. When Peggy finds out about us, I may lose her love and graces; however, I won't stay for her. You are my life and my future, and I appreciate your concern more than you know. But as long as I, we, have you and your love, guidance, and understanding, we'll be just fine, sweetheart. We will be happy."

"I appreciate what you've said, Sally, but I just want you to be sure and that you will have no regrets." Rusty needed reassurance.

"I'm sure, Rusty!" Sally hugged him tightly. She hoped his concern was resolved.

They continued walking, and Rusty mentioned his thoughts on the timeline for the future. Sally's divorce from Collin could be in six or seven weeks. She reminded Rusty about the boys' last day of school at the end of May. Rusty commented that he could be in Memphis right before then and could help Sally finish packing. They could hopefully leave for Connecticut right after the boys' last day.

Then came the *big, important* question: "Honey, when do you think you want us to get married?"

"Wow." Sally stopped walking. "Of course, I've thought about us getting married, but I haven't thought into the details of when yet. Let's go back to the house and look at the calendar," she said excitedly.

They grabbed each other's hands and ran as fast as they could back to the house. Rusty took the calendar from the kitchen counter and brought it to the table. He and Sally sat down and flipped the calendar pages to *May*.

"We need to have a little time to make arrangements, but I don't really want to wait too long. Do you, Sally?" Rusty asked.

"No, I don't. When do you want to get married, honey?" Sally asked as she turned the calendar page to *June*.

When Rusty saw the month of June, he looked at Sally and asked, "Would you like to be a June bride?"

Sally looked at Rusty and smiled. "That would be nice. I'd like to be a June bride!"

"OK. June it is!" Rusty declared. "Now, a date."

They discussed a preferred day of Saturday, so that narrowed it down. They agreed on the 21st; the 28th was too long to wait.

"Hey," Rusty started.

"Yes?"

"What about the 7th? The date would be . . . ." He paused.

"What? Tell me!" Sally said strongly.

Rusty spoke slowly: "6-7-80!" He looked at Sally "What do you think, sweetheart?"

Sally thought for a few seconds. "Yes! I like it," she shouted, and she grabbed Rusty's face and kissed his lips.

"What are y'all shouting about?" Todd said, entering the kitchen.

"Good morning, son. We're just making future plans," Sally explained.

"We're just very happy, Todd, and we're getting excited about when we will be more of a family," Rusty added.

"Say, would you and Pace like to stay with Rusty's folks for several hours this morning while Rusty and I run a few errands?" Sally asked, hoping for a positive answer.

"Sure, that'd be OK. Can we play pool, Rusty?" Todd replied.

"I'm sure my mom wouldn't mind," Rusty agreed.

"But now, Todd, you being the oldest, I expect you to mind your Ps and Qs and have your brother do the same. Please make me happy and proud of y'all by being very good boys. OK?" Sally wanted them to behave at their future grandparents' home.

"Yes, ma'am," Todd replied.

"Is your brother up yet?" Sally asked.

"Yes. I think he is in the bathroom," Todd answered.

Sally began preparing breakfast, and Pace wandered into the kitchen. She told him the plan for the morning, and he was OK with it too. They ate breakfast and dressed, and Rusty drove to his parents' home. They visited with Mandy and Russell for a few minutes before leaving. Sally cautioned the boys about behaving while she and Rusty were gone. She kissed them and thanked Mandy.

Rusty opened the pickup truck door for Sally, and she slid to the middle of the bench seat. They waved to the boys, who were standing in the glassed-in room, as they drove away.

First, Sally wanted to go to the school where the boys would be attending to make sure she would have the necessary paperwork needed to enroll the boys into school in the fall. All of that went well.

Then, Rusty asked Sally if it would be OK with her if the family's church pastor married them. Sally agreed, so Rusty's next stop was the church. Pastor Frank Taylor was in his office, and upon introducing him to Sally, Rusty proceeded to ask him if he would be available to marry them on June 7th. The pastor rejoiced for the happy couple, checked his calendar, and gave a thumbs up on the date. He asked for a time, and both Rusty and Sally stated 7 p.m.

The next stop was the bakery. The happy couple looked at several wedding cakes and chose the one they liked the best and put in an order for it. They wouldn't need it for several months still, but they figured they may as well get things taken care of for their wedding day while Sally was in town.

The jewelry store was just a block over from the bakery. Rusty and Sally walked into the store and looked at wedding rings and a matching engagement ring. Before the clerk walked up to help them, Sally looked at Rusty and said, "Sweetheart, it's so hard for me to believe we are doing this and that this is really happening for us. I'm just in awe, and I'm so happy! You've made me happier than I've ever been," she admitted with tears in her eyes.

"I know, sweetheart. I'm feeling the same way. You have made me a very happy man," Rusty confessed, and he kissed her.

The sales clerk approached them, and the two lovebirds began trying on matching rings that they liked, including a matching engagement ring for Sally.

After six sets of rings, Rusty and Sally agreed on a beautiful set, and the rings fit perfectly! The clerk slipped the ring boxes into a bag after Rusty paid for them.

As they walked to the pickup, Rusty asked Sally, "Do you want to look for a dress?"

Sally thought for a moment. "No, I'll have several weekends, and I'll look for one in Memphis. Honey, since I've been married before, it's fitting that I should not wear a white dress. I'd like to wear a light blue dress. Nothing fancy, but a little dressy. Is that OK with you?"

"I know blue is your favorite color, and carnations are your favorite flower. I know you will know the right dress when you see it! You'll be beautiful," Rusty said, complimenting her.

While they sat in the truck, Rusty asked, "Can you think of anywhere else we need to go or anything else we need to do? We won't have but, what, seven days before the wedding once I bring you and the boys here," Rusty stated.

"Well, there is one thing. I know you and your family know a lot of people. Will you and your folks be sending out wedding invitations? If so, you can go to a printing store and choose an invitation for us. Y'all can decide who you want to invite, and you should probably send them out no later than May 7th. I won't be inviting anyone." Sally paused. "Other than invitations, I can't think of anything else right now. The things we've done today are all time sensitive and needed to be addressed before I leave day after tomorrow. There is tomorrow, if we think of anything else. I guess we need to get to your folks' house. We've been gone more than two hours, but we have been very productive! Thank you, honey, for thinking about doing all this today," Sally said gratefully. "I sure do love you."

"Oh, Sally dear, you are so welcome, and I love you bunches." Rusty sighed.

Sally laid her head on Rusty's shoulder and rested as he drove to his parents' home.

When they arrived, the boys greeted them and were happy to see their mother. Mandy asked if they had eaten, and they hadn't, so right away she prepared ham sandwiches for them along with yesterday's potato salad. They shared with Russell and Mandy about their morning's activities. Russell and Mandy were glad the couple had accomplished a lot.

Todd and Pace told their mother and Rusty all about their morning. They played pool, had cookies and milk, and sang songs while Russell and Mandy played the piano, plus all four of them played cards. They had a good time.

As the four of them were leaving, Mandy invited them to an early dinner tomorrow afternoon around 3:30 p.m.

Rusty drove the short distance home, listening to the boys chatter on about their stay at his parents' home. He was so glad they had a good time. Sally was quiet, and once in the house, she took more pain medicine and told Rusty and the boys she was going to rest for a little while. Rusty followed her to the boys' bedroom. He was concerned. She explained that her time of the month made her tired, and it had been a busy day with lots of walking. But she reassured him that it was a wonderful day. She laid down on the bed, and he covered her with a blanket and left the room.

Since Sally was resting, Rusty had some alone time with the boys, which was good for all three of them. They went to the barn, fed the horses, and kept the horses company in the corral. The boys were getting more used to them. Prince and Princess enjoyed their time with the boys too.

After several hours, Rusty decided to check on Sally. So they put up the horses and came back to the house. Sally was still in the room, resting, so Rusty asked the boys about the card game they played with his parents. Rusty knew the game, and they played cards for an hour.

Not long after their game ended, Sally walked into the room. She said she was feeling better. Rusty had started dinner already, and it wouldn't be long before it was ready. They soon sat down to eat, and afterwards they all helped with the kitchen clean up.

Sally decided to join them in playing a game of cards. The evening passed, and the boys had their bath time and quiet time in front of the fireplace. They were soon off to bed. The boys said their prayers, and Sally tucked them in for the night. Then she went back to sit with Rusty on the couch.

When they were sure the boys were asleep, Rusty took Sally to bed. They cuddled and snuggled and fell asleep in each other's arms.

Rusty and Sally were awakened by the telephone ringing. Rusty dashed to the kitchen and answered the call. When he came back into the bedroom, he looked anxious. "There is a problem at the farm." He quickly dressed, kissed Sally, and left.

Even though it was too early for Sally to get up, going back to sleep was not happening. She was too concerned about what might be wrong at the farm to have such an urgent call so early in the morning. She was quiet as she moved around in the kitchen so as not to wake up the boys. She made coffee and fed the shepherds. When the coffee was perked, she poured a cup, wrapped a blanket around herself, and picked up the cup of coffee. The shepherds followed her out the back door. They ran and disappeared into the woods.

The morning air was cool but refreshing. Sally sat down on a metal bench just outside the screened-in room. She closed her eyes and thought of home. Rusty must have been pretty concerned about the differences in their two worlds for him to bring it up yesterday morning. Maybe he just wanted to make sure she was up for the challenges of making such a big change, and maybe he wanted to make sure she was ready to make the adjustments for him. There is a stigma between the two regions—the north verses the south. Yes, she did know her surroundings at home like the back of her hand, but she knew she could learn how to get around here too. As far as friends go—well, other than Peggy and a few church friends—there would really be none to be missed. Now, concerning the boys, that could be more difficult because of their school friends. But they're young, and they would be able to make new friends.

Soon there was an inner voice in Sally's mind that told her to *snap out of it!* That she was thinking too far down the line of the *family idea*. Besides, she's young, and her sons are younger; there is so much more life out there. Yes, there will be adjustments she'd need to make, but there's no sense getting cold feet now! This voice told her everything was going to be OK. She felt solace in thinking the Holy Spirit was reassuring her and calming her. *Just remember, God put you and Rusty together at the right moment, at the right place! You love him, and he loves you,* she thought. Sally felt a peace and comfort flow through her mind.

The sun started to rise, and the darkness faded. Sally walked down the gravel path toward the barn when suddenly the telephone started ringing. She ran back to the house.

"Hello?" she answered, almost out of breath.

"Sweetheart, are you OK?" Rusty asked.

"Oh, hi, honey. I was walking outside, and I ran to answer the telephone. Is everything OK with you? What was wrong at the farm?" Sally asked.

"I'm OK, just frustrated with equipment malfunction that has caused the milking process to be delayed, which then just backs up everything else. I might be a while yet. We're still trying to repair the equipment. The techs who installed the equipment should be here soon. I'm sorry, babe," Rusty apologized.

"I'm sorry for all the problems! Hey, you don't need to apologize. This is not your fault; things happen," Sally said, trying to ease the situation. "I know you're hungry. You want me to bring you something to eat?"

"No, but thanks. Mom's preparing breakfast now, and I'll grab a bite soon. Oh, wait a second." There was a slight pause in their conversation. "Mom just told me to tell you that she has plenty of food and you and the boys should come on over. Are the boys up yet?" Rusty asked.

"Yes, both of them are sitting at the kitchen table looking at me." She moved her mouth away from the telephone for a moment. "Do y'all want to go next door for breakfast?" she asked her sons.

"Yeah!" the boys yelled.

"Well, I guess you heard that!" Sally said back into the phone. "Please tell your mom *thank you*, and we'll try to be there soon." The call ended.

"OK, kids. Let's get dressed," Sally instructed joyfully.

Within ten minutes, they were dressed and on their way to the Summers' home. When they walked in the back doors, the aroma of breakfast made their mouths water.

The table was full of food. There were eggs, fried and scrambled, bacon, ham, biscuits, gravy, hominy, jams, and jellies. After the blessing over the food was said, the bowls and platters of food were passed around the table, and everyone enjoyed a delicious and filling breakfast.

When they were nearly finished, Rusty looked out the window and saw the repair tech's truck pull up near the house. "Got to go. Thanks, Mom!" He grabbed his coat and was out the door.

Russell needed to see what was happening with the equipment, so he raised up from the table and moved his walker to the coatrack. He struggled as he tried to put his coat on. Sally rushed from the table to assist him. He thanked her and walked toward the back door. Sally opened both of the back doors for him.

"Please be careful, Russell," Sally told him.

After they had cleaned up from breakfast, Mandy said she needed to go to the grocery store. Sally and the boys tagged along in their car, as she needed to gas up with a full tank for the trip back home tomorrow.

When they had finished their errands, Mandy, Sally, and the boys pulled into the Summers' driveway. Sally noticed the repair truck was gone. She hoped the equipment was now working as it should.

Rusty exited the house and helped his mom and Sally with the groceries. Once all the bags were brought inside the house, Rusty told his mom he needed to go home and clean up. But before he did, he asked if there was anything he or Sally could do to help with the preparation for their early dinner.

Mandy said, "No thanks. I've got it covered." She reminded them to be back to eat at about 3:30 p.m. Rusty gave a thumbs up and kissed his mom on her cheek. The boys and Sally hugged her, and they left for home.

Rusty briefly explained the equipment problem when Sally asked, but it was way too technical for her to understand. Maybe one day soon Rusty could explain more to her about the workings of the farm and its equipment.

While Rusty took a shower, the boys played with Prince and Princess in the backyard. Sally also decided to change into a pretty dress for dinner. She then went outside with the boys, and it wasn't long before Rusty joined them.

"Goodness, don't you look ever so handsome!" Sally exclaimed as she admired Rusty's looks and choice of clothing.

Rusty walked closer to her and kissed her lips. "Thank you, and you look very stunning yourself, my love," he said.

Sally asked the boys to come inside and take quick baths, which they did. While they bathed, Sally laid out their clothes. It was nearing 3:15, and soon the four of them left for Rusty's parents' home.

Again the smell of food filled the kitchen. Rusty and Sally helped Mandy with the finishing touches for their dinner. Everyone took their seats, the blessing was said, and eating began. Again, Mandy had outdone herself. Every bite of food was delicious.

Then, dessert was served. Rusty got up from the table and took several steps away. He retrieved a small box from his pocket, then turned toward Sally. He dropped to one knee, opened the top of the small box and said. . . .

"Sally, my sweetheart, I know this is too early, but I want to pledge my love to you now. Babe, I love you with all my heart. Will you marry me?"

Sally burst into uncontrollable tears. She struggled with her words. "Oh, my love, *yes!* I will marry you!" she replied through her happy tears.

Rusty removed Sally's beautiful engagement ring from its box and slipped it onto her finger. Sally stood up and wrapped her arms around Rusty's neck, and they kissed a forever kiss.

Russell, Mandy, Todd, and Pace clapped their hands in honor of the very momentous occasion and then gathered around the happy couple and congratulated them. Everyone was overjoyed. They continued the celebration by eating the dessert that had been prepared. Sally and Rusty couldn't take their eyes off of each other. They were so happy.

The time at the Summers' home came to an end. Sally, Todd, and Pace's goodbyes were sad because the next morning, they would be leaving to go home. There were lots of hugs given to Sally and the boys. Mandy and Russell told them that they would be praying for travel mercies and for their safe trip home.

On the way back to Rusty's home, Pace started crying. He didn't want to leave. Sally took him in her arms and explained to him that in a few short months, they would be back. That made him feel better, and he stopped crying.

The evening passed too quickly. Their last hours together were spent feeding and playing with the shepherds, feeding and being with the horses, and playing a few hands of cards. They were making memories!

The boys put on their PJs, and all of them sat by the fireplace one last time. Sally walked with the boys to their bedroom, kneeled with them to say their nightly prayers, and tucked them into bed with kisses and an "I love you."

Rusty, who was sitting on the couch, saw Sally slowly walk into the living area. She stopped in front of the fireplace. The fire was warm and inviting as the wood crackled and hissed. Rusty rose from the couch and went to Sally. She was admiring her new ring as the diamonds sparkled in the light of the fire.

"It's so beautiful, Rusty," Sally softly spoke.

"But the diamonds are not as beautiful as you are, sweetheart," Rusty said as he cupped her chin with his hand and raised up her face to kiss her warm, moist lips. "I love you so much, Sally. I wish I could tell you just how much I really do love you, but there are not words perfect enough to say. I wish you didn't have to go home. I wish the weeks that will separate us would be over and that time would be behind us. I will miss you every minute until we are back in each other's arms again." He wrapped his arms around her tightly, and she held him just as tight and sobbed on his chest. Rusty picked Sally up and carried her to his bed, and they slept in each other's warm embrace all night.

Chapter Twenty

T he dreaded morning sunlight began to filter through the window blind above Rusty's bed. Sally didn't want to acknowledge the day had arrived where she'd be leaving Rusty. Ten weeks without him was going to be so hard. She refused to open her eyes for the longest time. Rusty drew her body close to his, and she looked upon his handsome face with endearing eyes. They kissed each other tenderly. Rusty stood up and pulled Sally up out of bed and into his loving arms.

"Oh, Rusty dear, my heart is breaking!" Sally clung to Rusty tighter.

"Mine too, sweet Sally," Rusty softly whispered in her ear. "Mine too."

Sally breathed a deep sigh, and without looking at Rusty, she released her body from his and walked toward the door, trying not to cry.

In the kitchen, Sally attempted to prepare the coffee maker to perk their coffee. She could hardly see through her tears. She walked through the other kitchen door to the hallway to the boys' bedroom, grabbed some clothing from her suitcase, and went to the bathroom.

Back in the boys' bedroom, Sally began to wake Todd and Pace. She laid out their clothes and finished packing her suitcase. After the boys were dressed, she packed and closed their suitcase. The shepherds laid very still on the floor, watching the activity as if they were sad and knew the boys were leaving.

Sally sat their suitcases and pillows by the front door, then walked back to the kitchen with the boys following her.

Rusty stood at the back door, looking outside. He turned around, and Sally saw tears in his eyes. All three of them ran to Rusty and cried. The boys hugged his legs tightly.

"I don't want to leave you, Rusty! I will miss you so much," Todd expressed through his tears.

"Me too, Rusty," Pace agreed.

Rusty squatted down and took both boys in his arms. "I'll miss you guys too. I have grown to love you two. I can't wait to see you again, but in the meantime, you both have to promise me you'll watch after your mother for me. Now, I'm counting on you guys. OK?"

"We promise, Rusty," both boys said at the same time.

"OK. Good boys," Rusty said as he stood up.

"You want some coffee, honey?" Rusty asked Sally.

"No thanks," Sally remarked.

"Breakfast then?" Rusty encouraged as he tried to delay Sally's departure.

"No. I'll stop somewhere down the road, and we'll grab something to eat," she explained. "I guess we'll need to leave and get on the highways and byways."

Rusty didn't want to admit the time had come. "You be so very careful, and please call me if you need me. Call me tonight when you all stop for the night." Rusty's voice was breaking. He took Sally's hand, and they walked toward the front door. The shepherds were beside the boys, who were sobbing as they petted the shepherds one final time.

Rusty picked up the suitcases, and Sally opened the front door. A small picnic basket was sitting at the door with a note:

> You all have a safe trip. I'll be praying. We love you all, and we'll miss you very much. But we'll see you again soon.
>
> Love, Russell and Mandy.

"Oh, how so very sweet and thoughtful of them. Please tell them *thank you* for us," Sally said with gratitude. She held Rusty's arm as they walked slowly to her car. The boys held their pillows and walked by their mother.

Rusty put the suitcases in the trunk, then opened the back door for the boys and the driver's door for Sally. She sat the basket in the passenger seat.

"Boys, take care and be good. Remember, watch after your mother for me. I'll see you guys soon. I love you." Rusty hugged both boys, helped them in the back seat, and closed the door.

Rusty and Sally continued to fight back tears. "Sally, I tell you, this is tough! Seeing you leave . . . just, please, be so very careful," Rusty said.

"This is not easy for me either, Rusty dear. You be careful too, and you take good care of yourself for me." Sally threw her arms around his neck and kissed him passionately. "You hold that kiss for me, and when I see you the next time, I'll give you another one just like it!" Sally promised as she got in the car.

"You better, unless I give mine to you first! I love you, my sweet lady," Rusty said as he closed her car door.

"I love you bunches, my handsome hunk." Sally started the car, threw Rusty kisses, and began driving slowly away from him, tears streaming down her face. The car's windows were down, and all three of them waved until Rusty was no longer in sight.

Rusty walked back into the house with the shepherds behind him. He stood in front of the fireplace for a long while, sobbing. His love for Sally was so strong, and her sons had become very special to him. His new family.

Several miles away from Rusty's home, Sally had to pull her car over and dry the tears from her eyes so she could see the road. She took a moment to look at the atlas. She decided she'd like to take Interstate 84 back to Scranton,

Pennsylvania—a two-hour drive. She and the boys would grab some breakfast, then take Interstate 81 down to Tennessee, then Interstate 40 on to home.

Sally turned around to look in the backseat at the boys. They had stopped crying and were curled up asleep, hugging their pillows. She was glad they were resting. Now, she just had to stop crying so she could finish the journey home.

They ate a good breakfast in Scranton, and with the food Mandy had given them in the basket, they wouldn't need to stop again for food for a while. Sally needed to put the miles behind her.

After leaving Pennsylvania and Maryland, Sally started driving into and through the Allegheny Mountains. The scenery was beautiful, and there were many *oohs* and *aahs* from the car as each mountain seemed to be prettier than the last. Rusty had told her that Interstate 81 was very hilly and full of mountains, and truckers would rather not go that way. It was nothing but "drag and fly"—drag up the mountains and fly down the other side! Sally understood what he meant as she watched the truckers struggle up some of the steep mountains and then pass her quickly downhill.

After eight hours on the road with only one quick stop for gas, Sally and the boys needed to stop to stretch their legs. She looked through the picnic basket Mandy had given her and found several different kinds of sandwiches, a small container of mayo, cookies, potato chips, and several bottles of pop. She even remembered to pack a bottle opener. *That lady is so great and thoughtful, much like Peggy,* Sally remarked to herself. She and the boys ate to their hearts' content.

Sally referred to the atlas once again. Knoxville was only two hours away, and daylight was still good for at least another hour. She thought she could drive that far, then they would stop for the night. So it was back in the car and onto the super slab again. The boys had been so good, and she was thankful for that.

Once the sun set, Sally began to feel very tired. But she pushed herself. Near 9 p.m., she rolled into Knoxville and soon saw a motel sign. She stopped the car near the main office door and told the boys to stay in the car while she checked them in. After a few minutes, Sally returned to the car. Their room wasn't far from the office. Sally parked the car, took the overnight bag from the trunk, and unlocked the room door.

"I know y'all are hungry and tired. I saw a fast-food place next door. Do y'all want to eat or go to bed?" Sally asked the boys.

"I'd like to eat," Todd answered.

"Me too," Pace agreed.

"OK then. Give me a minute to call Rusty and let him know we are OK," Sally said. She went through the process of making a collect call, and Rusty answered.

"Yes, I'll accept the collect call. Hi, soon-to-be Mrs. Summers!" Rusty said.

"Aah, you know how to put a smile on this very tired face, sweetheart. Thank you." Sally smiled so big.

"Where are you?" Rusty asked.

"We're in Knoxville. I took Interstate 81 all the way down. You're right. It is very mountainous and beautiful, but we just putty-putted right along. Are you OK?" Sally asked.

"Yes, now that I hear your sweet voice and know you and the boys are OK. You've had a long day. You don't have but maybe six or so hours left until you get home," Rusty replied.

"Honey, please tell Mandy *thank you* for all the goodies in the picnic basket. Everything was very good. Saved us from having to stop for lunch! Baby, I feel so bad. Everything became so emotional when we were leaving that I did not tell you how much we enjoyed our days with you and your family. You were wonderful, and I'm so glad we made the trip. We needed that time together. The boys needed to meet you and get to know you. Everything was great! Our plans and our dreams came true and then some. My ring is beautiful! Thank you, sweetheart, and I love you so much. And yes, please thank your folks for everything too. They are great," Sally said sincerely.

"I will tell my parents. They think you're pretty great too. They love you and the boys, and they are so happy and pleased you all are going to be a part of our family. Yes, your ring is beautiful, and it's on the hand of a beautiful woman. I agree, everything was wonderful. You all get a good night's rest, and please call me when you get home. I love you, honey, and I miss you like crazy! Still praying for you to get home safely," Rusty said thoughtfully.

"I love and miss you too, bunches and bunches, my darlin'. I will call you. I always have you in my prayers. Love ya." Sally blew him a kiss.

"Talk tomorrow. Love you too." Rusty blew his kiss back to her. Then the call ended.

"OK, fellas," she said, placing the phone down and turning toward the boys. "Y'all ready to get something to eat?"

They were both fast asleep. Sally removed their shoes and scooted them under their bed covers. She hoped they weren't too hungry and that they would sleep well. She kissed their foreheads and prayed that the Lord would watch over them through the night. Then, she slipped on her nightgown and sat on the edge of the bed, looking down on her beautiful engagement ring. Tears of happiness rolled down her face. Rusty was the love of her life.

Sally and the boys slept in a little, but as soon as their feet touched the floor, they were ready to get on the road for home. After dressing and turning in the motel key, they grabbed breakfast from the place next door and got back on Interstate 40.

When Sally passed the city of Nashville, she thought back nine months ago to when she first saw Rusty's handsome face and fell in love with him. *How amazing life works out. God is so good!* Sally thought.

In Jackson, at the truck stop where Rusty and Sally saw each other again four months ago, she stopped for gas. Such sweet and precious memories she had of that magical day.

The next hour and a half, Sally couldn't put the miles behind them fast enough. Finally, she drove her car into her driveway, and she was home. She thanked the Lord for a safe trip home and for a wonderful week He had given them with Rusty and his family.

Once the three of them were in the house, Sally immediately called Rusty. He praised the Lord for their safe return. Sally immediately began to unpack their suitcases and do a load of laundry, and Todd and Pace unloaded their games and put them away. Sally would also need to go to the grocery store to restock on their food supply.

That night, Sally felt the loneliness in her bed. The last six nights had been blissful and full of love and happiness, and now she was all alone, and it was so quiet. The next ten weeks would be the loneliest season of her life. She clutched her right hand over her left hand to hold Rusty's ring and remember his pledge of love to her.

The next morning, as much as Sally didn't want to take Rusty's engagement ring off, she knew she was going to have to keep their secret a little while longer. With tears in her eyes, she slowly removed the precious ring from her finger and placed it in her mother's jewelry box.

Late in the afternoon on Sunday, Sally knew it was best to call Peggy and inform her they were home. When Peggy answered the telephone and heard Sally's voice, she was relieved to know they were home. Peggy asked Sally about the trip, and Sally told her they went north through a few states and came home down Interstate 81 through the beautiful Allegheny and Appalachian Mountains. Peggy was impressed with their travels. Peggy told Sally of her uneventful week and that she missed Sally and the boys very much.

After Sally's call to Peggy, she needed to talk to the boys about their trip. "I have to ask you two to kind of keep this trip to ourselves for now. I know y'all want to share with your friends and even with your Grandmother Peggy all about the fun, the people, and everything about our trip, but let's keep it our secret right now. Some folks just might not understand what's going on in our family. OK?"

"OK. It'll be our secret," the boys agreed.

Rusty called that evening, and his voice was warm, inviting, and very much needed. She could have listened to him talk for hours. She missed him so much. They had had a taste of life together, and they wanted more. But first, time would have to pass.

As Brother Hal had mentioned to Sally when she asked him for her week off from work, her timing was good because the following week leading up to Palm Sunday and then the week of Easter was truly busy. But that was good because the time passed by quickly, and soon it was April.

Not long after Sally and the boys had come home from work and school on April 1st, the telephone rang.

"Hello?" Sally answered.

"Hi, Sally. This is Hugh Cut. How are you?" he asked.

"Hi, Hugh. I'm good. How are you?" Sally responded.

"I'm OK. Thank you for asking. I have news. I spoke to the judge about your petition for divorce and explained your situation to her—that your husband left you high and dry and moved to Houston, Texas, because of a job relocation. I told her that your husband was not coming back to you and that he said he did not love you anymore and wanted you to file for divorce. Also, I told her that he did not want any custody or rights to your two sons. That he is moving on with his life without you, and he wants you to do the same. Upon hearing these things, the judge wants to expedite your petition. She suggested you overnight a non-custodial relinquishment form, which would give you full custody of your minor children, and also a request for release of his financial earnings statement. With the earning statement, the court will decide how much child support your husband will be instructed to pay as well as determine any alimony. The judge expressed that if she has this information in her hand at the trial, then there won't be any delays with the court's actions. Is this recommendation in agreement with you, Sally? I need to add that doing this will seal the deal for you and your sons. And it will eliminate added trial time. If she doesn't have this information by your trial date, which is set for April 22, the trial could be postponed until who knows when," Hugh explained.

"Yes, please do whatever you think is right," Sally urged him.

"OK. I thought you would agree. We took the liberty to prepare the letters and forms so that they would be ready to give to the courier who should be here by 5 p.m. today. Collin will receive the packet tomorrow. Hopefully he'll act on this new development right away and return the forms in a timely manner. Collin may call you with questions. Please do not elaborate on the details he needs to address. Give him my telephone number, and ask him to call me. It may take him a few days to fill out the forms as well as get the information needed from his employer. Do you have any questions?"

"No questions. I just hope and pray Collin will not procrastinate and just get this done!" Sally said. "The 22nd—that's just three weeks away! Surely you'll have everything you need by then."

"Absolutely hope so! OK, Sally, we'll let you know more when we know."

As Sally placed the handset back on its base, she praised the Lord out loud and prayed that Collin would do his part.

When Rusty called, she was so excited to tell him the good news. He was very delighted, especially the part about being officially divorced in three weeks. He told her the wedding invitation that he selected had been delivered to the store, and he would pick them up tomorrow and mail one of them so she could see it too. He hoped she would like what he chose. She said she was sure she would be happy with his choice.

A week later, Hugh Cut called and told Sally he had received the paperwork back from Collin, and he now had everything that was needed. He said he would be taking the paperwork to the judge the next day. Sally raised another praise to the Lord!

Sally helped Todd and Pace study for their six-week tests. Their schoolwork was getting harder, especially math. Sally wasn't good in math, and she felt like she was not much help—more so with Todd than with Pace. She prayed with them that they would do well on their tests.

When Rusty called and Sally told him the attorney had received Collin's paperwork, he breathed a big sigh of relief. He was very concerned that Collin would hold up the process of the divorce. Rusty had good news too: his dad was walking more and more without his walker and getting stronger. Sally rejoiced over the great news! She then told him she had received an envelope from him in the mail and was holding it in her hand. Sally preceded to open the envelope and pulled out their wedding invitation.

"Oh, Rusty! The wedding invitation is beautiful! I love it! You had to have chosen the prettiest one! And the engraving is very attractive. You did so good! Thank you for sending one to me. I'm looking forward to attending the wedding!" Sally giggled as she expressed her happiness.

"I'm glad you think it's OK, and I'm very proud you plan to attend! The groom is also very happy." Rusty laughed, then added, "Picking out a wedding invitation is not exactly a guy thing, but when I saw this one, I knew it was the right one," he confessed.

"Honey, it's great!" Sally reassured him.

"Mom agreed that we should send them out on May 7th like you mentioned, giving people a month to respond. That time will be here soon," exclaimed Rusty.

"Yeah, not long! I wish I could be there to help you with the invitations," Sally sadly said.

"I wish you could be here too, sweetheart."

The conversation continued a while longer before the secretly engaged couple kissed each other good night through the phone.

The next morning, Sally shared with Brother Hal that the attorney had called her to inform her that the divorce trial date was set for April 22nd. She didn't know a time yet, but she probably would need to take the day off. He understood.

That evening, Sally called Peggy and gave her the news about the court date and asked if she would be available to pick up the boys from school. Peggy said she would be able to get them. She asked Sally if she had heard from Collin, and Sally told her no, she hadn't. Peggy told Sally that she had not heard from him either.

Another week went by, and the attorney called Sally again to tell her that the judge was satisfied with all the paperwork that Collin submitted. That meant that all should go well for her on the 22nd. He also told Sally she would need to be at his office at 8 a.m. that Tuesday, and they would need to be at the courthouse no later than 9 a.m.

Two days before the court date, Sally informed Peggy of the timing for Tuesday, which meant she would need to leave the house no later than 7:15 a.m. She apologized to Peggy about the time change, but Peggy quickly told her not to worry about it and that she would be at their house by 7 a.m. to take the boys to school. Sally was grateful.

"Sally, will I need to pick them up from school that afternoon as well?" Peggy asked.

"I can't imagine being at the courthouse all day. Probably not, but thank you for asking," Sally responded.

On the night of the 21st when Rusty called, he could tell Sally had her mind on the next day. He knew he couldn't physically be with her, but he prayed with her over the telephone. Sally was thankful for his support, and she knew he'd be praying all the next day for her.

Sally was up earlier than normal after a very restless night. Too many thoughts about the trial. She decided to get dressed and be ready to walk out the door when the time came. By the time Todd and Pace got up, Sally almost had their breakfast prepared. The boys dressed and came to the table. Sally sat with them while they ate. She asked them to please remember the promise they made to her about not saying anything about their trip to their Grandmother Peggy. They again promised.

Peggy arrived at 7 a.m., and Sally prepared to leave. She reminded Peggy she'd need to leave about 8:15 a.m. to take the boys to school. Sally hugged and kissed the boys, and she thanked Peggy again for taking care of the boys for her. Peggy wished Sally well in court.

As Sally left, she waved to the boys who were standing at the living room window. She breathed a prayer that the Lord would watch over her little sons for her. The closer she drove to the attorney's office, the more nervous she became. She attempted to remind herself that people go to court and get divorced every day. It happens! So why, then, should she be so nervous? A divorce is what Collin wanted, and Sally wanted it too so she and Rusty could finally be married. *OK. Shake off this nervousness, Sally*, she told herself. But it wasn't working.

Sally parked the car in a parking space at the street's curb in front of Hugh's office with a few minutes to spare. Nervously, Sally opened the attorney's office door.

Hugh greeted her, and they walked to his office. He showed her the paperwork Collin signed and the earnings statement from his employer. Hugh saw Sally's hands shaking as she held the paperwork. He took his hand and laid it on Sally's hands. "It's going to be OK, Sally. There really isn't anything to be nervous about. I'll be doing most of the talking. The judge will swear you in and will ask you a few easy questions that you will answer. Then she will declare your divorce is final and rap her gavel. Now, she may discuss child support and/or alimony, but you won't have any input; I will. This is a slam dunk, kiddo. So relax!" Hugh tried to ease her nerves.

It was time to go. Hugh suggested Sally go with him because parking spaces were very few at that hour of the morning. She wasn't crazy about the idea, but she agreed.

Hugh kept the conversation going, trying to keep her calm. He talked about the weather. He asked her about the boys and their school. He mentioned his dog and that his parents wanted him to become a breeder.

Soon, they were near the courthouse. Hugh found a parking space after driving around the courthouse once. They walked inside, and Hugh looked at the docket board to find the information on which courtroom the trial's proceedings would be held and where Sally's name was on the docket. He turned to Sally as they began walking down the marble-floored halls toward the courtroom. "We're in luck. Your case is first on the docket. If there aren't any continuing cases from yesterday in front of your case, then the judge will hear your case right away. Here, this is our courtroom, Sally." Hugh opened the heavy wooden door.

Sally's nerves hit her hard as she walked into the somewhat intimidating room. Row after row of dark wooden benches filled half of the large room. There were four sets of paned windows that stretched from the floor to the tall ceiling behind the jury box. She saw the judge's bench, the witness chair, and the table and chairs where the counselors and plaintiff/defendants would sit.

Hugh approached the table, laid his briefcase down, and pulled out a chair from under the table for Sally to sit in. He took his place in another chair next to her.

More people came into the courtroom and sat down, even a police officer and a court reporter. Then the bailiff said loudly, "All rise."

Everyone stood up. The solid brown wooden door opened behind the judge's bench, and a lady dressed in a black robe stepped out and took her seat in a chair behind the huge desk. Then the bailiff announced, "The Court of the Thirtieth Judicial Circuit Court, Family Division, is now in session. Honorable Judge Joyce Lancaster presiding. You may be seated."

"Good morning," the judge greeted the people in the courtroom.

"Good morning," some of the people answered.

The judge began. "My first case is Sally Linfield Oldham versus Collin Edward Oldham in pursuant of a legal divorce. Counselor Cut, is your plaintiff in court today?"

Hugh stood up and placed his hand on Sally's shoulder, "Yes, she is, Your Honor."

"Is there a counselor for the defendant, Collin Edward Oldham, in the courtroom?" the judge asked.

No one answered.

"Counselor Cut, do you agree that this petition for divorce is non-contested?" the judge continued.

"Yes, Your Honor, I do," Hugh answered.

"Sally Linfield Oldham, please take the stand," the judge instructed.

Sally stood up and walked toward the witness stand as the bailiff approached her. She stopped.

The man instructed Sally: "Please raise your right hand. Do you swear to tell the truth, the whole truth, and nothing but the truth, so help you God?"

Sally answered, "I do." Then, she so nervously stepped up two steps and sat down in the chair.

"Please state your name for the court reporter," the judge prompted Sally.

"Sally Linfield Oldham," she announced with a shaky voice.

"Mrs. Oldham, you have come before this court today seeking a divorce from your husband, Collin Edward Oldham. Is that correct?" the judge asked Sally.

"Yes, ma'am," Sally uttered, asking God silently to give her strength.

"I have before me documentation that has been obtained from Mr. Oldham, stating that he has no desire to be married to you any longer and that he does not want any custody of your two minor children. In other words, he has abandoned you, his children, and his obligations. He will be held financially responsible for things such as child support and spousal support by my court order. Sally Linfield Oldham, your divorce petition has been granted. Your Final Divorce Decree will arrive in thirty days. Case closed," the judge ordered with the rap of her gavel.

Sally stepped down from the witness stand and walked toward her attorney. Hugh put all the paperwork into his briefcase and led Sally out of the courtroom. Sally was still shaking, but she thanked God that the stress of all the drama was behind her.

They walked out to Hugh's car. "You OK, Sally?" Hugh inquired. "It's mostly over!"

"I'm just numb, Hugh. I'm so glad it is over."

"Well, it really will be over in thirty days. I'll send you a copy of the Final Divorce Decree, and, if you want me too, I'll send a copy to Collin. Hey, I think we need some lunch. You hungry?" Hugh suggested.

Sally suddenly stopped.

"What's the matter, Sally?" Hugh asked.

"I am moving on May 22nd, a month from today. How will I get that paperwork? Do I have to sign it?" Sally said with worry in her voice.

Hugh was surprised. "I didn't know you were moving. You're going to stay local, right?" Hugh asked.

Sally got into Hugh's car, and he began driving. "No. I'm moving north to start a new job. Is there any way to get the decree any sooner?" she asked him with a distressed voice.

"Sally, do you want any lunch? We need to talk about this," Hugh insisted.

"No, I don't think so, Hugh," Sally answered.

"OK, so what's going on with your move?" Hugh asked. "I thought we might be able to see each other. I know Todd and Pace wanted to see Duke."

"The last day of school is May 22nd. I was hoping to leave that evening or early the next morning. I start work that next weekend. So what can we do?" Sally was frustrated.

"The only thing I know to do is talk to the judge. You're just starting a new job, right? Not getting married or anything? Because even though the judge declared you divorced, there is a required cool down period if folks decide they want to reconcile. In your case, I don't believe reconciliation is going to happen. And that may appeal to the judge to sign off earlier on your Final Decree. Plus, the fact you will be starting a new job out of state will help too. The only complication is calculating the boys' child support and your alimony. I'll try to talk to her tomorrow and see what I can do," Hugh said. Hugh drove his car into a parking space beside his office building.

As they exited the car, Sally remembered something. "Hugh, I need to pay you the balance of your fee."

Hugh opened the office door for Sally, and they walked into the office. Hugh pulled her paperwork from his briefcase. "Your balance is one hundred dollars."

Sally took her wallet from her purse and handed him five, twenty-dollar bills.

He wrote out a receipt and gave it to her. "Sally, this is Tuesday. I'll call you as soon as I know anything. It may be a few days. I really am sorry to see you move away. I really like you, Sally, but I truly do wish you the very best. You deserve it. You seem to have had a miserable marriage. I know you will meet someone very special who will honestly love you and those two fine sons of yours. We'll talk soon, Sally."

"Thank you, Hugh," Sally said as she turned and left the office. She walked quickly to her car and drove away. She felt flattered by his feelings for her, but all she needed from him now was to talk to the judge, hoping he would have enough influence to get the Final Divorce Decree and the support figured out much sooner than thirty days. Sally was starved from the long morning, so she stopped at a fast-food drive-through and treated herself to a burger and fries with a soda. She ate her meal as she drove home.

When she arrived home, she called Peggy and told her she would pick up the boys from school. Peggy asked if court went OK, and Sally told her that it did. She thanked Peggy again for taking the boys to school that morning.

Immediately, Sally called Rusty. Fortunately, he was home for lunch. She told him about court and the thirty-day wait for the Final Decree to be signed by the judge. She told him that she had told her attorney she was taking a new job up north and that she was leaving town on May 22nd. Sally continued telling Rusty that Hugh was going to talk to the judge to hopefully persuade her to sign off on it sooner. More time to wait, but was going to be OK. Rusty understood and was pleased that Sally told Hugh the reason she was needing to get the Final Decree done early. Fast thinking on her part, and it was the truth!

Sally picked up the boys from school and headed for a pizza place. They brought the delicious-smelling pizzas home for dinner and chowed down. During supper, Sally asked the boys if their secret was still safe. She was pleased when the boys told her it was.

After supper, the boys showed Sally their six-week report cards. Their grades were all As except for a C in math for Todd and a *U* for Pace for talking too much in class!

That evening, Todd and Pace shared the new desk while doing their homework. They watched some television, did bathtime, and then went off to bed. Sally, too, was ready for bed. It had been a crazy day.

It wasn't until April 29th before Sally heard from Hugh about the Final Divorce Decree. He had talked to the judge about Sally's situation, and she would need to come to his office on May 12th so he could take her to the courthouse to meet with the judge in her chambers in order to expedite her final paperwork. Sally was most grateful for his persistence in the unusual situation.

When Sally talked to Rusty that night, she told him about Hugh's call. He was so relieved that the judge apparently had agreed to finalize the divorce decree early. Sally told Rusty that she was thinking about calling her landlord on May 1st and giving him the required notice for moving out of the house. She also wanted to give Brother Hal her two-week's notice. That would give her a week to pack up their belongings. Rusty told her soon he was going to call the airlines to make his flight reservation to fly to Memphis May 21st, rent the moving truck the same day, and hopefully pack all her belongings that night and finish on the 22nd. If all goes well, Rusty said he'd like to leave that night or early the next morning on the 23rd. He expressed that there could be a lot of traffic on the road with it being Memorial Day weekend, but that would be OK. They all would be together.

"Oh, Rusty. I'm getting so excited! In three weeks, we'll be back together. I can't wait!" Sally expressed with such enthusiasm.

"I know, honey. I'm feeling the same way! I want to hold you in my arms and kiss your sweet lips," Rusty confessed with passion in his voice.

"Oh, you better hush! You're making me tingle all over, sweetheart." Sally could almost feel his strong arms around her.

"Soon, Sally. Soon. I love you. Stay safe. Till tomorrow." Rusty threw her his kiss.

"Got it! I love you too, my love," and she threw him her kiss.

May 1st was a *red letter* day. Before taking Todd and Pace to school, Sally called Mr. Waddell and gave him her thirty-day notice that they were moving out of the house. He was sorry to hear the news. He asked her to send him a written notice dated with that day's date. She agreed that she would put it in the mail that day. So she grabbed a writing tablet and wrote,

> *This letter will serve as my written notice to vacate your property at 3537 Tuggle Avenue, Memphis, Tennessee, no later than May 31, 1980. Today's date is May 1, 1980. Thank you for being a wonderful landlord.*
>
> *Sincerely,*
> *Sally Oldham*

While Sally still had the writing tablet in her hand, she also wrote a letter to Brother Hal:

> *Dear Brother Hal,*
>
> *I want to let you know that I will be resigning from my position as church office assistant at Cherish Baptist Church as of May 15, 1980— two weeks from today. I want to express my gratitude for the opportunity you have provided me during my time at the church. It's been a real blessing working with you and others.*
>
> *Thank you,*
> *Sally Oldham*

As Sally and the boys left for school, Sally raised the red mailbox flag and dropped Mr. Waddell's vacating property letter in the box.

At work, Sally kept a close eye on Brother Hal. Near eleven o'clock, the mailman came in to deliver the church's mail. *Perfect timing. Thank You, Lord!* Sally thought. As was one of her duties, she took the mail and walked toward Brother Hal's office. He was on the telephone, so she laid it on his desk. She placed her resignation letter on top of the pile. She then returned to her desk and continued her work.

About fifteen minutes later, Brother Hal came out of his office with her letter in his hand.

"What is this, young lady?" he asked anxiously.

Sally looked up from her work and said, "I didn't know how to tell you, so I wrote you a letter."

Brother Hal pulled up a nearby chair to her desk. "Why are you resigning?"

"I'm leaving Memphis and taking an exciting job in Connecticut," Sally explained.

"Connecticut! What? Oh, Sally, are you certain you want to do that? I'm sure you have prayed hard about this decision, right?"

"Yes, sir, I have. A lot!" Sally answered. "It's a job that will help my boys appreciate nature and grow in ways that are not available here. Yes, I don't like moving so far away, but I believe God is showing me a new path for me and my sons. While Todd and Pace were on spring break in March, we visited the area. It was a breath of fresh air, and it just felt right," Sally added.

Brother Hal looked sad. "It does sound like you've prayed about this situation and taken time for God to answer your prayers. We sure are going to miss you. You've been a special light to me, one that I've definitely grown to appreciate. I will miss you, Sally. But I will be in prayer for you, Todd, and Pace. If you ever need anything, please let me know. I mean that!" As Brother Hal got up, he returned the chair to it place.

Sally thanked him for his support and prayers. As he walked into his office, she saw him wipe the tears from his eyes. Sally's heart ached for Brother Hal's sadness.

Just before Sally's work day ended, Brother Hal laid her paycheck envelope on her desk and told her to have a nice weekend. She could tell he was still sad. Sally was sad too. She didn't mean to hurt him. She wondered if Peggy was going to be as sad and hurt. She needed to tell her tonight before she heard it from Brother Hal or someone else. She needed to be most thoughtful of her words to Peggy.

That evening, Sally was determined to be happy for the boys. After supper, the boys were watching television, so it was the perfect time to call Peggy. Sally took a deep breath and prayed the Lord would give her the right words to say. Like Rusty said, what she was going to tell Peggy was not a lie. She just wasn't telling the entire story.

Peggy's answered. "Hello?"

"Hi, Peggy. It's Sally. Are you busy?"

"Hi, Sally. No, I'm not busy. Just watching television. How are you and the boys?" she asked.

"We're good. The boys are watching television too." Sally took another deep breath. "I have something I need to tell you. I gave my two-week's notice to Brother Hal today."

"Oh, OK. You found a better job? Well, good for you! I know the church work opportunity came just when you needed it, but I knew you could find a better job. What's the name of your new employer?" Peggy inquired.

Sally paused. "It's Castle Hill Farm," Sally said.

Peggy was quiet for a moment. "I'm not recalling that name. Is it nearby?"

"No, Peggy. It's in Connecticut." Sally could have heard a pin drop. It was that quiet.

"Sally, did you say *Connecticut*?" Peggy asked slowly.

"Yes. You remember when the boys and I went out of town during their spring break? I went there and was able to find a job opportunity that sounded really good. It's a job that will help my sons appreciate nature and grow in ways that are not available here. I don't like moving so far away, but I believe God is providing a new path for me, Todd, and Pace. It was like a breath of fresh air, being there, and it just seems right. I've done a lot of praying about the move, the job, leaving you . . . but Peggy, I feel like this change would be good for us, and I believe God has opened this door." Sally knew leaving the part about Rusty out was important right now, and she hoped Peggy would understand later why she chose this.

Peggy slowly began to speak as if she wanted to be sure to say the right words. "Well, Sally, it will be very hard for me to see you and my grandsons leave. I wish it wouldn't happen, but since you believe God is opening the door for a new life and path for the three of you, you have my prayers to go before y'all, and I will always be lifting y'all up to Him. I say this in Jesus' name. When do y'all plan to leave?" Peggy was fighting back tears.

"In just a few weeks. The boys' last day of school is the 22nd," Sally said.

"I'd like to spend as much time as I can with the three of you then. Please, let's make plans to go to the zoo and to Libertyland, maybe even take the Memphis Queen boat ride—anything for us to make memories for us to always remember. We only have a few weeks together. Please, let's make the most of them. Please, Sally!" Peggy began to cry. "I've got to go. I love you and the boys so much," she said as she hung up the phone.

Sally had tears in her eyes as she felt horrible for Peggy. Sally knew Peggy was just trying to understand. She was still holding the handset in her hand when the telephone rang again. "Hello?"

"Uh oh, what's the matter, sweetheart?" Rusty detected sadness in Sally's voice.

"Oh, I just got off the telephone with Peggy. I told her we're moving," Sally said.

"I gather she didn't take it well?"

"No, not at all. I just feel bad for her. I hope she believes that God is leading us on a better path. She wants to spend as much time as she can with us over the next three weekends. She wants all of us to have lots of memories," Sally explained.

"I get it, and I understand. This news is very unexpected for her. Maybe her daughter and her family will have Peggy come and live with them. That would be an answer to prayer," Rusty suggested.

"That would be nice. Hopefully they will suggest that to her. So, how are you, sweetheart?" Sally asked.

"I'm OK. Were you able to give your notices to your landlord and Brother Hal?"

"Yes. When I called Mr. Waddell this morning, he said he was sorry to see us move. And Brother Hal was visibly saddened by my resignation. It's been a good day but a sad one too. But the worst should be over, at least for a while. I think I'm about ready for bed. I wish you were here to hold me," Sally said.

"Me too. We'd go to sleep in each other's arms. I so look forward to that again, but it will be soon! You go get ready for bed. I pray you sleep good. We'll talk tomorrow. I love you, my lady. Kissy kissy!" Rusty said, trying to lighten the mood.

Sally smiled. "I got your kissy kissy! You sleep good too. I have you in my prayers always. Talk tomorrow. Love ya. Kissy to you." And Sally hung up.

Sally and the boys called it a night and went to bed.

After church on May 3rd, Peggy, Sally, Todd, and Pace went to the zoo and had a wonderful afternoon looking at all the animals and exhibits. It was a memorable day for all of them.

The next day, Rusty's shared with Sally that his dad had passed a significant milestone. It had been four months since his heart attack, and his health was improving almost every day. He was able to relieve Rusty from some of his hard work. Rusty's hope and prayer was that in two months, his dad would be strong enough to manage the farm on his own, and Rusty could go back to driving over the road again. Sally wasn't sure how that was going to work out, but she knew God would show them the way.

Several days passed, and it was the evening of May 7th. Rusty called and was excited to report that the wedding invitations had been put in the mail and his flight reservation to Memphis was confirmed for the afternoon of May 21st—just two weeks away! He had also contacted a moving truck company and reserved a truck, and he would pick it up on his way to her house that evening. Sally was thrilled that so much had been accomplished that day. She was getting so excited.

Peggy called Sally and told her that on Saturday, May 9th, she had made reservations for all four of them to take the evening dinner cruise on the Memphis Paddlewheel Riverboat. Peggy said she would pick them up. Sally was looking forward to their time together.

That day came, and boy was it a beautiful and warm day. Peggy picked Sally and the boys up at four o'clock and drove downtown onto the cobblestone parking area by the river's edge. The boys were fascinated by everything they saw. Once on the paddlewheel boat, the boys wanted to go see the paddlewheel up close. Soon the boat was underway, and the paddlewheel began to turn and move the boat through the river's water.

After thirty minutes of cruising on the river and relaxing on the upper deck of the boat in the late afternoon sun, an announcement came across the loudspeaker, informing the passengers their dinner was about to be served so they should please take their seats in the dining room. The four of them descended down the steep, narrow steps to the middle level of the boat. Peggy held tightly to the handrail. They had to stand in line for a few minutes before entering the dining room. A crew member directed them to their seating location, which was next to a window with a great view of the river. Sally and Peggy allowed the boys to sit next to the window.

They were served the first of their four courses. The appetizers included potato skins, sausage balls, cheese sticks, small chicken fingers, and fried pickles. It was a super way to begin their meal. Next came the traditional salad for the second course. The boys weren't much on eating salads, but they did the best they could. Sally and Peggy helped them by taking a few bites.

By that point, the sun, which had been brightly shining all day, was close to setting. The sky was full of beautiful, vivid colors. It was very picturesque.

The main course was brought to their table next. There was fried chicken, a small slab of BBQ ribs, green beans, corn on the cob, and two dinner rolls. Just a good down-home southern meal!

Darkness had surrounded the boat, and the river's water had turned black. It was a little scary not being able to see anything past the window next to them.

As the dinner plates were being cleared from the table, the server arrived at their table with a large platter of desserts. They had a choice of a slice of pecan pie, a bowl of banana pudding, or a small plate of assorted cookies. The choice was difficult for Sally because she could have eaten all three! But she chose the pecan pie, as did Peggy. Todd took the banana pudding, and Pace selected the cookies. The dessert was a delicious conclusion to their four-course meal. It had met everyone's expectations and more.

The boys wanted to go up the steps again and watch the paddlewheel. The steps were steep and hard for Peggy to maneuver in the dimly lit stairway, but with patience and carefulness, she successfully managed the last step. She and Sally walked closely with the boys to the end of the boat so they could watch the wheel turn and turn.

As the boat was guided back to the dock, the four of them slowly took each narrow step cautiously until they reached the middle level. Several members of the boat's crew helped Peggy step from the boat to the moving wooden dock and then on to the cobblestones. Sally assisted Peggy up the cobblestone embankment to her car.

On the way home, the boys talked about every detail of the boat cruise. They really had a great experience, and Sally and Peggy had a wonderful time.

It was near ten o'clock when Peggy drove into Sally's driveway. Sally thanked Peggy for arranging such an enjoyable and memorable evening.

Sally assumed Rusty had tried to call her even though he knew she was going to be with Peggy. She called him as soon as she got home, and he was relieved to know she was OK.

It was May 11th, and Hugh Cut called Sally after she arrived home from work to tell her to be at his office at 10:15 a.m. the next day. He had arranged an appointment with the judge at eleven o'clock. She thanked Hugh for calling and prayed that the appointment would yield the Final Divorce Decree. She called the church and told Brother Hal that she had an appointment with the judge the next morning, so she wouldn't be able to come to the office in the morning. He understood.

The next morning, Sally arrived at the attorney's office, and soon after, she and Hugh left to go to the courthouse. This time, Hugh did not invite her to ride along with him, so she followed him in her car. He parked his car in the courthouse lot, but there were no parking spaces available for her. She had to drive around the courthouse twice before she was able to park her car. They walked into the courthouse together, and he knocked on the judge's chamber door. The judge opened the door and invited them into her office.

"Your Honor, Sally Oldham and I appreciate you accepting our request to see you," Hugh said to the judge.

"Please, sit down. Sally, your situation is a bit unusual. Granting a Final Divorce Decree before thirty days from your divorce trial is not normal. However, with your extenuating circumstances of your former husband living in Houston, having no desire to negotiate any reconciliation between you and him, as well as you and your sons' plans to move out of state, I'm signing the Final Divorce Decree today—ten days early. There will be a copy made of the original and given to Mr. Cut to be mailed to Collin, along with the order for child support for your two minor sons as well as your alimony. If and when you remarry, the order for alimony will cease. You will need to contact your attorney, then he will file a motion to the court to discontinue the alimony payments. The child support check will continue as ordered. You will also receive a copy of the order for child support and alimony. The child support and alimony will begin next month and will be distributed through the court system. When you know your new address, you need to contact Mr. Cut so he can notify the court clerk where to send the checks." The judge continued, "Sally, I'm very proud of your attitude in getting on with your life. Most women are not as fortunate as you are. I wish you and your sons the very best. Good luck."

"Thank you, Your Honor, and I'm grateful for you granting the Final Divorce Decree earlier than normal," Sally said thankfully.

"You're welcome. I'm happy it all worked out for you. Have a good day."

Hugh opened the judge's door, and both he and Sally left the judge's chambers. "We will wait here for the paperwork. Hopefully it won't take long," Hugh commented.

Usually Hugh was talkative, but he hardly said a word to her. She assumed he was still upset at her. The situation reminded her of Captain Hall, but Hugh was not as persistent. Hugh knew he couldn't and shouldn't date his client before the divorce was final. He might get into trouble.

After thirty minutes, a clerk handed Sally the paperwork, and Hugh was given the copies he needed to mail to Collin.

"OK, Sally. I guess this is it. I will need your new address. Just call me. Thank you for your business. I had hoped it might have turned into more, but I wish you the best of luck." He extended his hand, and Sally shook it.

"Thank you, Mr. Cut." Sally looked at him with gratitude but nothing more to say. She turned and walked to her car.

After grabbing some lunch, Sally went to the church and worked the rest of her time before getting the boys from school and going home.

Rusty was very happy she was granted the Final Divorce Decree. There should be nothing else standing in the way of their marriage.

Chapter Twenty-One

May 15th was a happy but sad day for Sally. She enjoyed her employment at the church. She felt like she was serving the Lord there, and Brother Hal was an uplifting person to work for.

Flowers were on her desk when she entered her office along with a "Thinking of You" card signed by Brother Hal and others. At lunch, Brother Hal and several church members, including Peggy, brought in a meal to celebrate Sally's last day of work.

At the end of the work day when Brother Hal handed the final paycheck envelope to Sally, he hugged her and told her he would ask God to be with her always. She thanked him, picked up her vase of flowers, and left the office with tears in her eyes.

The next day, Peggy, Sally, Todd, and Pace went to Libertyland. They rode rides, ate corn dogs, saw musical shows, ate funnel cakes, watched a magician do card tricks, ate cotton candy, and rode more rides. When the sun had set and the park's lights lit up the darkness, the park transformed into a delightful place of more excitement. What a wonderful, fun-filled day and evening they all had! They made more unforgettable memories to last their lifetimes.

On the way home, Sally asked Peggy if she had talked to Ellen and David about her and the boys moving away. Peggy said she had not talked to them, hoping that Sally would change her mind and stay. Sally encouraged Peggy to call them. There might be an opportunity for her to move in with them and still be close to family. Peggy said she'd thought about that, but she would have to sell her home, filled with so many fond memories of when her husband was alive. Sally understood but didn't like the idea of Peggy being far away from family.

Before Sally and the boys got out of Peggy's car, they made plans for Peggy to pick them up for church in the morning. Peggy asked Sally if she could visit with them some next week. Sally told her that would be OK except she was going to be packing, and the boys had to study for their final exams Monday and Tuesday night. Also, she told Peggy that the man who was going to help her move was planning on flying in on Thursday afternoon, and Sally would need to pick him up at the airport. The moving truck would be picked up soon after that and brought to the house. So Sally really couldn't tell her when a good time would be for Peggy to visit again. So Peggy asked if she could be at the house to see them off on moving day. Sally agreed to call her just before they were about to leave. Then Peggy started to cry. Sally tried to comfort her. Sally and the boys waved goodbye to her and watched her drive away. Sally felt so sad for Peggy.

After the Sunday morning church service, Peggy drove Sally and the boys around to the back of some stores, looking for boxes for Sally to use in packing their belongings. Then Peggy took them home and stayed all afternoon and into the evening. She left soon after supper. Sally could tell she was fighting back tears. That could have been the last time they would be able to spend time together. It was going to be an extremely busy and emotional week for Sally.

Sally asked the boys to sort through their toys and put the ones they *didn't* want in a pile and the ones they *did* want in another pile so they could pack only those they wanted. They began their project right away.

When the telephone rang, Sally was on a step-stool in the kitchen. She ran to the living room. "Hello?" she answered.

"Hi, honey. You busy?" Rusty asked.

"Well, I'm busy lookin' like this, talkin' to you! Whatcha doing?" Sally said in her southern drawl.

"Ahh, aren't you just so cute! But I guess I'm talking to you, looking like this too! We both are doing the same thing! Other than that, you OK?" Rusty inquired.

"Yip. I reckon so, honey!" Sally giggled. "I was in the kitchen packing some dishes from the cabinets, and the boys are sorting through their toys for me so I can pack the good ones. I really don't know how much of these kitchen things I need to bring with me because you probably have everything in your kitchen that we'll need. What do you think, sweetie?" Sally pondered.

"Well, go ahead and pack your things, and we'll sort it out when you get here," Rusty replied.

"OK, consider it done. Are you OK?" Sally asked.

"Yes, just missing you and the boys. But just four more days and we'll be together!"

"I know. It can't get here fast enough! I miss you so much too, sweetheart," Sally agreed.

The lovers ended their call with kisses and love.

Sally checked on the boys who were still going through their toys. She believed they were playing with some of them, deciding whether they wanted to keep them or not. She then returned to the kitchen and continued her task. After an hour, she had filled three boxes. All the kitchen was packed except for the items she would still need for the next several days.

The boys had finished sorting their toys. The old toys she placed in paper bags, while the good toys she packed in boxes.

"Well, I can't do anymore tonight. I have no more boxes. When I take y'all to school tomorrow, I'll search for more boxes. It's bathtime anyway. Thanks for helping me, kiddos," Sally said gratefully.

Bathtime was done, the boys were in their PJs, and they were ready to say their nightly prayers. They climbed into their beds, and Sally tucked them in and kissed them good night. Before she turned out their bedroom light, she thanked them again for keeping their promise about their trip to Connecticut. She explained to them that Rusty would be here in four days, and they could be moving in five or six days. But they had a lot to do before that time arrived. They would need to study tomorrow night and the next night for their final tests. Sally impressed upon them to listen closely to their teachers tomorrow and the next day so they would know what they needed to study. The school year was coming to an end, and they needed to do the best that they could.

"I love y'all. Sleep tight," she said, pausing at the door.

"We know, don't let the bedbugs bite!" The boys giggled.

Then Sally turned out the light and walked to her bedroom closet. She looked through her clothes. She took the suitcase and laid it on the bed and began packing her clothes. *No sense of carrying an empty suitcase,* she thought. Sally considered all she had accomplished that afternoon and night, and it was good. She called it a night and went to bed. She prayed and thanked God for all His blessings.

The alarm clock sounded as usual on Sally's nightstand, but it was a little different that morning. There was no rushing around, getting dressed for work. That felt good!

Todd's alarm clock had begun playing music as well, and the brothers were up and getting dressed.

Breakfast was prepared and eaten, dishes were washed, lunch boxes were filled with food, and Sally dressed in an old top and jeans. She walked to her mother's jewelry box, took out Rusty's engagement ring, and placed it on her finger. Oh, how beautiful it was! It was time to head for school.

As they arrived at school and the boys exited the car, Sally wished them to have a good day. The boys disappeared as the school door closed behind them. Then Sally went on her mission to find more boxes she could use to pack her things. She found many of them behind a convenient store. But before Sally went home, she stopped by Minnie Mouse's home. She knocked on the door.

"Well, look who's here! Cricket, come on in here," Minnie Mouse said. "How are you, girl? Been wondering about you. Don't hear you on the airwaves anymore. Coffee?"

"That sounds good. Thank you." Sally followed her into the kitchen and sat down at the table. "I've been thinking about you and wanted to come by and tell you the news. You remember the farmer from Connecticut, right?"

"Yes," Minnie Mouse answered slowly.

Sally continued. "We're getting married next month!" She raised her left hand in the air.

"What? Congratulations! Y'all found each other? That's great! Your ring is beautiful," Minnie Mouse rejoiced.

"Yes. He is a godsend! When Collin left me, I immediately filed for divorce. I was feeling down and went for a drive. I stopped at the truck stop in Jackson for lunch, and there he was! I could hardly believe my eyes. He saw me and, well, now we're about to be married," Sally said.

"Oh my gosh. You were at the right place at the right time! Wow. It was meant to be!" Minnie Mouse clapped her hands.

"This week will be crazy, but I wanted to come by and thank you for being such a good friend. You helped me so much. The Farmer, Rusty, will be here Thursday, and he is moving the boys and me to his home in Connecticut. So I wanted to tell you 'bye' before we left," Sally explained.

"Cricket, I'm so happy for you. I wish you the very best!" Minnie Mouse hugged Sally.

"Thank you. You and Firecracker been doing OK?" Sally asked.

"Yes, we're good. I've been learning how to drive an 18-wheeler, and I passed my driving test last week. I have my Commercial Driver License now, and Firecracker and I are going on the road together!" Minnie Mouse said excitedly.

"Oh, Minnie Mouse, that's fantastic! I feel your excitement too." Sally clapped her hands.

"Yes. He can't wait for us to drive as a team!"

Their visit and the conversation went on for an hour, and then, Sally left for home. She was very glad that she decided to stop and see Minnie Mouse.

Once she arrived home and carried in the boxes, she resumed the task of packing. When it was time to pick the boys up from school, she had almost packed the whole house. Tomorrow, she would need to pack the things that were in the building in the backyard.

As soon as the boys came in from school, they noticed how different the house looked. They were a little sad. After they ate their after-school snack, they hit the school books and began studying. Sally helped them where she could. Todd had taken lots of notes on what he heard his teacher say, hoping that would help him make good grades on his tests. Pace didn't have any notes, but he studied from the printout his teacher gave to each of her students.

Sally began to prepare a simple supper. When it was ready, the boys came to the table. Sally asked the blessing for their meal, and she also asked God to open Todd and Pace's minds to what they were studying and for them to retain that knowledge so they could make good grades on their tests.

After supper, the boys were back to the books until bathtime. They were tired, and after putting on their PJs, they were ready for bed. Sally could see the stress on Todd's face. When she covered him with his bedding, she told him she would say extra prayers for them that night. The nightly routine did not have the normal carefree, happy tone; it was more somber. Sally would be glad when all the studying and tests were over and done.

Rusty called Sally, but both had a long and busy day. They were ready for bed. Their wait time was down to three days! Rusty and Sally sent their love and kisses through the telephone line, and the call ended. Sally went to bed and prayed hard for Todd and Pace's tests tomorrow as well as for Rusty to rest well that night.

The morning of May 19th began as any other day. They got up, dressed, ate breakfast, and headed off to school. Before dropping the boys off at school, Sally prayed with her little men, asking the Lord to give them a good day and for them to do good on their tests. They ran to the school door, waved, and disappeared.

All the way home, Sally continued to pray for Todd and Pace. After arriving home and before she began her packing in the building out back, she called Matthew and Jodie. Her brother answered the telephone. They exchanged their greetings to each other and both asked about their families. Then, Sally surprised Matthew with the news of her divorce and of Rusty and their engagement. Matthew was happy for her until she told him she was moving to Connecticut that weekend and getting married next month. He was happy for her but sad about her moving so far away from them. Sally was sad too, but hopefully they would be able to visit them. She promised she would call them more often. Their goodbyes to each other were bittersweet.

Sally was remorseful for not being a better sister and for not being more forthwith to her brother about Rusty, but she felt safer by keeping him a secret until it was time for her to reveal Rusty to those whom she loved, for fear of them thinking poorly of her.

The morning was getting warm, and it was even warmer in the small, metal-roofed building out back, but there wasn't much in it to pack other than Collin's tools and a small plastic six-drawer organizer, with drawers full of screws, nuts, bolts, nails, and other miscellaneous hardware. Collin had stored their two bicycles in the building, Todd's small beginner's bike and Pace's Big Wheel, which he had outgrown. She was going to leave everything in the building, and hopefully she would remember to tell Rusty to be sure to pack what was out there. When she returned to the house, she wrote herself a reminder note. Then, she remembered the attic. Right away, she added "attic" to her note. Sally looked around the house, but she felt she had packed everything she could at that point.

The afternoon passed, and it was time to get the boys. They were happy their day was over, but more studying was ahead of them for the rest of their final tests tomorrow.

After their snack, they studied. After supper, they studied. Sally helped, especially Pace with his spelling words. At 8 p.m., Todd closed his school book and told his mother he was tired. Pace followed. They took their baths, put on their PJs, and went to bed.

Soon after the boys had gone to bed, Rusty called. Sally told him the house was packed as much as she could pack, and she told him about the building and the attic. Rusty told her he was packed and ready to fly when Thursday morning arrived. Sally mentioned to him that she needed to go to the post office and to the boys' school office tomorrow to give them a change of address. Rusty suggested maybe the landlord and the attorney might need that too. It would be a busy day for both of them tomorrow. They agreed it was time to call it a night. They gave each other their love, kisses, and good nights.

Todd, Pace, and Sally were up and at 'em, doing their normal get-ready routine for school. At the boys' school, instead of Sally driving through the drop-off car line, she parked the car and took her sons' hands as they walked inside the school. She stopped at the office door. She bent down in front of her sons and told them she would continue to pray for them and their tests. Then, the boys went to their separate classrooms. Sally entered the school office and told the lady behind the office counter about them moving, and she gave them her new address. Sally left the school and proceeded to the post office, the utility company, as well as the telephone company. Sally drove by Peggy's house and visited with her for an hour. She invited her to come over for supper that evening.

The boys ran out of the school full of happiness. Their tests were over, and they were so relieved. They picked up pizzas, and Peggy met them at their house. Peggy appreciated Sally allowing her to spend more time with them.

After Peggy left, it was bathtime, and soon after, it was bedtime. Just one and a half days left of school, and then their lives would change!

Rusty gave Sally important information when he called. The next morning, his parents were driving him to Bridgeport where he would board a nine o'clock flight to La Guardia Airport in Queens, New York. Then, at noon, he would be on Flight AA4733 bound for Memphis and would arrive at 2:30 p.m. Sally promised him she would be there waiting for him. She was so excited. Finally, the wait would be over, and the two of them would be together again.

After Sally dropped the boys off at school, she came home and washed several loads of clothes, readying them to be folded and packed. She stripped the bed linens and washed, dried, and remade the beds.

The time came for her to go to school and check the boys out and head to the airport. The boys were excited to be out of school and were also thrilled to see Rusty again.

Flight AA4733 was on time. As soon as they saw Rusty step his last step off the roll-up boarding stairway, Todd and Pace bolted to him and hugged his legs. When Sally reached him, they passionately kissed each other and hugged tightly. As they walked to the terminal building, Sally asked, "How were your flights?"

"They were good. No problems other than it seemed like it took me forever to get here. It's so good to see you all again," Rusty stated and hugged them again.

Once in the car, Sally drove off the airport property and steered the car in the direction of Getwell Road. They found the truck rental location, and Rusty took care of business, doing all the paperwork. Within fifteen minutes, he was ready to go. Todd and Pace were excited and wanted to ride with Rusty. The truck rental place was just a few miles from Sally's home, so it didn't take long before they had arrived. Rusty backed the truck into the driveway, and they went into the house.

"This is a nice home! Small but homey," Rusty commented.

"It has served its purpose for a number of years," Sally added.

"Not a lot of furniture, and that's good. I'm not sure where we'll put it at home, but we'll figure it out. I see you have done a great job of packing. Can I see the building out back?" Rusty asked.

"Sure, come on." Sally led him out the back door, down the four steps, and on the short walk to the building. Rusty opened the door.

"Ahh, this is a piece of cake. No problem." He sounded relieved. "How about the attic? Can I see it too?"

"OK," Sally replied.

Rusty closed the building door and followed Sally back into the house. Sally took the step ladder from the hall closet, and Rusty began to ascend the steps, opening the attic access cover. He was soon able to see into the attic.

"Sally, I need to bring these boxes out of the attic. Will it be OK if I set them in the living room and maybe even the dining room? That way, I won't have to do this in the morning," Rusty suggested.

"Yes, of course. Whatever is easiest for you," Sally agreed.

"OK." He disappeared into the attic. Then, he returned to the opening with a box and handed it down to Sally. He handed the next one to Todd, who was standing nearby, eager to help. Rusty handed them box after box until all the boxes and other items were out of the attic. Sally didn't realize so much was stored up there!

Rusty carefully descended the ladder, closed it up, and sat it in the dining room. "That's better because now I can see everything that needs to be put in the truck. It won't be too bad at all," Rusty calculated. He sat down on the couch to rest, and Sally brought him a glass of water to drink. She sat down beside him on one side, and the boys sat on the other side.

"You know, I tried picturing in my mind your home when we talked to each other. Is this where you would sit?" Rusty asked.

"Yes, sometimes. Other times, I'd go to the dining room and sit in one of the chairs," Sally answered.

"I think before the sun goes down and it gets dark, I'll go ahead and start loading the truck with these boxes. Then, instead of cooking, I'll take you all out to eat. How's that sound?" Rusty suggested.

"Sounds good! We'll help," Sally said. She propped the screen door open, Rusty raised up the door on the truck, and all four of them started to work. Box after box began filling the truck. In several hours, all the boxes were loaded, and there was still plenty of room for the furniture.

The temperature of the late afternoon and evening was warm, and all of them had worked up a sweat. As unusual as it was, the boys took *showers*! Rusty was next, then Sally. They dressed, and Rusty drove Sally's car to a nice restaurant where they enjoyed a delicious meal.

Back at home, the boys still had a half day of school to attend the next day, so they prepared for bed. After their nightly prayers, Sally tucked them into bed. She shared with them that that night could most likely be their last night to sleep in their room because tomorrow night they could be on the road, headed to their new home in Connecticut. The boys were a little sad, but they told her they were looking forward to all the new home had in store for them. Sally smiled. She kissed them good night, said she loved them, and, as always, she told them to sleep tight and not let the bedbugs bite! Rusty told them good night too. As she left their room, she turned out the light.

Finally, Rusty and Sally were alone. They hugged and kissed each other for a while. Then, they just sat on the couch and talked about tomorrow and their future together.

The telephone rang. Sally quickly answered it. "Hello?"

"I guess you should have called me and told me you were moving, Sally. Mom just told me. But it's OK. I received the Final Divorce Decree today, and now that we're not married anymore, you are free to do whatever you want to," Collin informed her.

Sally mouthed to Rusty that the call was from Collin. "Well, Collin, *you did*. You just up and left. And you're right; I am a free woman and am choosing to move on with my life, just as you told me you would." Sally tried to remain calm. Just hearing Collin's voice nearly made her sick!

"I did get the order for child support and alimony and that I have to submit the said amount within the first ten days of the month. It will be sent to you through the court. Sure hope your new life works out for you, Sally. Mine has." Collin hung up.

Sally didn't expect his call, but she was glad his mother told him. It saved her from having to deal with him.

"Sweetheart, are you OK? What did he say?" Rusty asked.

Sally took Rusty's hand. "Yes, I'm OK. Collin said he talked to his mom, and she told him. I guess Peggy thought she should let him know that the boys and I were moving. He did get the Decree and order for child support and alimony. He said he was glad I was moving on with my life because he has."

"He is such a *no good*." Rusty paused. "Well, you know." Rusty left the sentence open.

"I do know. And he is that, for sure!" Sally agreed. "I'm going to see if the boys are asleep. I hope the telephone ringing didn't wake them up. I'll be right back . . . and that's a promise!" She smiled seductively.

Rusty watched Sally as she walked away from him. She moved her body in a way that drove him crazy!

Within a few seconds, Sally returned. She bent forward slightly and took his hands in hers and drew him close to her. She kissed his sweet, warm lips very passionately. Rusty, as he had done at his home, swept her off her feet, held her in his arms, and carried her to her bedroom. He closed the door behind him, and they both laid down on her bed and intertwined around each other most of the night.

Sally woke Rusty up before both her and Todd's alarm clock. She wasn't yet ready for her sons to see Rusty and her in the same bed together. So Rusty got dressed and went to lay down on the living room couch, and Sally slipped into her robe as normal and began making coffee.

Soon, the boys were up and getting ready for school. Rusty decided to go to a nearby restaurant and grab some breakfast for everyone. That was different, and they all enjoyed the change.

Sally took the boys to school, and before they exited the car, she told them, "It's your last day. Have fun! I'll pick y'all up at noon." They waved, and off they ran toward the school door.

When Sally returned home, she found several cars parked in front of her home. As she got out of her car, she saw Brother Hal and several other men from church, taking furniture out of the house and bringing it toward the truck. Sally approached the back of the truck and peeked inside. "Hi, Brother Hal, Mr. Jessie, Mr. Carl. I appreciate y'all helping. How did you know?" she asked.

"Peggy called me and asked me to lend a helping hand with y'all's moving. I called Jessie and Carl to help too," Brother Hal explained.

"Fellas, I thank y'all so much." Sally was surprised and grateful.

"There really isn't much more to move from the house to the truck," Brother Hal remarked.

"I need to check the building out back," Sally remembered.

"Already done. The building is empty," Brother Hal informed her.

"Ahh, there you are," Rusty said, walking up to the truck. "I thought I heard your voice, Sally. Your preacher and the two deacons have been a huge help. The beds are all that's left. If you would take off the sheets and blankets, we'll break down the beds and get them in the truck."

"Sure, right away. I don't want to hold up progress now, do I?" Sally laughed. As Sally walked toward her house, she wondered how Rusty had introduced himself to the men of her church. When she stepped inside the house, the emptiness caught her off guard. Everything was gone! She suddenly felt sad, but she knew she could not get emotional, so she forced herself to walk to the boys' bedroom. She removed the bed linens and folded them. She proceeded to her bedroom and stripped her bed. The men needed to break down her bed first, then the boys' two twin beds. Sally still had several empty boxes, so she packed the bed linens in the boxes and took them to the truck. She took their pillows and placed them in the back seat of her car. She quickly packed the last items from the kitchen and gave the box to Rusty.

Sally looked around one last time, even in all the closets, the cabinets, and the bathroom shower. There was nothing left. She walked outside. "Thank you, Brother Hal, Jessie, and Carl for taking the time to help us load the truck so that we didn't have to do it all ourselves. We are so grateful for y'all's help." Sally hugged each one of them, and Rusty shook their hands. The men wished Sally a safe trip and Godspeed. They waved and left.

Rusty pulled down the door of the moving truck and locked it.

"I need to call Peggy and thank her for intervening for us," Sally said as she walked toward the house.

Rusty stopped her. "The telephone has been packed. I'm sorry, sweetheart."

Sally sighed. "OK." She looked at her watch. "It's almost time to get the boys from school. We can get the boys, then stop by her house and thank her for calling Brother Hal. And the boys and I can say goodbye to her. It would take but just a few minutes," she suggested.

"If it's OK with you, honey, I'll stay here and rest in the truck. You get the boys and then visit with Peggy. Try not to be too long, OK? Then swing back by here, and we'll head out. The sooner, the better. It's going to take us a few days to get home. How's that?" Rusty suggested.

"Are you sure, sweetheart?" Sally asked concerningly.

"Yes. This truck has a CB. I requested that, so we could communicate with each other on the road."

"Oh, you are so thoughtful!" Sally smiled. "OK, you rest. We'll be back soon. I love you." Sally kissed him.

Sally arrived at the school and was ready to pick up the boys. As Todd approached the car, Sally saw him holding hands with a cute young girl. He opened the passenger side front car door, and both of them bent down to look at Sally.

"Mom, this is Barbie. She's the one I told you I have lunch with each day," Todd said.

"Hi, Barbie! It's nice to meet you. I'm glad you and Todd have a sweet relationship. I hope you have a nice summer." Sally wasn't sure what to say.

"It was nice to meet you too. I really like your son, and I'm going to miss him a lot. I'll be praying for y'all." Barbie then turned to Todd, hugged him, and to his surprise and Sally's too, kissed him on his lips! "I love you, Todd. Please write me."

"I will, Barbie." As she began to walk away, Todd grabbed her arm, approached her, and kissed her back, right on the lips. "I love you too."

Sally had to gasp for air. She could hardly believe her eyes.

Pace was already in the back seat, and he shrieked, "Momma, did you see that? They kissed each other!" Todd entered the back seat all dreamy-eyed.

"Son," Sally began, "are you still eight years old, or did you grow up since I dropped you off at school this morning?"

"Mom, she is wonderful, and I do love her!" Todd admitted. Sally understood his feelings, but he was so young!

"She is a very pretty girl and well-mannered, too." Sally was impressed. "Are you OK?"

"Yeah, but I sure am going to miss her. But I'll write to her," Todd answered positively.

As Sally was driving away from the school car line, Pace shouted excitedly, "Momma! Here's my report card! I passed! I'll be in the second grade next year!"

Sally pulled into a parking space, and Pace handed her his very valuable folded card.

"Here's mine too, Mom. I made one bad grade, but I passed, too!" Todd rejoiced.

"Praise the Lord!" Sally looked at both report cards. "I'm so proud of both of y'all. It's been a rough and sometimes tough year for the both of you. I thank God for getting y'all through the difficult times, and these report cards show His love for you two. I'm so thankful and proud. Y'all are blessed!" Sally began driving again. She explained the plan of going by Grandmother Peggy's house to say a quick good-bye to her, then they would go by the house to join up with Rusty. She told them there was nothing left in the house so they were going to get on their way.

"It's really happening, Momma?" Pace exclaimed.

"Yes, it is! Are y'all excited?" Sally asked.

Right away, Pace yelled, "Yes!"

But Todd's "yes" was a borderline answer. Sally knew why.

When they arrived at Grandmother Peggy's house, Sally thanked her for calling Brother Hal to rally the troops and help load the moving truck. Peggy hugged her grandsons tightly and gave them big kisses on their cheeks. They hugged her right back. Then, Peggy began to cry as she hugged Sally.

"Please call me often, Sally. Let's not lose touch with each other. I love ya like you are my own daughter—even more. Please be careful. Call me when you get to where you're going to let me know y'all made it OK," Peggy pleaded.

"I will, Peggy. You take good care of yourself. Love ya bunches." Sally hugged Peggy with tears in her eyes. As she and the boys waved and threw kisses to Peggy, the thought crossed her mind that one day maybe Peggy could come live with them in Connecticut. Maybe it was a thought for a later time, but they were all crying, wondering if they'd ever see each other again.

Within minutes, Sally called Rusty on her CB radio, and he answered. At the house, they all used the bathroom before they started on their big drive. Todd and Pace had never seen the house empty before; they had always lived in that house. It was sad for them.

"Come on, guys. We need to go!" Rusty encouraged them.

Sally left the door key by the front door where Mr. Waddell asked her to leave it. She locked and closed the door for the last time. She had an awkward feeling, but it quickly passed once she got in her car, drove out of the driveway, and left all of it behind in her rearview mirror. She was stepping further out in faith and starting a new life for her and her sons. She prayed that God would give them travel mercies for a safe trip.

Sally followed close to Rusty, and the CBs transmitted perfectly. Todd and Pace decided to ride with Rusty, and they enjoyed chatting with their mother.

At the truck stop near Jackson, where Sally and Rusty first met up, they stopped for a late lunch. Their meal was good and filling. Rusty hoped they could make it near Knoxville before stopping for the night, but there was a lot of traffic on the super slab due to it being Memorial Day weekend. Plus, the rental truck didn't drive as fast as Rusty would have preferred, but that was OK. He was with Sally and the boys, and he thanked God that his prayers and dreams were coming true.

On the east side of Nashville, the travelers took a fuel and potty stop. As the rolling hills and mountains of the Appalachian were in front of them, the sun was setting, and darkness closed in all around them. Sally stayed very close to the truck Rusty was driving. They changed their CB channel to their usual channel 23 so they could talk more freely. Sally asked Rusty about seeing Brother Hal and what was said.

"Three men came to the door, looking for you," Rusty said. "I told them you had taken the boys to school and that I was asked to come here to help you move to Connecticut. One of the men, Brother Hal, introduced himself along with the other two men. He said they were from the church you attended, and they were there to help. Right away, all four of us got busy loading the furniture along with the washer and dryer onto the truck. I was most grateful for their help," Rusty explained.

Sally told Rusty that Brother Hal was the man who hired her for the church position.

"He mentioned you were a hard worker, a fast learner, and an added light to the church office. He said he sure would miss you and your pleasant disposition. Is he married?" Rusty asked.

"He said all of that? Wow! No, he's not married. He was, but his wife divorced him. She didn't like being straight-laced," Sally explained.

"I wonder if he had his sights on you?" Rusty speculated.

"Oh, Rusty, no! He's just a nice man." Sally shied away from his suspicion.

"Well, you thought *I* was nice . . ." Rusty continued.

"Yes, I did. I mean, I do, but it was different with us. God allowed you and me to be attracted to each other, and He encouraged us to step out in faith," Sally said.

"You are right, and this is true. How are you doing? Getting tired? It's after ten o'clock. You want to stop for the night? We're close to Knoxville," Rusty asked.

"Yes, only if you are ready to stop," Sally answered.

"I'm ready. I'll look for a motel."

Another five miles closer to Knoxville, Rusty saw an Interstate lodging sign. Several motels were listed. They exited Interstate 40 and drove onto one of the motel driveways. Rusty jumped down from the truck, went into the office, and several minutes later came out with keys. He drove the truck ahead and parked, Sally following behind. Rusty opened the motel room door while Sally managed to get sleeping Pace out of the truck and into the room. Rusty urged Todd to move to the passenger side of the truck. He picked him up and carried him to the room and laid him on the bed.

"Do you think we should sleep together?" Sally asked Rusty.

"No. One son with you, and the other with me," Rusty said with no hesitation. He understood and agreed with Sally's concerns.

"Good," Sally agreed. She took off the boys' shoes and covered them with their bed sheets. Then Sally and Rusty shared a kiss and went to opposite beds.

The next morning, all four of them were up early. They ate at a nearby restaurant and were on the road by 8 a.m. It was sunny and warm, and it felt good to have the car windows down with fresh air flowing through the car. The mountain scenery was beautiful.

Mile after mile, town after town, and several states in their travels were history. Traffic was heavy, but they maintained a constant speed. The necessary stops had to be made for gas, food, and the potty. Todd and Pace took turns riding with their mother and Rusty. They occupied themselves with their road games, talking on the CB, and visual games like the road alphabet game—anything to pass the time.

Near six o'clock that evening, they were on the outskirts of Hagerstown, Maryland. Rusty radioed Sally on the CB. "Honey, how are you doing?"

"I'm OK, but I'm getting tired. You sound tired," Sally said.

"Yeah, I am. There are lots of motels and eating places just ahead. I think we should call it a day," Rusty suggested.

"Sounds good to me. I'll follow you, my dear," Sally agreed.

Rusty made his turn off of Interstate 81 and chose a motel. Within ten minutes, they were in their room. The warmth of the day had made their skin feel sticky. It was shower time. Sally and Rusty waited on the boys to bathe first, but their time alone was occupied by hugs and kisses and lying on the bed next to each other. However, when the sound of the flowing water stopped, the lovers returned back to being prim and proper.

Rusty showered next while Sally helped the boys dress in clean clothes. When Rusty came out of the bathroom, he was dressed only in his underwear. The boys stared at him.

Suddenly Pace loudly said, "Rusty, you have a *hairy* body!"

"Yeah, that's the way God made me!" Rusty laughed and looked at Sally who was trying to keep from laughing out loud.

"They have never seen hair on a man's chest before." Sally glanced at him and voiced softly as she passed him to take her turn in the bathroom.

"Well, OK!" he replied in a deep manly voice.

Sally showered and dressed in the bathroom. When she opened the bathroom door, all three of her fellas were staring at her.

"Are you ready yet?" Rusty asked as if he was irritated.

"Yeah, Mom. We've been waiting on you forever!" Todd expressed.

"Yeah, Momma, forever!" Pace echoed.

"Well, I'm sorry." Sally was about to cry. "But I'm ready now. Is that OK?"

"Yes," Rusty laughed. "You boys better go hug your mother."

The boys ran to her and gave her a hug. Then they took her hands and walked toward the motel room door that Rusty already had opened, and they all walked out and together went to a very close restaurant for supper. It was a fun evening with lots of laughing as the soon-to-be family got to know each other better.

The next morning, the rain was coming down heavy. Fingers of lightning streaked across the sky above, and the thunder was loud. Pace held on to his mother's hand tightly as they watched the weather from the motel window.

"We'll try to wait the storm out before we make a mad dash to the car and truck. We don't need to get all wet," Rusty advised. "One good thing is we are only six hours away from home. I wonder if there is any news on the television?" Rusty walked toward the set and turned the knob. It took a moment for the screen to appear. He changed the channel several times with another knob and luckily, he found a news program. He watched it a minute, but the network went to a commercial.

Sally and the boys were still looking out the window. "The rain could be slacking up. Look, sweetheart," Sally observed.

Rusty joined them at the window. "You're right. It isn't raining as hard. Do we have everything ready if we have to move quickly?" Rusty asked.

"Yes," Sally answered.

The commercial was over, and the channel's programming was back on the screen, including the weather. But it was not for Hagerstown. Rusty turned off the television and stepped out the door.

"It's barely raining. We might get a little wet. Let's go for it!" Rusty decided. They grabbed their things, and out the door they ran as Rusty closed the motel room door behind him.

"Boys, get in the car with me for now," Sally yelled as she unlocked the car door and opened the door for the boys. "Rusty, I'll turn the CB on so we can talk."

"OK," he yelled back to her as he climbed in the cab of the truck. After a moment, Rusty asked, "You got a copy, Cricket?"

"I do, Farmer. Loud and clear," Sally answered.

"That wasn't too bad. I've got to return the key, then we can ease out. I'll find us a place to eat breakfast. It might be a little way down the road. OK?"

"We'll just follow you, Farmer from Connecticut," Sally replied.

Rusty drove near the office door, jumped out, ran inside, and soon arrived back to the truck. He made his way onto the street with Sally following close behind. He turned to the right and drove to the entrance ramp to Interstate 81 North.

Ten miles ahead was Green Castle, Pennsylvania. Rusty had been to a quaint little diner there before, and it had good food. So they decided to go there for breakfast. When they arrived, they went in and sat down at the counter. The boys were surprised at the way the diner looked inside; it was similar to the diner in Newtown.

They ate to their hearts' content. With their tummies full, they once again emerged on the super slab—and it was raining again. Rusty drove slower than he had yesterday, but each mile got them closer and closer to home.

To entertain the boys, all four of them played the alphabet game. Rusty kept the CB mic busy as he found his next letters for the game. The ride to

Scranton seemed faster than Rusty remembered it being. The game sure did help pass the time.

"Only two hours away from home," Rusty announced when they turned east on Interstate 84. "We should be clean and green all the way to the house." Rusty used a popular CB saying. "I know Princess and Prince will be so happy to see you boys," Rusty said to them.

"We'll be very happy to see them too," Pace said after he pressed the CB mic key excitedly.

Miles rolled by, and so did those two hours. As Rusty turned onto Old Castle Hill Road, he breathed a huge sigh of relief. He praised God for a safe trip home and for allowing his prayers and dreams to come true, being with Sally and her sons. When he turned into the driveway of his home, he pressed the key on the CB mic one last time and happily reported, "We are home!"

"Praise the Lord for *everything*," Sally rejoiced. "Look! There's Princess and Prince. They've come to say welcome home! Boys, y'all go see them!" As soon as Sally stopped the car, the boys jumped out and ran to the shepherds. They didn't need to be told twice!

Rusty met Sally as she opened the car door. He took her in his arms, held her close to him, and passionately kissed her. "We made it, Sally, honey. We're home, and our dreams have come true."

"And our prayers have been answered, my sweet Rusty." Sally hugged and kissed him right back.

Chapter Twenty-Two

As soon as Rusty, Sally, Todd, and Pace walked into Rusty's home, he called his parents to tell them they were back home. He also asked if they could send a few men over to the house to help him unload the truck.

Within minutes, ten men plus Rusty's parents were there to help. Hugs were given all around the family. Rusty's parents were so glad they were home and that they had made the trip safely. Everyone pitched in, and in less than an hour, the truck was unloaded. Rusty thanked all of them for their help. Sally and the boys followed Rusty to the local truck rental location to return their truck, then drove back to the house to begin the task of unpacking.

After an hour of sorting through boxes, the telephone rang. Rusty answered. "Hello?"

"Dinner is on the table. Mom says to come on!" Russell encouraged.

"OK, Dad. We'll be there in a few minutes. Thank you." Rusty accepted the invitation and hung up the telephone.

"That was Dad. Dinner's ready. You want to take a break and go eat?" Rusty asked his hard-working crew.

"That would be wonderful! Come on, boys. Let's wash up," Sally said, motioning to the helpers to follow her.

They all walked into the Summers' kitchen and all took their places at the table. Russell thanked God for their meal and for his family's safe trip home. Dinner was served.

"Mandy, thank you for thinking of us. You're always so thoughtful," Sally said.

"Well, I felt surely you all would like a home-cooked meal far better than . . . what's the saying truck drivers use, Rusty?" Mandy hesitated.

"It's *choke-n-puke*, Mom," Rusty told her.

"Oh, yeah! That just sounds so gross," Mandy replied.

"I'm praising God that you all are home safe and sound," Russell said thankfully. "And it's a good thing. So many people are responding to the wedding invitations. Looks like there is going to be a church full of people! It's wonderful!"

"That's great, Dad! The wedding is still twelve days away, but we need to discuss some things," Rusty said.

Sally suddenly stopped eating, and her countenance fell.

"Sally, dear, are you OK?" Mandy noticed the way she looked.

"I can't believe I did that. . . ." Sally recalled something she was supposed to have done in Memphis.

"What, sweetheart?" Rusty inquired.

"My *dress*," Sally sadly replied. "I was so busy, I did not look for or buy my dress for the wedding. I'm so sorry, Rusty!" she said with tears in her eyes.

Rusty quickly put his arm around her. "Hey, it's OK. Don't cry, honey. You know, I bet we can find one here. Isn't that right, Mom?"

"You bet we can. We can go shopping tomorrow. Problem solved!" Mandy stated.

"I just don't know how I forgot to do that!" Sally was so upset with herself.

Rusty gently turned Sally's face toward him. "Babe, you were so busy trying to take care of so many other things. It's OK." He leaned over and kissed her.

"Ahh, that's so precious," Mandy smiled.

Still, Sally felt terrible that she forgot something so very important, but she tried to regain her composure. *After all,* she told herself, *it wasn't the end of the world.*

Sally and the others finished their meal, and Sally helped Mandy clean up the kitchen. Todd and Pace ran upstairs to play. Rusty and his dad discussed a storage area for the things Sally wanted to keep and what to do with items that they really didn't need.

The kitchen clean-up was completed, and the ladies rejoined the men at the table. The wedding became the main topic. The cake was ordered, the rings were bought, Sally's dress was going to be found, the men would wear their suits and ties, Rusty needed a best man, and Sally needed someone to serve as her maid of honor as well as someone to walk her down the aisle.

"Well, it's a no-brainer! Dad can be my best man. Right, Dad?" Rusty said as he looked at his dad.

"Absolutely, son!" I'd be proud to be," Russell agreed with a hint of a tear in his eyes.

Rusty looked at Sally. "Now, Sally, I'm sorry you've not met more ladies of our community—"

"You don't need to say anymore. Mandy, would you be my matron of honor?" Sally asked.

"Oh, sweet girl, I'd be delighted. Thank you!" Mandy rejoiced.

"Thank you, Sally." Rusty smiled from ear to ear.

"So, who will walk your girl down the aisle? It can't be you, Rusty, and it can't be me either," Russell said.

"I know who!" Mandy declared.

"Who?" Rusty asked.

"None other than her two sweet little sons," Mandy answered.

Now Sally was grinning from ear to ear. "That's perfect, Mandy!" Sally reached across the table and took Mandy's hands. "Thank you!"

"Dad, can you ask several church men to be available to escort the guests to their seats?" Rusty asked.

"Sure, I can do that."

"I'll ask a few ladies at the church to oversee the reception," Mandy volunteered.

"What else?" Rusty thought out loud.

"What about flowers? The men and boys need boutonnieres, and Mandy and I need bouquets," Sally said.

"And we need some flowers for the church," Mandy chimed in.

"Oh, yes, some, but not a lot, right?" Rusty questioned.

"Some. We'll see," Mandy guessed.

"What about the rings? Who will have them?" Russell asked.

"Yeah, good thought, Dad," Rusty realized.

The four of them were quiet.

"Well . . ." began Sally as she looked at Rusty, "your dad could have your ring, and Mandy could have mine. Or Todd could have one, and Pace could have the other one. Just a thought."

"That's a thought! I don't know," Russell said.

"I know! That's easy. The boys! After they walk Sally down the aisle, we can have small pillows sitting on the first pew with the rings tied to them. After Sally takes her place beside me, the boys can get the pillows. Then, one can come and stand by Mom, and the other can come and stand by Dad. At the prompted time, each boy can present the ring. What do you think about that idea?" Rusty suggested.

"It could work," Russell agreed.

"Pastor Frank will have a rehearsal early the evening on June 6th, so he can walk all of us through the wedding procedure," Rusty said.

"That's good to know," Russell responded.

"So, Mom, do you and Sally want to go dress shopping tomorrow and go to the florist?" Rusty inquired.

"Yes, if that's OK with Sally. I know y'all have quite a bit of unpacking and putting away to do, but we probably should look soon so you know you have your dress," Mandy suggested.

Sally looked at Rusty.

"It's OK with me, sweetheart," he said.

"Yes. Thank you, Mandy," Sally replied respectively.

"I believe we have accomplished a lot for the wedding, and that's good. Thank you, Mom, for inviting us to dinner, but if you all will excuse us, we need to get home. I'll see you tomorrow, Dad, when Mom and Sally go shopping. Hopefully we can figure out what we can do with all the extra furniture," Rusty said.

"OK, son," answered Russell.

"Come on, boys. We need to go." Sally called them from the foot of the stairs. They ran down the steps and passed her like lightning, running out the door.

Sally hugged Russell and Mandy. "What time tomorrow?" Sally asked.

"Maybe 10 a.m. The shops will be open by then," Mandy suggested.

"See you then," Sally agreed.

Rusty, Sally, and the boys said their goodbyes, and Rusty drove them toward home. Rusty was glad they were able to discuss the wedding and that decisions were made. "Oh, Sally, I'm getting so excited!" Rusty expressed as he took Sally's hand. "I love you so much."

"I love you too, sweetheart. I think you're going to have to pinch me again. It's hard for me to believe it's really happening! All the wedding plans . . . yes, I'm excited too!" Sally leaned over and put her head on Rusty's shoulder.

When Rusty drove up to the house, Prince and Princess welcomed them. "They need to be fed. You boys want to do that?" Rusty asked.

"Yes, sir," both Todd and Pace answered at the same time.

Once the front door was unlocked and opened, the boys dashed toward the kitchen, the shepherds following right behind them.

Sally and Rusty had to make decisions about the added furniture. Sally wanted to keep the boys' beds and have them continue to sleep in one room for now. Rusty agreed. The bedroom with one bed was transformed into the boys' room with their beds, chest of drawers, and desk.

Rusty didn't want to change his bedroom, and that was fine with Sally. However, her dresser was moved into his bedroom.

There were empty cabinets in the kitchen, and Sally was able to easily fit her dishes and cookware. She stored away bath and hand towels, blankets, etc., on empty shelves in the hall closet. She hung up her clothing as well as the boys' in their closets. It was a late night, but all the boxes were unpacked.

"Dad and I will discuss where the best place will be to store your dining room table and chairs, the couch and chair, your bedroom suite, and the washer and dryer tomorrow. You tired, honey? I am. It's late." Rusty looked at his watch.

"Yes, I am tired. The boys were playing in their room. I'll check on them." Sally walked toward their bedroom. She found them already in their beds, asleep. She covered them with their blankets. The shepherds had taken up their normal places at the foot of the boys' beds. Sally smiled and remarked to herself, *Prince and Princess are precious to want to be near the boys.*

"The boys are already in their beds and asleep," Sally told Rusty as she walked toward him. She took his hands, and they retreated to his bedroom. He closed the door, and in a short time, they were in bed, cuddling and snuggling.

It was Memorial Day, but the cows did not know it was a holiday, and to dairy farmers, it was just another day. Rusty whispered in Sally's hear that he needed to go to the farm for a while and help his dad. He'd try not to be gone long. He slipped out of bed, dressed, and left quietly. A little while later, Sally got up and made coffee. The shepherds heard her and came into the kitchen. She fed them and let them out the back door.

Sally hadn't called Peggy yet since she arrived at the farm, so she needed to. With the telephone handset in her hand, the ringing sound began.

"Hello?" Peggy answered.

"Hi, Peggy. It's Sally. Just wanted you to know we made it OK. Hope you are OK?"

"Hi, Sally. I'm OK now and glad y'all are there. Are y'all OK?" Peggy asked.

"Yes, we are OK. You stay safe, and we'll talk again soon. Love ya," Sally said.

"Love you and the boys too. Thank you for calling. Yes, please call again soon, Sally." And the call ended.

Sally believed Peggy was about to cry. The call was short but necessary to keep Peggy from worrying about them. She needed to send Peggy her new address and telephone number so Peggy could call her too.

The coffee was ready, and Sally poured herself a cup. She decided to enjoy it by sitting in the screened-in room. It was a beautiful morning, but she soon heard the steps of her little sons. First, Pace entered the room, then Todd. They told her they really liked their new room, and they had lots of room to play.

Sally went back to the kitchen to prepare breakfast when Rusty came in with a basket full of breakfast foods. He was just in time. Rusty couldn't stay, but he asked for Sally to bring the boys to his parents' house, and he would watch them while she and his mom did their shopping. Sally agreed. They kissed, and he left again.

After they ate breakfast, Todd and Pace chose their own clothes and dressed themselves. Sally was very pleased! She dressed in some clothes that would be easy to take off, since she was going to be trying on dresses.

At 9:45, Sally and the boys left Rusty's house. She drove them to the Summers' home. Rusty and his mother met Sally at the car. Rusty opened the car door for his mom to get in, and the boys got out. The ladies waved goodbye as they headed off to shop.

Mandy suggested going to the florist first. The Flower Store was her favorite. Several of the staff attended Mandy's church, and she knew them well. When they entered the store, some of the staff approached Mandy and hugged her. Mandy introduced Sally as her soon-to-be daughter-in-law. The ladies were very friendly to Sally, and all of them congratulated her. Mandy explained that the wedding was going to be June 7th at the church, and she gave the ladies the flower list that they needed to order for the attendees. She asked for enough white netting for ten rows of pews on both sides of the church with blue and white bows with streamers. She also ordered two vases of flowers for the reception table. The florist employees had furnished flowers many times for weddings and such, so Mandy knew they knew what to do to make the special occasion perfect.

Sally felt like Mandy may be overdoing the flowers for the wedding, but it was not her place to say so. She was grateful Mandy was doing what she was doing. And what she was doing might be more for Rusty, since his first wedding was much different from his and Sally's wedding.

Next, it was off to the dress shop. Sally thought she knew what she wanted—nothing real fancy or elaborate, but no plain Jane either. The first and second shop had nothing Sally desired. But at the third shop, she spotted a beautiful full-length, soft-flowing, baby blue sleeveless dress with a white lace sequined bodice. It was a little pricy, but Sally really liked it, and it fit her small-framed body perfectly.

As Sally paid for the dress, she saw Mandy talking to the sales lady. Then, Mandy walked toward Sally.

"I hope you don't mind, Sally, but I asked the lady to hold the dress for you until June 6th. I know it will be safe here, and that way we don't risk Rusty seeing it before the wedding."

At first, Sally wasn't so sure, but Mandy explained that the old tradition was that the groom should not see the bride's dress before he sees it on his bride on their wedding day.

"I like your thinking, Mandy. Good idea. Thank you," Sally agreed.

Mandy motioned to the lady that it was OK.

On the way back to the Summers' home, Mandy mentioned several times how much she appreciated Sally allowing her to be a part of such an important day. It really meant a lot to Mandy. She added that when Rusty married before, neither she nor Russell were allowed to be involved in any way. So, to her and her husband, this was Rusty's first real marriage. They wanted to make it really special for him and, of course, for Sally too.

Sally understood, and she was glad that Mandy wanted to make it special for their son. Sally was just thrilled that she was marrying her knight in shining armor—the love of her life. She, too, wanted to make it perfect for Rusty.

Upon returning to Mandy's home, Sally found Rusty and the boys upstairs attempting to learn how to play ping pong. She heard Rusty saying that "they had to keep their eyes on the ball." When Todd saw his mother, he told her that playing ping pong was harder than it looked!

"Come on, Mom, try it," Todd encouraged her.

"Ah, not today, but soon. OK?" Sally replied.

"OK," Todd answered.

They all came downstairs and joined Mandy in the kitchen. She expressed to Rusty that she was most thankful that Sally agreed to let her go with her on their shopping spree. It was fun and productive. Then Mandy took leftover food from the refrigerator and put it in a basket to give Rusty and his family for dinner. They said their goodbyes, and Rusty, Sally, and the boys left for home.

As soon as they stepped into the house, Sally noticed her furniture was gone. Rusty explained that his dad had a small building inside a big building on the farm, and he and the farmhands moved her things over there. He told her the things were "double protected!"

Sally rolled her eyes.

Todd and Pace ran from their room, and Todd shouted, "Mom, come see this!" Pace grabbed his mother's hand and pulled her to his bedroom. Sally glanced at Rusty, and he just shrugged his shoulders and shook his head.

"See it?" Todd excitedly asked. Their television from their old house was sitting on the old telephone desk, and the television was on.

Rusty slipped in the doorway and watched. "You boys are surprised! I'm happy you are. Dad had an old antenna and some rabbit ears and, voilà—television!" Rusty explained.

The boys ran and hugged Rusty. "You're great, Rusty! Thank you." Todd was so happy.

"Thank you, Rusty," Pace echoed.

"OK, let's go eat. I'm hungry!" Rusty suggested.

Sally wrapped her arms around Rusty's waist. "You've got friends—no, let's make that *sons*—for life!"

Rusty smiled a huge smile.

After dinner, the shepherds and the horses were fed. The boys showered, and it was bedtime for all of them.

For the next five days, the routine was mostly the same. Rusty helped his dad at the farm, the boys and Sally went back and forth to the farm, the four of them ate dinner together, they fed Prince and Princess as well as Chief and Sundown, they played games, then they all showered and went to bed. But when Sunday came, it was church day. Todd, Pace, Rusty, and Russell dressed in suits and ties, and Mandy and Sally looked very prim and proper.

Sally and the boys were nervous about going to a new church, but they needed to get used to it. Bright Heaven Baptist Church looked much different on the outside than Cherish Baptist Church in Memphis, and oh, yes, it did on the inside too! But folks were friendly and pleasant. Rusty introduced Sally, Todd, and Pace to some of the church members before it was time to take their seats. Todd and Pace looked around at the congregation and saw some other kids about their age. The church service was about the same as their old church, but there was no children's church. It was a little hard for the boys to sit still after a while, but they tried.

Many people approached Rusty and congratulated him and Sally on their upcoming wedding, and they said they planned to attend.

After church, Rusty drove them home, and they changed clothes. Rusty then explained to Sally that every Sunday, his mother would prepare a meal, and they would spend the day together. Sally recalled her Sundays growing up. After church, her brother and his wife would join her mom, dad, and her for a meal her mother prepared. After the meal, the rest of the afternoon was spent watching television or playing games. Sally told Rusty it was refreshing that his family still does that.

The next morning, after Rusty spent several hours at the farm, he took Sally and the boys into town to visit the bakery and the florist to make sure everything was on schedule for June 7th. The storekeepers assured him all would be ready for the 7 p.m. wedding. Rusty breathed a deep sigh of relief. He wanted and needed everything to be perfect!

After a restless night, Sally quietly got out of Rusty's bed and went into the kitchen to begin her coffee. She looked at the clock on the stove, and it was only 2:30 a.m.! The shepherds slowly walked into the kitchen, blinking their eyes a lot as they were trying to get their eyes adjusted to the bright light. They may have realized it was too early to be up, so they walked out of the kitchen back to the boys' room.

Sally filled her cup with coffee, walked to the table, and sat down in a chair. She wondered what was going on with her. She asked the Lord to help her as she felt uneasy and stressed. But why? Could she be getting cold feet, or was it second thoughts about marrying Rusty? Sally knew she loved Rusty, but was she prepared for his lifestyle? He was at the farm almost every day, all day long. She missed being with him and doing things together. Then, she remembered he told her during their encounter at the Jackson truck stop that his life was driving over-the-road, and he was hardly home. Was this what her life was going to be like, and is it much different than what it was like with Collin? She felt very lonely. She attempted to reason with herself that if Rusty worked at a different job, he'd still be away from home during the day, so, what difference did it make?

Sally stepped out into the screened-in room, then out the door to the backyard. She breathed in the early morning air. It was refreshing, and in a way, it was consoling to her confused mind. She walked along the gravel path. Suddenly, she felt a cool breeze as it rustled the tree branches and leaves above her. She looked up and saw past the trees' canopy to a black sky dotted with bright shining stars. She realized God's blessings were all around her, and she was right where He wanted her to be. She wouldn't be there if God didn't orchestrate for her and Rusty's paths to cross months ago. She smiled as a calmness came over her. God revealed to her that she loved the man He planned for her, and everything else in her life was under His control. Her anxiety disappeared, and she felt the burden lifted. She glanced up at the night sky again and thanked the Lord for His mercy, grace, and answer to her prayer.

Rusty never knew about Sally's apprehension about marrying him early that morning in June, and the next several days went just as they should have.

Friday night's wedding rehearsal was perfect. Due to pre-marriage tradition, Mandy and Russell extended an invitation to Sally and the boys to stay with them so that the groom wouldn't be able to see his bride before the wedding. It meant bad luck if they were to see each other, apparently.

However, the 7th proved to be somewhat tricky as Rusty had to come to the farm to help his dad. Todd and Pace were told to keep an eye out for Rusty and alert Sally if he had to come inside the Summers' home. Sally had to stay out of sight!

Mandy went to the dress shop and picked up Sally's dress. Then, she needed to go to Rusty's house. With Sally's instructions, Mandy found Todd and Pace's suits, ties, shirts, shoes, and other clothing for the wedding as well as Sally's shoes, makeup, etc., for her special night.

The afternoon was fading away. It was time for Rusty to go home to shower and dress. Meanwhile, at the Summers' home, Sally helped Todd and Pace get dressed. Russell and the boys left the Summers' home, picked up Rusty, and headed for the church.

Mandy helped Sally get dressed. Looking at Sally, Mandy said, "You look beautiful, and your dress is gorgeous." Mandy turned away from Sally for a moment to open a box. "I asked the sales lady to fashion you a little something else." She unfolded an elegant light blue sequined veil with a light blue jeweled tiara that, when placed on top of Sally's head, would allow the veil to pour over Sally's shoulders to her waist.

Sally looked at her reflection in the full-length mirror. She was stunned at her appearance. "Mandy. . . ." tears filled Sally's eyes. "The veil is beautiful. Thank you so much!"

"No, my child. *You're* beautiful! The veil is just a shadow of your beauty. Come, we need to go." Mandy took Sally's hand. They got in Mandy's car and drove to the church. Mandy asked Sally to stay in the car. She was going into the church to make sure the coast was clear for her to enter the building. A few minutes later, Mandy motioned for Sally to come inside. Sally carefully exited the car and walked up the sidewalk to the door of the church.

Once inside, Mandy directed Sally to a side room where she could relax and wait for her turn to walk down the aisle.

During that thirty-minute wait, Mandy left Sally to check on the preparations for the reception. When she returned to the room, she had Todd and Pace with her. When Sally's sons saw her, their faces lit up.

"Mom, you are beautiful!" Todd exclaimed.

"You are really very pretty, too, Momma!" Pace added joyfully.

"Thank you both! You two look so handsome in your light blue suits. And I love the little boutonnieres!" Sally complimented her young men.

"Are you nervous, Mom?" Todd asked.

"Yes, a little," Sally replied.

"Are you?" Sally asked him.

"Yes, some," Todd answered.

"You and Pace did so well last night. Just do the same thing tonight. You too, Pace. Y'all will be fine. Let's say a little prayer." Sally took her sons' hands, and they bowed their heads. "Dear heavenly Father and our Savior Jesus Christ, we come before You, and we ask You to take the nervousness from my sons as they serve in my wedding. Please allow them to remember what they are to do. I thank You so much for them. They are special, Lord! We ask these things in Your Son's precious and holy name. Amen."

"Thank you, Momma," Pace said.

"Yes, thank you, Mom. I feel better!" remarked Todd.

They began to hear music playing. It was 7 p.m. A knock on the door sounded. Mandy opened the door slowly. One of the ushers softly told Mandy that it was time to begin her walk. Mandy stepped out of the room and took her place at the end of the church aisle. Then, she began to walk toward the altar.

The usher motioned for Sally and the boys to step out of the room. When Mandy arrived in her designated spot, the organist began to play "Here Comes the Bride." Everyone in the church stood up and turned, facing the church aisle. Sally placed Todd's hand around her left elbow, then she placed Pace's hand around her right elbow, and they began their walk toward the altar. Sally saw Rusty, and she smiled. He was so incredibly handsome!

Rusty saw Sally, and he smiled back at her. *She looks breathtaking and unbelievably beautiful!* he thought. Sally heard "awws" from the attendees when they saw Todd and Pace walking her down the aisle.

When she reached her spot, the pastor asked, "Who gives this bride to this groom tonight?"

"We do. Her sons," Todd and Pace answered together. The boys stepped away from their mother and sat down in the front pew. Rusty took his place beside Sally. Their eyes met with love and admiration. He mouthed to her that she was beautiful. Sally smiled at him. She then handed her bouquet to Mandy. Rusty took Sally's arm, and they walked together two steps up toward Pastor Frank.

"Let's pray," the pastor said. "Dear heavenly Father, our Creator and our Sustainer of life, we ask Your blessings upon Sally and Rusty as they pledge themselves to each other in holy matrimony. Allow their love and faith in You to guide them as they begin their lives together. We ask this in Jesus' name. Amen." Pastor Frank continued. "We are gathered here tonight in the presence of God to join this man and this woman in holy marriage. Romans 12:9 says, 'Love must be sincere. Hate what is evil, cling to what is good.' Colossians 3:4 tells us, 'And over all these virtues, put on love, which binds them all together in perfect unity.' Ephesians 4:2 says to, 'Always be completely humble and gentle; be patient, bearing with one another in love.'" Pastor Frank then motioned for Todd and Pace to come forward with the ring pillows.

Todd stood by his mother, and Pace stood beside his almost stepdad.

Rusty took Sally's ring from Pace's pillow, and he took Sally's left hand.

Pastor Frank said to Rusty, "Repeat after me. *I, Rusty Summers, take you, Sally Oldham, to be my wedded wife. To have and to hold from this day forward, for better, for worse, for richer, for poorer, in sickness and in health, to love and to cherish, until death do us part. I give you this ring as a symbol of these vows.*"

Rusty repeated the vows, then he slid Sally's wedding ring on her finger.

Then, Sally took Rusty's ring from Todd's pillow and took Rusty's left hand.

Pastor Frank said to Sally, "Repeat after me. *I, Sally Oldham, take you, Rusty Summers, as my wedded husband. To have and to hold from this day forward, for better, for worse, for richer or for poorer, in sickness and in health, to love and to cherish, until death do us part. I give you this ring as a symbol of these vows.*"

Sally repeated the vows, then she slid Rusty's wedding band on his finger.

Pastor Frank continued the service. "Let us pray. Heavenly Father, please help Rusty and Sally to be understanding and forgiving of human weaknesses and failings. Increase their faith and trust in You, and may You guide their lives and love. Bless their marriage with peace and happiness, and make their love beautiful for Your glory. Amen." Pastor Frank then looked up at the happy couple. "Now I pronounce you two *husband* and *wife*. You may kiss your bride!"

Rusty took Sally in his arms, and they kissed passionately.

Mandy handed Sally her bouquet as she and Rusty turned to face the people who came to witness this wonderful celebration.

Pastor Frank rejoiced. "Family and friends, I'm honored to introduce to all of you, Mr. and Mrs. Rusty Summers!"

Everyone began clapping as Sally and Rusty stepped off the platform and walked hand in hand down the aisle and out the front door, where they enjoyed a few more loving kisses with each other.

"Mrs. Sally Summers, I love you with all my heart!" Rusty declared loudly.

"Oh, Mr. Rusty Summers, I love you and will always love you totally and completely!" Sally cried with overwhelming joy.

"Come on, newlyweds. We need to do pictures!" Mandy said.

Rusty and Sally came back into the church. Sally hadn't noticed before, but the church was decorated beautifully, thanks to Mandy. The photographer began taking picture after picture of the bride and groom and the whole wedding party. It was all so exciting!

Finally, the couple joined the celebration downstairs in the reception hall. The hall was decorated just as Mandy had planned. It, too, was beautiful.

The bride and groom enjoyed meeting all their guests who came through the reception line. Then it was time to cut the beautiful wedding cake, and, of course, the traditional *feeding each other the first bites of the cake* was a must! The cake was then served to the guests, along with some punch. There were a few toasts given to the new couple, then the many wedding gifts were opened. Todd and Pace were so in awe of everything that was happening and were very happy for their mother.

As the newlyweds were about to leave the church, Rusty surprised Sally by telling her they were going to go away on a New York City honeymoon. Rusty already had their bags packed, and Mandy and Russell were going to keep the boys for three days while they were gone. Sally was so excited, but she wanted to make sure the boys were OK with that plan. They had already been told and were more than excited to be staying at their new grandparents' house!

Sally bent down in front of them and hugged them. "I'll miss y'all, but we'll be back in a few days. Please be good little men for your mother." She got serious for a moment. "I'm so proud of both of you. You two were perfect in the service. Thank y'all for walking me down the aisle. That was so special for me! We've gotta go now. I love y'all bunches!"

Rusty picked up both boys and told them that they'd see them soon, and he would take good care of their mother. Todd and Pace hugged Rusty's neck before he placed them back on the floor. Rusty's parents hugged the newlyweds. Rusty and Sally thanked them for everything they had done for their beautiful wedding.

Then Rusty grabbed Sally's hand, and they ran out of the church door. Immediately the well-wishers threw rice upon the couple as they ran to Rusty's truck, which was decorated from hood to tailgate with crepe paper streamers and tin cans tied on the back bumper of his truck. Once Rusty and Sally were in the truck and began to drive away, everyone yelled farewells to them. Sally snuggled close to Rusty as he drove toward the Big Apple. They couldn't stop talking about their wonderful evening.

Two hours later, they were settling into their hotel honeymoon suite, enjoying each other as newlyweds. New York City was full of so many things to do, places to go, and so much to see. And the newlyweds were eager to do everything they could while they were there.

After a beautiful night, Rusty and Sally awoke with lots of plans. Their first adventure was to see the Statue of Liberty. Rusty bought tickets, and they took the ferry to Liberty Island. They climbed the three hundred fifty-four steps to Lady Liberty's crown, and the views from the twenty-five windows were absolutely breathtaking!

The couple ferried back to Manhattan, and Rusty drove to Time's Square in Midtown. Finding a parking space was terrible, but Rusty finally found one, and he and Sally were fascinated by all the glitter and glamor of the high-rise buildings, the fancy billboards high above them, the many theaters, the sidewalk cafes, and the extremely fancy restaurants. They stopped into Joe's Pizzeria. The sign on the window read, "The Best Pizza on Broadway," and the couple were very impressed indeed. The pizza was delicious.

It was late afternoon, and their next stop was Coney Island. The Summers' strolled on the Boardwalk with the white sandy beach on one side as well as a bunch of food stands. On the other side was Luna Park Amusement Park, with an assortment of thrill rides, a few roller coasters, and lots of midway-style games. Sally and Rusty decided to ride a few of the rides, and they were thrilling! Rusty tried his hand at the games as well, and he won Sally several stuffed animals.

The sun had set, and the Island's many colorful lights came on. It was amazingly beautiful. Rusty and Sally's arms were around each other's waists as they walked on the Boardwalk once again, back to Rusty's truck.

By that point, the newlyweds were exhausted and were glad to be in their hotel room. They decided to order dinner by room service. It had been a long day but a very exciting one. They saw and did things for the first time together, and they made many memories.

It was the second day of their honeymoon, and the Summers' slept in for a while. But after breakfast, they were on the move again.

The Empire State Building is very famous. As Sally stood in front of the building, she read the sign out loud to Rusty:

There are 73 elevators, 103 floors with 1,860 steps from street level to the 102 floor's observation deck. At the top, there are 360 degrees of breathtaking views of the New York City skyline. On a clear day, one can see 6 states and a distance of 80 miles! It's one of the tallest structures in the world.

"Well, are you ready to go check it out?" Rusty asked.

"Yes! Let's go!" Sally answered.

The elevator ride was ear-popping, but when they stepped off and approached the windows, the views were, yes, breathtaking! It was a sunny, clear day, and Rusty and Sally could see what seemed like forever. An employee was telling visitors where the six different states were from different viewing places. It was amazing. Between the Statue of Liberty and the Empire State Building, the views from both were astonishing.

Back at ground level, they walked the twenty-five minutes to Central Park. While at the park, they grabbed several famous foot-long, fully-loaded hot dogs. They were really good but a lot to eat!

Central Park was huge at 840 acres, with eight lakes and ponds and beautiful bridges over them. There were big trees and lots of walkways. There were green areas where people were lying on blankets and children were playing. It was a peaceful place in a hustle and bustle city! Rusty and Sally relaxed on a bench and watched the people walk by and the squirrels play in the trees.

On the way back to the hotel, Rusty and Sally had dinner at a small café. The food was good, and the atmosphere was tranquil.

Back at their hotel room, they showered and then snuggled each other before falling to sleep.

When Rusty opened his eyes from sleeping, he saw Sally smiling at him.

"Good morning, my handsome hunk!" she greeted him.

Rusty smiled back and took Sally in his arms. "Good morning, my beautiful wife. I love you."

"I love you too." Sally kissed his lips. "I have had the most wonderful time with you on our honeymoon. Thank you so very much. I would have never dreamed of spending this time with you in New York City. Such an awesome surprise!"

"Honey, it has been great! I wanted to do something special for you, and I thought of other places for us to go, but I knew you'd never been to New York City. It's a fun place with lots to do. I'm sorry we'll leave today, but we'll come again. I'm so glad you've had a good time." Rusty drew Sally's body close to him and kissed her lovingly.

After a while, they were up and dressed. Rusty helped Sally repack their suitcases, and they left the room—but definitely not the memories they made. They would hold them dear to their hearts. Rusty knew of a quaint diner where they could stop for breakfast near Port Chester where the outdoor patio overlooked the water of the Long Island Sound.

The New York City traffic was hectic, but Rusty's driving capabilities got them safely through the city. After nearly an hour, Rusty parked his truck at the diner and helped Sally get out. Right away, Sally smelled the sea air and heard and saw seagulls flying overhead.

Upon entering the diner, Rusty waved to the person behind the counter and motioned with his hand. He led Sally out a door to an outside patio seating area. They sat down at a table that was nearest to the water's edge. The view was exceptional! The sun's reflection off the water made it glisten and sparkle with each ripple of the water. The water's action was almost mesmerizing!

A young woman hurried out the patio door and headed straight for Rusty with open arms. As she hugged Rusty, she joyfully expressed, " It's good to see you again! Where have you been? I've been missing you!"

Rusty looked at Sally who was a bit confused. "Kim, I'd like for you to meet the lady of my dreams! This is Sally, my wife."

Kim's face broke out into a big smile, and she immediately bent down and hugged Sally. "Congratulations, you two! That's wonderful. It's nice to meet you, Sally. You've got one great guy here." Kim leaned slightly toward Rusty. "She's beautiful," she spoke softly, but still loud enough for Sally to hear.

"I know. I'm blessed!" Rusty acknowledged softly.

"So what can I get you two to drink?" Kim asked with her pencil and meal order book in her hands.

"Coffee for both of us with cream and sugar, please," Rusty ordered. "And we'd like two of your delicious big breakfast meals too."

"Two coffees, coming up," Kim replied as she walked away.

Sally looked at Rusty with a look of wonder.

"I know. Who is this woman, right? No need to ask that question. I know that look you're giving me! Kim and I have known each other since first grade. And no, we were not lovers, just really good friends all these years," Rusty explained. "We're OK?"

Sally smiled. "We're fine, sweetheart."

Kim returned with their coffee. "I haven't seen you in a while. Everything OK?"

Rusty told her about meeting Sally, about his dad's heart attack that has had him grounded from driving, and about the bad snowstorm and how it affected the farm.

Kim was saddened about the news of Rusty's dad and the storm's setback, but she was very happy for Rusty and Sally's relationship. She went back into the diner, and within moments she reentered with their breakfast meals.

When Rusty and Sally had finished breakfast and paid the bill, they bid farewell to Kim and began their journey back home.

Their reunion with Todd and Pace was happy and cheerful. The boys were glad to see their mother and their new stepdad home again. Mandy and Russell hugged them and gave them welcome-back greetings. Mandy poured a cup of coffee for each of them while Sally and Rusty talked about their honeymoon and all the places they saw. As they were leaving to go home, Rusty told his dad that he would return after getting Sally and the boys settled at home. Russell told him to rest, and he'd see Rusty tomorrow.

When Rusty stopped the truck, he asked Sally to wait for him. He walked to the front door, unlocked it, and walked back to the truck. He helped Sally out of the driver's side, then he swooped her up into his arms. She wrapped her arms around Rusty's neck. He walked through the door, carrying her over the threshold. He kissed her tenderly and said, "Welcome home, Mrs. Summers!"

Sally looked at Rusty and told him she looked forward to a life full of love for her and her sons, but most of all, a lifetime of love, devotion, and caring for and with him.

Rusty was her knight in shining armor, the love of her life, and her handsome hunk!

Epilogue

As Rusty and Sally had done for nineteen years, Rusty, again, drove them to Midtown Manhattan, and they celebrated their twentieth wedding anniversary at the same quaint café where they ate on their honeymoon: The Sweet Carnation Café. But on this particular anniversary, June 7, 2000, they had the place to themselves. As they sat in the quiet café, Rusty and Sally turned back the clock as they reminisced about their life of many blessings, some sadness, and lots of excitement.

Just a few weeks after their wedding, Rusty's dad was cleared by his heart doctor to resume the duties of running the farm. It had been a very long and hard six months for Russell and Rusty, but the whole family rejoiced in Russell's full recovery and that life could get back to normal.

Rusty wasted no time returning to driving over-the-road, but not to Abilene. Rusty's boss gave him short runs as Rusty requested so he could be home more often with his family that he dearly loved.

Todd and Barbie exchanged "puppy love" letters and phone calls often for several years, but as time went on, there were fewer and fewer. However, they did see each other during a 1982 summer trip back to Memphis. Todd called Barbie and asked her to go to dinner with him and his family. She accepted. The couple seemed to enjoy each other's company, and he was glad he got to see her again.

Part of the trip was to visit with Peggy. Sally called Peggy at least once a week after leaving Memphis in May of 1980. To keep a friendly relationship with her, Sally didn't tell Peggy about her marriage to Rusty for six months. When she finally did, Peggy was surprised but happy for Sally. Peggy had decided to continue living in Memphis. It was good to see her and for all of them to spend time together.

After their visit with Peggy, it was on to Houston to introduce Rusty to Sally's brother, sister-in-law, and their children. They had recently moved to Houston from Dallas for better employment opportunities. It was a long drive, but it was great to see all of them. The family really liked Rusty!

The first summer was very different for Todd and Pace. When Rusty was home, they still helped out at the farm some, enjoyed riding their horses, spent hours at the beach, and learned how to keep their eyes on that ping pong ball.

For the first few months, each Sunday at church, Mandy made sure the whole family socialized. After a short while, the boys became friends with the other kids, as Rusty and Sally had become more active in church activities—such as picnic socials and the Founder's Day event, among others.

By the time school started that fall, Todd and Pace were excited about going to a new school.

With the boys back in school and Rusty's trips in the big rig, Sally had more time to spend with Mandy, working on church projects and helping her serve the Lord in their church activities. Sally saw how creative Mandy was, and she learned many things from her.

Sally asked Pastor Frank if she and Mandy could prepare and serve Wednesday night meals for church members who would like a meal before the evening prayer meetings. He took her request to the church board, and the suggestion was accepted. It was a huge success!

As more and more young couples with children moved into the area and began attending the church, Sally expressed her concern to the board and offered a solution for those youngsters who were becoming restless during adult worship service: add a children's church. She volunteered herself and Rusty, who was always home on Sundays, to teach children's church. The church board was excited about the idea and approved the plan. The children really liked having their own church time, and the parents were delighted as well.

Several years after Sally and Rusty married, Rusty asked Sally if it was too late to start a family with him. Sally knew Rusty wanted children, and she agreed. God heard their prayers, and within a year, Sally gave Rusty a son, Russell the III, who looked just like his dad and granddad! Mandy and Russell were more than thrilled to finally be grandparents. Little Rusty started getting spoiled from the day he was born.

Four months later, to Sally and Rusty's surprise, what they thought was several months of sickness turned out to be . . . another pregnancy! That pregnancy reminded Sally of the hard time she had carrying Pace, but all the health problems were forgotten when their daughter was born five months later. Rusty and Sally decided to name her Sadie, after his mother's first name (Sadie Amanda Summers), which made Mandy very happy. Todd and Pace enjoyed having siblings, and Rusty was thrilled to have children of his own.

Life for Sally and Rusty became very active with two babies and two pre-teen young men. Todd and Pace were doing extremely well in school, and they were playing in all sports. Rusty, Sally, Lil' Rusty, and Sadie went to as many of the boys' games as they could, and Grandpa and Grandma joined often. When the whole family was able to go to the games, the other parents would say, "Well, the gang's all here!" It was always fun, especially when Lil' Rusty and Sadie got older.

In September 1984, Todd entered into high school. That was definitely a *red letter day!* Just one year later, Pace entered into high school in September 1985. Both Pace and Todd were very active in all their high school sports.

The day after Thanksgiving in 1985, Sally received a dreaded phone call from Ellen, telling her tearfully that her mother had passed away in the night from a massive heart attack. Peggy had a heart attack earlier in the year, but even after she had surgery, she was always tired, and she never regained her full strength. In Sally's weekly conversations with Peggy, she could hear a difference in Peggy's voice. Her cute little sayings that had made Sally laugh were gone, and so was Peggy's interest in life. Sally longed for those wonderful times with Peggy.

Ellen called Sally several days later to discuss Peggy's funeral. Sally expressed to Rusty that she needed to go and pay her respects to her former mother-in-law. Rusty understood, and Sally made flight arrangements. Rusty adjusted his driving schedule so he could be home to take care of the children.

After Sally flew from Bridgeport to LaGuardia, the remainder of her trip was non-stop to Memphis. Ellen met her at the airport, and after getting caught up on family news over lunch, they went to the funeral home.

After a nice but sad service, Sally called for a cab. While she waited, she asked Ellen about Collin since she didn't see him at his mother's funeral. Ellen explained to her that when she called Collin to tell him about their mother's death, he thanked her for calling but said he would not be coming to the funeral. Then he hung up without another word!

Just then, Sally's cab arrived. She and Ellen hugged good-bye, and Ellen thanked her for coming to the funeral.

As the cab driver drove Sally to the airport, Sally thought about what Ellen had just told her and how truly uncaring Collin still was. She was so sad that he didn't seem to have changed and that he didn't even want to see his mother one last time, simply out of respect.

Sally boarded the plane and arrived in Bridgeport late that night. Her sweet husband was waiting for her with arms open wide!

January through May of the following year (1986), both Sally and Rusty taught Todd how to drive. In May, he passed his written driver's license test and received his driver's permit. He was so excited! It was a good learning experience for Pace, as his turn was coming up the next year.

Rusty and Todd went shopping for a vehicle soon after he received his permit. Several months later, they hit pay dirt. Todd drove home in a new, red 1985 truck. He was so proud of it! In the four months leading up to getting his real driver's license, Sally allowed him to use his portion of her child support check from Collin to fix up his truck the way he wanted it. On November 30th, Todd's 16th birthday, he drove his truck to school for the first time by himself.

In the months of January through May of 1987, Pace's driving skills came easy for him, and he passed his written test without any problems. The fanfare was just as exciting for Pace when he was given his driving permit. Again, Rusty took Pace vehicle shopping, and in no time at all, Pace drove up to his house and honked the horn. When Sally walked out the front door, she saw a new, shiny blue pickup truck. He had to take her for a ride in it. He was so excited! He got busy doing odd jobs to earn money to do a few modifications to his new truck. Sally offered to give him his share of her child support check, but he said he'd rather save that money for college.

Several days later, Todd graduated from high school. He was honored and celebrated for being a star athlete in all sports during all four years of high school. He also received a full-scholarship for football at the University of Connecticut but would ultimately choose to go a different route. Several months before graduation, Todd had received letters from colleges and universities, inviting him to visit their campuses. But his mind and heart were set on flying for the Air Force. He took a few weeks to enjoy being out of school and having fun with his friends before going to the United States Air Force recruiting office. Todd was greeted by a staff sergeant who asked him many questions. The sergeant needed to make sure and understand Todd's interest in joining the Air Force. The sergeant was satisfied with Todd's approach to joining the service and proceeded with the next steps. Several hours later, the sergeant shook Todd's hand and informed him that he should get a phone call or a letter in a week, instructing him of the Air Force's decision.

That week seemed like one of the longest weeks of their lives. But the letter and the phone call came. Todd was accepted, and he would report for basic training on August 1, 1987, at Lackland Air Force Base Basic Training Center in San Antonio, Texas. That date was five weeks away. Sally and Rusty were so proud of their son.

Todd decided to drive his truck instead of flying or taking a bus. Rusty and Todd looked at an atlas to determine the best route for Todd to take to San Antonio. It was much the same way Rusty drove to Abilene, except out of Dallas he would stay on Interstate 35 to San Antonio. Todd allowed four days to make the drive, and July 28th came quickly. His farewell was hard on the family, but that was the beginning of Todd's new life.

Todd called as often as he could, and after six weeks of basic training, it was time for his graduation. Rusty made arrangements with his boss to take a load of freight to San Antonio, and that one time was the acceptation for Sally and the kids to go with him.

Everyone was excited to get to go with Rusty in his big truck, and the trip went smoothly. Seeing Todd in his Air Force blue uniform was awesome. He was so handsome. He was all grown-up! Being able to see Todd and be with him for his graduation was worth the drive. Afterwards, they had lunch together. During that time, Todd told his folks he was remaining at Lackland to go to technical training school. Sally knew the military life from her dad, and she understood his decision.

All too soon, Rusty needed to get under his load and head north. Their goodbyes were tough, especially not knowing when they would see Todd again.

On November 19th, Pace turned 16, and he was proud as he drove his truck to school for the first time by himself, just as Todd did a year ago.

It was Pace's time to shine as he donned his cap and gown on a cool May evening for his high school graduation. When his name was called, and it was his turn to be given his diploma, the announcer acknowledged Pace's achievements in all sports, and, just like his brother, he graduated with honors and received a full-scholarship to Danbury State College. Rusty and Sally beamed with joy!

Even though Pace received invitations to visit different colleges and universities, Pace was only interested in attending Danbury State College. Immediately after graduation, he sought out ways to earn money.

Todd was doing well with his technical training, and he was learning a lot. He was getting closer to his goal of learning how to become an aviator. Several times he mentioned his girlfriend, Kate Amber, in his phone conversations.

Sally had mixed emotions when Lil' Rusty started kindergarten. He was very shy and almost teary-eyed on his first day, but after that, he was excited to go. His absence gave Sally and Rusty more time to spend with Sadie.

Pace was accepted into his choice college. On Saturdays and non-class days, he was busy being an entrepreneur. He definitely was a promoter of new business.

The holidays of 1988 came quickly, and when Todd took some leave time and came home from training at Christmas, he surprised his family by bringing Kate to meet them. She was very pretty, pleasant, and well-mannered, plus she was a major's daughter! Rusty and Sally noticed the look of love between the two young people. Todd and Kate's visit was only four days long, but their time together was special and valuable so the family could learn more about Todd's new very best friend. It was a wonderful Christmas.

The New Year of 1989 brought in illnesses to a lot of people, including the Summers' household. Lil' Rusty had been exposed to chicken pox, and he was sick for nearly a week. Another week passed, and Sadie began feeling bad. A few days later, her rash was noticeable. Even Sunday church services were canceled due to the children having chicken pox, and many adults also had influenza. Mandy and Russell didn't feel good, but they were not as sick as other folks.

By spring, most health problems had come full circle, and the community was getting back to normal. Todd called on Mother's Day with an announcement that he and Kate became engaged the evening before, and their marriage date was set for November 11th. He wanted Pace to be his best man, and he hoped all his folks would be able to come to San Antonio for their wedding. Sally told him that wild horses couldn't keep them away! She and Rusty were very happy for them.

School was out for the year, and Pace would be a sophomore in college, Lil' Rusty would be in first grade, and Sadie would start kindergarten come September.

Pace was doing well with his business, and Grandpa Russell allowed him to set up his office in one of the buildings on the farm to help him keep his overhead expense to zero.

It felt like all too soon the warm summer days were turning cooler as fall approached and school was back in session. And Todd and Kate's wedding was drawing near.

Arrangements were made for missing work and school, and Russell added on more help at the farm because Mandy and Russell told Rusty that they were not going to miss Todd's wedding.

Four days prior to the wedding date, Rusty rented a van so all seven people and their luggage would be accommodated. Early on the morning of November 8th, the van and all its passengers were en route to San Antonio. The trip was long, but lots of singing, game playing, and just talking made the trip bearable.

The day before the wedding, Todd took Pace to be fitted for his tuxedo. The Summers family enjoyed seeing the rehearsal for the wedding, and the rehearsal dinner was casual and relaxing. Kate's parents, Major Lee Amber and his wife, Lou, were southern-born and raised in Alabama. Sally instantly felt a connection with them.

Todd was able to secure lodging for his folks at the base housing reserved for out of town guests who were attending special events. Pace was invited to join the bachelor party that was thrown for Todd by some of his Air Force buddies.

That special fall Saturday morning was sunny and still warm in southern Texas. Everyone was up early and got dressed before heading to breakfast at a nearby restaurant just off the base property. Then, it was back to their rooms to dress for the 2 p.m. wedding.

Todd and Pace knocked on the door of their folks' room at 1 p.m. When Rusty opened the door, he was awestruck. The two young men he was looking at had grown up overnight and looked beyond dashing. Sally opened the door wider, and she became overwhelmed with emotion. Her two sons were looking ever so handsome. She couldn't help herself. She stepped toward them with tears in her eyes and hugged them with a mother's hug of love. When their grandparents saw the boys, they were amazed at how handsome they looked.

It was off to the base chapel for the blessed event. Upon arrival, Sally saw a storybook-like building. It was a very charming church. In the darkness the evening before, Sally could not see the beauty of it. Once inside, the fragrance of flowers grabbed one's senses. The decorator was most creative. It was beautiful. An airman escorted them to the front pew on the right side of the small place of worship. Sally took Rusty's hand as they lovingly looked into each other's eyes, remembering their own special wedding day nine years earlier.

Soon the chapel was full of mostly uniformed Air Force military women and men with their significant others. Then, from a side door at the front of the chapel, a man emerged with a Bible in his hand, followed by Todd and Pace. The organ began to play. A lady dressed in a short lilac-colored dress walked to the front of the church. Moments later, the music for the bride's entrance played. Everyone stood up and faced the beautifully dressed bride as she moved slowly toward the front of the church. Kate's full-length white empire-lined dress was overlaid with white lace. Her white netted veil dipped just below her chin. Her bouquet was made with white and lilac daisies. Such a beautiful picture of Todd's bride.

The young couple joined hands at the altar. Sally's eyes welled with tears of joy. Todd and Kate exchanged their vows and sealed them with their bands of gold. At the end of the service, the minister spoke those precious words: "Now, I pronounce you *husband* and *wife*. You may kiss your bride!" And did Todd ever! Rusty leaned over to Sally and whispered, "They need to come up for air!" Sally smiled and poked him in his side.

They all watched as the newlyweds walked quickly down the aisle and out the front door of the chapel. Soon, the photographer encouraged Todd and Kate to return to the front of the church where the picture taking would begin.

The wedding reception was held at the base's mess hall, which the major had reserved for the wedding guests only. It appeared there were more guests at the reception than at the wedding.

It was a joyous occasion, watching the couple enjoy their family and friends. Cake was served, toasts were given, and presents were opened. Then, the happy couple made their escape, and rice was tossed over them as they left the chapel. Todd had told his mother earlier that he and Kate's favorite place to go was Galveston, and that was where they were going to honeymoon for several days before returning home.

Rusty and Sally chatted with Lee and Lou for a little while before leaving the mess hall. The ladies exchanged addresses and phone numbers and promised to stay in touch with each other.

After another night in their rooms, it was an early start for their drive back to Connecticut. And after two long days on the road, it felt good to be home again. Lots of wonderful memories were made, and Sally would treasure them forever.

Soon, it was Thanksgiving, birthdays, Christmas, and a New Year, and 1990 brought excitement and new life into the Summers' household with the announcement from Todd and Kate. She was pregnant . . . with twins! Their due date was November 15th. Seven months to anxiously wait for those little babies to arrive.

Another year of school was over, and the weather was turning warmer. Pace added another year to his education, and his business was growing. He had been seeing a girl named Brandy for several months, but she moved away. Lil' Rusty and Sadie had gotten out of their toddler stage, and they were forming their own unique personalities, which was so exciting to witness.

Rusty and Sally's tenth anniversary was as loving and romantic as their honeymoon. As they walked hand-in-hand down Broadway in Midtown Manhattan, they felt so blessed to have each other and so thankful that God orchestrated their relationship in His timing.

Summer was fleeing, and Labor Day weekend set the stage for the kiddos to go back to school. Sally started marking off the days Kate and Todd had left before their babies would be born. Excitement was in the air. Then, on November 14th, the wait was over when Todd called and told them the twin boys were born. Kate was doing good, and the boys were healthy. Jerry, the first twin born, weighed five pounds, six ounces, and Eddie weighed five pounds, two ounces. Both babies were seventeen inches long. Praise the Lord, Mom and babies were OK! And the great-grandparents and grandparents were so proud.

Buying for Christmas was more thrilling that year. Thinking of those little ones always made Sally smile. She so longed to see her baby grandsons.

Another year had come and gone. When the school year ended, Rusty, Sally, Lil' Rusty, and Sadie made the trip to San Antonio to see Todd and his family. Pace's businesses kept him from going, and taking trips had gotten too hard for Russell and Mandy. Even though Todd had sent them pictures of Jerry and Eddie, seeing those little boys in person melted Rusty and Sally's hearts, and they loved them all the more.

During that visit, Todd gave his parents the news that he had received orders to report to Nellis Air Force Base in Las Vegas, Nevada, where he would further his flight training. But first he had to go to Maxwell Air Force Base in Montgomery, Alabama, for officer's training school. Also, he told them he had been promoted to cadet. He left for Maxwell ten days later. Kate and the boys remained in San Antonio in base housing. Then, at the end of August, they moved to Las Vegas. Sally hated to see them move so far away.

School for Pace, Lil' Rusty, and Sadie was back in session. Between school and work, Sally and Rusty hardly saw Pace. He had hired several trusted friends to help him operate one of his businesses. Even with all his work, he still found time to do his homework, and he made good grades. Rusty was proud of his ambitious son.

When Lil' Rusty and Sadie brought homework home, Sally's memories went back to the days when Todd and Pace were their age, and how she'd help them with their homework. She followed that same sweet routine with her younger children.

Several times through the year, Todd sent pictures of the twins to show how they were growing. Rusty and Sally missed them so much. The only good thing was that they talked to them often and heard about the things the boys were doing and learning.

On Halloween, the youngsters looked so cute. Lil' Rusty dressed like his grandpa, and Sadie dressed up as a princess. Very fitting for her! Rusty was on a run out of town, so Mandy went with Sally while the children trick-or-treated. They had so much fun.

A one-year-old celebration for the twins was a must over the phone. Rusty and Sally could hear them as they made sounds into the phone. Sally cried!

Sally helped Mandy begin baking for Thanksgiving and again for Christmas. There was always some activity going on at church between the two months, and Mandy's kitchen stayed busy and smelled delicious!

Todd called on Christmas Day and joyfully told his parents that Jerry and Eddie had started walking. Sally sure wished they could see them, all of them. Sally wasn't about to share her thoughts with Rusty or Mandy, but Christmases weren't the same without Todd. He always made the holidays so special. She tried very hard not to appear sad.

Pace surprised his parents and grandparents by bringing a young lady to Christmas dinner, Ava Lily. She lit up the room with her beauty and most gracious personality. Pace met her on his college campus last month. Sally and Rusty could tell Pace was fond of her.

The New Year of 1991 was ushered in by a bad snowstorm with high winds and blizzard conditions, but thank the dear Lord, it wasn't as bad as the damaging storm of 1980. The worst of the bad weather only lasted a few days, and the snow began to melt. However, before it did, Pace and Rusty helped Lil' Rusty and Sadie make a snow family made up of a daddy, a mommy, a big brother, a little brother, and a little sister. Memories rushed back in Sally's mind of the snow family Todd and Pace made years ago. Their snow family was very special.

The calendar pages turned quickly that year with the end of school, then suddenly, the kiddos were back in school. The twins turned two, and according to Todd and Kate, Jerry and Eddie were talking all the time! Thanksgiving cooking and baking had begun, and when Turkey Day arrived, the feast was placed on the table for eight people to enjoy. Pace was still dating Ava.

The cooking and baking started up again as Christmas was drawing near, and Mandy's kitchen was smelling ever so good. That Christmas Day became more blessed when Todd, Kate, Jerry, and Eddie walked into his grandparents' kitchen. What a wonderful surprise! It was a Christmas to remember.

Jerry and Eddie loved playing with their Uncle Lil' Rusty and Aunt Sadie. Sally and Rusty had fun just watching them play together. Todd had finished aviation training, was promoted to the rank of captain, and was being stationed at Wright-Patterson Air Force Base in Dayton, Ohio. His orders were to report to duty on January 15, 1992. The Summers family was surprised and thrilled! Todd, Kate, and the boys would be about ten hours away from the family. They all were very excited about the great news.

Todd explained that as soon as they returned home, packing would begin. He flew to Dayton and searched for a new home. Then Kate and the boys joined him. Sally reminded Todd that his grandfather was stationed at Wright-Patterson for five and a half years, from 1954 to 1959. He had forgotten that, and he felt fortunate to be where his grandfather's footsteps had once been.

Several days later and all too soon, Todd and his family had to leave. But what a special time and Christmas they all had.

The old year went out, and the new year came in. Todd found a new home in Dayton, and soon after, his family was together again. Todd looked forward to his new duty assignment as a pilot, flying in a squadron with other pilots. He was doing what he always dreamed of doing! Sally was so proud of him.

On Valentine's Day, Pace and Ava became engaged, but they decided to wait to get married until after her graduation in 1993. Rusty and Sally were pleased and happy for the young couple.

Pace graduated in May with a degree in business administration. Not long after graduation, he began building a new home on land just down the road from his parents' home. He was an owner of three businesses, and he had gained the respect of many other business owners. He had been approached to run for the position of a local alderman. Pace was honored, but he declined.

The year was slipping away, and celebrations of the holidays came to an end with another new year of 1993.

Pace finished his home. It was beautiful. Ava graduated from college with a degree in education and science. She planned to be a teacher. She and Pace married at the end of October of that year. It was a small but beautiful wedding in a church in Danbury. Pace was happy that Todd was there to be his best man. After the wedding and during picture-taking time, Sally and Rusty introduced themselves to Ava's parents, Joe and Raylee Lily. They were natives of Connecticut. He was an attorney, and she was a schoolteacher. Sally felt awkward around them, and Rusty said that they were a little too stiff-shirted for him. Sally prayed their relationship with Joe and Raylee would improve. The wedding reception was complete with dinner and champaign. Lots of toasts were given in honor of the newlyweds, cake was shared, and gifts were opened. Upon leaving the church, happy guests showered Pace and Ava with rice as they ran to Pace's decorated truck. Sally prayed for their happiness.

After Pace and Ava's memorable honeymoon in Gatlinburg, Tennessee, they set up housekeeping and began decorating for Christmas. They invited all the families for a Christmas house-warming celebration. Every room of their new home looked like it could have been in any popular home magazine. The house was beautiful!

Rusty arranged for Lil' Rusty and Sadie to stay the night at their grandparents' home on New Year's Eve so that he could take Sally to Bridgeport to dine at an exclusive supper club to celebrate the incoming New Year. The supper club was very nice, the food was excellent, and dancing together on the dance floor was so special. They held each other close during the slow music and did the rock-n-roll steps to the early sixties songs. At midnight, the two of them embraced each other as if they were newlyweds. It was a wonderful evening, and the night proceeded to get better after they arrived home, and their love spilled over through the rest of the night.

The New Year was a normal year of celebrating birthdays, anniversaries, and holidays. Rusty added another year of driving over-the-road, and Sally and Mandy continued serving the Lord at their church. Lil' Rusty and Sadie were making good grades in school. Russell was always hard at running the farm, phone calls were often made to Todd and his family, and Pace had opened an office and warehouse in town where he continued to be very successful. Ava had joined the teaching staff at the local elementary school and loved being a teacher.

The following May in 1995, Sally threw Rusty a fun-filled fiftieth birthday party at their church. Lots of church members attended as well as Russell and

Mandy, Pace and Ava, and Lil' Rusty and Sadie. Todd, Kate, and the boys wanted to come, but Todd was on a special assignment. He called his dad and wished him a big fiftieth birthday greeting.

School was out for another year, and Lil' Rusty would start junior high school next year. Sadie had excelled academically in her subjects and her grades, and she passed all required tests, so the school allowed her to skip the sixth grade. So she, too, was going to be entering into junior high school. Rusty and Sally were so proud of their daughter.

A lot of the days of summer were spent at the beach when Rusty was home. Their pre-teenagers and their friends played lots of volleyball and football. They threw frisbees a lot and did a lot of swimming and sunbathing. There was always food for picnics. It was a super fun summer.

The summer months changed Lil' Rusty and Sadie. They were growing up, being more sociable with their friends, and becoming less active with their folks. Sally was happy for them but sad at the same time.

Rusty and Sally had talked to Todd after Labor Day about them coming over to Ohio to spend Christmas with him and his family, but he called them at the end of October and explained that he had to go on TDY (temporary duty) in the middle of December and would not return for a month. So he and Kate suggested Rusty and Sally join them for Thanksgiving, and at the same time, they all could celebrate Christmas too.

It was a good plan, and no more encouragement was needed. Rusty and Sally packed their bags and headed for Dayton on November 21st. That was plenty of time to drive the ten-hour trip and for Sally to help Kate prepare the big meal, plus more time to spend with the twins and their folks.

Once at Todd and Kate's home, it only took the boys a little while to warm up to their grandparents. The next morning after breakfast, Kate and Sally began baking and getting the turkey ready for its long cook time. In between the cooking and baking, the men and the boys helped Kate and Sally put up the Christmas tree and decorate it, as well as the rest of their home. Rusty brought in from his truck all the colorfully wrapped Christmas gifts, and Kate placed them under and around the tree. The boys were so excited! Kate brought other wrapped gifts in as well. The area around the tree was hugged with numerous gifts of all shapes and sizes. Everything was beautiful and sparkled with the blessings and the love of God.

Thanksgiving Day was an extra special day, with the delicious meal, the excitement of opening all the perfectly chosen gifts, and the wonderful gathering of family.

Rusty and Sally spent one more day with Todd and his family, but sadly, their time came to go home to Connecticut. Todd's parents were most grateful for the awesome time they spent with him and his family. They hoped to see them again soon. The trip home was sad, but Sally and Rusty shared their memories together about their unforgettable visit with Todd, Kate, Jerry and Eddie.

Not long after Rusty and Sally's return home from their visit with Todd and his family, they both noticed Mandy was struggling to do her daily tasks around the house. Sally had always helped Mandy, but she was helping Mandy more and more. Russell took Mandy to the doctor and different tests were performed. The tests results showed her blood sugar was very high, and she had diabetes. The doctor immediately began insulin shots. But the worst of the test results revealed that her kidneys were badly damaged and there was damage to the blood vessels in her legs. The devastating news was that her body was not going to improve.

As the weeks passed, it became more and more challenging for Mandy to do everyday chores. She was getting so weak. Mandy's heart broke when her service for the Lord stopped. Sally helped as much as she could.

Near midnight on Sunday, March 16th, 1996, Russell called Rusty in a panic. Mandy had fallen. Rusty quickly dressed and rushed to the Summers' home. Sally heard the siren of an ambulance as she dressed. She woke Lil' Rusty and told him to watch Sadie so that she could go to Grandma and Grandpa's house. She drove fast the short distance between the two houses.

There was a flurry of activity going on. Sally ran inside the house. She found Rusty holding his dad in his arms, and they both were crying. Sally flew to Rusty's side. Then, she saw the ambulance people push the gurney into the kitchen with a covered body on it. Sally's heart nearly stopped at the sight. Russell collapsed to the floor. An ambulance attendant rushed to his side and called for another ambulance.

Rusty and Sally watched as the paramedics applied intravenous medication into Russell's arm. Another ambulance arrived. The attendants lifted and placed Russell's limp body on the gurney, then strapped his body securely before wheeling him out of the kitchen, outside, and into the ambulance.

"I'm going with Dad, Sally." Rusty did not hesitate and ran to the ambulance.

Sally stared at the ambulances as they sped down the long drive, heading for the main road. She was horrified. She trembled with fear. *God, please be with my family, and help me to understand what is happening,* Sally prayed.

Several overnight workers on the farm approached Sally and asked her what was going on. She told them what she knew. She asked them for their help as to who to call for more help with the cows. They gave her a few names.

Sally ran back in the house, found a personal phonebook, and located Pastor Frank's phone number. She dialed his number, and the ringing sounded five times.

"Hello?" a sleepy male voice answered.

"Pastor Frank, it's Sally Summers. I'm at the Summers' home, and something terrible has happened. Mandy has died, Russell collapsed, and Rusty's gone to the hospital with Russell in the ambulance, but I don't know which hospital they went to. How do I contact workers for the farm?"

"Oh, Sally! OK, let me think a second. The ambulances are most likely going to Danbury. I know some workers. I'll call them as well as a few dairy owners. Are you going to the hospital?" Pastor Frank asked.

"I want to, but I have the children," Sally explained.

"You need to go to the hospital." Then he voiced in the background to his wife, "Irene, you need to go to Rusty's house and watch the children. Sally needs to get to the hospital." Then to Sally, "OK, Irene is getting up and can be at your house in twenty minutes."

"Pastor Frank, thank you so much. I'll go home and wait for her. You'll call the workers and other farmers, right?" Sally needed to confirm what he had said.

"Yes, I'll take care of it. You, go!"

Sally quickly called Pace. She told him what happened. He told her he would go to the hospital. She also called Todd to inform him of what happened. Then she hurried out of the house. Another worker was waiting for her.

"Mrs. Sally, I just heard. I'm so sorry," Phillip said.

"Thank you, Phillip. Pastor Frank is making phone calls to get y'all some help. I'm going to the hospital. Y'all know what to do! I appreciate it," Sally faithfully said as she started the car and drove away.

When Sally arrived back at her house, Lil' Rusty met her at the door. "What's going on, Mom?" he blurted out.

"Your grandma has passed away, and your grandpa collapsed. He has been taken to the hospital. Your dad is with him. Pastor Frank's wife, Irene, is going to be here soon to stay with y'all. I'm going to the hospital. Please help her all you can. I'll call you later."

There was a knock on the front door. Sally opened the door, and Irene rushed in.

"Oh, Sally. I'm so sorry. You go on now, and be careful. I'll take care of everything here." Irene hugged Sally.

Sally hugged Lil' Rusty and left quickly. The short distance seemed longer than normal, but she finally arrived at the hospital. She ran into the building and inquired with the ER staff member where Russell Summers was. The staff member took Sally to his room. Rusty was very glad to see her and took her in his arms.

"Dr. Harrison is on call, and Dad's been taken to have some tests done," Rusty nervously explained.

"Was he awake? Is he OK?" Sally asked fearfully.

"The paramedics stabilized him in the ambulance, and he was talking to me before we arrived at the hospital. The doctor believes Dad's OK, but mainly he wants to check his heart with an EKG," Rusty further explained.

The door to their hospital room opened, and Pace peeked around the door, then stepped into the room. "Hey. How's Grandpa? I can't believe Grandma is gone! Dad, are you OK?" Pace walked straight to his dad and hugged him. Then, he hugged his mother.

Before Rusty could answer his son's questions, the door opened again, and Dr. Harrison entered the room.

"Rusty, I'm admitting Russell to the hospital. Everything looks good, but he's been through a lot tonight. He'll probably be OK to go home tomorrow. He is in a state of shock. Are you OK?"

"Yes, I'm OK, just in shock as well. I'm praising God that Dad's heart is OK. Did he tell you what happened?" Rusty questioned.

"He told me he was in the bedroom as they were about to go to bed when he heard a noise. When he came into the dining room, he saw Mandy lying on the floor. He said he tried to move her, but she was not responding. He called the police who in turn called an ambulance. He said he didn't think your mom was breathing," Dr. Harrison told them.

Rusty closed his eyes, thinking of the horror his dad must have suffered. How helpless he had to have felt! Tears began to roll down Rusty's face. He put his face in his hands and sobbed uncontrollably. Sally, crying as well, wrapped her arms around her grieving husband. Pace joined them, as well as Dr. Harrison, with a consoling hug, comforting all they could.

A nurse regretfully needed to interrupt the mournful moment. "Doctor, you're needed in Room 15," she anxiously requested.

"OK. I'll be right there," Dr. Harrison called to her. "Rusty, I'll keep a close eye on your dad. You can see him. He's now in Room 120," he said as he hurried away.

Rusty looked at Sally with sad, teary eyes. "What is happening? I can't believe this!"

"I know, sweetheart. Neither can I, but come on. Your dad needs us now." Sally took his and Pace's hands, and they walked together to Russell's room.

Upon entering the room, they saw Russell's eyes closed. Rusty, Pace, and Sally quietly stood beside his bed. Rusty took his dad's hand in his. Russell opened his eyes and reached for his son's hand with his other hand.

"Son, is it true, your mother has gone to heaven? I was just praying for her and for us who are now left behind. I can't believe she's gone!" He began to cry.

Rusty lowered the hospital bed rail and bent down to hold his extremely emotional father in his arms. All four of them cried.

After a short while, Russell drifted off to sleep. A nurse came in to check on him and told Rusty that Dr. Harrison had given his dad a sedative to help him rest and sleep.

The three of them sat down in chairs that were in the room. Rusty suggested Sally go home and call Pastor Frank. At that moment, a knock was heard on the hospital room door. The door opened slowly, and a person's head peered around the corner of the door.

"Pastor Frank! I just mentioned your name," Rusty said with surprise as he stood up.

"I know, I heard you!" he laughed softly and continued talking in a low voice. "No, Sally called me earlier to tell me about your parents. I'm so sorry, Rusty." Pastor Frank approached Rusty and hugged him, then Sally and Pace.

"I've called several other dairy farmers, and they are sending helpers to your dad's place. Everything is covered. So don't you worry about a thing. Irene is at your home, taking care of the children. So do you know what happened? And how's Russell? Ever since Sally called me, I've been praying for you all. The deacons are praying too, as well as members."

Rusty told him what the doctor told them of what his dad experienced, and then, Rusty added what he saw when he arrived at his dad's house. Pastor Frank shook his head at the tragic happenings. He then asked them to bow their heads while he prayed to their Father in heaven and to His Son, Jesus Christ.

Pastor Frank left as the sun was dawning and the hospital personnel were starting their morning rounds. Russell was awake and talking to the three of them and the nurses who were coming in and out of his room.

Rusty noticed and commented, "Dad, you seem to be feeling a little better this morning."

Russell looked at him. "Son, I'm trying to be more like myself on the outside, but on the inside, my heart is broken."

The hospital room door was partially opened, and Dr. Harrison walked into the room. "Good morning, Russell. Tell me how you think you feel this morning," he asked as he placed the ear portions of his stethoscope in his ears to listen to Russell's heart.

"I think I'm feeling pretty good, doc. Do you hear how broken my heart is through those tubes?" Russell asked sadly.

Dr. Harrison looked at Russell with his head cocked to one side. "No, but I do hear a good strong rhythmic beat, and that's what I want to hear," the doctor exclaimed. He continued checking Russell's vital signs, and he used encouraging words to lift Russell's spirits. "All your vitals are good. I'll begin your discharge paperwork, and after breakfast, all should be ready for you to leave and go home. I'm making a follow-up appointment for you on March 22nd at 11 a.m. I'll see you then, but in the meantime, please, take it easy. Continue to keep your dairy helpers, and let them do most of the work. Listen to me, Russell! Rusty, please, make sure he listens to his doctor!" He patted Rusty's shoulder and shook Russell's hand before leaving the room.

"OK, Dad. You heard him!" Rusty emphasized.

"Yeah, yeah, yeah! I heard him," Russell groaned.

Russell's breakfast arrived, so he ate some of it, then dressed with Rusty's help. A nurse with a wheelchair came into the room, and Russell sat down. The nurse helped him out to Rusty's truck, and they left the hospital. Sally and Pace followed behind them in their vehicles.

As Rusty drove down the road toward home, he had to bring up a subject he really did not want to discuss, but it definitely needed to take place. "Dad, we need to talk about Mom's funeral," he sadly stated.

"I know, son," Russell agreed. "Years ago, your mother and I talked to a lady at Newtown Funeral Home, and we pre-arranged our funerals with her. We need to go to the funeral home tomorrow."

"I did not remember that. I know that was a hard thing to think about and do, but now that Mom has passed, it's a good thing. Yes. I'll call and make an appointment when we get you home." Rusty breathed a sigh of relief.

The appointment was made, and Rusty, with Sally, took Russell to the funeral home the next day. In about an hour, all the arrangements for Mandy's funeral were planned for March 24th.

Russell struggled that whole week. Rusty and Sally, as well as church members, continued to surround him with as much love and compassion as they could. Church members flooded the house with food of all kinds for several weeks after the beautiful funeral and graveside service for Mandy. But then, life moved on, and not so many people visited with him. His days and nights were so very lonely and sometimes downright fearful. Russell prayed all the time for comfort, peace, and strength. He needed to do what he used to do, but he couldn't. The farm suffered as he had no interest in the cows anymore. Rusty tried his best again and again to encourage his dad but without any luck. And Rusty tried to work the farm, but it was just too much work for him to do too, even with helpers. Rusty was at his wit's end as to what to do.

Two months later, the unimaginable happened. Rusty came into Russell's house to check on his dad before he started to work on the morning of May 16th. He found his dad sitting at the kitchen table with his cup of coffee in front of him. Rusty spoke to him and received no response. Rusty noticed his dad was holding one of his favorite pictures of his mother. He greeted his dad again. Still, no response of any kind from his dad. Rusty approached his dad and placed his hand on his dad's shoulder. "Dad, are you OK?"

The picture fell from his dad's hands. Rusty froze in place, staring at his dad's still body. Rusty reluctantly touched his dad's hand. Rusty fell in the chair next to his dad and, as if he was in excruciating pain, cried loudly, "No, Dad, don't leave!" He continued to cry uncontrollably.

Upon hearing a loud scream, Phillip rushed into the kitchen and found Rusty with his dad. "Mr. Rusty, what's wrong? I heard a scream! Are you all OK?" Then, he noticed Mr. Russell's still body. "Oh no, Mr. Rusty! It can't be!"

Rusty looked up at Phillip in anguish. "Yes, Phillip. God has taken him to heaven." He raised up from the chair and walked to the phone. He dialed his home number. "Sally, Dad's gone to heaven."

Immediately Sally was there and was holding Rusty in her arms. They cried together. Rusty sat down at the table across from his dad while Sally called the police. Then, she called Pastor Frank.

Phillip re-entered the kitchen. "What can I do, Mrs. Sally?"

"Please, go to the others and tell them what has happened. I realize this is a very sad time, but please, y'all tend to the cows for Mr. Russell's sake, please,"

Sally answered as tears streamed down her face. Phillip ran from the kitchen and straight to the parlor.

The police and an ambulance arrived. Sally didn't want Rusty to watch the paramedics place Russell's body on the gurney, but he would not leave the kitchen. Rusty hugged his dad one last time before the attendant covered Russell's body. He then walked beside the gurney to the door leading outside. He watched from the glassed-in room as the ambulance drove away. His tears flowed even more. Sally wrapped her arms around his waist to comfort him.

After a while, Sally encouraged Rusty to come back into the kitchen. The police officer offered Rusty his condolences. He apologized for having to ask him questions, but he needed to complete his police report.

As the officer was asking questions, Pastor Frank entered the house and immediately walked to Rusty and put his arms around him. "I am so sorry for your great loss, Rusty. Your dad was one of the hardest working men I knew, and he'd give you his shirt off his back. He was a wonderful man. I will truly miss him. What can I do to help you all?"

Rusty hesitated for a moment. "I can't think of anything right now, Pastor Frank, but thank you for asking and for being here. I need to go check on the men at the parlor. Oh yeah, will you be able to do Dad's service for us?"

"Of course I will, Rusty. Please, let me know when. I'm here for you and your family," Pastor Frank reassured them.

Rusty left the house for the parlor.

Pastor Frank looked at Sally. "Is he OK? I'm concerned."

"Pastor Frank, no, he isn't. He is hurting and is in deep shock right now." Sally continued telling him what happened this morning when Rusty came into the house to check on his dad.

"Wow, how devastating. God works in mysterious ways, and He has a reason for everything. I'll be praying for all of you for comfort, peace, and strength. If there's nothing I can do at the moment, I'm going to my office to make phone calls to the deacons. Rusty's going to be lost without his dad. It was hard for you all when Mandy left us, but now Russell. . . ." Pastor Frank shook his head. He hugged Sally and left.

Sally thought about Pastor Frank's last words. Yes, Rusty would truly be lost without his dad and his best friend! She called Todd and Pace to tell them about the passing of their grandpa. They were shocked and very saddened to hear the news.

The next day, the funeral arrangements were made for May 25th, just two months after Mandy was laid to rest. Most people believed Russell died from a broken heart. He missed Mandy so much.

Todd and his family came in from Dayton to be with their dad, and Pace and Ava were by his side as well. Lil' Rusty and Sadie needed their mother's support. The service for Russell was beautiful but heart-wrenching for Rusty. Pastor Frank's eulogy for Russell was almost more than Rusty could take. There was not a dry eye in the church.

Todd, Kate, and the twins stayed another day before going back home, and Pace checked in on his folks often. But then, reality began to set in. Rusty and Sally were more lost than ever since Russell passed away. Their lives revolved around Rusty's parents. The whole family was heartbroken, but their spiritual belief allowed them to know from God's holy Word that all of them would see each other again in heaven.

Soon after Rusty's parents' deaths, he begrudgingly put the farm up for sale. In Russell and Mandy's will, Rusty was given ownership of their property. Rusty's Dad and Mom loved the farm and put their heart and soul into the work every day. Even though Rusty said he never wanted to be a dairy farmer because it was too much work and was way too time-consuming, Rusty's decision to sell the property was hard. He prayed that God would show him a way to continue running the farm and make it profitable, but Rusty didn't see a way. And the farm was sold.

From Russell's funeral until January of 1999, daily living was different and many times a struggle. But eventually, the Summers established their new normal as the family slowly settled in to the new life the Lord provided for them.

There were several times during those years when Pace and Ava believed they were going to become parents, but the doctor told Ava she was having false pregnancies. It was so disappointing for them and the family. Ava's symptoms occurred again at the end of February in 1999. Pace told his mother that Ava was vomiting in the mornings, but by noon, she was feeling better. She felt so bad that whole week and was unable to go to school and teach her classes.

Sally explained to him that it sounded like she was experiencing morning sickness and suggested they make a doctor's appointment soon. The appointment was made for the next day, and the doctor confirmed that Ava was indeed pregnant! Those words were the ones they so longed to hear for several years.

Pace called his mother late the evening of September 22nd and told her that Ava might be having contractions, and they were leaving for the hospital. Rusty wasn't home, and Sally told Lil' Rusty and Sadie she was going to the hospital to be with Pace and that Ava could be in labor. Sally wished she and Rusty had one of those new types of phones, that way she could call him to let him know he was about to be a *grandpa* again!

Sally arrived at the hospital at the same time Pace and Ava did. By the way Ava was walking, Sally suspected she was indeed in labor.

Once they were inside the emergency room, the staff wasted no time taking Ava by wheelchair to the maternity wing of the hospital. Pace and Sally followed close behind the nurse who was pushing the wheelchair rather quickly. The nurse briefly stopped and instructed Pace and Sally to go into the maternity waiting room. Then, the nurse continued on the journey with Ava.

Thirty minutes later, the attending nurse came into the waiting room and told them that Ava was in labor and doing fine. The doctor was on his way to the hospital and it might be a little while before the baby would be born. The nurse continued by saying Ava had just begun to dilate. As the nurse began to walk away, she said she would give them updates as they happened.

Pace looked at his watch. It was 11 p.m. Sally poured two cups of coffee from the refreshment table and gave one to Pace as she remarked that it might be a long night.

The two of them chatted a while, then Pace walked around. Sally could see anxiety was building up inside of him. He saw the nurse as she entered into the waiting room. She told them everything was moving along, but the birth could still be several hours away. Pace sat down and breathed a sigh. Sally encouraged him to rest, but he said he could not. He was too nervous.

Time passed slowly. Pace's watch indicated it was 3 a.m., and he walked again. Sally laid her head back on the cushion part of her chair and closed her eyes, but she did not sleep. She, too, was nervous and wondering how Ava was doing. She prayed.

The clock over the refreshment table had its hands straight up and down for 6 a.m. Ava's doctor rounded the corner of the maternity waiting room, still in his scrubs with a hat on his head. He walked up to Pace wearing a big smile. "Pace, Ava has delivered a healthy baby girl, weighing six pounds and thirteen ounces with a length of eighteen inches. Congratulations! Ava is doing fine. The nurse will be out soon to take you all to her room. Today is Thursday. Ava and baby should be OK to go home Saturday," he concluded as he walked away.

"Thanks, doc!" Pace said in a raised voice. He turned and looked at his mother with a very big smile.

Sally took Pace in her arms and hugged him tightly and said with tears in her eyes, "Congratulations, son!"

"A little girl. I have a daughter! How about that, Momma?" Pace had forgotten his nervousness, and he was rejoicing and praising the Lord with happiness he had never known before. He was such a proud daddy.

Sally smiled at the new dad.

The attending nurse showed Pace and Sally to Ava's room. Sally allowed Pace and Ava time to be together to celebrate their very special joy before she joined them.

Pace motioned for his mother to come into Ava's room. She hugged Ava and congratulated her on the birth of their baby girl. Sally hoped Ava's parents would come soon, but the thought was fleeting as they all enjoyed the excitement of the birth of their little girl.

On Saturday afternoon, Pace brought Ava and Abigail home. Rusty had returned home and he, Sally, Lil' Rusty, and Sadie went to Pace's home to see the baby. Abigail was a beautiful little girl. Joe and Raylee came in to see and meet their new granddaughter too. Even though Pace had built a nice-sized house, all of a sudden, it got crowded, and the Summers said they'd come back later. Pace understood.

Over the next six months, Sally and Rusty helped Pace and Ava when and where they could. After that time, the young couple got the hang of how to manage life with their baby daughter.

Rusty and Sally held each other's hands as they reminisced on the last twenty years of their married life that had gone by. They missed people who were there to see their ceremony. Russell and Mandy were in heaven; Todd, Kate, and the twins were in Dayton; Pace, Ava, and Abigail were in Hartford, attending a business conference; and since school ended several weeks earlier, both Lil' Rusty and Sadie had graduated high school. To celebrate their accomplishments, they, and some of their friends, went camping in the Green Mountains of Vermont for the week.

Their conversation turned to their future. Come fall, Sally and Rusty would become empty-nesters as both Lil' Rusty and Sadie would be college-bound. There was no one to care for. Prince and Princess were not with them any longer. When Princess died, Prince grieved so badly. Then, one day soon after Princess died, he disappeared without a trace. Chief developed cancer, and he had to be put down. Sundance lived two more years and died of old age. Sally shared with Rusty that she did not like the idea of being at home by herself. Immediately Rusty asked her to start going with him over-the-road. He'd ask his boss to put him back on longer runs. Or better yet, he'd teach her how to drive an 18-wheeler, and they could be team drivers! Sally liked his idea, and she agreed. She remembered her dear friend in Memphis, Minnie Mouse, who learned how to drive and joined her husband, Firecracker, driving over-the-road.

Rusty began teaching Sally how to drive, and soon she passed all her tests and was given her CDL—commercial driver's license. She thanked God for all His blessings.

By fall, Cricket was ready to share the ride with Rusty in their brand new burgundy Kenworth that they named "BUSTER." She was thrilled to be with her knight in shining armor, also known as . . .

the Farmer from Connecticut.